# A HOODED CROW

The latest compulsive adventure novel from the master of the genre, *A Hooded Crow* evokes a fascinating picture of the continuing rivalries and suspicions that colour the aftermath of the Cold War, as old enemies face each other on a new battlefield – southern Africa – and for the latest stakes – the smuggling of arms and high technology.

While Sir Kenneth Aubrey of British Intelligence recuperates from illness, his best men, Patrick Hyde and Tony Godwin, are obsessively in pursuit of proof of European infiltration of the electronics giant, Reid Group, whose former chairman is now a Cabinet minister. No one believes their accusations that Reid Group has been penetrated and its secrets stolen, and they are suspended from duty.

In a remote part of the Namibian bush, former British agent Richard Anderson discovers the wreckage of an aircraft belonging to Paulus Malan's huge MLC conglomerate. On board is Reid Group technology and the body of a KGB officer. When Anderson sends evidence of the cargo to Aubrey, Malan's men destroy his home in a faked terrorist atrocity, killing Anderson's beloved half-Bantu wife.

Aubrey is drawn reluctantly into involvement with Hyde's investigation and Anderson's desire for revenge, discovering that something much more sinister than high technology is on its way to Africa via a trade fair in Venice.

As Anderson begins to track down Paulus Malan, the reader is drawn into a world where the politics are new, the weapons of destruction even newer, but where the tactics and the risks are as old and as deadly as ever.

D0533324

# A HOODED CROW

# CRAIG THOMAS

Fontana

*An Imprint of* HarperCollins*Publishers*

Lines from 'The Whitsun Weddings' from Philip Larkin's *Collected Poems* published by Faber & Faber Ltd are reproduced with kind permission from the publishers.

Lines from 'Willful Homecoming' from *The Poetry of Robert Frost* edited by Edward Connery Lathem and published by Jonthan Cape are reproduced with kind permission from the publishers and the Executors of the Estate of Robert Frost.

Lines from 'Changing of the Guards' by Bob Dylan © Special Rider Music, are reproduced with kind permission of Warner Chapel Music Ltd.

Fontana
An Imprint of HarperCollins*Publishers*
77–85 Fulham Palace Road,
Hammersmith, London W6 8JB

This edition published by Fontana 1992

9 8 7 6 5 4 3 2 1

First published in Great Britain by
HarperCollins*Publishers* 1992

ISBN 0 00 647298 2

Set in Linotron Meridien by
Rowland Phototypesetting Ltd, Bury St Edmunds, Suffolk

Printed in Great Britain by
HarperCollinsManufacturing Glasgow

*this one is for*
Babs and George,    Joy and John,
Chris and Tony,    Beryl and Nev.
*for all the good times*

'But Eden is burning, either brace yourself for elimination
Or else your heart must have the courage for the changing
of the guards.'

Bob Dylan: 'Changing of the Guards'

'. . . sun destroys
The interest of what's happening in the shade.'

Philip Larkin: 'The Whitsun Weddings'

# PRELUDE

'. . . thus do we of wisdom and of reach,
With windlasses and with assays of bias,
By indirections find directions out.'

William Shakespeare: *Hamlet,* Act II, Scene 1

The noise of the official reception billowed out of the open doors of the St George Hall like a reproof as Andrew Babbington strode down the gallery towards Kapustin. The midday sun struck through the long windows which overlooked the Moskva. Kapustin's shoulders were hunched belligerently, his hands clasped behind his back as if he, too, flinched against the hubbub of the reception for David Reid and his entourage of British businessmen and civil servants, all come with their loans and their arrogance to help bail out the Soviet economy and preserve the status quo. Babbington realized that his mouth mimicked his disdain – and perhaps the ironic, shivery nervousness he felt. Should Reid turn now, he would recognize Babbington, even with his beard. Had the Deputy Chairman of the KGB summoned him for just such a small, bitter humiliation?

Rich stucco graced the walls behind the British Secretary of State for Trade and Industry and the Soviet President, and there were huge zinc columns supporting a row of statues of the goddess of Victory, crowned with laurel. What sort of victory was it, Babbington wondered, when representatives of the British government were entertained so obsequiously for the sake of some scrubby little trade deals and short-term loans? Marble slabs in niches commemorated the names and units of officers and men of the Russian armies who had been awarded the Order of St George – as he himself had been. Now, they might strike a new St George medal to commemorate what was happening in there at that moment! Perhaps Kapustin had intended this humiliation, because there was a certain, wormlike bitterness twisting in his stomach – people he knew, even some whose careers he had furthered, and the British Embassy across the river; he walking between the two. That room had celebrated the victory over the Nazis in 1945.

11

Kapustin's head snapped up, as if he had sensed rather than seen Babbington's proximity. Yes, he was aware of the irony of Babbington's presence, but had not engineered it for his humiliation. He was still – always would be – the traitor to his country who had fled to Moscow after Aubrey exposed him. Useful, promoted to the rank of general in the KGB. And *used*. Trusted only because they were certain he had no alternative. A constant diet of humiliation and rancour. Kapustin's broad, peasant's face was alive with anger, determination and the ubiquitous calculation. The old-fashioned suit he wore was generously bemedalled. Kapustin caught his glance, and grinned. 'Some of them I actually deserved, General,' he murmured, then tossed his head. 'Unlike some recipients I could name.'

'Deputy Chairman, why do you suddenly require my presence here – at this humiliating farce?' He caught someone in the room, near one of the doors, studying him, before shaking his head and turning away. Mistaken identity. As always, his habitual, aloof disdain of Kapustin was forgiven out of the benevolence of superior power.

'I summoned you because there is something that must be discussed now, at once. Walk with me – the noises of our respective countrymen grate.'

At once, they began to patrol the windowed gallery, Babbington keeping his glance towards the river and away from the doors. Even that much nervousness dismayed him. Glass-roofed tourist pleasure cruisers invested the river like floating greenhouses. The laughter and chatter boomed out at them as they passed each pair of open doors; empty, calculated gestures and the clink of glasses. He gripped his hands behind his back, as if parodying Kapustin – two starlings on a lawn, he thought, then quashed the Englishness of the image. Kapustin's blunt head moved beside him at shoulder height, pecking occasionally at present concerns and towards the doors. He appeared uncomfortable; angry, but wary. He looked up at Babbington. 'Andrew, I must instruct you to a course of action you will resent and mistrust – but which is necessary.'

'And that is?'

Kapustin's spadelike hand gripped his sleeve. 'Andrew, do not be languid with me. I have just spent a very uncomfortable fifteen minutes in an anteroom of that hall with a quorum of the Politburo.

I was summoned there and given my orders. It is a matter of *immediate* results. The business has become urgent.'

'Kapustin, what is it we are talking about?' Dealing with these people was often like another and more tense secret life than the one he had led in London, before Aubrey had exposed and usurped him. 'What the devil is this business?'

'We are talking about – toys, gewgaws, shiny objects. We are talking about seeing a *return on our massive investment*, as he put it to me.' Kapustin waved his hands in the air, as if engaged in some spell-casting or martial arts ritual.

'What do you mean?'

Kapustin's eyes were bright with anger, even as he squinted in the sunlight coming over Babbington's shoulder.

'I mean proving to them that we have not run off with the money!' His hand tightened on Babbington's sleeve once more. His words hissed. 'They are afraid – all of them, including our Chairman – of the amount of money and investment and goods that are about to be lost to us, since you informed us that Mr Shapiro is about to be arrested – and seems prepared to discuss a way out of his difficulties with the FBI and the CIA.'

'I've already made my feelings clear. Shapiro's usefulness is at an end. The material he supplied from the Reid Group has dried up. He can only do harm now, should he talk. I have already suggested that Shapiro be dealt with before he reaches that position. He's skulking in London now, afraid to return to America. So, let me remove him as an obstacle – '

'He is not the only obstacle! Much of our operation in California has been uncovered by the FBI – the companies in which we have an interest, the bank in Fresno, the banks and holding companies in the Caribbean ... And the fact that Aubrey's people have not been put out to grass, as you assured us they would, when illness removed Sir Kenneth.'

'Everything else is secure!'

'No, it is *not* secure.' Kapustin glared at Babbington. It was the accusing glance of a pedagogue severely disappointed in a once-lauded pupil. 'The London Rezident is monitoring the activities of that small group of people around Aubrey. They are continuing with their investigation of the Reid Group and its subsidiaries. And they are not as purposeless as a chicken with its head chopped off. Godwin, Hyde and the others might, at any moment, find the tripwire that sets off all the alarms, Andrew. *That* cannot be allowed to happen.'

The sunlight dazzled from the river's surface and from the floating greenhouses. Babbington rubbed his forehead, which prickled with the heat of his anger. Or perhaps it was a reaction to that heavy blanket of noise that kept billowing from the room as if orchestrated for his chagrin.

'You're panicking needlessly,' Babbington said.

'*I* am not panicking – but the members of the Politburo *are*. What they desire is the advanced wafer scale integration and transputer technology that could be obtained from the Reid Group – *now*, not when *you* feel the time is right.'

'You want to waste all those *years* with some operation that stinks of looting a bazaar?' Babbington involuntarily threw up his hands. 'I don't believe I'm hearing this, Kapustin. The material you require must be brought out piecemeal, if at all. You want to deliberately attract the attention of Aubrey's people? Why not *telephone* them, if that's the case!'

'They have fixed their minds,' Kapustin whispered fiercely, 'on acquiring this wafer scale integration technology from the Reid Group to assist our move towards a market economy, which has already taken us four years and shows no signs of working!' He bent closer to Babbington, so that the taller man had to lean down towards his mouth. 'It isn't any *easier*, now, Andrew, that our *friends* have the power. Do I make myself clear, Andrew?'

Waiters moved as in some vast hotel ballroom, with trays of canapés and bottles of champagne, refilling glasses. Guests rubbed well-cut suits against cocktail dresses, comparing mutual luxury. A blue cloud of cigar and cigarette smoke hovered over the vast room.

'I understand you – I don't agree with you, however. In fact, I violently disagree –'

Kapustin moved his hand in a flat, dismissive gesture. 'I am not concerned with your disagreement. There is to be no more continuation of risk. Just one final risk. You will get the richest, ripest pickings out of the UK, especially WSI and transputer technology. You will do it *now*, as quickly and ruthlessly as possible. Then you will shut down the UK operation until it is deemed safe to continue penetration of high-tech companies. You can move your focus of

14

operations to Germany or France, until it is safe to go back. Until Aubrey retires or dies . . .' He smiled grimly.

'A consummation devoutly to be wished,' Babbington growled.

They began to retrace their steps down the long gallery. The traffic seemed heavy on the nearest bridge, and the pleasure cruisers cut small wakes on the glittering river. Dots of colour strolled the far bank.

'See to it, Andrew. You have –'

'If we asset-strip the UK operation, then we will simply be shooting ourselves in the foot,' Babbington persisted with whispered, hoarse rage. His fist clenched and unclenched at his side in emphasis. 'We would have to start more or less afresh to penetrate high-tech companies –'

'Do it, Andrew. We intend to maintain our influence with the Politburo, and this – at *this* moment – is our way of doing so. Time presses. To minimize any additional risk, the timetable that has been proposed –' It was, so *evidently*, Kapustin's timetable! '– culminates in the VIATE fair in Venice, which will be your cover –'

'Impossible!'

'– culminates at that fair at the end of the month. It is *not* impossible. It must be done. Get rid of Shapiro, and then move swiftly . . .' He patted Babbington's sleeve. 'I'm sorry it has to happen, Andrew. The penetration of the Reid Group, the shareholding we have acquired so covertly . . . a great pity. But other priorities make their demands. For the present, we have to placate the Politburo, and they are more or less united in demanding a return on their investment. Where are the toys you promised us? they cry like children. We need them to perform an economic miracle! Ridiculous – but necessary.' He shook his sleeve again. 'You *do* understand, Andrew?'

Babbington nodded stiffly, after an interminable silence filled with the billow of laughter and chatter from the St George Hall. 'I understand,' he said thickly. Then, clearing his throat, he repeated: 'I understand my instructions.'

Kapustin smiled with knowing satisfaction, then he said: 'Of course you do. Good . . . now, off you go to get this business organized. Shoo!' He waved his arms as if to scatter chickens in some peasant farmyard. Babbington's cheeks were hot with anger.

15

Even with shame, he thought, as he turned away and began to walk down the long gallery with as much indifferent dignity as he could employ to stiffen his shoulders and his gait. *My orders come from* . . . those pug-faced generals and the *apparatchiks* we are forced to call our friends. Those *peasants* in braid-covered uniforms whose eyes and tongues have been slavering ever since they saw the first news footage from the Gulf. All those shiny *playthings*! All that obscenely-glamorous Western military technology. Get it for us, we must have it!

He reached the end of the gallery and turned out of sight of Kapustin, who he knew would be watching his – *retreat.* He retained the stiff, military posture.

The generals and the other hardliners – all the contemptible, powerful little people – had raised the game's stakes. They had to have this new technology. They'd been rendered ten years out of date by weaponry, tactics, skills in the Gulf, and they wanted, yet *again*, to catch up.

The stakes were dangerously high now – they would be ruthless with someone who failed them.

# PART ONE

# Selling England
# by the Pound

'I never think you should judge a country
by its politics. After all, we English
are quite honest by nature, aren't we?'

from Alfred Hitchcock's *The Lady Vanishes*

# ONE

## the envy of less happier lands

There were too many sensations in the room, too many people, all moving as black shadows against the summer light coming through the opened vertical blinds. He was angry, and his mood jolted against the smooth, closed business of the room, its finality. Shapiro was the only person missing, inactive. *For God's sake, how the hell had it been allowed to happen? The bugger was on the point of being arrested and extradited, and now he'd topped himself!*

Daniel Garrison, CIA Station Chief, signalled to him, and he stumped on his heavy sticks across the deep, blue carpet. Through the multiplicity of windows of the hotel suite's lounge, the traffic shunted or moved with matador grace and suddenness around the Wellington Arch.

Tony Godwin was there by virtue of a gesture, almost as if he was being rewarded – with a bloody consolation prize! – for good work; a star in his school exercise book. Shapiro had committed suicide in the bedroom of his suite at the Inter-Continental. The frock-coated management representative looked like a premature undertaker, especially since he seemed to find hand-wringing a comforting exercise. His look obscurely accused Godwin as he moved through the small crowd of Special Branch officers, a Customs official, the forensic team, others . . . He clapped his sticks together as if saluting Garrison and looked towards the half-open bedroom door. He glowered at Garrison's people posted there. Shapiro, to put it bluntly, had fucked up six months' work by topping himself!

And he had never appeared the suicidal sort. Only likely to be talkative, once he'd been pinned down.

'Well?' he snapped at Garrison, who shook his head lugubriously. 'Dan, how the hell could it have happened, just *now*, when he was about to have his collar felt? He was even putting out little feelers for a deal with us, for God's sake!' He rubbed a large hand through his fraying fair hair, catching sight of his untidy appearance in a long mirror; awkward and crippled, furiously angry like a frustrated child. He clenched his hand into a fist. The sun burned on the blue carpet and, despite the purr of the air-conditioning, the room seemed hot. 'Why the hell did he do it?'

His anger had fermented in the heat of the taxi that had brought him here from his flat. Hadn't even paused to feed Dubček, the black cat he'd brought from Prague years ago.

'Calm down, Tony – you'll blow a fuse.' There was no mockery in the remark. 'Look, we don't know why. He *was* sounding like he wanted to play ball, tell us everything he knew. Now, this –' He gestured at the two officers from Special Branch. 'Your people saw him come in last evening, with a high-class hooker on his arm and a smile on his face. She left about –'

'There was someone else here? Then he didn't necessarily help himself to oblivion! What does the doc say about time?'

'Anywhere between one and three this morning.'

'How?'

'Sleeping pills, washed down with Krug champagne. He'd had sex – the girl must have left and he must have got depressed. Perhaps he didn't like the idea of ten years on the prison farm, after –'

'The more he'd told us, the shorter the sentence. He understood that! Who was this tart he brought back?'

'No one knows. He didn't arrange anything from here or over the telephone.'

'She picked him up, then. Where did he eat last night?'

'Your people watched him. He went to some club, came out with her.'

'Then she could have killed him!'

'We don't *know*, Tony!' He rubbed his forehead. 'Look, I'm just as mad as you are. But it really doesn't look like she shoved a bottle of pills down his throat! I'm sorry, I guess the guy just chickened out at the last moment – who knows?'

'And maybe – just maybe – it's better for Langley and Washington he's said goodbye?' Garrison's eyes flinched at the accusation. 'No one really wanted another fuss about the KGB, did they? *Very inconvenient, a scandal!*'

Garrison ignored the blunt sarcasm and said: 'You want to take a look at him? He looks kind of – '

'You sound like a relative! Doesn't he look peaceful! There's months of hard, patient work up shit creek because fat Mr Shapiro of Shapiro Electrics of San José, California, has either killed himself or been done in. Nothing changes *that*, whatever happened to him.' The room had fallen silent, the shadows posed in stillness against the blinds. He was the actor, they merely the audience – too true, he thought bitterly. Their play was over, after a lengthy run, while his had closed for lack of support! 'Oh, *shit*!' he bellowed at the top of his voice. They could have had so *much* out of Shapiro. The details of the web, the methods of operation, the loans, the smuggling, the extent of KGB penetration of the Reid Group – bloody everything! Especially the details of the pipeline and how much Malan was involved ... Bugger it! The operation was dead now.

'Was there a note?' he asked.

'A short one – his handwriting, on hotel notepaper.' Godwin sniffed in disbelief. 'True. He blamed our harassment, business worries, the fear of prison – or worse. The usual paranoia.'

'He had nothing to worry about!'

'Maybe he was too scared to talk?'

'And maybe they killed him because he was about to.'

Garrison shrugged.

'Whatever, it's over now. We'll pick over the bones. Maybe we've frightened the Russians into laying off for a while. So long as we stay alert – '

'Christ, they'll own Saks Fifth Avenue before we get a better chance to see what they're up to!'

'I'm sorry, Tony – really sorry.' He cleared his throat. 'Look, I have to report to your Director General, Sir Clive – '

'Great. It's just the excuse he's been looking for to redeploy us – ever since Aubrey chucked us back in his lap and went on sick leave.'

'Sorry. I'll try to make it sound as if you should be allowed to go on with it. Do what I can.'

'It's stuffed, Dan – it's all stuffed!' He glared at the bedroom door. 'Thanks, Mister-Bloody-Shapiro – thanks for nothing!'


The sunlight glowed through the leaded glass of the pub window behind him and spilt across the faded, dusty carpet from the open door. Customers entering were solid black shapes without feature for a moment, as he glanced up from the *Evening Standard* as each one came in and took on slow substance in the yellow gloom. Godwin was wetting himself over Shapiro, and the phone call from Kellett had given him kittens. Patrick Hyde's attention was slow, incurious. He seemed more attentive to the soundless cricket on the television screen behind the bar.

David Reid, HM Secretary of State for Trade and Industry, occupied much of the newspaper's front page. There was a large photograph that seemed placed especially to irritate him. Reid was shaking hands with Alexander Dubček, in the Hradcany Castle in Prague. The frail, smiling figure of Dubček, more substantial than a mere ghost from the past, was potent, and a reminder of change. *Othello's occupation's gone . . .* Aubrey had said, being lugubriously clever when Hyde had accused the old man of seconding them to the DTI. All the real bloody good they were doing there! Letting them carry on smuggling microchips and maybe transputers and wafer scale integration technology, for all they knew, was not all that different from selling them laptop computers, telecommunications, microwaves and bloody fridges. Who *really* gave a stuff, anyway? Not even paranoid capitalists like the Yanks, it seemed, now that Shapiro was dead. Besides, in a year, we'll be *selling* them WSI and transputers and anything else they want, because they pay in hard currency bought with their massive gold reserves.

David Reid's picture . . . on his tour of newly-democratized eastern Europe, drumming up business. Hyde recognized the faces of at least four of the party surrounding Reid and Dubček. MDs and chairmen of large UK companies. Christ, what a comedown. He rubbed his stubbled cheek and sniffed loudly, turning to the back page then folding the newspaper at the racing section. Royal-bloody Ascot. He fished in the inside pocket of his grubby cotton jacket for a ballpen and began marking his selections from the afternoon's races. Glanced up at a shadow flung through the door – no – and then looked down once more.

Reid Electronics Group. If they were going to do the job properly, then they needed to bug the company offices in the NatWest Tower. But Orrell wouldn't let them. Hyde shook his head, smiling sardonically. Prissy old bugger. Can't upset a company like Reid, or its former major shareholder and founder, the Secretary of State for Selling England by the Pound. Reid had made another fortune when he'd sold his shareholding in the Reid group in the aftermath of the Harrell business. Of course he didn't know anything about it, and of course his shareholding was in the hands of his stockbrokers while he served in the government – all very proper – and he was even more decent and only made another ten million or whatever out of publically divesting himself of the family holding in Reid.

Oh, stop moaning. He looked up at the television behind the bar as he sipped at the glass of lager. Someone was walking back, head bowed, from the wicket, bat dragging. The scoreboard appeared, showing 57–4. It could only be England batting. He grinned. Against his lot, the Aussies, too. Perhaps he could skive off for a couple of hours that afternoon and watch some of it. Plenty of blokes he knew would be there, corks on their hats, the tinnies going down like ninepins. More of a laugh than waiting here for Kellett. He returned his concentration to his betting permutations. Godwin was obsessive about the Reid Electronics Group, but he wasn't wrong. His contact inside Reid, Kellett, was already – he looked at his watch – twenty minutes late. *Urgent*, Kellett had said. *I think I've really stumbled on something this time* . . . Kellett needed to, to justify the money that had been spent on him. Christ, I'm bored.

He rose in search of a refilled glass, then sat down again as Kellett, his contact, resolved himself from the black lump he had appeared in the doorway. Young, Yuppiefied, with too much expenditure on a salary required to stretch twice round the gasworks and once round Ros. Back in April, he'd persuaded Shelley to pay off the man's most pressing credit card bills and supply enough pocket-money to last a couple of champagne and smoked salmon weeks, and they'd had a man inside Reid Electronics' head office who couldn't be helpful enough. Falling over himself to offer them the gen – most of it duff. Until now? He willed the younger man to go

23

straight up to the bar. Instead, he hesitated, nodded to Hyde, then moved to order a drink.

Did Kellett have something, at last? He appeared tense, but that was usual when they met. Part of the game – the game Aubrey had worn himself out playing, so some quack in Harley Street diagnosed nervous exhaustion and a touch – *only a touch, mind, nothing to worry about* – of angina. *Take a month's rest.* So Aubrey was sitting, feet up, in his flat, or dawdling around the garden of his Oxfordshire cottage, while this operation he'd started trickled on, tired and aimless.

Another shadow in the doorway. Hyde hardly glanced at the man because he was with a young woman and they were talking loudly and laughing as they came through the doorway. His accent, as he asked for two glasses of white wine, was faultlessly upper-middle class, Oxbridge, Julian-and-Nigel. Baggy suit, loosened tie, fashionable haircut; there were another six just like him in the pub at that moment. The girl was smiling – too much, Hyde realized. And her eyes were hardly still for a moment; except when she glanced at his corner of the room. She leant against her companion as in sexual conspiracy. Kellett paid for his half-bottle of red wine and began moving towards Hyde – who nodded his head with one small, abrupt gesture and waggled his newspaper towards the open door. Keep away, the signal announced. Just in case. Was the girl anything but over-confidently vain, arrogant with money or narcissism? Trying to decide was like cleaning a rusty old garden implement suddenly and unexpectedly required. He gripped the newspaper tightly. Kellett went to a table on the other side of the doorway. The girl's head kept moving, smooth as a typewriter carriage. She seemed unconvinced by the distance between Hyde and Kellett. Yes, he *was* convinced. The man with her was her cover. She glanced across the pub once more at Hyde's corner. She was, presumably, one of Priabin's new intake, fresh from some Moscow training school. Priabin ordered ersatz Yuppies and Sloanes by the barrow-load to blend with his image of London. The training school was doing a good job. Hyde did not recognize her. No one really bothered any more. The Heathrow photographs arrived from the Branch, via MI5, weeks late these days – one long bloody holiday while the container-lorries packed with microwaves and televisions queued at Dover, all labelled Prague or Warsaw or Bucharest.

He picked up his empty glass, rose and walked towards the bar, even as the girl, chin raised, continued to scan the room as if seeking items for a gossip column. Her arrogance was a little too perfect, her condescension towards the pub's occupants clockwork in its precision. Hyde waved the newspaper stiffly behind his back, warning Kellett to leave. He reached the bar and placed his glass on it, ordering another pint.

The girl was in her early twenties, dressed in a wide floral skirt and black, shiny cotton top, her narrow shoulders and small breasts drowned in a baggy designer jacket. The cricketers drifted off the miniature green field of the screen, for lunch. The room seemed more smoky, noisier, and Hyde admitted the tension that the tiny, unimportant proximity of himself and the girl generated. A casserole hissed on a hotplate with the smell of cheap red wine. The girl's companion laughed at something she appeared to whisper, but the sound was tight in his throat. The girl studied him with deliberate indifference, then lit a cigarette. Hyde raised his filled glass to his lips, picked up his change –

– the lager poured over the designer jacket and the cotton top. The girl had nudged his elbow. He looked round momentarily. Kellett, alert, remained seated.

'You drunken pig!' the girl screamed at him, the accent perfect and perfectly outraged. She brushed frantically at her jacket, her cheeks reddened with anger, her eyes glittering with calculation. The man acting as her cover and minder moved purposefully closer to Hyde. 'Look what you've *done!*' There was an almost-silence in the pub.

'I'm sorry, I – my fault,' he muttered, drawn into the charade as the man pressed against him.

'It's *you* again!' the man shouted into Hyde's face. 'I've warned you before to stay away from Nicky!' His accent, too, was studied and under control, despite the simulated anger.

Serious. The artificially created situation was being hurried, deepened. Kellett was watching them now, bemused, hardly afraid – yet.

'I don't know you,' Hyde muttered thickly, swaying slightly,

25

half-raising one hand. The barman leant over and clutched his wrist.

'None of that in here. You've had enough, friend. Apologize –' He sounded puzzled, as if his expert judgement had been compromised. Hyde was suddenly drunk. 'You know this bloke, miss?'

' – neighbour. A drunk. Pesters Nicky all the time,' the cover man explained. He was taller than Hyde, his frame tensed against the necessity of sudden movement. He knew who he was dealing with, it was obvious – the type if not the individual.

Kellett had become just another member of the audience, who were beginning to settle as to an intriguingly unfolding drama. Sexual inadequacy, drunkenness; a soap opera in miniature. The two Russians were working to a good script. It had depth, needed an audience. Hyde, forced to comply, swayed more deliberately, aggressively, hoping that Kellett would understand, would leave.

'Piss off!'

'Watch the language,' the barman warned.

The girl had removed the designer jacket and was regarding it with appalled fascination.

'Four hundred it cost me! You've ruined it! Jimmy, get him to *pay* for it!' Someone laughed.

'You jogged my elbow,' Hyde protested.

'I did *not*! You lurched against me. Why can't you leave me alone – stop following me everywhere!'

'Is he – ?'

'Fuck off,' Hyde snapped at the barman.

'Mate, if it's trouble you're looking for –' A bulky figure rose from one of the bench seats under the window, purple, ruby and gold falling from the stained glass onto his clothes and face like diamonds, then sliding off like oil as he moved. No, there were two of them . . . not Russians, just the unofficial bouncers for when the Yuppies started throwing empty bottles and plates and throwing up.

'Trouble, George?'

Kellett was sitting like a rabbit in front of a car's rushing headlights. Go on, bugger off! Go home, go anywhere – I'll find you. It was more serious than he had recognized. It was a deliberate separation ploy, to get Kellett on his own. Isolate him.

*I think I'm really onto something. It's important – worth a lot – I know*

26

*it is.* Oh, yes, he'd replied, bored. Kellett had called him at Centre Point. Godwin had handed him the phone. Kellett exaggerated, they all did when they were on the hook and greedy. Now, he knew the man really did have something valuable. So did they, though God knew how. The information was so good they'd worked like mad to get this dangerous, complex charade organized in less than a couple of hours. Followed Kellett, yes, but they must have checked out the meeting place, even to spotting the potentially useful bouncers – who were paused on the lip of the inexorable progression of the situation as it moved on oiled wheels. *I'm sure it's what you've been looking for.* He hadn't believed Kellett –

– who had to get out now. While Hyde could still keep all of them occupied. Kellett was tense and bemused and suspicious but still seated. The girl was still dabbing at her sodden top and jacket, convincing Kellett that this was arbitrary, accidental. Hyde gripped the edge of the bar with one hand, lurching to attention.

'I don't know either of you.'

'You lying pillock! You hang around the flats, watching Nicky. You've been doing it for months. The police have even warned you off –' The man's eyes gleamed, darting once to the bulk of the two bouncers. Gog and Magog, the Brothers Grim. They looked eminently capable of inflicting efficient, brutal damage. It was almost bloody laughable, the way he'd been pulled into the situation.

'I bloody don't –!' he protested to the barman, extending the fiction, attempting to hold the Russians within the circumstances they had created for long enough to allow Kellett to decide to leave. Bugger off! He waved his arms at the room. 'I don't bloody know either of them!' The bouncers despised him and, where he had been comic to the rest of the pub a moment before, the sexual innuendo had made him arachnid, something that scuttled for the express purpose of being trodden upon. The girl glared at him, shaking her head violently.

'He does! He's known to the police – I had to report him to the police for watching me!' Oh, bloody hell, but you're *good.* Her voice was one a genuine Sloane would have had to practise assiduously to acquire. Perfect. It convinced the loose suits and vivid ties, the louche young men and the languorous girls. The trap was beautiful in its architecture, speed, manner of execution. The Russians now controlled the whole room.

'Oh, piss off, darling – I don't know you! Who'd fancy you, anyway, with tits that small?' He leaned towards the cover man. 'I don't know *you*, either!' The situation had to degenerate quickly into violence, which was inevitable, anyway. The bouncers intended to be the *deus ex machina*, the nemesis. They stirred like Rottweilers barely under leash. 'I'm bloody off, then, if my custom's not –'

He turned from the bar, staggered a little to giggles from the room, shoulders seedily sloped, acting the role they had created for him, even wiping a loose mouth with the back of his hand. He saw the girl and her cover exchange a quick, suspicious glance. The man looked towards Kellett. The sunlight glowed through the open door. Kellett was on his feet at once, but still hesitating, not realizing –

'What about my *jacket*?'

And the nearest of the two bouncers was in front of Hyde, large splayed hand thrust against his chest.

'You heard, mate. What about the lady's jacket?' The mock-Victorian veneer of the place came away like old paint. The bouncer's eyes were wary but confident, the swollen stomach bulging over his waistband irrelevant when dealing with a drunk of much smaller stature.

'Piss off – now!' Hyde growled, staring beyond the bouncer, directly at Kellett –

– who nodded, wiped his lips and turned through the door. Black in the sunlight. Now, just get past this drongo and catch up with –

He head-butted the bouncer, who staggered back, noise of breaking bone drowned by his squeal of pain. The second bouncer struck him in the kidneys before he could turn, and Hyde staggered and was hit again, then a third time. Glancing blows. No one believed he was drunk now, but it didn't matter. Blood covered the first bouncer's face, a larger, uglier badge than the lights from the stained glass on his clothes as he lay slumped near the door, a table overturned beside him, beer puddling on the carpet. Someone was complaining their trousers had been stained.

Hyde turned, but his legs were kicked from under him. The girl was struggling into the sodden jacket, and the man's shadow

28

already blocked the doorway. They were going after Kellett and he couldn't get out –

A heavy shoe in his ribs. He rolled away. Noises of an audience pleased at the violence happening to a stranger. His ribs burned, his kidneys ached. The first bouncer staggered to his feet and came lurching towards him. As his foot swung, Hyde grabbed and twisted the man off-balance. The second bouncer kicked him in the thigh as he climbed to his feet, and he lurched against the bar. A glass fumbled itself into his grip. The barman was already on the telephone, the damage mounting to unacceptable levels, too high just for the pleasure of seeing him get a kicking. Hyde broke the glass and thrust it forward. The bouncers hesitated, then someone encouraged them. The girl and her cover had disappeared. Christ, what a cock-up –

'Come on, sport!' he taunted. 'I'll have your face off!'

Hurry up, you berk! he yelled silently at the barman who was gabbling at the receiver and staring at him. Beyond the bouncers, there were others stirring now, like the beginnings of a pack, as if they wore fur, not suits and frocks. Everyone wanted a little taste of the concoction the Russians had manufactured, the dangerous, heady flavour of violence. Except for the broken beer glass in his hand, they'd be circling him now.

Hurry up . . . Godwin's last lead into the Reid Group has just walked out of here with the KGB on his tail! Bloody hurry it up –

'Look, I couldn't get here any sooner!' Godwin roared at Hyde, lurching round on his sticks to face him. 'Terry Chambers has the Malan surveillance, young Darren is otherwise engaged, and I've been trying to cobble together a report which will persuade Orrell to let us carry on with this bloody, cocked-up investigation! All right?'

On the television screen behind the station sergeant's desk, a late news programme was repeating film of David Reid toasting his Czech hosts in an ornate room, beneath chandeliers. Everyone was smiling, and appeared content to the point of smugness.

'I've been sitting in a bloody cell all afternoon, for Christ's sake – because PC Plod and his mates didn't believe me without ID. And I didn't have my bloody ID, did I?' Hyde tugged his jacket over his shoulders, wincing at the renewed pain in his kidneys and ribs.

'Are you all right?'

'Nothing broken,' the sergeant at the desk murmured without looking up from his newspaper. 'The doc had a good look at him.' He glanced up then, malevolently. 'That car got there before *he* did any more damage – to himself or anyone else.' He glowered at Hyde. 'You will tell your friends you *can* find a copper when you need one, won't you?' Then he tossed his head and returned to his crossword, sucking the end of his pencil. A drunk sat slumped against the opposite wall, smelling of beer and vomit, his face grey with stubble and decline.

'What's what, then?' Hyde asked, then called back over his shoulder: 'I peed on the blanket before I left!' and laughed.

'Christ, Patrick, no wonder you put people's backs up!'

'Look, I was in there for hours and no one was in the slightest bit interested. They were too busy looking for witnesses!'

'Shame about democracy, isn't it? Gets in the way.'

'They were about to charge me with actual bodily harm, for Christ's sake!'

'Oh, calm down. What happened to the Russians?'

'They went after Kellett. What would you expect? What have you done about it?'

Godwin looked intensely glum. 'Nothing, yet – except get you out of choky.'

'Christ, I sometimes wonder about you!' Hyde exclaimed. 'Either Kellett has information – a lifebelt – or he hasn't. But we'd better grab hold of something! Come on.'

The car that had brought Godwin was parked fifty yards along Old Jewry from the police station. The driver sat upright from his dozing slouch as Hyde opened the door. Godwin struggled into the rear seat and Hyde slumped in beside him.

'Kellett's flat – Docklands.' Hyde gave the address. 'I told you on the phone, when I finally managed to reach you and you deigned to take my call, that he might need protection. But you've been too busy watching your arse to bother!' He sat back against his seat, feet thrust up like a child against the front passenger seat, and looked at his watch. Eleven.

'I didn't do anything because I was too busy trying to salvage something from this bloody mess!' Godwin snapped.

'All right – don't throw a wobbly. Kellett is about all we can salvage from this bloody fiasco, mate. You should have realized that.'

The bulk of the Bank of England disappeared in the wing mirror.

'Is he in any real danger?'

'God knows. He got out of there, eventually, as if his trousers were on fire. But, they went after him. Let's hope they didn't catch him. Christ, it was a smooth enough operation.'

'And you fell right in.'

'Kellett didn't call the office until ten-thirty. By twelve-thirty, they had the whole thing up and running.'

Eastcheap, then the Tower, strange as a dream, a folly beached amid the concrete and lights.

'What could he have turned up, all of a sudden? He wasn't just scared, was he?'

'What of?'

'I don't know! It's just that he hasn't been much use to us before.'

'How did they even *know* about him?' Hyde asked. 'Unless they've got the tap into Reid Electronics that we're not allowed! What a bloody laugh if that's true. Turn Sir Clive purple, that will – have to order an extra-strong chota peg before dinner.' Hyde turned to Godwin. 'It's fucked, isn't it, if Kellett's dead?' Godwin nodded lugubriously. The Royal Mint loomed ahead. 'Shit.'

Eventually, Limehouse intruded on their oppressive silence. New flats along the river, which was skeletal with lights, the blocks crowding above newly-fashionable streets and smart alleys. Hyde was wound like a spring as the driver turned right and began to patrol the walls, the ornamental gates, the brick-paved causeways and mock-jetties. Porsches, though fewer than before, BMWs clustered like flies, the noise from wine bars and discos coming to them through the window Hyde had opened. Smell of the river. Hyde sniffed as a leggy girl sprang from an Escort cabriolet, laughing, long hair moving as in a shampoo advertisement.

'This is it,' he announced, tapping the driver on the shoulder. 'That one over there.'

The driver rasped on the handbrake opposite a geometrical, subdued-brick block of flats, jutting and crenellated like the wall of a castle; as if the place required defending from the surrounding countryside and its inhabitants. Hyde got out and breathed deeply.

31

Kellett lived on the seventh floor, overlooking the river. He couldn't afford the flat and his lifestyle, especially his cocaine intake, not with high interest rates and the BMW and the very expensive hi-fi. Godwin stumped along beside him towards the foyer. Hyde pressed the video-entryphone for Kellett's flat – again, then a third time. He looked darkly at Godwin.

'Police ID?' Godwin nodded, and Hyde pressed the resident porter's bell. Eventually:

'Who is it?'

'CID. Let us in. We want to see Mr Kellett. He's not answering his bell.' Godwin dutifully held up the warrant card at the eye of the entryphone.

'Very well.' The doors buzzed and Hyde pushed against them.

'Careless sod – either that or he's got wonderful eyesight.' A closed, stale-cooking scent in the foyer, and in the lift. 'I'm glad he's not my porter.'

'Ros hardly lets *you* back in.'

The lift sighed up. Hyde said, quietly: 'I should have warned you – you're right. I should have.'

'We're here now,' Godwin replied, acknowledging what appeared to be a grudging apology. The door of the lift soughed open, then clunked, the noise announcing the silence of the carpeted corridor. Another stale smell. 'Which one?'

'Flat 62 – this is 61 –' Hyde walked down the corridor.

'You look like a man dying for a pee,' Godwin remarked, leaning against the wall.

'Here we are.'

The noise of music more appropriate to the lift sounded in Hyde's ears as he pressed the bell of the flat. Coming from inside. The bastard was in. Godwin clumped softly towards him across the carpet speckled with marks and a lack of Hoovering. Black dustbin bags outside a farther door. The noise that could come only from satellite television from somewhere else – an American football commentator. Hyde pressed the bell again, and heard the buzzing just above the volume of the hi-fi. Twenty thousand quid to play that rubbish, he thought. A right drongo, hardly in the real world, just holding on lightly to it by his fingertips.

'He hasn't put his bags out for the porter, then.'

'He bloody hasn't.'

Hyde knelt down and lifted the letter-flap.

'Well?'

'Fancy half-stairs – can't see a bloody thing.'

'Well?'

'Smell gas, can you?'

'Quite possibly.'

Hyde kicked the fragile door – compressed shavings, by the look of the inside of the letter-flap and no Banham locks. It opened at the third attempt, and he stumbled into the flat. Four stairs led up directly into an open-plan lounge. The smell of still-new carpet and half-dried plaster, and the whiff of static in his nostrils from the hi-fi, and something else. Pictures on the walls, posters and prints.

'Who in hell told him to invest in this stuff?' Godwin asked. 'No wonder he's hard up. All from Bond Street and Mayfair galleries – look, all signed, limited editions.' The enlarged, monochrome print of a moonrise over an open field which Hyde had noticed and which Godwin now recognized. 'You know how much the old bugger sells prints of *that* for, don't you?' he murmured. 'Whatever his bloody name is . . . ?' Hyde shrugged.

Hyde glanced at the room. Leather furniture, Chinese rugs that were hardly less expensive in Hong Kong than Mayfair. The hi-fi's large speakers and perhaps a dozen boxes to produce the noise that was coming from them. And the limited edition prints and posters on the walls . . . and the old, leather-bound books – he picked a Dickens from a shelf and checked its date; first edition, naturally. The room was a library, a gallery, a means of exhibition and invest-ment. With borrowed and overspent funds. Hedging against a rainy day and creating bad weather at the same time. The room was – greedy, too. An octogenarian's pride belonging to a boy of twenty-five who couldn't wait. Perhaps his parents in the country had endowed him with the taste, and the appetite. It was empty, too, and silent except for the noise from the hi-fi.

'What sort of life does he think he's living?' Hyde asked. 'Who is he trying to impress?'

'A string of birds or doting parents?'

'Or not doting – or not even well-off,' seeming to gain some other insight from the room. Before he saw Kellett's ankles and shoes protruding from behind the huge leather Chesterfield. 'He won't be doing much of either any more, will he?'

'Oh, shit,' Godwin breathed, his look accusing.

Hyde knelt by the – body it certainly was. The young features stared up at him uncomplainingly. There was a spillage of nausea and his whisky glass near his cheek and dribbling on his chin. No pulse. Flesh warm, soft. The small sheet of foil, the lighter and the inhaler were not on the coffee table simply casually or of necessity, then. They were evidence, they were deception. The smell of the crack in the room was deliberate – that bloody Russian-actress-Sloane-cow!

Godwin loomed over him, breathing heavily.

'He'll have had a heart attack, as well, I expect, just to complete the trinity – it's so bloody clichéd who could resist believing it?'

'Not Orrell, that's for certain,' Hyde murmured.

Godwin stumped away on his sticks, muttering: 'Someone's nailing up the exit doors one by one, before they set fire to the cinema.'

Hyde stared at the pale, young face, then turned towards Godwin, who was dialling a number on the cellular phone he had picked up from the coffee table, where it had been lying beside the silver foil and the inhaler and the white granules that looked like chips of almond.

'What did the tart look like Shapiro took up to his room?' Hyde asked.

'What? Oh, a tart – white – about catalogues the description in detail.'

'In this case, tell that old fart Orrell he'd better let us bug Reid Electronics – or find us something else to do!'


It was a DC-3, an old Dakota, in desert camouflage, still and broken. The starboard wing was cracked like a fractured arm. A gouge in the red earth of the Bush stretched behind the wreck, stencilled by a line of broken trees and spreadeagled bushes. The crash was recent. A thin, last skein of oily smoke rose from the port engine.

Richard Anderson slowed the Land Rover some sixty yards from the shattered aeroplane, on the crest of a dune-like rise, and leaned his forearms on the steering wheel, studying the Dakota. He was prompted by no sense of possible survivors, certain that the crew were dead. His beard scratched his neck as he repeatedly shook his head. He could picture the plane's interior vividly, ribbed, skeletal, half made-up. Birds climbed into the heat of the early morning, and his arms were reddened by the sun rising behind him, throwing the bulky shadow of the Land Rover and himself down the slope towards the wrecked Dakota. There was dust on the fuselage, dulling the glint of metal and glass. Eagles and their prey, songbirds and hunters, moved above him. He heard the noises of wings and throats as the shock of his discovery became tangible. Why had the plane crashed out here? There had been no storm the previous night in Windhoek. The old aircraft lay as if beached by some great wave on the reddish, sandy soil. He could smell the slow, safe leakage of aviation fuel on the hardly-stirring morning air.

From the vantage of the rise, he could see for miles in every direction. He was alone in that part of the Bush. The gouge that the plane had excavated pointed west, towards the coast and Walvis Bay. Curiosity finally itched in his frame, and he put the Land Rover into gear and the vehicle bumped and heaved itself down the shallow slope. The blue flash of a lizard crossed his path and disappeared. A long, dappled neck swerved away from the far side of the DC-3 then the giraffe sailed into view, only half-startled, loping away with an easy stride. He passed dry, baked, grey trees.

A white blob that was an expressionless face hung as if thrust against the pilot's side window, staring blindly down at him through the dust-smeared perspex. There was a dark stain across the man's cheek, from his ear. He was alone −?

The Dakota's camouflage paint might have been military, but the fuselage carried no insignia and no company logo. Where had it been heading, then? It was at least a hundred miles off-course if it was flying from Walvis Bay to anywhere in South Africa, carrying whatever freight. Black hair draped stickily across the broad forehead of the dead face in the cockpit.

Anderson climbed out of the Land Rover, muscles creaking. His right hand stroked along the fuselage. Dust on his fingers. He moved to the starboard engine. The pool of leaking aviation fuel was still wet. The aircraft must have crashed just before dawn, little more than an hour earlier. He studied the sky with a movement as involuntary as a nervous tic. Empty. Cautiously, he moved around the silent plane until he reached the main cabin door, which had lurched open during the crash. He gripped the door frame with both hands and pulled himself into the hold. No one. Only boxes and crates emerged from the gloom as his eyes adjusted to the blackness of the interior. Stencilled lettering on the lashed-down cargo, even torn labels. As he remained poised in the doorway, the silence of the hold seemed more oppressive than that of the Bush around the wreck, as if a great charge of electricity had been left unearthed. The hair on his forearms and neck prickled with it.

A lizard, already intruding, scuttled away from his boots as he moved forward towards the cockpit door. His hand hesitated on the handle. Scraped-away words and instructions on the metal, in Afrikaans and English. Military –? Carefully, he pushed open the door and ducked into the narrow cockpit.

There were two of them, he realized, flinching against the mass of flies that rose from the bodies then settled slowly again to feed. The pilot's face was pressed against the side window while the co-pilot's body was folded over its seatbelt like an abandoned ventriloquist's dummy. His head was down, his neck resting on the cup of the control column's wheel-like grips; a man waiting for some imagined guillotine blade's descent. The flies were congregated around the mouths and noses and ears of the two men, making the streaks of blood black and viscous. He studied the infested faces, and the almost identical clothes on the bodies. Sandy-coloured bush jackets; pale corduroy trousers on the pilot, grubby cotton slacks on the other man. Not military, then. He leaned forward, his hand hesitating above the co-pilot's bush jacket. Flies drifted towards him, inspecting the perspiration on his forehead and beneath his arms. It was many years since he had seen any dead body other than that of the occasional elephant poacher shot by the patrols. Swallowing, he patted the pockets. A small bulk in the co-pilot's back pocket. He raised the body, growling as if to keep the flies at bay, and removed a scuffed, misshapen leather wallet. Then, with the flies and the smell of blood slowly nauseating him, he searched the pilot's body. Nothing. Strangely, nothing at all; no identification.

Growling again at the flies, he flailed his arms at them and slammed the cockpit door behind him. If the clock on the instrument panel had been stopped by the impact, the Dakota had crashed no more than forty minutes earlier. The flies that had accompanied him slowly dispersed. It was hotter in the hold, now.

Nothing on the instrument panel appeared to explain the cause of the crash. A dry breeze puffed and threw dust in through the cabin door.

He knelt on the floor of the hold beside a crate stencilled in English. A name and a company logo had been all but obscured with a smear of black paint. In the light from the open door, he opened the wallet. Namibian currency, some high-denomination rand notes. A snapshot and a piece of folded card. A photograph of a young woman holding a baby in her arms, with the drab, wide desolation of some city square behind her. He turned the snapshot over. The woman's name, that of the child, and the place and date, all recorded in a flourishing hand. Church towers, he had noticed, onion-domed in the distance behind the woman. *Novgorod, 1989.* The snapshot quivered in his hand. The piece of folded card was red. The co-pilot's photograph and name, the same as that of the woman. A sort of passport, or warrant card. He understood Russian. He'd seen such things before. It was a KGB warrant card.

The legend on the crate nearest him was distinct enough to recognize. *Reid Electronics Group, plc. United Kingdom.* His eyes glanced from the snapshot to the KGB identification, to the crate – snapshot, card, crate –

The pilot, presumably, had been intent upon concealing his identity. Was he South African? The Russian had not wanted to leave his wallet or his wife's image behind, nor his official identity. *Novgorod, 1989. Reid Electronics, United Kingdom.* He stood up stiffly and quickly, thrusting the card and snapshot into the wallet and the wallet into his back pocket. He was seized, momentarily, by a desire to escape from the hold, to leave the place; only slowly did he understand the resurrection of old impulses, old instincts, as if his present self had been elbowed roughly aside by the younger, trained person he had once been. He was sweating again and could hear his heartbeat in the silence of the hold.

Calmed himself, gradually, breathing deeply. The crate had been loosened from its restraints by the impact, had moved and become damaged. It contained television sets, the inscription claimed. Colour televisions. Other crates contained microwave ovens, others portable hi-fi sets . . . ridiculous to find a mystery here. He glanced at the cockpit door. A KGB guard for *microwaves*, televisions? He pulled at a long splinter of wood on the damaged crate, then another, exposing –

Not television sets. What, he was not certain. He snatched the emergency axe from its clips on the fuselage, and chopped crudely. The wood splintered, came away.

Stout polythene and polystyrene chips protecting the contents. Their unfamiliarity, as he tugged and ripped open one package, disappointed him. Transistorized units, a tiny personal computer-like keypad. Another package – something like a transceiver. *Infra-red*, he caught on one package. His younger self urged him. He snatched up packages wrapped in bubbly polythene or in cardboard.

He did not know what they contained, only that they were –

– proof. Of something untoward. The temperature was becoming unbearable in the hold of the Dakota. His present, fifty-three-year-old self attempted to protest, *this is simply a crashed old aircraft filled with civilian freight*, but he was aware of the bulge of the Russian's wallet in his back pocket. Ridiculous, this, he told himself as he carried the armful of packages to the Land Rover, his frame slightly stunned from the small jump onto the reddish, sandy soil. He flung the packages into the back of the vehicle and whirled round giddily. Hot. An eagle soared, but the sky was otherwise empty. They would be looking for the aircraft.

He hurried back to the Dakota and climbed with a great effort into the hold. Stumbled forward to the cockpit door, hesitated, then opened it onto the ascending cloud of flies. He searched the pockets of the doors, the nets above the dead men, the shelf beneath the instrument panel – nothing. No flight plan, nothing. Further proof. He looked balefully at the Russian, obscurely blaming the man for his panic. He swatted and flailed at the flies, then fled the cockpit and jumped down once more onto the sand, aware for the first time of the crowded scuffings of his footprints, of the tyre tracks of the Land Rover leading down the rise to the Dakota. He brushed his forehead, at a loss.

Soon, they'd be here. The black dot in the sky was still an eagle or a vulture, not an enlarging aircraft or helicopter. A KGB officer as co-pilot for a civilian flight carrying freight without a flight plan. He had no idea what it meant, though he did know he was afraid, was panicked by what he had found. He shook his head like a wounded bull.

The dry breeze rattled hard dust against the flank of the Land Rover. He knew, despite the seductive attractions of panic and flight, that he must stay. He had to hide the vehicle and find a vantage-point, and school himself to wait. Not for long . . . they'd be desperate to find what the Dakota contained. And he had to know who came looking for it. High-technology disguised as televisions and microwaves. Deliberation and forethought. Disguise. A KGB officer in Namibia, dead in the cockpit of an old Dakota –

He breathed deeply.

The pale sky seemed to tremble with heat, like a piece of cloth moving in the breeze. Wipe out the tracks of the vehicle and his own footprints, and then hide. No, first go back and replace the axe in its clips, wipe the edge of the blade free of wood chippings. Make the damage to the boxes and crates – so much of it and unnecessary, it seemed now – look as if it was the result of the impact. After *that*, hide.


'Sit down, Godwin.'

The view from Sir Clive Orrell's spacious offices as Director General of SIS looked out over the river, and always seemed, once he had begun a conversation in his habitual, blunt, authoritarian way, to face deliberately in the other direction from the Palace of Westminster. The offices were eyrie-like. Christ, I'm beginning to sound like Duncan Campbell or the *Guardian*, he realized. On the other hand, Hyde had once called this place Berchtesgarten-over-Thames, though only after Orrell had taken up residence as DG.

Orrell gestured to a chair drawn up in front of his massive mahogany desk, then wandered briefly to the window. A pigeon looked, in the hot morning light, more than usually supplicatory. Perhaps it was used to Orrell's lack of open-handedness. Know how you feel, son. Aubrey had handed them back to SIS and Orrell's control when he went off ill; but he'd resigned all real interest in the investigation when they'd been unable to find anything suspicious in February, when they'd gone through Reid Group like bloodhounds. Orrell, too, was about to renege on any interest he'd ever shown. Pilate soap, the scent of the season.

'Thank you, sir,' he murmured obsequiously. Orrell never wearied of deference.

He glimpsed his report to Orrell on the desk, together with one headed Grosvenor Square and with the CIA symbol in the corner. Not a promising sight.

He placed his sticks behind the chair and lumped himself down into its squeaky protest. Leather, like the furniture of the entire office, as if Orrell had once seen some televised drama of Whitehall life and specifically noted only the appointments and furniture the sets had displayed.

'You wanted to see me, sir?'

Orrell, apparently irritated by the importunate pigeon, turned from the window and walked to his desk.

'Yes, Godwin – simply to tell you that I have –' Here he tapped at the sheaf of papers on his desk. '– a full report from Grosvenor Square regarding the suicide of that man Shapiro, and on the basis of this report, I'm – about to stand down your unit.' Without even looking at Godwin, he held up his hand for continued silence as he patrolled the wall behind his desk where the obligatory portrait of the monarch looked rather glumly at the print to its right, apparently disapproving of the arrangement of dead pheasants and fruit; though that idea was as peculiar as Orrell's taste in art. 'It is my decision, Godwin, and not taken lightly –' Or inadvisedly, sir, like marriage with the CIA? '– indeed, taken after the most careful consideration and advice.' He paused at the window once more. The pigeon was persistent in its puzzlement and pecked at the glass, slightly startling Orrell with his dark suit and ample bulk, outlined against the hot blue sky. 'I think you have – with the utmost care and diligence, of course – taken this matter as far as is possible.'

Godwin thought of Shelley, to whom Aubrey had originally handed him and Hyde and Chambers. Shelley had been immediately sidelined on some high-sounding European security service amalgamation in Berlin. Orrell, recognizing Aubrey's acolyte, had – he thought – avoided being stabbed by posting Shelley back into Europe. After that, it was evident that the wind of scepticism was blowing through SIS – or the limp breeze of all-eyes-on-the-pension and the GCMG!

Orrell was a caretaker – or care-avoider, depending on how you looked at it – a gentleman-in-waiting until the Cabinet Secretary got round to deciding the future shape and purpose of the service.

Still, pompous old sod, the Yanks liked him. He was even more stupid than *their* Director.

'I see, sir. You've, er, read my report on the death of Mr Kellett, the man we had inside – '

'The employee you suborned – to no good purpose, as it turns out.' Orrell glowered. 'A drug addict with a ridiculously expensive lifestyle! You have wasted thousands of the service's funds on that worthless little man, just to have him overdose on you!'

'Yes, sir.' It was hopeless, as he knew it would be. Orrell wouldn't feel the shock of the new or unexpected if it hit him between the eyes, like a garden rake he'd absent-mindedly stepped on. He removed the beginnings of the smirk from his face.

'You must admit, Godwin, that this pernicious and wrongheaded crusade of yours against the Reid Electronics Group and its associated companies has now come to a halt. That it has run out of fuel? This man Shapiro had evidently been hounded to the point of suicide by the heavy-handed methods of the Americans, which you seem so much to admire. Thus, the service is left with one suicide, one drug overdose, and your unwarranted suspicions that the Russians must be up to something big because they're murdering half the population of the capital!' The rhetorical flourish was evidently one he had rehearsed, he seemed so delighted with it.

'No, sir – '

Orrell turned to face him.

'The CIA is admitting they are at a dead end, Godwin – *you* are not. Why, pray?'

Surprising Orrell and himself, Godwin yawned. 'Sorry, sir – sleeping badly.' Orrell nodded his acceptance of the fiction.

'I have talked with the Foreign Office and with the DS, and I have come to the conclusion that I have no choice but to desist from wasting the service's funding on this operation. It is stood down from this moment in time.'

'Sir – ' he pleaded.

It was the tone that Orrell seemed to have been awaiting. He burst out righteously:

'You exhausted Kenneth Aubrey's patience and probably his health, and now you seem determined to exhaust mine! Godwin, this business is becoming an obsession with you. The Malan group of companies has withdrawn from Reid, entirely. There is no, repeat *no*, connection even hinted at between the Russians and the Reid Group. Your own theories become more bizarre the moment they are confronted by any facts. Now, we have two so-called murders on the same day, to support your continuing with this farce! It will not do, Godwin – it simply will no longer *do*.' He waved a hand in Godwin's vague direction.

'That's all I have to say. You would appear to have a few days' leave due – I suggest you take them and report to your section head at the beginning of next week. I commend your diligence, and deplore your lack of rationality. Goodbye, Godwin.'

'Goodbye, sir.'

He collected his sticks and stumped across the acres of carpet to the door. The pigeon had already departed. Presumably, it had witnessed Orrell rehearsing his outrage before Godwin's arrival. He heard Orrell squeak into his leather chair and then the rustle of papers and their deposition in one of the desk's drawers. End of story. His last six months' work. Christ, was it really *easier* to believe that the KGB had suddenly become neater and cleaner than the Mormons?

He avoided all eye-contact with Orrell's secretary and the young aide who leaned over her desk, long hair flopping, rugby club tie bristling. More prop forwards in SIS than a British Lions touring party, Hyde claimed. Adding that all rugby players were closet poofters, just by way of a variation of prejudice. Lady Orrell evidently hadn't yet inspected the new secretary, who was good-looking, a class act. Dumb as a Swiss finishing school could make her, of course.

He reached the corridor and even the lift before his face collapsed into anger. He realized he was sweating. His tie seemed about to throttle him, his shirt as enclosing as armour.

Give it up? Sod *you*, sir!

TWO

# the isle is full of noises

The sun was high now, no longer dust-tinged a nightmarish red as it had been at dawn when he had discovered the DC-3. The dust hung in the distance now, like an horizon, solid-seeming as a range of distant, hazy hills. In the nearer distance, zebra and gazelle and wildebeest were no more than moving specks; much less real than the crashed aircraft and the tiny figures moving around it.

Anderson looked down from the branches of an acacia tree, once more refining the focus of the binoculars. He was already certain of their leader's identity, but just to make sure –

The man's face jumped into clarity, half-shadowed by the port wing. A strong, square face, clean-shaven; a man of about forty. Dark glasses hid his eyes, but Anderson had seen their remote, hard paleness on previous occasions. A thick neck, broad shoulders. An unquestioning, confident set to the body, even though it was relaxed and unmoving. The mouth and jaw were marked with a similar confidence, and it was not too fanciful to recognize them as the stigmata of a violent past.

It was Blantyre. Colonel Robin Blantyre, ex-Rhodesian Selous Scout, ex-South African Reconnaissance Commando – now what was he? An employee of Malan-Labuschagne who controlled the Walvis Bay area and its trade and minerals, or simply an ex-soldier who had stayed on in independent Namibia because he loved the peace of the Bush and leading an anti-poaching unit made up of identical veterans? Blantyre had been – was still? – both. He was also the veteran of two dozen raids, into Angola, Mozambique, Zimbabwe, Zambia; the glamorous, fêted, be-medalled, dangerous Robin Blantyre.

Recognition had shaken him in his perch high in the acacia like a sudden wind buffeting through the branches and the concealing leaves. Blantyre's presence there was charged with meaning – and

43

danger. No mere accident had brought him to the crash site in answer to a scout plane's signal as it had buzzed over less than half-an-hour after Anderson had concealed the Land Rover. It was in a dry water hole amid sparse, stiff grass taller than himself. The crate he had broken open lay on the sand, where they had thrown it from the hold, together with the damaged boxes from which he had also removed – evidence. Of what? *Novgorod, 1989*, and a KGB pass . . .

Anderson shivered. Blantyre knew him, probably knew who he had once been. They wouldn't believe he was a . . . naturalist, he had decided. Watching the game from the acacia. Slightly eccentric, well-meaning, harmless. He lifted the binoculars quickly and Blantyre seemed to be looking across the sand and the small teats of the dunes towards the tree and him. His growing unease during the hours he had been alone in the Bush, waiting, was now usurped by a chilly fear. Blantyre had killed more people, in all likelihood, than he himself had; and his killing was more recent. Suddenly, it was as if a leopard dozed at the foot of the acacia, cutting off all escape.

The two American XR 311 scout cars, the barrels of their machine guns pointing skywards like salutes, were parked close to the wreck's cold shadow. Blantyre was addressing the four men of his unit, his arm sweeping, pausing, pointing, making a grid of the landscape. They'd already searched the area of the wreck for tracks and signs. Blantyre knew – he was certain of it – that someone had visited the wreck, and broken open the crate and the boxes. His only problem would be happenstance or design? They had reacted quickly and expertly, not to the wreck itself, but to the intrusion into the cargo.

Anderson leant back against the bole of the tree, his feet planted firmly on two thick branches. He could not be seen, could not . . . He inhaled and exhaled slowly, rhythmically. The small breeze rustled the dark leaves. The five men who had arrived fifteen minutes earlier were, doubtless, South African Defence Forces commandos in the thinnest of guises. He sipped water from a plastic bottle. Warm. The telephoto lens of his camera rested in the crook of his arm, the body of the camera against his hip. Despite the scream that seemed to louden and deafen at the back of his head as he had worked, he had still photographed the interior of the

Dakota, before wiping out his tracks and those of the vehicle . . .

To leave a darker stirring of the red sand. No detail, but nevertheless the certainty of some kind of intrusion. An armful of contents from the crate and boxes was stowed in the back of the Land Rover, and now he had Blantyre and the others on film. He had the Russian's snapshot and ID card. There was nothing else. He could leave.

He looked down at the foot of the tree. The grass and sand there had the dappled coat of a leopard or a cheetah, and he felt unnerved. He could climb down now, walk back to the vehicle, start the engine, head north back towards Etosha. Home. Contact someone . . . anyone.

The unit spread out with the suddenness of stones setting off an avalanche. The four men, two to a vehicle, started engines, manned the machine guns, spread out in a billowing cloud of dust, accelerating away from the epicentre of the Dakota. Now, he must stay. He felt cold, then hot. The two scout cars rode the terrain like insects skittering, throwing up clouds of dust. If he tried to use the Land Rover now, they would find him. He raised the binoculars with reluctance. A zebra dashed ahead of one of the scout cars as it circled towards the water hole where he had hidden the vehicle. Distant gazelle were startled into motion by the other scout car.

He forced his attention back to the DC-3, picking up Blantyre sitting beneath the shade offered by the port wing. Cigarette smoke hung in the air. Blantyre had instructed them to discover any sign of the intruder. The dry water hole was a convenient focus. And, heightened as his senses were by tension, he caught the distant, insect drone of aircraft engines, from the west. Events had long overtaken him, he realized, cursing the stupidity of that younger, reckless self which had prompted him to linger as if he could *do* anything! The dust rose above the dry water hole from the swinging curve in which the animal-like scout car approached it. The flash of an elephant's grey bulk lumbering through the tall, dry grass.

Through the glasses, he ensured that the scout car halted and its crew of two descended from it. The still-invisible aircraft droned slowly closer . . . He was moving more quickly than any of them now, as he slid and tumbled through the branches of the tree like a small monkey still inheriting its kingdom. Then he dropped the

45

last few feet to the ground from the lowest branch, scored by leopard's claws. His breath vanished for a moment, and he bent like a half-started sprinter, on fingers and toes, recovering it. The binoculars and camera dangled from their straps around his neck.

Then he cautiously stood upright. The Dakota was out of sight in a small fold in the land. The water hole was closest, and he should, in all innocence, return to his vehicle rather than head towards the wreckage. He began walking.

Naturalist, naturalist, naturalist – to explain the camera and the glasses. Blantyre knew him, thought him eccentric, all but despised him as a *royneek*, English. And living with – *married* to – a half-caste, a Namibian *coloured*.

Perhaps the sum of all those little contempts and dislikes would render him harmless in Blantyre's eyes. He reached the crest of the dune that sheltered the dry water hole, and found them inspecting the Land Rover, looking in the glove compartment, the door pockets, one of them unfolding a map as if to shake sand from it, then inspecting it for marks, incriminations, intent.

He stood on the crest for a moment, watching them, calming his body, sensing and measuring the perspiration beneath his arms, across his brow, timing his breathing. Then he began to move carefully down the slope, a lizard sliding out of his path across the tiny avalanche of disturbed sand. One of the two, a corporal by the uniform bush shirt he still wore, whirled round, hearing him.

He was squinted at by both men, neither of whom had produced a pistol, then the corporal removed his stained bush hat, revealing a line of white skin like a bandage between his ruddy tan and his dark hair. His face abandoned alertness, inquisitiveness. Just a middle-aged white bloke, a lot of them in the Bush. It was as if he had spoken. Then he did say: 'You saw us coming? Heard us, man?'

The accent was Afrikaans. Undeniably the corporal had been SADF – might still be, for all Anderson knew. Who knew what the South Africans were up to in Namibia? Certainly, Malan-Labuschagne Consolidated, still operating in that Exclusion Zone along the coast from Walvis Bay to Oranjemund, used none but ex- or current SADF personnel for security duty. 'Eh, man? What you doing out here? You see the crash?'

He shook his head. 'It must have happened before dawn. I've seen the wreck, though – through the glasses.' He patted the

46

binoculars on his chest. 'I was about to –'

It was as if they had heard nothing of his careful alibi, his tone of voice, his innocence.

'You been over to that crash, man? Take a look-around, maybe?' the corporal enquired, scratching his beard, his eyes alert amid their tiny lines and wrinkles. There was a quick, experienced cunning in his expression. 'Why're you out here, man, and not on the road – uh?'

'Anti-poaching patrol?' Anderson asked as casually as he could, stilling a small tremor that had begun in his left leg.

'Maybe – you?'

'As you see, watching the local wildlife –' He patted his camera, still slung across his chest. 'Taking a few photographs. You seem to have scattered most of the game, however.' He was conscious of the Englishness of his voice and syntax; another mask.

'Did we? A pity that, man,' the second soldier commented. The corporal grinned, shading his eyes with his bush hat.

The second soldier had climbed back into the scout car, and his fingers were tapping a disbelieving rhythm on the steering wheel. Or perhaps simple, dismissive impatience. A small group of zebra shuffled and browsed beneath trees some hundreds of yards away. He attempted to concentrate upon them, slowly raising the glasses. The aircraft was visible now, moving in a wide circle. He tossed his head and asked: 'Looking for you?'

'Interested? What are you doing way out here, man? Apart from taking pictures? Where are you from, Englishman?'

'Okaukuejo – in the Etosha. The game lodge. I run it.'

'What's your name?'

'Anderson – Richard Anderson.'

The corporal was silent for a moment, then nodded.

'Heard the name. You're from Jo'burg – a few years back?'

A breeze chilled against Anderson's drying shirt.

'That's right. And you're from the Transvaal, too, by the sound of your voice?'

'Maybe. Our colonel – he's back at the crash – would like to talk to you. Anyone we find, he said.'

'You have authority? From whom?' The effort at normality, at being *white* as much as innocent, was wearing; to think himself back into South-West Africa, to forget the recent independence of

Namibia. These men didn't have the minds to admit change. And they believed – since he was all they had found – he must have visited the crash site. 'Doesn't matter. I have the time. I'll talk to your colonel, even though I didn't see what happened – and I haven't been near the wreck. Saw it through the glasses only some minutes ago . . .'

'Ag, man, the colonel isn't going to bite you!' the corporal said roughly. The suspicion in his eyes had been damped down by Anderson's innocuousness, his comfortable middle-age; hard though the latter was to admit. 'Come on, then.'

The corporal glanced up at the circling, dropping aircraft, a small-ish two-engined passenger plane. Anderson watched it, too, as it levelled and seemed on its final approach. Smoke rose from where the Dakota must lie, presumably a flare to indicate the direction of the breeze. It bent like the beginning of a question mark. Then the corporal climbed up beside the driver of the scout car, indicating that Anderson should start up the Land Rover. The aircraft dropped behind low dunes, out of sight. Come to collect the cargo and the two bodies. He started his engine, feeling the perspiration of relief and anticipated tension cover his body. Dark stains on his shirt. His forearms quivered as he gripped the steering wheel and followed the scout car slowly, lurchingly, out of the hollow of the water hole. Over the lip, he fell into convoy behind the XR 311, to its left to avoid the dust its fat, low tyres churned up. The machine gun mounted on the vehicle was hypnotic, despite its being pointed at the empty sky.

The acacia rose over the Bush like an accusation. He should never have stayed. They hadn't, it appeared, searched the Land Rover – but what he had taken was hidden in the tool box and the film in his camera was betraying . . . they can't *develop* it out here, you bloody fool! he told himself. The corporal was none too bright, taken in by appearances. Knew only what he was and had recently been, not his more distant past.

The Land Rover bumped down the shallow rise towards the Dakota. The two bodies were lying near Blantyre's feet, in the shade, tidily and like a premonition. The small aircraft had come to a halt, the dust of its touchdown settling slowly. It bore civilian markings. Along its flank, disturbingly, Anderson read the acronym, MLC. The aircraft was from Walvis Bay. He attempted to prepare his features with an expression of confusion, mystification. The small plane sat innocently on a flat stretch of sand. Blantyre had risen to his feet and was standing with his hands on his hips, intently watching the approaching Land Rover. He was beside the open cargo door of the DC-3, as if indicating the evidence of a crime to its perpetrator. Anderson drew to a halt beside the Rhodesian.

'What's this, Corporal Uys? Where did you find this man?' His voice was clipped and precise, quiet.

Uys nodded behind him as he climbed from the scout car.

'Dry water hole over there, Colonel.' Uys moved close to Blantyre and began speaking rapidly in Afrikaans. Anderson assumed a look of incomprehension, of attentive bemusement, under Blantyre's casual scrutiny. He felt hotter, the Bush seemed no larger than a box, a cell, the midwinter heat oppressive and confining.

When Uys had finished speaking, Blantyre nodded and approached the Land Rover, holding out a large hand, a smile disarmingly exhibited, his dark glasses removed. His eyes were crinkled against the sunlight with sceptical intensity.

'Good morning, Colonel,' Anderson greeted him, taking the man's firm grip. Where his hand had rested on his shorts, there was a faint smudge of nervous perspiration.

'Mr Anderson. You're a long way from Etosha – a long way south?' Blantyre put his hands back on his hips, continuing to squint much as a bird of prey might have done into shadows and thin cover.

'Back from a trip to Windhoek. I left early this – I presume this happened before dawn. I saw no sign, heard nothing. Sorry I can't be of more help.'

'Watching the game, Uys says?'

'Yes.'

'I'd heard it preoccupied you, Mr Anderson. Lately. You don't like people, or something?'

He shrugged. There was the faintest scent of contempt in Blantyre's voice, like the after-odour of a meal he had eaten; a halitosis of arrogance and invulnerability. It assisted his heartbeat to calm, his sweat to dry.

'I – not many of them. Perhaps I've been unfortunate in those I've had to deal with.'

The small aircraft was one of the Riley adaptations of a Cessna model that the South African Defence Forces had favoured for years when engaged in border surveillance, or cross-border intrusions against Frelimo and SWAPO. Twin Avro Lycoming engines, advanced avionics. Something in him continued to compile the report, despite his tension – no, his *fear*, confronted with Blantyre.

'What brought it down? Who were they?'

'One of our regular supply flights spotted the wreckage from the air. They must have – as you said – come down before dawn. No emergency call, nothing.' He nodded at the bodies. 'They were killed in the crash. Must have been making for Windhoek. It'll have been established by now.' He looked at his watch. 'Public relations, Mr Anderson. It looks good for us if MLC flies the bodies out.'

'You work for MLC at Walvis Bay now, Colonel? A little tame for you, I should have –'

'Sometimes.' Blantyre was suspicious but not dismissive of the vague obsequiousness of his tone. The man liked being thought of as a hero; thought of himself that way, too, perhaps. A tinge of contempt in Anderson's mouth, strangely exhilarating. 'You must know what it's like, even after wars like yours, I mean?'

He smiled, shaking his head. 'That was too long ago. I've forgotten –'

'Why don't you get down, Mr Anderson? I'm getting a pain in the neck looking up at you.' He heard Uys laughing as he climbed slowly out of the Land Rover. 'That's better.'

They were almost of the same height. It was, he admitted, like looking at an old photograph of himself. Blantyre seemed to recognize something latent in him. He hoped not.

Blantyre's touch on the skin of his arm was cool, light. He guided him away from where the pilot of the Cessna and two other men, working silently and methodically and without instruction, had begun unloading the cargo from the Dakota. Blantyre was smiling, relaxed. Uys began talking in Afrikaans behind them and Anderson was careful not to tense at the sound of his name and the disparaging description from the corporal. *Old* royneek *fart, married to a Bantu, living up north like a fucking hermit.* The obligatory expectoration by way of emphasis and dismissal.

'You know me, Mr Anderson, and I know you. You were still practising law in Jo'burg until a few years ago. You were out here before the – elections, and stayed on, or came back. Married, I heard . . . ?'

'I am. She's half-German, half-Herero, and her name is Margarethe. I'm very lucky. Of course, I could even live in the Republic with her now, but I don't have any desire to go back.'

'Why not? Smoke?' Anderson shook his head. A battered American cigarette lighter appeared, its cap clicked open noisily, its flame smelling of lighter fuel not butane. A beer advertised dimly on its scratched, dulled side as Blantyre showed it to him, smiling. 'I found it years ago. Its previous owner didn't have any further use for it. Why don't you go back, then?'

'People. I prefer it here, as you surmised.'

'Don't your liberal friends miss you? Not to mention all the Bantus who used to be on your list of clients – eh, man?'

'They could all pay, Colonel.' He turned from Blantyre's scrutiny towards the XR 311 which, loaded with crates and boxes, was dragging a curtain of dust behind it out to the Cessna. Blantyre's cigarette smoke was acrid around him. Distant zebra. The glare of the sun on salt pans, insubstantial undulations in the far distance, beyond which lay the Namib and the coast – and Walvis Bay and MLC; South Africa's private enclave sealed off from the remainder of Namibia; the naval base and the factories and the secrets. 'They could all pay.'

'A lot of your liberal friends – they liked humping the black dollies, I hear? You defended a few of them.'

'Yes. Before they scrapped those stupid laws and the Immorality Act.'

'You defended white women who had the hots for what the kaffirs keep in their ragged-arsed trousers, too?'

'Yes. One or two.'

Blantyre laughed, loudly, slapping him across the shoulders. 'No wonder you left, man! Who needs friends like that, eh?' He continued laughing, then said quickly: 'And you ended up marrying a Bantu yourself?'

He nodded slowly. 'Yes. I'm happy to be able to report that I did.'

'No offence, man. But when pressure from people like you got rid of the pass laws and the immorality laws – uh, the end of civilization! A lot of people didn't like you, back home.'

'I was aware of the fact.' He realized that the slightly formal, rather prissy image of an English solicitor, was good cover; his liberal ideals concealing him within Blantyre's bigotry.

'No offence, man.'

They stood together at the top of the rise. The bodies had been zipped into long plastic bags. He shivered. He'd seen so many. SWAPO guerrillas went into them, ivory poachers, black miners killed underground on the Reef because of carelessness or lack of safety precautions. He shook his head, then said, 'I'd better be going. I shan't make Okaukuejo until midnight or later if I don't get off. You don't want me for anything, Colonel? I'm sorry I couldn't help.'

'No, man. You get off. There's – no need to report this, yourself that is. It'll all have been done at the Bay, the paperwork. OK?'

'Thanks. A bother, having to give evidence to any investigation. Especially when one didn't see anything, anyway.'

'Sure. Any tourists staying at the lodge right now?'

'One or two.'

'I might drop by for a beer one of these days.'

'I'll keep some cool, pending your arrival.'

'You watch out for me, then, man – I'll be seeing you.'

'Fine.'

They had returned to his Land Rover. He climbed in. Blantyre ground out his cigarette, shook Anderson's hand. By the dust that was approaching, it was obvious that the second scout car had been summoned back. Uys watched him with dim contempt. Blantyre's suspicions were allayed, if not dismissed.

He started the engine, waved, put the vehicle into gear and pulled away from the wrecked Dakota in a wide circle, raising as little dust as possible. He bumped up the rise and over it, dropping immediately out of sight of the wreck. He rounded a clump of thornbush and suddenly the shaking began; his mouth filled with sweet saliva. It was like some malarial attack. MLC was involved, through Blantyre, with a KGB officer and – what, stolen technology from the UK? It was incredible, but Blantyre had forged the link, some chain of conspiracy. Paulus Malan, he knew, had Russian links – gold and diamonds. Everyone in the Republic knew that . . . but this? What did it mean?

Damn stumbling on the wreck and damn even more the stupidity of old, unpractised instincts that had made him hang around, just so that he might encounter Blantyre – who threatened, that was the word, to visit the game lodge. He must *do* something –

– and that something was to inform Aubrey. There was nothing for it but to fulfil those old instincts and contact the man who had helped him escape to South Africa in the first place ... Why did he so *willingly* drift into memory? Aubrey was old now, but still empowered. Aubrey, who had accepted, even assisted in, his killing of a senior intelligence officer of his own service – his own superior. That had been after he had got back from East Germany, his fingernails pulled out by the KGB, his body exhausted and mind inflamed, having escaped from the imprisonment and torture his superior's betrayal of his network had visited on him. 1966. He had been a young man. Aubrey's man loaned to someone else, a double agent. He had never been able to decide whether that had been Aubrey's purpose, to expose the double through him. He'd thrown the man from the third-floor window of his own flat, one dark night in November – and Aubrey had helped him flee.

Aubrey. Had to be. He must send *him* evidence of the things he had taken from the wrecked Dakota.

The Bush spread out silent and vast around him, devoid of life, it seemed. Isolated, he was a speck to be glimpsed by an eagle. He had to pass the information to Aubrey, then he could forget his past and return to the present.


'Look, there isn't going to be any sound of bugles!' Godwin snapped. 'Pass the hoi-sin sauce – ta.' His mouth full, he continued: 'Look, Terry, I tried my *best*! No one wants to listen any more – and Patrick's subject to a disciplinary enquiry over what happened in that pub. *If* we go any further, then we're on our own. It's definitely *unofficial*. It's a right fucking mess!'

Hyde opened another can of lager. Godwin's cat, Dubček, was seated on his lap and he occasionally slipped it fragments of Szechuan beef. The cat seemed to appreciate its spiciness.

'I don't doubt you were rude to Orrell on top of everything else,' Chambers observed.

'Who could resist it?' Hyde replied, spooning more fried rice from its foil container onto his plate. 'Have you had *all* that roast duck, Chambers?'

Godwin's kitchen table was littered with containers from the Chinese takeaway in the next street, his small, untidy, unrenovated kitchen filled with the scents of the meal. Hyde looked up at Godwin.

'Well?' he asked. 'What are we going to do? You've got a few days' leave, I could skive off, Chambers could go to his granny's funeral . . .' He smiled, as if taunting Godwin.

Godwin looked down at the table. Half a dozen cans of lager, emptied and on their sides, another dozen or more waiting. For most of the meal, nothing but the sound of their eating and, from Hyde's lap, the cat's purring. Their mutual resentment was almost comfortable, reassuring, characterizing them as victims, and therefore blameless. Godwin opened another can of lager for himself, then motioned it towards Chambers, who shook his head and swallowed from the can in front of him; belching.

'Pig,' Hyde murmured without malice or irritation.

'Are you going to get off this enquiry?' Godwin asked.

Hyde shrugged. 'God knows. Depends who has it in for me at the moment and whether they're on the enquiry – or whether Orrell thinks it's fun to screw some of Aubrey's old workhands. Who knows? I'm not staying awake worrying about it.'

'It's all been such a bloody waste of time,' Chambers muttered.

'So you said – many, many times, sport.' Then he looked up at Godwin and asked: 'Why haven't you called Darren off the surveillance he's on?'

Godwin flushed and snapped back: 'How do you know what he's doing?'

'He'd be here, otherwise – wouldn't he? Who's he watching – Malan?' Reluctantly, Godwin nodded. 'Thought so.'

'You'll drop a real ballock, Tony, if anyone finds out.'

'I know that, Terry. Look, perhaps I didn't make out the best case to Orrell – !'

'Who ever does?' Hyde asked. Then: 'What's Malan been doing today, while we've been in the shit?'

'Business as usual. Just like yesterday and the day before.' He wiped his hands on his shirt and lumbered up from his seat. From the draining board of the sink unit, he passed Hyde a large buff envelope. It was smeared with cat food. Empty tins and washing-up littered the draining board. 'Have a look.'

Enlargements, taken from a distance with a telescopic lens. Monochrome, paled by brilliant sunlight. Malan had been in London for the past two days, attending to the concerns of Malan-Labuschagne Consolidated and its European subsidiaries. He had been nowhere near any Reid Group company, nowhere near . . . oh, but he had been naughty, hadn't he! Godwin was grinning as Hyde looked up, then passed the enlargements to Chambers.

'Where's Darren now?'

'Outside some theatre in the West End. Malan's taking in a show. Remember when we first saw those snaps of him at the Bolshoi with the head of the Narodny bank, years ago . . . ?' His voice sounded as if he were indulging some puntlike drift into sunlit memory.

'Why did he see Priabin? Where?' Chambers asked.

'Darren's scribbled on the back – what does it say?'

'Kensington Palace Gardens,' Hyde said. Then he looked up at Godwin, a sliver of beef speared on his fork, his mouth filled with rice. 'What's on your mind, Godwin?'

'I rang the limousine service Malan uses, this evening. Just to check, on Mr Malan's behalf, what time it was booked for tomorrow, were they sure of the address. Tomorrow, at eleven, he's going to see MacPherson, CEO of Reid Group.'

'And –?'

'Don't you see? If we had a bug in Reid, or we still had –'

'Kellett? He wouldn't have been invited to the meeting, would he?'

'Are you *really* thinking of an unofficial surveillance op?' Chambers asked dubiously, his eyes searching the littered kitchen as if for a bolt hole.

'You've worried our Terence already,' Hyde sneered. Then added: 'And me. We're deep enough in the shit as it is, Godwin. You're getting paranoid about Malan and Priabin.'

'I *know* something's going on, and we have to find out what it is!'

'Who's this *we*?' Hyde snorted. 'Your bloody living room is littered with stuff. Any trick-cyclist given five minutes in there would have enough to have you put away. This business is eating you up, mate!'

'Doesn't the fact that the girl was there as well as Priabin even interest you – just a bit?'

'I can't do anything about that tart, Godwin. Look, we've been pissing about being SIS, DS, Special Branch, DTI inspectors, Customs and Excise – we don't even know who we are any more or what we're really supposed to be doing!' He chewed on a piece of dry-looking duck, crunching the peanuts that came as its dressing. He waved his fork in emphasis as Chambers nodded his agreement. 'No one's bloody interested – I don't think *I* am any more. This has been stuffed up a dead possum's bum for too long. It's a waste of bloody time. Why don't we just say sorry to Orrell and behave ourselves?'

'Look, just one surveillance, on the Reid offices in the NatWest Tower. There's an empty office across the street. We can use a van and the laser eavesdropper.' He was red with desperation. 'Look, if it doesn't work, and we come up empty, then we'll forget the whole thing – I'll just shut up about it. OK?'

The cat climbed from Hyde's lap onto the table and began sniffing Godwin's fingers, then his plate. Godwin absently stroked its back as it began eating his remaining prawns. Hyde burst out laughing.

'You're so involved with this, you can't see what's happening in front of your nose!'

'What? Oh . . . !' He shrugged and allowed the cat to continue its quiet, methodical assault. Then he once more looked up exasperated. 'Well?' He pointed his fork like an angry baton. 'Your bloody cynicism gets up my nose, Patrick – it really does! We're not talking about bags of bloody marbles or toffees here! These transputers and the WSI chips can go into *anything* – super-computers the size of a vanity case, missile guidance systems, bomb detonators, satellites – it's *important*!' he ended almost apologetically, his features red again.

Chambers said: 'Look, if we're caught, we'll really be in it –'

Hyde interrupted, studying his plate. 'All right. Just tomorrow.' He looked up and grinned. 'Since it means so much to you. Darren's just about clever enough to keep his mouth shut – are you, Chambers?'

'Look, I might just have a career left in the service, unlike you two mad buggers. Tell me why I should risk it, if no one wants to know, anyway?'

Hyde clenched his fist slowly, but Godwin burst out: 'It's supposed to be our *job*, Terry! Whether we're SIS, DS, or Avon ladies, we're supposed to concern ourselves with the operations of foreign intelligence services on British soil. This *is*, in case you hadn't noticed, a foreign intelligence service operation.' Hyde pretended applause.

'See?' he said to Chambers. 'It's just somewhere to go in the morning, instead of staying in bed and growing your toenails.' Godwin grinned in complicity. Hyde was hooked. A *mad bugger*, as Chambers had observed.

'After all, Terry,' Godwin murmured. 'We are assisting in the investigation of two murders. Can't get much more moral or patriotic than that, can you?' Chambers snorted derisively.

'You'll get rice up your nose, doing that,' Hyde remarked. Then he snapped at Godwin: 'Can you get the stuff early tomorrow morning – on the q.t.?' Godwin nodded. 'Right, let's do it, then.' He paused: 'Any more of that stir-fry veg left in the oven?'


A hundred yards from the main lodge, something moved through the Bush and unsettled him, though he guessed it must be a lion rather than a trained man. Stars pricked out softly and quickly, hanging like lamps against the velvet evening. The voices from the bar behind him seemed distant, his attention entirely focused on the darkness and what might emerge from it at any moment.

*Only in Africa, peace* . . . He'd read that line in a volume of third-rate poetry in a second-hand bookshop in Jo'burg, years before. Written by a Lutheran missionary a century ago, before the Bush had finally driven him mad. He had found that feeling out here, in Etosha with his wife, having sought its promise for years.

Blantyre and the DC-3's wreckage shook his thoughts like a rough hand waking him from a dreaming, satisfying sleep. Nerves jumped along his forearms, and he resented the sense of an old excitement that unsettled his stomach and made his whole frame itch with its new insistence. It was as if he had brought some ailment back with him from the crash site, something contagious. He had given up his legal practice for this place, this peace, picturing himself as a man able to grow old with diminishing regrets. A privileged hermit, Margarethe had called him. Or, ruthless in his enjoyment of peace.

Margarethe . . .

Anderson half-turned, sensing his wife reach his side, and put his arm around her shoulders. She held on to his body with her arms, resting her head against his side.

'What is it, Richard?' she asked at once, as she registered his tension. She looked up at him, but he could not see the vividly-blue eyes in the darkness, just the slight re-arrangement of facial bones beneath smooth skin that indicated her mixed parentage.

'I'm – going to have to find somewhere to hide . . . what I brought with me, yesterday.'

He squeezed her shoulders. Tenderness with her was always easy; he had grown used to it.

'But it is hidden –'

'Somewhere better. Blantyre is no fool, and he's dangerous.'

'Couldn't you have left it there, then? Where you found it?' There was blame in her voice, but she did not release her grip on him. Her hands were cool through his shirt.

He shook his head. 'No. It's important. To people I used to know in London. I'm sure it is. The Russian, especially.'

'Important to you, too.'

He shook his head with a vehemence composed of desire and denial. She moved away from him, then reached out and touched his beard, his mouth.

'I didn't think,' he said. 'I wish I had left it, I'm sorry.'

'Richard, you are not the man you were – that was a long time ago. You must be *careful*, if he comes.'

'He'll come. At least the letter's gone to London.'

He reached out and stroked her hair, which she wore in long, tight ringlets, beaded and woven like rope. She held tightly to him.

'It happened,' he murmured against her head. 'I wasn't looking for it, didn't want –'

'It doesn't matter.' Margarethe shivered, moving away from him again, rubbing her arms. 'I will be glad when he has come, and gone.' There was a trace of her father's German accent, amid the high, birdlike clicking of the Herero language she had inherited from her mother. There was hardly anything, when they spoke together, of the Anglicized, professional voice she employed as a

58

visiting nurse. She waved her hand, as if warding off insects. 'You are certain he will come, aren't you?'

'I don't think he really believed me. I wasn't practised enough to fool him.' He sighed. Her small, light frame seemed enlarged by his responsibility for her. 'Look, it'll be all right, if we just keep up appearances.' His hands took hold of her bare arms, which were chilly, goose-fleshed in the warm night. 'Help me hide this stuff, now.'

'Where?'

'Down by the dam somewhere – even under the water?' he suggested. The urgency in his voice was a passable imitation of a former confidence. Margarethe, catching his tone, stared at him as if he had become a stranger. She shook her head.

'Be *careful*, Richard.'

'Mm.'

'Very well, down at the dam. I'll tell Joseph to attend to the bar, and check on the cook.' Then she smiled vividly. 'Would this Colonel Blantyre be expecting to see me wearing a goatskin frill on my head and smeared from head to foot in butter and ochre? Would that deceive him?'

Anderson laughed softly. 'You're not afraid of him, are you?'

She shook her head. 'Only for you.' The braids of her hair moved across her face and shoulders. 'Go and fetch the things you must hide. I'll speak to Joseph – hurry!'

There was a renewed outburst of laughter from the group of guests near the bar, and the noise struck against them as if in derision. He nodded to her, squeezing her upper arms, then she moved away as he released her. Anderson descended the three steps from the verandah that surrounded the main lodge, skirting the warmly-lit restaurant and bar. Moonlight showed already on the thatched roofs of the line of guest huts down by the waterhole, raised on stilts and platformed to support large tents. Nightlights glowed like faint planets through the canvas of the three closest tents. He heard the grumble of a lion some distance off, and farther still the muted bellow of an elephant; both noises startled him like sudden intruders. The Bush had constricted around his urgency, bringing everything, even Blantyre, closer.

He opened the door of the storeroom and groped for the heavy canvas bag without switching on the light. As he bent, he heard his

59

muscles creak and the noise of his breathing. Blantyre was almost fifteen years his junior, and he was a killer.

He hefted the lumpy, murmurous bag onto his shoulder and relocked the storeroom, pausing in the darkness but hearing nothing but the laughter from the bar and the gabble of conversations mingling with the smell of cooking from the kitchen. A springbok he had shot earlier in the day. He walked slowly back towards the light from the restaurant as Margarethe came running lightly out of the glow. He called softly to her. She clutched his hand the moment she joined him.

'OK?' he asked.

'Yes.'

They hurried down the moonlit path towards the faint sheen of placid water and the fuzzy globes of light shining through the canvas.

'What equipment is it – do you know? Won't the water damage it?'

'It's wrapped in polythene – I don't really know. Electrical equipment from a British company. But it's the Russian who was with it – who must have flown from Walvis Bay . . . that's what's wrong with it all. I don't think it should be here, *or* in the Republic.'

They reached the water. The evening exhilarated, the stars enlarged to soft blue, white and red globes, looming overhead. There was gentle, secret movement on the other side of the dam. Anderson breathed in deeply, as if he had come to the last moment of some extended holiday and was on the point of departure.

'Where?' Margarethe asked him.

They patrolled the edge of the water. Tall reeds, trampled, open stretches of sandy earth, stunted acacias.

'Here.' He paused and unslung the canvas bag from his shoulder.

'What if the water should damage it?'

'The look of it will be enough – it doesn't have to work.' He did feel elated, it was true, at the ease with which he could make himself and Margarethe innocent, above suspicion.

He gathered up some heavy stones, then knelt with the bag at the edge of the water. He submerged it gently, the bag disappearing in a bouquet of bubbles. Carefully, he lowered each of the stones on top of it. Disguise and anchor. The water was above his elbows. Reeds rubbed against his arms and shoulders. It would do – he flashed his torch. The settling sand masked the canvas bag. The stones appeared to be naturally there. The reeds hung over the water. It would do very well.

He looked up, startled as a drinking animal, at the noise of a vehicle approaching the game lodge, grinding and heaving up the rutted track. Headlights flared on the evening as if against a dark screen, bucking with the ground's undulations. Then the lights halted and the engine died, somewhere in the general glow from the lodge.

'Him?' Margarethe asked, gripping his arm with wet fingers. She had carefully, delicately re-arranged two of the stones, then stirred up more sand that would settle on them and the bag.

'Quite likely. We're not expecting any other guests. Seems he's alone – only one vehicle.'

'Then we should get back –'

He grabbed her arm in restraint.

'No,' he warned. 'We don't want to burst in on him like a couple of kids who've been caught at the jam. We'll circle around the lodge and come in from the opposite direction.' He felt a quivering in her arm and pulled her against him, stroking her braided hair, his lips on her forehead. Her whole body was trembling. 'It's all right, sweetheart,' he soothed. 'It's all right . . .' He pressed her closer, kissing her. 'Come on, all we need is a bit of nerve to get us through.'

She swallowed and nodded vigorously. 'Yes.'

He dropped one arm and held her shoulders in the crook of the other, walking slowly as he clutched her against him. He wasn't afraid of Blantyre, not here, not now. Only afraid for her and already angry at the contempt Blantyre would display towards her. Yet there was, too, an old, familiar prickle of pleasure on his cheeks and lips, a recognized dryness at the back of his throat.

'I love you,' he said. She pressed against him.

'This is just a game to you – I know that.'

'I love you.'

They climbed the slope, heading away from the lodge. He strained to hear but did not catch Blantyre's voice amid the renewed babble from the bar. Then, as they came to the head of the slope, he saw Blantyre standing at the bar, a glass of beer in one hand, his head moving slowly, methodically as he assessed each of the handful of

61

guests – and seeming to look for him and Margarethe, too. She shivered against him, but only momentarily.

'That's him,' he said unnecessarily, as they skirted the lodge in the darkness beyond its glow. 'Leave the talking to me – and, remember that to him you're half Bantu.' He squeezed her against him as they turned back towards the lodge. 'He'll be curious, he'll envy me your bed, but you won't be real.' They separated as they climbed the steps to the long curve of the verandah. Blantyre saw them immediately.

Anderson ducked his head to avoid the low, thatched eaves. A bird rustled above him like a whispered caution. Blantyre was already coming towards him, hand extended, a smile on his large, square face. He studied Margarethe admiringly, much as he might have surveyed a prizewinning dog or farm animal. Anderson stilled his resentment. Yet she seemed exposed and vulnerable as she moved behind the bar – entirely his fault.

'Mr Anderson – I told you I'd look you up . . . and the beer is cold. Thanks.' He was at ease, grinning. 'Nice billet you have here, man.' His arm indicated the lodge before coming to rest on Anderson's shoulder; who steeled himself not to shrug instinctively against its pressure. Blantyre raised his glass and swallowed an ironic toast.

The other guests were evidently aware of his identity and reputation. There was an almost instant camaraderie with fame, obsequious and titillated.

'I'm glad you could come . . . Margarethe, this is Colonel Robin Blantyre – we're honoured, my darling.' Blantyre's eyes twitched as if to pounce upon sarcasm, but Anderson knew his expression was carefully arranged. 'You must have heard of the Colonel's reputation, darling.' Again, suspicion was fended off by his practised, legal blandness. Blantyre's esteem had impressed all of the guests, with the possible exception of the two elderly American ladies. The party up from Windhoek and the wildlife photographer from Port Elizabeth made Blantyre the centre of gravity of the room; or the still, deep centre of a small whirlpool.

Blantyre held out his hand and took Margarethe's fingers in his large grip. 'Your husband told you how we met?'

She nodded, her strange blue eyes alert, the sharp angles of her face stretching the skin, masklike. Blantyre turned. 'Been out for

62

an evening walk without a gun, Mr Anderson?'

'A short step. There's not much out there likely to attack a man, Colonel. You know that.'

Blantyre grinned, looking out into the darkness for a moment. 'Maybe.'

Conversation stuttered into life at the occupied tables as people settled for the evening meal and assumed that their host would monopolize the conversation of the dangerously glamorous Robin Blantyre. The two elderly Americans were listening as the wildlife photographer explained the newcomer's identity. Fascination spread like a pale, fungoid growth on each face as he spoke.

'Mm, that cooking smells good – you really do have something special here. I'm not surprised you left the law for it. Though how a man like you could have become a bloody solicitor beats me, eh, man?' He slapped Anderson's shoulder as if exposing some professional cover which had now been penetrated. Then he called to Margarethe: 'You got a spare tent or room for tonight, Mrs Anderson?'

'Just for one?' she asked coolly, exciting his admiration, reaching for the register.

'Just for one.'

'One of the tents down at the water's edge, Colonel?' Anderson asked nonchalantly. It was like a remembered role in a renowned drama, not difficult to recapture. Careful –

'Fine.' Margarethe offered him the register and a pen, and he scrawled his name with an expected flourish, though the letters were surprisingly neat.

Margarethe said: 'You're attached to Walvis Bay, I gather from my husband, Colonel?'

'That's true, Mrs Anderson – that's true. Then there's the ivory poaching patrols. We get called out on those occasionally. Knowing the Bush as we do.' William the cook appeared from the kitchen and caught her attention.

'Excuse me, Colonel –'

'Of course.' His courtesy was mocking.

As she walked away, Anderson announced to Blantyre, so that she could hear his voice: 'My wife was classified as Coloured, before such terms lost their meaning. I could, through contacts in Pretoria, have changed that. She didn't want me to. We met when I came out here on holiday.'

'And stayed.'

'Not at once. She came back to Jo'burg with me, but she . . .' He smiled sardonically. 'She didn't like city life, not even in our liberal suburb. We came back here – to do this, in my advancing years.'

'You're not that old, man.' Blantyre seemed nonplussed by intimacy.

Anderson could smell the barbecueing springbok meat, and he looked towards the spit turning above the fire. The scent of paraffin, too, and William and Joseph's faces lit like those of hunted animals – Margarethe was there, too, and he suddenly disliked the imagery of hunt and pursuit and danger. His peace waved like the distant flag of a lost cause in the sensuous impression of the place at that moment.

The old past was breaking in, Blantyre was still wearing his fixed and conditioned look of contempt for Margarethe. Kaffir, black dolly, et cetera. Like the neighbours in Jo'burg, on the hot, dry lawns, moving in their print frocks among their gardeners and maids, struggling to forget that her hair was braided and her face and arms dark. They'd had to come back to the Bush, to avoid that, however apologetically remarked or avoided in the white suburb.

He gestured Blantyre to a table, then sat down opposite him. William and Joseph chattered like nightbirds around the roasting meat. Margarethe consulted the orders for wine and beer at the bar, her face tightened in concentration; almost as if she were flinching against a peremptory knocking at some invisible door. He smiled at Blantyre, who finished the last of his beer. This man is – bad. Thoroughly bad, he reminded himself. Be careful . . .


'Well, well, look who's here!' Chambers announced breathlessly. 'Right on time and right outside the NatWest Tower. Mr Malan in his hired Roller – shit, here comes Michael Aspel with *This is Your Life*!' Chambers laughed at his own joke while Godwin shook his head.

'He's here, Patrick – are you ready yet?'

'Look, you'll have to be patient, the traffic down here is bloody awful!' Hyde's voice emerged from the transmitter sitting heavily and black on the folding table. 'BMWs and Golf GTis up to your eyeballs!'

The excitement was infectious – like a bloody school outing, Godwin observed. The morning sun glared beyond the dark-tinted windows, against which a fly buzzed, as if decorating or weaving something around the barrel of the laser eavesdropper, which angled down towards the windows of the Reid Group offices. No one was alert to surveillance at that kind of oblique angle. The eavesdropper would have to be moved now that the window they had selected as their dry run had proved the equipment's veracity. *He took me to a wine bar – and then tried to climb into bed with me . . . a bloody wine bar!* And where Fiona and Sally were going for their holidays, and who with, and where they were meeting tonight and with whom, and that dishy man in sales . . . Sleep-inducing, with hardly a prick of interest because they were unaware of being over-heard. MacPherson's secretary and some other Sloaney girl. The fly buzzed irritatingly on the windowsill. The windows were spotted and dusty on the outside. The office had been empty for some months, he had been lucky to find it. Who would pay the bill for the month's rental, he could not imagine, and cared even less.

The venetian blinds on the focus window leaned threateningly, as if they might collapse at any moment. If they did, then the eavesdropper couldn't pick up the infinitesimal vibrations of voices against the window's glass. *A wine bar dinner, and he even showed me the packet of condoms, to prove he was taking it seriously!* Godwin tossed his head. Chambers, peering down into their office, had admired the speaker's legs.

Which was the problem, though neither he nor Hyde had remarked it – how close to the windows of MacPherson's office would Malan and whoever was with him be seated? They would need the group to be sitting as close to the windows as possible for the video and stills cameras to operate successfully. Most of MacPherson's smooth, rosewood desk was visible. He checked once more.

There was a breathing like ether from the transmitter, and the grunt of gears being changed. Godwin did not bother to peer out over the precipice of the windowsill to watch Hyde, in the van that wore the necessary POLICE labelling, shuffling back and forth within its row of orange-and-white cones marking off its parking spot in Copthall Street below him. The van had to be precisely placed if the eavesdropper was to be exactly aligned with the receiver in the van, picking up the bounced laser signal and its collected aural vibrations.

'– think Mr Kellett in Exports had AIDS?' he heard over the speaker.

A glimpse of printed cotton as a woman moved round Mac-Pherson's desk.

'That's it, Patrick!' he shouted, flicking down the transmit switch after lumbering across the room, intercepting Chambers. God, it was hot in this bloody office, the sun streaming in through windows that looked as if they were coated with nicotine.

'You don't *drop* dead from it,' came the answer from the speaker, relaying someone's reply from the office via the van.

'Hold it there!'

'Are you sure?' Hyde asked.

'Hang on . . .'

'What about selling your flat, then? Any offers?'

'Yah, just one. But I think they're serious – people from the Midlands wanting a London base. Cheek – nothing *fancy*, they said, this will do! God, who are these people? No mortgage or anything.'

Silly cow.

'Patrick, that's fine. You can come up now – Darren can look after the equipment.'

'Anyone want any lunch from round the corner – the Yuppies' sandwich bar?'

'A ploughman's with a French stick round it,' Chambers called out. 'Bring some beer, too.'

'I'll have salad in a French stick,' Godwin murmured. The sense of company, of identity, was suspicious, and he disregarded it.

'I'll just write all that down, sir,' he heard Hyde reply, then murmur something to Darren in the back of the van.

'Thank you, Sally,' he heard the speaker linked to the equipment in the van burst out. The movement-responsive camera clicked and the film wound on. He pressed the start button on the camcorder. A babbled murmur of greetings, assurances, welcomes, some laughter as trousered legs and MacPherson came into view through the lens of the still camera. Malan, presumably, someone else, and a woman's legs that didn't belong to the secretary. Even he'd taken that much notice, despite the monkishness induced – or suffered – because of his useless limbs. He watched the other legs walking and shuffling, then –

Malan, then another man – oh, yes – and then Patrick's nasty little female acquaintance from the pub. They'd managed to identify her as Valentina Malenkova, assistant Trade Attaché at the Soviet Embassy – what the bloody hell was she doing in the Reid offices? What a fucking *nerve*.

Godwin checked the calibrating lights on the eavesdropper's control box, made tiny adjustments, then switched on the back-up tape recorder. Outside, the financial towers jutted out of an oily haze. MacPherson's Glasgow accent resonated, and then he distinguished Malan's accent. The second man was van Vuuren, CEO of MLC's EuroConstruct subsidiary; building the Bucharest TraveLodge and dozens of other hotels and factories and sports centres and blocks of flats in eastern Europe. Even undercutting the Japs with their quotes, so the story went.

It was proof, if proof were needed except for idiots, he thought, as MacPherson gestured his guests to a group of armchairs near the windows. Valentina – what the hell is a KGB agent doing with the CEO of Reid Electronics? *Oh, probably making the tea, Godwin*, would no doubt be Sir Clive's reply!

From the speaker, pleasantries, mutual congratulation, expansion plans, common business concerns, the pace of orders and dates of supply. Then MacPherson coming bluntly to the point.

'Paulus – I know how hard you've been lobbying the board members you've been approaching, and I know they think you're right – *I* think you're right, for Christ's sake. But, I just have to tell you that we have to stay whiter-than-white –' A burst of laughter from Malan. 'Sorry . . . but you know how careful David had to be in disposing of his own shares. We can't be seen to be entering any joint ventures with MLC, and that's the end of it. Everyone's watching us –' Godwin smirked. '– just to catch us getting back into bed with you. I can't do it.'

The door opened behind Godwin. Then Hyde was beside him.

'What's Priabin's tart doing in there?' His curiosity was feral, angry. 'Is MacPherson crooked, then?'

'I doubt it. He even refused to join the Masons twenty years ago, though his father was one. She's there as Malan's personal assistant, according to the introductions. They don't half give them good diction at the KGB school these days. She's even got a notebook on her lap.'

'Talk about two fingers.' Godwin heard the sound of a can being opened, then it was thrust into his grip. Then two other plopping noises. Hyde flicked the ring-pull against the window.

'Don't disturb the bloody machinery!' Godwin growled.

'Sorry, darling.'

'Not that MacPherson won't do business with Malan if he can – he's doing plenty now – but he wants to keep his nose clean. Too many defence contracts won't come his way if he's seen to be sliding down the crocodile's throat.'

Below, they laughed and the girl scribbled something in her notebook. Polished as a Swiss finishing school, these days, that KGB academy outside Moscow.

Malan.

'I just want to help both Reid and MLC. Interest rates are high, you won't borrow heavily. You're jogging behind the rest of the waggons in the gold rush.'

MacPherson was holding up his hand. Godwin, Hyde and Chambers were all crowded against the tinted window.

'I know it's in the company's interests, Paulus, you don't have to convince me on that point. But they went through this group of companies like pest officers after rats. I'm not having that again, not ever. It would do more damage to profits than any deals with you I have to turn down.'

'It's a pity you have to sit on your expansion schemes, Mac.'

'Don't I know it. But you haven't had the trouble we've had just hanging on to the few subsidiaries we still have in common. On the other hand, Paulus, I see no harm in cooperation in as many areas as possible – that aren't sensitive.'

'Good. That's why Piet's here, to talk about that very subject.'

'God, this is really fascinating,' Hyde remarked and wandered away to a corner of the office and squatted on the floor. Chambers glanced at Godwin and smirked, tossing his head.

Van Vuuren was speaking now, his laptop computer on his knees, his fingers tapping. Something struck Godwin, but it vanished almost at once as he realized that the camcorder video-tape had slowed to a halt.

'I told you to check the bloody tape in this!' he roared at Chambers. 'Oh, shit!' The idea that had glanced across his imagination had returned, whole and visible, tangible enough to grasp. 'Get another fucking tape in there, *now*! Oh, *no*!' he wailed as the noise of the movement-activated camera ceased. He slapped another cassette of film against it. It began clicking comfortingly once more. Van Vuuren was still tapping at his computer.

'. . . discussed this in outline before, Gordon,' van Vuuren was saying as he typed into the laptop. 'I'll just call up the outstanding orders.' Christ, he was into MLC's mainframe computer in Johannesburg, connected to it by MacPherson's telephone line. God, have we *missed* anything? They'd be able to read the unfolded screen of his laptop, in enlargement. What had they bloody missed?

He glared at Chambers, who shrugged apologetically, as the camcorder began whirring once more. Again, there was that idea in his mind – not clear any more, and not necessarily the one he thought he'd entertained, but something.

'Labour costs in Namibia are eleven per cent below those in South Africa, and in the eastern bloc they're twenty per cent below, even with our generosity.' He could see van Vuuren smiling.

'Oh, you've found yourselves some new niggers, have you, son?' MacPherson observed drily. Malan laughed.

'As you say,' he replied. 'This is why you'd be mad not to come in.' MacPherson was shaking his head.

'It's not a moral objection,' he assured them.

'In which case, we want you working at full stretch,' Malan remarked. 'We have a huge order for consumer electronics – '

'Oh, is that the one the Koreans can't meet, Paulus?'

'I – I'm afraid so. We need you – I'll be open about that.'

'You want the stuff in a hurry, do you, son? It'll cost you, you realize that?'

'We'll have to pay what you ask – within reason.'

'Oh, I'm reasonable, don't you worry. How long?'

'Three, four weeks, for the bulk of the order.'

'Christ, you wouldn't like just to buy us out, would you? Hotels, leisure centres, factories, homes – almost every project you have under way at the moment . . . is that right?'

Malan nodded. His face appeared severe and cornered – was it imagination to believe he was satisfied, even pleased? There was something fishy about the whole conversation. As if it was an elaborate pretence . . . no, not quite that. As if *Malan* was pretending. Pretending that he no longer had any influence over the Reid Group, that he came to them merely as a customer. Almost as if he could hear the South African purring like a cat. Was he still somehow in control of Reid, had he hooks in the group, despite his public and publicized withdrawal? There was something about his face – he'd have to look at it in close-up.

'Christ,' Chambers murmured. 'Talk about winning the pools – that order's huge, I mean *vast*. How did Malan get let down by those little yellow buggers in Korea?'

'I don't know, do I?'

'We thought we'd have the component factories up and running over there,' van Vuuren was saying. 'But, we haven't. They can't even work like blacks.' He giggled. The girl appeared to be smiling, too.

'Then you'll be wanting supervisory personnel, computer programmes – the whole works – eh?'

'I'm afraid so. Look, Gordon, can you be in a position to talk fully with Piet here tomorrow?' MacPherson nodded. 'Good, then I'll leave you and him alone together to break this thing down, then you two meet again tomorrow – OK?'

'Fine by me, son.'

'Jesus Christ,' Godwin murmured. 'Did you hear that?' He sighed orgasmically. 'An order so big they'll need a fleet of planes to get it out – all bound for eastern Europe.'

'Bloody hell, you think we've –?' Chambers began.

'Oh, yes, I really think we have found something.' He felt hot, flushed with some as yet unidentified success.

Malan wanted to increase the pace of supplies from the Reid Group companies to his own eastern European subsidiaries. Soon, *now*. After spending yesterday afternoon with Priabin, and now having that girl alongside him. It had to be – just *had to be* – a KGB operation which also happened to suit Malan's book! He gripped Chambers' arm, who grinned, then winked.

'Go on,' they heard Hyde call out, 'tell Uncle Tony how clever he is. He likes that.'

'Well, aren't I?' Godwin asked, turning around.

Hyde raised his beer can ironically. 'Oh, you are, mate, you are. Did I ever say otherwise?'

The door of the office opened. A young man in the uniform of an office cleaning company poked his head and chest round it, opened his mouth to speak, but evidently saw the range of equipment beside which Godwin and Chambers were posed. Then saw Hyde squatting malevolently in the corner.

'I – this office is being rented. I –'

The vacuum cleaner stood beside his slim form, as if he were anchored to it. His eyes moved robotically, but with quickening intensity and recognition from them to the equipment, back to them, then to the cameras, to the amplifier from which voices still came, to Hyde . . .

Who was on his feet quickly, in his crumpled police uniform, murmuring: 'Listen, my son,' and pulling the cleaner through the door. 'Yes, before you ask, we're the coppers, but you can't see the warrant card because we're not supposed to be here . . . mm?' He propelled the young man down the corridor with a firm grip on his elbow. The vacuum cleaner squeaked along behind them like a dragged child's toy. 'We'll be gone in a half-hour or so – OK? You just go and empty someone else's waste-baskets and forget what you saw.'

'Look, I don't want any –'

'This is official, but then I'm not telling you how or why.' They reached the lift and Hyde punched the button. 'You've suddenly come over all dizzy, sport, and will have to go home for a lie-down. OK?'

The cleaner nodded. The doors of the lift soughed open. Hyde pushed the man in ahead of him and kicked the vacuum cleaner away. He pressed Ground Floor/Reception. The lift moved with American swiftness and silence. The man was nervous, still bemused, the after-images of what he had seen all but visible on his dilated pupils. Hyde remained silent, gripping the man's elbow, which had adopted a slight tremor. The doors opened.

'What about –'

'You just go home and forget. That's what you do.'

The foyer was cramped, and empty. 'There,' said Hyde as they reached the revolving glass doors where the street already appeared goldenly hot. 'Off you go, sport.' He propelled the cleaner through the doors, following him, standing with him for a moment on the steps.

'Sorry,' the young man offered, a belated excitement now appearing on his features. 'I – right, I'll go and have a drink. Can I come back later? I – new on the job, see, don't want to risk – '

'Yes. Half an hour.' Hyde was squinting against the slant of the sun, looking towards the parked van. The final jigsaw-piece of conviction slipped into place when the cleaner saw the van and glanced back at Hyde's unbuttoned police uniform with a new acceptance of its pretence.

'Cheers.' He went down the building's steps to the pavement.

Hyde shaded his eyes and looked up towards the windows of MacPherson's office. Godwin might even be right . . . something was certainly happening. And soon. He rubbed his hands through his tightly curling hair, then stretched luxuriously. Better check on Darren the Wonder Dog while I'm –

On the steps of the NatWest building, directly opposite him, stood Malan and the girl from the KGB. They were both looking at him, the girl bending close to Malan, then looking at the van with POLICE on the side and shaking her head vigorously. She was talking rapidly, her hand making small, definite chopping motions. She'd seen him, and recognized him. The surveillance was blown.

Oh, shit –

Too late, he turned away.

# THREE

## Africa and golden joys

Blantyre pushed aside the heavy, round stones and then lifted the waterlogged canvas bag clear of the reeds, which rattled stiffly against his forearms as he disturbed them. The water was cool on his hands and wrists. He turned to Uys and grinned.

'Easy,' he said, shaking the dripping bag so that its contents slithered against one another in their polythene wrappings like woken snakes. 'Now, let's just make sure.' He wrestled with the straps and buckles and freed them, then settled on his haunches. The other members of his unit stood idly, like spectators or automatons. Except for Uys, who said in a hoarse whisper:

'I thought you said this bloke used to be an agent, sir.'

'A long time ago – not long after you were born in that shed on that Christ-knows-where farm, Uys. He's obviously forgotten his training.' As if he had tickled a great fish onto the bank, he held up a sodden cardboard box, then a miniature keypad, then held up a water-filled bag containing small, still shapes. He remembered carrying a goldfish thus home from a fair, or was it after that circling of the wagons at the Boertrekker Memorial, during his childhood?

'Transputers,' he explained. 'Don't hurt your brains worrying about what they're for.' The bag was dripping over the small selection of items he'd arranged on the wet sand like runes. He put it down. 'He's forgotten everything he ever learned, by the look of it, man.' He checked the articles, rubbing his chin, the light of Uys' torch remaining steady. A lion snorted and grumbled on the far side of the dam. 'It must be all here,' Blantyre decided. 'Just waiting to be found.'

'Has he told anyone?' Uys asked.

'Who's to tell, out here?' He sighed and shook his head. 'Bloody *amateur*! I don't even begin to know why he took the bloody stuff, uh?' He got to his feet, holding the empty canvas bag like something he had severed from a body.

'What do we do now?' Uys asked. He was the only one of the unit facing Blantyre. Its other three members, armed, now faced outwards to give protecting fire into the night; scanning the lodge, the dam, the raised line of thatched platforms and their closed tents, the paths leading to and from the artificial waterhole. 'Sir?'

Blantyre smiled, and he saw Uys' white teeth answer his expression in the darkness. The stars hung heavily as if poorly suspended in the velvet darkness, and something slight and innocent slid through the water near them.

'How many of them, sir?' Uys asked.

'Eight guests, Anderson and the black dolly, maybe as many as six kaffirs. They all sleep away behind the lodge . . . easy to just set fire to the place, or put a rocket into it.'

'Just about the right number to make it an atrocity, Colonel,' Uys observed.

'Ah, well, so many of these kaffirs are still running round Namibia with guns and grudges. Who can tell what they might get up to, in the dark?'

'Then we'll – '

'We have to, Corporal. We can't leave Anderson alive to talk about what he found, can we? And therefore we can't leave any witnesses.'

'No, sir. When?'

'Just before dawn.'

'Then we just happen to arrive, just after daylight, having seen the smoke?'

'Exactly, Uys. Christ, what we might find – the mutilations and everything. Horrible!'

'Should never have let the South-West go independent, sir. Just proves the point.'

Blantyre said: 'He might last a week in the headlines, poor bastard. The atrocity at Okaukuejo Lodge . . .' He sighed. 'Right, change the ammunition to Russian issue, black faces for you blokes, use knives wherever and whenever you can. Make sure the bloody place *burns*!'

The others in the unit had turned round and drawn closer to him, as if he held out a bowl of food to hungry cats.

'OK, Pelzer,' Uys said, 'you collect up the evidence.'

Blantyre looked at his watch.

'It's just after one now. I want the raid mounted and over by six-thirty, so let's get moving.'


The long signal from Priabin was – satisfactory. Babbington spread his fingers on it as he stood beside his desk, the cool early morning light falling on the decoded pages instead of the lamplight which he had switched off as he came to the last, unrelated item in the report. Turned it off as quickly as shutting a door against a gale. He'd stood up, too, quite suddenly and strode about the room. His fingers drummed on the pages now, but even then he felt obligated to snatch them away.

Once more, he walked to the high window overlooking the Arsenal. The morning was fine, almost cloudless. Below, he watched the falconers, two of them carrying goshawks on their gauntleted wrists and looking up towards the roofs of the Council of Ministers building which contained his office. His head slightly to one side, he heard the cawing of a flock of hooded crows on the roof above his window, as if they mocked the two young KGB guards and their birds. He watched as the hood of one of the birds was removed, then its jesses loosed. The falconer's arm flung wide and the bird rose into the morning sun, becoming black, then almost ghostly white, finally golden. It moved purposefully, as if aimed directly at his window, then it disappeared above him into the raucous, already fading laughter of the crows. The hawks hardly ever caught or killed any of them as they moved from roof to roof around the Kremlin. It was a sport without purpose or result. The young falconer near the row of Napoleon's captured cannon was already beginning to whirl the lure to summon the futile hawk back to his wrist.

Without purpose or successful result . . . It was not an omen, that vain pursuit, but it did, somehow, force him to recall the final paragraph of Priabin's report. Babbington's wife had fallen from a horse, some miles from her home, and had suffered brain damage. The information had been gleaned from a report in *The Times*. Doubtless, that Murdoch rag that had once been a newspaper had gloatingly recollected what they deemed his *treachery*. She,

Elizabeth, was in a coma and not expected to come out of it . . . no doubt his son, the unamiable Richard, would soon switch off the life-support and inherit her money.

He did not understand why Priabin had included the information, or why it niggled at the corner of his awareness like grit in a mental eye. He cordially hated her, as she did him – though she would not be aware that she hated him now, he imagined. Had he wanted to return, to be at her bedside – even switch off the machinery of her living himself – he could not have done so. Not that he wished it. Richard could not lay hold of his money, only the house and what she had retained of her family's poor resources and the money he had deposited in her accounts and the shares in her name. He'd drink and roister it away in a year, probably.

Babbington rubbed his beard and moved from the window with a slight smile as the goshawk returned to the falconer's wrist. It looked grumpily dissatisfied. Perhaps his son would not even wait a decent interval before ending his mother's unconscious existence – his daughter, who hated him with all the venom of her mother, would not restrain him, though out of pain rather than cupidity or indifference. No, Priabin should not have sent that item of information. It belonged, like so much else, to a past life, a former self.

But, the remainder of his signal was – satisfactory. Aubrey, as they knew, was still on sick leave. Orrell was a clod. Godwin a technician who had no inkling of what might in reality be happening, merely that someone had their hand in the petty cash! Malan had hurried the schedule competently. If the Reid Group had to be abandoned, then so be it. It would be stripped of everything that wasn't nailed down before the UK operation was closed down. He ground his teeth. Kapustin had, he was forced to admit, been right. No smoke without fire, the finger of suspicion, mud sticks, et cetera! The symmetry and secrecy of the Reid operation was compromised. It was wisest to abandon the UK, for the moment – once they could replicate the transputer and wafer scale integration technology successfully. However, he should signal Priabin and instruct him to obtain whatever information he thought Godwin and the damnable Hyde had obtained by eavesdropping. Though it must be done under deep cover, it could not be *their* interest that was revealed. Orrell was a clown, but then Godwin might run to Aubrey with his snivelling little tale and that perfidious old man might, just might, be well enough to take note. It was, of course, easily containable. A surprising piece of enterprise by Godwin. But then, suspension could not be any farther than around the very next corner, if the matter of obtaining the material was handled subtly.

Priabin was clever enough for the business. It was – satisfactory. It was, simply, a pity that Reid and especially Inmost and its advanced microchip and transputer research programme, would be lost to them. Temporarily. They would have to go back to America in a big way when the dust of the Shapiro business had settled.

Then he shivered, unexpectedly. For some unfathomable reason, he recalled waking, as a young bridegroom-to-be, at four in the morning, horrified that he had forgotten to write his damned speech of thanks for the wedding reception. He had scribbled feverishly in the dawn light, and it had gone well. Elizabeth had looked – charming that day, yet already complaisant and resentful, knowing she had been bought and sold; his family's money for her family's ancestry. An exchange surely, rather than a sordid bargain? He remembered now. She had looked charming for others, merely sullen for him, even on their wedding day.

He breathed deeply. Perhaps her paintings would increase in value with her death. It would help keep Richard in the style to which he had early determined to remain accustomed.

He reached the window again. The falconers had gone and the crows were back, scrabbling and cawing and sharpening their beaks on the tiles and guttering above his head. The sky outside was clear and blue with every prospect of a fine day. He turned over the last page of Priabin's report then picked up the telephone.

'Yes, I want to dictate a signal for Codes, to be transmitted immediately to London. Come in now, would you?'


As he slipped from the bed, he suddenly felt his whole body bend beneath the freight of that other person in the bedroom; Margarethe. He had endangered her. He looked down at her tiny frame, apparently peacefully asleep, the sheet and single blanket pulled up around her, one arm exposed, its dark skin sheened by the yellow moon.

He had been unable to sleep. Blantyre meant him and his wife harm, the fact was inescapable. He swallowed a hard lump in his throat as he looked at Margarethe, then padded across the rugs scattered on the wooden floor, pausing only to put on his shorts and a thin sweatshirt, then his boots. The floor creaked, Margarethe moved and murmured, then slipped back into a deeper sleep, her arm now stretched across the white space where he had been lying. He reluctantly closed the bedroom door behind him, having taken the old Browning CP-35 pistol from the chest of drawers with little or no conscious thought. The butt was already warming in his hand; he clenched it too tightly, as if he had never before held a gun.

The pre-dawn air was chilly after the bedroom and living room, but not necessarily the cause of the shiver that enveloped him for whole seconds, until he shook it off as a dog might have done water. Then, head cocked to one side, he listened. Someone snoring loudly, the hum of an unseen insect. The fingertips of his left hand prickled with heat and gradually his body seemed to become more alert, thinner-skinned, its network of nerves closer to the surface. He went quietly down the steps and along the sloping track towards the tents silhouetted against the sheen of the water. He was pressed – compelled – to check the safety of the canvas bag and its contents, the proof that Blantyre and MLC were in collusion with at least one KGB officer who had spent a holiday – or came from, or had relatives living in – Novgorod the Great . . . There was little or nothing else. The cargo didn't mean anything to him, it might even be legal. Except that Blantyre was there. He walked with a swift, crouching lope.

Before-dawn was already beginning to pale into the day, making the eastern darkness royal-blue, dimming the stars. The moon was almost at the horizon, tiredly jaundiced. A bird rustled in the thatch of the closest tourist tent. Floorboards creaked as someone turned over in bed.

For there was some kind of collusion, some illegality – he smiled at the prim, solicitor's tone of his thoughts – in the adjacence of a KGB ID card to British technology, in the shell of an old Dakota in the middle of the Namibian Bush. Otherwise . . .

Otherwise, he would have been dealing with some thick-necked, dim sergeant of police, even a black man. *That*, of course, was the confirmation. A *whites-only* recovery of goods from a wrecked aircraft. The stone had struck the water and the ripples had begun moving outwards – which made him thankful he had dispatched the airmail letter to Aubrey in London.

The relief in his breathing unnerved him as he inspected the little sandy stretch beside the dam and found no footprints. Blantyre hadn't been here then –

– the canvas bag was gone, and the stones had been moved. It and its contents had been taken away. Anderson gasped with fear, uncertainty. He looked around wildly, his arms waving as if in protest. Blantyre's tent was lightless, and the scene around him was empty of people . . . hadn't just happened, then. Distantly, he heard Joseph or William rattling pans or buckets. The royal-blue of the day filled almost half of the sky now. The eastern horizon was paler. A kudu stepped innocently from the low trees on the other side of the dam, then paused, sensing his presence. Its horns were like silhouetted branches. He could not avoid staring across the expanse of grey water towards the animal, recognizing its nervousness as his own, knowing that both he and the big gazelle were potential victims.

He stood up, wiping the water from his arms and hands with hard, rubbing strokes. The kudu crashed back into the cover of the stunted trees. He ran wildly, then, dragging the pistol from the belt of his shorts, towards Blantyre's tent. He clattered up the steps, disregarding the noise, and tugged open the flap and the mosquito netting, plunging into the darkness –

– to find his bed empty. Slept-in, but now empty and cool. Fear seized his chest with a chill implosive force, making resolve smaller, allowing hesitation to hurry against him. He had not even *thought* of the consequences of bursting in on Blantyre, had the man been there and roused from sleep. His instincts were uncertain and unpractised. He was no longer the jewelled and cogged piece of machinery he had once been. He was something rusted, abandoned in long grass and weeds, and no match for Blantyre.

Where was he? He had the evidence, obviously – he *knew*. Anderson whirled around in the narrow tent. Insects had already entered. He lit the oil-lamp because he needed to perform a small sequence of physical actions to calm the shiver he felt mounting through his frame. At once, in the smoky lick of the flame, he saw thick-bodied insects as large as toffees throw themselves against the glass of the lamp. The tent was as tidy as a soldier's abandoned billet. As if

79

Blantyre had merely left without paying his bill –

The first explosion shook him like thunder; realization was almost immediate. Fear flooded his present self, but there was a resurgence of that former self, already moving and assuming control of him. He dragged aside the tent flap. From the house, a gout of flame burst out of part of the thatched roof.

The tent's platform clattered beneath his hurrying boots as the house erupted again in a second explosion – rocket, he realized, remembering the puzzling fizz of noise just before the crump of the explosion and the surge of flame.

He careered down the few steps, then ran wildly up the long slope towards the house, his hands and chest already bathed in the orange light of the fire as he raced against its progress along the roof. He was aware of every passing second, every millimetre of the fire's advance; aware of where the rocket had been directed, towards the house itself, towards the bedroom where he – she . . . the fire would be inspecting then swallowing each piece of furniture, each rug, each door, entering the bedroom, reaching the *bed*. Their primary target was himself – his room, his wife. A third explosion terrified him into halting for a moment, stunning him with the certainty that he was already too late.

He whimpered with terror and anticipated, certain loss, cursed his body for being too slow to get to the house. The thatch over the verandah caught, rustled like living grass for a moment, then roared upwards.

People behind him were waking, calling out to one another like dolphins separated and hunted; small, chirruping cries of alarm and incomprehension. There were others in the main house, too . . . would they kill them all? Or only those who were dangerous to them? Margarethe –! He was forty yards, then thirty, then twenty from the raging thatch. Something staggered across the verandah as he reached it and rolled down the steps, burning, at his feet. It might have been one of the elderly American women. He coughed on the smoke that the dawn breeze thrust towards him. William was dead on the verandah, his throat slashed. Burning gobbets of thatch rained down on him as he crossed the restaurant, flinching against the noise of the flames and the falling thatch. He flung open the first door. Another explosion, near the dam – no time for them now.

He was calling out; screaming her name, his eyes watering, his throat raw and lungs filled with the acrid smoke. Behind him, bottles in the bar exploded. The narrow corridor of unpainted concrete was as smoke-filled as a railway tunnel. He shouted, yelled, pleaded for a reply.

A dark figure, a blackened rather than black face, the strange-familiar outline of a rifle, something stubby and foreign. The menace, the immediate threat, absorbed all his subliminal concentration. He killed the unidentified figure at once, with two shots, as he might a mamba he found in the house. His concentration was so finely focused that he saw the shots rip the shirt like the fingers of an angry mob, saw the white flesh before the red gouted. The body fell back behind a bloom of red fire that erupted from the floorboards at an open door towards the end of the corridor. He stepped over the flames and the body.

Joseph's bedroom door. Joseph lay half on his bed, destroyed by the frenzy of a long knife. Wild, disappointed men from the Bush, ex-SWAPO or some other extreme remnant; it happened, still. Here, it would appear the convincing lie of an atrocity carried out by local blacks against whites. He rushed on down the corridor, the smell of burning flesh too close to belong to anyone but himself. He dared not look down at his clothing, his exposed skin.

The bedroom door was as he had left it, closed. What remained of it. Flame licked at the dark wood and slid along the door's panels. He kicked at it, thankful he had put on the heavy boots. It sagged inwards. The walls of their bedroom were orange with leaping fire. It was difficult to see the bed; smoke filled the room, flame shimmering through its rolling cloud. The whole bedroom seemed on the point of a single, massive combustion.

Coughing, he crawled towards where the bed must be ... gun jerking forward at each movement of his right hand, the weight on his raw hands and knees hurting, splinters dragging into his skin, the heat scorching ... He inched on, his chest tightening, his awareness concentrating more and more narrowly on the certainty of choking in the smoke if he stayed in the bedroom even moments longer ...

Touched what he immediately knew was her hand and which did not touch his but merely rested there on the floor. The absence of any pulse in the wrist he held in his fingers prompted the terror of certainty. His whole stomach heaved and he fought the desire to vomit, swallowing again and again, concentrating solely on it . . .

Slowly, fragmentedly, he realized that the smoke was no thicker than when he had entered the room and that the flames were dancing sinuously in the breeze that was coming through a great gap torn in the bedroom wall. Her hand did not move, her wrist did not pucker with a pulse, her body did not stir. His hand climbed her arm like the touch of a blind man, then felt her small, delicate features, her cheekbones, lips, nose. The back of her head was slippery with blood. She would not move again, ever. He remained on his knees, doubled up by the scorching of his skin and the effects of the smoke; immobile with grief. She had been killed by one of the rockets, impacting with the wall near the bed, flinging her across the room with the force of the explosion. He realized that he had not been making for the bed, but had been drawn to this spot in the far corner of the room where her body had been flung.

Smoke billowed. His throat was raw and his eyes streamed. His mind was quiescent, in traumatic rest, his limbs felt weaker and heavier. Slowly, he collapsed onto his side, near her, his hand holding hers. He could not see her body and could not bear to imagine the destruction that had been working on it.

Nagging like a sore, like the pain of his scorched flesh . . . survival. His fingers were numb, gripping her hand. His mind was numb . . . survival. Blantyre. Strangely, the letter he had sent to Aubrey. The Dakota. Survival . . . Blantyre, who had done this to Margarethe. Blantyre, who had intended it . . .

. . . revenge, the illness of which he thought himself cured forever. *Blantyre*. Out there, somewhere, the architect and designer of this . . . her murder.

Part of him cried out as he began crawling, wanting not to leave her, protesting at his desertion. But the other self found the shattered door and the corridor and its rough floorboards, found the restaurant after the signpost of the South African he had shot. The smoke seemed to lessen, then increase once more. The thatch above the restaurant had collapsed into a dozen small fires. Bottles continued to explode like guns. A line of flames down by the water. No survivors. The fires were the exact, mocking shapes of the guest tents.

He hopped, staggered, jumped across the small distance from the verandah to the ground . . . fell. He rolled down the long, shallow slope, feeling as if he had not survived; that his real self was dead, burning beside her body. And yet he knew some other self lived more violently and truly than he had thought possible. He was already beginning to ignore the last of the screaming, the noise of explosions and killing. He was concerned only with concealment, escape. Until he could seize his opportunity, take the chance he knew *would* come.

Water. Stop the pain with water. But his pain was increasing and his grief was seeping back, the horror of knowledge and the touch of his fingers on her slippery, wet skin and her broken head . . . Hatred of Blantyre, whom he saw as clearly as if the man stood over him holding a pistol, drove him on hands and knees down towards the water. Dawn impressed itself even on his blurred, wet vision. Otherwise, his awareness became blank except for the palpable form of the man who had murdered Margarethe.

Renewed gunfire prompted him like a cattle-prod. Things rattled agonizingly against his raw skin, then he was drowning. A terrified bout of coughing and vomiting, the noise in his ears of water being thrashed by desperate arms. The water seeming further to inflame his skin. He wanted to scream with infinite pain and rage.

Slowly, stroke by clumsy stroke, he swam out from the bank, his mind already unconscious, even her face distant, then gone. Blantyre's face, too – small and indistinct, then absent. Then her face coming back, as he tried to swim . . .

. . . unconscious, he opened his mouth, not sensing the water that rushed to fill his lungs.


Hyde was staring down at the Charing Cross Road and the early morning crowds at the junction with Oxford Street. The slumped, dozing shapes of young and ancient had removed themselves from the doorways of the sex shop and the pub. The city looked normally untidy now, not desperate or abandoned as it sometimes did just before dawn.

Godwin was, as if a voice on an interminable tape-loop, arguing with Chambers.

'It can be done, Terry – it's all in *there*!' They were sitting in front of the huge television screen, quarrelsome and yet as unmoving as two old women in a residential home. Less active than the bag-lady down there, near the traffic lights, intent on a crumbling lump of something in one dirty hand which she kept pressing to her mouth. A stale, abandoned pasty or pie, probably. 'And we can get in there, if we can gather the whole access code from the stills and the videotape.'

'We'd have to get *everything* right – every single letter and number,' Chambers warned. 'And we had to change the films at one point – look, I'm not saying it's impossible, just that we'll be bloody lucky. And there's the fact that it's bound to be a secure laptop. There'll be an ID signal sent from his machine to the main-frame, to identify it, even if we knew the access codes. We couldn't use another machine –'

'No, we could bloody well use his, though!'

'How the hell could we do that?'

'Never mind, for the moment. Let's hurry up those enlargements of the stills and start picking the bones out of this tape with the help of the freeze-frame.'

'Do you two want anything as mundane as breakfast?' Hyde enquired.

'What? Oh, yes . . . I'll tell Jim –'

'*I'll* get it. Jim stays on duty downstairs. Priabin knows about us. Ten to one, he knows what equipment we used and what we might have found out from Malan – which is bugger all, but he won't see it like that. I'll get breakfast.'

'Suit yourself.'

'Lock the doors and keep your eyes on the security camera.'

'We're safe up here,' Godwin remarked breezily.

And perhaps they were. He'd check for surveillance when he got downstairs. The special lift could only be operated with a key, the two floors were sealed off from the rest of Centre Point, there were alarms, security cameras. And it was the middle of London and broad daylight. Perhaps Godwin was right.

He turned to look back at the television screen. A frame had been frozen. He recognized MacPherson's desk, the telephone attached to van Vuuren's laptop computer, the man's slim fingers poised over its keypad, about to insert himself into the MLC mainframe in Johannesburg. God alone knew how Godwin thought he was going to do the same.

He closed the door behind him. The corridor was glowing with dusty light coming through the fire door window. Twenty floors up, a sealed unit within the building, in effect.

But the silence from Priabin was deafening.

'There,' Godwin sighed in the darkness. 'Perfect.' He held up the last of the enlargements, close to his face, then added: 'OK, turn on the lights.'

The darkroom lights sprang out against the beige walls and the lowered, black blinds, glanced off the enlarger, the liquors in the trays and the rows of prints that gleamed like washing-lines arranged for some detergent advertisement. The room seemed suddenly warmer, almost foetid, with their efforts, and Godwin turned to grin at Chambers – who hurried forward between the festooned outer garments and lingerie of the lines of prints.

There were hands suspended everywhere in the room, dangling from the clips and pegs along the cat's cradle of cords; hands poised, hands working, hands at rest. Fingers extended like those of a pianist, fingers clawlike or drawn back as if to pounce again. Van Vuuren's hands and fingers, van Vuuren's keypad, his screen folded open on his lap. Everything was – potentially – there. Godwin glanced at his watch. Four-thirty in the afternoon. Van Vuuren was back at the InterContinental Hotel. He had booked a table for dinner in the hotel restaurant, and the high-class call girl was half-caste, as beautiful and desirable as something gleaming from an advert for coffee or rum. Van Vuuren's suite would be unoccupied for perhaps as long as two hours, from eight until ten. And he would be certain to leave his laptop in his suite – not take it with him to the restaurant.

Godwin rubbed his hands like a miser or someone moving closer to a fire. Once they had solved the sequence of the still enlargements, he had power over van Vuuren, and thus power over Malan – and the satisfaction of a solution beckoning.

'OK,' he announced, 'let's start taking them down.'

They were as eager as two children raiding an orchard, reaching up, pulling prints out of the grasp of their clips, gathering them into ordered sequences. Chambers hesitated. 'We're not going to get enough detail off these.' He inspected the enlargement he had

85

plucked from its clip, as if short-sighted. 'His hands were moving too fast –'

'I know that,' Godwin replied sarcastically. 'But look at the screen he's using, the VDU – clear as a bell. Try getting that quality from a freeze-frame on the video. Besides which, we had to change the bloody cassette halfway through. There'll be stuff missing – so don't get anything out of sequence.'

'OK,' Chambers muttered, pulling down the last of the enlargements, then holding them against his chest. 'Set, then?'

Godwin grinned. 'Set.' He looked at his watch. 'Four-forty. Let's get to it.'

As they left the darkroom, the distant sighing of lifts was audible above the hum of computers and amplifiers. Late afternoon, home time, Godwin thought, but then the image of his unkempt flat and the sole company of the thin black cat appeared, and the noise of the lifts faded. Chambers lowered the blinds and closed them. The afternoon light was smoky at the edges of the windows. Chambers was whistling softly as he tugged the huge television screen into the centre of the room, inspected the video cassette and slid it into the VCR. Godwin busied himself arranging the sheafs of enlargements on a long table, as if he were laying places for an important dinner party. Van Vuuren was dining at eight. Perhaps he'd climb on the half-caste call girl before dinner, perhaps not. He looked up. Chambers was fast-forwarding through the arrival of Malan, van Vuuren and Priabin's girl in MacPherson's office. Trust Hyde to blow it all, appearing on the steps just as Malan left!

'OK?' Chambers enquired.

'OK . . . bit more – oh, ah, just there. He's dragged the laptop onto his knees – right.' There was a hard, bright light pooling down on the long table, gleaming off the prints. The image on the screen was clear, detailed. Chambers, waving the remote control like a flag, seated himself in front of the screen and switched on a tiny pocket recorder. Settled with a pad on his crossed leg, pen poised. 'Ready for dictation, Miss Chambers?' Godwin enquired.

'Not sitting on your knee though, Mr Godwin.'

'OK, let's watch this video nasty.' He settled himself to comfort, poised against the thrust of his sticks, the table neatly laid with enlargements, in their proper sequence. Outside, he heard a distant church clock thinly chime the hour. Five. The lifts sighed downwards with gratitude. They had their own private lift, key-operated like the fire doors at the end of the corridor. They were isolated within the huge office block. 'Right . . . Open Sesame.'

On the screen, van Vuuren's hands opened the laptop computer. Chambers flicked a switch, and the conversation recorded by the laser eavesdropper filled the darkened room. Van Vuuren and Malan attempting to prove to MacPherson that Reid Electronics needed their business. They'd already listened to it so many times, it was becoming subliminal. Van Vuuren's fingers were poised, like some tricksy shot of the bent arms and legs of a row of sprinters waiting for the starting pistol. Chambers stirred on his chair and Godwin felt tense, ludicrously on his mark, ready to move. Chambers held the tiny recorder to his lips, poised.

Van Vuuren's right hand attached MacPherson's telephone extension to the computer, then his fingers began jabbing at the buttons.

'. . . South Africa . . . that's Jo'burg, MLC's main building,' Chambers murmured as Godwin shuffled along the table, under the hard light thrown down on it from the ceiling, the fingers of one hand touching and arranging the enlargements as if he were making the final, fussy inspection of his place settings. 'Now we're into the mainframe.'

The room was oppressively silent behind the thin murmur of electricity and machines, behind Chambers' whisper and the scribble of his pen and even the tiny whirr of his pocket recorder. The still photographs caught most of the numbers – especially on the VDU screen, repeating everything like a prompter in a theatre.

The screen recognized van Vuuren – at least, the fingerprint of his personal computer – in the photograph under Godwin's splayed fingers, which were white and coarse like anaemic sausages under the light. *Access confirmation required,* spilt the VDU.

'Kruger,' Chambers muttered, snorting. 'Christ, how bloody original – they might have made it Krugerrand, I suppose,' he added derisively.

'Kruger it is,' Godwin confirmed. The photographs, and the video, were even better than he had hoped. Piece of cake, as they used to say . . . Remembering ominously, the panicky moment when he and Chambers had changed the video cassette in the recorder *and* the roll of film in the camera . . . there had been an overlap of whole seconds. He tried not to think of it, attending to Chambers and the sequence he was following, piece by piece. 'Then these words – Afrikaans, Terry?'

'First one is . . . B-o-e-t-'

'-e . . . new word.' Godwin skipped a number of enlargements. 'Yes, here we are. Boete Erazmus. Who was he? Friend of Paul Kruger?'

'Doesn't matter, does it? Next?' Chambers began muttering but Godwin, elated and anxious in the same moment, was halfway along the table now, approaching what he knew to be a blank place setting. He skipped heavily on his sticks and announced.

'E-l-l-i-s . . . Park. Ellis Park.'

'Agreed. Why am I the straight man again?'

'Because, Ernie, you don't look as comical as I do,' Godwin muttered. 'What have you got next?'

Chambers pressed the Play button of the remote control, then said: 'Where's Ellis Park?'

'Who knows?' Godwin thudded around the end of the table, his fingers measuring the display on the photographed VDU as it changed letter by letter by –

'Shit,' Chambers murmured. 'End of tape.'

Godwin had reached the gap he superstitiously hadn't left empty. Even crowded the prints there, as if to compensate.

'N-e-w-l-a . . .' Chambers recited, pressing the slow-motion button each time, inspecting each frame, leaning forward on his chair, straining at the screen. 'Then the new bloody tape says – what?' Godwin was watching the jerk of the images on the TV screen, mesmerized. '-s-v-e-l-d . . . Shit!' He rounded on Godwin, his chair bucking like that of an angry child refusing to eat. 'What have you bloody got?'

'Newla, like you, then I don't even have the end of the next word, or words . . . was that being eaten as you got back?'

Chambers flicked on two frames. 'Yes, the next one's -e-l-d . . . it's being gobbled. Then he's in. *Menu*'s the next thing to appear. You?'

'Menu,' Godwin announced heavily, his fingers stirring on the print, as if to conjure something more from it. 'Oh, balls.' He waggled his sticks in exasperation, while Chambers sat gloomily with his chin on his arms, which were folded along the back of his chair.

The building around, above, below them was silent now, but the room was no longer cleverly secretive, comfortably engaged in exposure.

'Have we got the rest of it?' Godwin snapped. The names had not even begun to niggle, or suggest. English and Afrikaans – they speak *both*, he reminded himself. Van Vuuren's access code – probably common to all MLC executives, at least the senior ones who would have been issued with fingerprinted laptops and allowed to access the mainframe's voluminous files – had a hole in it. If they couldn't decipher – *guess* – what it was, then they couldn't access the computer in Johannesburg, down the telephone line in van Vuuren's hotel suite – that evening, or ever. Van Vuuren was leaving for South Africa the following morning. 'Oh, bugger.'

'Just number sequences,' Chambers commented, having relayed them to his tiny recorder. 'Then we get into the business. After the numbers – he used only the ones to access the project and shipment files, didn't he? – we could have anything we wanted. The mainframe asks, you tell it in simple words –'

'Afrikaans?'

'No, English.'

'So, we've got it all, except for – what? One word, two, three –'

'God knows – I don't. Oh, there's one joke, did you spot it?'

Godwin scanned the prints. 'Yes – to confirm the Menu, keep it on the screen – must be a failsafe device. The trick answer – *Mandela.*'

'Cheeky bastards.'

'Everything – *almost*. God, we've got MLC's mainframe lying down with its legs open, and we can't get a hard on!' Then Godwin looked towards a corner of the silent room as the alarm sounded. The security man's features appeared on the small close-circuit screen, intercepting the usual images of Centre Point's foyer or the emergency staircase in an unceasing, secure and discounted sequence. Godwin heard the distant wailing of a siren from beyond the lowered blinds. Chambers had risen from his chair and was approaching the screen. The room seemed isolated beyond the point of comfort.

'Mr Godwin, there's been a bomb alert – might I suggest you evacuate, like the rest of the building?'

'I thought they'd gone home –' Godwin began. Five-forty now.

'Mr Godwin, most of the building was empty – a few people were left. They've gone now, I've checked. The Bomb Squad has been summoned – telephone tip-off, looks like some Middle East connection. Can you come down now in the lift? I'm being evacuated like everyone else.' There was a police uniform half in the picture behind their security man.

'Bloody hell –!' Chambers began.

'Yes, Jim, we'll be down at once.'

'Very well, Mr Godwin.' The screen went blank, then reasserted the images of the foyer and the staircase. A couple of people were hurrying through the foyer; the stairs were blank.

'Well?' Chambers asked.

'Well? Let's collect the stuff we need – just in case.'

'They saw Hyde on the steps yesterday. Do you –?'

'Don't ask – just collect the gear, the videotape, the recorder.'

'Right.'

Godwin began to gather up the stills, shuffling them expertly into a heap, struggling along the table, while Chambers expelled the cassette, collected sheafs of computer printout, their notes, other papers. Christ, Godwin thought, let's get a move-on, there's so much bloody stuff here. He glanced round at Chambers once more, his arms full of still-tacky photographs, Chambers' embrace filled to overflowing – two paediatric nurses saving babies from a ward.

'Have we got everything – well, *enough*?' he burst out.

Chambers was stuffing sheafs of material into a loose bag, then kneeling to fill another, glancing wildly towards littered tables, shelves of videotape.

'Another couple of minutes!' he blurted.

The evening sun struck hotly at the edges of the lowered blinds. Suddenly, the room was menacing. A bomb scare. There was no way it could be counter-activity, no way it was simply a ruse. It was a real device . . . rush hour, crowded streets, corner of Oxford Street. Whoever it was, they were really in business. Godwin scooped videotapes into the open mouth of a sports bag, sweeping his arm along metal shelving as if he were engaged in some lunatic supermarket competition.

90

'Ready?' he shouted in a high voice that didn't seem to be his.

'Ready!' Chambers called back in a voice similarly distorted.

'Then let's bloody well go. Let's get moving before they cut off the power to the lift!'

On the screen in the corner, an empty foyer, empty corridors, empty staircase. In another minute, they'd be isolated up here, with the bomb likely to go off. They hadn't burned the codebooks or collected them; there was a hundred thousand quid's worth of equipment in the rooms as well as all the secrets, lying around like dandruff now.

Godwin scuttled after Chambers, through the doors and into the corridor towards the lift.


Hyde paused at the corner of Oxford Street and the Charing Cross Road, the polythene bag of jazz records banging against his knee. He knew that Ros would want to add up the little sticky labels that betrayed his extravagance, and then berate him with the total before he could peel them from each record sleeve. Jesus . . . The traffic was glutinously still as he came out of the side-street, a few horns tooting impotently, already more than half-accustomed to an emergency. Red-and-white tape fluttered in the early evening breeze, clots of frocks and shirts and suits had collected on the pavements as the shops emptied and their cargoes stilled into observation. Oxford Street was taped to a standstill, as was the Charing Cross Road. Clutters of black taxis amid the Smarties of queues of cars, all collected in front of the dais on which the real dignitaries of the occasion would be seated. Centre Point. Suddenly, police everywhere, TV cameras, the first of the fire engines almost discreetly parked, the ambulances . . .

And the crowd began to move against him, backwards, as the police swept at them like a stiff, new broom, brushing them away from the steps of the office block. He began struggling forward, no one looking at him, no one staring towards him, all of them gravitationally tugged in their concentration towards Centre Point, their heads craning upwards, waiting for the movie-like shattering of glass and the spill of rubble from a damaged tower. He elbowed two girls aside, then a man in a fawn suit with sweatstained armpits, then an old man – righted him, apologized, pushed forward – then more shoppers, more bags colliding with his own . . . which he dropped on the tarmac, and managed to ignore after an initial pang.

A police uniform, a hand aimed at his chest deterringly.

'I'm sorry, sir, but –'

Crowds milling – the last of them, really – on the steps, people in ordered flight. He glimpsed Godwin and then Chambers, stooped with the weight of bags, papers protruding, a bulky laptop computer in Chambers' right hand; as if they had looted a shop. It couldn't be a bomb scare, not with those two carrying out their luggage. Too accidental to be real; it was arranged. He glanced up more than twenty floors. The blinds were down all along that secure floor. He waved his ID card.

'Just let me through – you've seen one before?'

The policeman winced, became angry, then nodded him through, tight-lipped with disdain. He sensed the crowd's sudden interest in him as he began mounting the steps, waving his ID now like a flag at anyone who moved towards him. Top of the steps, and Godwin almost bumping into him as he balanced himself for the short descent to the long-shadowed street and the expectant crowd.

'Where's Jim?' Hyde asked.

'You're bloody *late*!' Chambers snapped, sweating under the effort of his bags and computer.

'Where's Jim, Godwin – why isn't he with you?'

'What –?' Godwin's head turned towards the smoked glass doors and the dim foyer beyond them. 'He – I assumed . . .'

'He'd be *here*, waiting for you, you pair of pillocks! What's happened to him?'

'I forgot Jim –'

'Oh, *shit*!' He glared at Godwin, then added: 'This is no bomb scare, sport – or didn't you realize that?' He hurried towards the glass doors and the policeman nervously posted there. He flashed his ID card, then thrust the doors open. A police inspector moved to intercept him, his reflection sun-dimmed and slanted by the movement of the door. The constable shook his head at the inspector, who slowed, then turned to Godwin. Hyde pushed into the empty, silent foyer of Centre Point.

He glanced back towards the crowds, being shunted like retreating waves by a tidemark of blue uniforms. There were more ambulances now, the first fire engine had become a small flock, and he heard the wail of nearing sirens. No one would enter the building now, because his ID had told them that he, and whoever he sought, did not officially exist and wouldn't need to be explained away. Silence and emptiness in the vast foyer; deserted security desks, boards filled with engraved nameplates signifying emptied offices.

He began to run, because of Jim, the security man who should have been outside with Godwin and Chambers – Jim *would* have been, ex-Special Branch sergeant. Jim and his bank of screens monitoring the rest of the building, the lifts, the emergency stairs –

– because of yesterday, because Malan and Priabin's clever bitch had seen him opposite the NatWest Tower. He wriggled the key in the closed door, found it unlocked, opened it. His face brushed against the swing of a jacket hung up behind the door. On the console's desk, the *Sun* lay open like a cliché at the racing pages, pencil-marked. The chair was empty –

– no monochrome images of the stairs, the lift doors closed, the foyer and the secure floor . . . Jim's hand open like a flower, his face bland in death, eyes staring at the ceiling. A small leak of blood from the back of his neck, near the hairline. The collar was damp with it, hardly wet, really . . . A cigarette still smouldering in a tin ashtray. The screens had been switched off, but they'd been in a hurry. There was no pulse, no heartbeat; Jim's stubble against his temple as he listened to the man's chest. He perched on the edge of the chair and flicked at the console's switches. Screens enlivened, suddenly filled with empty corridors, blank walls, lift doors, the silence of the secure floor, some scraps and sheets of paper littering the corridor, dropped as Chambers and Godwin scuttled for the lift. The emergency stairs – fifth floor, sixth, seventh – secure lift doors closed . . . where was it, up or down? Should be down –

– inside the SIS offices. Three of them, blurting onto the screen, scuttling in their black outfits and ski masks, fingering papers, machines, collecting with furious, controlled haste. They'd been inside when the fake bomb scare alert began, waited until they could kill Jim – Hyde glanced down at the pale expression and the blank, open eyes – then gone up in the secure lift almost immediately. In five minutes, they'd be out the same way.

Priabin's people, armed with Uzis, dressed like the SAS at the Iranian Embassy siege. Neat, all of it . . . fingering whatever Godwin

93

and Chambers hadn't had time to snatch up. And that was, undoubtedly, a lot. Clues to exactly what they were doing, how far they were into the maze.

'Stupid bastards,' he murmured, slipping from the chair and closing the office door behind him. Locking it. Then he ran to the bank of lifts in the foyer. They'd hear the SIS lift going down and coming back up, they'd be waiting if he used that.

The floor below – no, above them, two floors to be safer. The lift soughed upwards, seeming noisier to his nerves. Priabin's people, had to be, not Malan's . . . he wouldn't get his fingers dirty handling rubbish like himself and Godwin and Chambers. Priabin had to follow after Malan's pet dislikes with the pooper-scooper.

Two floors above the SIS offices, the lift stopped and the doors opened.

Christ, why did Godwin and Chambers have to believe the *Independent* and the Yanks when they were told the Cold War was over? He stepped out into the corridor, gingerly as a cat. Sirens from below, distant and unreal. Godwin and Chambers no longer believed that people meant them *real* harm, for Christ's sake! People would still come through doors, waving guns, even if their reasons had changed. Three men with Uzis – he took the Heckler & Koch out of his waistband and pulled the slide back, jerking a round into readiness. They had begun stuffing material, machines, computer printouts and tapes into soft canvas bags as he had left Jim's office and Jim's body. Not long now. They wouldn't hang about.

He went through the fire doors and down the staircase. He looked from the window down towards the diminished and shadowy street, to the army vehicles and purposeful movement of uniforms away from them. The crowd was welded by the hot glow of the evening sun into a variegated mass of shabby, faded colours, cordoned by a thin, dark line of policemen. He reached the SIS floor and its silence, his fingers touching out at full stretch of his arm at the fire door. He pushed at the door, trying to remember if it squeaked – silence as it opened, then the clicks and bumps like an old, damaged record amplified as he heard their noises. He held the gun two-handed, vertically in front of his face, elbows bent, as he shuffled silently along the corridor, back sliding along the wall.

The storeroom door was unlocked – fortunate sloppiness by Jim or someone else. He slipped into the darkness, closing the door behind him, hearing his breathing at once, magnified above their noises from the two main rooms of the floor. He flicked on the light. Dust, metal shelving dulled with it, a litter of old files, papers, tapes stacked like pram wheels, bins of tape waste and shredded printout. Unspooled tape and confetti-like shreds of paper scattered over the floor. They'd searched the storeroom already, and abandoned it as an unyielding mine. He moved across the floor, listening, sidling by a trolley on which an old TV monitor rested. His hand fondled the shredded paper as if he were dipping into a bran tub, feeling grain. He patted his pockets for the lighter –

– the lid of which clanged noisily, imitating old American lighters. He shovelled armfuls of tape spool and paper into the waste-bin, then lifted it onto the trolley. Removed the TV, hearing every tiny noise louder than their noises from beyond the door. If it's locked . . . ? Can't be, they opened it. He flicked at the igniter, flame spurted. He dropped the lighter in the bin as the flame adjusted into a tall, willowy column. Flare –

He heaved at the trolley and it moved with weak, squeaking protest towards the door.

'What was that?' he heard in Russian.

Door –

– open. Trolley . . . Christ! Through into the room, dim with closed blinds, one man near the windows, another very close, the third swinging around, the Uzi coming –

– *alarm*. The high-pitched, sinister threat of an alarm wail. The flame and smoke belched out of the bin. He slammed the storeroom door behind him. The woodwork nippled near his face, then split and tore from the impact of bullets. He opened the door into the corridor – empty. Twenty seconds. Flame glaring from an open door, reflected on the walls more orange than the sunlight. They might guess, when there were no sprinklers in operation, realize it was a computer room, no water allowed, that it would flood with an inert gas in a matter of seconds, after the doors locked.

One of them had. Hyde was kneeling, hand flung behind him as if in protest or remonstrance, pistol extended stiffly. Two shots. The black-garbed man bucked backwards, flinging up his hands, then fell back into the room – popping out into view again like some huge, comic puppet as the force of another man's rush expelled him. Already the air-conditioning would have shut off and there were only seconds before the security doors and the lift doors all locked shut and the room was pumped full of the inert gas.

Hyde blundered through the fire doors onto the staircase, stumbled and rolled, scraping his hands and knees, the gun hurting his hand as he collided with the wall. He caught a lurching view of the street below, then he shook his head and turned, waiting for them to come.

The doors must be locked. He could hear faint banging, like distant central-heating pipes rumbling with intruding air. No air in there, not now. No one was coming out.

Then, no further banging. Silence. He went down the stairs slowly, replacing the gun in his waistband in the small of his back, adjusting his loose tie, straightening and brushing his jacket in small, obsessive movements. They were dead by now; asphyxiated. *Choked to death*, if you prefer, he admitted to himself. Murdered.

He pushed open the fire door on the floor below the sealed SIS offices and walked towards the lift doors. There'd be a captain or major somewhere and a chief inspector who could be told it was a hoax, a false alarm. Then, when SIS's forensic team went in, they'd find IRA or Lebanese or Iraqi papers on the bodies – Priabin would have covered all the angles. He felt tired, a little dizzy; as if with a summer cold.


'Yes, that's exactly what I mean, Valentina! He set off the fire alarm in a secure computer room and activated the safety system. It pumped the air out and left them to asphyxiate – you wonder why I do not underestimate these people!' Priabin banged his desk with his fist and all but rose out of his seat. Then he rubbed his face as if washing and settled back into the chair.

The evening paper was blazoned with a photograph of Centre Point and fuddled and hysterical with rumours – *SAS had been sent in* down to *it was all a hoax*. The television screen in a corner of the room, sound turned down, was jogging its images through crowds around Centre Point – he'd heard it already on the commercial channel news, then at six. The official version was that it was a hoax. Their final position would probably be – to counter the telephone claims of responsibility from his invented Iraqi vengeance squad – that the intruders, who may or may not have been from the Middle East, must have set off the security system. Committed suicide, as it were; an accident. Without the telephone calls to the news media which had been necessary to clear the building, they'd deny anything at all ever happened!

Dear God-in-Heaven, what an unholy bloody mess! Three good men – as important as their skills, men who could pass for Arabs – were dead and they knew no more now than they had done before he'd sent them in. Christ, he'd even glimpsed on one news item Godwin and Chambers standing on the steps, arms filled with bags and files and cassettes, like two women on the first day of Harrods sale! He glowered suspiciously at Valentina, who was watching the television screen intently. She appeared as shocked as he. She was, of course, wholly ambitious – she even suspected how bored and adrift he really was. She might, at some point, consider how this could be used to her advantage. She couldn't hope for his posting, but she could hope for a higher rung of the ladder.

Priabin shuffled through the reports on his desk; the girl watched him, alert as a cat. Sir Clive Orrell had rushed to the Cabinet Office to see Longmead, together with the ministers and their advisers who formed the anti-terrorism Cabinet Committee. They were still in session, judging by the comings and the absence of departures. The emergency at Centre Point was being wound down, returned to normal. Heavy police presence. The bodies had been smuggled out of the basement garage in an unmarked van. No doubt, any film of Hyde's presence had already been requested from the broadcasting authorities. At least they'll buy the deception that it was some Iraqi retaliation for the Gulf War, and they'd be left having to explain why the security services had offices in Centre Point. Then both his people and theirs could go back into hiding – a draw. Nil–nil, after extra time! Hyde would be debriefed – they'd probably be grateful he did it in such a publicity-avoiding manner!

'Where's Hyde now?' he blurted. The girl twitched as if awoken, then turned to him.

'Vanished – for the moment. Being debriefed, I presume, sir.'

'I doubt it. Godwin and Chambers?'

'They've been debriefed. They're at Godwin's flat in Kentish Town.'

'They're being watched?' She nodded. 'Then double up the

teams. Godwin and Chambers won't go far without their *minder*, Hyde. They'll lead us to him.'

He banged his fist on the desk again. 'Listen to me, Valentina! I'm not interested in *revenge*. I may indeed feel guilty we lost three men today, and I may appear to be over-reacting as a consequence, but believe me, I'm not. We have to know what they know. To do that, we must isolate Godwin and Chambers, and it must be done carefully – *accidentally*.' She was nodding in agreement, plucking her lower lip between a long finger and her thumb, red-nailed. 'But Hyde has to be out of the way first – he *is* dangerous.'

He turned to the window. Outside, the evening was heavy with retained light over the city, and the trees were dark beneath the warm sky, entertaining a twilight of their own. He scrabbled on his desk and lit a cigarette, the girl refusing his offer. He blew smoke at the ceiling.

Perhaps he needed to be this angry to be sufficiently decisive and ruthless. Centre wanted people eliminated, at least rendered harmless. He was – always had been – squeamish of gripping the cobras and milking their fangs. Not only was it messy, it was dangerous. They usually bit back. But now, the old deadly game was back, with a vengeance. The gentle city evening, to which he had long become accustomed, settled as lightly as birds on the embassy lawns. Dmitri, he instructed himself, move on to the cruder, simpler decisions that made you successful for so long. You cannot afford to be seduced by London. He turned to Valentina, smiling.

'I'm putting you in command – not because I think there's a can to be carried – but because it's urgent. I'll think, you decide.'

'I . . . yes.' She rubbed her forehead. Priabin remembered that there was one, just one, female Rezident in the service, and she was fifty-five and in Guatemala because not too many officers with aspirations spoke Spanish, because any future postings were limited to the outer circles of the inferno, Latin America. Valentina intended to improve the ratio, and probably before she was forty; that much had been evident within a week of her being posted to London.

And she was quick, alert and ruthless, and this was her kind of operation. He'd organized Kellett's death, of course, to keep him quiet, but Valentina had played Shapiro's whore for all it was worth – then overdosed him after sleeping with him. That she had shrugged off, finding his oblique and hesitant questioning little more than ludicrous. So, she could be put in command of the removal of Hyde, to open up Godwin and whatever he possessed or knew.

'We're fighting over different bones, it seems to me, General – but we're the same dogs. Or we are expected to be the same. This man Hyde certainly is.'

He nodded, and turned again to the window. The orange sky was like the glow from some huge, beneficent conflagration.

'Very well, let's locate him and take him out of the game, Valentina. But Foxhunt rules apply. Since we must retain secure cover, the death must be perceived as an accident. Other than those strictures, you have a free hand in getting rid of Hyde.'

# gentlemen of the shade

'Right, van Vuuren's in the restaurant, with the girl. He hasn't got the laptop with him. It's in the suite.'

Hyde slipped into the seat beside Godwin. The coffee shop was all but empty. Chambers was visibly excited, like a kid – the bouquet of flowers was on the chair beside him. Godwin's briefcase, bulging and shabby, was beside Hyde's foot. The table was littered with printout paper and Godwin's sheets and notebooks, scrawled in his big, untidy handwriting.

'I haven't got the answer, not yet,' he offered.

'Oh, for Christ's sake, Godwin –! Van Vuuren's having dinner before he has a bonk, not on holiday for a bloody fortnight!' He leaned forward and, in a glaring whisper, addressed Chambers. 'Have you ordered the champagne at the desk?'

'Yes. And fruit.' Chambers was inordinately pleased with himself.

'Is that in case van Vuuren overdoes it and has to go to hospital?' His fist ground at the woven table mat. 'Look, when I bumped off the three Marx brothers this afternoon, I didn't expect Priabin not to notice. Orrell's trousers are on fire because he can't find me – I checked with Ros. I *have* to report in tomorrow morning, so let's get it right tonight, shall we? We haven't a lot of time to spare before they send someone round checking that all their doors are locked – and that means tipping off van Vuuren. And by the look of the tart he's with, he'll be rushing his dinner just to get back upstairs with her! Understand me?'

'Yes!' Chambers snapped.

'Right – now, what's the access code?'

'There are five words, or groups of words, no group longer than two. Some English, some Afrikaans. The numbers we've got – look.' Scribbled in the notebook, like some old, simple addition sum from his primary school.

'But, the *words*?'

'Darren and I can't make head or tail of what might be missing. Dictionaries, guide books, maps, newspapers – I'm bloody knackered, the effort we've put in since . . .'

'Since three hours ago. Oh, shit.'

'Darren's still using the computer, to try to come up with the answer. He'll call if – '

'Look, why not just pinch his bloody laptop? I'll bring it back later – or make it look like a break-in. You can't use it yet. So, let's keep it until you can?'

'As soon as he sees it's missing, there goes everything. Jo'burg will change all the codes, immediately.'

'All right, Chambers, stop smirking.' Hyde glanced at his watch. 'You – get yourself into the suite, then let Godwin in. I'll watch van Vuuren. And you've got until nine, at the latest. It's eight-ten now. If you haven't cracked it by nine, then bring the bloody machine out with you. And that's *my* decision as case officer.'

'Very well,' Godwin agreed.

Chambers scowled, but Hyde merely tossed his head, indicating the door of the coffee shop.

'Right. Give me ten minutes, then follow me up.' He made an attempt to ignore Hyde which, to Chambers' increasing irritation, produced no more than a sarcastic smile from the Australian.

He stood up, collecting the bouquet. To his back, he heard Hyde remark: 'Don't forget to go down on one knee when you give her the flowers.'

Piss off! he thought violently. The foyer of the InterContinental was crowded with guests; one or two fur coats, even in midsummer, the occasional drift of Arab robes. Luggage and movement. Hyde claimed there was no one keeping van Vuuren under surveillance except himself. He began feeling hot as soon as he paused outside the doors of the lift, the flowers now as foolish as Hyde had made them sound, the adrenalin unfamiliar and coarse, like some powerful, cheap foreign drink. Piss off, Hyde, I'm going to get this right, he thought.

The doors opened. A Chinese girl, too much make-up, a bloated European or American with her, his neck boiling over the collar of his shirt, his jacket draped over his stomach like curtains at some ugly, convex window. Chambers shivered as he entered the empty lift. Then a porter held the door and a luggage trolley was thrust in beside him.

'What floor, sir?' in some barely decipherable accent. Chambers mumbled the answer.

The lift stopped at the third floor and the porter departed. Then it stopped at the fifth. For a woman in late middle age with too much heady, expensive perfume and stretched skin around her mouth and along her jaw. She got out at the sixth. From along the corridor, the noise of a television and a bellowing American voice. Chambers sighed, rubbing at his forehead. The doors opened again at van Vuuren's floor. Chambers blurted into the corridor.

Empty. Trays littered with the debris of afternoon snacks outside some of the doors, notices warning off staff already on some of the door handles. It would have been easier with keys, but the InterContinental used those bloody plastic things programmed to the lock of a single door, *for your security, sir* . . . He moved rapidly down the corridor towards the fire doors, hesitantly passing van Vuuren's suite as if it were the location of an ambush. Godwin and he had it, surely, but the words wouldn't come out right; like a drunk's lips moving loosely, they couldn't pronounce the access codes! With the bouquet in its cellophane and bearing the inimitable label of Moyses Stevens, he scuttled gratefully behind the fire doors, peering back through the wired glass at the empty corridor. How long did it take them to provide a bottle of champagne, for God's sake, when most of the guests were rushing out to four hundred quid restaurants to meet million-dollar deals?

*Squeak*, just as he was remembering the gaps in the access codes . . . *Kruger*, to begin, then *Boete Erazmus*, then *Ellis Park* – what did that mean, where was it? Then, oh, then *N-e-w-l-a-* and nothing else except *s-v-e-l-d* . . . Except for the jokeword, *Mandela*. He agreed with Godwin, there was time for only two more letter-groupings . . . the end of one word, the beginning or first word for the second. *Squeak* –

The trolley dragging the slow, huddled room service waiter down the corridor from the service lift towards the door of van Vuuren's suite. The neck of the champagne bottle thrusting from the ice bucket, the bowl of fruit wrapped in cellophane, like the bouquet that rustled against his cheek as he began to breathe more quickly. Then a door opened and an open-necked shirt and bulging flannels

102

appeared, at once berating the waiter, who shrugged expressively and doubtless struggled with English.

'What kind of craphouse *is* this hotel, anyway?' Chambers heard in a muffled roar through the glass.

A door slammed, taking the striped shirt out of view, and the waiter struggled on behind his trolley. Napkins, some wrapped cheese, an erect carnation in a thin vase. The waiter knocked at the door of van Vuuren's suite, waited, then knocked again. Cursed silently, the bent head and moving lips eloquent. Knocked – rang the bell ... come on, *come on!* The bouquet rubbed against his stubble. The door opened to the programme of the waiter's mastercard, and the trolley dragged him into the suite. Chambers swallowed, but there was no moisture at the back of his mouth, then stepped through the fire door, releasing it with exaggerated caution. Hurried the two intervening doors to van Vuuren's suite – door still *open*, thank God! The waiter fussing around the trolley, transforming it into a table near the window.

Chambers held the bouquet of orchids and carnations in front of him as he stepped into the room. The waiter looked up over the parapet of the paper and cellophane at him, surprised.

'Ah, thank you, yes,' Chambers mumbled. *Don't forget the tip,* Hyde had said. *It makes you legit.* How much, he had wanted to ask but had not dared, confronted with Hyde's anticipated contempt. He thrust the two pound coins into the waiter's hand, scribbled awkwardly *van-something-scrawl* at the bottom of the receipt, stared at the window and the first prickling lights of the city beyond it until –

He whirled round. The door had shut behind the waiter. He was inside. He flung the bouquet into the bathroom, where it slithered down the side of the bath, spilling leaves and petals inside its wrapping. He looked at his watch. Eight-twenty, Jesus ...

The suite had all the warm-lit emptiness of temporary accommodation, the scents of carpet and polish rather than lives. Table lamps, standard lamps, subdued downlighters and wall lights. Yet the room was little but the small hillocks and valleys of furniture. Two three-piece suites in the main lounge, two kingsize beds in the bedroom. Christ, a second bedroom, two bathrooms, it was a bloody house, not a hotel room. Fruit in bowls and cellophane was strewn across the various tables and chests. Chambers opened a sliding cupboard door and saw van Vuuren's suitcases and bags, his clothes. Began to open drawers, discovering ties, handkerchiefs . . . drawer after drawer, a packet of Mates, taking no chances, even with a high-class working girl – his whole behaviour like that of an obsessive, endlessly checking that things were tidied, drawers were shut.

The telephone rang. He stood rigidly still. Twice, three, four . . . seven, eight. Christ –! He was sweating freely, caught as in a spotlight in the middle of the lounge, the low edge of a coffee table pressing against his calf. Thirteen, fourteen –

Silence. He collapsed into an easy chair. *Don't sit anywhere unless you plump up the bloody cushions!* Hyde shouted in his head. He jumped to his feet, unsteadily, almost dizzy. His hands – God, his hands were *shaking*!

Doorbell –

Oh, no –! Godwin, must be. He squinted into the little convex hole in the door. Godwin's features, distorted as in the back of a shiny spoon, glowered at him. He opened the door.

'Well?' Godwin shook his head glumly. 'Oh, no –'

'Don't start, Gladys!' Godwin snapped. 'Darren hasn't got a clue, neither have I. What's the bloody time?'

'Eight-twenty-three . . . sod it.'

'So, we'll just make ourselves comfortable, shall we, and wait until nine o'clock? Then we can lift that –' He nodded towards the opened wardrobe, where the laptop computer stood on its edge beside a suitcase. '– and bugger off. Because, Terry, I don't have the bloody answer and that's a fact that can't be avoided.'


There was a huge African moon looming like a bland, puzzled face just beyond the open slats of the blind. The smell of ether, of ointments, and the immediate pain, as if awoken by the scents, in his hands and on his stretched, stiff cheeks. He was lying down – lying on a hard bed, near the window through which the moon rose and glowed. He gingerly flexed his fingers. They remembered heat, pain, and the long time before the relief of cool water. Then the images came – and the constriction in his throat, and the choking sensation, the smoke in his lungs and the smell of burning flesh that might or might not have been his own. Then he began to hear his own cries as they gripped his scorched and raw skin as he was

104

dragged from the waterhole, to collapse on the bank and immediately discover the country of unconsciousness. He hardly sensed the present hold of his bandages and the ease of salves.

*. . . very lucky, Mr Anderson,* he heard the Indian doctor saying once more, though the moonlit room was empty, and quiet except for his own strained breathing. *Superficial burns . . . no lung damage, I am pleased to say . . . you might well have suffocated, even drowned, Mr Anderson . . . very lucky indeed, sir . . .* And then the doctor had drifted away from the edge of eyesight, and he had remembered Margarethe was dead. It was inescapable . . . but he had not asked for tranquillizers or sleeping pills, just stared into that storm until it abated a little; out of weariness, perhaps. He felt he was poised at the eye of the hurricane, in a pool of calm that was too shallow.

*Very lucky, Mr Anderson . . .* The doctor's voice had faltered at that point, understanding that he was conscious, and remembered. Or perhaps he had reacted to his glaring eyes, staring out of what he knew must be a blackened face. The doctor had turned away with a movement of delicacy, and removed and wiped his glasses. In so doing, he had released Anderson's weak hold on consciousness.

*Very lucky . . .*

Christ, she was *dead*. Blantyre had burned her to death, had others killed or shot them himself. *Lucky . . .* The word blew away like a scrap of burnt paper down a long tunnel which had become his perspective on events. People had survived the attack and the fire – they had dragged him from the waterhole where he must have been floundering like something half-dead. But no one who had become important to his limited sympathies had survived, merely a few customers of the company that managed that area of the reserve for which he was responsible. *She* was dead. To his first, uxorious wife's painful, agonized death from cancer, he had been remarkably indifferent. Nature and disease could not be regarded as things to be opposed, and the woman had long ceased to have any meaning other than humiliation for him. But Margarethe was dead now, his second wife, his – *black dolly*, as Blantyre had called her.

. . . someone had said, as he had drifted back towards unconsciousness, as the quick African dusk striped the room because of the blinds, that *Blantyre hadn't been able to get there on time, they'd seen the smoke, his patrol . . . disgruntled ex-SWAPO people, communists or something like . . .* He might have groaned aloud then, because they had come rushing to the bedside, assuming pain rather than protest.

Most of the day, he had lain in the back of the truck because the medical aircraft was grounded and he had had to be driven the hundred and thirty miles to the clinic at Otjiwarongo. He remembered only the jolting and lolling of his head, as if he had become some kind of idiot – and as if all thought of her was being shaken loose, allowed to drift like the cloud of dust behind the truck. Even his screams had been vengeful, occupied with losing thought of her, and the clinging image of Blantyre.

His body was numb with bruising and sedatives, constricted by plasters and bandaging. The moonlight filled the room, imaging the blind on the far wall. A drip glinted beside his bed, there was the faint noise of a fan, the occasional howl of a night animal from outside which made him jerk and shudder as if it voiced his pain. He remembered the pressure of one of the guests' mouths against his own, attempting to revive him – but that was too imitative, too easily evocative of his dead wife's mouth, and he blotted it out. He did not know whether or not Blantyre knew he had survived the attack. Blantyre had apparently re-arrived, in all pretended innocence, two hours after dawn. By then, he had been on his way. Probably one of the survivors had explained that he had been taken to the clinic. A guest had accompanied him and the woman who had died beside him during the journey. He shook his head feebly, and the pain returned. Blantyre would know, somehow, in some way . . .

He felt the night and the *out there* pressing against the window, against the flimsy walls of the room in which he had been left. He could remember nurses, attention, the relief of pain . . . but mostly now he was aware of the weakness of his body and the death of his wife. He felt shrunken, as if the fire had shrivelled him like a fruit, so that she and himself and the past few years were no bigger than seeds – waiting . . .

. . . for nothing to come back out of the tunnel into which she had been blown like a scrap of paper. His cheeks felt wet. The image persisted, of her as a scorched, brown scrap of paper, nothing more . . . A still, tiny body in the corner of the shattered, burning bedroom. His bandages felt tighter. Grief welled through him like a huge wave.

Eventually, his cheeks stung as the tears dried. He felt emptied, like a spilt vessel, retaining only the knowledge that Blantyre undoubtedly knew he had survived and where he had been taken. She had been swallowed by silence and the darkness for the moment. Blantyre would come to Otjiwarongo soon. He must conserve what energy he possessed, to be ready. He flexed his fingers painfully, sensed his bruises and burns. How could he kill Blantyre, a wounded man like him? How *could* he . . . ? If Blantyre walked into the moonlit room now, it would be over in less than a minute with nothing more deadly than a pillow. He squirmed with mounting rage. Even his grief disabled him like another physical injury; the ink from some frightened squid, surrounding and enveloping him. Repellent, immobilizing. Blantyre could appear at any moment – at *that* moment, and he was helpless.

'Look, I can't touch the bloody thing – you know that!' Godwin protested as he stumped about the room and Chambers was reduced to following him, scuffing over the indentations made by his heavy sticks; having plumped up the cushions, for Christ's sake! Godwin turned at the windows overlooking the Wellington Arch and continued: 'Patrick's right – we'll have to take the thing with us and hope for the best!'

Eight-forty. Chambers gathered up Godwin's scattered notes, formulations – guesses! – then straightened with a start as the telephone rang – two, three . . . Ended. Then began again. Chambers snatched up the receiver, knowing it was Hyde and resenting Hyde's realization that their game was going down the bog.

'Yes?' he snapped.

'Have you two buggers got anywhere, for Christ's sake?' Hyde whispered. 'The girl's just picking at the meal because she wants to get it over as soon as possible with that little shit and he's already ordering his pudding because he can't wait to get her up to the room. He's bloody *drooling*! What have you got?'

'Nothing, bugger it – nothing! Satisfied?'

'Look, I wouldn't work with you again on pain of excommunication, Chambers. Pull yourself together. If you can't get into the mainframe, then bring the laptop out with you – but get on with it, either way!'

Chambers listened to the purr of the disconnected call, then replaced the receiver, which was filmed with perspiration.

'It's got to be two other names – places or people!' he all but wailed.

'We've been through the Boer Wars, both of them, we've been through the map of South Africa again and again, the guide books – it's like bloody Mastermind. But there's no *logic* to it!'

He stumped past Chambers towards the opened wardrobe from which they had not even bothered to remove the laptop computer. Godwin stared at it, as if willing it to confess and threatening it with pain if it remained uncommunicative. He poked at it with one of his sticks, poked at van Vuuren's Louis Vuitton luggage, the South African Airways labels still attached, the flying springbok gold against blue. Still flying the long way, via the Cape Verde islands, but that was being renegotiated. Soon, they'd be able to land at Nairobi, Harare, wherever they wanted. Why am I wasting my time thinking about it? he reprimanded himself, knowing precisely the virtue of distraction. They couldn't solve the riddle, they'd have to risk exposure by taking the laptop and hoping they could get into the mainframe in Jo'burg before van Vuuren or Malan had all the access codes changed. Hence the focus on the labels, the luggage . . . the springbok . . . the labels – the *springbok*? They were even talking about the England rugby team touring South –

Christ, the bloody Springboks! No one had been to South Africa for years, no wonder he –!

'Give me the phone – quick!' He lurched across the room and collapsed into an armchair, dabbing furiously at the keypad. 'Yes – sports department!' he snapped. He was grinning weakly, feverishly at Chambers, who seemed afraid of him, as at lunacy. '*Evening Standard*,' he muttered in a breathless voice. 'Bloke I was in Uni with, writes on rug – Yes, Gareth Jones, please! Yes, it's very urgent. Tell him it's Tony Godwin – *Tony God-win.*' He clicked his finger at Chambers, whispering: 'Give me those names – quick! Come on – *there*!' Chambers handed him the list of names . . . Ellis Park, that's the one that rang a bell – well, now it did! After recollecting the springbok badge on a green jersey. The bloody South African rugby team! 'What. Where is he? What? What's the number of the bloody pub, then? No, I'm not his wife, you cheeky sod. It's a matter of life and death, so it couldn't be about his wife, could it? What?

Yes, got that – thanks.' He cut off the call, redialled, looked up at Chambers and winked. His heart was thudding in his chest. Chambers held out his arm, pointing at his watch. Eight forty-five. Enough time, just enough, as long as the girl downstairs wanted a brandy before facing up to van Vuuren! 'Yes – is that Boswell's Wine Bar? One of your customers, he's there at the moment . . . Bugger that, love. Police, OK? Now, will you get Mr Gareth Jones to the telephone, please. Thank you.'

He began to drum on the arm of the chair with his broad fingers, as if already typing out the access codes on the laptop's keypad. Chambers shrugged a request for an explanation, but he waved postponement. He could hear his own breathing hoarsely loud in the earpiece. Then: 'Gareth – Tony Godwin . . . yes, and you? How's – er, is it still Tracey? Oh, sorry to hear that. Look, can you do me a favour – just a couple of quick questions . . . yes, now. Look, you were on the last British Lions tour to South Africa for one of the newspapers, weren't you? No, it's not official, just a stupid bet. Well, doesn't matter if you do, just answer the questions, Gareth. If I read out these names, can you tell me the two that are missing – and spell them out? Yes, crossword, that's it. Yes, half the winnings. I've got Ellis Park, Boete Erazmus, and part of a word, New – what is it? Newlands . . .' Godwin scribbled, gesticulating with the pencil at Chambers as if to ward him off. 'And the other word – Yes, the four Test grounds of the Springboks, must be –!' He felt the perspiration of relief dampen his forehead. 'And the fourth . . . L-o-f-tus . . . what's that? V-e-r-s-veld – yes! Thanks, Gareth, I owe you a pint. See you –!'

He sat back in his chair, exhausted. Chambers remained motionless, as if in shock, in the middle of the room.

'How?' he managed eventually.

'The labels on his luggage – a springbok. Badge of the South – oh, never mind now, get the bloody machine and attach it to the phone. We're in bloody business! *Kruger – Mandela –* the four Test grounds, four bloody rugby venues – and we're in to MLC's mainframe!'

Eight forty-seven –


The girl shook her head, refusing an after-dinner drink. Van Vuuren evidently didn't mind – there'd be booze in the room, even ignoring

Chambers' champagne. His head was already swivelling for sight of a waiter, his hand poised to wave. Eight-fifty, no, almost fifty-one. Christ, why do people have to rush their bloody dinners in expensive restaurants? Looking at the girl, on the other hand, Hyde thought, rubbing his chin, who could blame van Vuuren, even if he was paying for it?

The waiter arrived with the bill. Hyde was leaning back in his chair, craning to see into Le Soufflé restaurant from the hotel's cocktail bar. Van Vuuren signed it with a flourish. Does she take Amex? he wondered. That'll do nicely?

Hyde finished his lager and stood up, moving quickly to the telephone at the door of the cocktail bar. He dialled van Vuuren's suite. Waited . . . Engaged. Engaged? He held on. Were they in? Or was Godwin ringing up pimply Darren for the answer! He dialled the number once more. Still engaged. The waiter had been satisfied with a twenty-pound note. Van Vuuren's impatience was evident.

Hyde hurried to the lifts.


'Bloody hell – Captain Flint's buried treasure, map and all!' Godwin breathed. Behind him, Chambers photographed the laptop's screen while the hard-copy printer they had coupled to the machine continued to grumble and cough out the information. Eight fifty-five. 'Look at it. God, with a couple of hours and a bit of luck, we'd be able to open everything up on computer-predicted number sequences. Namibia – that's interesting. France . . . Jackpot time. Terry Chambers, come on down!'

Fifty-seven . . . Patrick would just have to wait, it can't be choked off now. He dabbed at the keypad, drawing the number sequence from the notes balanced on his knee.

'What are you after?'

'UK companies whose pass-through trade has doubled, even trebled in the last few months . . . export companies, shippers.'

'Why that area?' Chambers murmured, absorbed now in checking the printout, having tidied Godwin's papers back into his briefcase.

'It has to be leaving the country somehow. Who's sending it out, and where to?'

'Could be useful to –' There was a loud, insistent banging on the door of the suite. 'Oh, no –!'

'You buggers – get moving! He's on his way up with the tart, for God's sake!'

'Hyde –'

Chambers hurried to the door and Hyde spilt into the lounge, waving his arms.

'Come on, you stupid buggers – let's go!' He unplugged the printer and Godwin scowled in protest. Then he snatched the telephone receiver off the laptop and replaced it. 'Come on – he's on his way!' He snapped the lid of the laptop shut. 'Where does this go?'

'Patrick, another *minute*, for Christ's sake!'

'No! Get moving.'

Chambers took the laptop and replaced it in the wardrobe, closing the louvred door on it. Hyde was plumping up cushions while Godwin was staring at his bulging briefcase and the printout as if he had walked into his own home to discover it burgled by strangers. Then he gathered his sticks to his sides and Chambers collected the case. Hyde was smoothing the carpet with hands and feet, moving disturbed furniture back onto its indentations in the thick pile.

'That'll have to do . . . Wait!' He passed Chambers and eased open the door. The corridor was empty. 'OK, through the fire exit. We'll wait until he's shut himself in. Bring the bloody flowers, Chambers! No, not the bloody champagne, that could have been left by the hotel, just the flowers!'

Hyde closed the door behind them, then the fire door. Looked back through the Georgian-wired glass. Corridor . . . no longer empty. Van Vuuren, shorter than the long-legged girl, coming down the corridor beside her, she holding his arm. They paused outside the door of the suite and then van Vuuren let them in. The door clicked shut. Chambers and Godwin, red-faced, were sweating – Hyde wiped his sleeve across his brow.

'Don't bloody do that to me again!'

'Christ, we did it.' Chambers patted the briefcase and the printout under his arm, smirking. Then he threw the bouquet down the emergency stairs. Petals flew, stems snapped. 'We bloody did it!' he announced.

\*

111

He came up the noisome staircase because, once again, the lifts were inoperable. The cosy officialese disguised his guilt. In reality, some little bastards had sabotaged the lifts yet again, isolating dozens of pensioners and Asians and children in their fortress-like block of flats. He passed a black man who was wriggling and grunting his way to sexual climax at a turning of the stair. The girl behind the man's shoulders was all but invisible. Her spread and braced legs indicated custom and acceptance. As he rounded a turn of the staircase, he heard a quick gasp and a few quick-drawn breaths.

But ninety-year-old Aunt Vi wouldn't move out to sheltered accommodation or even a nice little bungalow somewhere, would she? Not bloody likely. *Lived here all my life, I have, in this street . . .* Street? It had disappeared in the sixties under the tons of concrete and infill required to raise these monstrosities . . . at the behest, he always felt, of developers and architects who either never set foot in the country again or lived in Georgian mansions just outside Bath. He tossed his head. *Here I stand*, said Aunt Vi, who was one of the two middle-aged aunts in their mothball-smelling overcoats who'd come out to Woollongong to see him and his mother, and the one who'd come to Southampton to collect him from the boat, a ten-year-old orphan in a strange country.

Guilt drove him to see Vi once a week. Ros, he suspected, came quite often, though she never mentioned her visits. But chocolate fingers and Jaffa cakes were often about the place, in their opened packets – and Vi didn't spend her pension on luxuries. Gladys was dead and Vi was alone, marooned sixteen floors up in this dump. *Gött strafe England* – but this had been erected just where the bloody Germans had helped to clear the slums!

He reached the long, dark concrete corridor with its low balcony to one side and the disfigured row of doors on the other, where she lived. The cries of yobs, black and white, like the calls of wild animals, echoed around the four sides of the block and across the littered courtyard with its two burned-out cars and other rubbish. FORT APACHE – STEPNEY had been spray-painted on the wall at the turning of the corridor, though he could hardly read the letters now. That movie was years old, anyway. No one had touched up or repainted the joke. Mindless *fucks* and *ballocks* and a lot of swastikas were more in tune with the times and the vandalism and the educational level – around here, the graffiti should be at ankle-

112

height, if its distance up the wall was any measure of the level of intelligence. Youths called like lost souls as he reached her door; no, more as if they were locating other members of a pack prior to the hunt. Fort-fucking-Apache! He knocked loudly on the door, calling out at once: 'Vi – it's me, Patrick. Open the door.'

He could hear the television blaring vainly at her deafness from inside the flat; a wall of sound, like those erected in at least six of the flats along this landing, fending off the noises from outside. 'Vi – open the door, it's Patrick!' he shouted through the letter box.

In the moments which followed, he heard the television, the calls, high laughter, even some more covert noises from the court-yard – robbery or crack retailing. Eventually, her shadow loomed behind the reinforced, frosted glass and he heard the drawing back of the bolts and the opening of the security lock he had had fitted. In the hierarchy of the block, she was safer than most. There were black yobs, brown ones, and enough whites to find her some kind of deaf, dotty object of amusement rather than persecution. In simple terms, the shit went through the Asian letter boxes. And, of course, he had broken one yob's arm, two years ago, *pour encourager les autres.* He pecked at Vi's raspy, leathery cheek as she presented it to him, then locked the door behind him and followed her into the minuscule lounge. Good decorative order, Mayfair estate agents would claim, had they dared take a Stepney flat onto their august books. He'd wallpapered the place last year. The furniture revealed the geological layers of Vi's life and that of her sister, who had married better than Vi: comfortably solid Victorian, inter-war util-ity, post-war appalling and some bits and pieces of the sixties. And the television, herded into a corner by the massed furniture, thun-dered out some inane game show.

She sat down like a slowly collapsing sack filled with bones and little else. Her eyes were rheumily bright, and her lips still becoming accustomed, it seemed, to the dentures she had had for as long as he'd known her. His entire family, she was, since Glad had died. Her eyes wore their cataracts like acquired wisdom.

'You all right?' she shouted, leaning towards him, the familiar amalgam of foster mother and schoolmistress in her cracked old voice. And something survived of the stranger who had met him off the boat from Sydney almost thirty years ago. She watched the bottle in his pocket as if it was a pistol. Shaking his head, he tugged it from his jacket and placed it on the scarred Victorian dresser that dominated one entire wall of the lounge.

'*Yours*,' he emphasized. 'Your nightcap.' She shook her head, but he noticed that the other bottle, the last he had brought, was almost empty.

She had been his first memory of England, the mothball smell of her cardigan as she crushed him against her ample bosom comforting but strange. The leaning, skeletal spires of the port cranes had risen insect-headed behind her. He remembered the chill of the port, the greyness of the sky. Remembered, too, that she had smiled continually during the train journey across the snowbound countryside between Southampton and London, her mouth even in those days filled with the dentures that seemed to move independently of her lips and will. He patted her hand and sat opposite her after reducing the volume of the television; settling into the comparative peace of the next hour, punctuated more by noise from outside than it would ever be by their conversation. Vi watched the television absorbedly, no longer able to hear the contestants or the quizmaster. It would make the game no less comprehensible for her.

He looked at her. Her brightness of eye was an illusion of comfort. Normally, she berated him about the neighbours – *those blackies and darkies* – or his unshaven appearance; she had blossomed during the time when he couldn't control the drinking, seizing upon him like a raptor upon a carcass, re-invading his life. Re-fostering him, he supposed.

'I wonder what he wants?' Vi enquired, as if addressing someone else in the room. Not the cat. The yobs had thrown that from the balcony one day, turning it into a shapeless little lump that leaked down in the courtyard. That had been when he had broken the arm of one of them, after threatening him with joining the cat from the same altitude. Eventually, the cat's body had been kicked somewhere out of sight and Vi had had no pets since then. 'Always bringing me something. I don't want *things* at my time of life!' she continued, apparently to the television.

The yobs drowned her words, running past, banging against doors like ball-bearings. Black and white loiterers, off to mug their neighbours who didn't dare use their garages after dark. He detested Stepney with a deep loathing, probably because he had once lived in this flat with Vi, before he had gone into the army. Then into *that special regiment, what did they call it – SAS? Now, he's got a proper office job, in Whitehall.* That was how Vi explained it loudly to the Asian grocer . . . *quite respectable, for a darkie, him.* She was sometimes suspicious that Hyde hardly ever appeared in a suit, of course, having a *proper office job and all that.* SAS probably, like garlic on the door, kept at least some of the vampires that roamed the corridors and staircases of the block at bay, so he didn't mind her broadcasts.

Someone rattled the letter box. Vi hadn't heard, of course. Hyde tossed his head and watched the almost-silent screen with her. She'd get up and drag herself across the room soon, to turn up the volume – when the next set of contestants smirked and posed. The letter box rattled again. He turned his head to look along the passage. A shadow loomed beyond the reinforced glass. The letter box rattled again. Perhaps they did bother her, then, but she didn't hear so couldn't inform him? Rattle, rattle, a more persistent rhythm. A light outside flared, making the shadow more bulky and solid –

Jesus! The letter box. Vi's head turned slowly as he clattered his chair back against a tea trolley wedged between the dresser and a Victorian table with a potted plant on it.

A gobbet of lighted cloth or paper was pushed through the letter box and flared on the doormat. He ran down the passage as the shadow disappeared and stamped on the tiny fire, grinding it out. The smell of petrol and smoke and the singed doormat. Nothing really damaged – oh yes, just kids. They're bored, you know, unemployed. Fuck them!

'Vi!' he shouted. 'Come and lock the door behind me.'

He was forcibly reminded of how old she really was as she struggled into the passage, muttering: 'Little buggers . . . not for months –' The keys rattled softly in her hand.

He opened the door and looked out, then kissed her cheek, shut the door behind him and heard it lock. Heard the bolts. The corridor appeared empty. Rap music blared up from the courtyard. Distant voices and raucous laughter echoed amid the concrete canyons like the neighing of horses. Beyond that, he heard something smash with the quick sound of breaking glass. He'd have to fit a fireproof letter-holder behind the door some time, if this was the new game. There was nothing for some seconds except the usual noises of the block and the smell of overcooked vegetables and dog or human urine close by.

Then, from the opposite ends of the long, sixteenth-floor alley-way, shadows. Two whites at one end, perhaps three blacks at the other, both groups intent upon convergence. He listened to Vi retreat and the volume of the television increase, then thrust his hands into his pockets and began walking along the concrete corri-dor, past door after door, towards the two whites. One of the blacks behind him was carrying a ghetto-blaster which boomed tinnily off the concrete. *I Shot the Sheriff.* Laughter, tinged with anticipation –? He wasn't sure, but some electricity in his spine made him shiver. There was something about the burning cloth through the letter box, something about the silent emptiness of the corridor by the time he had opened the door – and about this pincer movement now. Something about faces on the Tube. Bob Marley's amplified, dis-torted voice trailed him along the corridor and the two whites had slowed. Faces on the Tube, shadows in the dim streets, footsteps behind him on the staircase? Yobs? The two whites were ten yards away now, and had stopped, apparently outside a door. Then one of them began urinating through the letter box while the other laughed and pulled open a can of lager. Bob Marley's voice had halted, too, bellowing some twenty yards behind him. Yobs? Organized, with a specific target? He touched at the pistol in the small of his back, then slouched forward towards the two whites, adopting the vague weave of a drunk – plenty of practice there, my son – and at once the urinat-ing youth turned to face him, zipping his jeans. White faces, white designer trainers, white hands. A mindless giggle from one of them. Specific target – himself. The fire – he could faintly smell petrol on one of them – had been specific too; to draw him out.

He felt the dryness of his mouth and sucked saliva from his cheeks. Why? *Who?* Priabin . . . ? Bob Marley had begun moving closer, stealthy footsteps shunting him forward. Five of them. He reached out a tentative hand, leaning against the rough-finished concrete that was the place's *texture*, for Christ's sake, a bloody *visual amenity*, shaking his head and laughing to himself –

– disconcerting them. The blacks had paused. Then he kicked the closest white just below the kneecap, hard, doubling him up with a cry of pain. Hyde brought both hands, linked into one fist, down on the back of his neck. Then the second white – gleam of a blade? The youth was watching his feet, trying to watch his hands at the same time, was about to open his mouth to call out to the blacks.

116

Hyde brought his forearm down hard just above the gleam and something tinkled metallically on the concrete, then drove his elbow into the youth's stomach and his extended knuckles into his face in a short jabbing movement. He felt bone break.

'Aw, fucking *Christ* – !' the youth screamed, holding his nose. As he doubled over in his stunned pain, Hyde punched him on the side of the head, kicked the knife along the corridor, then turned to study the three blacks, carrying the ghetto-blaster and perhaps pickaxe handles. Guns? he wondered, feeling the cold electricity shiver through his frame again. He touched his own gun for reassurance, then shouted: 'Whatever it is, you three – fuck off! Unless you want what these two got, piss off!'

He paused, then moved to turn away, not needing to hurry until he heard them move. Groans rumbled from the two white youths, curses and aggressive breathing. No, they wouldn't move, not for the moment, not until he reached the head of the staircase – sixteen floors up.

Then he heard a whistle's peremptory summons from one of the blacks, and knew that it was no longer a confrontation, a swatting of violent, mindless flies. It was a pursuit. The whistle sounded for a second time, more urgently. He began running for the stairs.

The half-kaffir girl was kneeling on the bed like a bitch so that he could enter her, doglike. White suspender-belt, white stockings, smooth brown buttocks. Van Vuuren allowed her hand to guide his penetration. He was sweating as his movements accelerated, as the litany of crudities hurried through his mind towards the climax. Kaffir bitch, kaffir bitch, kaffir . . . The telephone.

'Christ–!' He shuddered as he withdrew, splashing the girl's buttocks with semen. He snatched up the telephone, angry at the evidence of his humiliation which had not quite become hers. The girl turned lazily, then smoothed her buttocks dry on the bed-linen. Then she rolled across the bed and pulled the top sheet around her, waiting with the patience and impassivity of machinery. '*Yes? What–?* No, no you weren't interrupting me, Paulus.' He studied the girl's fine-boned face for some reaction to his accent and to his subservience. There was none. 'Yes . . . good. Oh, you've spoken to him. No, the shipment's cleared for tomorrow night, yes. The money's been deposited as usual.' He replaced his glasses. The girl's breasts beneath the thin sheet. He picked up the champagne flute from the bedside table and sipped at it. 'No, there are no problems . . . no? What—? Oh, I see . . . yes, I understand. *Their* suggestion? No, yours, sure, Paulus. Yes, I'll give it some thought, begin making arrangements, yes . . . Goodnight.'

He put down the receiver and, as at a signal, the girl peeled back the sheet with a mechanical absence of sexuality, down past her suspender-belt to her thighs. He walked away from the bed and lit a cigarette, standing at the window as he watched the traffic clotting around the Wellington Arch, brake lights shining out in protest and rebuff. The shipment was organized, almost on its way. There had been the usual division of the spoils . . . on to France, then to Namibia. Yes, things would change now, obviously, since the bloody Russians wanted their stuff to go direct, more or less, in the planned build-up to the VIATE climax.

He heard the girl rubbing her arms as if cold. He knew that he could ignore her until he was ready. She would remain until she was paid, whatever the humiliations along the way. He picked a shred of tobacco from his tongue.

That guy Babbington waltzed with Paulus, and Paulus let him do it – that was the real *pisser* in this whole set-up! Reid Electronics was too valuable to lose, that was the real point at issue. And it was *coitus interruptus* so that Paulus could relay his orders from Moscow, from that English bastard who'd gone over to them!

The French company . . . now, that *was* too good to lose. But it was close to Reid. Malan was playing dangerous games, risking exposing Reid, but trying to protect the French company. If he opened the can, everyone would see the whole box of sardines in there. He puffed angrily at his cigarette. Panic, that's what it was, because they had to stay in Europe now that South Africa might – God help it – end up in the hands of the kaffirs, and that woolly-headed old bastard Mandela might one day step up on the President's podium in Pretoria! Christ, he'd kill some black buggers the day that appeared on the bloody television news . . .

*Coitus interruptus* . . . that phrase? Oh, yes . . . he remembered masturbating to Havelock Ellis' dry, analytical, unerotic prose, as a boy on the farm. His sexual education.

Kaffirs. He turned suddenly to the girl, angry, desiring only her

118

humiliation. She rose mechanically onto all fours on the bed, with suitable subservience. Van Vuuren pulled off his dressing-gown and moved towards her.

He could hear Blantyre's voice and that of the nurse at the door of the room, heightened whispers magnified by the silence of the night as the moon declined.

'. . . under sedation, Colonel, two sleeping pills. You can talk to him in the morning, not before.'

'Yes. A pity. He could help me . . . sleeping, you said?'

Anderson lay in an icy perspiration of terror. He was something that Blantyre could despatch with consummate ease and without the slightest hesitation. The perspiration seemed to be soaking the pillows and the sheet beneath him. He stared at the ceiling, where the declining moon rendered the blades of the fan as big and dangerous as the rotor-blades of a helicopter. Light seemed to stream in as Blantyre opened the door, but it retreated into a wide vertical band as his eyes adjusted. Sweat ran down his temples, as if the sense of his own scent were betraying him to the hunting animal who blocked out the band of light at the door. Blantyre seemed to inspect him minutely, for whole minutes, before –

'That's enough, Colonel. He's obviously sleeping.'

'Yes. Obviously.' The door closed and the moonlight slowly became stronger and cooler.

He was shivering now, his whole body shuddering with relaxed effort, and the anticipation of terror and terror experienced. Blantyre would wait, patient as a hungry lion, until morning. Then he would come in, check, assess, and decide that he must be eliminated. The shivering would not subside. It pained him with a violent disgust beyond the vivid sensation of helplessness. Once, he might have broken Blantyre like an insect on a wheel. Now, Blantyre was his nemesis. His violent past had simply bided its time, until he was unable to resist his enemies – then betrayed him to them.

In the morning, doubtless with the appropriate papers, Blantyre would remove him from the clinic, take him gently away as if he were leading a friend, and then kill him out in the Bush.

And there was nothing he would be able to do to prevent it.

# not for the fashion of these times

Surreal. The assault upon the senses of the noisome staircase of the block of flats, and the familiar-alien scratch of an R/T and the pounding of heavy footsteps. It was bloody *Stepney*, for Christ's sake, and totally alien. He cannoned off a turning of the stairs – fourth floor? – and skittered quick as a stone down the next flight to the half-landing. His own breathing was loud, and he quelled it for a moment, pausing against the wall, shuddering like the black man who had been fornicating against the wall as he had arrived at Vi's landing. Distantly he heard their voices, the calls of animals reasserting the identity of the pack. The R/T –? He heard the call of the whistle again – answered, this time. He felt weak with exertion and the aftershock of the violence he had inflicted. Four floors –

He launched himself with calculated incaution down the next flight. The smell of curry and urine and vomit assailed him. His foot slipped in something and he righted himself, scraping his cheek against rough-cast concrete – the bastards who designed and built this are sunning themselves in the Bahamas, he told himself, encouraging the light delirium of movement and adrenalin. Second floor. He was near the bottom, he snatched the pistol from his belt and brandished it, scraping his knuckles against the wall as he careered downwards –

Bullied a body out of his path at another turn of the staircase, hearing the quick grunt of exhaled breath as he turned the corner. No one, not dangerous, but he had hit the soft, dark body anyway – where were they?

He floundered out into the courtyard and at once a car's headlights glared on in the dusk, sweeping across the concrete and rubble and litter and the burned-out wreckage, brightening eyes and bodies. He stood in the headlights, frozen like a rabbit. An R/T crackled, but the car's engine merely idled expectantly. Then a second car appeared – to a whoop of anticipation from one of the landings where the four sides of the block gloomed up out of eyesight all around him. Grass, thrusting through cracked flagstones near his feet, was made white and dead-looking by the light. A line of washing jerking in the wind like a row of hanged matchstick men.

The place was as bleak as anywhere in eastern Europe, only a mile from the Bank of England. He was totally isolated and their numbers were unknown. Urgency from an R/T in shadow quite close to him. Then the two cars, facing each other with horns of light stretched out, moved forward across the concrete towards him.

The line of grubby, optimistic washing draped itself as if in protest, leaping on to the bonnet and windscreen of the nearer car. Hyde rolled away from the light, across splintered glass and dog excrement and polystyrene rubbish which cracked under him.

The cars had halted as if pawing the ground with hooves, only yards from each other, their headlights out. But it was too late, they would already have temporarily blinded each other. A car door banged, but he did not pause to look, he was already scuttling away, almost on all fours while torches flashed weakly down from the landings and balconies and more and more lights went on around the amphitheatre of the block. The sky above the flats seemed to lose the last pale wash of daylight. If he broke out, then the city would become alien like the courtyard, more dangerous to him than most other cities. He collided with a motorbike, sending it sprawling, handlebars like flailing arms.

Voices, calls, responses. Location. One of the cars sprayed light towards the direction of the noise he had made. It was a vulgar, conspicuous consumption of manpower and effort. Oh, yes, it was Priabin, and probably the girl – intent to make matters even after the fiasco of Centre Point.

He was standing upright behind a pillar with its small tiles long since peeled away to expose the stained, gummy concrete. He pressed his gun against his nose and lips like a holy relic. They'd want an accident, wouldn't they? Someone had to be in touch with Priabin direct – he was on the end of some cellular phone line, prodding, dissuading, agreeing.

He heard a cry of despair from somewhere a long way up. An

121

old, cracked voice. 'Why can't you bugger *off*?' Oh, yes, why can't you . . .

The cars' engines stilled into silence. No lights. A black shadow slipped down the alley near him and he whirled on it. A terrified Asian face stared back, eyes wide, hands raised palm-outwards, almost white. Then the face and its body disappeared as he shivered himself back into concentration – madness of a controllable kind. Silence and lightlessness invested the courtyard, except for the scratching of R/Ts and the whisper of voices. The sudden, curious lights in the block had vanished, taking with them all the other windows. No one wanted to know now, certain it was dangerous. Gradually, he heard his own stertorous breathing again, and realized that they might, too.

Shadows began to flit, like bats at dusk, small and quick and fluttery – three, four. The slap of training shoes on concrete, the whisper of their sudden halts and movements. He calmed his breathing, listened beyond the adrenalin and pounding blood, heard them scrabble and slither like rats. Closer.

Then he heard the blurt of noise, very close, from a telephone or R/T, a voice questioning excitedly. He lowered the gun towards the deep shadow and almost squeezed the trigger, as if it was Priabin hiding there.

'Valentina?'

She heard Priabin's whisper mount in excitement. Their mutual elation was as intimate as congress in the darkness where she pressed against the wall.

'Yes?' she snapped back hoarsely, knowing how close she was to Hyde. 'It's all right.' Ridiculous, their conversation, as if they were two commodity brokers or estate agents fixing some obscure movement of money or property; not quite real. Only Hyde was real, over there, behind one of those pillars, visible in the last grubby exhalation of a lamp's light from the street. Had it been winter, she would have been able to see his breath palely clouding and to fix the target. She shivered with excitement. 'Leave it in my hands,' she added and cut the connection. Sorry immediately. If Hyde heard the ringing of the cellular phone in her pocket, he'd fire at once.

Hyde's weekly visit to his aunt's flat. Tonight's the night, she had said, almost smirking across the desk at Priabin. Let him go into that Afghanistan on Parliament's doorstep, but don't let him come out. And their people and the louts they'd used before and the other louts those louts had recruited would have made it as simple as a fall from a high ledge. Except that Hyde had been quick and clever and brutal and no one had got to the upper landings before he had made the courtyard. She'd let him come down because the real numbers, and the real expertise, were down here.

Which pillar? She raised the small nightsight monocular viewer to her eyes again, sensing her bodyguard shift his weight on his haunches beside her. The courtyard became grey and white, and ghostly shadows slipped through it as insubstantial as net curtains, her people closing in on the direction they knew Hyde had taken. Her gaze slid across the spilt motorcycle towards the pillars. Nothing. He would glow in a thermal imager, but there was no whisk of movement in the viewer. Her people were in control now, keeping the louts and yobs away from the smell of the quarry because they were too noisy, too clumsy. Another shadow moved, then another. It was like those scenes in old Western films, the Indians creeping up on the wagon train or the fort.

A shadow loomed against the pillar she suspected; arm held out, it fired a single shot. One of the net curtains in the monocular viewer blew more violently in the breeze of the gunshot, then fell. Immediately, Hyde's shadow was moving, away down the colonnade of cheap, scarred pillars towards the alleyway to the street.

She snatched the R/T from her bodyguard's hand. 'Target is on the move. He must be making for the Tube station. All units, all units – follow.' She spoke in English. Some of the louts had wanted R/Ts, and she had supplied them. It was all useful adrenalin and power.

She rose from her crouch, shrugging off the bodyguard's hand and his subsequent apology with equal indifference. Then she, too, was running, ghostly as the last glimpses she had had of her people in pursuit of Hyde. No caution now, only the hunt and its exhilaration. Hyde –

He turned once, at the corner of a street mean as anything in Prague or Berlin and now more dangerous. The Wall was down there, rebuilt here. Acres of concrete, the great bulk of the block of flats, the few working streetlamps, the few parked cars – one of them already up on bricks, wheels missing. Two figures flitted from shade to shade, through grubby light into shadow again. Mile End

Tube station. No police cars round here. Even if there were, they'd never stop for someone flagging them down, they'd just report it to the station. He pushed the gun into his waistband, against his stomach, then gripped the door handle of an old Ford, rattling it until the whole body of the Cortina moved and rust pattered into the gutter from the nearside sill. Locked. A single shot, then the high, distant cry of orders over an R/T . . .

People waiting, then. He was coldly certain of that as he ran down the shadowy sidestreet, his shadow looming out ahead, then diminishing suddenly, guillotined by his passing beneath the street-lamp. Two more streets, then the Tube station. He heard the blurting of a car at speed, loudening as it turned the corner and the lights glared down the mean houses towards him. A television's blare from a strengthened glass window close to his face was lost in the roar of the car's engine. A BMW. He ducked into a doorway, then abandoned the idea of cat-and-mouse. He couldn't let them get ahead of him – not more of them than there were already. His shadow again, fleeing with the hopelessness of increasing size and lack of substance as the car closed on him. The cracked pavement treacherous as ice. Then the car slowed, as if scenting the ground. Another corner, the shabby lights of shabbier shops, the curl of spicy food and sitar music from an upstairs window, pots, pans, clotheshorses, apples and strange, bulbous fruit ranged along a shop's reinforced window. Other shops already grilled against the night. A dog snapping at his ankles, its owner half-amused, half-restraining. Black youths on the opposite pavement, shouting louder than their ghetto-blaster.

The Tube station. Evening traffic on the Mile End Road. Normality. The BMW and the other car queueing behind it now at the crossroads. Stuck. He wiped his forehead and his hand was wet as he rubbed it on his thighs. Jesus . . . Shops open, a McDonald's, a video-parlour, the boozer. Cars parked, cars moving, light. He dashed across the road at the first glimpse of green from the pedestrian traffic signal.

In the entrance, just beyond the portico of the Tube station, he saw a yob clutching an R/T against his cheek, as if struggling with some alien life form which had battened on to his skin. Was he an amateur, or had he turned away in professional discretion? Did it matter? The BMW had turned on to the Mile End Road and was

124

already drawing to a halt at the kerb, twenty yards from the station entrance. A drunk lying in vomit on the footstepped tiles, a black rifling his pockets while others laughed and the drunk grinned solemnly. A legless beggar with a dog, a cap at the feet of his crutches into which someone had thrown a crushed lager can, at which the cripple stared. Crowd – a claret-and-blue scarf, then another. Rowdy yobs, young couples, pimply and washed-out, girls in shapeless black. Someone jangling on a guitar somewhere nearer the platform, the thin noise coming up out of the stairwell of the escalator. His heightened senses welcomed the assault of impressions even as he glanced at the Underground chart on one tiled, urinal-like wall, then watched the hunched man . . . professional, he decided. Luckily. The blacks completed their asset-stripping of the amiable drunk and jived towards the escalator beyond the ticket barrier, grinning and raucous.

The man with the R/T turned as if surprised in some covert, impeachable act and found himself confronted by Hyde, who opened his cotton jacket to display the pistol's grip, then smiled. A young couple passed him, then an elderly, hesitant man, then five, six youths. Hyde moved on, knowing the man could and would do nothing, since the Transport Police constable and his sergeant were directly behind the group of roaring youths, as if shepherding them with a long, invisible cattle-prod. He glanced back as his ticket was spat out of the machine. The man's face was angry. Hyde passed through the barrier and descended the escalator. The men from the BMW had been passing beneath the portico of the station entrance as he lost sight of the Transport Police. One of the yelling youths ahead of him vomited theatrically across the division between the two escalators, and ascending passengers flinched away in disgust, and were intimidated by hard laughter and rhythmically waved gestures. He watched the escalator behind him. How many of the amateurs could they get to the station before the next eastbound train? He could take the westbound Central Line to Notting Hill . . . but he wouldn't.

He saw the man with the R/T and the two from the BMW; all three casually dressed, indistinguishable from other users of the station. He shivered as he imagined himself being thrust off the platform and falling against the live rail or in front of a train . . . crowds, he reminded himself. His pursuers no longer possessed the

125

advantage of the neat, discreet, anarchic darkness of the block of flats where they would not have been noticed, never suspected. Where was the girl? He paused at the bottom of the escalator's slatted movement, looking back. There she was. He waved and turned away, apparently heading down the westbound tunnel of the Central Line . . . they'd not know this station, even though they'd had it covered. Embassy and Trade Mission professionals didn't frequent Mile End and Stepney. He doubled through a tiled archway, retracing his steps, and descended the short escalator flight to the District Line, eastbound platform . . . northeast, actually, old chap. Upminster at the end of the line, Hornchurch before that. Quite nice in parts, truly . . .

And then he was afraid again, because the platform was all but deserted. Quiet, so that he could hear the distant guitar and the plaintive, almost tuneless voice of the busker. How old was he, for Christ's sake – *Blowin' in the Wind*? God, the innocence. Two people, kissing as if their appetites if not their lives depended on it; silent, gobbling desperation. Fifteen yards away. Adverts for underwear and a tedious intellectual comedy Ros had made him take her to. Further ads for mineral water and lager. The Underground map. Someone slumped in sleep on a bench below a hideously masked, grinning image of some unknown pop singer on a poster. A youth with a Walkman standing close enough to the edge of the platform to be tipped onto the rails with minimal effort. Otherwise, emptiness. Next Train, the overhead display admitted. Upminster. How long? The tunnel was silent –

– the girl, at once delighted with the stage onto which she had hurried, finding it all but deserted. Two men with her, one of them the man he had passed in the station foyer, stepping over the drunk and the black with exaggerated care. The girl waved at him mockingly and one of the men grinned, then bent his head to his R/T, talking quickly. Hyde pressed his back against the curved wall behind him, against a poster advertising Andrew Lloyd Webber's genius. Hyde tossed his head. Chuck me off from in front of a Proms poster, at least!

His head swivelled like one of the loose, bulbous eyes of a chameleon, back and forth along the platform. If they could get the yobs here in time – why wait? – there was no one watching.

The young couple devoured each other with silent, undiminished intensity and the drunk on the bench snored and smelt in his filthy clothing, emitting wind noisily. The girl looked disdainful but the second man giggled with excitement.

Then the girl was on the cellular phone – would it work down here? Christ knew. The tunnel was silent. His hands pressed damply behind him on the dryness of the poster. His temperature soared. They'd be armed, for certain. But they wouldn't want that kind of noise, would they? They *were* Soviet Embassy people, *he* had the high-card hand, surely, on a London Underground platform?

At a gesture from the girl, the two men moved closer, sidling gently as rising water along the platform towards him. He rested one hand on the gun in his waistband. He glanced along the platform. Two others. Pincer movement. If he fired, they'd kill him at once.

The platform and the tunnel remained silent.


You know this place – don't be afraid, you *know* this place. Its name is Otjiwarongo – you know it well . . . he repeated it to himself over and over, as the huge moon slipped sideways beyond the window and its zebra-striped image moved across the wall opposite his bed, tiredly declining. He had discovered a simple, complete thought, and clung to it. He had gripped at the moonlight at first, then began measuring its progress, like a man under sentence, his nostrils widened for the first scent of the breakfast they would bring . . . the prisoner ate a hearty breakfast, wasn't that what they once reported? Clinging to the passage of time had weakened him, absorbed much of his diminished energies. Then he had imagined the town, because of the barking of a dog or some other animal, the snatch of a drunk's song, the engine of a vehicle.

Clung to – Otjiwarongo, to knowledge of it, tracing it on some mental map, rebuilding a ghost town in his imagination; peopling it, too. People he knew, people who might help. The dog must have got loose from somewhere, for it nuzzled close to the wall outside, he had even heard it relieve itself against the wood. It barked occasionally, reminding him, prompting, nudging.

He had accepted the dog's admonitions as the late night grew towards the brief cool of dawn. So, he was seated on the edge of the bed, in his vest and shorts, weakened and sweaty with the efforts of discovering his clothes and remaining silent, repeating to himself again and again, *you know this place.* You knew it when its white area and black matchbox township were entirely distinct, before they began to melt together. You know where there are vehicles, food, supplies, weapons. But he could not avoid, or resist, remembering the place as it had been before independence, however partial and cosmetic that process had been. It was as if he was black, and hunted by the old power, by Blantyre, who would be coming back.

Anderson watched his arms shivering as his hands gripped the edge of the bed and he pressed the soles of his feet against the linoleum to still the tremors of fear that seemed to possess his whole frame. His breathing became louder. *Otjiwarongo.* In the township, the scrubby, dusty place . . . Joe Tsumis, who had a 4WD, more than one, and who had been a tourist guide up to Ovamboland . . . you *know* him, for Christ's sake, so get on with it and stop thinking of Blantyre!

He pushed himself weakly to his feet, fumbling cotton shorts out of the bedside locker, hovering uncertainly and almost with desperation on one leg, then the other, breaking out into a sweat that the night's cool could not allay. Then his shirt over an already sticky chest and shoulders, then his boots – breathing puffing and snorting in his ears, as if he were having some kind of attack, for God's sake! Trying to calm himself as he tied his bootlaces.

Afterwards, things were easier, as if he had recuperated in his anger. Bandages, the painkillers, his papers – because he wouldn't be allowed where he intended going without the papers that proved he was really a white man under his pale skin – and his wallet. Joe Tsumis wouldn't take credit cards, but others would.

Then he stood looking at the square of the window as the sky began to lighten. Distinct pinpricks of lights in the dawn from the town. Was then horrified at the thought that Joe Tsumis might have left or been killed in the three years since he had last seen him . . . Slowly, deliberately, he wiped his forehead, then wiped his palm on the shorts. He hurried to the window, gripping the fine mesh screen with his fingertips. The air, already tired at the prospect of the day's heat, was only slightly cooler against his forehead as it leaked through the open window. He rattled the mesh softly. It did not yield. Pull, push –? He inspected its fixings, the screws rusty in the chipped, peeling wood. Push –

A squeak like that of a small animal caught in a trap came from the screen. The quiet ripping of loosening screws. His sweating increased. The noises were unnervingly loud. Then, as he began shivering with indecision, the dog barked again, the noise peremptory, and he pushed at the rusty screen and it fell outwards. He clung to it with his fingertips, bending out over the sill and lowering it against the wall quietly. Breathing noisily but regularly. Carefully, he climbed through the open window and dropped to the ground.

No one. He began walking, stiffly towards the few scattered lights of Otjiwarongo, along the dusty street lined with wooden, two-storey houses, a few shops, a small hotel. The mission church's spire black against the first, quick greyness of the dawn. It was an image of a frontier town; like so many towns and villages and settlements in Namibia, frozen in the last century. Small aloes, patches of desiccated lawn, the tidy, packed earth of white-owned frontages and yards. A few lights were on behind still-drawn curtains or mesh screens – the lights of servants. Anderson passed the hotel furtively, on the other side of the wide, empty street. Blantyre must be staying there, there was nowhere else.

Then the township, half kraal, half battered petrol can assemblage of sheds and huts. Leaking light as if the original contents of the cans was seeping into the town itself. Sheds in the back gardens of the last of the colonial houses, tents erected in the street. The boundary of black and white gradually blurring. Trees and plants and scrubby lawns became dirt patches growing vegetables. Independence and suffrage ... but the invasion of the suburb that was so out of place on the high plateau scattered with native kraals was under way, like grass growing up through paving stones; irresistible.

But the township failed to distract him from the idea that Joe Tsumis was no longer in Otjiwarongo, or from the creeping sensation that, voyeur-like, he could sense Blantyre waking, stirring in his bed, getting up in order to cross the few hundred yards to the clinic, to find him gone and raise the alarm. Joe had driven him when he had first come to discover Namibia, to find somewhere to settle and escape; driven him northwards with enthusiasm perhaps half-a-dozen times, because a white man had been the perfect cover for his gun-running to SWAPO units in the Bush. Then Anderson had found Etosha, place of dry water, and the wardenship vacant, and not seen Joe more than two or three times since.

Black men and women, mostly Damara and Nama, headscarved, language clicking in the suddenly lighter air as the sun was about to lift itself above the horizon ahead of him. The men soberly black-trilbied, white-shirted. There were only domestic jobs, but they were slightly better paid now. The dawn flared up, and the sky was deep blue directly overhead. He must hurry now, through the servants drifting towards the white suburb. Joe Tsumis – *be there*.

Tethered goats, chickens scrabbling in the dust. Children in dim doorways with huge eyes, curious and perhaps no longer afraid. He hurried on, down another nameless, shapeless street, then turned past a garage littered with old tyres – Joe's? – and with a single old-fashioned pump. He was unsure. Squinting, he could see no 4WDs in the interior of the dilapidated barn beyond the pump. He spun around, dizzily studying the place, vainly orientating himself.

Then he saw it. Pink in the early sun, its chrome blazing, an elderly American Cadillac, open-topped, palely upholstered. It was parked next to the garage, outside a more substantial, all-wooden hut of one storey, but extended at the back, curtains at the windows. He was hot and sticky with gratitude, turning on his heel to study the street behind him. One ancient truck, bicycles, no white man's vehicle. He hurried past the Cadillac, past the vegetable plot and the three tethered goats – it was Joe's place. Grinning, he banged on the door, calling at once:

'Joe! Joe Tsumis! It's Richard – Richard Anderson.' He banged again. 'Open up, Joe!' A boy on a rickety bicycle stopped in the street to watch him, and he realized his knocking was like a visitation from the past; white, demanding, official. 'Joe – sorry to disturb you –'

It was at that gesture to equality that the door opened. A young woman, Himba by her features, a cotton frock draped over her slim body, a baby at one exposed breast. A new wife? She appeared unsurprised, and unwilling. Then Joe appeared behind her, one hand behind his back, his beard greyer, his eyes suspicious, quick – then softening as he recognized Anderson. He pushed the young woman back into the house and the long-barrelled pistol appeared harmlessly from behind his back. Pots rattled somewhere at the rear of the hut, which was dirt-floored, but with bright Himba rugs and perhaps Herero weaves, too, in the matting. Tsumis watched him now, detached but curious.

'Joe –' he said.

'What is it – Richard Anderson? What do you want from me?' Anderson rubbed his beard and shrugged, disarming Tsumis, making himself nothing more than a harmless white man who hardly noticed the pistol hanging slackly in Tsumis' hand. 'What is it, so early, too?' Tsumis assessed him; dress, sallowness, bandaging.

'I – want . . . can pay – for your help, Joe.'

The old, habitual glance either way along the dirt street, then: 'Come in, man – come in.'

He ducked his head to enter. Table lamps, rugs, a low table, a dining table and chairs; beginnings of substance. Voices sounded from a back room and the noise of people leaving. Empty bottles, cards on the low table.

'Sit down – Richard, man.' Tsumis gestured to a chair, which creaked and tilted as Anderson lowered himself into it. His hands gripped the wooden arms as he understood change in the place, furtiveness and power crowding the corners of the room. Tsumis saw his disconcertedness and said: 'Times have changed.' He put the gun on the low table amid the playing cards. Quick as thrown water, sunlight splashed in through the open window, making the dirt floor rich and the rugs vivid. 'You want a laugh, Richard?' Anderson shook his head bemusedly. 'You want to shake hands with the local MP?' Tsumis held out his hand, then roared with laughter that possessed a cynical top register. He slapped his thighs. 'Yes, man – got elected at Independence.' He leaned forward. 'Got the job, got as corrupt as hell straight away – got power, Richard.'

'Congratulations.'

'Ah, the voice of the public schoolboy – I recognize it. From the advisers they send us. Still, man, better than that accent that says *keffir* – eh?' He studied Anderson, then asked in a former voice he might have specifically summoned: 'What happened to you?'

Anderson shook his head, but was betrayed by weariness, and murmured: 'She's dead, Joe – murdered.' The shock on Tsumis' face was real, sufficiently so to turn the leaking tap. He sat, chin resting on his sunken chest, and told Tsumis how, why, when – everything except the motive for Blantyre's enmity.

131

'Why?' Tsumis asked, eventually.

'I – something from the past, something old, that happened in Jo'burg, a long time ago.'

Tsumis shrugged dismissively. 'And now – what for you? I'm sorry, by the way -'

'Thank you.'

'I know Blantyre. A pity you do.' Tsumis spat. 'A bastard – a real bastard. I saw him once . . .' Anderson hardly listened to the atrocity Tsumis had witnessed in the Bush, years before. He banked the pain of his emotions and waited for Tsumis to finish speaking. The sunlight hardened, drying like paint on the wall, and the low, long room was filled with slow motes. Tsumis, he guessed, would turn him in if it suited him – he'd always been capable of it – or he might help him, sell him what he needed. 'So, he wants you?'

'Yes. I need to get away. A vehicle, supplies. I can pay.'

'I don't take American Express – money will do nicely.'

It was his shrunken, defeated condition, he decided, despising himself, that would make Tsumis help him. A harmless, bemused man, not worth much to Blantyre. And Blantyre was unpredictable, hated blacks, liked killing them. He controlled his sigh of relief at the realization, gripping the arms of the old chair.

'I can pay you, Joe – no favours, just business. A 4WD, some supplies – food and water.'

'For how long?'

'Just for long enough to drive a long way away from here.'

Tsumis nodded. Anderson heard a timid knocking at what must be the back door. The Himba girl appeared, tossing her head in the direction of the noises. Tsumis got up.

'Excuse me – business.'

He watched the motes dance to Tsumis' movements in the slabs of sunlight crossing the room, hardly listening to the altercation over the instalment of bribery or extortion at the rear door. Tsumis entered the room again, angrily waving a small wad of bright Namibian currency.

'See?' Tsumis challenged. 'Corruption's damn' inefficient round here since the whites handed over!' Then he laughed, and announced: 'This is a dirt place, it always will be. Expect no better. There's nothing here but a bit of money. I'm collecting it, as much as I can – then we go to Windhoek or Swakopmund, and buy more power – I'm a Marxist who's corrupt as hell! Maybe one day, I'll be President, who knows? Then I'll do the right thing. Meantime, Richard man, I got to get connections.' He waved the money.

Confident he could not offend Tsumis or lose his help, Anderson said, 'You're not a Marxist, or anything else, come to that, Joe. You never were.' Tsumis looked angry for a moment, then a past self grinned from behind the recently acquired actor's mask. 'At least you're consistent, still being in it for the money.'

Tsumis flung the notes across the room in assumed disdain. They fluttered to the packed floor like feathers from a bird.

'OK. I'll send one of the boys for supplies – three days, no more – don't want to arouse suspicion. They'll tell you how much. You want to see the Land Rover now?' The sun warned, climbing the wall opposite the window.

'How old is it?'

'No more than twenty years – think I'd cheat you?'

He slapped Anderson's shoulder, making him wince against the pain. They walked through the sprawling untidiness of the kitchen, Anderson hardly remarking the Himba girl. The children were scuttling like puppies, their gradations of age careful as calculation. Tsumis' hand remained on his shoulder even as they entered the yard and the morning sun struck him like a blow on the side of his face as they trod amongst the chickens and goats towards the garage. The sun unnerved him more than Tsumis' words.

'That Blantyre, he's a deep bastard, the worst. You watch out for him. I don't wish you dead, Richard.' Anderson watched his shadow stride more confidently ahead of him, acting casual indifference far better than the skin on his cheeks. 'Let's get you out of here. More comfortable for both of us, uh?'

The inky blindness of the garage shed was claustrophobic after the brightness of the yard. He had thought of obtaining a vehicle and supplies as a complex, difficult task. Joe had made it easy – and thrust him towards his future with a large hand on his shoulder.

The Land Rover, emerging from the gloom, seemed drab, forlorn. Don Quixote's old nag. He clenched his fists, remembering the burning; squeezed his fists tightly, hurting himself. What could he

133

do? How could he even begin to imagine he could survive, never mind succeed against Blantyre?

Silence from the hole of the tunnel. Hyde dragged his cotton jacket open so that the gun would be evident. They hesitated, so that he knew they would not close in further, but merely wait, shepherding him like dogs to some quiet, final place. The girl – that bloody imitation Sloane! – was utterly confident. A nerve jumped in his wrist, potent as a hand across his face.

He calmed his breathing. *Next Train*, where the bloody hell are you? He surreptitiously glanced at his watch. What time did the boozers turn out – eleven, eleven-thirty? It was ten fifty-eight. A bag-lady stuttered into view, two supermarket bags in each frail hand. She arranged herself on a bench –

– train, sighing like an ugly voice out of the tunnel's mouth, rushing towards him. The bloody cavalry almost missing the final reel! The bag-lady ceremoniously arranged her plastic sheet and her newspapers: dozens of copies of the *Christian Science Monitor*, she must have lifted them from the Reading Room. She bore no resemblance to Vi; nevertheless she reminded him of his aunt. The train, as it slowed, was disappointingly empty. Eleven o'clock. They'd keep him on the streets until dawn, be in every pub, café, bus shelter and alley with him, always pressing close. The train came to a stop and he hesitated because any sudden movement might panic them, make them use a quick, small knife.

He boarded the train. Two more now . . . the girl and her two minders got into the same carriage, the others into the one behind. Up-bloody-minster . . . if he went all the way, it would be goodbye in the suburban dark. The bag-lady, reposing like the carved effigy of some baron's lady on a medieval tomb, was whisked out of sight and the tunnel walls pressed against the glass, then vanished in the reflection of his own face as he strap-hung near the end door of the carriage. He watched his face, watched them, one lolling, the other man more tense, the girl revelling in the mounting tension. She'd been there before and liked the sensations.

Slowing – Bow Road. Blacks, a tramp, a Transport copper looking along the platform. No one left, two people got on. Signal from one of them? No, he didn't think so. But she must have told them where he was going, what he was doing, before she got into the uncommunicative Tube. The train lurched out of the station. Posters and graffiti mocked, then the tunnel. Almost at once, Bromley-by-Bow, and still no more bloody people than before – shit. A few stragglers got off, a handful joined the train. Eleven-five. For Christ's sake, what time did the bloody boozers turn out in this part of London? The girl was watching him proprietorially while the men watched her and himself in turn, heads nipping back and forth mechanically. His legs felt shaky.

West Ham station. Transport Police in twos – a good sign. He clung to the station name as the trickle of boarding passengers attempted to fill the carriage by spreading themselves along the seats. Two high-voiced, raucous, harmless blacks, two old ladies, a couple of young scrubbers. The girl flinched from their tasteless mock-leather and studs and earrings and stiff hair. He smiled at her, shaking his head; attempting to regain control, confidence. The girl glared back.

Plaistow. The train stopped. A busker's saxophone from some-where, the blacks in the carriage swinging their loose hips to its rhythm, then roaring with laughter. No one suspicious boarded. If he could just get off the bloody train! He staggered against the restraint of the strap to which he clung as the train surged into the tunnel. One more station, just one more, and then the move would be entirely his, and probably fatal. It would be without distraction. Eleven-ten. The boozers, oh the boozers emptying, *please* –! One minute, then two . . . the train rushed on, swinging around a slow curve of the track, then the lights and the first of the signs, Upton Park. *Please* –

– yes. As the train slowed once more, the platform's muddle became a crowd. Claret-and-blue scarves everywhere, around almost every neck. Drunks, the merely happy – a *crowd*. Hyde felt weak with relief, then he bunched and stiffened with tension as the train slowed and the crowd pressed to the edge of the platform, a landscape of grinning, hot faces and moving arms. West Ham had been playing a summer friendly against some Spanish club at Upton Park. This mob was on its way back to Dagenham or Barking or wherever.

The two men were distracted by the crowded platform as the train came to a stop, and were disarmed by the crowd's pressure

135

against the unopened doors. Hyde was imprisoned. The girl seemed doubtful, watching him from beneath a furrowed brow.

The door began sliding open and he thrust at the blocked escape route with a panic of adrenalin as they realized he was attempting to use the crowd. He was buffeted backwards, one foot still on the floor of the carriage, then he lowered his head and burrowed at them like a boxer with a shorter reach, lighter but more determined. Complaints, a struggling leg aimed in his vague direction, the bellowing of *I'm forever blowing bubbles*, and then he was five yards, then six, from the open door and turned, pressed against the curving station wall, to see one of the men swept back into the carriage and the girl's face pressed against the window like that of a furiously disappointed child. Even as the press of football supporters dragged him like a tide's undertow, off-balance, he waved at her, then elbowed and swam through the remainder of the crowd towards the exit sign. Way Out – oh, yes . . .

The platform was now empty, except for the Transport Police, looking relieved – six, eight of them – and one of the two men who had boarded the carriage behind his. And who weighed the situation as he hovered near two of the policemen. The girl's face, caricaturing anger and disappointment, slid past him into the tunnel as the train gathered speed.

He ran up the steps. The lone KGB man wouldn't move without back-up or new orders. He'd probably claim Hyde had identified himself to the police, rendering him powerless to accomplish the mission.

Hyde ran blithely up the escalator, a grin in command of his mouth. Centre Point, he thought. They'd try to head him off at the pass, any way they could. So, he couldn't go back to Centre Point. And they'd put a team in Philbeach Gardens, to wait for him. There wasn't anything to smile about, really. Still, he couldn't help the immediate sensations. Good old Hammers –


Van Vuuren watched the limousine chauffeur carrying his bags across the foyer of the InterContinental towards the bright heat beyond the glass doors, and put his laptop computer down at his feet as he glanced at his bill. He smirked to himself – flowers, champagne, yes . . . breakfast. The girl was not on the bill. Paulus drew the line at that . . . charge this, charge that. OK. Telephone calls, room service . . . He made to pass the bill to his assistant, who was already fishing his company Amex card from his Filofax. Then he snatched it back and said to the Chinese girl behind the glass of her kiosk:

'I didn't make that telephone call – the one to Johannesburg. Will you check on it, please. These, yes – but not this one. When was this?' His voice, he realized, was already slightly shrill with suspicion. The girl assumed it was directed at the hotel. 'Please be accurate. Find out what time the call was made.'

'Anything wrong, sir?' his assistant asked. One of those more-English-than-the-English voices from Natal. A disparagement of his own heavy Afrikaaner accent in every syllable, even in his height and longish fair hair. Bright, though.

'No. I – this girl's checking something. I want to – may want Paulus on the line. Get hold of a telephone in one of the offices. Do what you must – get it.'

His assistant moved along the Reception counter, thrusting himself in front of two Arabs, and bent to murmur to the frock-coated desk manager, who at once began shaking his head. But the movement slowed like the coming to rest of one of those Russian dolls as the young man touched a breast pocket and van Vuuren was indicated with a gesture of his head.

The Chinese girl. The number was too familiar – and too secure – not to be recognized immediately.

' – call was made a' eight-fifty, sir. Sorry to –'

'I didn't make it. Who used the phone in my room?' he snapped. The tremor of suspicion now had its epicentre somewhere in his stomach.

'Sir, you must ha' used the telephone. Staff are –'

'Who *used* it?' he snarled.

But, at once, it no longer mattered. He glared at the laptop at his feet as at an animal that had bitten him, after kindness. Someone had got into his suite and used it, linked it via the telephone line to MLC's mainframe in Jo'burg, asked it for information –

– bastards, those bastards who'd had MacPherson's office under surveillance. The British bastards.

His assistant was gesturing success.

'Pay my bill!' he snapped. 'And look after *this*!' He held out the

137

computer as if it had betrayed him. 'Where?' he barked at the frock-coated manager, and was shown into a cubbyhole brimming with a small desk, a telephone and an old filing cabinet. 'Get out!' he shouted and shut the door. The airless, windowless cupboard of a room was hot – *he* was hot, for Christ's sake! Hot and terrified by the certainty that they had the codes and they had got into MLC's mainframe.

His finger paused in stabbing out Malan's number. God, Paulus would . . . He wiped his forehead with his fingertips and they came away damp. He inspected them with repulsion, inspected the receiver with an identical dislike. Then, reluctantly, he continued dialling the Johannesburg number, glancing at his watch. Malan would already be at work, in his office in the mansion. Jesus – it was too bloody awful to contemplate! Priabin and his jokers should have got hold of anything and everything. Instead, that mad bastard Australian had killed them, *three* of them –! They had the bloody codes, they must have ripped the guts out of the mainframe! He ought to call the mainframe, access what it had been asked, what it had given away –

He moved the receiver away from his ear, but then heard the connection made and Malan's voice.

'Paulus, it's me.'

'Piet, what is it?' Paulus already knew something was wrong. Like a lion scenting a flesh wound a mile away, he was so bloody sensitive to tones of voice . . . or just to the possible urgency of an international call from himself at that time in the morning. 'Is anything wrong?'

There was no easy way to –

'Paulus, someone's – someone's been into the mainframe, using my –'

'Wait!' Malan snapped. Then he heard another line being used, and Malan's demand for a check on requests made by van Vuuren's computer. 'When was this?'

'Last night, just before nine –'

Malan relayed the time, then: 'What happened?'

'They must have broken into my room – no sign of forced entry – I don't understand how they –'

'Photographic equipment, Piet. Surveillance by camera. You've heard of it? They must have photographed the screen as you tapped in in MacPherson's office. We were told these people would be *stopped*, and they haven't been! Wait – ' A telephone was ringing distantly, and he heard Malan on the other line, repeating: 'Yes, yes . . . yes – *yes.*' Then: 'Stop all new shipments, Piet – stop them *now.*'

'Paulus, what did they get?'

'They accessed anything and everything you opened up for them in MacPherson's office, Piet! Do I need to explain? From what they have, they could pinpoint the company and the airport. As with everything, it was only clever while it was secure. Get it stopped or changed, then call me.'

The receiver hummed in his ear. The relief that shivered through him was unavoidable. Just because Malan had not panicked – as he had, in this shitty little room, preparing to grovel! His hands were clammy. The noise in his head was thunder-like. *Think!*

Stop tonight's shipment, that was the first thing. They'd had no time to respond while he slept. They might have arranged surveillance in Birmingham – no, couldn't have . . . because Priabin assured him they were working unofficially, they had no back-up, few resources. Just sufficient to get them into MLC's mainframe, that was all! Stop the shipment, then, get it changed for something harmless, something it was *supposed* to be on the Customs forms and the manifest. If that could be done, then those people could do what they wanted, go ahead as stupidly as they wished, and it would blow up in their faces. The more *fuss* they made, the more they'd be borne down on. Hauled off, like a dog from a child it was savaging. All the sympathy with the child, whatever it had been doing to annoy the dog.

He grinned, inspected his idea as carefully as he might have done a contract worth billions of rands, then nodded to himself. A knock at the door. Gert, the assistant. He waved him away and the door closed again.

Ring their man – make him, in turn, sweat as freely as he had done. Grab the bastard's balls and wrench on them. Then call Priabin. Consult him, get his people moving in on these bastards who'd made him sweat. Priabin should have taken – what was his name? *Hyde* – should have taken him *out*!

He was sweating again. These people had to be removed – fucking Communists, couldn't organize a bloody thing!

He dialled a Birmingham number – 021? 021 . . . The ringing

tone, twice, three – then the answerphone. ' – not able to come to the phone, please leave – '

Where was he? He glanced furtively at his watch, as if he were being observed.

Then he remembered, the man was on a flight from somewhere, still on his way home. Christ, who did he ring *now*?

Godwin opened the curtains – he must have dozed for half an hour, perhaps longer, since daylight first surprised him – then he glanced around his littered lounge; cramped, in need of decoration, the old furniture. Chambers was lying on the lumpy sofa, soundly asleep. The Centre Point offices were strictly out of bounds to them, they'd had to bring everything back – home? Peculiar word, it seemed, at that time of the morning and with someone asleep in the room he occupied, often for weeks or even months, alone. Chambers looked like a Yuppie fallen into a drunken doze rather than an exhausted sleep. Dubček was lying against Chambers' stomach, legs extended over his waist as he lay on his side. The cat had already snagged threads from the fat, paisley-patterned tie that hung loosely around his neck. Godwin tossed his head, disturbed by company; pained by it, too, for some indefinable reason.

He inspected the street below the window: a milkman, a few early pedestrians, the first cars nudging or sidling out of their cramped residents' parking slots; and houses still blinded by curtains, the thinner material letting grubby light soak into them.

He turned to face the room, rubbing his stomach because of the indigestion of hunger. The previous evening they'd had only sandwiches of stale bread and corned beef because, by the time they had realized their late evening hunger, the takeaways had closed. After that, with the regularity of beer and the occasions of scotch, they had worked until three. Flipcharts still sat propped on a ladderback chair, and the mass of hard copy printout lay dismembered and seemingly flung about the room by a wind. There were also the reference books, and the sheaves of paper scribbled on or screwed up and discarded without being tidied. He rubbed his temples. It had been strangely mindless, some intellectual equivalent of an acid house party or disco, where the throb of the work had been like emptying music, so that nothing else mattered. They

140

had never been outside the experience even for a moment – except to find the takeaways closed and a lack of TV dinners in the freezer.

But, on the displayed sheet of the flipchart folder propped on the chair, they had it, the letters dim in the subdued light that sidled around the too-close buildings opposite. The place, the company. Birmingham airport. SwiftEx, bulk shippers to Europe, including eastern Europe. Simple as that. Both of them chasing through the mass of detail extracted from the MLC mainframe, making sense of it, cross-referencing with months of other material . . . sensing the acceleration and the pattern of shipments to meet a recent, unexpected increase in orders. And the orders coming more and more from verifiable MLC subsidiaries or associated companies. TVs by the thousands, microwaves, cookers, cellular telephones, air-conditioning – anything and *everything* manufactured by the Reid Group subsidiary, Reid Davies, in Birmingham. And the stuff went out from Brum airport, via a Brum shipper. Jesus, they'd cheered, laughed, almost cried, had a large whisky each and crashed out. Knackered.

Worth it.

Godwin, grinning, lit a cigarette. Chambers' nose twitched, he growled his throat clear, and opened his eyes, stirring helpless as a baby for a moment before blinking at Godwin's shadow outlined against the window.

'God, what time is it?'

'Seven.'

Dubček stirred, clung on for a moment, making Chambers wince at the claws in his skin, then slowly and reluctantly abandoned his human pillow. 'God, my mouth! Like a lion-tamer's armpit!'

'Coffee?'

'Uh? Oh, right. Even if I do begin to slop noisily when I walk –' Then his head turned to the flipchart, as if he felt he might have dreamed the effort and the success. He grinned at Godwin, rubbing his eyes. 'We did do it, then?'

'Yes, I really think we did!' Godwin returned Chambers' grin, rubbing his hair and brushing cigarette ash from his grubby shirt-front. He pointed towards his own computer, resting on the littered, scratched surface of the dining table. 'And it's all in there. The whole beautiful arrangement!'

'That can't be all of it – can it?'

Godwin shook his head. 'Just *our* bit – the UK pipeline.'

'And only where the stuff comes from – not where it goes. Well, except that French company.'

'Dumas Electroniques. The mouse that swallowed the elephant.'

'They don't own Reid Group, they're just the largest single shareholder since they bought David Reid's personal shareholding.'

'But who owns Dumas?'

'God knows – the bloke who wrote *The Three Musketeers*?'

'But, if we find out,' Godwin pressed, 'we might have the next length of the pipeline, then the one after that . . . all the way to – wherever. Malan's being used by the KGB, obviously.'

'Why obviously?' Chambers called from the kitchen. Godwin could hear the gradual boiling of the kettle.

'He can't be getting the major share – so he's being used.'

'Why?'

'Why would he agree?' The kettle boiled and clicked off. Dubček had followed Chambers. Godwin heard the scraping of a fork round a tin of catfood. 'Because of the *concessions* in eastern Europe and Russia? He's worked with them for years over gold and diamonds – they trust him, insofar as they trust anyone. Who else would they work with?'

Chambers brought the mugs through and handed him one. Then Chambers stared, unimpressed, out of the window. On the other hand, Chambers had an unsaleable flat in Docklands – a lot tidier and a lot more expensive to run. Kentish Town could become fashionable before Docklands emerged from its slump. Godwin tossed his head. He just wasn't used to company.

'OK,' Chambers said, 'but what do we do now? No one who's afraid of Orrell is going to listen to us. Anyway, most of them are too thick to understand this.' Then he added: 'I can't see any suspicious vehicles out there – did you notice anything?'

'Wishing Patrick was here?' Chambers looked scornful, but uncertain. 'No, I didn't see anything. Anyway, from what he said over the phone, they want him removed first, then they'll come for us.' Chambers shivered.

'He's a pillock.'

'He's a dangerous animal.'

'Why don't we talk to Aubrey?' Chambers was holding his mug in both hands, as if warming himself; looking somehow shrunken.

'The old man's *ill*. He's not even back at work yet. If he ever comes back. He might listen, but what could he do, with Orrell's nose so far up the Cabinet's collective backside?' Godwin shook his head. 'I *want* to talk to Aubrey, but I don't think there's anything he could do, not at this stage.'

'So, what do we do? That acceleration in there –' He waved towards the flipcharts. 'It'll break the bloody sound barrier if it gets any faster!'

It was true. The volume of goods passing through Reid Davies, the orders they were fulfilling, the shipping done by SwiftEx – it was all like a boil coming to a head. It had to be soon. Malan had just piled new, even bigger orders onto Reid Group. It was like that runaway merry-go-round in the Hitchcock film, spinning out of control, blurring into a rush and whirl.

And Patrick . . . they wanted him dead, and quickly. There was no doubt things were about to jump.

'You say it isn't Davies?'

Godwin shook his head. 'Doubt it. He used to work for us, courier, sideliner, people-carrier. Aubrey wouldn't believe it was him – I don't.'

'Then there's a lot of people he's employed who are in it. Have to be, to bring it off – sending the high-tech stuff out disguised as TVs and microwaves!' Chambers put down his mug and thrust his hands into his pockets. 'What do we do then?'

'I'm going to ring Customs, and *pretend* we have Sir Clive's authority for surveillance on SwiftEx at Brum airport.' Chambers nodded and smirked approval. 'Meanwhile, you and I are going to drive up to Brum and sit outside Reid Davies' gates and wait for the latest order for an MLC company to roll out on its way to the shippers. Today, tomorrow – couldn't be later, could it? Then we'll send Customs in to open the boxes. Like it?'

'A bit. Orrell will have a heart attack – Christ, that sod Bannister, our glorious deputy DG, was pretty rough last night!'

'Bannister's as thick as only a confidant of Clive Orrell's could be – don't worry about him. As long as we kept saying we knew nothing and we were sorry for any inconvenience caused.'

'This will be different. We're supposed to be on leave, pending investigation.'

'Do you want to do this, or not?' Godwin snapped.

'Yes, yes –!' Chambers protested too violently.

'Look, don't chicken out now, after all the bloody work we've put in,' Godwin raged, crossing to the telephone with an admonishingly loud noise from his sticks. He picked up the receiver and brandished it in Chambers' direction. 'If Orrell and Bannister don't give a stuff, then I *do*! Look, it's going to take weeks, maybe months, as it is – with what we've got – to get inside Reid Davies and clean it out. Don't give me any lily-livered worries about your fucking pension now, Terry – just *don't*!'

He began dabbing out the number, feeling hot but pleased with his outburst. They needed to catch a shipment, that was *all* they needed, to open up the whole can of worms.

The Special Branch man inspected Hyde's unshaven, weary features, and his antagonism became contempt. The morning was hot, even though it was only just after seven. Already, the shrill of a child exploded from the gardens, followed by the splutter of birds as they accelerated into the morning like small vehicles. He'd trailed around London, mostly on foot – one early taxi, a bus filled with people heading for work and resenting their impending separation from the bright day. There was a smell of petrol everywhere in the windless air. No one had tailed him or picked him up, not even as he ate at a breakfast caravan parked beside a railway bridge. He belched. Indigestible sandwiches filled with bacon and fried egg, and the aftertaste of sweet tea. He glanced up at Ros' window. She wasn't there, but who had she already let in who occupied her attention?

Because Priabin's people weren't here. Special Branch had frightened them off, parking outside his door.

'Can I help, officer?' he asked insultingly, hands in his pockets.

'Hyde – has to be, doesn't it?' the Special Branch man commented. 'People waiting to see you.' He nodded towards the flat before he got out of the Granada. The policeman was taller than Hyde, bulky and confidently smirking. Agent of the civil power – unlike, his expression remarked, the small man who confronted him. Another of those spooks, as the Yanks called them, getting his come-uppance. 'Would you care to accompany me, sir?' He warily offered his cupped hand towards Hyde's elbow.

'I wouldn't.'

'Yours is about to drop on you,' the SB officer observed, sniffing the air like a large dog.

'Was there anyone *here*, when you arrived?' Hyde asked impatiently.

'Look, there's no one hiding in the bushes, not even your bookie.'

'Oh, those important files you keep in Curzon Street. Any people in cars – you know, ones who didn't drive straight off to work?'

The car's driver looked angry and leaned belligerently across the passenger seat.

'Take clever Dick upstairs, Dean,' he said.

Hyde spluttered with laughter. 'It's true – the policemen are getting younger.'

'Just let me see you laughing upstairs.'

'Why – who are my houseguests, Constable?'

'Sir Clive Orrell and Aubrey, the –'

'– old fart, you were about to add? OK, we'll go inside – just get your mate in there to have a look around the gardens, will you? As a last favour for a dying man?'

Christ, *Aubrey*? He'd come off sick leave to his flat with Orrell? Serious was not the word . . .

There was sufficient professionalism latent even in their situation for the SB man to nod to the driver and murmur: 'Just play up to him, will you, Jack? Have a look for Mata Hari in a parked car, would you?'

Hyde clicked his fingers. 'Glad to see you covered yourself there, *Dean*,' and shrugged off the attempted grip and strode across the pavement to the three steps up to the front door. He glimpsed Ros' volume fill the window of her flat, even the warning round O of her mouth opening, before he passed under the porch.

The birds vied with the traffic from the main road and the periodic coughing of engines starting up in Philbeach Gardens. Then Ros was at the door, the habitual *where-have-you-been* expression on her face collapsing quickly into confusion, into *what's-going-on?* He kissed her cheek in passing, shrugging his ignorance. Even though he could no longer pretend, even to himself. Aubrey was prepared to arrive in tandem with Orrell . . . *Goodnight, ladies* . . . It was all about to fall in on his head. He climbed the staircase to the first floor, then the second, with Ros behind him, silently shooing him up towards his suspension. She seemed impressed, angry and reluctant at the same moment concerning the two august civil servants who were waiting for him. That's what they were, and it's *your* pension that's on the line!

As he pushed open the door of his flat, Aubrey whirled round in front of the French clock on the mantelpiece. Hyde appraised him, like a surgeon a patient. The old man leaned heavily on his stick, but he seemed fitter than the last time they'd met. His skin was less waxy, almost tinted with health. But there was no sense of Aubrey's support for him, merely irritation, suspicion – distance between them. The bellicose bad humour of an old man galvanized into reluctant energy and purpose. Hyde felt his stomach sag. There'd be no help from Aubrey, just the ballocking and the suspension – dismissal? – from Orrell.

Aubrey seemed almost contemptuous of Hyde's own unshaven, highly-odorous self, and at once began to pace the room, as if he had been waiting for some theatrical cue, his stick jutting out just ahead of him at each step, as if in control of him. Orrell watched with a bluff kind of calculation. Neither of the two new cats had gone near him. Both of them at least feigned sleep. The Burmese stray stretched itself, its legs too long for its body. It always walked as if it had a sore backside – like Orrell, except that he rolled. The other one, the tortoiseshell with the black mask, was asleep on the windowsill outside the open window, one ear idly attending to the birdsong from the few paltry trees in the back garden. Even now, he tried not to be interested in them. Ros had brought them home from some rescue shelter. Instead, he tried ever more violently to remember Layla, six months' dead and buried in the garden.

As if at some invisible tug from a string Orrell held, Aubrey said: 'Patrick, where the *devil* have you been? I have been dragged – requested to come here – because you could not be located on the express orders of your own Director-General!' The formality was strange and awesome; pathetic, too. The last refuge of an old man. He glanced at Orrell and saw nothing but satisfaction on his large, uncharactered face. Then Aubrey let fall, amid his dry officialese, something of himself as he said: 'Why Sir Clive required my presence, I have no idea. You are no longer attached to me by anything, not even some imagined umbilical cord!' He turned his back on Hyde immediately.

Orrell seemed to consider his remarks as sufficiently reprimanding, for he said: 'You were ordered to report to Century House yesterday for a full debriefing. DDG Bannister –' Hyde maintained a stony inexpression. '– issued that order at – well, never mind. But, after an incident of the *significance* of that at Centre Point, you must surely have realized your report would be required at the most senior levels?'

Aubrey's shoulders were twitchy, uncertain within his light-weight suit. The Burmese, Hyde noticed, had stretched one paw out towards Aubrey's straw hat, lying on the sofa. Another few inches and she'd become animated and destructive. To some extent, Orrell was inhibited by Aubrey's presence – authority, rather. What should he do? Authority haunted the corridors of Orrell's labyrin-thine mind. Empty labyrinth, though. No Minotaur in there. Get rid of Orrell, then. Signal Aubrey with –

'Sir, I'm sorry.' Aubrey's head cocked like that of a bird. Orrell, too, seemed suspicious if not surprised. Apology was his due, after all. Hyde flicked his hands, then rubbed his unshaven face. 'After that – sir, you know how it is for field agents, afterwards . . .' He collapsed into one of the armchairs. Ros, in the doorway, he realized for the first time, emanated a puzzlement that he gratefully accepted. If she was bemused, then Orrell had no chance.

'Hyde, what are you saying to me?' Aubrey snapped.

'Sir, I'm saying that I went in there, gung-ho if you like, because I thought . . . well, didn't think, really, but I *knew* the bomb scare was a hoax, I *knew* someone was in there. When I found the security guard dead, I – just went over the top, sir.' No speech he had ever made had been so studied. Out of anger, really, coming face to face with Aubrey and the old man's irritation . . . and out of his con-tempt for Orrell, of course.

Orrell cleared his throat. His eyes cast about on the dark carpet. 'I see, Hyde, but we need to *know!* No time to allow you to wind down, get it out of your system, you know that. Not in these circum-stances.'

'No, sir.'

'Very well.' The sofa squeaked and the Burmese muttered in its sleep as Orrell stood up. 'All right, Hyde. Get yourself cleaned up and get along to my office by two this afternoon. The heat's off this business, as from now. Make sure you are on time.' The sarcasm was heavy.

'Yes, sir.'

'Thank you, Miss Woode, I'll see myself out – Kenneth?'

'No, Clive. I think you have been far too magnanimous. I think someone should explain *accountability* to Patrick; I believe that was why I was asked to come?'

'Yes, of course, yes.'

Hyde looked up as he heard Orrell's heavy tread retreat down the first flight of stairs. His grin faded as he saw the look of outrage on Aubrey's face, the quick, unstudied movements of his body, the flicks of the stick beside him. There was infinite reproach in every minuscule gesture.

Strangely, however, Hyde's anger at Aubrey seemed to sputter out almost at once. There was something self-accusing, even guilty, about Aubrey's expression. Hyde said: 'In case you're wondering, it was Priabin. Not a gang of murderous wogs, but the KGB in there. Understand?' His tone was sullen, and Aubrey all but glowered at him. Behind that, there was something else, the abstraction of someone looking at old, mildewed, sepia prints of his childhood or some early love affair. 'What's the matter with you?' Hyde prompted.

Aubrey glanced around the room and then sat heavily on the sofa near his straw hat. 'I was contacted by the Commander of Special Branch,' he murmured, holding up his hand for silence but not looking at Hyde. 'My real, day-to-day authority now appears so slight that the Branch feels no compunction about waking me at five-thirty in the morning to ask your whereabouts. At six, Clive Orrell was on the line, requesting in an unavoidable way that I accompany him here.' He sighed. 'The Commander's request was, incidentally, as to the whereabouts of that *devious little bastard.*' He looked up and essayed, almost successfully, a tired and wintry smile. Then he said: 'I'm sorry, Patrick.'

Eventually, Hyde murmured: 'What?'

'I'm sorry –'

'I survived, you mean?'

'Don't be paranoid!' Aubrey snapped, so much in a caricature of his waspish, professional self that Hyde almost grinned again, rubbing his hands through his hair.

The tortoiseshell had vanished from the windowsill at the moment of Aubrey's snapping comment. Ros had slipped back into the room and seated herself in the armchair nearest the door. The Burmese had invaded her lap and at once began kneading her sleeve with its paws and sucking at the material of her voluminous frock. Her broad forehead was creased with puzzled confusion, her eyes in sympathy with the small, old man on the sofa. He sat upright, clasping his stick.

'Coffee, Sir Kenneth?' Ros asked. The silence seemed to swallow the words.

'What? Oh, no thank you, Ros. Very kind of you, but no.' Then he fell to studying Hyde, who felt himself obscurely reprimanded and admired at the same moment. 'What is going on, Patrick? What is happening?'

Hyde blundered immediately into a summary of the previous evening and night, glancing in sudden rushes on Godwin's theories, the surveillance on Reid Group. Malan's name worked like a cattle-prod on the old, upright body. Aubrey's pale blue eyes seemed to search Hyde's face for signs of deception or imagination. Then he murmured: 'Malan's behind it, then. He's there, behind everything? You're quite certain?'

Hyde nodded. 'He's holding hands with Priabin. He's in everything up to his neck.'

'And Priabin's intention is to remove you and open up the way to Tony and Chambers? You're equally sure of that?' The tortoiseshell re-appeared on the windowsill, regarding the old man with a mild, steady curiosity, its head to one side. Aubrey said: 'I am expected to add to the official reprimand you just received. Which will precede your official suspension this afternoon.' Hyde snorted, but Aubrey held up his hand. 'It was evidently felt to be chastening, for both of us, if I were to be the one who administered six of the best to someone whom they regard as a favoured pupil of mine.' Again, the sad, wise smile. It was an Aubrey Hyde found difficulty in comprehending, as if he were seeing both too much and too little of the man's nature. Aubrey looked up. 'You two will understand me – my confusion and perhaps guiltiness. I am barely recovered, I think. It wore me out, like any obsession, any passion.' He shook his head. 'But it seems fated, does it not? It cannot be let alone – nor are we to be let alone by *it*, apparently.'

'We?' Hyde mocked.

'Oh, yes – the plural. We – *us*.'

149

'What can you do?'

'I don't know. I might be able to prevent you being suspended, who knows? At any rate, I must put my hand to the business. I agree with your assessment. They intend something very soon, something crucial to them, of huge proportion.'

'Then get me out of *here*,' Hyde insisted. 'They'll have those two drongos parked outside to make certain I don't go anywhere except Century House this afternoon. Get them called off – talk to Godwin, let me talk to him.'

'For the moment, do nothing. Stay here. I mean that. Do nothing in *addition* to invoke Sir Clive's mastodon dislike. Because he will tread you under, if you go any further with this on your own.' He stared at Hyde. 'Do you understand me, Patrick?'

'Look, there may not be any time left to sit on our arses!'

'I realize that! But *you* must do nothing more to bring down Orrell's wrath. You will attend him this afternoon, you will be polite – you will *remain* polite, you will appear to accept your fate, whatever it is! No, Patrick, you will do as I *say*.'

Hyde eventually slumped back into his chair, waving a dismissive hand. 'Oh, bugger off to your club and have a couple of early scotches.'

'Hyde,' Ros warned, but Aubrey smiled.

'You make not only a virtue but a style of living out of truculence, Patrick. Conserve it, for the moment. It will be needed. Now, I must leave – there is much to do and as you reminded me, little time in which to do it. Meanwhile, you are to do nothing on your own account – *nothing*.'

# this night's great business

It was the old house, still little more than a bungalow, white-painted with a broad *stoep* and a deep shadowy verandah, which his great-grandfather had built. The house was surrounded by the imitation English parkland that his grandfather had brought back in his imagination from his public school and his weekends at friends' country houses. Malan stopped the Range Rover and, as the air-conditioning sighed into silence with the engine, the heat of noon seemed to clamp itself upon the vehicle, claiming and isolating it. For a moment, he sat, both hands still gripping the steering wheel, looking at the shadows on the verandah, at the dim mesh of the screen door and the vague landscape of the cluttered hall through the open inner door. Malan felt an habitual reluctance to leave the vehicle, cross the short, hot patch of sunlight, and go into the house. His father's house – retreat, nursing home; place of abode and imminent demise.

He half-opened the door and hesitated once more. Music; probably Beethoven . . . yes, coming from inside. He shook his head, but he was unsure of his disapprobation – the music, the anticipated encounter, or the midday news he had angrily switched off. A lengthy report of the progress – and success – of the constitutional talks between the de Villiers government and the kaffirs – Mandela and the other ANC leaders. The document of surrender was the joke – sourly repeated – in the Automobile Club and the half-dozen boardrooms he had occupied during the past day or two. Within a year, Mandela would be mounting a dais in Pretoria with the Presidential ribbon around his neck. At least, that was what the pessimists claimed – along with the Conservatives and the AWB extremists.

The newspapers on the front passenger seat were full of the same stuff, and they caught his eye now as he hesitated to confront his father – then their headlines and photographs of smiling blacks and whites shaking hands seemed to thrust him out into the hard, hot sun. His shoulders hunched against its heat and force, then he was under the verandah roof, in its deep, humming shadows. Hanging baskets of flowers, two old rocking chairs, a white, wrought-iron table and chairs, the hammock at the far end of the *stoep*. This place, where he had always met men older than himself – great-grandfather, though he was difficult to recollect except in his white massiveness, grandfather, and now father. This place. It tugged, though; hurt, sometimes. He hated it. He hurried through the screen door and it banged behind him, startling footsteps at the other end of the hall, because it was, for an instant, as if his dead sister waited to pounce out of the *stoep*'s deep shadows. His wife hardly ever came back to him from the sailing accident that had drowned her and his sister, Diana. Nor did his sister as an adult, herself married; twice divorced . . . she only threatened to come back aged seven or eight, his little sister.

The footsteps had been those of the black nurse, and she clicked across the parquet flooring towards him now, a respectful suspicion and distance in her eyes. She was carrying a tray of medicine bottles, pill bottles – all of which were mere placebos now, with the disease so far advanced, its full invasion force moved out from his stomach, occupying much of his body.

'How is my father?' he asked awkwardly, as if not knowing her language.

'Resting, sir.' It was all she ever said, that and what she now added. 'Do not stay long, sir – you'll tire him.' His father, he knew, spoke to her for hours, especially when her husband came to collect her and the night nurse came on duty. Even spoke to her children. He was angry with that, as at a trick of charm possessed by another man which made his way with people smoother, easier.

'Very well.' He nodded. Dusty footprints behind him on the gleaming wood of the floor. Great-grandfather's animal heads glared dimly down from the walls, grandfather's faded watercolours were there, too – and the dozens of photographs, even some of himself, growing older. Maps, books, old furniture, rugs. A littered and comfortable place, like the main house had been until he had rendered it newly antiseptic, office-like. 'Very well,' he repeated, but the nurse had disappeared, presumably into the kitchen.

Shrugging his shoulders, he knocked on the open bedroom door and heard his father murmur wordlessly. The music ceased at once. He went into the room that smelt of bedlinen, old heat, his father's age and shrunkenness, and the oppressive scent of roses brought down by one of the gardeners, fresh every day. Books littered the counterpane, his father's spectacles were near his shrivelled, narrow hand, liver-spotted and long-nailed, and the swivel stand on which his books were piled was pushed aside from the wide bed. Jeppe Malan was propped against big pillows, his hair tidied, his features decoratively glazed or varnished with attention to his inward self – then the eyes flickered wide, recognizingly. Malan bent and kissed his father's forehead, which was cool, and his father's hand caught at his wrist for an instant, lightly as a girl's touch. Malan pulled a chair to the bedside and sat down, unrelaxed.

His father smiled with saintly, ascetic lips narrowed and made bloodless by the progress of the disease. His face, once much like Malan's own, broad and confident, was deeply lined, pale; beatific. He could think of no other image that fitted the dying man or explained the new, farther distance between them. It described Jeppe's assumption of some kind of *moral* superiority, for Jesus' sake –!'

'What are you reading?' he asked, clearing his throat. The floor was untidy with newspapers in English and Afrikaans. 'Besides the papers?'

'Some poetry, Paulus. Some philosophy, some history . . .' His voice was extremely weary, detached; again that bloody sainthood imposed by the cancer! His father was bravely resigned, but it wasn't that he disliked or resented. It was this suddenly contemplative man – no, he'd been that for years. Ever since the war . . . ? He'd come back, so the legend claimed, reluctant to run MLC – there were no surviving Labuschagne children – and taken up wealth and power like a burden.

'I see. I heard –' Again, he cleared his throat. 'I heard that Mandela was here, while I was in Europe?' It was not an accusation, though it was more than conversation to occupy time and the gloom. 'Did you discuss philosophy?'

Jeppe Malan nodded. 'Not that we agreed,' he observed. 'He was sorry for me. My illness –'

Malan watched his hands, with the freedom of independent

agents, clenching on his thighs. That fucking kaffir! He felt *sorry* . . . ? Sorry he might be in a position to nationalize, break up or ruin MLC in the next year or so!

'Did he apologize for his Marxist attitude towards us?' he asked involuntarily.

His father's hand seemed to float towards his own, and touch it carefully, as if exploring for a moment before wearying and withdrawing again. He said: 'I didn't ask him to apologize. He might have done.' The old man sighed. The bed seemed too big for him, like adult clothes on a child – Diana in her mother's frocks and high-heeled shoes and make-up, at six or seven . . . He shook his head as if plagued by flies. The fan whirred softly about them, old-fashioned, hardly stirring the thundery air of the room.

'He'll ruin us – that's the only outcome.'

'Unless there's no MLC left in South Africa.'

'What?'

'That's what Mandela fears. You don't think he came because I was dying, do you? Well, not entirely.' His breathing was ragged, his eyes wide and staring at the ceiling, as if he were absorbed in the movement of the fan. He continued: 'He's afraid you'll get out, take everything.'

'It's ours to take, Pa. What does Mandela want to do with it, uh? Nationalize the bloody mines, the gold and diamonds, the Oranjemund operation, the car plant, the chemicals and pharmaceuticals – *everything*. You know he hasn't wavered from that since the bastard first went to Robben Island.' He shook his head. 'That bloke makes me sick. Coming here to see a dying man just to persuade . . .' He shrugged.

'Persuade what? Persuade you not to continue with your European operations?' His father was silent for a moment, then nodded gently. 'Perhaps he did.' He smiled. 'Millie was impressed when she found him at the door. Father of South Africa, and all that. Since Mandela came, she has read the papers with greater enthusiasm than ever when I've felt too tired.' His head moved slowly and his eyes focused on Malan. 'What are you doing, son?' His hand fluttered, but Malan's wrist was out of reach. 'MLC is an *African* company, whatever interests we have abroad, in the rest of the world. It is *not* European.' His father's face was blotched with a trace of colour, near the cheekbones. It seemed a further exhibition of his illness. Malan shook his head.

'I haven't kept things from you,' he said sullenly. Perhaps his sister always threatened to appear in the shadows because he was always a child, coming to this place. 'The company's *my* responsibility.'

'Agreed. So is this country.'

'Not the way it will be!' he burst out, then calmed himself, breathing deeply. 'Not the way things will be – ' But his father was nodding with a strained attempt at vigour.

'Whatever happens. Do you think this country will be *better* if the company leaves? Do you think that?' It was an entire and onerous disbelief rather than a challenge.

'Your paternalism's old-fashioned, Pa. They don't want it, the kaffirs – '

'They will *need* us. Don't you think Mandela and the others realize?' He was tiring, as if the house and its past bore down on him more heavily than upon Malan.

'My concern is the future of MLC.'

'MLC – my company, yours now – *is* this country. What will you do to *our* country? Have you thought of that?' His frail white hand was patting the counterpane, plucking at it occasionally, as if a small, trained animal lay near him on the bed. His idea of the kaffirs, Malan thought. To be patted on the head, stroked, made a fuss of. He just doesn't understand. Too old. Dying. 'This is *your* country – what are you doing to it, son – what?'

The movements of his hand had become dismissive, as if he were shooing away his weariness, or the future. Malan stood up, seeing his father's exhaustion. As he bent forward to kiss his cheek, the old man's eyes were alight and unforgiving. He stared like the portrait of his great-grandfather, Jeppe's grandfather, out in the hall. Patriarchal, certain, old. And out of date, out of touch, as the country changed out of all recognition around them. Yet he felt pained as he straightened up, looming over his father. It was difficult to come, painful to leave. Always.

His father lay there, surrounded by the family detritus of the bedroom, its dried proteas in bulky arrangements on the sideboard and a dark table, the flies at the mesh of the screen, the hot sunlight leaking around the closed blinds. Malan was suddenly aware of the strangeness of the room rather than its overpowering familiarity. His father belonged in that white man's African room, but he did not. No longer. The main house was like a series of offices, an agglomeration of hotel suites. European, international; stateless. He shook his head and announced softly: 'I'll come this evening,' but his father was apparently asleep. Slowly, he turned away, passing Millie in the hall without remarking her presence as she hurried into the bedroom to inspect –

What? Her prize? Her tame white man, fallen? No, perhaps not.

The sun struck down and the interior of the Range Rover was as claustrophobic as the distance between the *stoep* and the vehicle. He started the engine and turned up the air-conditioning. It blew coolly against his flushed cheeks. The wheel was hot under his palms. He glanced at the bungalow. It had taken three generations of Malans, before himself, to build MLC. It mustn't be lost. It couldn't remain just African and *not* be lost. *He* couldn't remain South African without surrendering the company, watching it decline, be split up . . .

Which was why Jeppe could watch with indifference while it happened. Death had already shrunk the world to the size of that bedroom, MLC was no longer important to him.

Malan revved the engine loudly and careered away from the bungalow, dust filling the driving mirror.


'No, it's Ros' phone. It isn't bugged. I checked. Mine is.'

'Good. What's the old man got in mind?'

Hyde shook his head. Ros was out shopping. The branch of the tree bending towards the open window of her lounge at the rear of the flat was moving as if to encourage the last cool air to enter the room.

'Something that'll take too long. Has he talked to you? Well, he will. I can't bloody move, anyway. They're sitting in a car outside.'

The Burmese on the brocaded sofa appeared sublimely indifferent. Ros did not encourage them onto her furniture, but the suite was already plucked and puckered from the exercise of the cats' claws. She fussed at it then forgot.

'Look, Patrick, nobbling a shipment is the only way out for us, if we can't wait for the old man. I've contacted Customs –'

'Christ! I suppose you used Orrell's authority?'

'No, Bannister's name was sufficient.'

'That unforgiving bastard.' He sipped at the can of lager, which had already warmed to tastelessness.

'Come on, Patrick, we *need* you.' Godwin had known to ring Ros' number. She'd summoned him from his flat down to hers.

'I just told you, I can't bloody well move! Those two outside, Mutt and Jeff, will just whisk me down to Curzon Street or Century House if I so much as put the empty milk bottles on the step.' He glanced at his watch. 'I have to be in Orrell's office at two – it's almost one now.'

'Patrick –! Terry and I can't do everything by ourselves, and I can't bring Customs in until we're sure a shipment's left Reid Davies for SwiftEx. I've just explained all that, for God's sake!' The line was hollow, crackly, occasionally fading as they presumably passed under a motorway bridge. 'I've left Darren behind just for the purpose. Now, can't you climb out the back bloody window or something?'

Involuntarily, Hyde glanced at the open window and its partial mask of leaves. The tortoiseshell cat, itself masked as if to mock secrecy, appeared, head on one side.

'What if I did?' he asked.

'Darren can pick you up – where? Outside Earl's Court? Would that do?'

'Look, I should see Orrell. If I don't turn up, they'll be after all four of us. Aubrey warned me.'

'Bugger Orrell! If we nobble Reid Davies, we're all in clover –' The call faded momentarily, then: '– don't you see?'

'Christ, I don't –'

'Look! If we get suspended for finding nothing, it'll all have been a right bloody waste of time, won't it? At least this way we might get the job done!'

'Oh, stop bloody shouting, Godwin! You're beginning to sound like my mother!' He lowered his voice. 'Right, call Darren the Wonder Dog and tell him to pick me up in fifteen minutes, outside Earl's Court . . . the exhibition building, not the Tube station!'

'Good. He'll drive you to Bickenhill. Terry's dropping me off there before he goes on to Willenhall, to Reid Davies. See you.'

Hyde put down the receiver and stared at it, shaking his head.

Godwin simply didn't want to listen to anything. Aubrey's direct order was a fleabite. Godwin had already been bitten by his bloody obsession with Reid Group, Malan and all the other buggers in the game. It was like an affair, it wouldn't let him go until he'd seen the woman in bed with his best friend, or she'd left taking all his money. He crossed to the window and looked out. Over the garden wall, nip down past the church to the railway lines, bingo . . . simple, son. Except for when it turns out to be a wild-goose chase and Orrell appears snorting like a bull and pawing the bloody ground! And you'll have fucked up any chance of Aubrey bailing you out.

He shrugged. What have you got to lose? Most of it's already gone, mate. Where's the gun, your wallet?

Shit, it was like Butch Cassidy jumping off the cliff. No, it bloody wasn't. It was Redford and Newman dashing through that door into the final, frozen frame of the film, with two thousand sharpshooters waiting – *that*'s what it was like!

Absently, he stroked the cat, who seemed offended at the unwonted, intrusive act.


Richard Anderson stopped the grumbling, rusting Land Rover in the patchy shade of a scrubby acacia, switched off the engine and at once clamped his hands beneath his armpits, cradling them gently against the pain. Each burn and bruise tormented him. He slumped over the steering wheel, exhausted. The early afternoon heat clung around the tree solid as a horde of insects. The engine of the Land Rover clicked and protested in the heavy silence. The last of the dust along the tarred highway settled. He heard the call of some hunting bird, a half-hearted scream in the heat. He emptied his mind, letting the towns through which he had passed, or bypassed – Omaruru, Karibib, Usakos – settle like the dust on the road and disappear. Let the slowly descending road ahead disappear, too, and the narrow, gleaming strip of sky along the horizon that might be the sea. Behind him, the escarpment had retreated into the haze, brown and grey, indistinct.

Eventually, he sipped water from the flask and splashed a palmful of it onto his face. His hand came away brownly from the dampened dust in his beard and skin. As he looked up, the Erongo mountains seemed insubstantial in the heat. Turning his head, the northern edge of the Namib nibbled at trees and plants ahead of him, promising low dunes and sand all the way to the coast. Swakopmund. Then Walvis Bay, both within the enclave still controlled by South Africa.

The goal was illusory, he realized. A small, bright bird settled in the decayed branches of the acacia, seeking absent flowers. He stared at it, the back of his neck aching. Walvis Bay was where the DC-3 must have begun its flight, and MLC had operations in Walvis Bay. A lizard slipped through the few poor fronds of tough grass that had sprouted in the shade after the minimal winter rains. Illusory. What did he hope for? That his letter had reached Aubrey, that Aubrey would arrive with the nightlight and the comfort blanket for his childish grief and incapacity? He lowered his head. Perhaps that was what he did really want . . . a way of escape – at least a sense of *others*, of not being alone.

Something wet his wrist. The water would have dried from his face moments earlier . . . again. A cold, metronomic ticking of damp spots on his wrist, continuing regular as a clock. She had come out of the dark behind his eyelids and surprised him, her face close so that he was able to catch her scent amid the sensations of heat and dust. He had stopped the 4WD, and collided with his grief. To halt movement, even for a moment, was too long.

He looked up, sharply, as her image retreated once more. No dust rose above the tarred road, not even in the distance towards the hills. An aircraft trailed its white signal across the high blue. Blantyre would be in pursuit, however slowly or carefully. Guessing where he would go, knowing his history too well to be mistaken about his dreams of justice – and revenge. When he arrived in Walvis Bay, Blantyre would either be there already or close behind. All schemes of mounting some kind of surveillance on MLC's private airstrip in Walvis Bay or sniffing out and around their factories and offices were – ridiculous. Prompted by the impotence of his insatiable revenge.

He breathed deeply, time and again. Gradually – so gradually – calming himself, becoming nothing more than a man parked at the side of a road which led to an airport and flights out of Namibia. The mountains maintained their distance, the phosphoric, burning strip of sky that was the Atlantic or the coastal dunes remained

159

narrow, distanced. The birds in the acacia chirped with lulling regularity. He sniffed loudly. Survival was paramount – and that meant buying a ticket and boarding an SAA flight to Jo'burg or Cape Town or even Windhoek . . .

To demonstrate that he had given up, that he was no longer any threat to them. To simply get out. Blantyre was intent upon his death. He would thwart that. However far he might be forced to travel, and however unmitigated the grief he might find when he once again halted, he would thwart Blantyre's necessity to kill him.

'OK, I'm just down the street from Reid Davies – are you *sure* this is the right place? It's just a poky factory site in a backstreet!'

'Terry, this is the West Midlands – welcome to the home of tin bashing.'

'For God's sake, they can't be smuggling transputers and WSI from here!'

Chambers watched the narrow, sloping street. It was lined with closed – or open – wooden doors, some of which bore signs that explained the mysteries that occurred behind them. What he had expected, he had no idea – perhaps something on some industrial park that patronized the district into believing it was no longer in the last century . . . maybe. But, somehow, not this weirdly quiet street with a jazz record shop, some fenced-in units, a canal bridge halfway along its length, and all those stable-like doors, on one of which was proclaimed the headquarters and factory space of Reid Davies, a subsidiary of the Reid Group, plc. And it was peaceful, even with the window open, on a sunny late afternoon, as if the place was dozing in the warm light like a cat. Christ, were they all on strike or out of work, or something?

'Oh, yes, they can. That area's full of little firms that turn out just the nut and just the bolt – or just the transputer or just the WSI circuit you need. Reid Davies owns most of the companies in that street, or didn't you pay attention when I told you?'

'Sorry. How are you doing?'

Tower blocks disfigured the afternoon. There *was* a Porsche parked along the street – no, two, neither of them the cheaper models. Godwin might be right.

'I'm hovering by the railway bridge. I've walked up and down,

160

sat down, pretended to be waiting for a bus . . . when the hell are Darren and Patrick going to arrive?'

'Anything doing?'

'Sod all. SwiftEx has had deliveries and shipments from lots of clients, but not from Reid Davies. I've checked the airport, without causing a fuss, but nothing. If we want to check – *later* – then we'll have to lean on them.'

'What about Customs?'

'Reluctant and sceptical – what would you expect? They'll cooperate – but I don't want to put them on alert until the Reid Davies shipment leaves the factory. Any sign of it?'

'I hope to God they don't check with Bannister,' Chambers observed sourly. 'I'll go and have a look. Ring you.'

Chambers opened the door of the car and thrust the cellular telephone into his trouser pocket. It bulked awkwardly. He locked the car door and stood with his hands on his hips. The sidestreet traffic was light, pedestrians few unless overalled, or briefcased like reps. Grimy windows, some of them broken, old, warm brick sooted and crumbling; corrugated, tiled and slated roofs. He felt hesitant, undecided. He rubbed a hand through his hair and checked the parking meter, then his watch. He began walking along the uneven tarred pavement with its surviving cobbles outside many of the closed doors. Those that were open exposed narrow alleyways or cobbled courtyards. He shook his head. It was difficult to reconcile this set-up with transputer manufacture. More like the setting for quick respray jobs on stolen cars. As for wafer scale integration technology, the next generation of chips and microcomputers – forget it.

Reid Davies, across the street. A single-decker bus in blue-cream livery slid past, exposing like a drawn curtain the glimpse of two large lorries, both emblazoned SwiftEx, one with its rear doors closed. The other was being fed by a forklift truck, lifting a stack of crates on a pallet into the shadowy mouth of the lorry. He perspired with reaction – and excitement – and fumbled the cellular phone from his pocket, dabbing out Godwin's number.

'– here,' he blurted out. 'Two trucks, both SwiftEx.' Another forklift truck trundled to the lorry and fed it. 'I think one of them's already been loaded.' Cars obscured the courtyard, then: 'The second one's almost stuffed to the roof – TVs, by the look of it –

161

microwaves, VCRs – the usual stock-in-trade. What do you –?'

'Hang on there for the moment. Let me know when they leave. I'll get over to Customs in the meanwhile and get things set up. TVs and bloody microwaves! That's what they make in there, and another of the companies in that street is part of the WSI manufacturing for Reid Electronics, and a third does packaging work on the transputers.' Godwin was gloating, but Chambers felt no resentment. 'They switch the boxes, simple as that, must be.'

'Reid Group packages its stuff here?'

'I wonder how much? There's certainly some, from Darren's checks on those subsidiaries of Reid Davies – Christ, when we've opened the boxes at this end, we might be allowed to go all the way through that street like a dose of salts! OK, hang on until they leave, then tail them here. See you –'

Chambers switched off and tucked the phone under his arm. He leant against the crumbling brick of the grubby wall behind him. Transputers, WSI, packaging – the smell of a small foundry like burnt bread on the air. Christ, it was coming together, it really was. If enough Reid Group packaging and shipping was done from here, then it made it so bloody *simple* for them! He glanced furtively around him as if the grimy windows would betray their interiors, and he would see clues like flags. God, it could be a real bonus, this one –

Cars obscured his view of the courtyard of Reid Davies, then he saw the tailgate and the doors of the second lorry being closed and noisily bolted and locked. A blue saloon passed slowly. The gates were opened to their widest extent and he felt his heart thud as the engine of one of the lorries was started up. A man in overalls strolled out into the street and the lorry's reversing lights came on and its warning horn began sounding.

Chambers turned towards the car. The blue saloon had slowed to a halt beside it.


'For God's sake, what are they doing about it? What are *you* doing about it?'

Babbington had been on the point of leaving his office when his assistant had called him back – bawled down the corridor like a fishwife that Priabin was in secure telephone contact and was declaring an emergency. He had snatched the remote telephone from the young man's hand and slammed the door of the inner office behind him. The delays and grumbles of encoding-decoding by the encryption unit in the outer office further irritated him.

'I – suggest, General, that it may be too late to do anything but show our hand.' Priabin was concerned, his confidence ebbed.

'Where is *Mortimer*? Why can't he be reached?'

'He's been out of the country on business. I'm not certain when he's expected – van Vuuren claims he returns today, but he's vague about –'

'Forget *Mortimer* then. I expect it's too late to change the shipment in any case.'

'It has been loaded.'

'You've surveillance there?'

'Yes.'

'Good. Then employ it. Chambers is there, you say, and Godwin at the airport? How far is Hyde from Birmingham? It must be where he is heading.'

'An hour and a half, perhaps more. The traffic's heavy on the M1, there are roadworks.'

'Keep Hyde away. Stop the others – as *discreetly* as is possible in the circumstances. But *stop* them. Meanwhile, *I'll* speak to Malan. He must find a way to irritate MacPherson with the news that the consignment may be delayed. Someone, at least, must prompt Century House to wake up and notice what some of their finest are doing! As for you, there are no excuses for delay. Keep those damned people away from that shipment!'


'Look, we're stuck in a six-mile tailback and there's sod all we can do about it!' Hyde snapped. 'Listen to the bloody travel news, why don't you? Some lorry jack-knifed and overturned. Bloody French apples or something all over the northbound carriageway! Gloria Hunniford just told us!'

Darren Westfield grinned, then attempted to appear gravely concerned, like a poor actor's too-sudden change of mood. Hyde grimaced at him and banged the parcel shelf of the Escort. The fact that he suspected they had been tailed by a Renault all the way from Earl's Court was now irrelevant. The other car was stuck half a mile back as glutinously as they were themselves. A police car, siren wailing and blue light winking palely in the bright afternoon, passed them at speed on the hard shoulder. Hyde wiped his forehead.

'Watch your back, Godwin. We were tailed.' He glared at Darren, who appeared more likely to break out in acne than perspiration. 'Darren here didn't realize it –'

'Neither did you until we reached Watford,' Darren observed quietly.

'If they're watching us, then they must be watching you and Chambers. If you move, they might too.'

'OK, got you. I'll watch out. The consignment's loaded and about to leave – Terry just called in with the news.'

'Right. Let's hope to God the traffic clears and all the incriminating evidence is on that lorry. Otherwise –' he glanced at the dashboard clock. Two-thirty. 'Otherwise Orrell, who is probably chewing the office carpet by now, is going to have my balls devilled for tomorrow's breakfast.' He heard Godwin chuckle.

'We'll save your virility, Patrick. I'll keep in touch.'

Hyde lowered the cellular telephone to his lap and drummed his hands on his thighs.

'Got any good books?'

'No. Want the paper?' Then Darren's attempt at Hyde's mood vanished, and he asked naively: 'Is this going to be all right?'

'I should think so. They're just watching us. I spy with my little eye something beginning with . . .'

Chambers reached the car and inserted the key in the lock. The blue saloon must be waiting for a parking meter to become free. Two men. He opened the door – one of the men was using the carphone – and put his own telephone on the passenger seat. He looked up. The first SwiftEx lorry was backing out of the narrow archway of Reid Davies, reversing horn sounding continually like a burglar alarm –

Slamming of a door behind him as he bent to climb into the car. Hand on his shoulder, jerking him round. Men from the blue car –?

'What's the –?' he began.

'It's him,' one of them, the taller, bulkier one, confirmed.

The flash of the knife and a searing sensation in his side as he attempted to wriggle free. The nerves becoming instantly numb against the anticipated pain, his hand grasping feebly at the knife-blade, cutting itself across the palm, then the knife entering him again, somewhere in the area of his stomach. Difficult to tell, the pain of the first wound made him cry out, made their activities indistinct. As he slumped to the pavement, his back against the car and his legs spread out like an abandoned doll, he heard little more than the noise of the lorry's continual horn as it reversed into the narrow street. Felt only their quick, rough search of his pockets, his jacket – which was then thrown down beside him. Saw a hand with his wallet . . .

Mugging. They didn't want his wallet, just the credibility it would give to this pretended street crime. His hand was red as he pressed it against his stomach, and he stared down, gaping, at the sight of his blood. Then he heard someone shouting . . . *after* the noise of their car. Feet on the tarred pavement, close to him, a shadow bending over him . . . Minutes, by the clock-spread of his blood, after the car had gone. Overalls bending over him, the noise of the lorry's horn silent now. Things becoming dim, all except the pain, which seemed to be everywhere, even behind his eyelids, which were red as he closed them, then dark, empty . . .

Van Vuuren listened, for perhaps the dozenth time, to the engaged tone from *Mortimer*'s carphone. At first, it had been a surge of relief to hear that the phone was being used, that the man had returned, must be in his car driving from London or wherever. Now that he could talk to him, he could alter the consignment or get it stopped. But it was continually *engaged*! Angrily, he slammed down the telephone. Three o'clock. He had been stuck in MLC's offices in the Strand, staring at the walls, at the river and Charing Cross station from the high windows of ShellMex House, since eight in the morning and he'd accomplished nothing – *nothing*! Paulus had been on the line four times, pushing, carping, instructing, threatening – all to no bloody purpose, he couldn't get hold of the only man who could alter the damned consignment! Because they'd got into his suite, used his laptop, rifled the mainframe in Jo'burg, *knew* what they were looking for. Must know . . . they were in Birmingham, for God's sake!

He pushed the remnants of his lunch away from him across the borrowed desk. The telephone blurted and he snatched it up.

'Paulus – yes! No, I can't get – what? Oh *no* – can't it be turned back?'

'Listen to me, Piet. Priabin's been given specific instructions regarding your new friends –'

'But if Customs –?'

'Customs won't. I've had Babbington on the line. I've made a call. Customs are satisfied.'

Van Vuuren wiped his forehead with his crumpled handkerchief. Relief was immediate and made the image of the grey handkerchief, newly damp, something repellent and shameful.

'But what if –? I mean, *how*?'

'Calls can be made that purport to be from Customs at Birmingham airport, Piet. To Special Branch, enquiring as to the legitimacy of their instructions from a Mr Godwin – who seems to have the right credentials, sir, just checking. Do you understand now, Piet?'

Jesus, why didn't he think of this before? Or did he, and just left me to sweat it out?

'Then you don't want me to –'

'I want you on the evening flight home. Here, tomorrow. OK, Piet?'

'Yes, Paulus.'

The telephone was replaced in Malan's study, or the office or wherever he was. Van Vuuren replaced his receiver and sat back in the leather chair, which was hot against his buttocks. The sun glittered on the river, a dead light because of the tinted windows. His hands were shaking . . . it had been close. He held up a trembling thumb and forefinger, almost touching each other. That close. Waterloo Bridge in the tiny gap of tinted air between his quivering fingers. Oh, *Jesus*. He slapped his hand down on the desk. Three blokes, or was it four? Didn't matter, they'd blundered against the whole bloody applecart, man! Almost tipped it over. One consignment that wasn't what was claimed on the manifest and the Customs and insurance forms, and they'd have had as much assistance and back-up as they wanted and a new set of burrowing tools to go after the pipeline . . .

. . . and now, they couldn't. They'd be stood down, disciplined. Locked up for all he knew, which would be satisfying, for all the fucking sweat and nerves he'd used up over the last eight hours!

Paulus' cool cleverness – he envied. Usually, he could ignore it, he was autonomous in MLC, trusted and good. Now – ?

Paulus wouldn't harbour . . . he'd let it go. It wasn't really his fault. He recalled the half-kaffir girl, the restaurant meal, and felt queasy. Paulus would know why he'd left his laptop in the suite.

The river and the sky did not look cool through the tinted glass, merely without vitality, despite the movement of trains and the craft on the water. From behind the windows, the weather appeared thundery, dully yellow like clouded brass. He poured water from a jug with a nerveless movement of his wrist, and the water splashed on the leather surface of the desk.

But it was *over*, he reminded himself. They wouldn't be allowed to issue parking fines after this! Those English bastards were finished.

Gradually, his nerves settled. The plastic cup was empty of water, the traffic thickening up across the bridge. Over . . . pity the Russians hadn't murdered the bastards and bugger the indiscretion!


Two of them, then eventually three – those he could identify, or had become suspicious of. He attempted to relearn old tricks, tried to think like Hyde, between the recurring, malarial bouts of terror which had begun the moment he had called Chambers' number. The phone had been answered, hollowly, from inside a vehicle – the ambulance in which Terry Chambers had just died, on his way to hospital. Two stab wounds. Dead. He was still quivering with shock – fear. Unbelievable – *true*. They'd killed Chambers, just like that.

It was five-thirty. Just so long as he patrolled the upper gallery or the ground floor of the terminal, alongside or beneath the biplane suspended from the ribbed roof, he might remain safe. He did not dare use the toilets, or one of the bars, or the bookshop or boutiques. Nor become too enmeshed in the milling herds of holidaymakers who had flooded the building in search of their charter flights and packaged familiarities. They'd taken Chambers out with the ruthless efficiency of machines. Customs and the police were of no avail . . . *please, sir, they might want to kill me, those men over there.* They'd just laugh, anyway he was there against orders, and nobody had sympathy with that sort of behaviour.

God, he was shaking like a leaf! They'd *killed* Terry, just snuffed him out. And they were here now, looking for the chance to do the same to him. Hyde had been right, too right! He swallowed saliva, almost choking on his fears, then tried to concentrate, pick them out –

One young man loitered for the umpteenth time against the garishness of book racks outside W. H. Smith's. The second man, middle-aged and conspicuously holidaymaking with a bright shirt and tugging his suitcase on a folding metal trolley. It went everywhere with him, up and down the escalators and round and about, like a large, awkward dog. The third man had taken him a long time to spot – but were the difficult ones dangerous, or was it the man you saw first and eventually discounted who did the bloody job in the end? Terry hadn't had the time to find out. The third man was impatient, clock-watching, stridently silent as he studied the Arrivals board again and again. He drew attention to himself, but only as someone meeting a friend from one of the many delayed flights. Greek air-traffic controllers or Spanish Customs on strike, it made little difference to the neat terminal suddenly becoming a dosshouse filled with truculent victims. He had no idea whether there were more than three – whether the man who had used the knife on Chambers, *Christ, a knife in the street to look like a mugging*, was in the terminal building. He could have entered it in the last hour, as the passengers for the evening flights flocked in, ambushing or assaulting each other with their luggage.

Five forty-five. He could at least avoid the toilets with some degree of comfort, as a trained, disciplined cripple.

He planted himself firmly on the escalator and descended from the gallery, watching the main floor of the building adjust itself to his balance, knowing that the man with the impatient glare at the Arrivals board was behind him now, and seeing the man with the doglike suitcase at the bottom of the flight of moving steps . . . He glanced wildly round. The third man was on the stairs, just starting down. The suitcase, tartan-lidded, seemed to crouch at the bottom, waiting to pounce at his ankles. Christ, they'd got fed up, they'd been told to move in.

The escalator was steep, smooth as an icy slope as it moved him towards the man with his doglike trolley. Even he, with his lack of tradecraft, understood the eagerness on the face above the bright shirt. The man in the suit behind him no longer attended with the slightest pretence to the Arrivals board. His eyes were attentive only to Godwin and the man with the trolley.

In one bound, he was free . . . ? With two fucking *sticks* in place of a confident stride? Why – why now? Had the bloody lorries arrived at last? When he had enquired earlier, Customs had pronounced there had been delays on the M6, holiday traffic. Three hours from bloody Willenhall!

'Passengers for Suntours flight to Malaga . . . served with sandwiches and other light refreshments in the . . .' floated past his head as he reached his conjunction with the inevitable and the dog-trolley was thrust under his sticks, tripping him. The Russian was immediately on him like a dog himself, apologizing with:

'– didn't see you, please, I'm so sorry,' in good English. A woman watched and was reassured. 'Let me help you –'

'Need any help?' The man in the suit. 'Let's get him on his feet – saw the whole thing, accident –'

Godwin lay sprawled on his back, having turned so at least he was able to watch what they intended doing to him, his sticks spread out on either side of him like extra legs, as useless as his own. The two Russians bent over him – one of them reassured passers-by, then the other did so, explaining his clumsiness. They held his arms all the time as they crouched beside him, one of them kneeling on the stick still attached to his right hand and elbow – the other stick removed, held upright, then their hands reached under his armpits.

'– coffee, tea, something stronger, set you up, so sorry.' They were both smiling solicitously, much like a vet and his nurse, one holding the animal, the other the final needle, they were that confident. Needles –? Here, now, something to keep him quiet?

He was dragged to his feet and their proximity hemmed in the strength of his shoulders and upper torso. He gripped the sticks they thrust back under his elbows, disabling him anew. He was sweating violently, almost dizzy as if they had already sedated him, shaking his head like a wounded bull, their aftershave and cool skills both heady. Oh, shit, he was bloody *useless* at this, bloody hopeless! They'd caught Chambers in a quiet street and opened up his guts, now it was his turn –

– moving. They held him slightly off-balance, so that he teetered ahead of his sticks and his dragging, clumsy feet. Just quickly enough to control him, make him concerned not to stumble and

169

entirely lose his balance, making him stare at the floor as they moved him towards the sunlight where the automatic doors of the terminal ushered in new crowds. Almost at the doors, colliding with a luggage trolley, hearing the Brummy apology fade behind him, the air outside a hot breath on his face.

Collision with another trolley, the apology, his stagger because the man with the bright shirt had released his arm – cried out? Apologies again – Christ, bloody apologies, *apologies* –! Australian accent.

'Oh, sorry, mate, didn't mean to –'

The trolley deft as a sword, shunted into the suited man's stomach and shins, then Hyde's hands under his right arm and around his waist and they were outside. Godwin whirled round clumsily, dizzily. The Russians were on the other side of the tinted, sliding glass doors, revealed and masked as trolleys towed brightly-dressed groups into the terminal. Then Hyde was shaking him.

'You OK? Christ, you don't half need looking after, mate!'

He nodded, managing to adjust his weight on the newly assured sticks and calm his breathing.

'All right,' he puffed. 'All right.' Then, squinting at the tinted doors: 'What will they do now?'

'Sod off if they've got any sense. There's three of us –' Darren's young features were pleasurably alarmed. 'How many of them?'

'I saw three – Terry's *dead*! They killed him in the street,' Godwin blurted. 'I – couldn't tell you over the phone. They killed him –'

'Bastards,' Hyde muttered, visibly shocked, running his hands through his hair. 'Both of you – *watch* yourselves. Now, where's the bloody shipment, since they've told us it's not kosher. Bastards,' he finished softly.

'It's not here yet. Held up on the M6 at Spaghetti Junction.'

'Or waiting until you'd been scraped off the floor. What about Customs?'

Godwin felt a warm lassitude of shock now, with Hyde and Darren beside him and with his weight heavy on his sticks. 'Oh – they haven't checked my authority. At least, they hadn't. They'll do the consignment as a spot check. The SwiftEx plane's on the tarmac. They'll try to take it straight aboard, since the lorries are late.' The two Russians had drifted out of sight into the slow, muddy crowd moving beyond the glass. 'Where are they?'

170

'Probably calling Priabin to ask what to do next. If we wanted proof, you and Chambers are all the evidence we needed. Not even Russians kill for microwaves. Let's go and see Customs, Godwin – and *you* –' He glared at Darren. 'Keep your *eyes open*. What does the third one look like?'

'Young, five-ten, dark hair, yellow polo shirt, yellow slacks.'

'Poof, is he?'

The Customs officer came through the doors the moment before they reached them, recognizing Godwin at once, his face suspicious and dismissive of Hyde.

'The trucks have arrived from SwiftEx, Mr Godwin. However, there's been a – complication. Can you come along now and sort things out?'

'*What* complication?' Hyde snapped.

The Customs officer looked to Godwin for illumination. There was an air of irritation, of having been somehow deceived by callers at his door who mentioned their Mormon sympathies only after –

Hyde said: 'What complication? You look as if you've just been sold a Timeshare.'

'If you're all together,' the Customs man murmured after Godwin had supplied their names, 'then would you all come with me.' It was no longer a matter of request.

'What else has gone wrong?' Hyde hissed as they entered the terminal.

Godwin shook his head, the tremor in his arms only stilled by the movement and pressure of the sticks. His legs, insofar as they responded to anything, felt weak. He was shivery. What *had* gone wrong?

'Can't see anything – yellow shirt and slacks? That him?'

'That bloke's nearly fifty and the scrubber leaning on the trolley's his daughter.'

The corridor they entered was quiet, occupied by occasional uniforms – airlines, police, Customs.

'– for Majorca, there has been a further delay . . .' faded behind them.

'In here,' the Customs officer indicated, holding open a door. 'My superior would like a word – yours, too.'

Godwin bundled himself into the office, aware of the hum of the air-conditioning, then of the airport's chief Customs officer; then, finally, aware of Deputy Director-General Edward Bannister as he rose from a small sofa.

'Shit,' he heard Hyde murmur behind him as the door closed.

'Godwin,' Bannister acknowledged. 'And Hyde . . . would you like to call Sir Clive now and apologize, or wait until you have a more formal opportunity?'

'I should think the DG's gone home by now, sir,' Hyde replied.

'Westfield, I think you can leave. I shall, of course, require a statement from you in the not-too-distant future.' He waved his hand in dismissal. The door closed behind Darren.

The Customs officer, Warren, appeared at once satisfied with Bannister's icy tone and his command of the situation. He smiled momentarily as Bannister said: 'Don't sit down, gentlemen – ah, Mr Warren, might I prevail on you to loan us your office for a few moments?'

Warren stood up. 'Certainly, Mr Bannister. Good job we –' He glowered at Godwin with a new rage prompted by a sense of consequences avoided.

'Yes, indeed. Thank you, Mr Warren.'

' – serving an evening meal in the . . .' for a moment before the door closed once more.

The room shrank around Godwin now that Warren had departed and he burst out: 'Sir, you've got to act now! Terry Chambers was killed this afternoon. The lorries are here now! You have to get Customs to –'

Bannister seemed baffled not so much by his words but by Hyde standing stiffly to attention at Godwin's side. It was pure mockery and Bannister knew it. Not now, Patrick, *please* not now.

'I have not journeyed here in the noisiest of helicopters to open crates of television sets, Godwin,' Bannister said sarcastically. He was venomous, narrow-minded. A former civil servant in MoD . . . army intelligence. *Displays army levels of intelligence all the time*, had been Hyde's observation, months before. Above all, Bannister devoted himself to hierarchy and its expression throughout SIS. 'And neither have either of you,' Bannister added.

'Sir?'

'Yes, Godwin?' Bannister regained his position on the sofa and studied them with the glance of a barrister assured of the jury's verdict.

172

The window behind Warren's desk was one-way glass and over-looked the tarmac. As Godwin watched, the SwiftEx aircraft, a small Boeing, was approached by the two lorries Chambers had seen leaving Reid Davies in Willenhall. There was a Customs van there, too, but it suggested laxity, even indifference, one man leaning against its bonnet. There was something overpoweringly unflurried about the scene that enraged Godwin.

'Sir, you have to order – request – Customs to inspect that con-signment from Reid Davies –' Godwin sensed Hyde's silent, stiff tension beside him, strong as a charge of static. Bannister's features were a mirror of the calm, unhurried scene beyond the deadening effect of the window. ' – they killed Chambers, sir!' Godwin blurted, attempting to bludgeon action. His own danger made him shiver in recollection.

'Muggers, so West Midlands police inform me.' Bannister was untroubled, imperturbable. 'They have, quite rightly of course, begun a murder enquiry.'

'Sir, they killed him because he was on surveillance outside –'

Bannister held up his hand. 'Unauthorized surveillance. Specifi-cally *denied* surveillance. We are not dealing with impropriety here, gentlemen . . .' The tone was housemasterly, ironic. 'We are deal-ing with something that equates to paranoia – to persecution of legitimate businesses by members of the intelligence service.'

He leaned forward as Hyde murmured: 'This is a fucking waste of time.'

Bannister's cheeks wore two spots of colour for a moment, then he observed drily: 'I'm sure you will regard this matter in a different light, Hyde, once I have finished what I came here to say.' He sat back on the sofa once more. The back of one of the lorries was open, and the sole Customs man had entered its interior. 'The effect this could have in the left-wing media, on television particularly, is something I would have expected you to make strenuous efforts to avoid.' The Customs man, clipboard and a sheaf of documents in hand, re-emerged into the tobacco-coloured light, scribbling on forms, then handing papers to, presumably, a member of the aircraft's crew.

All over.

'Oh, shit!' Godwin exclaimed.

'Ah – precisely what you will discover you have been standing in, Godwin.' The Customs man got back into his small, white van and the vehicle turned and sped away from the Boeing. Oh, *shit*. 'It is almost my pleasant – certainly my necessary – duty to inform you, gentlemen, that your careers in the intelligence service of your country –' The aircraft was being loaded now from a forklift truck which chugged out of the rear of the first lorry towards the flank of the plane. Godwin stared at it as at some lost vision of contentment. '– are over. From this moment, I am not too sorry to say, you are no longer on the staff of the service.' He cleared his throat. Hyde was wound tense as a spring beside him.

Then Hyde burst out: 'Christ, Harrow has won the Wall Game, or is it Eton this year? Doesn't bloody matter a toss, though, does it – *sir*? *Your* lot has won, either way!'

It seemed all that Hyde wanted to say – or, perhaps, could say.

Bannister murmured, as if brushing a speck from his shoe: 'Your class attitudes are nowhere near as fresh-minted as you seem to think, Hyde. Fortunately, this service is no longer to be run on such maverick and impeachable grounds –' A spark of genuine outrage then: 'Do you have no *understanding* of how the nature of our work has changed?'

Hyde was still waving his arms, as if he vainly expected to fly out of the situation. Then, slowly, he moved them back to his sides.

'You will deliver to me now,' Bannister intoned in a dignified, marmorial voice, 'your official passes and documents, and in your case, Hyde, I assume a weapon –? And any and all other materials relating to your recent activities such as you may possess. We cannot have – *I* will not tolerate – maverick operations that are aimed at the fabric of society or which may undermine the state –!' The man's anger was genuine, Godwin realized. Christ, *another* bloody idealist! 'Therefore,' Bannister added, recovering his sang-froid, 'it is necessary that we dispense, entirely and for good, with your services. Both of you.'

Beyond the window, the forklift truck raised its third or fourth load towards the cargo hold of the small Boeing without the slightest effort or hindrance. Godwin, removing his passes and other ID from his wallet as he leaned tiredly on his sticks, blinked back tears of disappointment, and rage.

# PART TWO

---

# The Merchandise
# of Venice

'The world is too much with us; late and soon,
Getting and spending, we lay waste our powers:
Little we see in Nature that is ours;
We have given our hearts away . . .'

William Wordsworth: Sonnet

# forms and visages of duty

He allowed Mrs Grey to serve the coffee – silver pot; her favourite bone china – while his head whirled with Chambers' death and the dismissal of Hyde and Godwin, who sat opposite him now, over-awed by Mrs Grey's silent ordering of the crockery. And there was that other matter, flying in his head, over *there*.

He glanced towards the Georgian tea-table where he habitually left his opened letters until Mrs Grey enquired as to their provenance and destination. The curled, opened edge of the Jiffybag lay there still, its small gape like a sifting mouth, as large as a whale's in the effect it had upon his memory and his present concerns. *From: R. Anderson* it had claimed on its reverse side. On the obverse, the postmark had proclaimed *Namibia* – a place he had promised to visit in a foolish, expansive moment. He had opened the slim package with a smile, in anticipation . . . to find –

A KGB identity card and a photograph of a woman holding a child, on the reverse of which was scribbled *Novgorod, 1989* . . . and a note evidently written in haste and with hardly a mention of their mutual past. A Dakota aircraft . . . electronic goods on board labelled *Reid Group, plc* . . . plunged into the Namibian sand. And MLC involvement – and Blantyre, who tried to kill Ros to cover up the affair of his murdered niece.

The past was like an animal, ignored or perhaps beaten into a corner, and which had all the time been waiting its chance to attack, seize him by the throat. It had allied itself with an equally violent present, the moment they had struck Chambers down in a quiet Midlands backstreet, pretending that robbery was their casual motive. And it infuriated him, creating a towering rage against Priabin, Bannister, Orrell . . . but most especially against Malan, whose hand was in this violence. Who had had Chambers murdered just as surely as he had been responsible for Kathryn's death.

Damn them, they were *still* killing his people!

Hyde was noisy with his coffee, recalling his attention, but he was unable to forbear rubbing his temples for an instant before clearing his throat and saying: 'I – am sorry – and concerned – at the manner in which things have been done.'

Hyde's eyes had already become glazed with indifference. Godwin seemed eager for a reprieve. Aubrey wondered if he might be offering no more than scraps to what one otherwise-sober journal had called *The Dogs of Yesterday?* He studied them both. In Godwin, the fire of obsession still flared, together with a sense of fear, now that Chambers had been summarily disposed of. Hyde, of course, was incapable of reconstruction – though he could as easily leave this business as remain within it. There was one further consideration – his own exhaustion. And his *angina pectoris*, which had elicited for an old man the professionally wise sympathy of a specialist in his middle years and good health. The unspoken *What do you expect at your age?* He refrained, with a conscious effort, from touching his chest above the heart. Kathryn's death had worn him out; the impotence and rage of unsatisfied vengeance against Malan had exhausted him. And these two – one politely, the other without illusions – knew as much. He glanced once more at the tea-table and the eloquent mouth of the Jiffybag. A temptation and a goad; perhaps more of the lash than the inducement in it, so accustomed had he become to his semi-invalid condition and the ministrations of Mrs Grey over the past weeks. Nevertheless . . .

He had to admit the contents of the Jiffybag were sufficient to rouse an old conscience. Namibia – MLC – Malan and the KGB. Godwin's so long-sought pipeline, the connection, the *link*. He could not, under any circumstances short of his demise, ignore the contents and implications of the letter. Clearing his throat, he announced: 'I have received information that convinces me not only that we must act, but that our speculations were, in large part, accurate.'

Godwin's head snapped up from the fingers he was moving indecisively among the biscuits provided by Mrs Grey. A custard cream fell onto the carpet in response to his surprise. 'Sir? Information from where? Who?'

'Totally unconnected with our enquiries. Pure happenstance. But which encourages me –' At once, like a conjuror certain of his audience's attention, he took the ID card and the photograph, folded within the brief letter, from his breast pocket. He had donned a jacket as he might have done chainmail when the doorbell had sounded. 'This is the confirmation.'

Hyde snatched the letter. 'Where's this from?' He inspected the signature, then looked up. 'Christ, isn't he –?'

Godwin, peering across at the pasteboard card, the photograph and then the letter, exclaimed: 'Namibia? An old transport plane – MLC . . . Jesus Christ – sir!'

'Is this proof? Does it convince you?' Hyde snapped. 'This Anderson – he is the bloke who got out of East Germany in 'sixty-four, came back and killed a Deputy DG he claimed had betrayed him –?' He hesitated. There was another aspect to the legend, one that no one ever voiced publically. Certainly not in Aubrey's hearing.

Aubrey nodded. 'The very same.'

'Did you –?' Hyde began, at once disappointed, as if he had encountered a passion already preoccupied by another.

'Off the record, that rumour might not be without foundation – there may have been an arrangement.' He had helped Richard Anderson escape to South Africa and supplied him with sufficient funds to buy himself into a legal practice. Because the man he had killed *had* betrayed him, *was* a double agent. It was the simplest solution.

And the partial admission, he realized, finally closed the circle. He could do no less for Hyde and Godwin and for Chambers' memory; or for his dead niece. Richard had repaid his debt with a reminder of newer, more pressing obligations. So be it.

There was, however, the problem of Richard's whereabouts, even his continued health. He had rung the game lodge in Etosha. The line had been restored, but the voices had been distant and masked, yet clear enough to inform him that Anderson had been taken to hospital, after an – *atrocity* was the word that recurred. Counter-activity was more accurate, he suspected. Just as they had killed Chambers, attempted Hyde's life, threatened Godwin – they had tried to kill Anderson. Had they succeeded?

'Where did this come from?' Hyde asked, waving the ID card.

'One of the bodies in the aircraft.'

'It's that neat, then? What does Anderson say?'

'I can't contact him. There was an attack on the game lodge

179

where he was warden. He was alive, afterwards. But I tried the hospital – he'd discharged himself, through a window at dawn, and hasn't been seen since. I don't know where to find him, I'm afraid.'

'Too good to be true, then – isn't it?' Hyde scoffed.

'Or too bad.'

'That bastard Blantyre – he's in it.'

'Yes.'

'So – Anderson encountered Blantyre, Blantyre's bright enough to be suspicious, he torches the game lodge. How many bystanders died?'

'Anderson's wife, for certain.'

He glanced towards the door. Mrs Grey would not come out of her kitchen unless summoned. He was glad for the absence of her narrow rectitude, her solicitous, mummifying care. Not that he was ungrateful . . . it was simply that he must do without it now.

'Then you'd better bloody well find Anderson – or give him up now,' Hyde observed. 'If Blantyre's after him, on Malan's orders, he's got the life expectancy of a Para going over the top – sir. Christ, he's just something Blantyre wipes off his shoes!' Hyde was animated by venom. 'I know Blantyre! He didn't get brutalized, he was born like it.'

'I can do nothing – for the moment. I must wait until Richard gets in touch. He will, if he's alive.'

'The pipeline went through Namibia, then,' Godwin remarked.

'What? Oh yes. Does that surprise you, Tony?'

'No. It's clever. Their old long way round the Cape. Now, they're using their Suez Canal. The stuff has to be going direct via EuroConstruct and its subsidiaries – via Paris, and Dumas Electroniques.'

'Why are they still using Namibia – since 1989 made things so much easier?'

'This has to be Malan's share of the proceeds, I assume.'

Hyde whirled round from the tall window. 'Look, we know they were using Namibia as of last week. It doesn't matter why. What matters is – are we going to do anything about it? Reid Group is being robbed blind and the stuff leaves Reid Davies in Willenhall disguised as tellies and microwaves. Anderson confirms that much. So, are we going for it, or just going down the pub for a pint and a sandwich?' He glowered at Aubrey. 'Are we going to go on picking this like a spot, or are we going to *do* something?'

Softly, Aubrey announced: 'We are going to do something about it.'

Godwin sighed aloud. Hyde eventually relaxed his shoulders and his grim expression. He had searched Aubrey's face for confirmation, and at least found no contradiction in his studied lack of expression.

'What first, sir?' Godwin asked with perennial enthusiasm.

'All the material you have, Tony, stored in that computer of yours.' He rubbed his hands as if at a fire. 'I want everything you have on, or suspect of, Reid Davies. Meanwhile, more coffee, I think,' he added briskly.

Hyde tossed his head, but more in recognition than derision. Aubrey smiled to himself.

'You old bugger,' he heard Hyde murmur, his back to him.


The moment he left the air-conditioned foyer of the Mermaid Hotel, the sun struck down on him and it was as if his skin was immediately permeated with the nauseous smell of fish. It was impossible to assimilate or ignore, hanging over Walvis Bay like an invisible cloud, heavier than the sunlight. There were deep, purple pools of shadow on the opposite side of 7th Street. His new clothes made him itch and the back of his neck, exposed by a haircut, crawled. He touched his shaved cheek gingerly, checking his new face and identity. Then he saw Blantyre, climbing out of a Mercedes, thirty yards further down the street which was divided almost racially into sunlight and dark shadow.

Anderson wanted to flee back into the plant-ridden foyer among the drifting whores and their pimps and the businessmen and middle-class blacks, just to get off the naked street, out of the sun.

Blantyre crossed the broad pavement and entered an office block. MLC had offices on some of the upper floors. He'd discovered that two days before, within hours of his arrival. There was no one else in the Mercedes. His body quivered, and he sweated inside the new bush jacket and the neat, pressed shorts. His face was hot and exposed, and he suddenly felt more recognizable. Then he uprooted himself from the moment and hurried back into the foyer.

He sat down in an armchair that faced the side windows, his back to the doors, and stared unseeingly at the mats and the half-filled ashtray on a low table, his hands blurred but visibly trembling at the edge of his eyesight. It had happened as he knew it would. While Blantyre was absent, he had engaged in half-hearted surveillance and a kind of recuperation; a brief remission – until Blantyre's tall, broad shape emerging from the long, pale car had proved that the disease had not been eradicated. It was stronger than before. He could do nothing, he realized. He had learned nothing since his arrival; the MLC warehouse complex to the north of the town, with its own small airstrip, hadn't revealed anything. No one – until Blantyre – had arrived at the MLC offices, other than the regular staff. He'd sat at a café table opposite the building for hours, pretending – yes, *pretending* . . . He was terrified of Blantyre, afraid for his life. Which is why he had not called Aubrey from Walvis Bay; had not checked whether his packet had arrived, or whether it had intrigued the old man in London. He didn't want Aubrey's interest now! Anything but . . .

In this town – South Africa's last frontier they called it – he was forced to admit the fraudulent manner in which he had spent the past two days. Amid the coffee-coloured or white whores and their minders, the drug pushers, the businessmen – he was an alien. The place thronged against him like the passengers in a crowded bus, the kind of place he had fled for the emptiness and animals of Etosha. He was a bird of passage, less at home than the flamingoes on the lagoon to the south of the town. There was nothing he could will himself to accomplish.

He looked round at the reception desk. His packing would take mere minutes. He could leave the old 4WD in the parking lot and take a taxi out to the airport. Checking out would take moments, they weren't busy. His name was assumed, he would pay in cash drawn by credit card on his account in Windhoek. Blantyre would not know he had been here.

There was a flight to Windhoek at noon, another to Jo'burg that afternoon. He could take either one, if he hurried. While Blantyre was still in the MLC building. He stood up stiffly, and felt dizzy for a moment, before his head cleared.

When he stopped, it would be time for Margarethe to confront him accusingly. He hurried to the lifts. Getting away from Blantyre was all that really mattered.


Aubrey put down the telephone in the hall of the flat. Mrs Grey seemed disapproving as she glanced from the open door of the kitchen where she was preparing lunch. The junior minister at the Foreign and Commonwealth Office had appeared disappointed at having his lunch appointment with Aubrey cancelled at short notice – much as Mrs Grey seemed to resent having to prepare cold salmon and salad for himself, Hyde and Godwin. Aubrey felt a mischievous pleasure in the sudden rearrangement of his day. He re-entered the broad lounge. Trees and Regent's Park lay beyond the net curtains at the tall windows. A faint breeze shifted the curtains carefully, like a frail hand.

'That young man needn't be too concerned at failing to attract my patronage,' he announced. 'He's a protégé of Geoffrey Long-mead, and therefore bound to travel far.'

The green carpet was littered, to Mrs Grey's intense annoyance and silent deprecation, with printout sheets containing the infor-mation Godwin had extracted from his computer, via the laptop which was coupled to Aubrey's hardly employed electronic type-writer. The littered room, further untidied by the presence of Hyde and Godwin, pleased him. Sombre, anxious, urgent, but yes, defi-nitely pleasurable. A homecoming of sorts.

'Well, Tony?'

Godwin gestured at the carpet. Hyde, peculiarly posed in a chair near the window, sheets opened and untidy before him on Aubrey's occasional table, was studying the unfolding sheets and making notes on a pad.

'The stuff went to Dumas Electroniques. Dumas owns a large shareholding in Reid Group – thanks to David Reid selling them *his* shares. But there aren't any details on Dumas. It's still a small company. It's expanding, yes – but not as much as you might expect. It's all wrong. Dumas shouldn't be behaving like a *minor* company any longer.'

'Or receiving dodgy shipments from Reid Davies,' Hyde remarked.

It was as if he had been given the task of minding two truculent, easily bored children while their mother, some vague relative, had taken herself off to the Harrods sale.

'What about Reid Davies?' Aubrey asked.

Godwin pointed to a hastily heaped collection of printouts and scribbled notes torn from a pad, lying on the floor. 'Staff roll, recent contracts and shipments – as much as we have, sir.'

Aubrey picked up the sheaf.

'Look, it's obvious they must have been using Namibia when things were normal.' Hyde smiled involuntarily. 'Malan took his share off the top, then no doubt shipped the rest on via Mozambique, even Ethiopia. To Moscow. Now, though, MLC has subsidiaries sprouting like bloody mushrooms all over eastern Europe.'

He scratched his temple with a pencil, looking much as a puzzled child might have done. Aubrey dismissed the thought. Hyde's survival instincts included intelligence. Others had discovered that an instant too late, on occasion.

'So?' Godwin muttered, leafing through a notebook, noisily flicking pages in frustration.

'So – it's easier now – that's all. That stuff went to Dumas, and Dumas must be sending it on. Both through Namibia and direct. So, whatever Dumas is or isn't, it's doing the KGB's job for them. Either they own it or Malan does – at least they have to control part of it. They couldn't do it any other way.'

'And *did* that shipment go to Dumas?'

'It did, sir,' Godwin replied. 'I checked.'

'Then what, in heaven's name, *is* Dumas?'

'Naughty,' Hyde remarked. 'Very naughty.'

Aubrey returned to his chair, skimming the material on Reid Davies, which was immediately intractable. There was nothing in Richard's letter regarding any French company. Willenhall in the West Midlands seemed unpropitious territory for any grandiose and covert scheme –

– except that Chambers had been murdered in that quiet backstreet, and the shipment from there had been whisked off to Dumas last Friday evening with Orrell's blessing!

He knew what he must do and that was to talk to Michael Davies, who part owned and completely ran Reid Davies. Get in there and root out the method of the thing.

He pondered Anderson. He had fled the clinic rather than been discharged, and had disappeared. Much to the chagrin of Colonel Blantyre, he gathered from the administrator of the clinic, who had been most helpful. Where had Richard disappeared to? He felt chilly with the sense of Anderson's violent past reinvigorated. But he was twenty-five years older now, what could he do? Blantyre unnerved even Hyde.

Mrs Grey appeared in the doorway and seemed at once appalled and unable to announce lunch. She reproved him for deliberate, self-induced over-excitement with a small, sharp glance.

'Wine, Sir Kenneth?'

'I think Mr Hyde would prefer beer, Mrs Grey. You did get some?' She nodded tightly as if she had been forced to admit to some demeaning act like shoplifting. 'Some Chablis for myself and Mr Godwin . . . thank you, Mrs Grey.'

She retreated like the survivor of a defeated army, with enormous reluctance. Her gaze was firmly on Hyde and Godwin at the table in front of the window, shuffling papers, muttering together like children engaged in some complicated game.

Then Hyde burst out: 'I bloody *told* you I recognized some of these names! There *are* old STB people on the boards of these companies that are MLC subsidiaries or associates in Czechoslovakia! Look, that bastard *Novak*, for example. How the hell Havel didn't have him buried alive I'll never know — see? There!' He tapped the sheet with his pencil, holding the continuous paper under Godwin's face.

Who nodded his head.

'And they've got contracts oustanding with Dumas — Christ, it's the bloody pipeline, isn't it, going through Czecho to Moscow — Dumas, these Czech subsidiaries, the KGB.' Godwin turned to Aubrey with a beaming smile. 'We've got them, sir — I really think we've got them!'

'I'll bet bloody Husak himself is on the boards of some of these companies. Oh, Jesus — all we have to do is tie everything up in one neat parcel.'

'Can we?' Aubrey asked eagerly.

'We'll bloody well try!'

\*

The Namib Desert stretched away southwards and to the east, the monotony of the plateau nibbled at by the huge, reptilian mounds of the dunes, beyond which the sea glittered pale as the hazy sky. The tinted windows of the departure lounge seemed barely to reduce the glare and the openness that unnerved him. Anderson felt heated and drained, as if he had wandered in from that landscape.

His ticket was crumpled in his fingers and his one small bag rested beside his feet as he sat slumped forward, appearing to be preoccupied with the book in his other hand. Smudged print from his damp thumb at the bottom of each turned, unread page. The flight to Jo'burg was scheduled to take off in another hour . . . the plane had just landed, a small Boeing, and taxied towards the terminal building, whiter than the dunes against the dulled glare of the sea and sky. The plane and the place pressed against the windows of the lounge.

The handful of passengers who had disembarked and trooped like trained chimps across the hot tarmac drifted into the air-conditioning of the lounge, divided from himself and the waiting emigrants from Walvis Bay by a single barrier. Another handful waited for them, a few children in anticipation, one uniformed chauffeur holding a scribbled placard, a few women –

– Blantyre. Anderson shuddered. The pillar against which he was seated concealed him but seemed insubstantial as he flinched against the recognition. The man must have followed him –

– no, could not have done, he'd already raised his arm to attract the attention of one of the disembarking passengers. Which man? Blantyre, standing beside the uniformed chauffeur, was obviously meeting someone, and assumed his role in attracting the attention of . . . a small man, light glinting on spectacles, slightly balding, squat-figured, and carrying a briefcase, which he at once handed to the chauffeur. He shook hands with Blantyre. The figure of the man –? The strut and arrogance of his stride, the turn of his head? Anderson struggled with an old, mental image, attempting to super-impose it and match it with the man's walk, and face. He shook his head. He knew – had known the man . . . but no longer. Years before, somewhere – Jo'burg probably.

A couple of days and he would sever himself from Africa and Blantyre. He would release the money still in the bank accounts, sell the few shares, then head for the UK, or some still-underdeveloped corner of Spain, up in the Pyrenees, perhaps. But he did know that man . . . he bent forward gently, carefully, following Blantyre and his companion as remotely and curiously as a telescopic lens. He stood up, keeping close to the pillar, the book dropped unnoticed onto an adjoining seat, his bag stirred by his foot. Blantyre was an employee of –

Was it MLC, something to do with Malan? He couldn't remember, so why try? He realized he had moved out of the shadow of the pillar and past the first few rows of tip-up seats in the wake of Blantyre and the shorter man in the sleek suit and the glinting spectacles. He moved carefully, as if through a darkened room littered with furniture arranged to distress the unwary. Pillar to pillar, eyeline blocked by passengers, by the newspaper stand, by –

Shriek of a child beside him, startling him as if the girl had pointed him out. Blantyre and the other man were paused inside the doors while, presumably, the chauffeur brought the limousine to them. Desultory talk. As he hovered against a coffee machine, his passport pressed against his left breast importunately. His ticket was still in his left hand and he thrust it into his jacket pocket. He was hot again, tense yet less fearful. Especially as he moved among white faces and white security guards and the black faces were reduced to their former lot, bending above wide brushes or mops being squeezed in buckets. A big black woman was working behind the news-stand.

Anderson watched Blantyre and the other man from behind the newly-arrived morning edition of *The Afrikaaner*, knowing the safety of reading without buying as the black woman studied him from the corner of her eyesight. He cracked open the broadsheet, shuffled it straight, appeared to read. Blantyre and the other man conversed easily, but with much the same distinction as might have been exhibited between the black woman and himself. Flashes of cloud rather than sun fled across Blantyre's face. Anderson began to feel he would not be recognized, even with a direct and angry glance. In the newspaper, history fleeted. Mandela and the South African President, de Villiers, shaking hands at yet another meeting. Proposals for some sort of proportional representation, more promises to control the rumbling township violence, and the ANC acceding to a lack of nationalization – Malan there suddenly, in the newspaper, flanked by lieutenants.

187

Flanked by the other man – he raised his head, then looked down again, then up again – yes. *That* man – van Vuuren? And the recognition tailing off like the fall of a firework from the night. Van Vuuren. MLC Senior Vice-President, the caption read. He repeated the name, again and again . . . and nothing. Certainty in one sense, but the past refused to come out of its locked, rusted box.

At least he knew his name. He cracked the newspaper together and folded it. Van Vuuren. An MLC lieutenant. The connection. He put the paper down, and saw another flash of angry, thunderous cloud on Blantyre's face. Blantyre was being given distasteful orders. Anderson looked down at uncertain fingertips, resting on a South African propaganda magazine, government inspired in the old days. *Panorama*, or something. He flicked pages because Blantyre's head was beginning to move as he was unsettled by his subordination to van Vuuren. Plants, landscapes, proteas, jackals and leopards – anything but human realities . . . hospitals, black nurse and white child, ringlets, starched uniform, small figure within it –

Rage. The photograph of the hospital had brought back, as in a comet's orbit, the only bright thing in his night, Margarethe.

Van Vuuren moved towards the doors and the uniformed chauffeur beyond them as they slid open. Blantyre, the underling, servant, followed in his casual slacks and bush jacket. He knew van Vuuren belonged to his past, when he had crept through the Bush of the apartheid laws, the marriage forbiddings and the Group Areas Act and the instances of rape and insult and attack by white upon black. He clenched his fists. He almost had hold of the man, almost knew him . . . Then it vanished again, so firmly had he determined to put that life behind him, out of mind. Offices and ploys and information. The lot of a man, which he had first learned to become in Johannesburg, in a lawyers' office.

He shut the magazine with a jolt of his hand. Van Vuuren and Blantyre were climbing into the long, dark Mercedes beyond the tinted doors. How?

*Avis*, like a beacon. Avis. Car hire. A minute, two. He hurried to the doors and saw the Mercedes head towards the main road to Walvis Bay. A flock of pelicans turned gold in the light of early afternoon. If he hurried, he could pick them up, find out where they were heading.

Surprise and exhilaration ambushed him as he approached the Avis desk, but he did not even pause to consider the sensations.

'Well, what do you think? Back in the game, mate, and it's the *old* game, too!' Hyde's challenge was almost blithe, and strangely welcome. 'There's Novak, and, besides him, a colonel in the STB, two captains and a couple of oiks as union conveners – Jesus! You know these names as well as I do.'

Aubrey pursed his lips and plucked at the lower one, aware that the action loosened his half-dentures. The list was provocative precisely because it was so familiar. Hyde leant over his shoulder, his breathing excited, his pencil tapping at each name in turn. All were staff of three Czechoslovak companies formerly owned and operated by the state and now . . . *now*, co-operative ventures with two Western organizations, Malan-Labuschagne Consolidated of South Africa and Dumas Electroniques of Paris. Both those companies had invested heavily, supplied managerial skills, improved efficiency, modernized, just as hundreds of Western companies had done with thousands of antiquated industries and companies in the former East. Except –

MLC and Dumas had, presumably, either encouraged or at least allowed former Czech intelligence personnel to work in, even control, the companies in question. Novak was brutal, but clever, an expert in industrial espionage – irony that – and once deputy rezident in their London embassy. Novak had disappeared, presumed gone to Russia to some safe KGB haven, soon after Havel and Dubček had stood together on the balcony of the Hradcany in 1989. Now, he was back. Sanitized, trusted, powerful once more: Antonin Novak.

He looked up. Regent's Park lay golden and green under the late afternoon sun beyond the net curtains. Novak's presence as joint managing director of one company and senior director of the other one Hyde had located was neither happenstance nor coincidence. It was enemy action. 'We anticipated this sort of thing in Rumania, possibly Bulgaria – not in Prague or Plzeň.'

'Christ, sir, where do you think all these people *went* when Havel brought his scooter and Frank Zappa into the Hradcany? Intelligence and security were their only growth industries over there – the Czechs' biggest employer! If you put *them* all out of work, it

189

would be like closing down ICI and BP over here. They knew where all the bodies were buried – how could they have been got rid of, unless they'd agreed to go quietly? And Novak bloody didn't, that's obvious.' Hyde was patrolling the room, hands waving above his head. 'If you looked at Poland, Hungary – anywhere – I bet you'd find the same thing. The police *economy* after the police state!'

'I agree – jobs for the boys does not fully describe it, does it?' He smiled. There was an itch in his palms and a nervous excitement unsettling his stomach. His chest felt tight, but he no longer considered such intimations as those of mortality.

'Business as bloody usual,' Godwin announced happily, with the grin of a man entirely, finally justified. 'Except now it's real businesses they're into.'

'We have neither the time nor resources to expand our field of enquiry – understand that, both of you.' Aubrey's hand indicated the litter of continuous paper, notepads, the typewriter they had rigged to Godwin's laptop as a printer. 'We have found sufficient indication that certain individuals and organizations are engaged – in collaboration with known operatives of a foreign intelligence service – in activities directed against this country. We are committed to the defence of the realm, and it is on that basis that we shall proceed.' He smiled.

'We're no longer empowered to defend the fucking realm,' Hyde announced sourly.

'Ah, yes. I shall have to see Geoffrey Longmead and have that little matter put right.'

'How?'

'By worrying him. Dumas bought David Reid's shares – David Reid is the great white hope of the government. Geoffrey approved the laying-on of hands, the anointing of David Reid as eventual successor. Any breath of scandal that might touch David should be investigated.'

'Kept quiet, you mean.'

'Exactly, Patrick. So, Geoffrey will want me to look into this, very quietly – just in case. And I will need both of you. Indeed, it was what you were attempting to do all the time, against the most wilful obstruction.'

Hyde was smiling, shaking his head. 'You crafty old bugger,' he murmured.

'Precisely. Now, Tony, what *is* Dumas?'

'From one angle, little more than its Lichtenstein holding company and a couple of small factories producing consumer electronics, even electric can-openers and toothbrushes. From another, it controls, works with, has joint ventures in common with, owns shares in, has bought out – dozens of companies, here, there and just about everywhere.' He shook his large head. 'I doubt we can crack that nut in time, sir.'

'Then we'd better concentrate on the other side of the coin and the Channel, hadn't we? The people who sent that shipment to Dumas – Reid Davies. Mike Davies in particular.' He snapped his fingers. 'One other thought – since Novak came back from Moscow, he presumably came back with KGB approval, even instruction. Correct?' Godwin nodded. 'Then Malan's connections with the KGB are even more pronounced than we thought. These people are all tied together – Malan and the faithful van Vuuren, Priabin, Novak – Dumas, MLC, Reid Group wittingly or unwittingly.' He smiled cunningly. 'MLC and Dumas are deeply compromised by having people like Novak on the boards of companies with whom they do business or which they even part own. Oh, dear – Geoffrey Longmead will be *delighted* to have us hush this up with a quiet little investigation!' He sighed with a deep satisfaction, then felt his eyes prick. They'd killed Chambers – this was the way back at them.

There was a polite, perhaps even reluctant knocking at the door of the drawing room.

'Yes, Mrs Grey?'

She moved like a blindfolded child in order to ignore the condition of the room.

'Sir Kenneth – while I was out, um, shopping for the things you requested –' Hyde's lager '– did the window cleaner call for his money? I'd like to make a note. He was next door when I went out and gone by the time I came back.'

Hyde was standing beside her. She appeared a little agitated.

'How long does it take him – usually? Back and front?' Hyde asked. Aubrey sensed the tension and alarm beneath the calm, careful words.

Mrs Grey nodded. 'I insist on back and front being done. Perhaps forty minutes, what with moving his ladd –'

'How long did it take you to find and buy my beer, Mrs Grey?'

His eyes glinted. Mrs Grey seemed embarrassed, yet disarmed by his manner. Aubrey began to suspect.

'No more than twenty minutes. Which is why I enquired whether –'

Aubrey made to rise, speak – but Hyde flapped him back into silence.

'And he'd gone by then. No other flats, houses in the block – how many does he do?'

'We're always last on his round. Once every two weeks.'

'Van or bike?'

She seemed puzzled for a moment, then nodded.

'A small van.'

'Think carefully, Mrs Grey – no, look at me –' He held her arms gently. 'Did you see or even pass the van when you went out?'

The angry, determined concentration of the elderly. For a long time. Then, with certainty: 'No, I didn't – just the ladders and him at the top. I remember wishing him a good morning, but he often doesn't reply.' Aubrey found the tension of suspicion increasingly unbearable, but Hyde seemed possessed of infinite patience.

'But, you recognized him?'

'Well, yes, he – I didn't look closely, of course. He was wearing the usual overalls. Perhaps the van was parked beyond the corner?'

'Thanks, Mrs Grey,' Hyde murmured. 'That's all, love . . .' He went to the windows and tugged aside the net curtains. The sunlight on the park reflected through dusty glass. Mrs Grey glanced at Aubrey, who smiled reassuringly and nodded her towards the door. She moved like a supplicant.

When she had closed the door behind her, Aubrey said heavily: 'Well? Damage?'

By way of reply, Hyde pointed towards the top corner of the left-hand window. Then he slid it upwards and climbed onto the windowsill, balancing there for a moment as if on the point of some acrobatic, backwards dive towards the street below, then he climbed back into the room. He held out his palm, in which lay a small metal button, across the lines of his hand. He nodded fiercely, his breathing loud. Godwin crowded against Aubrey and him. Then Hyde turned to the open window and flung the button towards the Park.

'Catch some married bugger fornicating in there after dark,' he muttered.

'You mean – ?'

'Oh, everything. I mean *everything* we've said. This room's been bugged ever since we got here. They know the bloody *lot*!'

A collection of child's building blocks, scattered to some vestigial sense of order across the reddish sand. Anderson studied the Malan-Labuschagne Consolidated (Walvis Bay) factory site through his small binoculars, neat as those used at a racecourse to pretend interest in the event. Van Vuuren had been taken in the Mercedes to the Mermaid Hotel in the town, then, within a half-hour, had been brought out to the factory complex that sat uninterestingly behind a high fence. The flat, low units cast lengthening black oblongs of shadow towards each other. Van Vuuren and Blantyre had disappeared into the bronze-glassed, six-storey building that evidently formed the office accommodation. There were garages, fuel pumps, sheds, single-storey factory units, and a large car park, almost full, presumably with staff vehicles. Any subsidised business park anywhere in the world and no longer out of place on the edge of the Namib, though this only nibbled unconvincingly at the desert. Unlike the leached, dug, transformed wilderness created by MLC and Anglo-American further down the coast at Lüderitz and Oranjemund; the diamond coast. A man-made lunarscape, dead, bitter, grey. There was a small airstrip, too, on the far side of the complex, with a miniature control tower and two large hangars.

He scanned the place once more. The first few figures emerging beside their stretched shadows, heading for the car park. Almost five in the afternoon. The drift at once became a loose crowd, and the first cars turned out of the car park, bringing up dust from the gravel road towards Walvis Bay, behind him. The sea was already turning gold and the pelicans and other birds were almost blood-red or black like scrawled, charcoal signs against the evening sky. A flight of seabirds, goitered pelicans, then something moving with less grace and more purpose; a small aircraft, coming in over the narrow peninsula across the lagoon from the town, dropping lower, the sunlight silver and glinting on its glass and metal. A fire tender had appeared from the mouth of one of the hangars. Anderson waited, content with his merely observing self. The camera lay beside him, its lens still capped. Nothing had happened and he was satisfied with the sensations of routine, of undemanding purpose.

The aircraft, a small jet transport, was audible now, gradually drowning the noise of the cars. The fire tender took up a position near the airstrip. The plane turned in the distance and seemed to hesitate, as if balancing itself on a sloping wire it would slip down towards the narrow runway. It then slid lower, tentatively at first, then with a seeming hurry, its flaps fully lowered, the clean lines of the wings broken into the geometry of deceleration. It touched the runway and the engines howled with reverse thrust. Then it slowed quickly, turning gently down the taxiway towards the larger of the two hangars. The fire tender slinked away in disappointment. The car park was all but emptied – presumably only security people remained, plus those who would unload the aircraft's cargo. Its flank turned towards the sun behind him. *St Michel, Paris.* A flare of logo, some winged horse or something like. Paris. It slowed docilely at the mouth of the hangar, where overalled men gathered and the first forklift truck appeared, bright yellow and blue, blazoned with *MLC.*

And van Vuuren and Blantyre, getting out of an open 4WD, van Vuuren in shirtsleeves, Blantyre still like a film extra stranded by the financial collapse of a jungle epic on the fringes of some modern, suburban drama. It was easier, each time, to caricature the man – especially from the crest of this stray, small dune that had wandered off from the vast herd of them a few miles to the south. It was no more than a dozen metres high, a dozen in length. The sand had been firm enough to allow him to leave the gravel road and circle behind the dune, where he had parked the hired car. The cargo door of the aircraft was opened from inside, and steps were lowered. Blantyre followed van Vuuren into the cargo hold. The evening grew more vivid in the sky, with purple nibbling at the eastern horizon.

Photographs? The aircraft was . . . proof of what? Nothing, at present. The pursuit of profit, the business of trade. He lifted his hand from the barrel of the lens and excised the thought that this was time-wasting, vacationary from revenge and grief alike. Blantyre emerged from the black doorway, then van Vuuren. Anderson still could remember nothing about the man . . . some kind of professional dealing – but then, some of his partners had prepared tort and contract work for MLC companies. He had been the token liberal, and done the token liberal things in defending

194

black men and women. Won just once, ruining the defendant's nervous sanity even as he achieved the demotion of a police lieutenant to corporal for a two-month disciplinary period. Rape.

Blantyre signalled the forklift trucks forward. A crate appeared in the doorway, to be speared through its pallet and hoisted away into the light. Anderson adjusted the focus of the small binoculars, straining to read the stencilled name on the crate, the imagery of the crashed DC-3 and its cargo suddenly stinging him alert. Like the sand pattering against his shirt and exposed neck, lifted off the dune by a small, cool salt breeze. The dune's shadow stretched towards the wire-enclosed compound. The forklift turned into the sunlight and he attempted to identify the lettering. Hardly legible at this distance.

R – L, there, the smudge of *Ltd*, presumably. R – E – I . . . the second word isn't GROUP, it ends in an S, he thought, blinking away eyestrain. Was it even REID? D and S, first and last letters – REID DAVIES? Birm – *ingham*? The forklift passed into the hangar and then a second trundled away from the aircraft with a pallet of boxes. Indecipherable writing. Perhaps the size of box to contain a television set, something of that kind . . .

He placed the binoculars on the sand and took up the camera, uncapping the lens and focusing. The forklift – stupid not to have thought of it before – leapt closer than through the binoculars. Television sets. REID DAVIES Ltd., BIRMINGHAM. In smaller letters, on each of the boxes, something-something. There seemed no distance now between himself and the aircraft, or the men's faces. He avoided aiming the telephoto lens at Blantyre. Van Vuuren was still a stranger, distant as the image in the newspaper. The other faces were anonymous. On the crate that now filled the cargo doorway, he read *Part of the Reid Electronics Group*. He heard the camera click and the motor whirr on, as if someone else had depressed the button. Click. The crate would be sufficient, he decided, as the breeze against his neck and shirt awakened nerves, demonstrated his isolated exposure. REID DAVIES was clearly visible on the television sets, but he'd missed that with the camera. On the crate now he could make out both the name and its association with the Reid Group. The neat, gleaming aircraft *was* the DC-3, a second chance –

'What are you doing here, man?' The voice, behind and slightly below, startled him. He had heard no vehicle, no laborious ascent of the small dune, or slippage of sand. 'Hey, man – I asked you a question. What are you doing here?'

'I recognized the bloody woman!' Hyde exclaimed. 'Two men in a van – *not* the window cleaner's van – and her in a Golf GTi. She was off like a rat down a drain when she saw me.' He slumped into an armchair, rubbing his face, then tugging at his hair with his fingers. 'Oh, ballocks! We look such bloody *mugs*!'

'I – I agree we might have been more secure than we were,' Aubrey murmured, 'but it was not to be anticipated that they –'

'They've had the bloody jump on us all the way.'

'I told you they were worried, sir,' Godwin offered apologetically.

'Then what do you suggest we do?' Aubrey asked. 'If there is anything to be done? I suggest we continue, now we are guaranteed a degree of privacy. You have an alternative, Patrick?'

Hyde merely glared, then shook his head. The room was sombre with more than the early evening.

'Right – we'll have to move swiftly then,' Aubrey remarked. 'We must get into this business, break through on the narrow front we have – Reid Davies to Dumas, to –' He thought of Anderson. There was no help there, not until he could talk to Richard. Was he even still alive? 'Tony – that material from your surveillance on Reid Group's offices?'

'Yes, sir?'

'You – what was it you said about this VIATE exposition in Venice?' He clicked his fingers impatiently.

'Wonderful cover story – I think, sir? Or was it wonderful opportunity?'

'Exactly. Either will do. Get hold of a list of exhibitors, and examine their connections with one another. If something very big is about to happen, and – Chambers' murder and the attempts on Patrick would confirm that – then *volume* and *bulk* increase in proportion. And VIATE is concerned with the most advanced high technology, *not* microwave cookers. If *I* were Malan or the KGB, I would very *much* want to get my hands on a great deal that will be exhibited at the Venice International Advanced Technology Exposition . . . Wouldn't you?'

196

# the ladder to all high designs

He was wearily angry. No, he decided with a great effort, he was weary *and* angry. The long evening dipping into night had worn at him in successive, creeping waves of information, response and indecision. When he had finally rid the place of Hyde and Godwin, it had been close to one o'clock. Mrs Grey had come out of her room in her dressing-gown to ascertain his condition and digestive requirements, but he had shooed her off like a small, aged hen and gone to his bed, stubbed and extinguished like a smoked cigarette. He'd lain for most of the night in that semi-sleep that seemed, at his age, his moments of greatest clarity. Unaware of the time, he'd tottered into the drawing room now, the morning seemingly advanced across the grass of the park. He paused to open the window because of the cheap cigar Godwin had required in his depression and one of those sweet, crumpled cigarettes Hyde continued to smoke, then he picked up the insistent telephone. The previous day's incursions by unmannered barbarians had evidently reduced Mrs Grey to a foetal desire for sleep.

'Yes?' he snapped. 'Yes, Kenneth Aubrey speaking . . . Richard, is that really you?' He seemed close, over one of those crystal intercontinental lines.

'Kenneth, you got my package?'

'Richard, I tried to get in touch –'

'Doesn't matter, had to keep moving.' The breathless exchange of urgencies, the focusing of imagination and attention into his awakening thoughts. 'You got the package, Kenneth? Make any sense?'

'Richard, your wife,' he could not help blurting.

'Man called Blantyre. Not important, for the moment. You understand the package? I'm not sure I do, except that none of it should have –'

'One of our concerns, Richard – one of our concerns. You'd left the hospital, disappeared – where are you?'

'Swakopmund – boarding house. Cheap, out of season. I'm in the enclave. They're still flying British stuff in, Kenneth, I have photographs. Same company or companies. *Reid.* I know who he is – I don't know why the Russians are involved or why – they killed my wife. Do *you*?' The anger and the half-contemptuous demand stung.

Mrs Grey appeared at the door, and he waved her innocuously out of the room.

'Richard, I'm not quite certain – there's some sort of pattern emerging at this end, into which your information instilled a great deal of clarity. But you, why Swakopmund? A holiday resort, is that right?'

'I've seen another flight, another cargo, Kenneth. Same people – at least, a subsidiary. MLC's plant in Walvis Bay took delivery last night – Paris air shipper flew it in. I had a bit of contact, not much – ' Aubrey realized that he and Anderson used old jargon so precisely that the words were like signals of recognition between members of a clique.

'Which subsidiary?'

'Some company called Reid Davies.'

It had to be part of the shipment that left Birmingham for Dumas, that Hyde and Godwin had failed to stop and which had been the cause of Chambers' death. His breath caught, then, almost unwillingly, Aubrey continued with the debriefing charade, which was easier and more convenient for both of them.

'What contact?'

'Patrol. I was on surveillance. Convinced them with an ornithologist routine. I *hate* the ease with which it works, Kenneth, my new harmlessness!'

'I do understand, Richard. Reid Davies – yes, we know them. We've had – contacts here, too.'

'Then it's real – I mean, not just local. It's widespread and important.'

'Appears to be, Richard.' He sat down with a surprising degree of gratitude, facing the net curtains and the day beyond them. Invigorated though, not tired. But he was dizzy with the unexpected exhilaration and the swirl and rush of conflicting priorities.

Richard alive, Richard's proofs, his possible danger –

'This man Blantyre?' he blurted.

'Yes?' Anderson replied warily.

'What – imminent risk is he to your safety? To the safety of the agent-in-place,' he added, an involuntary smile seeping onto his old, dry lips. 'Are you all right, Richard?' he insisted when there was nothing to interrupt his reflections.

'Oh, I'm OK, Kenneth – just OK. As long as this isn't something of no importance. I haven't got the time or energy.'

'No, I don't think it's that, Richard. Indeed, far from it. What happened?' And after Anderson's brief narrative, he asked anxiously: 'This man van Vuuren. To *us* here he seems very significant. But you can't recall in what context –?'

'No. I know who he is now, not who he was. Sorry. I don't think it's important to me. I want Blantyre, but it seems more complicated than that. So, I'll work with you. Kenneth – now that I've foolishly aroused the guard dog. You tell me what it's about. Why the secrecy about these shipments? Who's robbing who blind now?'

'As far as we can make out, Richard, there's Russian involvement, together with MLC. Malan himself, this other man van Vuuren, Blantyre of course . . .' He hesitated, sensing the silent rage at the other end of the connection. 'It's high technology, as you suspected. We're nibbling at the edges of this thing, Richard, but I want Malan!' His anger seemed like an echo of the silent cry from Anderson. He thought of Kathryn, his dead niece.

'Why?' Anderson asked bluntly.

'I, like you, lost someone. Blantyre was not involved, but Malan was.'

'Very well. What do you want me to do?'

'Will you go back for me, Richard, be my agent-in-place? Keep them under surveillance, discover what you can, report to me regularly. Stay out of contact for the moment. Just surveillance, arrivals and departures, goods and individuals. Will you do that?'

The silence was lengthy. Then: 'For the moment – couple of days, perhaps. Yes.' He paused, then added: 'I'll rack my brains about van Vuuren, perhaps there's some hold I might have if I did remember.'

'He's important, Richard – very. It would help greatly.'

'Then I'll try,' Anderson replied heavily.

'Resources – money, Richard?'

'I can buy what I need. I'll get myself organized, Kenneth. I'll report this evening. Seven, your time.' Again, he hesitated, then added fiercely: 'I *want* them, Kenneth. I won't be sidetracked into something nebulous and long-term. I want – ' There was something that choked in his voice. ' – bodies, Kenneth. At least one. Understand that. And if *I* can't do it, then you'd better send someone to do it for me. Do you agree, Kenneth?'

Heavily, Aubrey murmured, 'Yes, Richard. Your fee. I understand.'

'Then I'll get moving. This evening.' And the connection was at once cut. Aubrey shivered and fumbled for a cigarette and lit it, his hand quivering. Somehow *too* close – the past *too* insistent with that casual pact between them that a man should be killed. He paced the carpet, tugging at his lip, failing to enjoy the cigarette. Perhaps he was unprepared for such a brutal rush back to those violent times.

He stubbed out the remainder of his cigarette and returned to the window, hands once more in his pockets. He thought of Priabin and the fact that he had bugged the flat, *his* flat, and knew all they now knew; as Babbington surely would. He realized then that their knowledge would precipitate action. He clicked his fingers in impatient summons of an idea. In his old age, ideas were reluctant, sullen servants at the best of times, but now, when he needed them –

Anderson was keeping MLC and van Vuuren under surveillance. Hyde and Godwin must get into Reid Davies today, tomorrow at the latest. And what was it he and Godwin had said about Venice – *all canals lead to Venice*? VIATE – Venice International Advanced Technology Exposition, *They'll all be there. It would be like pinching the takings at M & S, Marble Arch, on a summer Saturday, if Priabin and Babbington could have their pick of what'll be there.*

What a conduit, a *confluence*, Aubrey thought. All those Reid and MLC and Dumas companies and associates and subsidiaries, flowing goods into that meeting of many waters – oh, indeed, what pickings in that cash register!

He snapped his fingers with pleasure. He'd see Mike Davies. An idea began to gleam like uncovered gold. Venetian gold.


'*Think* about the implications, before you alert Babbington. Think about *him*.' He sighed. 'Aubrey is the most cunning and alert of old men. Put him in one of these private rest homes and he would be running the place – and making a larger profit – within a month. Because the man on the street, the field agent, has a peculiar accent and kills without compunction, don't assume that Aubrey – or even Hyde for that matter – functions by mere impulse or out of old habits. We've woken people who didn't want to sleep in the first place, and now they know we haven't slept either!'

'General?' she remarked sullenly. 'They have a critical path direct to Reid Davies, and the VIATE build-up is happening there!'

Priabin rubbed his chin. 'I can't alert SIS again, not by any route. Even *they* might think there was something wrong. We shall have to rely on *Mortimer*. There's no other way.'

'I don't trust him!'

'Why? Because you don't know him, or because he isn't a believer, only a mercenary?' he snapped back, spreading his arms wide in a dismissive gesture. 'Most of them – even *us* – are not believers, whatever ideology you choose as a yardstick. *Mortimer* is reliable. If not, his life is in ruins. He knows that. And Aubrey has no suspicion of him. Which is why he needs coaching and why he's flown down to London today. I shall brief him.' Her flicker of doubt stung him, and he growled: 'Listen to me, Valentina! Mark me well, young woman. Babbington is focusing everything in VIATE, *risking* the whole enterprise, when it is not really necessary. If Aubrey rolled up the entire Reid Group tomorrow, we would be back in the UK and in business within twelve months, through Dumas. General Babbington is jeopardizing the *whole* of European operations for the sake of a coup, one stroke of daring. Remember that if you are tempted to send any unauthorized signals to Moscow Centre marked EYES ONLY – Babbington! Now, Valentina, do you *understand*?' His fist banged the desk, only partially for theatrical effect. The girl flinched bodily in her chair.

Finally, she nodded.

'Good,' he remarked. 'The VIATE snatch is too greedy, there's too much. Like looting a jewellery shop. It's dazzled Babbington. He won't listen to reason any more, not on that subject.' He spread his hands on the desk. 'Please understand that, Valentina. Babbington is as dogmatic, even fanatical, as Aubrey himself. Whatever the size or significance of the bone, they will fight to the death over it.

That is their mutual past, present and future. I sometimes think if you scratch the surface of each of them, nothing really exists for either except the prospect of defeating the other.' He grinned. 'Meanwhile, our company, Dumas Electroniques, is gathering in the harvest Babbington ordained. *We* have to keep Aubrey's nose and Hyde's fists and boots out of the caviar for a week at the outside. Let's concentrate on that, shall we?'


The fog lay around the dune, damply chill, writhing like great, slow funnels of smoke, all but obscuring the MLC factory complex. To Anderson, perched on the dune's crest, it was like being in a small boat. In another hour, the mist would have lifted, exposing the complex and the dune. He heard the noises of vehicle engines, the putter of forklift trucks, the heavier throat-clearing of articulated lorries. He heard the occasional, illusory call of an invisible voice. There was no other cover except the dune, no other vantage point, despite the risk of discovery – *re*discovery.

From the sounds of activity, coming blindly out of the swirl and heave of the sea mist, he imagined that a shipment was being made ready to leave by road, presumably southwards to the Republic. He glanced down at the folded map in its polythene sheath, then rubbed his bare arm with his free hand; it was too cold not to be warmly dressed. He hadn't expected fog.

They'd take the gravel trunk road east, then join the tarred road south to the border and eventually, Cape Town. He presumed it was the shipment of Reid Davies stuff the French transport plane had flown in the previous day. Yet it could be something else entirely. Whatever, it was a long trek. Perhaps that was what attracted the Boer, van Vuuren, to the overland route? He tossed his head. There had been no transport plane in either of the hangars. One of their aircraft was missing, he thought bitterly. And capable of claiming lives long after it had crashed in the Bush. The voices coming infrequently out of the mist, even though male, were ghostly hers. He shivered.

The mist, twitching rather than moving with the great, majestic indifference of the sea, rolled more quickly as it thinned and warmed. The dunes to the south thrust through it, ochre-coloured now in the strike of the sun. The voices diminished, as did the mechanical noises and the putter of engines. Beyond the wire, as it emerged from the fog, four articulated trucks took on shape and bulk, together with their yellow, attendant forklifts. He raised the more powerful binoculars he had bought and focused them. So far as he could discern through the grey conjunctivitis of the failing mist, the crate was labelled *Reid Davies*. His chest tightened and he dipped below the crest of the dune, lying on his stomach. A small, bright lizard slipped away from him in a miniature avalanche of damp sand. He raised his head and the binoculars. A set of doors was slammed shut and locked by an overalled driver. Each truck bore the logo *MLC*. He scanned the scene, but there was no sign of Blantyre among the scattered men. The cars emerged from the car park, the first windscreen and strip of chrome catching the early sun. Heavy engines were being revved and the gates of the complex clanged hollowly as they were opened. The first of the huge Volvo trucks lumbered towards and through the gap.

He glanced back down the dune towards the hired 4WD. He should tail them, ensure their route south or perhaps east into South Africa . . . it was at least a thousand miles to Cape Town, more than twelve-fifty to Jo'burg. MLC had extensive manufacturing and distribution – and R and D – facilities in both cities. How long? Two drivers to each truck, he saw as the second Volvo lurched through the gates onto the gravel road and turned east. Dust billowed, yellow, and thicker than the remaining mist. If they drove without stopping, he wouldn't be able to trail them successfully. He wouldn't be able to stop for supplies, water, rest – for two days.

He was not equipped, not in any way. The third and then the last of the trucks rumbled through the gates, which were shut and locked behind them. The column of dust hovered over the road, drifting eastwards towards the checkpoint at the boundary of the Walvis Bay enclave. Anderson experienced an urgent, sharp disappointment. He lifted the binoculars reluctantly and scanned the complex. Van Vuuren emerged from the office block with a chauffeur, who carried his briefcase. Two other men accompanied van Vuuren, their postures suggestive of subordination – hunched shoulders, eager smiles, waving hands. Van Vuuren, short and bulky in the well-tailored light topcoat, was oblivious of their deference. He climbed into the waiting Mercedes limousine.

Anderson glanced towards the retreating column of dust, his pillar of cloud that should be going before him. He wrenched himself away from the convoy, from his angry disappointment, back to the Mercedes. Van Vuuren – that *something*, the *past*.

The Mercedes headed towards the gates, the two men watching it, one of them with his hand raised. The gates were opened.

He was sliding down the shallow dune towards the 4WD before he considered the purpose of the action, the map thrust into his shirt, and binoculars in his hand. He could hear the Mercedes, which had turned towards Walvis Bay, purring along the gravel road. It emerged from the bulk of the dune, retreating beneath its own pillar of dust. The sun struck down, making the concrete of distant buildings gleam like a Mediterranean village. The glass fingers of hotels and office blocks shone. He started the engine of the 4WD and drew out of the shadow of the dune onto the road, maintaining his distance behind the limousine. That *something* hurt like a flesh wound, a thorn under his skin. If only he could remember! He had shut out so much of his past that it was like an attempt to relocate his home in a drowned village beneath a new reservoir, years after the event. But it's *there*, he told himself, some hold on van Vuuren, something he is – or was – something he did, some connection with that bloody law practice that had wasted so many years of his life!

The outskirts of the town, his thoughts maddening him like insects around his head. Scrubby bungalow plots, a few scraggy bushes and flowerbeds, washing on a line. A garage . . . then the wooden buildings becoming concrete and brick and glass and climbing into the morning, the gravel road becoming a street. The drive-in cinema and then the sports stadium. Van Vuuren was not heading for the airport – the railway station? The MLC offices? Hotel –?

He followed the Mercedes down Thirteenth Road, then turned after it into Seventh Street. The perpetual stink of fish from the harbour oppressed him through the open window of the Colt 4WD. The Mercedes drew up in front of the hotel, and the chauffeur opened the rear door for van Vuuren. A consultation of watches, then a nod from the driver. Anderson halted at a parking meter thirty yards behind the Mercedes and watched van Vuuren enter

204

the Mermaid Hotel. Then he got out and walked towards the tinted glass of the foyer doors.

The doors sighed open upon palms and greenery and air-conditioning. He shivered at the drop in temperature, and located van Vuuren almost at once, collecting his room key at the desk. Anderson sat down on a long, curving bench seat behind a miniature rockery bright with flowers and tiny shrubs. Van Vuuren consulted his watch once more. Anderson looked at his – nine-thirty. The foyer echoed to footsteps on the polished wooden blocks. A few businessmen, all but outnumbered by staff. Then the billowing noise of a vacuum cleaner from somewhere just out of sight. A tall woman came through the doors and removed her sunglasses. Dark-skinned, but not black. Half-caste, as they had called all of them – still did in private – or Coloureds . . . like Margarethe. He swallowed drily, his throat tight and dusty. The woman looked around with a casual, professional glance. Early for a whore, but then . . . Perhaps he was wrong. Was he accepting stereotypes, the idea that she could not be as well groomed and dressed and confident without having seen white men reduced to paunches and bulging erect penises – their socks still on, even their trousers ridiculously round their ankles? Couldn't she just be a businesswoman?

She seemed to recognize a glance among glances and at once walked towards – van Vuuren, who had ordered coffee and gestured her to a seat without himself rising to his feet. The girl smiled – yes, professionally, he decided with a recollected lawyer's eye. He'd dealt with them, with the futility of their complaints against white men who had abused them, refused to pay, beaten them. Glamorous black and Coloured whores.

The girl accepted coffee, but the image was indistinct beneath the confusion of other images. Van Vuuren's face, the girl – *other* girls . . . *one* other girl . . . her face against the light coming through his office window. Behind her permed-straight hair the crowded high buildings of Johannesburg, shadowing her features. She'd chosen the seat deliberately to hide her bruising and split lip and swollen eye from him as best she could. Rape. The girl wasn't a whore, and that had been important – why? Van Vuuren's face, the light coming off his spectacles as he sat – sat *near the window of Anderson's office*, glancing out occasionally as if bored and preoccupied, the same high Johannesburg buildings behind his profile.

205

Coloured girl, bright, utterly beautiful beneath the bruising, he imagined . . . worked for –

Confusion of images, like a multiple exposure of the same frame of film. Van Vuuren, the girl, *this* girl now, the waiter, the girl in Johannesburg, accusing van Vuuren of raping her at, at – *his office*, late on a Friday afternoon as she was on the point of leaving to catch her train to whichever township . . . van Vuuren's lawyer smiling blandly, a man Anderson knew . . . his senior partners' faces, all leaning grotesquely towards him as into the lens of a camera . . . and –

– the case disappearing. The girl disappearing, contempt of her healing face, weeks after the assault. Vanishing into unemployment and the township. The case had never come to court. Van Vuuren had been in the Broederbond, van Vuuren had been important, he had been white and rich. And he liked a *touch of the tarbrush, so what? That's not a crime, Richard* – and laughter dismissed the event. But it *was* a crime, wasn't it? Back then it would have been – not against the person but against the *law*.

Van Vuuren finished his coffee and dabbed his lips with the handkerchief from his breast pocket. He stood up at once. The man had bluffed his way out of the accusation that he had raped the girl on his office sofa, and Anderson's law firm had assisted in keeping the matter quiet because the police might, just might, have wanted to talk to van Vuuren about his infringement of the Immorality Act. Even if he had wriggled out of any charge, it would have ruined him with the Bond. Hence the Anglicized law firm. Van Vuuren had chosen to discredit the girl or bribe her or whatever had happened after the senior partner had taken it out of Anderson's hands. Had it become public, the Afrikaaner community would never have tried him; they would merely have punished him with ostracism.

He felt queasy with recollected and now more vigorous guilt. And angry as the girl stood up, her purse tucked into the crook of her arm, and followed van Vuuren towards the lifts. Anderson shook his head and the images separated then dimmed. He rubbed his hot, damp forehead and pressed his fingers against his temples. Van Vuuren had raped – had had intercourse with – a black woman. Social and perhaps even business banishment. Malan – the son at least – would not have approved or remained supportive. A divorce would have been pressed upon the wife, and the case would have risen into the sunlight like a weed. The girl had had to be kept quiet, the case made to disappear like a thin stream in the dry season. The girl had been brave to consult a lawyer – and stupid. He had been guilty, handing her over to the senior partner and allowing him to dispose of the corpse of the case.

Van Vuuren and the whore entered the lift.

Anderson sat back in hot relief at the feat of recollection and the sense that the pillar of cloud from the Mercedes had been real, the one from the Volvo trucks no more than an illusion. He breathed deeply.

Now what?

Imprecisely, and in another hot rush of images and scraps of thought, he saw Mandela's face, saw the President, de Villiers, shaking Mandela's hand, co-signing acts of repeal with Mandela and other ANC leaders . . . van Vuuren's crime disappeared. No! Only his *immorality* disappeared. Now, his *crime* became real. The rape of a Coloured girl, however long ago, by a prominent white South African businessman, was more than ever intolerable, scandalous. Anderson closed his hand into a holding fist. It could put van Vuuren there, just there –


'No, Tony – that is my decision and it will be adhered to. I am not requesting authority – or granting it – to examine Reid Davies from top to bottom. Not at the moment. It would scare too many people into flight. Any frontal assault, any *direct* approach – is likely not to be successful. Geoffrey Longmead has agreed – out of sheer panic – to your temporary reinstatement, to your working for and with me. Which means the greatest *care* on our part. We are in business, but our working capital is small – don't waste it, either of you. By the way, were either of you followed here?'

Aubrey stepped carefully across the pentacle-like outline of a human form still visible on the carpet tiles. The midday sunlight streamed down into the Centre Point office, into which Aubrey had let all three of them with his personal set of keycards. The walls were scorched as a result of the fire Hyde had started to operate the inert-gas fire-extinguishing system which had killed the three Russians. The offices had been casually tidied, superficially cleaned.

Apparently, Century House had no immediate use for them. Electricity, the telephone and fax machines and the computer equipment remained functional.

'We could gut that place like a fish,' Hyde observed.

'*Any* approach to Michael Davies must be oblique, unsuspicious. Patrick – do you see?'

'I suppose so.' The response was sullen. 'If we get much quieter, creeping about like this, they'll think we've died anyway.' He shrugged. 'What's the plan?'

'VIATE – the exposition. Tony, what do you have thus far?'

'At least fifteen of the exhibiting companies are Dumas subsidiaries or associates, or they're linked to them or Reid by large co-operative ventures, especially research and development work. There are a few others –' He was posed by a flipchart on an easel, and turned over one of the heavy, squeaking folds of chinograph paper. A lopsided piece of complex genealogy occupied the uncovered sheet. '– who've borrowed some very funny money from a couple of banks we're interested in. Or from connections with the dubious bank in California in the case of the Yank firms who are coming. That do you, sir? It's all I've had time to get round to.'

'Fine, Tony, fine.' Aubrey approached the flipchart, rubbing his smooth chin. His hand, moving like that of a casual magician, detailed the lines and boxes and company names, as if to make them disappear or enlarge. 'I see. The core of our operation.'

'What operation?' Hyde asked from his chair near the window.

'Ah. You and Tony are going to VIATE – as accredited members of the sales or scientific delegation of Reid Davies Ltd. You will be *inside*, fully entitled to be there, unsuspicious.'

'And –?'

'You move through the bloodstream of that exposition until you find what we need, evidence of disease.'

'Wonderful! How do we get employed by Reid Davies in the next couple of days? I mean, I know Godwin and I are rare birds, but they might – just might – not want us on the payroll.'

'That is what we must settle with Mike Davies. This evening. We're having dinner at his home near Birmingham, all three of us. You'll like it, Patrick – he has quite a good cellar *and* stocks Australian lager!'

Hyde slapped his thighs.

'Look — you don't want to arouse suspicion, right? Now what bloody story have you told him? And how do you know he's one of the good guys?'

'He was one of ours — one of *mine*.'

'People change.'

'Not in this case.'

'Then why don't we ask him to let us look inside his company on the q.t.?'

'Because someone in there may run to Priabin or Malan, and there might be telephone calls to others and the net result would be that the rumblings in the Cabinet Office become an eruption! Please understand the likelihood of that, Patrick, if you stamp around in your loudest, most inquisitive shoes.'

Hyde shrugged once more. 'Just testing you,' he muttered.

'Good. Finally, a quorum. Excellent!'

'What's the cover story — for Davies?'

Aubrey glanced at Godwin, who cleared his throat and said: 'We've information received, from one of our sources on the other side of what-used-to-be — *somewhere* over there — that undesirables like Novak seem to have infiltrated some of the companies that have invested or set up in eastern Europe . . . oh, make it up as you go along, then!' he burst out in response to Hyde's cynical grimace.

'Just so long,' Aubrey said, 'as we have the story straight in our minds before this evening — that former intelligence and security people in eastern Europe are milking *funds* from companies in the UK. A sordid little *financial* scandal. It should have everyone patting us on the back and shouting their encouragement for us to continue.'

'It sounds too much like the truth,' Godwin commented.

'It would have to, would it not? To be convincing to those who know something of our activities. I have cleared this with Century House *and* with Longmead. Davies will no doubt check with Century House. Thus, the parallel with the truth.' Aubrey turned from his contemplation of the traffic at the junction of the Charing Cross Road and Oxford Street. A shirtsleeved, frocked crowd, busy as lemmings, surged across the pedestrian crossing as the lights changed.

Longmead and Orrell, like most career politicians and administrators, enjoyed machinations, complexities, office politics. Such exercises had often seemed glutinous as mud to him, and with little reward to the spirit. Cleverness, mental agility, the arts of deception – for the purposes of probity, and good, of course – were truly pleasurable. His was not the deception of princes; rather, the jester's detached, vigorous, mocking intelligence.

'Clive Orrell will be rather unnerved, I imagine,' he observed, preening, 'when he realizes that all those reports and digests he's so assiduously ignored might have some foundation.'

'Scared shitless,' Hyde cackled.

'Unnerved at the prospect, since he's disregarded all these people and their new legitimacy for months. But he won't demur at our investigation. Longmead all but had the vapours. Filthy lucre always excites his disapprobation, probably because he married it unhappily. You agree, Patrick?'

Hyde grinned.

'Then let us extrapolate – add conviction to outline, shall we? *Before* lunch.'


Anderson approached the boarding house, which huddled behind smarter, larger houses, some of them rest homes for the wealthy, others with pretensions to the status of hotels, all of them confronting the white sand of Swakopmund's North Beach. He had found a vacant parking space in the next street. Long shadows of the two-storey wooden houses lay across the street like heavy, velvet cloaks. It would take him little time to pack. He would be in easy time to catch the evening flight to Windhoek, then a connection – probably the following morning – to Jo'burg. Van Vuuren had flown out of Walvis Bay on the afternoon flight, direct to Johannesburg, so he had returned to the boarding house immediately.

He climbed the three steps to the porch and opened the screen door, walking through the open inner door into the cool of the small, dark hallway. The landlady, German by descent like so many in Swakopmund, was invisible, but there was a smell of onions and overcooked vegetables from the rear of the place. When he brought his bag down, he would call her and pay. He looked at his watch.

Four. He should call Aubrey – from the airport if not earlier – and inform him of his change of tack, of the new, vigorous breeze at his back. Van Vuuren, who had raped a Coloured girl. In the present climate of the Republic, even his membership of the Broederbond wouldn't save van Vuuren from scandal, ignominy and prison. Or exile from South Africa. It would be a very public way to demonstrate the best of intentions by the government and all prominent whites – to wash their hands of van Vuuren in public.

Nor would it save him from Anderson's blackmail. Once the old evidence had been obtained, and even the woman found.

He reached the first floor landing and paused outside the door of his room. He touched the door with his fingertips, to find it unlocked. The key – he stared at it in accusing disbelief – was in his right hand. The landlady –? The hair was rising on the back of his neck, an old itch flaring between his shoulderblades. He listened, knowing that hesitation betrayed his caution. Nothing. He glanced back down the staircase, which had creaked his presence at every step. The afternoon flooded through a stained glass window at the end of the corridor, haloing some early German missionary or explorer. He hesitated, then flung open the door to its full extent, flattening his body against it as he heard a screech of pain and the clatter of something heavy onto the floorboards. He wrenched the door back and slammed it hard against the man behind it a second time, then a third. A hand – white, fingers curled like a claw – appeared at the edge of the door, as if to resist his attack, then slid down towards the lock, then lower –

Anderson sprang behind the door. Above the mask of blood and the empty, unconscious eyes was the white band across the forehead against the deep tan. He recognized that, more than anything else. Uys, the corporal, from the Bush, one of the people who –

He knelt on the man, fingers at once at his throat, knees into his chest so that the breathing he wanted to stop became more jerky, coital in its surges and rough movements. He squeezed the throat, harder, the blood pounding in his ears as if he heard Uys' blood rather than his own, his vision confined to Uys' tightening, gagging face . . . slackening, head lolling as soon as he released his grip. Anderson lifted his head, himself gagging for air, breathing for the first time, it seemed, since he had flung back the door. He crawled away from the body on all fours, shaking, nauseous.

211

Then he dimly took in the room. It had been ransacked without noise but without care. Entry had been through the open window, from the side of the house. His few new possessions were scattered on the bed and the rug, linings were torn in his suit, trouser pockets turned out. Uys had found nothing because there was nothing to find. He had his passport and credit cards with him.

Shakily, he climbed upright, holding onto the edge of the bed. Then he sat down and listened to the rattle of pans from the kitchen, the noise of German from a radio or gramophone, the creak of the house in the afternoon sun. Weary. Empty. Calm, too. Margarethe had hardly been present, except as a recollection thrusting him on to do what he had done to Uys. Now, she seemed absent altogether, as if having withdrawn her approval or consent. He did not know which –

– *time-wasting*. Stand up, get your things.

Suddenly, he was violently gathering his clothes and camera into the empty sports bag. The film had been exposed to the light by Uys – he glanced at the sick, bloody features that lolled above the stained bush shirt. Then he crossed to the window. Uys could not have been alone –

Blantyre?

Not now . . . please.

The 4WD could be reached from this alleyway below him, between two of the wooden houses, without re-entering the street onto which the boarding house fronted. They would be watching from that street, must have alerted Uys . . . ? No R/T or earpiece. He ran his hands over the body. Nothing, except the gun tucked half beneath the bedside rug by the twitching of Uys' foot as he had died. He snatched it up. Spare clip? No time. He hefted the bag, his hearing intent upon the betraying staircase. Nothing. Then the screen door slammed, as if to warn him.

He swung one leg over the windowsill, his shoulder looped through the sports bag's handles so that it swung across his back as he climbed out of the window and began lowering himself down the iron drainpipe. He was sweating profusely. He'd killed a man and Blantyre might already be climbing the staircase –

# in what glory once he was

The old man was reconstructing the past, that much would have been obvious to a child. Hyde sat in the bay of the drawing room, on a narrow, moiré-covered Edwardian settee beside the french windows. Aubrey was perched like a comfortable owl on a small sofa while Davies relaxed on a longer brocaded sofa to one side of the marble fireplace. In a moment of silence, Hyde could hear the French clock's tick from the mantel. Godwin hunched grumpily in an armchair, cuddling a small whisky tightly to his chest. Aubrey wove the fantasy of the room and his shared past with Davies – with all of them, really.

Outside, Davies' children ran and whooped across the broad lawn beneath the birds. The swallows neatly scissored the evening air as the rush of swifts cried about the Victorian house, calling through the open windows before they climbed vertically into the darkening blue. Hyde sensed himself lulled, and probably excessively mistrustful of Davies. But Aubrey seemed assured and confident of Davies, even though the man hesitated and vacillated and failed to register quite the degree of shock the old man's revelations deserved. Swifts paddled violently through the air away from the house as a small girl held onto a reluctant cat's tail and was dragged behind a rosebed – the small cry of minor injury occurred a moment later.

Hyde felt himself to be little more than a brooding presence, a stilled machine awaiting implementation. He stood up at the thought and wandered through the french windows into the garden, standing beside the sundial on the terrace as the children immediately attended to him. Pink entered the evening sky, remarking the outline of more distant clouds, giving the evening a shape, perspective. The swifts' hooliganism seemed at once more urgent.

Davies was concerned – yes. He seemed to want to assist. He'd worked as a valuable courier for the service a number of times. Hyde began to wonder whether it was not the peace of this place, its evident satisfaction, that irritated him – which irritation he directed at Davies. Maybe he was just slow on the uptake, confused, his first thoughts being of the problems caused to his business. Davies had changed, though Aubrey hadn't noticed . . . but perhaps he'd just grown a few years older, his borrowing was too high, he just *liked* success and didn't need Aubrey coming around like a death's head. *Memento mori.* Pointing the finger and recreating the old, Faustian bargain. Hyde sighed. Whatever, nothing mattered until they got to Venice, he and Godwin in suits and smarmed hair, salesmen.

The swifts were three hundred feet up now, calling urgently to one another as they gorged. Black, sooty fragments at one moment, then reformed and rushing with undeniable purpose. Davies' wife had called the two children in. In their stead, two pigeons bumped across the lawn. Hyde glanced towards Aubrey –

– Aubrey looked through the french windows. Hyde seemed tensely angry, almost as if disappointed. Inwardly, Aubrey sighed, then turned to Michael Davies, who appeared suddenly ill at ease, as if discovered drinking his whisky too quickly for taste or sense. It was like trying to recall a swimmer well out of his depth, or one become adventurous who no longer required the certainties of the shore. Davies had been one of his best couriers and observers, but that had been in his youth, like prowess at games or with women; he was married now, and had given up women and cricket for the sake of his business. The change of times and circumstances jolted.

He leaned forward on the small sofa in his most confiding manner. 'You see, Michael – and I know it's an imposition – but I'm concerned at these Old Guard people popping up at every hole in the box . . .' He smiled disarmingly. The increase of dentures had meant, humiliatingly, practice before a cheval mirror to perfect what had once come so easily! But, Davies was unsuspicious; reluctant, but unsuspicious. 'If a couple of my people – Tony here and the more anthropoidal example on your terrace –' Don't flinch, Tony, you should know my tricks by now. 'If they could somehow slot into your operation at VIATE, feel their way around, it would be so helpful.'

Davies nodded and sipped his whisky, attentive to the noises of his son and daughter, who seemed again to have invested the garden. Aubrey saw Hyde stroking one of the two cats and talking, on his haunches, to the children. Perhaps his was a lulling exercise, too . . . ? With Michael Davies, it was that strange and unexpected exercise of taking spies and couriers out from the warm, back to the cold. Davies might well consider Aubrey's proposal as an illegitimate intrusion.

'Unfortunately, Michael,' he remarked, 'my companions and myself remain the children of darkness. However changed the times. Ours is a traditional calling that hasn't yet lost all its purpose.'

'Kenneth? I don't understand.'

'These rather distasteful people with their distasteful pasts, Michael. They come within my bailiwick, I'm afraid. To see such people gaining a new credence, perhaps new power – what with the rather naive governments elected in some of those countries – is of legitimate concern to the service. We must therefore explore the possible dangers. Many of these people will undoubtedly be at the VIATE exposition.' He turned to Godwin, who rustled paper in his briefcase beside the armchair, nodding in vigorous support.

'There's a list here somewhere –' Aubrey began, but Davies interrupted with: 'I believe you. I can't say I've come across anyone who stuck out like one of the old sore thumbs.' He smiled engagingly. 'But then I'm rusty and a lot of them look as if they might have been in their secret police at some time! Except for Havel and Dubček and Walesa, one or two others . . .' He sipped at his whisky. 'Another, Kenneth?'

Aubrey shook his head and declined. Godwin held out his tumbler and, with a grin, Davies refilled it from a decanter on the Victorian sideboard.

'Thanks,' Godwin muttered, reassuming his affable grin.

'Well, Michael? Can you see your way clear to assisting? Without too much disruption to your business in Venice, I mean. I shouldn't want to –'

'Kenneth, you always were irresistible!' Davies laughed. 'There were plenty of courier jobs I really didn't want to do for you – but did anyway. Tell me, does Hyde possess a suit? Otherwise, you'd better buy him a double-breasted example of the species. I take it you do, Tony?'

'One suit, interviews and weddings,' Godwin returned.

215

'Good.' Davies rubbed the hair at the back of his neck. 'I'll have to think carefully about what role I cast Hyde in. He doesn't look too bright, does he? Au fait with the kind of stuff we make, I mean.' Godwin's bland smile reassured Davies that he had not underestimated Hyde. 'As for you, Tony, you shouldn't be any problem. I'll put you with someone on our computer-based exhibits, OK?'

'Fine with me.'

'Thank you, Michael. I expect this little adventure to have a great many spin-offs — for the service and perhaps elsewhere.' Aubrey smiled, then said innocuously: 'And how is the business, Michael? Prospering, it would seem, since you're exhibiting at this VIATE thing?'

'Doing quite nicely, thanks, Kenneth. Not the same —' He was shaking his head. '— not the same as running your own show, but Reid Group's about as comfortable a senior partner as you could get, so —' He shrugged. 'Wolf from the door, that sort of thing. You know.'

'Good, good. You fit nicely into their set-up then?'

'A lot of subsidiary work comes our way — plus a lot more in the way of funds for R and D. It's OK.'

'I was concerned at the time, when things looked so bad. What with that single MoD contract cancelled and seeming to spell the end of so much of your hard work. You might so easily have gone to the wall.'

'Things are OK now, thanks, Kenneth — so stop worrying about me.' Davies' confidence was vigorous, even blasé. 'It wasn't your responsibility, just because I'd worked part-time for you. You didn't owe me anything.' Shade of resentment there? Aubrey wondered, but Davies' smile disarmed his curiosity. 'Anyway, Reid Group came along at just the right moment and they didn't want to asset-strip the company, just help it expand. Great.'

The door of the drawing room opened and Carole Davies appeared, hot-faced from the tropicality of the kitchen.

'I'm just about to serve dinner, Mike — Sir Kenneth. I just hope the meat's still *pink*!' Aubrey did not demur at the employment of his title. Carole Davies seemed to derive such a genuine pleasure from its audible announcement. 'Would you take our guests in, Mike?'

216

Davies was on his feet.

'I'll just get the kids in —'

'The au pair can do that, Mike. Take Sir Kenneth into the dining room. Must dash —'

Davies shrugged at her retreating form as they moved into the panelled hall.

'Ever been to Venice, Tony?'

Godwin had just had time to wink at Aubrey. Behind them, Hyde drifted through the open french windows, hands in his pockets.

'No, I haven't. Looking forward to it, Mike.'

Aubrey's attitude had been dubious, hesitant and dismissive by turns, Anderson thought as the taxi took him, less reluctantly than might once have been its wont, along the Soweto Highway towards the township. The road elbowed its way between golf courses, sports complexes, neat, tree-enveloped suburbs and the omnipresent red-earth dunes of Johannesburg's history and wealth. White wooden, stuccoed, brick, even pillared houses attempted neatness and an assertion of values, which the vast barrows thrown up by the deep goldmines of the Reef, the Witwatersrand, diminished and even mocked. The neat, still-white suburbs huddled together amid the red-yellow, acid-looking mounds as if to suggest the alienness of the place that surrounded them.

Aubrey . . . Anderson tossed his head and glanced into the driving mirror, then into the offside wing mirror, shuffling on the hot plastic seat of the taxi like a schoolboy with a weak bladder. Nothing — no car had followed them from the city centre. He had shaken off Blantyre, then. He'd been there, at Jan Smuts airport as Anderson had disembarked. *Seen* Anderson as Anderson had seen him. Nothing in the newspapers during the two days since he had left Swakopmund — no dead bodies in boarding-house bedrooms, no white fugitive sought for questioning by the police. Only Blantyre, knowing he would come, or at the least expecting him. Waiting patiently as a porter at the airport.

He shivered with recollection. Lurking, hiding, waiting — for hours, until he had deemed it safe. Booking into a hotel under an assumed name, watching for surveillance even as he studied the office block that housed his former legal practice. Knowing that

217

Blantyre knew he was in Jo'burg, fearing that he also knew why he was there.

The highway became dustier, the dust reddening the late afternoon light ahead of the taxi and glaring through the tinted windscreen. The sun's great ball disfigured by pylons and electricity cables and the huddled outskirts of the township. Woollen-hatted youths, men wrapped in blankets and wearing trilbies, women in cardigans and wide skirts. The taxi passed the station, waiting to accomplish its day with the return of hundreds of thousands of black faces. He shrank inwardly. It was Soweto. Even more than the Americanized, high-rise centre of Johannesburg, it bluntly confirmed that Etosha and the game wardenship – and his dead wife – were elements of an illusion. Was that why he had left those things he had deliberately not wanted to take with him, wanted to abandon, with his old housekeeper, Mary M'tebisi? Somehow, he had not wanted to toss them into one of the dustbins they had filled with the detritus of the white suburb and the white life to which neither of them could successfully adapt. His dark suits he had given to Mary's husband, half his size, much of the furniture too . . . but he had made Mary keep, like some dangerous talisman, the office keys and some of his old papers and a handful of other things that typified what he so desired to leave –

– and yet had not left, and hadn't been able to throw away.

The taxi driver turned to him, asking the address once more. Yes, there was less reluctance, but no less disdain on his face than there might once have been.

His great escape . . . he tossed his head, angrily baffled by his own former actions, and his present luck – in leaving keys, cards, files with Mary. Had it been pretence when he had claimed that the amulets might protect her and told her that she could send for him if she or any belonging to her were in trouble with the police or BOSS? Had he *known* he would, one undetermined day, be forced back? He directed the driver and attempted to settle back into his seat; alive with nerve-endings, anticipations, the sense of having once more become a player rather than an observer. Aubrey evidently felt he had a stronger hand in Europe, better cards – for the moment. Aubrey might even be using technique, goading him into activity by a display of mild indifference. It was possible, though it hardly mattered. His own motives drove him, not any priority of

218

Aubrey's. He shook his head, dismissing the idle speculation.

'You read about that explosion, man? In the papers?' the taxi driver asked, old contempt and enmity thick as his accent. 'Bet those kaffir bastards are hiding out in here, someplace – uh?'

Anderson murmured something noncommittal. One of the more lurid newspapers lay on the hot plastic seat beside him. *Atrocity* was the headline. A damaged bank near the MLC building. *Extremist elements*, Communists within the ANC, even a left-wing White connection . . . the usual witch-hunting, carried out these days even in Johannesburg and Pretoria in a reedy, plaintive and ineffectual voice. It was over, almost – and without a final bloodbath of white against black. There were murders in the townships, Zulu against Xhosa, there were terrorist outrages and dire warnings from the far right. But it *was* going to be done, and done without the chaos that had been predicted for twenty years.

A police patrol, unheckled and unstoned, passed them, travelling out of the township. White driver, black partner. No SADF vehicles or uniforms. Youths playing football on a scrubby patch of waste ground near a derelict petrol station, a single goalpost erected. Barefootedly assured, even brilliant. The contrast with the newspaper was strident, reassuring.

Eventually, narrower streets, after a crowded African market. Some large cars – but the place had been thick with cars, whether old or new. The place was – what? *Generally* better off than in the old days, when there were rich blacks, but small in number. There were taller buildings against the lowering sun, too, rather than just the pylons. There were businesses – white businesses – here now, factories and office blocks. Telephone wires criss-crossed the street and orange sky.

Then Mary's tiny breezeblock bungalow, with the vegetable strip in place of a parched front lawn, a goat bleating somewhere behind the house as he opened the taxi door – and a new, extended section attached to the house. An old woman was shelling peas into a colander beside the front door. He paid the driver and the cab turned unhurriedly round and moved away into the orange-glared dust. He stood, hands on hips, inhaling the dusty air and the scent of cooking as the old woman watched him before scuttling inside, leaving the colander of black peas beside the stool on which she had been hunched. In another moment, Mary's bulk was in the doorway, her eyes shaded by her hand as she attempted to make out his features. Then she seemed to wobble into a jelly of excitement and surprise, almost flinging her apron over her face, placing her hands there instead, as if he had come back from the dead for no benevolent purpose.

'Mary?' he said, moving forward to the kerb of planted stones that marked the boundary of the property. Children squealed like wounded animals in some game at the back of the house.

'Mis'r *Richard*–!' Her voice rose into a wail of welcome. She hurried forward and took his extended hand, holding it much as a fortune-teller might have done, turning it in her own pale-palmed hands. Then she looked sharply into his eyes and appeared to know everything. At least, that there had been trouble. She looked back at his palm, then his face. 'You' welcome – *welcome* . . . in, in!' She shooed him forward, towards the door. He ducked his head on entering, his movements awkward since she still held onto his apparently revealing – and welcome – hand. The old woman might be her mother, her husband's mother, he did not know. She returned to the colander as soon as he entered, deferential as if nothing had changed. Probably it hadn't in her mind, after a life of invisibility. The children he could see through the rear window of the living room, beyond the plain wooden table where the setting sun spilt on its cracked, scratched, deeply polished surface. Linoleum covered the earth of the floor. A door was opened onto a . . . he peered and Mary giggled like a child. A bathroom in lurid pink. Bath and washbasin and toilet bowl. Through the window, he could see that the tiny, decrepit shed that had been the outside privy had disappeared. Ritually burned no doubt, he thought with a smile. He went, respectfully, to peer into the bathroom. Soft white towels, soft toilet paper, new linoleum on the floor. Mary continued to giggle and he turned to face her.

'I'm glad, Mary, so glad.' As she nodded agreement, her flesh wobbled. Her bulk made the living room seem tinier than it was. Two small faces appeared at the back door, curious, unrecognizing. He remembered the girl as a suckling baby, the boy as a sullen two-year-old. Mary gestured him to a chair and he nodded his thanks. The children drifted away. 'Where's Thomas?' he asked lightly, as if trying to distract her now studious gaze. He remembered, Margarethe had once said . . . *our passivity only* looks *like folk wisdom, Richard – just remember that. It's really just the patience of dumb animals, waiting.* It had shocked his liberal pretensions. Watching Mary watching him, he was uncertain Margarethe had been right.

He had betrayed himself now, knowing his eyes glistened, seeing his barely hidden distress on Mary's mirroring features. But she, mercifully, did not enquire, and he asked quickly after her husband, then the children, then the old woman and the extensions of her family and her husband's family whose names he could recall. A litany of success, at least that was how she made it seem, as she bustled at the stove in the galley-sized kitchen and rattled saucepans and cutlery. As she had done when she and Thomas and the new children had lived in the most generously-sized wooden hut he could place in the grounds of his house without arousing the ire of the neighbours and the curiosity of the authorities. Not very brave, he thought sourly. One room and a toilet did not necessarily compensate for his pleasant manner when she served him breakfast, or the bonuses and occasional treats and clothes he had bought the children and herself. The fact that she retained a gratitude that might be described as eternal was a silent, poignant accusation.

He shook hands gravely with Thomas, who took off his black trilby as he saw Anderson rise from the chair at the table. Thomas, too, was indebted, reminded of small kindnesses by his presence; so that they were both like pet cats or dogs, their response out of all proportion to the attention lavished on them. Yes, Thomas' job was in the township, a concierge at some new office building . . . there would be black executives, doubtless, but not Thomas among them. His lack of education.

He ate with them, accepting the offer of beer from Thomas. The children seemed incurious, as if he, a white man, was no more than an aspect of the landscape of their lives, to go largely unnoticed, as blacks had been in a former white landscape. Mary cleared the dishes and returned to the table. Thomas' voice could be heard clicking and chuckling in Xhosa with the voices of neighbours, which Anderson snatched at imperfectly. He spread his hands on the table.

'I need what I left with you, Mary,' he announced, at which she clutched his hands in her moist palms, her face distorted with concern.

221

'What trouble is it?' she asked.

He shook his head.

'White trouble.' He smiled bitterly. 'White mischief.' She seemed both puzzled and anxious.

'Why you come back here?' She sounded as if she were pleading. 'Why?' Shaking his hands in hers.

'I had to. Things – things didn't work out, Mary.'

'– so *tired*,' she said. 'Nothing here for – you mean harm.' It was as if she had accused him of some crime; reluctantly but of necessity.

He began shaking his head, but then nodded. 'It's something that has to be done – *I* have to do. For which I need my stuff. The keys and papers.'

The quick dusk had gone and the vast township glared with neon and street-lighting through the windows. The rumble of vehicles was louder, more persistent than when he had last come to Soweto. They sat in the unlamped darkness, her eyes staring brightly at him, her round, double-chinned features wearied by his mood.

'Where's Missis?' she blurted, as if to dissipate the tension like a gathering storm in the room. She seemed planted on her chair, determined not to bring him the things he had asked for. 'Where . . . ?'

'Dead,' he announced. 'It's why I've come back, Mary. That's all you need to know.' He could see the snail-tracks of tears on her black face, the glitter of her wet eyes. She might even keen for Margarethe later, after he had gone. For the moment, she was restrained in subordination to white reticence. 'Thank you,' he murmured throatily, now shaking her hands gently. 'Please, Mary, the papers and the keys. Bring me the box – I won't need to trouble you again.'

She sniffed loudly and wiped her eyes and nose with a large handkerchief. She disappeared into the one bedroom, and he heard rummaging, scraping noises. Then she returned with a metal box such as a film cameraman might have carried. Thomas' and the other voices chuckled like a stream outside the door. The occasional insect cruised the room, as if searching vainly for a lamp against which to incinerate itself. She placed the box on the table, its locks and clips closed.

'Thank you, Mary,' he said, patting the box with the nervousness he might have shown a strange, growling dog. 'I – where's the nearest taxi driver, Mary?'

She nodded, understanding that his visit was completed and she was divorced from him now by the box placed between them. He had returned to his past and she had a fearful inkling of his dangerous purpose; of which she disapproved. But, he suspected, she also wished him gone, so that she might sit alone and mourn Margarethe.

Traffic sounded outside, drowning the conversation of the men on the front step. Their voices continued, as the flicker and wash of headlights entered the room through the door and windows. He glanced round at the door as the conversation hurried and became alarmed and Thomas' head appeared in what might be accusation in the doorway. Mary was concerned, her hand on the box.

'What is it?' he asked, and was answered by the noise of a siren outside and the screech of brakes, then something bellowed through a megaphone in distorted English.

*Terrorists . . . police . . . remain in your homes*, he snatched from the bellow. The newspaper's image of a bomb explosion, the cry of *atrocity*. ANC disclaimers, counter-accusations from the Conservatives, a breakaway extremist group, white and black. Satisfactory scapegoats or inventions –

*Stay in your houses, this is a security operation*. The megaphone was closer now, other vehicles were coming to a hurrying stop and there were running footsteps and the bemused outcries of surprised innocence. He heard the breaking of glass, the shattering of wood. Cries, orders, the greatest of haste. Thomas re-entered the room, glaring at him. The other men had dispersed. Thomas spat on the floor, to Mary's outrage. Feet could be heard pounding towards the house. Mary grabbed at his hand as he clenched the carrying handle of the box, and she tugged him through the rear door, her son at once appearing, to be gathered to her, then whispered to.

'*White man* – have you seen –?' he heard shouted. 'Terrorist! A *white* man, *him* we want!' Mary had heard even before he had, and dragged him away, understanding simply because of his wife's death and his request for the box. Behind them, Thomas' voice was raised in supplicatory protest and denial. Anderson hoped to God Mary's neighbours wouldn't give him the lie. Somehow, they *knew*!

223

They'd traced his former life like a neat, clear path, the names and the people . . .

He turned to Mary and kissed her cheek clumsily. Then the boy took his hand reluctantly and dragged him towards the teetering fence at the end of the patch of dirt behind the house, clearly visible in the haze of lights from the front. If Mary and Thomas told the truth, they probably would not be hurt. They couldn't, any longer, simply disappear into the police cells and re-appear falling from a high window – could they? Behind the lithe, small boy, he slipped through a gap in the rickety fence, dragging the box after him, its weight surprising in his panic. There were raised voices behind him, Mary's protests vigorous and loud. There seemed a sense of abashed pause, perhaps the running down of the impetus of the snatch operation.

'No white man here, no boss here – boss,' he heard fade on the air. Their search would, perforce, be brief. They'd have a riot on their hands if they weren't careful.

He was sweating profusely, shivering with avoided danger. The boy led him on, turning gleaming eyes on him from time to time as they wound their way through huddled lanes of shops and drinking shibeens and open-doored brothels and gambling parlours. The smell of urine and drink and refuse assaulted him, the past kept alive. The boy's pale palms waved him on, despite his weariness and fear and the increasing weight of the box.


Under other circumstances, it might have been entirely amusing, this charade of inspecting Hyde and Godwin and their transformed appearance. *Washed behind the ears, clean fingernails?* It was on his lips to say the words aloud, just for a moment. Instead, he nodded and said: 'Very well, sit down, both of you. Your next-to-Godliness is intimidating me!'

Godwin grinned and Hyde at once tugged his tie loose and unbuttoned his collar. 'Christ,' he muttered.

It was, or promised to be, a hot, clear morning. Already the pecking birds and drifting first visitors were slightly masked by a haze in Regent's Park. He glanced at *The Times* folded neatly beside his plate at the window table. David Reid had announced in the House the previous evening – fortuitously in time for *News at Ten*

224

– an EC aid package to the Soviet Union which would, conservatively, be equivalent to $10 billion, *to unfreeze the transport and distribution services* and avoid the shortages of previous winters. Another costly effort to keep the Soviet Union on the rails, avoid chaos. Unless some of the people they had identified as having legitimized themselves, joining companies, banks, even PR companies, were very swift, they would miss the gravy before it poured away like water in the desert!

Godwin, too, glanced at the headline.

'Bloody stupid move,' he muttered. 'It'll just disappear.'

'Exactly my sentiments,' Aubrey remarked. 'Now, you have whatever you need in terms of secure communications.' He handed Godwin a small, folded piece of paper. 'The Italians have been very helpful. One line in your hotel, another at the exposition itself, both entirely secure. Checked twice daily. My own telephones will be similarly checked. You've drawn whatever else you need, Tony?'

'Yes, sir.'

'Don't fuss, sir,' Hyde remarked with a kind of buoyant sourness.

Godwin looked at his watch. 'We'd better be going, sir. The car's got to get us to Brum airport before ten-thirty. Any news from Anderson, sir?'

'He's shifted his operation to Johannesburg. Something he thinks worth pursuing as far as our friend van Vuuren is concerned. He should have reported in last evening, but didn't. I'm sure there's nothing to worry about . . . Yes, yes, you two get off. And find something. Find out what they're moving or hoping to move. And remember our Italian colleagues will supply as much support as you need the moment you request it.' He shook their hands. There was a small current of excitement running between them. Despite his sombre thoughts during the night, of his dead niece and Malan's ultimate culpability, this had something of an adventure about it.

'We'll try, sir.'

'If we can catch them with evidence in their sweaty grasp, then we can go through the whole of Reid Group, Reid Davies' peculiar packing operation, even get the French DST to go through Dumas like a fever in the blood.' Godwin was openly grinning. 'Which is what we all would wish – *but* . . .' He raised his finger portentously, knowing that he must impress them with theatricality. 'But . . . whatever grandiose visions we may entertain of foiling Babbington, or any sense of personal revenge or justice –' His voice faltered for an instant, then he continued: 'Whatever the prizes would *seem* to be, there is only one real prize. I've looked very carefully at Reid Group's R and D programme. WSI and transputer technology – *both* well down the line towards production. I have no inkling as to how much has already gone missing, but I want whatever is supposed to change hands in Venice – *stopped*. I want it traced, halted, accounted for. *If* they are using the VIATE exposition to smuggle material, then those are the things they will be smuggling. Locating the next stages of their pipeline, even implicating Novak and people like him, come second to this. This is – no more and no less – an intelligence operation against the security service of a foreign power. Do I make myself absolutely clear? At no time and in no manner is the recovery of the smuggled technology to be jeopardized – not even . . .' It was so *difficult* to reconsign her to the back of his mind, out of mental sight! So difficult, too, to attempt to ignore Babbington and the everlasting enmity between them. But he must. 'Not even in order to catch Babbington or Malan red-handed! Or to unearth Novak. Not at the moment. Understand?'

Eventually, and with marked reluctance, they sobered and nodded. Aubrey felt relieved. It *was* possible to operate within distinct boundaries.

'Good, then I'll keep my desk and diary as free as I can. Westfield will be assigned as my aide for the duration. Yes, yes, you must hurry –!'


'Valentina, what the *hell* is going on? I find this request for more of these –' Priabin's hand wiped across the monochrome enlargements spread over his desk, his other hand curled into a fist on his hip. '– placed by *mistake* on my desk this morning. A request from Centre. Your secretary was trying to recover all this stuff when I walked in! What the hell is this?'

The noon sunlight thrust down through the trees along Kensington Palace Gardens as he turned to the window. His anger was mingled with dismay, even nerves, and he did not wish her to identify anything other than his rage and superior rank. But, dear *God*, what games was she playing?

He turned back to her before she could reply. She looked hunched and fearful on her chair, as if there was jam still around her mouth!

'You've been reporting, behind my back, to Centre – to Babbington! To the extent that you've kept this information from me. Godwin and that bloody animal Hyde leaving from Birmingham airport, with the *Reid Davies* party, on a flight to Venice.' His anger was so genuine his voice did not even suggest falsetto. He banged his fist on the desk – a picture of Hyde slid onto the carpet, Hyde in a suit! – and the girl flinched gratifyingly. She wasn't yet nerved to duplicity, at least not against her Rezident. 'Well?'

She burst out with: 'You know I disagreed with your decision not to inform the Centre!'

'You *disagreed*? I gave you an order! You want to play the old games, do you, you stupid arrogant bitch?' Her eyes flared, but Priabin had no wish to restrain his insults. 'You want to play the old games of deceit with one hand, but you want it all to be above-board and respectable on the other! You can't hand me or yourself over to Babbington as you've done and expect to be promoted on *merit* at the same time!' He rubbed his hands through his hair. 'Besides,' he added, turning again to the window, 'you don't play the game well enough. You've only learned it second-hand. You can't *play* with these people, you give nothing but hostages to fortune! Kapustin is an unreconstructed Stalinist and Babbington is paranoid about Aubrey and England. Did you expect sense from either of them?' He turned back to her. 'My God, I'm so bloody *disappointed* in you. When Babbington sees these pictures and whatever piece of meaningful prose you attached to them, all he'll wonder is why you and I didn't get ahead of the game, why they were already leaving before we noticed. Ten black marks, Valentina!'

The girl's eyes glittered with angry, humiliated tears, but she snapped back defiantly: 'We *didn't* know.'

'Oh, grow up, Valentina. The world hasn't changed!' He brushed aside a sense of regret. 'It's business as it always was for the KGB, for Christ's sake!' He slipped into his chair and leaned across the

desk. 'All that happens now is that we're held to be incompetent –
me primarily – and your career will be blighted, you'll be *used* rather
than employed. Is that what you wanted?'

'Of course it wasn't.'

'My bloody job, then? You fool – Christ, I thought you were
cleverer than this.'

'Oh, for God's sake, don't keep playing the same bloody song!'
she yelled, her cheeks pink. She swept her hair out of her face and
glared at him, her hands quivering as if she were registering a minor
earthquake. 'Look, I did what I thought best. I thought you were
*wrong.*'

'Evidently.' But he smiled shakily. 'But why the hell haven't we
heard from *Mortimer* about this? He's on the bloody spot, for God's
sake! Why hasn't he told us that Hyde and Godwin are part of the
Reid Davies team heading for the expo?' He waved his arms in the
air. 'Dear Christ in heaven, is the whole bloody thing going up like
a flare?'

'You want me to talk to him?' she began, then added, penitently:
'I can't, can I? He's on the plane, too.'

'Maybe he's scared – or thinks he's too clever for them. Aubrey
must have enveigled him into it. Davies, I mean. Old loyalties, old
favours. And what is Aubrey after in Venice? He's within a touch
of the whole scenario. Why is he *bothering* with Venice?'

'Proof. A way in?'

He nodded. 'Probably. If he could expose the expo operation, he
would be given carte blanche, and then some . . . must be that.' He
looked up, and smiled. 'But you have dropped us in the shit. We'll
be lucky to climb out. Unless we can sew this up in a bag and drop
it in the river. Think we can take Hyde and Godwin out *before* they
do too much damage?'

Her eyes widened, then she nodded. 'What about Babbington?
He's due to –'

'He won't be able to stay away now, will he? Now you've told
him who's at the party. Sorry. But, we'll have an audience.' His
features glowered. 'If we don't secure the consignment's free passage, then we're finished, both of us. Me for not knowing, you for
not acting on what you did know.' He rubbed his cheek. It was,
appallingly, like explaining something to a child, and a rather naive
one at that. 'If I hadn't found out, I'd have been for the chop. But

*you* – you would have been regarded as little brighter than an idiot.'
He spread his hands. 'There always *were* vampires and werewolves,
Valentina. Nothing's changed!' He grimaced. 'So, now we both
know what's going on, we're about to do what we should have
done in the first place. Pull the rug from under Aubrey, who's
always been *our* responsibility.' He waved his hands towards her.
'So, let's get organized. I want to be in Venice tonight – tomorrow
morning at the latest, with everything in place.'


He had slept in the main railway station, his head nodding on his
chest, his presence as unremarked as that of the handful of drunks
or blacks or the few Boer farmers from the veldt waiting for the
morning trains. Mary's boy had taken him to the Soweto station
and at once abandoned him in the swirl and crush of disembarking
passengers from the crowded trains from the city. The few police
had not noticed him. There had been something almost – what?
*Polite?* Something restrained, anyway, about the police raid, the
care they had taken to isolate the object of their search as a white
man, their calls for calm . . . their later politeness to Mary and
Thomas – he had rung Thomas at his work. Mary's husband had
been puzzled at leniency, the immediate abandonment of the
search. None of their neighbours had informed them of his visit.
Thomas' silences eloquently voiced the hope that he would not
return.

His hotel was under surveillance, however. Hence his return to
the Central Station, his bag at his feet, the metal box beside it. He
had used the service lift to get to his hotel room, packed his few
things, left the same way. He had recognized no faces, only gestures,
postures. Perhaps they had not been looking for him, but it was
wiser to assume they were. To have mobilized the police, even for
a low-key incursion into Soweto, was unremarkable, but in it he
sensed their evaluation of him as a threat.

He aimed the directional microphone through the thorny
branches of the bush behind which he was crouched, then adjusted
the volume of the sound. The buzz and chatter and deep male
laughter from the *braaivleis* at the rear of van Vuuren's house
seemed startlingly loud, and he reduced the volume. Snatches of
conversation sounded in the earpiece he now plugged into the

recorder. He raised the binoculars to his eyes. The African dusk flared in the neat, tree-enclosed garden from the two barbecue fires. Van Vuuren's face was reddened by the coals of one of them. He was nodding and grinning with a bearded man at some remark or joke. Bright print frocks drifted like clumps of moving flowers through the increasing, soft gloom of the garden, or were grouped like small rockeries. High chatter, the Boer accents almost de rigueur, like the presentation of credentials.

The surveillance equipment was easy to purchase, most of it at discount prices, even in closing-down sales heralded by signs of hope white-painted on shop windows in large letters, as if to declare the shutting down of a repressive state. Fifty per cent off the apparatus of control . . . he smiled grimly. The place was changing.

Not down there, though. There were faces he recognized from the Conservative Party, even one or two of the thicker-necked compatriots who belonged openly to the AWB. Strangely, he was invigorated by the images in the lenses and the voices in the earpiece, as if he were inspecting specimens in glass bottles, museum artifacts. Buying the rifle and pistol had also been a simple matter. Gun sales were up. There were one or two boastful holsters down there, slung around paunches and astride bush jackets and khaki shorts or slacks. Polished, bearded faces, unabashed and still loud. One or two businessmen of the Broederbond variety, a sportsman or two – van Vuuren was wearing a shirt that might, in the dusk, have passed for a Springbok jersey. Anderson remembered now that van Vuuren had once been a promising rugby player, until a knee injury. Not international material, but with enough kudos to begin his business career amid publicity and good wishes.

The large, white-painted wooden house at the far extent of the garden was located in a winding, tree-lined avenue littered with traffic impediments and discreet surveillance equipment in the suburb of Bryanston. It was close to the *Buiteklub*, the country club, whose grounds and golf course he had crossed, as if walking an invisible dog, to reach the knoll above van Vuuren's property. The carefully planted trees and bushes that marked the club's boundary provided excellent cover and the gently rolling ground placed him *above* the man and his guests and his house.

He realigned the microphone after a gentle, rhythmic sweep of the garden. Steaks and *boerewors* sizzled amid the soft explosions of beer cans, the heavy or high laughter, the certainty expressed in the small noises and movements of the guests. The evening darkened as van Vuuren's voice murmured like a point of focus amid the wash of noises, in reply to his bearded companion's remark.

'You leaving for Europe tomorrow, Piet, I hear.' Van Vuuren had confirmed the information. Anderson swallowed, then dragged his fingers across his lips. The exultant noises of golfers killing a snake at the side of the fairway behind him, struck against his back like a mocking, urging hand. Then, in front of him, through the binoculars, Blantyre's form drifted into the smoke and glow of one of the barbecue fires, against a background of printed frocks and the occasional flicker of a white-shirted black servant. Blantyre made directly for van Vuuren, and the bearded man at once drifted away. Anderson pressed the earpiece with his fingers, but the conversation was like a distant broadcast interrupted by the renewed ether of the party.

'– sign of him, why are you worrying?'
'You leave tom – won't follow –'
'– interested in me, man?'
'– idea. Just be careful –'

Gusts of laughter and intoxication, and the barking of a dog that was gambolling between the gouts of frocks and pale shirts and the flames and smoke. Rottweiler or something of the kind – remember that, he instructed himself amid surges of disappointment. Van Vuuren was leaving for Europe the following day. Blantyre understood that he, Anderson, was interested in the man, was cautioning him. They must, somehow, have discovered he had followed van Vuuren to the airport in Walvis Bay. He looked at his hand as it shivered just in front of his face. Behind him, the last golfers climbed into their buggy – they must have been hunting for lost golfballs or even for the snake, rather than playing in the quick gloom – then they turned their vehicle around and climbed a slope towards the distant clubhouse.

He felt isolated by their departure, rather than confirmed in his raptor's posture above the unsuspecting *braaivleis*. He could no longer group or hold these people in the palm of his contempt. Blantyre had suggested their retained power to control and hurt. Margarethe sprang up like the evening breeze, making him shudder.

231

Then Blantyre was leaving.

'– good flight, man.'

'There's nothing to –?'

'Don't worry, man – don't worry. It's taken care of,' he heard in a burst of silence while the dog was rubbed fondly and the next helpings of steak and sausage came off the busy griddles.

Blantyre walked up the garden towards the house, nodding to the round form in almost-white that hung like a ghost near the patio; van Vuuren's large wife. The small, obnoxious son's tones had piped intrudingly in his ear since he arrived, demanding attention, food, more attention. Van Vuuren's daughter seemed as plump and uncertain as her mother. Then Blantyre disappeared around the side of the house and almost at once a car's engine sounded above the noise of the barbecue party. Anderson shivered, but he could not regard the involuntary spasm as one of relief. Blantyre occupied space with such utter certainty, even on a darkened lawn and lit only by the occasional spurts of barbecue fires.

He gathered up the recorder, pulling the earpiece from his head. He had much to do. It had to be that evening or night, there wouldn't be another opportunity. He realized now how hollow his stomach felt, how shrunkenly cheated his whole body felt. Van Vuuren was leaving for Europe in the morning. He had to break into his old offices that evening, had to get hold – physically hold – of van Vuuren that night . . . he had to *know* his place, the spread of the golf course, the streets leading to van Vuuren's front door. Whatever Blantyre knew or did, he must concentrate on van Vuuren.

He gathered the awkward bundle of the microphone, recorder and camera in his arms and galloped breathlessly down the slope, across the adjacent fairway, towards the nearest green and its limp flag.

The big stars had begun to emerge – he had to hurry.


The lagoon was being boiled in the sunset colour of the water and the few buildings he could briefly glimpse and at once recognize were dyed with its agitated, surreal colour before the aircraft dipped too low towards Marco Polo airport for him to take in any more. A few spires and towers half-submerged in an orange sea was his impression as the wheels touched. The engines produced reverse thrust and the airport buildings blurred from a string of lights then re-emerged as dull, low shapes sprinkled with separate, weak lamps. The sky was pale and the few clouds deeply pinked like flowerheads. Priabin glanced at Valentina in the business class seat next to him. The Rome Rezident should have flown up by now, so should the back-up team from Milan. As many as a dozen people – another six in economy class behind the dragged-across curtain that had separated this compartment from the bulk of the passengers. Venice. The flight was two-thirds full, mostly with businessmen; a few tourists in short-sleeved shirts and slacks or frocks appeared misplaced. The plane slowed and then turned onto the taxiway towards the terminal building. An announcement in Italian and English instructed them to remain in their seats, then that infuriating, rubbishy musak broke out again. He always hoped that, if ever trapped in a plane plunging towards a mountain or the winter ocean, the music would be more appropriate during his last conscious moments.

He tossed his head and grinned at her, loosening his seatbelt against instructions. Already, the insatiably business-like were at their overhead lockers or clambering into their creased jackets.

It was quite simple, even ordinary. Babbington himself had been obliged to admit as much – see the matter through Priabin's eyes. The shipments must be protected; inspected, approved, then sent onwards. Other than that, there were two matters, intimately connected. Siamese, really, in their oneness. The liquidation of Hyde and Godwin. The prevention of their learning, uncovering, reporting anything – anything at all – and their certain and permanent retirement from the scene of activity. Full stop. Period.

He looked at his watch. Eight. The flight was on time. Hyde and Godwin were already under surveillance by the first group he'd managed to get sent in from Milan – emergency activity, overriding priority. Babbington himself was due in Venice the following day. If he inspected the operation and found everything to be in order, then he'd let matters drop. His career and that of Valentina would be back on the rails. There had been a minor rant, defused in part by the flatness of tone induced by the encryption unit on the telephone – but in Babbington, too, there had been a little fever of excitement, a welcome for the *familiarity* of what was a small-scale, *traditional* wet operation.

Valentina stood up as the aircraft came to a halt and the door at the front of the fuselage was opened by the stewardess. He slid into the aisle – she had not permitted herself to accept the window seat, of course. He grinned.

Full stop; dead stop – for Hyde and Godwin.

# TEN

## quick and in my arms

Hyde moved with the casual hurry of the last tourists coming out from beneath the porticos of St Mark's. He glanced up at the gilded images of greater dramas and meanings. But he was relieved, and challenged. It *was* the old game, however finessed and with altered priorities. It was still the old game –

– had been from the moment they had picked him up, two of them at first, then three. He had been watching Harry's Bar where Michael Davies was entertaining some prospective buyers from the united Germany, Czechoslovakia, France and even the most liquid African nations. A drinking session that had already begun to bore Hyde, sipping a small beer beside the Grand Canal where one of the day-trippers was wobbling into the first of the evening gondolas. Even the Italians didn't seem to be insulted by the leering grasps and mockery of the gondoliers. By leaning wearily on the table beneath the awning which welcomed the flies from the canal, he had been able to see the door of Harry's Bar. When Davies' cluster of employees, clients and prospective customers had emerged into the narrow *calle* that ran between the bar and the hotel up towards the Piazza San Marco, he had drifted behind them – only to find that they had moved, in a laughing, hand-to-shoulder group, into the cathedral. The pigeons had lifted like puffs of grey smoke in seeming protest out of the flocks of tourists in brighter plumage. Hyde had followed them into St Mark's –

– knowing that one of them was already behind him, because the man with the newspaper who had floated along the waterside near Harry's Bar was the man from the pub in London, before Kellett had been murdered. His newspaper reading was too avid, too deliberate. And he had been watching Hyde as well as the bar.

Someone in Davies' group was important to Priabin. The man with the newspaper had not been demoted to a cushy posting like

235

Venice or Rome, he had been despatched to this place like a plumber, plugging leaks, tidying up cracks in the supply.

He had known for certain as he had shuffled and weaved behind Davies' half-bored group, diminished beneath the ornate domes and alcoves and blocks of celebratory marble. There were two others, and one of them was the girl, Valentina, though at first he had not recognized her behind the huge sunglasses and the bright yellow false hair. Eventually she had defined herself by her walk, her posture, and the authority that peeped from beneath her assumed anonymity. One of Davies' group was to be protected then – from him.

When they had moved out from the sultry, gold-struck gloom of the cathedral into the piazza once more, Hyde became certain of their intent. Their entire concentration had turned to him. He shrugged his shoulders into a slouch they would take for unawareness, even boredom, and became more aware of his surroundings. As he moved through the flocks of pigeons and tourists, he was aware, too, of the gun thrust into his waistband. The sky had darkened overhead and the shadows filled the piazza, so that the café lights sprang out as if it were an earlier, winter's evening. He slid between drifting and strolling sightseers, past the exhibited daubs of art students as the public buildings and their archways gloomed about him.

Shouldn't be there, of course. Should be at the expo site with Godwin, checking the Reid Group subsidiaries, the exhibition stands, the warehouses. But Mestre and the site were across the causeway and Davies was here, entertaining in the dining room – booked for half an hour's time – of the Gritti Palace. And he wanted to see Davies when Davies wasn't aware of him, when the man wasn't on guard. He wasn't sure, but there was *something* . . .

He passed under the archway of the Ala Napoleonica and into the Calle dell' Ascenscion, knowing they were drawn with him now as a comet by its tail. The Davies group, pausing occasionally to glance into shop windows, make conversation, slap shoulders, was ahead of him, and he matched his pace to their casual saunter. The narrow shoplit *calle* was crowded, slow-moving as a snake in hot sunshine. He did not look behind him, not even when he stopped to glance blindly into shop windows, or hesitate as if deciding his destination. They, too, were enclosed by the narrow street's

236

tall buildings and would be unwilling to make a move without a clear escape route.

Davies, shepherding his group like a tour guide, headed them towards the rear of the Gritti Palace. Hyde turned after them. Suddenly, there were fewer people as they drifted towards the narrow little hump of a bridge. A church's high, stained wall was rough and cool against his palm, as he halted, watching the group. Laughing, they moved towards the lights from the hotel's foyer. Another small humped bridge, another church, gold-tipped by the last of the sun, and they had disappeared. He lounged against the wall of Santa Maria, hands in his pockets, indecisive and apparently bored. Casually, he scanned the tourists and one thin dog, two cats, a group of Japanese towed behind a guide with a wand, the flash from their cameras blinking out repeatedly. One flare caught the girl and she flinched, as if identified. One of the men was still with her, but the one from the pub – who might even have killed Kellett, he did not know the man's capacities, yet – was on the opposite side of the narrow bridge, ahead of him.

The Japanese disappeared into the gloom of the evening towards St Mark's Square. The crowd was diminished by their absence. He tossed his head, looked at his watch, then moved towards the foyer of the Gritti Palace, peering in, seeming satisfied. Then he turned and crossed the bridge – the man he knew inspected postcards in the gloom with sudden intensity as he passed him. Nerves began, the tickling of the hair on his neck and scalp, the itch in his palms – but it was controlled, even satisfying. The narrow streets and tiny, toylike bridges were sparse with people, quiet, until he reached the Campo San Stefano, knowing that they would guess he was heading for the Accademia bridge; pulling them away from the equilibrium of confidence and numbers, into quieter and quieter streets and squares. The sky showed the first stars. A scrubby, long *campo*, dotted with a few trees and washing thrust out from windows with drunken shutters. A man smoking in one window, in a vest, a woman leaning her huge, melon-like breasts on the windowsill of another apartment, hair straggling untidily around a weary face. He came to the Grand Canal and ascended the wooden bridge, pausing in the middle of it, absorbed into the stretch of palazzos, churches and darkening water. He glanced casually from side to side.

The girl was not yet on the bridge but her companion was, his yellow shirt identifying him. The man from the pub, dressed in pale slacks and a loose blue shirt, drifted past him to the other side of the bridge. He signalled recognition and stillness to another man at the far end of the bridge, beneath the shadows of the Accademia di Belle Arti, where pigeons minced and fussed between the students and sightseers on its flight of steps. Four of them now –

– split them, hurry the process. He turned his head with deliberation and stared directly at the girl, nerves jumping in his palms as he gripped the balustrade of the wooden bridge. She halted as if accused, then turned to look down at the canal. He grinned and swallowed the unexpected excitement that had risen into his throat. He felt lightheaded, slightly dizzy. He hoped Godwin wasn't under the same threat, should have thought of that earlier. As long as Godwin stayed in lighted places where there were people erecting stands and moving machinery and electronics – too late to worry now.

He moved away from his apparently absorbed stance in the middle of the bridge, and descended to the *campiello* in front of the Accademia. And began to walk more briskly down the broad, almost deserted street beside the gallery. Away from the Grand Canal, away from other people, always certain they were behind him, waiting for them to close the gap.


Anderson turned off Commissioner Street and up the ramp of a multistorey car park, the old Ford rattling. He snatched out the ticket from the lips of the machine and the barrier rose. The car climbed the slope as wheezily as an old man. The wound-down window brought him the echoes of his own car's asthmatic, gargling exhaust and the occasional, distant screech of tyres. He climbed floor after floor of the car park, until the vehicles had become no more than a scattered few dots over-awed by the empty, muggy space of concrete. He pulled into a parking bay and switched off the engine. Silence, at once. The warmth of the evening came through the open window. He rested his head against the back of the driving seat, smelling petrol, the close atmosphere and the queasy scent of fried frankfurters and onions from far below.

Anderson got out of the Ford and locked the door. Then he went to the boot and brought out the metal box. The mike and recorder lay like unusable fishing tackle. He slammed the boot shut. Enjoyable, the emptiness of the place. There was a retained blaze of light from the Marshall Hotel and the adjoining shopping mall and a patchwork of light and dark from the tower of the MLC building.

He knelt by the metal box and examined its contents once more, as he had done on the half-empty train from the township and in the station concourse, whenever woken from his drowse by a cleaner or a raised voice. Keys – he knew every one now and touched each of them like separate runes. He had not kept the file on the young black woman who had been raped; he had surrendered that to compromise and failure almost from the beginning – when the senior partner, Seaward, had informed him that such and such would be done for such and such reasons . . . *all right, Richard? I don't see a problem here. Could do us much good, indeed . . .* Truth to tell, the litigation and conveyancing and tort had come in from MLC and he had, indeed, not seen any great problem.

If he could find the file, and find the girl – or anything he could bring to bear on van Vuuren, no excuse would be accepted. Match to straw, it would go up in fire. He held the keys in front of his face. There was nothing else in the box that was of any immediate help, just old combinations, telephone numbers, storeroom codes. He thrust the sheets into the inside pocket of his jacket, smelling the scent of arid grass on his sleeve as he did so. Stood up, reopened the boot and replaced the box. Ready?

Ready . . .

He checked that the car door was locked, window closed. Then walked towards the lift at one corner of the acreage of concrete which seemed now scented with old oil leaks and the omnipresent onions from the street vendor's stall ten floors below. He looked over the edge of the car park's concrete sill. Commissioner Street was a blur of light and neon and crowds. On the other side of the car park, where its fumes must not intrude, was the glow of the shopping mall under its huge expanse of toughened glass. The great greenhouse which cultivated rich white children and token middle-class blacks. Though even that might have already changed, he corrected himself. Changed a little, anyway. He descended in the lift to the concourse of the Marshall Centre.

The lift doors opened and closed swiftly, as if the shabby, metal interior regarded itself as unsuitable for display before the opulent garishness of the concourse's boutiques, stores, advertisements. He stepped out onto the intricate, immaculate tiles. Three terraces of expensive shops, discreet supermarkets, enveigling, seductive windows. A huge baobab tree arched upwards from the ground floor towards the dark, sullen glass of the greenhouse roof, and exotic blooms and broad, glossy leaves sprouted everywhere; an ordered jungle, unlikely to reclaim the ground beneath the tiles. He crossed the crowded concourse, moving more purposefully than the drifting, relaxed crowds in bright shirts and frocks. The place was neither alien nor familiar, merely a landscape against which he moved. The entrance to the office block which contained his former law firm was diagonally opposite the lift doors from the car park, but he felt little familiarity in retracing old steps. The vast, tinted glass doors of the MLC building were two glittering boutiques closer to him. He bumped into a young couple, who were polite, but seemed amused at his urgency. He shrugged off the impression, and moved towards the doors – sighing open – and into the foyer of the building that contained the offices of Bright, Seaward, Seaward, et cetera . . . Their former junior partner, bought in by money Aubrey had supplied after he had fled England, was returning. He smiled grimly, clasping the keys in his pockets. The foyer was virtually empty. A large black woman was being dragged behind a huge, pincer-action broom. Lists of nameboards hung like scrolls of honour at some university between each set of lift doors. He glanced behind him. The world of the concourse seemed dimmed, was silent, beyond the nicotine shading of the doors.

There was a security man in the basement of the building, alarms, security locks, key-coded locks on the doors. If any combination had been changed, the location of any infra-red sensor altered, he would be discovered. The alarms would trip, sounding in the nearest police station, three blocks away. Breathing deeply, he summoned the lift with a single, determined jab of his right forefinger.

The lift's silent, rapid ascent to the fifteenth floor, dizzied him. He was sweating as it slowed quickly and the door opened onto –

A silent corridor; empty. He paused in the lift for an instant, then let the door close behind him. The corridor was familiarly strange; something of the past remained, but that was, in reality, only the reluctance with which he had come to it each morning. Driven to some sort of radicalism by mere boredom? He shrugged the idea aside.

The offices of Bright, Seaward & Seaward lay at the end of the short corridor, beyond the blackwood doors with their ornate, brass doorknobs. He faced the doors and the gleaming brass with an ironic smile, and jingled the keys in his pocket as he moved towards them. There were no security cameras on this floor, though the files he needed would be on the floor below, where cameras –

He flinched at the ease with which he had contemplated the burglary of his old offices. Once, it had been a momentary exercise to examine the layout of the cameras and the way in which they reported to their screens in the basement, supervised by one doltish, idle individual. He touched the brass doorknob of *Bright, Seaward & Seaward*, then pulled out the keys with his other hand. A passing amusement, to spot the blindspots, the angles, the *inefficiency* of the expensive security system his partners had been sold! Now, though, the idea unnerved him. He glanced towards a long slit of a window set in the angle of the corridor and saw the streetlamps far below him and the fuzzy, caterpillar-like running-together of car head-lights on one of the motorways. He shivered.

Carefully, with a touch that seemed ineffectual, he inserted the key into the lock. He turned the key in his fingertips, sweating profusely. The lock gave in easy surrender, its slight click drowned by his exhalation. He pushed open the door, which protested slightly against the thick pile of the carpet inside. He was confronted by glass doors and a box on the wall with a code keypad. No card had to be inserted, just the number. He shut the outer door softly behind him. One wrong number and the alarm would sound in the basement and the idle Afrikaaner, kept on by his Anglophile part-ners as a kind of house *white*, would wake himself and struggle up to this floor in the lift, gun ready. His fingers hovered above the keypad. Two-nine-zero-three . . . why had he employed the anni-versary of his first marriage, when he had been in the process of starting anew, forgetting and erasing the past? He began dialling.

*Cancel!* His other hand had been on the handle of the glass doors, pushing as he completed the number. Nothing – no yielding. *Cancel.* He redialled his number and listened. Silence outside. The alarm light remained dead. He was sweating again.

Bright's number – what was it? Not a date, part of a number . . .

too complicated to remember. Seaward – the old man, not the son who was dead from the neck up and totally alive in the region of his loins. The old man, Dick Seaward . . . ? He smiled, almost gently.

Death of someone, the strangest choice, as if he never wanted to forget. Death of his daughter in a car accident. Anderson flushed at the memory of the prematurely old man thrusting his photographs upon him, of the grave and the headstone and the girl's age, together with the immediately immaculate quality of the girl's life. The girl, who had come to *him* because she knew no one else who would help her – who had the expertise – to obtain her an abortion. The girl had not been particularly promiscuous, simply uncaring and unlikeable. Unlikely sanctity visited on her after her death in a motorway accident in Europe, on a day unimaginable for old Dick Seaward. Teeming, driving rain and a partial fog and the spray from forty-five-ton trucks – and the car driver's head filled with the afterglow of cannabis. Outside Frankfurt. He knew the details so well because the Frankfurt police had been helpful and discreet and he had received the official and the unofficial mail, while Dick Seaward in the next office – that one there, at the end of the corridor – had been erecting his shrine.

He bit off all recollection, realizing its ability to evoke and threaten. Except for the date, on the police report, on Seaward's lips so often – the sixteenth of February. Seaward's entry code because he had discovered love in a blinding moment of guilt and loss, and would never let her slip his mind again. He dabbed the numbers out carefully on the keypad, holding his breath.

Pushed at the door – stiff – *open.* He stumbled inside, a prickle of perspiration along his forehead, closing the door behind him with a nerveless hand, remembering that the alarm would sound if the door did not relock. Leaned against the glass, surveying the familiarly strange. The rectangle of blue carpet and the receptionist's desk, the corridors leading off in three directions, like *points of our peculiar compass, one quadrant missing,* as the senior partner, Bright, had announced, to the obsequious smile of the receptionist, the day he had first seen these offices. And he had spent years in this place, accommodating to its peculiar compass. Until he had tired of it, one morning and for no apparent reason. It might have been the tie Seaward's son had been wearing, or a sick joke, or the polish gleaming on Bright's shoes. By that time, *anything* would have done it, however trivial.

He padded across the thick carpet. The window in this inner foyer looked down towards the gleaming city, its lights lying confidently and carelessly about like the first South African diamonds. He shook his head, passing the offices with the nameplates. His own – he ignored the door. He was here to render his account, and *his* ex-solicitor's fees were horrendous . . .

He thought of old Seaward and his daughter as he passed Seaward's office and imagined its dishevelled appearance. Seaward might not be dead of drink or guilt; more like undead, but with no way for Bright to be rid of him. Seaward had enough money to remain in the firm as long as he chose; equal partner. He followed a turn in the main corridor to its junction with a single door, blank of names or description; the door to the lower floor and the file room and security safes. He fished out a small bunch of keys, inspecting them almost lovingly, as if his memories of this place were all pleasant. He rattled them, then held out the remembered, correct key and jabbed it into the lock. There had been no alarms connected to this door. The cameras and the poorly-sited IR beams were at the bottom of the stairs, waiting for a moment's unwariness. A knitted cat's cradle of a trap which had its blindspots, gaps and weaknesses. He glanced back along the empty, pictureless corridor, but it was impossible to convince himself that anything would be found in Seaward's office, or even Bright's. Everything he would need – if it hadn't been shredded or thrown out – would be down in the secure room. The decisions to do nothing, the statement by the girl, van Vuuren's account of the attempted rape in an office in that building over there . . .

He glanced behind him as if expecting a window to open in the blank walls of the corridor. Then, with a grunt as if weightlifting, he turned the key.

Open. Easy. Down there, silence and the almost-dark. Smiling as he recalled old habits, he reached beyond the door and switched on the lights . . . Stepping onto the first tread of the stairs, then beginning to descend, carefully testing the steps, furiously remembering the angles and compass of the minimal number of infra-red beams, and the blindspots of the cameras. Once he got beyond the first door, the bleak little foyer of chequered tiles on which an

243

African rug had always seemed to have been spilt like paint, he wouldn't have to worry about the cameras or the beams – well done, Bright, you old bastard, saving money everywhere you could –

Christ – oh sweet Jesus Christ! His head turned and he looked back up the stairs at the light-switch. You bloody fool! The lights going on would have registered on the security cameras. The guard would know someone was down here, his screens would be lit up like a bloody Christmas tree . . .

There were six of them now, and he knew their faces – would be able to identify each one of them. He had been trailing around, even down to the Quartiere Santa Marta where the tourists never went and the whorehouses leaned against poor apartments – the first bit, everyone hoped, that would slip into the lagoon, so that La Serenissima could make a dignified exit. Trailing them by the nose, to ensure that there were no more.

He shivered even now, at the recollection of one of Michael Davies' group. Novak, Antonin Novak, former senior colonel in Czech Intelligence. Novak was *here*, with Davies. He needed to call Aubrey but now dare not risk it. Novak had been a name he knew instantly, but a face he recalled only with difficulty.

The six men and the girl had him hemmed in now on the Fondamenta delle Zattere, opposite the island where the Venetians had put the Jews, La Giudecca, with its dim lighting and few poor spires, over which the lights from the Lido could hang like the glow of stars.

He'd dragged them through the dock area, then back along the Záttere, as they began slipping through deeper shadows and he had begun to hear, above radios and television sets and raised voices, the noise of R/Ts.

Hyde shivered. Time to get out of it. As he crouched inside the small, enclosed, paved courtyard of a neat old palazzo that had been converted into flats and which blinked out modestly towards La Giudecca, he heard the shuffle and skid of a pair of training shoes beyond the wall. They were using the radio transmitters, co-ordinating their activities. Trouble was, his head was filled with recollections of Novak. He shivered again as a training shoe

244

squeaked like a weasel out on the canalside promenade. The lights from the Lido's chock-full hotels, boarding houses and cafés glowed behind the Church of the Redeemer, outlining its dome and cross – and the figure that slipped across the gap of water-lit moonlight, gun in hand.

He twitched as he heard a television set switched on in one of the flats, blaring out strident Italian voices. He settled himself down again onto his haunches, clutching his arms across his chest, chin resting on his forearm. The moonlight gilded the water in lines of pale gold braid. A stunted tree grew out of a pot, like a rebellious houseplant amid the courtyard's paving. A cat had wandered incuriously past him ten minutes ago. Novak's features kept coming out of the evening, taunting him. What could he be doing here, in Venice, kissing bums with people like Davies and the Africans and Germans? He clutched his upper arms with his hands, squatting in the darkness, listening for –

Crackle of an R/T or cellular phone. He heard it, then another and a murmuring voice, sensing its location was betrayed by having to answer. The girl, undoubtedly. He slid his torso up the rough brick wall until he was standing pressed against it, his head cocked. He couldn't make out the words, only the urgency of the whispered reply. Gradually, as if teasing at a tiny knot in silk with numb, clumsy fingers, he sensed the location . . . just – *there*. He breathed shallowly. On the other side of the wall, in the next courtyard –

– sweat along his forehead. They'd search this one next. He was aware of the girl's higher-pitched voice coming through the R/T, the urgent whispering of the man, then a male voice at the other end of the channel, replacing the girl's. He heard the tone of authority, the voice somehow familiar, even though the words were indistinguishable. Then the noise of a *vaporetto*'s engine, heading out towards the Lido, drowned all other noise and his fingers twitched like a pianist's against the wall behind him. Damn. The darkness was hot, breathless, the moon had lumbered above the wall, spilling silver light into the courtyard, onto the tree that leaned drunkenly and on the gleam of the cat's eyes at the corner of the building. Slowly, the noise of the *vaporetto* diminished.

Out of the growing silence rose the murmur of voices from one of the flats, then the sharp, small cry of a baby. Then the absence of the crackles and spurts of static and the whispers from the other side of the wall. Hyde forced himself to slide noiselessly to its angle, then towards the entrance to the small, hot courtyard. Then, startling him, as the moonlight threw a shadow towards the tree, he heard the phone or transmitter spurt again.

Priabin's voice, had to be. That had been the familiar one. He swallowed carefully. Kept his moist palms pressed against the wall at his sides. Watched the shadow hunch into secretive reply. The man was still on the broad paving of the Zattere. Hyde strained to hear the exchange in Russian.

'– here, I know it, General. I need back-up.'

'I'm calling this off,' Hyde heard in reply. *Why?* 'All units –' Where was Priabin? With the girl?

No. Her voice exploded in the stillness, almost as if she was beside the man throwing his shadow into the courtyard. '– must be *removed*!' he heard, then Priabin's reply: 'You want to explain to *him*?'

'Five minutes!' the girl pleaded, enraged. 'Just five minutes! Maxim, are you sure?'

'– saw him go into one of these courtyards – back-up. Sir, we can –' *Shit* – Priabin was going to give in.

'Where *exactly*?' Priabin was teetering on the edge.

'About a couple of hundred yards from you, sir. Opposite the church – directly opposite.'

A silence, then: 'Very well – five minutes . . . he's arriving in an hour.'

Another silence, then: 'All units –' And something like *converge*. Then the shadow, which clutched its transmitter against its head in a gesture of toothache, began whispering, and Hyde edged to the end of the wall . . . judging the length of the shadow, the distance of the whispering voice, listening beyond it, too, for the first quick footfalls of the back-up.

Decision. Movement. The shadow became unwrapped, stretching in shock as Hyde moved the few paces, closing on the man, striking him across the face with his forearm, hitting him in the stomach with curled, hard knuckles. Chopping against the side of the falling man's neck, the transmitter rattling on the flagstones.

Footfalls. His head turned rapidly. Two men running towards him from the direction of the Old Customs House –

– and the *boat*. Suddenly, the *vaporetto* he had thought heading out towards the Lido was a small motorboat idling in the braided reflections of moonlight, thirty yards or so from the Záttere's edge. Its engine started up with a gunshot noise, then a growl as it sprang towards him like an animal. He saw the girl and Priabin, presumably, in the bow. There was a third man, marginally in profile, head slightly cocked. Hyde couldn't see the rifle. He ducked and wove towards the next courtyard entrance. The first bullets plucked dust from the wall above his head, then he was in darkness again, his breathing louder than the noise of running feet, themselves almost masked by the magnified insect noise of the boat's engine. He threw himself towards the courtyard wall, dragged himself onto its top then dropped at once down the other side. The narrow canal that linked La Giudecca and the Grand Canal became visible as moonlight occupied the darkness as dimly and hesitantly as a mist.

He paused, pressed back against the wall, two or three feet opposite the reflected square of a window from which a light burned. Something – a rat – scuttled near his feet, then moved into the narrow canal with a small swallowing noise. He shivered. Listening, he detected voices urgently moving about beyond the wall. He hesitated, then began walking quickly alongside the canal, past the occasional thin dog and narrow alleys, skirting a tiny bridge, moving carefully away from –

A blare of light from the searchlight on the bow of the boat. He saw the outline of a rotting, wide-waisted gondola in its gleam. It washed the walls of grubby buildings, then seemed to search him like fingers through his hair and clothes, spilling over him as loud as a cry of alarm. And the girl's voice, he was certain, through a distorting megaphone, all caution abandoned.

He ran on, scraping his hands and body against the wall as if trying to become part of it. Ahead of him, there were lights from the hotels and palazzos along the Grand Canal, but they seemed to retreat down the tunnel of the narrow canal and its buildings. The noise of gunfire crackled again.

His hand went from him and he staggered – an opening like a slit in the night, the narrowest of alleys. He lurched into it, off-balance, then continued as chips of stonework came from the wall close to him. The whistle of the bullet, nothing of the explosion. Priabin had ordered the marksman to fit a silencer. There were footsteps and shouts, too.

A church loomed mockingly in a weed-strewn little *campo*. Other spires and domes rose beyond it like mountains. The lights of Venice were brighter. The noise of the motorboat had stilled, but the footsteps were more urgent now. He drew the gun from his waistband, and sighted at the exit from the narrow alleyway, his shaking forearm stilled by the rough, grubby stone of the church wall. He fired immediately there was a shadow-figure visible – he did not consider which, until it rolled on the ground, screaming and clutching its thigh. A second shadow dodged back into deeper shadow.

Lights were coming on in upstairs windows with the stuttering regularity of people rising for work. But there was clearly alarm in the way curtains were drawn back. He could not have sent a clearer signal of distress than by wounding the man who now thrashed about in the moonlight. Hyde grinned and fired two more shots at the open mouth of the alleyway but there was no returned fire. A woman screamed from one of the open windows. Then the first two unannounced shots from the sniper's rifle plucked out stonework, scarring the grubbiness with pale scuffs. Hyde ducked back. Waited. The woman went on screaming, even behind the shutters her husband had reclosed. The man on the ground still writhed and cursed.

Hyde listened to his own breathing. Any route he chose which did not attempt to double back on them would drive him away from the bridge across the Grand Canal and towards the narrowing spit of land that was the Old Customs House Point. They'd make an easy kill of it there.

The man on the ground was being encouraged to drag himself towards the shadows of the alleyway. White hands flapped into the light, urging him towards their batlike fluttering. Then hands grabbed him, there was a squeal as he was dragged upright and his cursing began to diminish rapidly, then became more strident, violently protesting against pain –

– and haste. They were going . . . He breathed with relief, leaning his head back against the angle of the wall. Hearing now, as they must have done, the siren from a police launch, rounding the point by the Customs House or already in the Giudecca canal. *I want to report shooting* . . . in Venice? Lucky they came at all, it might have been the Cosa Nostra, and then what would the cops have done? Someone was leaning furtively out of a nearby window, a thin man in a grubby vest, who saw him and called out, pointing, only to be dragged away by a large woman in a tight spotted frock –

– then Hyde had flitted across the square, into the moonlight and out of it again, into the shadows of the nearest *calle* which gave way suddenly to another *campo* and its inevitable church.

As he jogged towards the Salute landing to find a *vaporetto* or a water-taxi, he wondered who was arriving within an hour who was important enough for them to pass up the chance of killing him. Christ, whoever it was had real pull, and had to be from Moscow Centre. Interesting. Was he flying in or coming on the train? Flying . . .

Marco Polo for you, then, my son – and those bastards will be there, too, though not necessarily expecting you.

He began shivering with the nausea of reaction as he reached the Salute landing and a *vaporetto* chugged and wheezed towards the side of the canal.


The last of the sunset was streaming across the net-curtained windows, as gauzy and sight-hampering as the nets themselves. Young Darren Westfield was made as comfortable as Mrs Grey's immediately maternal attentions could render him. He was perched on the edge of an easy chair in the drawing room of the Chairman of the Joint Intelligence Committee. Aubrey would have smiled inwardly at the boy's discomfiture, had not his anxieties precluded it. There had been a wasp in the room early in the evening, and he had trapped it between a Spode cup and saucer and ushered it back through the open windows. A pity he could not do the same with his worries.

He looked down at the litter of notes and files around his feet. It did not seem to diminish his imperial significance as far as young Westfield was concerned, but to himself it made him an old man, comfortable in disarray. But there *was* something –

What possible kind of *expertise* did Novak have to offer MLC and Dumas that was *not* illegal? Novak was among the most cunning and brutal of the old school. He had ordered killings with ease, was a masterly interrogator in his brutish fashion, had controlled people with ruthlessness and consummate skill –

He tossed his head. Perhaps he qualified as a born-again capitalist, after that c.v.!

Rubbish. Either he retained covert power that Malan could still employ and exploit in partnership with Babbington, or – what?

The phone rang, startling him, and he snatched it up from his side.

'Patrick, yes.'

'I haven't got long – someone's arriving in about an hour, someone important. I'm tailing Priabin – the gang's all here.'

'What of Tony?'

'No idea. I'll check with him later. I thought you'd like to know. He's here. *Former* Senior Colonel Antonin Novak of the STB. Dressed in a business suit and taken out to dinner by Michael Davies. OK? Be in touch.'

Aubrey switched off the receiver and stared in surprise and satisfaction at the ceiling. Novak. He smiled. A *business* expert! He had controlled liaisons between the IRA, Gaddafi, and the remainder of the terrorist groups in Europe. He'd even been photographed with Saddam Hussein once. He shook his head, as if to clear it. But, Novak – with Davies? In Venice on *business*?

He clicked his fingers, startling young Westfield.

'Darren, check those surveillance photographs that either you or poor Chambers took. The various contact ones, not the NatWest Tower surveillance.' Westfield put them into his hands in a glossy sheaf, and he flicked through them. Eventually, Priabin and a man still recognizable despite new clothes, hairstyle, moustache – Antonin Novak. Priabin, the girl, Novak and van Vuuren. In a restaurant, out of doors, the girl squinting in the sunlight, having removed her huge, fashionable sunglasses. Aubrey all but purred.

'Curiouser and curiouser,' he murmured. There was *something*, though. Nagging at him. Something he had glimpsed, or with which memory had made some brief connection, causing a fitful spark. What was it? he demanded angrily of himself.

'Darren, where are the names of those companies Colonel Novak now serves with such capitalistic fervour? Find them for me . . .'

'Companies connected with Dumas – companies with which Novak has a connection?' Darren murmured, shuffling through heaps of paper. He consulted his notes, checked through another pile.

Aubrey sighed with impatience, and his chest felt alarmingly tight, as if his angina were about to revisit him. He rubbed at it, his other hand tapping nervously at the arm of his chair. It was something to do with one of Novak's former areas of expertise, with Libya perhaps, or the IRA – the connection was there somewhere, but it wasn't yet clear, dammit!

Then Darren handed him Hyde's scrawled note. 'Here, sir – sorry it took me so long.'

He stared at the names, both of them, as if they were crystals that only slowly sank in a thick fluid. Diamonds sliding deeper into amber. Oh, my God, my dear God . . .

One of the companies produced Semtex explosive and had, in the past, supplied Libya who had, in turn, supplied the IRA and the other dark angels of European terrorism . . . the second company was a manufacturer of very modern, very effective small arms, mortars, anti-tank weapons, rocket launchers. The circle closed with a loud, ringing snap. Malan, Reid Group, Dumas, and now Novak. Shipping arms to – *white* South Africa? Weapons and explosives – and people in South Africa who would use them, and others against whom they would be used. *Plus ça change*, et-damned-cetera!

'Darren – quickly! I want these two companies examined, top to bottom – everything they produce and have produced or even *might* be producing!'

My God, he recollected, then saw on the page he still held in his hand . . . nerve gas. One of these damnable companies had once been a producer of *nerve gas* for the Warsaw Pact.

'Yes, both companies – the one outside Prague and the one in Plzeň. And get me Tony Godwin on the line, I must talk to him and Patrick without delay! Hurry, young man – *hurry*!'

251

# in such a night as this

Twenty-three minutes. He'd *wasted* that much time . . . The guard had not been alerted by the light he had stupidly switched on, then clicked off again in his panic, having stumbled back up the stairs to the switch. He'd waited in the dimness at the top of the stairs for the door to open, for the noise of an alarm or the siren of a police car – had heard one which had made his heart bump with a wooden, knocking sound in his chest, but the siren had faded away somewhere as he held his breath; a faint insect noise lost in the dull murmur of the traffic below.

Wasted, *wasted* . . .

His rage made him slipshod, careless. Files were already spilt on the cool, chequered tiles of the secure room, their contents lolling like white and pink tongues. Filing cabinet drawers gaped like jaws. He couldn't find what he wanted, even though no new filing system seemed to have been introduced – other things were in their old places; the partnership profits, shareholding details, tax returns, staff salaries and bonuses . . . all where he remembered them to be stored. And the old files – the sensitive, the erroneous, the political and the unscrupulous – were where they had always been. His keys had opened the cabinets, his fingers had riffled through the files, recognizing the names of plaintiffs, clients, masquerades and deceptions – but *nothing on the girl or van Vuuren*! Not in these cabinets, or in the Malan-Labuschagne files. He'd found stuff that would send Bright and old Seaward to prison for years, and not so much as a traffic violation by van Vuuren!

Anderson paused, wiping his brow with the back of his hand. Then he gripped the edges of the open drawer, which was at chest height, as if needing sudden support. The lighting was subdued in the sterile, cool room. He had dodged the single security camera which focused on the foot of the stairs outside, and the two infrared beams that backed it up. Sliding along the wall, then dropping into a crouch to scuttle like a large rodent to the inner door. Once inside the room itself, there was no security that the correct keys could not compromise; as his had done. For *what*, though? For bloody *what*? His fists banged the edges of the drawer in a fury of disappointment. Twenty-five minutes since he had first descended to the lower floor. He was in that bloody place where he had sworn he would never set foot again, shoved on by a clever *scheme* that mocked him now like hollow laughter. Like the cold sweat on his forehead and beneath his arms. He lowered his face until his forehead rested on the edge of the drawer, which creaked metallically with his weight.

Where, for God's sake? Had they shredded them? Not like Bright, that, though Seaward might have done it in one of the sudden fits of rectitude he had suffered ever since his daughter's death. A fitful, apologetic morality which might have prompted him to sanitize portions of these confidential files. He shook his head. He didn't know. There might be other files missing. He thought he recollected others, mostly involving abortion arrangements, liaisons between black and white that had turned sour or possibly dangerous. There were other cases like van Vuuren's – even the deaths of girls or black servants, killed in sexual or authoritarian rages. He could find some but perhaps not others. He didn't know half of what had gone on in Bright's office over the years, or out at his Parktown home, the murkier side of the practice . . . or the things in which Seaward had colluded before his daughter's death had broken his world like an eggshell.

Breathing deeply, he unlocked other cabinets, pulled out the drawers and desultorily flicked through the files; aimless cross-checking, mere occupation of a decent interval before admitting failure . . . where, *dammit*, where? Thirty minutes, thirty-five . . . the tiles were littered with strewn files and sheets. It did not matter. Who would guess it was him, anyway?

Forty minutes. Nothing. He had opened a hundred confidential files, and found van Vuuren's name twice, as a character witness. Character witness!

He slammed the drawer back in and turned away from it, kicking aside papers and files as he made his way to the door. Frustrated pride nipped at him like a dog at his ankles. The anger of disappointment, of impotence, was fiercer. Cautiously, he opened the door of the secure room, studying the IR boxes positioned on opposite walls, and the single camera; saw on the floor the imagined marks of his knees and hands and back as he had outwitted the security system. Bright's expensive, incompetent system . . . Mockery was no palliative. He got to his hands and knees and prepared to scuttle across the floor, looking up all the time at the IR sensor focused in his direction, whose beam he must not break by movement, looking at the little blank eye that would flash if he −

Light on.

Temperature. Not just bloody movement, *temperature*. It had never functioned efficiently. To register the rise in temperature required a bloody *gang* to enter the place, not just one intruder − but he was *hot*, with rage and frustration. He *burned*, for God's sake!

He ducked beneath the camera's limited eyesight and tugged open the door. Was the alarm connected to the police, or just to the basement? He couldn't remember, so he slammed the door behind him and bolted up the stairs, fleeing down the deep carpet past his old office, past that of old Seaward. He'd have to take the stairs, the idle bastard in the basement would use the lift. The heat of his body mocked him.

He blundered against the glass doors, his hands leaving hot prints that shrank as the glass cooled again. Seaward's office . . . the guard . . . lift coming up . . . Seaward's office − the old man's bouts of guilt, of purging, the moral laxative of his daughter's death. The thoughts came quickly, out of the waves of fear and panic. Seaward drank himself stupid most afternoons, in his untidy office, behind the closed venetian blinds. Guilt . . . expanding like the effects of a pebble in a pool. *Seaward would end up feeling guilty about everything* − how many times had he said that? He glared round in his panic, and the distance to Seaward's office seemed immense. He could almost hear the lift sighing swiftly up to that floor. Seaward would have taken the files on cover-ups, on payoffs to injured or assaulted blacks, especially young women. Three of the files he knew of, beside the girl who had come to him, had been missing. Young black women either dead or abused or both. There could have been fifty more, for all he knew.

He blundered back along the corridor and wrenched at the handle of Seaward's door. Then he glanced back towards the glass doors and the dark wood doors beyond them, still closed. Sirenless hum of traffic from below. Locked. He stepped back and kicked at the veneered door – kicked again, then a third time, and the lock burst. Another alarm would have sounded now – if Seaward had bothered or remembered to set it. Anderson staggered into the office, coughing with effort. Then he flicked on the lights, which subduedly exclaimed on the wreckage of the room. Untidiness, the smell of cigars and whisky in the sterile air. Blinds closed, desk littered with papers, cabinets open, drawers unlocked. He moved behind Seaward's desk, after closing and wedging the door, and opened the few drawers that were closed. Photograph of the dead daughter, looking sullen in sunlight, in an ornate silver frame. He shuffled the untidy heaps and mounds of papers, then hunched down behind the desk so that he would not immediately be seen by someone opening the door, forcing the wedge. Seaward's decline everywhere. Bottle in one drawer, glass in another, as if that minimal separation was all he could maintain. Nothing, nothing –

The faint buzz of the security lock sounded as someone punched in the correct code. He paused, waiting; looked down at his hand resting on a heap of files in the bottom, right-hand drawer. Silently, his nerves jumping, he fingered them one by one, reading the African names on the tabs. Three, four, five – that one he remembered, he'd found them – then the girl's, Veronica Mokesi. *The Mokesi girl is lying*, he heard van Vuuren reciting in his head, his lips contemptuous as they easily spilt the lie.

The door of Seaward's office was pushed an inch open and met the resistance of the wedge. Seaward hadn't needed the wedge for years, his door had always been uninvitingly closed against the world. Then the door was thrust awkwardly, hesitantly open and an Afrikaaner accent – same voice, Roets the anthropoidal security man – called:

'Is that you, Mr Seaward? Set off the alarm again –' Then the error was discovered as the door handle rattled loosely in Roets' grip and his breath exclaimed surprise and suspicion. His voice, a moment later. 'All right, you bastard, come out where I can see you!' Roets' bulky, potbellied figure was posed as a heavy shadow in the doorway, then took on colour and form as he entered the room. *Veronica Mokesi*. The file was under his damp fingertips.

Then Anderson stood up, his hands in the air, suddenly calm

and decided. He smiled at Roets' surprise and the slow dawn of realization that the intruder was known to him.

'What – man, what the hell are you doing here, eh?' he scowled.

Anderson glanced down. The black girls in their files, the abused and the bribed and the seen-off-the-premises . . . and Veronica Mokesi. The picture in the file would be of a bruised face.

'Good evening, Roets. How unfortunate.' His accent had always irritated Roets. The man's face twisted with contempt and the gun was hefted in his hand. 'I came back for something. Just a few years late, that's all.'

'You broke in, you mean! Well, we'll wait for the police now, man. The alarm goes through to the station, see. They'll be here in a minute. You can talk your way out of it with them.' He laughed. 'Sit in the chair,' he ordered as Anderson was already lowering himself into the capacious leather swivel chair. It creaked in the hot, stale-scented silence of the room. Roets pushed his cap back on his head and heaved his belt higher around his stomach.

'Thank you, Roets. Some of Mr Seaward's whisky? You don't mind if I do?'

'Hands on the desk!'

Anderson shrugged. There was a pleasure in his own calm lack of nerves. Contempt still came easily, a kind of emotional back-up. He moved his fingers as if playing a piano on the edge of the desk, near the blotter and the heavy silver picture frame and the set of pens inscribed to commemorate some charity work. The file of Veronica Mokesi stared out of the pile as if the girl herself watched him.

'Christ, man – what are *you* doing here?' Roets asked, as if he felt compelled to break the heavy silence.

'Old business, Roets. Unfinished business.'

'Seaward doesn't keep any money in the office, man.'

'I know that, Roets.' The dismissal in his voice angered the man. His head was cocked to one side, listening. Anderson tensed against the first distant whine of a police siren. Yet was still calm, imperturbable. Roets was sweating. 'It's not money, Roets. That would be too easy.'

'Don't tell me, man – save it for the cops. I don't care. I just caught you breaking in here. Lucky I didn't shoot you!'

'Wrong colour, Roets. There might have been questions.' His hands continued to tap out some run of silent notes on the desk, as if miming to a recording. Picture frame, blotter, paperknife, pen set – paperweight.

Roets shrugged his shoulders by way of reply and glanced down at the pistol in his fist. Evidently, it bolstered his chronic sense of inferiority. Paperweight. Some rough-shaped rock that sparkled like fool's gold mounted on a small black base. It was beside the sullen, unsmiling girl's photograph. He would have to rise quickly and snatch it up in the same moment and –

Siren. Roets' smile confirmed it.

'Must be the taxi you ordered, *Mr* Anderson.' He laughed.

Concentrate . . . let him wind down from that little pitch first . . . concentrate. He would have to snatch it up, rise, throw. Roets was seated ten feet away. He couldn't miss. Veronica Mokesi's file watched him from the drawer and he felt prodded by the success of finding it, by the prospect of van Vuuren –

Siren louder now, descending through the scale like a recorded voice slowed down. Roets was still sweating. Rise and throw, rise and –

He threw the heavy paperweight at Roets, who ducked instinctively, and quickly for a big man, but whose bulk toppled the chair in which he was perched. He went down on one knee and remained there long enough for Anderson to rush from behind the desk, and kick out at Roets' head, catching the man on the temple with the toe of his heavy boot. Then he kicked again, more deliberately, his left foot clamped down on Roets' wrist so that the fingers loosened around the handle of the pistol. Roets' eyes whitened and his head flopped sideways. Anderson picked up the pistol and hesitated only for a moment. The file. He snatched it out of the drawer, clasping it tightly against his chest. A keepsake for van Vuuren.

Outside, the siren's note dwindled into silence. They'd use the lift, too, but they might block the stairs at the bottom. He caught sight of himself in the glass of the girl's framed photograph. White enough, clean enough. Walk with confidence, go with God. He smiled at Roets' unconscious chins and white eyeballs.

Then he hurried from the office, clutching the file, the pistol left harmlessly on the desk beside the framed picture.

*

'Yes, it's him all right. I'm not likely to mistake *him*, am I?'

Hyde's voice was masked and small, as if he was whispering. The shock of his identification of Andrew Babbington arriving in Venice failed to strike with any clarity; distant and diminished like the effect of the international telephone call. Aubrey continued to stare at the most recent clutter around his feet, holding the crystal tumbler and its second small whisky in his right hand, the receiver feebly against his cheek. Babbington, after all these years, was fixed in the past, in embalming fluid, his image cold. He rubbed his temple meditatively with the tumbler, at a loss really, for any response. Darren Westfield's gloom seemed real enough, but it might have been politeness and nothing more. After all, there was no *proof* that Novak's connection was as sinister as Aubrey conceived it to be. There was only circumstantial evidence, littered around his chair. Mrs Grey had retired to bed, her glance reproving him for depriving young Westfield of his sleep . . . *growing boy and all that*, he supposed. The supper she had prepared had been substantial, on Westfield's behalf.

'You don't seem very interested,' Hyde remarked. 'I'm in this shitty little airport, wearing overalls and trying to look like an Italian, and I see Babbington get out of a Russian jet, and you're not gloating – sir.' He paused, then added: ''They're all here for the divvy-up.'

'What – oh, apparently so,' Aubrey murmured. Circumstantial evidence. Giles Pyott's late-evening help and curiosity over the telephone had only added to the weight of Aubrey's intuition, not to the evidence. 'Er – well done, Patrick. Priabin is there, too, you say?'

'Three cars, out on the tarmac. Still sitting there. Tinted windows, full security cover. The gang's *all* here.'

*It proved impossible to keep tabs on such stockpiles, Kenneth,* Pyott had said. *In the end, we had to take the word of Czech ministers, Russian assurances, Polish promises . . . you know the form. We never had any real figures, any real idea of the scale of the problem. If they say they've destroyed such and such a warhead or launch vehicle, we accept their word . . . No, Kenneth. There were factory inspections, records, of course. Whether they were accurate, who would know?*

Pyott had, at long last, learned to refrain from questions of his own, however intrigued he might be. Aubrey had dismissed the possibility of such enquiries airily. *Bee in my bonnet – not important. Good night, Giles.*

But the bee had become a little swarm of anxieties and forebodings. He all but glared at Westfield, seated on the sofa, eating the last of the sandwiches Mrs Grey had prepared for him, a glass of beer on the occasional table beside him. He knitted his brow defensively, even helpfully.

'I – something *else* has come up, Patrick. Something that might be – more difficult, dangerous perhaps. Something that is of concern to us, of *intrinsic* interest.'

'What?' Hyde replied after a moment's silence. 'Will you want me to tail Babbington?'

'Probably – why? Are they leaving?'

'Not yet. He must be having his papers inspected out there. Customs van – the Fat Controller's put his top hat on for this. What's wrong?'

'Something has to be established – Novak's motive for attending the exposition.'

'Collecting his fee – supervising for Babbington? Who knows? Does it matter, except that it ties people neatly together?'

'It may well do. It's a matter of the companies – are they moving yet?'

'No. Get on with it though.'

'Novak's companies, those with which he has a recent and significant connection – among them are an arms manufacturing company and one of those nasty little businesses that produced nerve agents for the Warsaw Pact, back in the Dark Ages. I –'

'And you think –? Why? Who to?'

'Malan. South Africa. Even van Vuuren . . . ? The Middle East, Third World countries – I do not know, Patrick. In *this* case, possibly the far Right in South Africa. The *white* Right. Van Vuuren is a Bond member, has AWB associations –'

'Van Vuuren isn't here.'

'But scheduled to arrive tomorrow.'

'I can't swallow that lot.'

'Then help me to dismiss my fears. The possible scenario is worst case. Nerve gas and arms supplied to the supremacists who loathe the de Villiers government, the new constitution, Mandela – everything. Find out whether Novak brought anything with him apart from a change of clothing, Patrick. Indulge me – put my mind at rest.'

Was it ridiculous? He looked down at the carpet. In the subdued lighting, the scanty evidence seemed insignificant. Or perhaps through the mellowness of two malt whiskies! Was there a heart of darkness here, something obscene, or was there merely the matter of KGB penetration of the Reid Group?

'That's what you want?' Hyde persisted. 'You want me to concentrate on Novak – not Babbington or Davies or anyone else, just Novak?'

'For the moment – yes,' Aubrey replied heavily. 'I can't *ignore* it, Patrick! If there is anything, anything at all, to my fears, then it is *that* which must be stopped. At any cost.'

'OK, you're the boss. I – wait, they're moving!'

Hyde slapped the receiver back onto its rest and skittered through the few remaining passengers near the luggage carousel. There'd been no familiar faces among the passengers. Babbington had come alone. Hyde thrust open the doors and the warmth of the night created immediate perspiration, wrapping itself around his face like a heavy towel. He hesitated in the shadows of the terminal building as the procession of three black limousines moved slowly past, their passengers invisible behind tinted glass. As they headed for the airport exit, Hyde ran to the hired car. If they were driving, then they weren't going directly into Venice.

They could be, he corrected himself, dragging open the door of the small Mercedes and thrusting the key into the ignition; the windscreen fogging with his excitement. Trust Aubrey to spoil that! Babbington arrives, tying the whole bundle into a lovely prezzie, and the old fart is dreaming about bloody nerve gas!

He reversed out of the line of parked cars, heaved the wheel round, then headed for the airport exit and the main road to Mestre and Marghera. There was little traffic, the occasional headlights bumping and swerving towards him in the other lane, the tail-lights of the three-limousine convoy nearing slowly, then settling as he maintained an exact distance behind them, then dropped back, then moved closer, dropped back again. One other car's headlights splashed on the road behind him. Out on the lagoon, Venice burned like a small, hilly island whose vegetation had caught fire in dry weather. Old fart . . .

They were all here, that was the point, surely? Even Babbington in his excited greed couldn't wait to open the parcels, he had to come and look for himself! And Davies and Malan and van Vuuren would be on their way. It was exactly as the old man had predicted, as Godwin had guessed. It was happening, like the movements of a precise, predictable mechanism. All he had had to do was to link them together – and find, among the warehouses, the evidence, the *proof* . . . And stuff the bloody lot of them. Now, Aubrey was talking about nerve gas and the white nutters with the Nazi-style symbols and salutes in South Africa, for Christ's sake!

He slowed once more, dropping back from the convoy, which was moving at no more than fifty. Slow, bright ships moved across the lagoon. Nerve gas, arms? Novak was there on a jolly, had to be.

The cars turned north towards Mestre. Must be the exposition site. He couldn't believe Babbington would be staying in a seedy, second-rate hotel in Mestre – not his bloody style, that. If they were heading for the Piazzale Roma, across the causeway, they'd have turned left. He slipped behind an old Fiat as he turned north. Babbington wouldn't have to worry about being spotted now. It wasn't risky to come out of the Centre and swan around Europe any longer, was it?

Mestre's grubby suburbs, the rubbish dump behind the gleaming billboard of La Serenissima. There *was* a rubbish dump, too . . . landfills they call them now. A parked bulldozer, some gulls still scratching and hovering and no doubt efficiently opening plastic rubbish bags in the dark. The town centre glowed ahead. Then the little convoy turned left, towards the exposition site. Hyde slowed and followed.

The occasional gleam of light from a gated villa, patches of poor housing, the twists of new roads and their pale concrete verges in the headlights. The warm air hurried into the car through the open window, Mestre glowing off to the right like something irradiated. Aubrey had no idea what he was talking about. The convoy turned again. The exposition site, for certain. Dark trees dimly throwing back the headlights of the Mercedes. Aubrey *could* sense things, while he sat in his drawing room, reading philosophy or Dickens. But, *this* . . . ?

But, they had committed atrocities, the AWB, the Afrikaaner Resistance Movement, led by that fanatic bigot, Terre Blanche. And

261

there were other insects under the stones nastier than the AWB, now that the government and Mandela were holding hands.

Lights glaring from around a swimming pool, people cavorting and the snatch of loud musak. Then the car was past the open gates of the garish villa and the road ran through a few new stunted trees, before the darkness opened out. The low, hangar-like buildings of the exhibition centre – the site of VIATE – were visible as they huddled against the big, warm stars. The convoy of limousines passed between two of the exhibition halls, nipped through an open red-and-white barrier, and made towards the warehousing complex. Hyde was aware of the quiet beyond the engine, and switched off his headlights after turning the car at right angles.

Gradually, night sight. The stars burnished, the sky was no longer black but glowing and patchily dark. A few loose, high clouds stretched thin as extinct striplights. He listened to the slow retreat of the three limousines, then the sudden silencing of their engines. A moment later, the slamming of a door. He could walk from where he was, the Mercedes slouched against the side of one of the smaller halls. The warehouse complex was a couple of hundred yards beyond it.

Voices from a group of people, men and women, crossing the concrete towards the exhibitors' car park. The noises of other cars, the slitted glow of lights from the halls containing the exposition. Godwin would probably still be in there somewhere, winkling out facts like a chimp extracting termites from a nest with a thin reed. Hyde tossed his head, then wondered what Godwin would make of Aubrey's cloudy fantasy of nerve gas and arms to Terre Blanche and the rest of the white supremacists. He slipped along the side of the hall until he reached the angle of the building. There was a sliver of moon, low down, but the concrete was pale and betraying. He could see the tail-lights of the three cars, drawn up neat as docked ships, near one of the warehouses. Warehouse 14. A row of parked vans, various emblems on their flanks, two forklift trucks. A small huddle of figures around the limousines, near where light spilt extravagantly from the open door of the building. Hyde raised the night-sight binoculars to his eyes and waited for the starlight to accumulate and the shifting curtains of grey and white to solidify into distinct ghosts.

Eventually, Babbington, Priabin and the smaller figure of the girl.

The heavies – including those who had pursued him through the *calles* and *campos* – disposed themselves according to instinct or training or orders from Priabin . . .

. . . who was talking to – what a load of balls Aubrey was talking! There he was, shaking hands with Babbington, hardly nervous at all, dear heart . . . *Davies. Michael*-bloody-Davies. One of *us* is he, you old fart? One of theirs . . . Ballocks to nerve gas, he had Davies shaking hands with Andrew Babbington, and that would do as the underpinning for a successful operation . . . and Warehouse 14, which had nothing to do with the Reid Group or Reid Davies. Warehouse 14, and fucking Davies shaking hands with Babbington – oh, you *beaut* . . .


The twisting, tree-shadowed street was quiet and deserted, except for one old lady walking a toy dog which seemed more arthritic and reluctant than herself. A bowed, slow figure moving through an element she remained certain of; not even the paving slabs were irregular or in need of repair here. Anderson jolted the car over another humped speed-deterring barrier – perhaps they might even begin calling them *sleeping policemen* here, soon? He smiled away an onset of nerves, then slowed the car on the opposite side of the street from a house well set back behind a high hedge and drooping trees, its security light shining through slowly-swaying branches. Van Vuuren's residence. One in the morning. He backed the car quietly until he could see, through the wrought-iron high gate, that there were no interior lights still on. He listened. No noise or pad or snuffle of the dog. Was it inside, too? Had to be. He switched off the engine and the headlights as the silence settled lightly around him.

The night was cool, the large stars seeming close against the fly-speckled windscreen. Big cars or fun cars drawn up in long drives or under carports. The occasional noise of dogs, the blurt of a cat across the silent street. The security firm's patrols were lax, and they still looked for black faces in old and garish cars. Lack of imagination assisted him, a white man. Just as it had as he had entered the foyer from the second floor stairs and passed the two policemen with a friendly nod and a slightly quizzical glance on his way out of the office block. By now, they might have related his departure to Roets' description, but it mattered little. Stories of revenge and a need of cash would be all too convincing to Bright, who they would have awoken by now. Seaward would be unwakeable before nine or ten in the morning, and unfocused before noon. Veronica Mokesi's file, in the boot of the car, would not be missed for a week, if ever.

Now, van Vuuren.

He got out of the car and crossed the street with studied casualness, touched the wrought-iron gate near a spider's web, then pushed it open, hesitating at the slow creak and waiting for the dog. After ten seconds, still nothing. As he walked up the flagged path beside the gravel drive, he could see the tiny shapes of moths and insects in the halo of the security light. The lawn was dark under the stars.

His fingertips tingled and his heart raced. He felt elated amid the wealthy normality of the street and the suburb. As he neared the house, the knoll from which he had watched the barbecue vanished. Then he was in the light and the insects circled him. The camera stared cyclopically. He listened once more for the dog, but there was only silence. He stood on the single step, within the porch's arch, and pressed the bell.

Dog, loud enough to be outside, and he jolted back from the door before realizing it was barking inside the house. The smell of the watered lawn seemed fresher in his relief. A light had flicked on in the inner porch as he had rung the bell, and he looked up at the camera, knowing his expression would be distortedly benign, even respectful.

Van Vuuren's harsh voice.

'What is it, man? It's bloody one in the morning!' The dog continued to bark. 'Shut up, you bloody dog!' van Vuuren shouted. A murmur that was more distant, presumably the plump wife.

Anderson leant close to the entryphone.

'Mr van Vuuren? I have the right house?' The Afrikaaner accent was understated but unmistakable. 'I have a packet here for you from a Mr Malan. You are Mr Piet van Vuuren? This is the address on the package.'

'Yes, I'm van Vuuren. From *Paulus* Malan?' There was the soft grunt of someone bending to put on slippers or struggling into a dressing-gown. So much the better, in pyjamas or dressing-gown, for what was to come. 'Who are you? I don't recognize you.'

'Secure Messenger Service, Mr van Vuuren.'

'Why didn't he use *our* people?'

'I'm sorry, Mr van Vuuren, I don't understand. The office gave me this package to deliver here – is there a mistake or something? I only do as I'm –'

'Yes, yes!' van Vuuren snapped. 'Wait a moment.'

A form beyond the leaded glass, illuminated from behind, the dog's shape padding towards it. Anderson tensed involuntarily as van Vuuren's squat shadow enlarged and then shrank again as he reached the door. The noise of bolts being drawn, a secure lock being turned by a key. The dog's snuffling excitement around van Vuuren's legs. The door opened on a safety chain and van Vuuren peered blearily out without his spectacles. The Rottweiler's snout thrust through the gap at knee height.

'What package, man? It's one in the morning – you only work at night, or something?'

'I was told it was urgent, Mr van Vuuren. The office told me to collect it –'

'Yes, yes! Do I sign for it?'

He was holding the Jiffybag out of reach of van Vuuren's first, exploratory grasp. The dog nudged at his wrist and, in his irritation, van Vuuren loosened the chain and snapped at the animal, which slunk away with a quiet, sullen whine. The door opened wide –

– as van Vuuren's bleary eyes cleared and focused on the pistol that Anderson thrust into his flinching, rotund stomach.

'Step through the door, Mr van Vuuren – *quietly*,' Anderson whispered. 'At once.'

Van Vuuren gargled: 'What do you want, man? Who are you?' The pale, stunned face was as empty as a moon.

'It doesn't matter. You'll learn everything in time. This way, Mr van Vuuren – please.'

For a moment – just a moment – van Vuuren hesitated, his bulk almost protected by the door, his hand still gripping its edge. But the pistol was still thrust into his stomach . . . so that he slumped into a smaller, deflated shape and came through the door. His stomach gingerly inhaled against the pressure of the gun as his hands flapped loosely above his shoulders. Only his eyes glared and resisted.

'Who the fuck are *you*, man?' he snarled.

'Nemesis.' He was pleased at the portentousness of his tone. 'Richard Anderson – do you know the name?' He slipped behind van Vuuren, closed the door softly, and prodded the man forward with the gun; even as van Vuuren flinched to one side, then steadied himself, hands still raised. 'I think you'd better appear a little more casual. Hands down.' They reached the gate. 'That's my car over there. Please get in and drive where I tell you.' Amusingly, he saw van Vuuren glance down at his soft leather slippers, then up again. 'It will be all right. It's not far.'

'What do you want, man? Money – what?'

Anderson shook his head. 'Something more precious – information. Don't shake your head. You don't want to be the first, do you? Even before Blantyre?'

He pushed van Vuuren into the driving seat, then rounded the car and got in. The dog had begun barking again inside the house and lights had gone on upstairs.

'Who are you – *what* are you, man?' van Vuuren demanded, perspiring freely.

'Your gaoler. Your interrogator.' He grinned and handed van Vuuren the ignition key. 'Switch on and let's go. As we travel, I'll tell you about my wife's murder, shall I? I remember it – vividly.' He nudged van Vuuren in the ribs, and the car jerked away from the kerb, almost stalling. 'Very vividly,' he sighed.


Hyde all but slopped coffee from the plastic cup as he spread his hands.

'Babbington was taken to this villa, behind cypresses and high gates, on the Padua road –' He tossed his head. 'North of Mestre. Davies went with him, they must have had half a bottle of something, then Davies was driven back to the Piazzale Roma and caught a late water-taxi back to the Gritti Palace. That's it – that's what they did, after they'd obviously gloated over whatever was in Warehouse 14.' He shrugged again. 'Now you know why *you're* not allowed to talk to the important customers – it isn't your image, it's Davies. He's up to *here* in it.'

'Then I'd better tell the old man, hadn't I?' Godwin asked.

They were seated behind a fold of the washed-grey screen of the

266

Reid Davies stand in the main hall of the exposition. Hyde regarded his business suit with suspicion, while Godwin seemed about to erupt from his, the waistcoat riding up over his stomach as he slouched on his chair. The hall's constant noise of air-conditioning, talk, laughter, intruded.

Hyde scratched his nose. 'What about this bloody nerve gas scare?' he asked. 'The old fart sounds more and more like the *Sun* every day.' He grinned. '*Our boys go in – and cover themselves with sores*. I can see the headline now in the Brighter, Bonkaway JIC Digest.' He shrugged. 'I don't see that, do you?'

A tall blonde whisked past them, draped as elegantly and efficiently as a matador's cloak in front of two French businessmen heading for the upper level of the stand and the champagne. It was ten-thirty in the morning. Hyde squinted after them, then shook his head.

'I don't suppose temporary, forced-on-him staff get privileges, do they?' he enquired of the plastic cup. 'Unfair, really, having her first, when we're going to stuff him – wouldn't you say?'

'Am I to tell the old man, or not?'

'Why bother at the moment? I'm going to have a look in Warehouse 14, just to make sure. Then we'll tell Aubrey his nerve gas scare is just that. OK?'

'What if Davies wants to know where you are?'

'Tell him you saw me wandering off with one of the tarts on the Yamaha stand. He'll like that. It'll suitably demean me and convince him. Not that I wouldn't mind –' He finished his coffee. 'Anything else you want me to look at?'

Godwin shook his head.

'There's a lot of warehouse space – much too much, if what they're supposed to be showing is anything to go by.' Godwin flicked through a notebook. 'You can have a go at some of this stuff if you come up empty.' He grinned, looking up again, then added: 'I don't like the old man's dark hints about nerve gas and this bugger Novak, though. I can't discount it as easily as you do.'

'All right, then – *you* watch Novak. You suck up to Aubrey while I solve the mystery. I don't really care.'

'You obviously didn't get much sleep last night.'

'You know me so well, darling.'

'Not that well!'

'Watch out,' Hyde cautioned, still smiling as he squinted through

267

a gap in the folded screen. 'Here's Sonny Jim with a gang of Japs, waving his hands about. I'll fuck off before he sees me.'

'OK – see you. Have a nice day.'

'Do your tie up. Anyone would think you weren't a proper salesman!'

Hyde smiled, then slipped behind the screen, out into the main hall, a structured, designed maze of stands and exhibits. Huge computer mock-ups in plastics or polystyrene, the subtle gaudiness of every known and many unknown electronics companies in the consuming world. Hostesses and salespersons glinting and winking like silver fish in a great pool. The ubiquitous business suits cramming the aisles. The smell of used electricity sharp as saltpetre. The assault of noise.

Everything faded in the stark Venetian sunlight outside the hall. The lagoon shone like a mirror along the horizon and the churches of Venice nudged incompletely, sketchlike through the mid-morning haze. The interior of the Mercedes was hot, plastic-scented. He threw his jacket into the rear and undid his tie. A group of businessmen debouched from a long black limousine outside the hall and patted and laughed each other inside.

Warehouse 14, then . . . Hyde rubbed his face. Davies, eh? He allowed the thought to repeat itself for perhaps the fiftieth time, and bring the same smile to his face. Gotcha. Davies must have been caught in the same expansive, rouble-filled net that had caught Reid Group and Dumas. Just another fish hauled up. No wonder the Russians had a hard currency problem. And a supply of some of the best high-tech in the West. He ran his left hand through his hair. Snapping Davies like a stick would be fun.

He started the engine, pausing for a moment at a thought of Richard Anderson. Not much left for *him*, was there . . . ? He put the car into gear and pulled away from the illusory shadow of the main hall out into the glaring sunlight. A coach from the Piazzale Roma decanted thirty or forty suited men and women into the sun's blows. Hyde watched the rituals of laughter and back-patting and initial salesmanship in the driver's mirror. And, almost in the moment they disappeared, the warehouse was ahead of him. He drew against the side of the hall where he had masked the car the previous night, got out and opened the tailgate. Quickly, he tugged overalls up over his trousers, snapping the clips on his chest, throwing his tie into the well of the boot, then changing his shoes for rubber-soled boots. He collected the loose, oily-looking workman's tool bag which contained the camera and the spare film and the pistol, and strolled across the piazza-like, aching sunlight. He slouched effectively. There were transport vans drawn up in front of the warehouse, and two men lounging in one of them. They disregarded his small-framed, overalled lack of threat. Jesus, I don't even need to get myself tattooed to complete the disguise.

A radio playing old hits, clear enough to make him skip to remembered lyrics and rhythm for a moment, the sunlight heavy on his shoulders, then he was innocently round the angle of the building and hidden from the men in the van. Shale, pebbles, weeds, cracked concrete, the occasional discarded beer or Coke tin; cigarette stubs. He continued to the next corner, and found the ladder to the angled roof, complex enough in slopes and gulleys to have belonged to a Gothic cathedral. Checking his isolation, he began to climb. The building's steel was warm even on this shaded side, the corrugated metal of the roof hot on his palms as he grasped its edge. He looked down. No one. Venice floated offshore like a gaudy, phantasmagorical oil platform.

Skylights . . . oh, *sky*lights . . . He scuttled, his hands and feet making crablike, bony noises on the corrugated roof. He ran doubled up along a gulley, startling pigeons into the air. Swallows moved like needles weaving an intricate piece of embroidery close to the roof, then up into the air, plucking out the thread. Discarded cans indicated sunbathers. He looked at his watch. Still not eleven. He imagined Godwin embarrassedly explaining his absence, and grinned. Venice seemed to have moved in the haze, like a great ship drifting with the tide, the masts of churches, the fo'castles and poops of palazzos and cathedrals and museums merging into one another. Beyond the city, the Lido was lost in the sun's consumption of the water.

Skylight. He dropped to his haunches and peered through the bird-specked, grimy glass. Any warehouse on any new industrial park anywhere. Dusty, sunlit concrete, the movement of a forklift truck, the drift of two shirtsleeved men. He rubbed at the glass gently, his hand wetted with perspiration from his forehead. The sun was angrily heavy on his neck and back, like an animal that had pounced only half in play.

269

He looked up again, not towards the illusory city, but more immediately down at the acres of concrete and other warehouses and exhibition halls. He was invisible, except to the returning pigeons and the flicking swallows. Good . . . he settled back and using the binoculars through the smudge of half-cleared glass, glimpsed Reid Group on two of the crates down there, beneath the skylight.

He stood up, hardly curious, and saw Novak . . . Well, sensed it was him and swung up the glasses and was certain. Getting out of a big BMW with two evident minders from one of the very old schools. Novak, coming towards Warehouse 14.

His disappointment was momentary, but sharp as a child's, as Novak disappeared through the opened doorway of an adjacent, smaller warehouse, followed by the two minders. The door closed behind them and the noise of it arrived a moment later, small as a touch. Hyde, hands on his hips knotted into fists, stared at the glinting BMW, at the closed door and the small warehouse and its low roof.

All in a day's work . . . but I don't . . . I really *don't* – believe there's nerve gas.


The aircraft seemed to wobble slightly, as if adjusting its livery to make the best impression when it landed at Marco Polo. Malan looked down, even as he picked up the telephone from beside his deep seat, and pushed aside the remains of his cooked breakfast. Venice, a city he found attractive for only the briefest stopovers, seemed to be slowly boiling in a silvery, saucepan-like lagoon, so that it threatened at any minute to disappear into the gleam and haze of light.

'Malan,' he announced, picking a shred of bacon from between his teeth. 'Yes?'

It was Blantyre.

'Sorry, Paulus – it's van Vuuren.'

'Yes?'

The city passed beneath the belly of the jet. Mestre's ugliness seemed less well concealed by the heat, then he glimpsed the airport ahead and below.

'He – he's disappeared. Someone came to his house last night – a messenger that stupid wife of his claims – and van Vuuren went off with him.'

'Someone – who?'

'The wife saw a white man's face, she says, on the entryphone screen in the bedroom. Says she watched. Saw nothing, though.'

'A white man?'

'I think it might be Anderson.'

'What does he *want*, Robin?'

'To get even?'

'With *whom*, man? With MLC, for Christ's sake? Robin, you didn't do that well. He even killed Uys – don't ask how I know, I *know*.' The runway was distinguishable now, a narrow strip of concrete savoured by the water on either side of it. The aircraft straightened, its nose down. Then it seemed to plunge at the airport.

'He wants blood, Paulus – or maybe information. He was connected with Aubrey.'

'Twenty-five years ago!'

'Nevertheless, Piet knows everything. I would have said Anderson would have been looking for me, not Piet.'

'You'd better find him, Robin. Quickly. Use all the influence you must, but find him.'

He put down the receiver and stood up, to be assisted into his jacket by the black manservant. Then his seatbelt was deferentially fastened. He attempted to relax, but the moment in which the wheels encountered the runway was unsettling, as if a shiver of apprehension ran through the aircraft and his body. He clenched his right hand as the terminal building emerged from the oil-like slide of deceleration. Anderson had van Vuuren. Why? For Aubrey . . . ?

He began to dismiss the idea, then remembered Aubrey's niece, Kathryn. *He* was blamed –

That bloody old *man*! He clung to things like his father clung to the last scraps of his life. Clung to memories and revenges. His hand continued to clench and unclench.


Anderson looked out of the grimy, cobwebbed window to the derelict forecourt, weed-strewn, and the listing, tired old petrol pumps that remained. The roof of the forecourt sagged wearily. The owner of the petrol station had abandoned the place two years before, heading for Australia and away from the dread of a black majority govern-

271

ment. The forlorn, mistaken little site was on the edge of Diepkloof, where the suburb straggled away towards the great-backed mounds of spoil from the mines. A distant dam's white concrete gleamed in the noon haze. He swallowed Evian water from a big plastic bottle. Behind him, van Vuuren shuffled in his restraints, the legs of his upright chair squeaking on the linoleum that lay cracked and contoured on the floor. A rack still half-filled with nibbled, mouldy paperbacks, a few empty shelves, the smell of disuse. Behind the one room was a tiny kitchen, but the water, electricity and gas had long been disconnected. It was a sad, meaningless place which slowed down, even stopped, the passage of time.

It was perfect.

'Do you want some water, Piet?' he asked, turning to face the man tied on the chair. Van Vuuren scowled silently, wrestling with the rope that held his hands behind him and his feet to the legs of the chair. His thin strands of remaining hair were awry, his pyjama shirt open and sweat-stained – the heat in the place was suffocating.

He was nowhere near collapse. Concerned, yes – especially with regard to his interrupted business life, his trip to Europe. But not unnerved. 'Suit yourself. It's hot for the time of year, I think. Cooler in the Bush.'

'Why don't you fucking well go back there, then?' van Vuuren raged, struggling with the ropes and moving the chair with small protesting squeaks. 'Why did you come here, man? What do you want with me – why don't you *tell* me what you want?' His reddened face glared.

'You want to talk?' Anderson asked.

He had left van Vuuren alone, gagged and immobilized, while he had driven to a supermarket in Diepkloof for supplies. He'd taken his time, then driven around. He had been silent for the most part while they were together. But van Vuuren seemed incapable of working through his outrage, his snatched-away comforts of large house, money, family, and arriving at isolation. It was as if Anderson was still the outsider, the not-quite-real; the kaffir presence that was little more than a shadow or a dream. Even now, he remained defiant, glancing at the window each time a car passed, with certainty rather than with fearful, desperate hope. There was only the occasional car. A new motorway had taken most of the traffic years before. Perhaps the garage owner hadn't left merely out of bigotry and fear, after all.

'You want to talk, Piet?' he repeated.

'Don't you fucking call me *Piet*, man!' he shouted back. '*Mister* van Vuuren to you!' His accent grated as he raged, straining against the ropes and his circumstances.

'OK, Piet – you don't want to talk. Not yet.'

'*Mister* van Vuuren, you bastard!'

Anderson smiled and shook his head.

'Mr van Vuuren. You don't seem to think I'm in earnest. This – ' He gestured at the decaying room. ' – isn't real to you, somehow. I assure you it is.' His own accent was more deliberate, dismissively aloof. 'We are safe from discovery here, for a long time. I have supplies – enough for myself for twice as long. If you wish to drink and eat, you must learn the art of compromise.'

'You English bastard – what do you *want*?' It was the outrage of Afrikaanerdom, of membership of the Broederbond, of sleek wealth and real power. This could *not*, in *Johannesburg*, be happening to him; he refused to believe it.

'Information,' Anderson sighed. Van Vuuren wasn't ready, but his own impatience prompted. He dragged a chair opposite van Vuuren and straddled it, leaning his forearms on its ladder back, the bottle in one hand. He stared at his prisoner. 'Information that will enable me to destroy Blantyre – pull the house down around even Paulus Malan. I want to know about the shipments and the KGB officer who died in the DC-3 and who owns what and what is being smuggled. *And* why my wife was murdered.' He watched van Vuuren as he sipped at the bottle's narrow neck. Clicking his tongue in satisfaction, he stared at the man once more. 'I am deadly serious, but you're beginning to sense that, aren't you?'

'You think *you* can take us on – take on MLC – and *win*?'

'I am –' He swallowed. '– a man without a future, van Vuuren.' He spoke with soft, plausible menace. The involuntary brightening of his eyes added its penn'orth of conviction. 'I am – bereft, lost. I don't suppose you understand, do you – not with that plain wife of yours and your habits of occasional congress with good-looking blacks and Coloureds?' He stood up suddenly, as if his emotions were too betraying. Facing the window, he said: 'My wife was classified as Coloured, van Vuuren – did you know that? Ironic, isn't it? Having lost her, I have lost, as the poet said, the better half of myself.' He turned to face van Vuuren, the light from the window behind him. 'I have nothing more to lose, and a single purpose. Justice, revenge – you may use which term you prefer. And I will have that justice . . .' He was leaning over van Vuuren now. 'I doubt you've ever killed anything bigger than a gazelle, van Vuuren. I have killed a lot of people. Recently, I killed Blantyre's man in Swakopmund. Discovered it could still be done, quite easily. Therefore, either you assist me or I destroy you, and bury you behind this shed, or throw you into one of the underground storage tanks out there –' He gestured at the window. ' – or, I don't. An alternative would be to allow the first kaffir-dominated government to bring you to trial for rape and assault –' He turned his back quickly and moved again to the window. 'That would *ruin* you utterly. A fate worse than death, surely?' He chuckled softly, then listened, his back still to van Vuuren.

Eventually: 'I don't know what you mean, man. You won't kill me.'

'I might have to, if you're not afraid of disgrace.' He stared at the reddish earth lying like a range of low hills in the haze. The Reef; the power. He turned. 'You really have forgotten, haven't you? Forgotten *me* and forgotten Veronica Mokesi, too.'

The girl's name evidently was forgotten. Van Vuuren strained towards Anderson in the gloom of the hut, which creaked softly in the sun, then shook his head.

'You've got some grudge against me, man – why didn't you say? I don't even remember you! I get you the sack, you lose your pension rights, or something?'

'Nothing like that. Bright, Seaward, Seaward and Anderson, solicitors to the powerful, white and wealthy. You really don't remember?'

Slowly, van Vuuren shook his head, in disbelief rather than at a failure of memory. Anderson sighed.

'The Englishman? The house *Englishman* in that firm? *You?*' He could hardly believe it. 'So, you're that bloke? So *what?* You've got a bill I haven't paid?' He laughed, but his voice was becoming more hoarse. Anderson offered the bottle and van Vuuren shook his head vehemently.

'Suit yourself. Now you remember me, do you recall Veronica?'

'Who? Is that your wife's name? Might have guessed you'd have married a kaffir girl. Yes, I remember Bright told me they kept you on as the firm's conscience. The respectable, liberal front man.'

'You think I was unaware of that?'

'Doesn't matter. Your efforts weren't worth elephant dung, man – and you know it. You were just salving your English conscience.'

'Agreed. It was a wasted time. No, Veronica Mokesi was not the name of my wife. Veronica was one of your secretaries. She didn't work for you for long. Didn't enjoy the little attentions you paid her.'

Van Vuuren's face was puzzled, and he frowned for memory like a child. When he did remember, his confidence seemed undiminished.

'I remember something.' His smile was lascivious. 'So what, man?' He shrugged in his restraints.

'So what? I have the files – from Bright, Seaward & Seaward, no less. Her statements to me, photographs which were taken at the time – she was very bruised. *Your* statement, transcribed from a tape recording.'

'What can you do with them?'

'Ruin you. Paulus Malan would be deeply embarrassed – MLC would be outraged. The boys in the Bond –' He smiled. '– oh, dear, wouldn't they be upset. Mandela and the ANC would press for your arrest in a *quid pro quo* for dear Winnie's misbehaviour and her sentence, mm?' Van Vuuren's eyes began to see, quite lucidly, the possible future. 'At the least, your wife would have to sue for a messy and public divorce. Things have changed, Piet. You would be a *cause célèbre*, as they say. A fate worse than death?'

Van Vuuren shook his head. 'You don't mean it.'

'Oh, but I do. I assure you I do.'

'*Why?*'

'Oh, you mean – why should I *care*? I don't really. I admit that. It serves my purpose. The ANC would care, though, wouldn't they?'

Van Vuuren's mouth opened slightly, like a widening settlement crack in fresh plaster. The slow, inexorable subsidence had, perhaps, begun. Then he shook his head defiantly.

'It would be hushed up, man – it would *still* be hushed up.'

'Perhaps.' Anderson shrugged. Van Vuuren's voice was very hoarse now, and he tilted the bottle invitingly in the man's direction. A few drops of Evian fell to the linoleum, disturbing foraging ants. Who returned to inspect the droplets. At Blantyre's insistence or even that of Malan, the police would already be scurrying like the ants, looking for him. 'Perhaps.' Van Vuuren could not be disabused of belief in a rescuing cavalry bugle which would sound at any moment. 'I shouldn't count on a burial other than your own – unless you cooperate. The files are in my briefcase, on the counter there.' Van Vuuren's head swung quickly, possessively. 'You may take them with you when you leave. If you give me what I want. If you don't, of course, then you won't be leaving at all. I couldn't risk my own safety by letting you survive. Could I?'


Godwin sat in the rear of the taxi, behind the indifferent driver who lit another cigarette as soon as he tugged on the handbrake and picked up his newspaper. The dust settled around the car – *English private eye, uh? Divorce?* Godwin's nod had been sufficient to still any vestigial curiosity. The cypresses and cedars were dark against the sky, reaching back from the high, closed gates towards the white stuccoed villa. The dark green shutters were opened back, and there was a glint of distant water from a high fountain.

The limousine had turned in, after the gates had opened electronically, taking Malan and Michael Davies inside. The dust was settling from the vehicle's passage along the ochre drive.

Godwin got out of the taxi and lumped himself to comfort on his sticks. Thus propped, he studied the gates, the dark stains of the trees and the large, elegant residence beyond them. In the distance and the midday haze, the Eugenean hills struggled to possess more substance than in a painting of themselves. The villa was on the Padua road, fifteen miles from Mestre. Hyde had suspected it might once have been a KGB R and R house. It might well have been. Certainly, Babbington was now inside, awaiting his lunch guests. Godwin rubbed his sheened forehead and pushed back his hair with a large hand. The traffic was light off the main highway to Padua and Verona. He'd followed Davies out of the exhibition hall, and recognized Paulus Malan – grabbed the taxi, *follow that car* – and it had drawn him all the way out here, to the place Babbington had been brought the previous night.

Not that he was going to creep up to the house for his evidence.

A photo-opportunity beckoned whenever they left the villa again, as the limousine turned out of the gates.

He reached back into the rear of the taxi with a smile of satisfaction and lifted out the cellular phone. *I've told you not to ring me while I'm at work*, Patrick would probably complain. Still, he shouldn't be in a position to be overheard talking. He dialled the number. No ringing out, just a flashing light. If he couldn't answer, he wouldn't. The tiny answerphone in the casing of the receiver would tape his message. *I'll get back to you.* Wonderful thing, science. He leant against the bole of a stringy-looking sycamore at the side of the road. There were other villas dotting the landscape, small as cattle in their neat grounds, behind their tiny fountains. Vineyards and orchards stretched away towards the bruise-coloured hills to the west. He scented lemon on the slight, dust-sifting breeze. He stretched luxuriously. Naughty Mike Davies – shame, really. He quite liked the guy. Must have had some bad breaks, needed funds to save the company – been photographed with another woman, a man . . . ? Whatever, Babbington and Malan had got their hooks into him. And Aubrey would have to decide what to do about it, not him, thank God. Come on, Patrick, check the light on your phone, you berk. Aubrey could gut Davies like a haddock, get every shred of proof they needed. Now, it was just a matter of stopping whatever was in Warehouse 14 from going any further east or south. He leaned his cheek against his shoulder, the receiver trapped there, and rubbed his hands. Look at your light, you silly bugger – or switch on the answerphone. Science might be wonderful, Hyde's inattention to detail wasn't. Poor old Davies – it could be his last nice lunch for a long time. Perhaps the old man would fly out –

'Yes? Where the hell have you been, in the bog?'

'I'm on the roof of a fucking warehouse, watching our old Czechmate pissing about below me. Arrived with a couple of minders half an hour ago.'

'Where? Number 14?'

'No, next door. I wonder why?'

'I'm out at that villa – Davies is here with Malan.'

'Tell Aubrey. He'll have apoplexy.'

'Listen, I got our Italian friends to check on Novak's room, his reservation, tickets, et cetera.'

'Yes?'

'He tried to get hold of van Vuuren – his home number, office, carphone, anything he could think of – more than two dozen times this morning. Must have got into a panic when he couldn't find him.'

'Is van Vuuren on his way here?'

'Room's booked at the Cipriani, same as Malan. Expected today some time.'

'That's all right, then.'

'Novak wants van Vuuren but not Malan – he hasn't been near him.'

'So?'

'I just wondered. Novak did have a call from Johannesburg, just before he left for the warehouse. It was Blantyre. What the message was no one knows. Blantyre and van Vuuren, mm? Makes you think – what with *another* warehouse being used. I wonder if Babbington knows?'

'Doesn't matter, does it?'

'I don't know – but you'd better find out what's in there. Perhaps there's something wrong with van Vuuren?'

'Maybe. Anderson was going after him. Perhaps the bugger got to him?'

'Just see what's in that warehouse, will you, that's so important to van Vuuren, Blantyre and Novak?'

'Don't give me the nerve gas story, please.'

'It's a side deal, whatever it is. And there are people who'd like it on hand – even like to use it – in South Africa.'

'All right, all right. *You* take some pictures and ring the old man. Find out when he wants us to lift Davies, what we do about Babbington – and Warehouse 14.'

'OK. See you.'

He switched off the phone and then stared at it. Time to call the old man, then. He wouldn't like it. Apoplexy was right. Poor old Davies – Aubrey's disapproval would make him squirm more than the thought of twenty years inside!


There was a moment, seated in van Vuuren's study, with the gazelle-skin rugs on the deep carpet and the kaffir bric-à-brac clinging to the panelled walls, when he realized that he detested van Vuuren. As well as most of their mutual associates in the Bond, even Paulus Malan. It was little more than a moment, but very real, like an indigestive pain. Then Robin Blantyre continued dialling the number of Novak's carphone, having failed to contact the Czech at his hotel. It was all slightly unclean – no, not that – it had been unclean for a long time. He had retreated south from Rhodesia to South Africa and had spent years in the South-West fighting SWAPO with the Defence Forces and the Selous Scouts. Even then, he felt his integrity had been soiled, by others. It was nothing but the protection of profit, of gold and diamonds.

The phone rang in Novak's car.

Van Vuuren's wife had slipped through the study door like a black servant, leaving him alone. The police had been briefed, they had Anderson's picture to distribute, his own people were mining the man's background and raking over abandoned buildings. They knew what car to look for, *who* to look for. The rest was a matter of time. He would be run down, dug out and got rid of. Van Vuuren . . . ? It would depend, he thought, as he forensically examined the study and its whispers of money and self-satisfaction. Even Anderson had the right idea, the Bush was better than all this.

'Novak? Blantyre,' he said when the phone in Novak's car was answered. He listened for a moment to the Czech's earlier nerves being regurgitated, a twist of contempt on his mouth. Then he said: 'The money's *there*, man. No, van Vuuren's got stomach trouble, I told you. He's been delayed. The plan goes ahead – yes. *You* do what's necessary, man – do it. Yes, tonight. Everything's arranged. *Then* I release the funds, yes . . .'

He looked at the ceiling. It was a constant process of corruption, backsliding, impropriety. Novak had a villa in Majorca, he was renovating a palace in the Czech countryside, he had the Swiss account. And, like van Vuuren, it was always *more* he wanted. Van Vuuren's arrangement with Novak was bringing them money – that was their shared motive. Fuck the Republic, fuck South Africa and the white man – so long as we have the money to get out!

It applied to Paulus, too, he reacknowledged as he murmured to Novak: 'Yes, that's right. Once the shipment touches down and I've inspected it, the authorization will be sent to Zürich.' Don't worry, you bastard, you'll get the money.

Paulus, too. Cosying with the fucking Communists and a traitor, Babbington – thinking about moving MLC out of South Africa because he wouldn't stay and fight for what he'd always believed.

'No!' he snapped at Novak. 'You watch out for Hyde, and for the cripple, Godwin. You've been sent the photographs. Don't get near them, or let them near you or the shipment. Other than that, Novak, I don't give a fuck with a gazelle what you do or what happens to you. Yes, that's right. Just business. If this first shipment's good, then there'll be new orders. Sure.'

He put down the receiver and glanced around the room. These white men who filled their places with African rubbish. Did they think that made them *belong*? Paulus and van Vuuren . . . running out, one way or another. Not him, though – oh no, not him.

He almost admired Anderson, and his motive. You killed my wife, I'll get back at you any way I can. It was clean, comprehensible. It had nothing to do with money, or traitors, or servants of the Crown like fucking Hyde, who he would like to meet again, just once more . . .

Mrs van Vuuren sidled her face around the study door, as if she might be asking whether he would like tea or when he would be leaving. Blantyre stood up. Look at her, he thought, fat, white and forty-five. Needs a hair-do, some make-up, and she'd still be ugly as sin. No wonder van Vuuren preferred the kaffir girls, the little shit.

'I'll be going now,' he announced, passing her. 'You've got my number if he calls. And –' He turned, looming over her. '– if he calls, make sure you tell me. Understand, Mrs van Vuuren?' The woman nodded dumbly, terrified by his bulk in her hall, reflected from the polished mahogany floor.

Blantyre went outside, squinting in the noon sun. When and if van Vuuren called, then it would be neater, tidier, if he died. Anderson could be blamed. A sudden and only half-expected rage of contempt for his acquaintances rose into his chest. They rocked the secure cradle of his world more violently than the ANC and Mandela and the de Villiers government had ever been able to do. Bastards –

He'd find Anderson and van Vuuren and kill them.

# strike on the tinder

'Yes, Westfield and I will be with you by late afternoon . . . yes, yes. No, I'll use our Italian friends when it becomes necessary — you say there's no sense of immediate removal of the goods from either warehouse?'

Godwin squinted in the afternoon sun, across orchards, vineyards and olive groves stretching away towards distant hills.

'No, sir, I don't think so.'

'Then Patrick has time to make a closer inspection, if he can gain ingress to the target area. Is that possible?'

'He thinks he can get in from the roof.'

'Then let him do so. In safety. For yourself, I see no real necessity for photographs of anyone except Davies, so you'd better hang on there in the hope of obtaining something picturesquely incriminating. Then you may detain him. At least restrict his movements until I have a chance to confront him. That other warehouse, by the way . . . ?'

'Patrick's still sniffy about the nerve agent scenario.'

'Naturally. I wonder if Michael Davies can help us there?' There was a pause, then: 'I would *not* have believed it of him.'

Godwin grinned. Nothing like righteous indignation. Davies was up shit creek. The old man's wrath and technique would fall on him like a ton of bricks.

'No, sir. He might have got stuck in the mud like Reid himself —'

'Perhaps, perhaps.'

'Are we rounding them all up, sir? Making a big splash?'

'I — the Cabinet Secretary and — other informed opinion, would prefer not. Arrest whom we must, but quietly.'

'There's a bloody warehouse full of high-tech, sir. It'll take more than a Ford Transit —'

'I have a thought regarding that aspect of the matter. It would be better if it – disappeared. *Not* east or south, of course. I'll consider. Where is Priabin?'

Godwin looked at the tall gates. Priabin had got out of a small, hired Alfa half an hour earlier, bent towards the entryphone, grinned up into its lens, and the gates had been opened for him. The girl had been driving the car.

'He's here, too. Nice lunch laid on, I expect.'

'But there is no sign that matters might be coming to an immediate head – *no* sign?'

'No, sir. I'd say tomorrow.'

'Priabin must have been *running* Davies!' Aubrey suddenly burst out. 'Clever young man!'

'Aren't they all, sir? But we've got them by the short and curlies now.'

'Tell Patrick that the warehouses are of the utmost importance. And tell him to be *certain* what they contain. *Each* of them.'

'Worried it's going too smoothly, sir?'

'Perhaps. Ah, the car is here. Maintain contact. But get hold of Davies as soon as he is separated from his friends.'

The receiver purred and Godwin switched it off, letting it dangle from his wrist by its strap. Hyde was certainly going to *love* his afternoon on a hot tin roof.

Distantly, Venice floated in the haze and glitter of the lagoon. Mestre sprawled, its thrown-together ugliness softened by the heat. The Lido lay like a sandbank across the steel-coloured water. Godwin brought a plastic packet containing cheese sandwiches from his pocket, ripped its film covering and began eating. The taxi driver had had wine, salami and thick, crusty bread – without offering him any.

It'd be better if they burned the bloody warehouses down ... not if there's nerve agent though. Patrick had better check the sprinkler system, if there is one. Chewing on the indigestible, soapy bread – did the Italians import British white sliced for these bloody sandwiches? – he dialled Hyde's cellular phone.


'Keep down!' Anderson whispered fiercely as van Vuuren struggled in his grip like a frightened cat, his eyes bulging and his lips attempting to form a shout behind the gag. He drew the pistol and pressed it against van Vuuren's temple, and the man's efforts subsided into still resentment, a lassitude of desperation. 'That's better.'

He raised his head and looked over the grass-clumped sandy knoll, back down towards the abandoned petrol station. The police car had passed, then slowed and turned on the dusty road, heading back towards them. He had stifled van Vuuren's first attempt to cry out, gagged him, released his legs and dragged him out of the rear door and up the slight rise behind the hut. Their footprints were as big as those of some huge, maddened animal in the soft sand. If the two policemen – one of them was still in the patrol car – searched for signs, they'd find their tracks at once.

Van Vuuren squirmed beside him, belly-down on the sand. Anderson pressed the barrel of the pistol harder against his sweating temple. Quietude almost at once, except for the shiver of fear that trembled through the man's body. The policeman peered through the cracked, grimy windows, then pulled open the door. He paused on the step – Anderson could just see him, around the edge of the long hut. The supplies he had bought were in the kitchen behind the main room, the empty Evian bottles lay on the floor. There was the chair . . .

The policeman disappeared, then almost at once reappeared around the corner of the building, his cap pushed back on his head, his stride unsuspicious, unhurried. He glanced up at the knoll, shading his eyes for a moment, then turned on his heel and headed back to the patrol car, drawn up under the dappling shade of the forecourt's decaying roof. He shook his head as he climbed back into the car.

Anderson's relief as the car pulled out towards the road was a cattle-prod to van Vuuren, who rose to his knees and bullied Anderson aside. He toppled himself over the lip of the incline, rolling before getting to his feet and beginning to run, his head flailing from side to side and his legs floundering, as if they were waving to attract attention because his arms were still tied behind his back. He raised the pistol, then realized the danger of the noise and the risk of killing van Vuuren. Instead, he tumbled after him, leaping on the man's back and dragging him flat. Sand was in his eyes and mouth as he looked up. Blinking away wetness, he saw the police car begin to hurry away down the road towards Diepkloof. He was breathing violently as he rolled off the man and lay facing him, the pistol aimed at van Vuuren's face. The eyes died as if some light had been switched off behind them.

Now, Anderson told himself, now, while's he's deflated, feels his last chance has gone. He stood up, dragging van Vuuren to his knees by gripping his pyjama collar; then dragged him by one bound arm towards the lee of the building, thrusting him inside as if throwing the man away like a sack of rubbish. He slammed the rear door behind them, pushing van Vuuren ahead of him into the main room and onto the chair. The violence of his breathing was an added terror to the South African as he was tied to the chair. Anderson stood back, making sure the pistol was in plain sight as he deliberately opened another bottle of water and swallowed greedily, then used more of it to wash the sand from his face and eyes. Van Vuuren watched with impotent malevolence, as Anderson poured some onto the floor, then shouted: 'Listen to me, you Afrikaaner *shit*!' His body was bent towards van Vuuren, the pistol waggling beside his thigh, as if it might accidentally fire at any moment, discharged by the force of his rage. 'Listen to me! I want to know things, and I want to know them *now*. Understand? Either you start telling me, or I won't wait to ruin you the legitimate way. You'll be reading about your divorce from your wheelchair! Understand me, van Vuuren?' He moved closer in a quick, pouncing step. '*Understand?*'

Van Vuuren was terrified, as if he believed Anderson insane. His eyes flicked from the pistol to his face, to the pistol. He tried to swallow, even attempted to speak, but only hoarse, tired gobbling noises came from behind the gag –

– which Anderson roughly removed. There were no words, even then, only louder scrapings and swallowings. Hefting the Evian bottle from the counter, he tilted it to van Vuuren's lips and the man swallowed greedily; then he snatched it away.

Narrow hatred flared in van Vuuren's eyes. 'What do you – *want*?' he wailed hoarsely. 'Why are you doing this to me, you bastard?' Veins stood out on his temples, and the cords of his neck were drawn taut.

Anderson realized he must possess the appearance of some malevolent ghost, and employed even that to his advantage.

'I want *you*!' he bellowed, his own neck tautened, his temples throbbing. 'If I can't bring down Malan, then I'll settle for you – and kill Blantyre from a distance some dark night!' He held up his hands in front of van Vuuren, palms inwards. 'See these fingernails? My partners always asked me to keep my hands out of sight whenever we had important clients! The KGB pulled the nails out in the cellars of the Lubyanka – they never grew straight or clean again!' Theatrically, he dipped his hand into the briefcase and pulled out a pair of pliers, still polythened onto their manufacturer's cardboard rectangle. 'You'll be luckier, van Vuuren! Your hands are behind your back. You won't have to watch while I do it to you!'

He paused and drank from the bottle again. What had Aubrey wanted to know, precisely? It was, of course, difficult to recall everything he and Aubrey had discussed over the telephone, from that call box half a mile towards Diepkloof. There was so much detail. How long, how much, by what means? It seemed to have very little to do with justice, with *his* satisfaction.

'I lost my first wife to lovers and finally to cancer. I lost my second to a *faked atrocity meant to kill me!* Do you think I give a fuck what happens to *you*?' He grinned, then took up the pliers and pulled away the polythene case. He held them up, then picked up the file on Veronica Mokesi, waving them both loosely in his fingers. 'One or the other, van Vuuren. Of course, choose the wrong one and you won't even be able to *hold* the other when I hand it over – will you?'

Aubrey had said it was urgent – there was something he could hardly bring himself to speak of. Nerve gas, for van Vuuren's friends? Whoever they were – the boys in the Bond, the AWB. Yes, he had replied, they'd like the insurance of something like nerve gas – they'd like to wear a VX canister slung under their potbellies instead of a mere pistol. Oh, yes . . .

All the moments he was silent, he stared at the ceiling, dragging in large, threatening, unstable breaths. Then he looked down at his prisoner.

'See? Who *cares*, van Vuuren? I can do it. I've killed men with guns, explosives, booby traps, piano wire – anything I could lay my hands on.' He snorted. 'Who's the nerve gas for?'

It was *true*, he realized, in the betraying instant before van Vuuren shook his head.

'Don't know what you mean!'

He laid down the file and kept the pliers very visible, as he said: 'But we know that's a lie, don't we? How can you convince me you're telling the truth?' He made a dart behind van Vuuren's back, the pliers extended and open in his right hand.

'*No* –!'

He closed them firmly on the nail of the right forefinger.

'No – no!'

He leaned caressingly against van Vuuren's shoulder and cheek, like a lover.

'Tell me, then . . . tell me,' he whispered.

Van Vuuren's head dropped, shaking from side to side, but the denials meant nothing. 'How did you know?'

He smoothed van Vuuren's hair and neck like a whore, then tilted the Evian bottle against the man's lips. Van Vuuren's frame shivered, like a frail dwelling in a violent storm. When he had finished drinking, he took the bottle away gently, then patted the man's shoulder.

Nerve agent. Last man in the *laager*. While ninety per cent of white South Africans were either resigned, accepting or even optimistic, the other ten per cent would do *anything* to change their world back to what it had been. Nerve gas, guns . . . it fitted.

'Now – *why* did you get involved?' he asked.

Van Vuuren stared at the floor.

'They're selling us down the river, man.' He looked up, glaring. 'Who could expect *you* to understand? This is *our* country, man!'

'Theirs, too.'

Van Vuuren snarled: 'Most of the kaffirs have been here less time than the English. You think – man, you really *think* – they'll play by the rules, once they get their hands on power? They're shooting each other in the townships because they're Zulu or non-Zulu right now! You think *we* would stand any chance?' He coughed, and Anderson nursed the bottle to his lips. Best to leave him to fulminate. He stepped back, and van Vuuren glared at him, straining forward against the rope.

'Man, you English are so bloody *ignorant*! *Years* now since they let that kaffir bastard Mandela out of prison, and there's more people dying every day – *blacks!* – than during the state of emergency. That's what you call progress, is it?' He shook his head in contempt. 'You think we're all pig-ignorant Afrikaaners with rotten fucking accents, I know your kind! But we – we *know*, man. We know how it will be, people like me and Robin Blantyre and some of our politicians and businessmen. Unless the kaffirs can get their house in order, then we're not prepared to hand everything over to them, just like that! Whatever it takes, whatever we can get our hands on, we'll use – just like you English would if it was *your* bloody country!'

The silence which followed seemed endless, punctuated only by their mutually ragged breaths and the droning of some large insect up near the corrugated roof of the hut. Eventually, recalling Aubrey's conversation, Anderson said: 'And this is where Novak comes into the picture, is it? You met him through EuroCon – you realized he had things you could make use of. At least, hoard against the rainy day? Is that it?'

'You know a hell of a lot, Englishman.' Van Vuuren was genuinely disorientated by the extent of his information.

'You think I'm entirely alone, van Vuuren?' He shook his head. 'I sent some evidence from the crash to London. To people I know. It tied in with what they knew. I said you'd be able to fill out the picture, in exchange for your life. So, nerve gas is the answer, is it? To *all* our problems?'

'You think we'd use it if we didn't have to?'

'I've no idea. It'll be stopped in Venice, anyway.' Van Vuuren appeared dumbstruck. 'Oh, yes, it's not coming here –' Pray God. '– it's dealt with. It's the penetration – extent, persons, purposes – that people want from you in exchange for your life. Get it now?'

Van Vuuren's features were charted with conflicting fear, doubt, contempt – and the overriding sense of being tricked.

'You don't know anything!' he snapped, straining forward, the rope across his chest imbedded in his flesh. 'You're just piss-arsing about, hoping to catch something on the end of the line!'

Anderson had no notion of how much bluff there was in his defiance. He said coldly: 'You think I'm just an *agent*, do you, van Vuuren? The people in London – you think I'm restrained in some way. People to answer to, that kind of thing. Well, maybe I was once –' He had begun to circle van Vuuren's chair, not touching him, rather abstracted and diffident, if anything. But as regular and inexorable as the ticking of a clock towards an explosion. 'I was something like you imagine – once. A long time ago . . . but you

287

know that. I don't work for them now, haven't for years.' Van Vuuren had sunk back on the chair, uneasy with the pedagogic tone. 'It was pure accident – finding the wreckage. Maybe I sent them the stuff because of auld lang syne. But I'm *here* because *I* choose. Understand? I want to ruin Malan and Blantyre for what they did to *me*. To begin with, there is a great desire in me –' He turned to face van Vuuren, stopping in front of him, holding out the pliers once more. '– to do it now. *Your* schemes, the ones you've admitted to, killed my wife, van Vuuren. There really isn't anything more to say, is there?' The gleam of his eyes was hardly pretended. It was true, he could strike out this moment, hurt and humiliate and revenge himself. 'Why don't I have fun with you, for my wife's sake?'

Van Vuuren appeared to be listening. There was the hard, sharp intrusion of birdsong for a moment from outside, and the mutter of a receding car. Almost half a minute later, another car. Anderson watched the plump, collapsed figure in the chair. More quietly, he said: 'I have nothing more to lose. I am one of those desperate people usually encountered in fiction. I have nothing left, van Vuuren.'

He did not even look at the man, rather stared at the fly-specked ceiling and the still fan and grubby striplight; then at the abandoned, empty shelving and the greasy counter and rusty till. He could almost hear the termites in the structure. Another car passing outside, as if its noise was funnelled from a great distance, then in the ensuing silence, the sift of sand against the planking of the walls. His throat was dry with talking, constricted with memory, and his eyes felt tight, squeezed. Margarethe was coming back, out of the tidy darkness at the back of his mind.

Looking down, having blinked his eyes wide, he murmured: 'You see, van Vuuren, I'm everyone's fantasy of freedom of action. No consequences.'

Then he moved swiftly, gritting his teeth as he passed behind van Vuuren, and gripped one of his fingers with the pliers, tugging at once at the nail, wincing against the scream as blood poured from the damaged hand. He let the freed nail drop from the grip of the pliers, themselves bloody at the bright tips, then clamped his hand over the open, screaming mouth, shuddering at what he had done. The cellars of the Lubyanka; he'd crossed more than a Rubicon.

Then he remembered nerve gas and Veronica Mokesi and Margarethe. His stomach began to settle, and eventually van Vuuren's shudders lessened and there seemed to be no stifled noises vibrating against his wet palm. Then he released the man and moved to confront him, bending over him, the Evian bottle tilted against his lips. His dampened hand patting the man's flinching brow.

'Now?' he asked, eventually. 'Without any more of it.' He felt cold in the foetid air of the shedlike building which smelt of rat-droppings and sand and van Vuuren's loosened bowels. He suppressed a shiver.

Van Vuuren was sobbing with pain and shock. And nodding, rhythmically as a pendulum, without thought. For the moment, he would do anything. It was time to disinfect and bandage the finger. The flies had deserted their sweating foreheads – they'd already have settled on the blood. Time to put the savage away until required, for Blantyre and Malan.

Now that van Vuuren would talk, he could feel a certain narrow sympathy for him. And relief, too . . .

Godwin slapped his insensitive thighs with his large hands, and glared at the camera he had thrown down on the rear seat beside him. Bloody waste of time! Bloody tinted windows that half-obscured Malan – and Davies travelling back on his own with that bloody girl Valentina! They already had pictures of those two cosying.

The taxi drifted in the settling dust behind the small Alfa which the girl was driving. Godwin looked at his watch again. Three-thirty. Hyde still on the roof, complaining about the heat and the delay – and the security that prevented him from going through a skylight and checking either warehouse. The old man had said Patrick could go in. He just couldn't *get* in, that was the trouble; too many people about.

Which meant Davies. The road straightened from its twists, and emerged from beneath ranks of oaks then dipped towards a Venice becalmed and glittering. Davies – he'd have him in straight away – might even be able to persuade him to cooperate, let them see inside at least one of the warehouses.

He sat back against the hot plastic, feeling his shirt stick to it and slide greasily as buttered paper around a baking tin. He grinned. He did feel hungry, in fact. Coffee and a piece of rich cake wouldn't go amiss. Davies could have room service bring some up while they discussed his immediate future.

The Alfa reached the causeway out to the city and the taxi followed, after Godwin waved the driver to proceed. His shrug was stereotypical. It was too hazy to make out the airport to the north from the Ponte della Libertà. The islands of Murano and San Michele were basking whales, without contour or feature. A train, pulling out of the city, passed them on the parallel railway bridge. Then they had reached the first campanile and palazzo, and modernity threatened to vanish until they reached the Piazzale Roma and the vast car parks. The Alfa drifted away beneath a barrier as his driver pulled into the taxi rank. Godwin heaped bright Italian currency into his hand and got out of the hot interior into the humid afternoon. Davies wouldn't walk in this – he'd take a water taxi or even a gondola. He'd meet them there, save looking for the Alfa in that crowd.

However, he waited until he saw Davies, attentive to the Russian girl, perhaps overly so, leaving the car park, the jacket of his suit trailing over his shoulder. The girl seemed indifferent, even as if she were pretending not to be his companion. Godwin hobbled after them, obscured by a crowd that had debouched from coaches, down a narrow *calle* towards the landing stage. Presumably, Davies' efforts at ingratiation implied they were returning to the Gritti Palace – Davies was not described as monogamous in his file. The girl looked as if she wouldn't be spending the afternoon in his suite. Godwin hesitated. The *vaporetti* and the smaller *motoscafi* ran every ten minutes from the Piazzale Roma. He could afford to wait for the next one, whichever route they took. He waited, in the narrow entrance to the *calle*, behind the milling passengers.

Thought so . . . Davies was taking the *accelerato* route along the Grand Canal – give the girl a sightseeing tour, soften her up, probably. If he took the *diretto* route via the Rio Nuovo – no scenery – he'd reach San Marco before them, maybe even get as far as the Gritti Palace before they did.

He shuffled forward on his sticks as the *vaporetto* pulled away from the landing stage towards the first long bend of the Grand Canal. He reached the end of the queue, hot, but satisfied. Anticipating the shocked look on Davies' face – *who's been a naughty boy, then?* – as he opened the door of the suite. He touched the pistol in his pocket. Just in case. The *motoscafo* churned the languid grey water of the canal and bumped against the landing stage. Godwin shuffled behind a jabbering family – three children who communicated only in high-pitched screams – up the gangway onto the deck.

The tired dusty trees of the Giardino Papadopoli, then a stretch of dank, high houses before the single church until the Rio Foscari emptied them into the Grand Canal. The city eventually reassumed its weary beauty and much recorded face as he looked ahead from the stern of the *motoscafo*, over heads and lenses. He saw Santa Maria della Salute like a mound of grubby snow in the haze and the palazzos that had become hotels lining the route towards the church.

Godwin disembarked at the San Marco landing stage and struggled through the heat and crowds past the artists and their daubs, and into the crowded narrow *calle* up to San Moisè. Finally, he reached the rear entrance of the Gritti Palace, and the chance to lounge in brief shade as gratefully as one of the thin dogs or thinner cats. The crowds drifted past, most of them organized, some in smaller groups, even couples. Suited men entered the Gritti Palace, and one or two sleek with more casual wealth. He hefted the sports bag on his broad shoulder and was content to wait.

Eventually, Davies and Valentina. She was laughing now, even touching at his arm as at something she might examine more closely. The girl who had tried, very hard, to murder Patrick. Good job it was him, not Hyde, standing in the shade of Santa Maria, as they went into the foyer of the hotel. Godwin was puzzled. The girl had demonstrated the indifference of a taxi driver. Now, rearing its ugly head, the beast with two backs. On the other hand, maybe they had mirrors on the ceiling in the Gritti Palace, or something else just as intriguing . . . or perhaps a canal-view suite and a drink heavily iced was sufficient for her to be pleasant to Davies. What's a bonk between friends, after all? He prepared to wait, looking at his watch. Four-ten. The old man would be landing soon, flustered, dark-suited, insistent as a Dalek that his enemies be exterminated. Godwin laughed aloud, to the alarm of a Japanese with a huge lens and a small woman.

Four-fifteen . . . four-twenty. *Have another, why don't you? Are you trying to get me drunk, Mr Davies?* Four twenty-five.

291

And then, the thought of Shapiro ... as the girl, Valentina, emerged with studiedly casual haste from the hotel and turned right over the little hump of a bridge towards the Via 22 Marzo. Shapiro's death was superimposed upon a sense of her professional persona and her proximity to Davies – and there was the hotel, the imagined suite overlooking the Grand Canal and now, very vividly, Shapiro's dead face looking up at the ceiling of his London hotel room. The girl had done it, to stop a leak.

Godwin all but started after her, then shambled violently towards the foyer doors, which slid open to receive him. Take Davies in now, anyway, assuming he wasn't ... Jesus, he couldn't be, could he? He jabbed the button of the lift. Suite 302–303. The lift doors opened. An American voice behind him complained at the price charged at Florian's for two coffees. His wife seemed unimpressed. Godwin grinned shakily when silently appealed to, then lurched out of the lift as it reached the third floor. He knocked on Davies' door and waited then rang the bell before knocking again.

'Mike – are you OK? Mike, open up. Tony Godwin – *Mike?*'

He pressed his head against the door and listened. Nothing. No running of a shower, no splashes from a bath. Then the noise of a *vaporetto* through open windows. On the balcony –? He glanced wildly around. A maid appeared from another room, her arms laden with soiled towels.

'Quick – please!' he called. 'I think my friend may be ill – Mr Davies. Open the door for me, would you? Please hurry!'

Startled into compliance, the sticks an emblem of Godwin's harmlessness, she turned her master key in the door and Godwin blundered past her. Shapiro was so strongly in his mind he looked into the bedroom first, expecting to find a body. Davies was, however, lying face down on the floor of the suite's sitting room, his legs twisted one beneath the other, one arm stretched out as if he had sought some last support from the armchair near which his head lay. His other arm was beneath his body, his hand spread against his chest. The maid was quietly appalled. Godwin managed to turn over Davies' body. The spread hand fell away from the chest. Beautiful ... a heart attack. A half-empty bottle and his breath smelt of the spirit. Oh, you *cow*!

'I want to see the manager – *manager*,' he repeated to the maid. 'Go and fetch him – *prego*.'

She nodded and left the room. Godwin heard her slithering hurriedly along the corridor to the service lift.

He closed Davies' eyes. His face was twisted with pain. There was no harm in the local police being called in. An autopsy wouldn't find anything if Valentina's skills were up to their usual standard! No connections. He looked at his watch. Just after four-thirty. The ancient Dalek would soon be getting off the plane with young Darren, to find he'd been beaten to it.

To find that it was all in danger of being up the spout again, bugger it! Davies had been the best way in. Which left Patrick, perched up on the warehouse roof like one of the bloody pigeons. He'd wait for Aubrey's OK, but Patrick had to go in now, whatever the risks.


The first heavy drops of rain splashed against the rear window, beside Aubrey's cheek, and bounced on the bonnet of the limousine put at his disposal by Giovanni Calvino of Italian Intelligence. A nightlike darkness had spread across the lagoon, and the city seemed subdued. Suddenly, it was lit by a jagged flash of lightning, as the rain intensified, drumming against the windows.

'Yes, Tony, yes,' he murmured through the storm's static, the receiver of the carphone pressed against his ear. 'Quite damnable . . . and, yes, I agree with your assessment. Matters are coming to a head. Patrick must go in immediately, if he can do so with safety. No, I'll talk to him myself.' He scribbled the number on a pad on his knee. 'No, Tony, you simply cooperate. I'll inform Giovanni Calvino. Stick to your story –' He flinched at another yellow-blue streak of lightning and the sudden image of La Serenissima as a ship in distress. Then only the afterimage of the light remained as the darkness of the storm crowded back. 'It must be stopped,' he added. 'No, Tony – I have nothing positive from South Africa. I feel I'll have to drag someone unwillingly from some cocktail party, to protect Richard and his prize. Our only prize, as of this moment. Goodbye, Tony.'

He put down the telephone and glanced at Darren Westfield, who seemed fascinated by the storm and the sudden, defenceless appearances of Venice out of the darkness. The rain beat on the limousine as on corrugated iron. Hyde, up on the roof . . .

293

It *was* at a head, like some monstrous boil to be lanced. Priabin and Babbington must intend sudden action; they had precipitated the situation by murdering Davies, who was evidently of no further use to them and too closely watched by Hyde and Godwin. He rubbed his cheek. Anderson was a narrow thread, with Blantyre doubtless seeking him with efficient desperation, at Malan's orders. Tony had echoed his own decision when he had suggested that *destruction was the easiest choice, sir.* Once they were certain of what the warehouse contained, then it should be put to the torch.

He picked up the receiver once more and dialled Hyde's number.

'Christ, about fucking time!' he heard almost at once. 'It's *pissing* on me, Godwin!'

'Patrick – Aubrey.'

'At bloody last!' Hyde repeated. 'I've spent the bloody afternoon roasting up here, hopping from roof to roof like a bloody pigeon, and now I'm being drowned! Have you seen the *weather*?'

'Can you go in, with any degree of safety, Patrick?'

'Which bloody one?'

'Warehouse 14 – I think the urgency lies there. I want identification of just *one* smuggled item of equipment from Reid Group – one photograph, one piece of evidence . . . then it may all be put to the torch.'

'You think it would burn in this bloody weather?'

'You must advise me.'

'You've got the authority?'

Hyde's voice sounded filled with effort, and seemed to move too, as if it were a weak, drifting radio signal.

'Longmead and Orrell have been informed that Babbington is here. They fear the mocking laughter that would be occasioned by *his* getting the better of us – and of them. I am commanded to do what must be done – to be *tidy.*' A gasp from Hyde. 'Are you all right?' Aubrey blurted.

'Just fucking slipped on the bloody ladder, that's all!' A few moments, then, 'Down now.'

'Is there any sign of urgent activity?'

'Couple of lorries drew up a few minutes ago. Outside 14. There's no hurry, though. Not at the moment. I'm crossing open ground now – hang on –' Aubrey could hear Hyde's rapid, hoarse breath-

ing as he sprinted what must be the space between the two warehouses. Then, breathlessly: 'OK – it's OK!'

'Davies is dead, Patrick – the girl killed him.'

'Great – oh, fucking great! No wonder you want me to have a
look inside. We've got bloody nothing at the moment, then, have
we?' His breathing was stertorous, concentrated again, from the
effort of climbing up to the roof of the larger warehouse. Lightning
flashed once more over the lagoon, the dotted islands looking like
spars and fragments ripped from the city by the storm's violence.
'Bloody gang of wankers, my old granny could do better,' he heard
Hyde muttering. 'Right, I'm on the roof. There's one skylight at this
far end. I might be able to get down behind some of the crates, or
even the container load that's intact. With *luck*. Look – *sir*, am I
getting any back-up? I don't really like to ask, but it might help.'
The sarcasm was elated, almost wild. Hyde was, as they said, psych-
ing himself up. 'There's another container arrived. Three now – the
drivers are still in their cabs. I guess at four people inside, at most.
I've loosened the studs holding the skylight . . . yes, I can get down,
*if* they're at the other end of the warehouse.'

'Our interest must have provoked Babbington to action. It won't
be long. Go carefully, Patrick –'

Aubrey replaced the receiver, then tapped the driver's shoulder.

'Take us to Commander Calvino now,' he said.

Lightning poured like the rain, making the whole area of the
lagoon blaze for a moment. Then the thunder bellowed.

Once Hyde had firm evidence that the smuggled material was in
Warehouse 14 – that which had left Birmingham airport or had
reached Venice via Dumas or other MLC subsidiaries, then he would
have the place surrounded. One of Calvino's people could discharge
some kind of incendiary device, destroying as much as possible in a
terrible *accident*. So much neater, with so much less to explain. He
closed his hand. The operation was in one place, almost in one
dimension. He was suddenly impatient at the blinding rain, hardly
disturbed by the wipers, the flashes of lightning and the booming of
the thunder, and the slow traffic in which they were caught up.

\*

He flinched against another tumult of light, hunched against the
beat of the rain and then clapped his hands against his ears as the

295

thunder came. The rain stung, even through the black waterproof cape buttoned around his throat, that had been with the equipment in the boot of the Mercedes. He felt immersed. Anything was better than the jagged stab of the lightning or its sudden, repetitive incandescence; and the deafening thunder. Glimpses of Venice were of a liner tilting bow-first into the lagoon.

He had padded to the other end of the warehouse roof, then returned. The three lorries – two cabs and only one with a trailer – were drawn up in front of the warehouse, the windows still fugged by their drivers. For the moment, no one was interested in loading. The rain ran into his ears and eyes and his hair was flattened against his skull. He looked down through the wet skylight, rubbing it continuously like a windscreen wiper. No one. He'd seen three different people, one older than the other two, and one of them recognizable as one of his pursuers from the Zattere. Priabin's people, then. There was no one at this far end of the warehouse, now.

Carefully, he eased the glass and frame of the skylight away from its base, dragging his cape over the empty little rectangle, and peered in. Rain from his hair and neck dropped away into the hard-lit gloom as he lowered his head. He stared like a bat along the dustily illuminated ranks of crates and boxes, past the intact container, then strained to see beneath the lighting suspended from the roof, and could just make out the offices inside the main doors. Listened as well as he could –

– shuffled the glass back into place as the lightning flashed again and the thunder rolled immediately after it Shivering, he clasped the edges of the skylight frame in his hands, until the thunder had rolled away inland, towards the Eugenean hills. He clipped the rope to one of the struts just below the skylight, and dropped it away into the dusk. He hesitated, then balanced the tool bag on one shoulder and lowered himself through the hole of the skylight, dragging his cape across the opening to keep out the rain as he slithered through, clinging to the strut and the rope.

Hung there, turning slow as a top above the crates and boxes and the regimented alleys of concrete between them. The rain drummed on the cape, which seeped but which wouldn't have to matter – better than half an hour working the glass back into place, ballocks to that. But the acreage of the warehouse seemed artificially silent,

296

dumbstruck by the weather outside. Gradually, he heard a radio reedily piping at the far end of the warehouse, smelt the cardboard and wood and plastics and polystyrene and oil, and began lowering himself into a gloom –

– which became hard-lit, spotlighted, as soon as he passed beneath the nearest of the rank of shaded bulbs strung from the roof, so that his throat constricted. He dropped quickly down the rope until he became masked by the high-stacked crates labelled *Reid Davies* – adjacent to *Dumas Electroniques* stencilled on other crates and vast cartons. Recognitions warmed him. He looked up at the rope, and heard the occasional drip of water before the cry of thunder. As it rolled, he tugged the rope on its clip along the strut, into the shadow against the warehouse wall. Dumas, Reid Group, Reid Davies, springing out of the dusty gloom and his memory like emblems. He looked down at his feet. Water surrounded them. Never mind. He opened the bag and removed the camera, then the jemmy and the screwdriver. Then he padded along the corridor formed by the crates and the outside wall. Old packaging littered the floor and the dilapidated, grubby shelving. Signs of haste in disturbed dust, handprints, footmarks, the untidy stacking of shelves, the lack of system. No one was coming here to draw exhibits or samples, this was all going somewhere else.

He levered one plank of wood out from its crate, then a second, exposing . . . nothing much. He moved on quickly, his footsteps no longer slippery or audible, opened the side of another crate, and found anonymous wood beneath it which he also jemmied into splinters. Found his treasure. Godwin would have wet himself at the sight. Transputers and WSI microchips, neatly boxed and labelled. Stepping back, having tugged out a single box and opened it, he photographed the package and the crate's labelling. The lightning would account for any superfluous flashes of light. Then a Dumas crate, hardly recognizing the French on the boxes it contained, except that Dumas wouldn't legitimately be supplying those avionic parts to anyone except the French air force. He felt elated, an excitement that was at last tangible. *Eureka*. The flash of the camera detonated in the gloom. Nice, neat –

The buzzer of the main doors sounded beelike through the warehouse, startling him. Through another small canyon of crates and shelving, he saw that the intact container rested in an amphitheatre of dull light. He shouldered the camera and climbed the stack of crates until he was looking over the top, towards the doors. And *she* walked through the small judas door in her shiny raincoat, shaking her spotted umbrella, as casually coming from a death as a prostitute might have come from a client. She shook her wet hair like a dog, in all innocence. Priabin was behind her, then the sloping shoulders of overalled or T-shirted men, the drivers. The door closed behind them with a distant clatter. Lying on the crates now, flattened and tense, he recognized the shadow who had closed the door before the man walked into the first dusty hardness of light. *God bless you, Sir Andrew.* Babbington, unused and uncomfortable yet also commanding, expecting and receiving deference.

Where was Malan?

The drivers of the three container lorries drifted away into shadow. Through the skylights, lightning gouged at the warehouse and the thunder volleyed behind it, deafening. Babbington began a processional, towards the undisturbed container. It had been backed into the warehouse – would be driven out, presumably, by one of the trucks. The girl and Priabin clung to Babbington's progress like moths drawn after a torch. The divvy-up needed Malan, but then perhaps Babbington, prodded by Davies' execution, wouldn't wait, would just order the stuff to be loaded and taken to Marco Polo, or even overland through Yugoslavia, seals intact.

If Aubrey wanted this lot put to the torch, easiest would be one of the American portable flame-grenade launchers. No setting of charges, fuses, just fire away. Babbington reached the container and leaned towards Priabin in intent conversation. Beyond the two men, and the container beside which they had all halted, was a second container. A forklift truck, arms laden with crates, was resting at the lip of its tailgate. Christ, he hadn't seen that second load from the skylight. They must have been loading that container most of the afternoon. Babbington was inspecting its interior now, hands on his hips, face pursed into disapproval. He motioned to Priabin, who called back along the corridor of shelving and crates. The drivers slouched into a distant light, followed by other overalled figures and two men in shirtsleeves. Babbington waved his arms, then spoke in a chill, authoritative voice. One man climbed onto the forklift and started its engine humming. It lurched into the interior of the container and almost at once Hyde could hear its hydraulics lowering the crates. The bloody thing was well over half-full already. Lightning flashed again and the lights in the warehouse flickered, like the waving of fragile old hands, then their light steadied again. Babbington looked up towards the whalelike ribs of the roof. The truck came out of the container's stomach and nuzzled away towards more crates, as Priabin and Babbington directed it. The increase in tension was tangible, the hurry unmistakable. Fuck a fire in here, Hyde thought, there wasn't going to be time. He must get closer.

He began lowering himself down the cliff-face of crates towards the concrete floor. Then he slipped along the narrow corridor between them and the corrugated wall, then through stacked boxes, more crates, moving with exaggerated caution, as if stepping through thick mud. The forklift passed close to him, along another alleyway, then a second truck nudged the crates behind which he had paused. He ducked and moved on, then found himself down on one knee, peering through dusty boxes on metal shelves at Babbington and Priabin; their legs and shoes confronting one another. Babbington's replies were hesitant and soothing. Hyde could get no closer.

'. . . had to be done,' he heard Priabin assure.

'– acceleration – don't like . . .' from Babbington. '– what we can, then!' he burst out, his rain-wet shoes striding a pace or two away, then returning.

'. . . most, anyway.'

'– *dislike*!'

Then Babbington's shoes strode away towards the tyres of one of the forklift trucks. Hyde breathed steadily, quietly, then looked down at the bag beside him. Call Aubrey, get the place under surveillance, sealed. Too late to be tidy.

Footsteps, even as he made to move. His hand, in the mouth of the bag, closed around the Browning automatic's grip. He turned, and confronted a man opening his mouth, one of the shirtsleeved KGB men. Hyde fired twice. The shells spat on the concrete, their glasslike noises drowned by the clatter of nuts and bolts from an open box, as the man collapsed against the shelves. He fell face down on the floor and Hyde stood up as if in response to the first shout of surprised alarm.

He ducked through one alleyway of shelves, then another. The noises of the forklift trucks ceased, and he heard his own breathing and the blood racing in his ears – then he heard someone shouting orders before all noise was drowned by thunder.

He had to call Aubrey. They had to come now –


It was as if the airbed which Anderson had brought from the car and inflated with a foot pump was some species of psychiatrist's couch; a confessional. His detachment, too, was a pastiche of some professional manner. Van Vuuren had drunk the whisky greedily, and now clutched the bottle against his chest with his bandaged hand. Through the grimy window, the quick African dusk settled over the forecourt and the dusty, empty perspective beyond it; at least, it seemed to. It might be a storm darkening the sky, he thought, as he looked at his watch as if measuring van Vuuren's pulse.

It had been a rambling confession – more a denouncement, a cry of betrayal accompanied by the catalogue of infidelities and compromises of the government, MLC, Paulus Malan . . . all except a few brave white spirits who would not let the past go. Self-justification, ego, bigotry, hatred, anger and despair.

Arms had been brought in, from eastern Europe, for some months, mostly rifles and handguns, grenades, even flame-throwers . . . not in great numbers, Anderson surmised, but with a threatening acceleration and growing recklessness. *Some of us are prepared to resist . . . I began to realize it could be done, there's so much stuff just lying around over there, man – cheap, too.* Van Vuuren had become voluble with the drink, its effect magnified by his body coming out of trauma after the –

Anderson avoided looking at the bandaged hand, the occasional grimaces of pain on his face, his nursing of the hand against his chest.

*. . . then I found Novak, made it easier . . . Never used MLC money, only our own,* he affirmed with incongruous rectitude.

There was nerve agent – *make the buggers blink, that will* – waiting to be transported. *Why I was needed in Venice,* he had complained as if some kind of small domestic crisis had detained him, ship-wrecking his plans. He had glared as he made the pronouncement.

300

*Novak will get it here.* He seemed certain of that. Anderson had learned from the rambling, oblivious denunciations and accusations, that Malan was not implicated in the arms or nerve gas smuggling.

Such had been Anderson's borrowed detachment that he was hardly stirred by the information. He would, eventually, pass it to Aubrey, who would stop the consignment, but there were no images of twisted black shapes on the ground or poisoned water supplies or Armageddon blackmail ... just his own, narrower concerns.

Eventually, van Vuuren had admitted, *Malan ordered your killing. Blantyre would have done it anyway, but Malan gave the order. You'd stumbled on the pipeline for MLC's share of the profits.* Now, he did see the bodies – one body, really, just one. At that point, it had been only Blantyre to satisfy his revenge. Interrupted, and surprised by the question regarding the faked atrocity in Etosha, van Vuuren had eventually nodded, confirming Malan's part in Margarethe's murder.

Nothing else mattered. The Broederbond and the AWB and the Conservatives and the tinpot white resistance groups ... only Malan's guilt, Blantyre's culpability. He had found the man *behind* things, the only things that were of any significance.

He would inform Aubrey, after dark when it was safer to find a telephone, of the consignment of nerve gas – VX or Sarin or whatever filthy rubbish they had got their hands on in Czechoslovakia. And, with that call, resign; walk away to confront his own concerns, *his* probity, *his* demand for justice. Malan and Blantyre. He would kill them both.

Van Vuuren continued to mutter confession and contempt and rage and cunning, more distantly and intermittently now, as if his transmitter was fading, its batteries run low. Anderson paid him no attention. He had learned everything he wished. Van Vuuren, should he have attempted to escape, might have been allowed to walk out, wander off down the road.

A ragged blind blew in the increasing wind that rattled sand against the grimy window. The dust was a dust storm, the spoil from the Rand blowing over the Johannesburg suburbs. Ashes to ashes ... It might take months, certainly weeks, but it would be done. *Lex talionis.* The sand sifted in through the rotting window frames and loose planking. Van Vuuren appeared not to have noticed the approaching storm.

Occasional, bleary headlights passed on the road. Anderson turned his future in his hand, like a child's glass ball. Upside down, the snow fell on the tiny scene within the glass. Whichever way he turned the prospect of his future, it invariably bore the same distinct outline. There was nothing, absolutely *nothing*, to stop him. An eye for an eye. That would give him the illusion of peace, make sense of it, give her rest . . .

Headlights turned off the road and splashed through the flying sand and dust over the forecourt. The shadowy vehicle behind them slowly came to a halt. The headlights remained on, probing the building.


Hyde was crouched near the office inside the main doors, in deep shadow. The doors were opened to the storm, and the torrential rain diffused the headlights of one of the truck cabs as it turned towards the warehouse. A KGB man, in overalls, stood beside the open door, the headlights illuminating the Makarov pistol in his left hand. Inside the hutlike office, another man peered over his spectacles as he completed the faked inventories of the container loads. His hesitations, his small, neat handwriting and figures, prompted needle-like on Hyde's arms and neck. It was a salvage operation now. Snatch up the goodies, the alarm's gone off. He shuffled back into the shadows. The truck rolled into the warehouse, its lights blazing.

He edged his way along the wall, hearing nothing other than the engine and the renewed drumming of the rain after organ-like thunder. When he was wedged between two small steeples of crates, he fished the cellular phone out of the bag and dialled Aubrey's number. You'd better have the cavalry organized, sport –

The red light on the phone blinked its ringing-out rhythm, then was interrupted.

'Just listen!' he whispered fiercely. 'I'm identified. The target area's about to be abandoned. Get here with the troops. *Now.*'

'Yes,' Aubrey murmured from a great distance. Hyde thrust the phone back into the bag, then considered leaving the bag, but knew

302

he might need the phone again, and *would* need the spare clips of ammunition. Better hang on to it.

He listened now that the truck's engine was no more than idling, and heard Babbington's raised voice, urging matters ahead, Priabin calling to his people, then the girl's higher-pitched reply. It wouldn't take long now. Lightning through the open doors, then the thunder, now perhaps a couple of miles away. The girl would be commissioned with killing him while Babbington and Priabin organized the looting. Two containers –?

Yes, they were still loading the second one. He breathed as steadily as he could after climbing skeletal shelving and peering over it at the amphitheatre glaring in the headlights of the truck shunting in reverse gear towards the waiting, loaded container. The warehouse seemed denuded, far less full, as if to deliberately mock his surveillance. He clung on, scanning the remaining columns of boxes and crates. The logos were familiar even if indecipherable now – Reid Group, Reid Davies, Dumas. Being cleared like Harrods on the first morning of a sale. The forklifts could hardly get off the ramp of the second container now, Santa had stuffed the stocking so full. One of them chugged backwards, then the other mounted and deposited its crates. Sweating men shuffled them more closely together, Babbington waving his arms like a maddened traffic warden, while Priabin was hurrying towards the office. Through the doors, the second truck was nosing inside, as if looking for its companion, its engine noise obscuring everything else.

Metal dented near his hand, and was hot as he touched it, but he had not heard the bullet or its ricochet. Wildly, he glanced around. One man knelt atop a heap of crates thirty yards away, with his arms stiffly extended, gripping a pistol in his curled hands.

Hyde dropped from the shelves and buckled into a crouch while the gunman's shouts, eager as those of a huntsman, rang through the warehouse. This was Brum-fucking-airport all over again, having the bloody stuff snatched away from under his nose! He scuttled to the end of the shelving. Pausing for a moment, he opened the bag and withdrew the two extra clips of ammunition. Then left the bag. The telephone was useless now.

He heard the next shot, but had no sense of its direction. Then a third. He could see no one, not even the man on top of the crates. He heard calls, back and forth, from invisible hunters, heard the

303

directions being given to the truck driver as he attempted the link-up between his vehicle and the container, heard the idling of the second truck's engine. Then a glare of blue light burst through the open doors and the skylight, and the preliminary rasp, then growl, of the retreating thunder. In which noise he moved, scurrying like a rat for deeper shadow, seeing one figure briefly from the corner of his eye. Whether the man had seen him he had no idea. Another flicker of lightning, less dazzling, and a breath of thunder. The rain struck more reticently on the roof.

He crouched beside cardboard boxes. *Reid Davies, part of the Reid Group plc.* Fax machines. He wiped his forehead with the back of the hand that held the Browning, then rested the barrel against his heated cheek. He couldn't stop the container lorry leaving, not even by shooting the driver. To do that, he'd have to be exposed and they'd kill him easily. Boxes falling somewhere made him start, his hand gripping the edge of a damaged crate — neat stacks of mainframe computer tapes, cushioned in polystyrene wedges, wrapped in polythene; huge programme spools.

One of them, a man's footsteps by the sound of it, was moving towards him. Then, at a shout, the footsteps halted. ' – bag here!' he heard. Then, more loudly and clearly: 'Camera, telephone!' The footsteps that had been approaching hurried away.

Closer than he had guessed, he heard Babbington's voice, realizing the significance of the telephone. Stupid sod, leaving it for them to find. It would invoke greater urgency in them, an almost manic scramble to find and destroy him. Possibly Priabin's voice, but distorted by a megaphone. Then scattering noises, like the barks and scampering of eager dogs. He shivered. The walls had shrunk inwards and the zealous voices seemed louder, the calling back and forth of the small expert pack. The rain was lessening and the thunder was grumbling away inland. The chugging truck engines were impatient to move. The second container's doors slammed shut in a kind of panicky triumph.

– footsteps. He turned, shaking, arms extended in front of him, and fired. The man ducked back, then something tore a sliver of wood from a crate near him. He watched, with a kind of slowed-down, filmic shock, as the splinter of wood cartwheeled out of the light into shadow. Then he turned and fired again, swivelling on one knee like someone in a training demonstration.

Arms up, the second man fell back, gun skittering on the concrete. He swung back again and fired a third shot. The man ducked out of sight once more without being able to fire. Then Hyde scrambled up a stack of cardboard boxes, treacherous as a loose dune slope, and rolled as he felt the impact of two bullets into the untidy, slipping mound. Bright coins of transputer chips spilt into the dusty light like a fortune lost. More shots, but he was rolling, amid boxes, then he was half-buried by their weight. He struggled free, gun extended, turning even as he sat amid the wreckage, firing again two-handed. At no one, he realized, when he had the composure to look. He scrabbled away on hands as well as feet, into the shadow of high shelving.

Then she was there – Valentina, less surprised than himself, her hands seeming to move more quickly, but her features distracted between the megaphone in her left hand and the gun in her right – so that it was he who fired first, twice, then once more, like someone beating a venomous snake long after it was dead. Then the cold frenzy of a fourth shot. The girl was quite still, her right leg twisted under her body, her skirt rucked to her thighs, her hair gleaming with rain.

Calls were shouted out again, but they were less confident, quietened by the succession of shots he had fired. He tugged out the empty clip and thrust a new one home, jerking the first round into the chamber. He was shivering, sweating profusely. Then, slowly, he backed away from the girl's body and into deeper shadow, while her name was called – even her rank – but there were no sounds of Babbington or Priabin, no assumptions of command. Then he heard the noise of the truck's engine growling forward towards the doors.

He began running. You'd better shoot the driver, sport, even if it only holds them for a couple of minutes. Shoot the driver, shoot the driver . . . over and over as he raced along one of the long corridors of shelving, all but oblivious to voices behind him. If someone came out of a side passage behind him, they'd have a running target, could take their time – perhaps they'd paused having found the girl's body, been subdued into indecision . . .

He was at the doors, as was the truck with the first of the containers –

He raised his gun, aiming at the high window of the cab. The driver wasn't even looking at him, he was looking directly ahead to – where the doors were blocked by an artic. In front and to either side of which men with Uzis and rifles were waiting for the driver's decision . . . which was to halt, pull on the brake loudly, and raise his hands in the cab. Hyde sank into a squatting position on the concrete, shivering uncontrollably.

Even before the driver had had time to obey the order, in Italian, repeated in English, and then in Russian, to climb down from his cab, Aubrey was bending over him, shaking him as if he had failed some test, been a disappointment to a doting parent.

'Who emptied the other warehouse – *when*?' Aubrey demanded. 'Patrick – there's nothing *there*. Novak has cleaned it out!'

# PART THREE

## Only in Africa, Peace

*'Ex Africa semper aliquid novi'* –
(There is always something new out of Africa)
Pliny the Elder

## THIRTEEN

# another lean, unwashed artificer

The sunlight streamed in on the intent, concentrated, vivid faces of the loadmaster and her crew as the rear cargo ramp opened like the tailgate of a huge lorry. The engine noise from the Hercules was louder, but there was a strange illusion of windless silence, too. Then the drogue 'chute cracked open behind him with an explosive sound and his head was jerked against the vehicle's seat. He was flung backwards, away from the aircraft's cargo crew, the Land Rover hurtling out of the diminishing tunnel of the C-130's dark interior into the African sun. Then he felt nauseously jolted as the shock-absorbing pallet struck the sand of the Kuiseb Canyon. The scene was obscured by the dust storm thrown up behind it by the aircraft's passage at no more than fifteen feet above the desert. The wild, surreal sense of the impact followed, then the pallet slowed, slewing sideways and braking in the reddish sand – sand which settled on him, on the Land Rover, and above which the Hercules would lift lumberingly into the dark blue of the dawn.

London to Brighton in four minutes – Jesus Christ, it had been just like that. Coughing in the chill, dust-laden air, he released the straps that had secured him in the Land Rover's driving seat. Jesus, the things I do for England . . .

He squinted above the slowly settling dust, picking up the Hercules as it levelled after its turn and came back towards the flat, ages-dry riverbed they had selected for the drop. The aircraft would, after its second drop, recross the Namibian coast and drift up into radar view once more, pursuing its journey from Ascension Island to the Falklands. It had flown below radar height most of the way from Ascension across the darkened ocean, while he slept. It came on again, dropping lower, undercarriage lowered, ramp open. It was slightly to starboard of the original track – *I don't want to be dropped on from a great height, everyone else has already done that* – and then it passed, the dust roiling behind it, into which a 'chute vanished, a gleaming metal canister dragged out of the cargo bay behind it. He thought he saw a hand wave whitely, then the ramp and the undercarriage both came up together and the Hercules banked away towards the coast, south of the Walvis Bay enclave, its engine noise diminishing into –

– a silence that seemed to press on his ears, palpable as the pressure created by a small concussion. He jogged into the settling dust and dragged the canister towards the Land Rover. He released the cords of the parachute and wrapped it into a bundle, then heaved the canister into the rear of the vehicle – *not to be opened before Christmas* – and then began releasing the 4WD from the restraints that attached it to the pallet. Straightening at last, he looked around him. He was perhaps three or four miles from the C14 road to Aruvlei and Walvis Bay, which was sixty miles north-west. A fingernail of sun rose above the closest lip of the canyon. The low escarpment's edge became gilded, and the worn, desiccated, empty hills reddened lividly from their bruised night colour. Hyde shook his head. *Welcome to Mars.* The sun struck warmly and immediately in its milder winter anger. A lizard scuttled away across the coarse, gravelly sand towards the shade of rocks. As he started the Land Rover, the noise of the engine bellowed back at him from the low canyon walls, shapeless and gradual as a mudslide. The vehicle bucked across the uneven ground, and he looked back at the forlorn pallet and its half-buried drogue parachute. Anyone who saw it would think it was South African Defence Forces equipment, abandoned after some exercise. *Who* would see it? Empty as the moon. He nudged the vehicle, in four-wheel drive, up the twisting, low incline, heaving on the wheel as he followed the bed of a sometime stream which had once emptied into the dry riverbed of the Kuiseb. A few stunted acacias, the discolouration of lichen – or perhaps even minerals – decayed on the rocks. As he reached the canyon lip, he looked west towards the frozen march of dunes out in the Namib; more solid-seeming than the pale, stunted hills around him.

He looked down at his shorts, heavy boots, the already sweat-stained bush shirt with its faded corporal's insignia. The bush hat

was clamped down on his forehead. SADF. Corporal-bloody-Hyde
. . . couldn't give him an officer's uniform, could they? He slowed
the Land Rover and switched off the engine. There was a streak of
dust along the northern horizon which might have marked the
passage of a heavy truck along the road. The silence pressed around
him once more, heavy as a blanket, and as disorientating as the
loss of hearing.

*Stop it at any cost*, Aubrey had impressed upon him, forbearing to
add, *to yourself* – but it was what he had meant. Anderson said it
was nerve agent, so nerve agent it was. *Stop it inside Namibia. By
any means.*

Short of blowing it up, of course, and releasing the nerve agent.
Slight drawback to that. Priabin and Babbington had got away from
Venice without a hitch, and that same night someone had Sem-
texed Warehouse 14, reducing its contents to scorched and melted
rubbish. Under the noses of the Italians . . . it destroyed a man's
faith in the EC, really. So, it had all gone back under the carpet,
and was no longer a matter of proof, investigation or counteractiv-
ity, just of stopping a consignment of Czech nerve agent reaching
the lunatics on the fringes of Afrikaanerdom.

Hyde tossed his head, squinting in the hard light to where the
road passed across the endless, bleak gravel plains of the northern
desert. He looked down at the map again. The MLC complex outside
Walvis Bay was where they would have shipped the stuff from
Venice, on the Italian cargo charter that had taken off half an hour
before he and the Italians had reached Marco Polo in the cool
aftermath of the storm. Two days ago. Find the plane, which hadn't
reappeared despite being scheduled to return to Milan with
imported MLC nuts and bolts or whatever. Aubrey assumed it was
still sitting on the airstrip. Expensive way to find out, hiring a whole
aircraft to get him there. The aircrew had been highly amused at
the idea of shooting him out of the back of the Hercules – and more
excited than they would have been pushing grain out over Ethiopia
or supplies over Kuwait. They'd looked at him as at some exhibit
in a museum; a reconstruction of a dinosaur – a *spy*, what's that?

He studied the terrain, nodding to himself, then started the
engine. The bonnet of the Land Rover dipped as he began
descending a shallow slope towards the flat, drab gravel plain. If
it's all that's left – and Aubrey wasn't going to get far now with

311

Longmead and half the Cabinet trying to keep the boat steady and HM Secretary of State for Trade and Industry shitting brick-sized lumps in case anything nasty stuck to his untarnished image – then he'd better give it his best shot. At least stuff van Vuuren and Blantyre and their plan!

The Land Rover bounced and crabbed over the gravel and small, pebbly boulders. Aubrey was back on the fringes again: over-zealous behaviour, the blight on his career. Hyde grinned sourly. The old bugger was, really, immensely naive, always assuming that people wanted to hear the unpalatable truth. More dust hanging in the air a little to the north – the road, for sure. Reid Davies was going to carry the whole heavy can – David Reid was going to go on smelling of roses because there were too many people who saw him as the heir apparent, and no one wanted to rock the Pretoria boat just now, with Mandela and de Villiers engaged in their long courtship dance.

Then he shivered slightly in the hot air, his hands gripping the wheel more fiercely, as if for reassurance. It *was* nerve gas – Jesus. And you're the night-soil man, come to clear up the fucking mess.


*Nothing of this must touch David Reid*, Longmead had pronounced with unctuous gravitas. *None of it is of* his *making, and none of it should cloud his career* . . . Though, for certain, David had long known where the funds and orders that had rescued Reid Group had originated – with Malan and even the KGB!

Aubrey glanced through the aircraft window as the 747 banked over one of the neat, dusty suburbs of Johannesburg and began its approach to Jan Smuts airport. His empty glass of orange juice – *no champagne, thank you, a little early for my stomach* – had been taken away by the attentive stewardess, and his small table folded beside him into its slot. First Class was all but full, mostly British busi-nessmen confident and legitimate in their business trips to the new South Africa. Champagne? There was nothing to celebrate.

Some kind of botched blackmail scenario would be attached to the uxorious Michael Davies, Reid Davies would be *cleansed*, to use Longmead's word, and Malan would remain at large . . . *can't rock any boats at the moment in South Africa*. From the snatches of conver-sation he had overheard during the flight, he understood the reluctance of the Cabinet committee to implicate Malan. Such pressing *business* reasons, such imperatives of *trade*.

The aircraft began sliding through thin, gauzy morning cloud towards the gleaming city below. A cricket team would undoubtedly follow the businessmen within months, with the MCC's blessing.

*Malan will be forbidden all dealings with Reid Group – that should satisfy you, Kenneth . . . ? Connections between Reid Group and this French company will be severed – the French can clean their own house. If necessary, Reid Group will be broken up.*

Longmead at his most obsequious, most Victorian. Close one's front door and there was no way the plague could affect one, mm? It was all such *rubbish*. He heard his dentures grinding and glanced at the seat beside him. His travelling companion – a machine-tool manufacturer from the Midlands – had evidently vanished to the toilet, to return smothered in expensive aftershave, no doubt. Aubrey's embarrassment dissipated. *Embarrassment to the de Villiers government by activity directed at MLC is inconceivable. There is always a point at which to stop, and that point has been reached.*

For two days and nights he had pressed his own imperatives, only for them to be dismissed, overruled. His claim regarding the shipment he believed to be nerve agent had been ridiculed, and time had made David Reid innocent. There was nothing more to be said –

– except, *Stop it, at any cost.* To Hyde. He had abused the last of his authority to place Hyde in Namibia. It had been a desperate, final decision. His reputation and career would, in all probability, never recover from it – it simply *had* to be done. It had to be stopped because disbelief in Whitehall would not make it go away. It was not a nightmare to be avoided by putting heads under safe blankets; it was real. It would be used to kill. Even to destabilize South Africa. He could not let it happen. Even to the extent of coming to Johannesburg himself, to confront Malan – to attempt to bend him to his will. Blackmail him.

The Midlands businessman slipped back into his seat, clouded in aftershave, his cheeks shinily smooth, almost accusatory of Aubrey's own lack of toilet. He smiled and Aubrey returned the expression, before glancing down towards the nearing city with a sensation of fluttery nerves in his stomach.

313

The seatbelt and No Smoking signs were illuminated. Tiredly, he fiddled with his seatbelt. Richard Anderson was out there somewhere, utterly free and entirely dangerous, with a single purpose – to kill Malan. Nothing except his own demise would stop him. Malan had to be blackmailed and used to prevent a catastrophe before Richard got to him. Malan had to help him locate, and stop, the consignment from Venice – stop Blantyre and whoever else might be in on things, especially van Vuuren.

After that – he nodded grimly – Richard could have Malan or anyone else he wished to kill.


The Zil swept past the television tower and the uglier older domes and crosses of the Donskoi monastery, down the M4, the Lyusinov-skaya ulitsa, towards the M5 and Domodedovo airport. Babbington stared sullenly at the bright noon beyond the passenger window, the sun gleaming off the monastery's inevitable, barbaric onion towers. Determined as he was not to glance in Kapustin's direction, for fear of betraying his overwhelming sensation of relief, he continued to stare through the window. Having collected Kapustin from the glass-surrounded offices of the KGB's Chairman, they were beyond the Sadovaya ring road and making good time. Another monastery reflected in a loop of the river. They were like confrontations with upbraiding spirits.

'– behind us,' Kapustin was growling, staring at the back of the driver's neck beyond the glass partition of the limousine. 'When it came to it, we were recognized as *indispensable* . . . even *you*. Someone who understands how they think, who was once one of them –' He'd survived because of a former identity, because he was *still* the Englishman, *Sir* Andrew Babbington. 'So, the failure in Venice was easier to pass off than I expected.' The sense of favours done, obligations incurred.

'Thank you,' Babbington murmured.

Kapustin shrugged. 'It was necessary. Get rid of that interfering old shit, Aubrey. Make sure what is done is done under *your* auspices, not Malan's. We need Malan – and power over him, as before. You assure me the British will drop this business like a hot stone without Aubrey. Prove your case.'

Babbington looked towards the vain towers of churches which

had become museums. The traffic towards the airport was thicker, wilder, as it always was on Moscow's motorways. The courts filled with drunken drivers and petitioners for dead men's pensions – *killed in a road accident, your honour.* The traffic clotted, swerved, raced. Their driver's shoulders were stiff with concentration and anticipated avoidance. A minor collision between two old Moskvas resulted in upspringing bonnets and steam from burst radiators, and an almost immediate scuffle in the motorway's slow lane. Less than a quarter of a mile farther on, another car, burned out, lay on the side of the road. Babbington was unnerved by the insistent evidence of *accident*, of disruption.

'We have been blamed – *you* have been blamed – for that appalling cock-up in Venice – but Priabin may be made to carry some of your temporary burden. *If* you get rid of Aubrey.' He shook Babbington's arm roughly, so that he was obliged to turn his head and look at Kapustin. The burning eyes seemed retreated into innumerable lines of age and cunning. 'Andrew, do your job. Malan's asked for our assistance and advice. Render him the necessary service.' He laughed throatily, shaking Babbington's arm now as if in apology, even affection. 'We are indispensable. They can't run the show without us. Malan helps us to sustain our crucial importance. Let nothing happen to him. Just get *rid* of Aubrey.'


It dropped slowly, almost elegantly out of the hot, windless afternoon sky, like a pale seabird seeking the coast behind him. Then it emerged into an aircraft and he heard the note of its engine – almost the first noise since the retreating engines of the Italian cargo plane had vanished eastwards a little after twelve. Gradually, the aircraft became a Cessna wobbling in the air currents as it floated above the airstrip and then landed, throwing up a cloud of dust behind it. It slowed, then taxied, and the cabin door opened before it came to a halt. A stubbled man slewed to a halt in a 4WD beside the aircraft and – oh, yes . . .

Blantyre, saluted with cheerful mockery by the driver of the Japanese 4WD. Blantyre returned the salute with a grin. The Cessna taxied away to its hangar as the vehicle bristled towards the administrative building of the MLC compound. Hyde watched through binoculars, squinting against the glare from chrome and sand, until Blantyre had passed into the air-conditioned, enviable interior of the main building. The driver lit a cigarette and the first exhaled smoke hung above his head like a small cloud. Then Hyde rolled on his back on the isolated dune and stared, satisfied, up at the sky. Until that moment, he had merely hoped that nothing had left by road. Now, he knew for certain. Blantyre had arrived to supervise, command. The consignment of nerve agent and small arms was in one of the low warehouses. The Italian plane that had brought them had been the same one that had taken off from Venice, just before they'd got to Marco Polo, with a flight plan filed that would bring it to Walvis Bay. The registration tallied. The shipment had come in, but it hadn't left – oh no, no show without Punch, and Punch had just arrived. Beaut . . .

The Land Rover was hidden half a mile away, in the shallowest of gravelly depressions, overhung by a sorry, lean clump of desiccated bushes. Clever old bastard, Aubrey – good guesser, anyway.

Then the sense of the desert and the glittering ocean and the silence now that the 4WD's noise had died – all impinged, then pressed. Dunes to the south, the escarpment to the east, the gravel desert to the north, the sea to the west; himself on the solitary dune. Blantyre, two container trucks at least, perhaps three in each cab, escort of maybe two vehicles, three or four to each 4WD – and they might drive non-stop, taking turns at the wheel. He would have to follow alone, and without rest. Until they were all isolated enough by desert or mountain or canyon for *no* alternative arrangement to be made. No plane, no other trucks, no helicopter, no boat . . . so that there was *no way out.*

He shivered. It wasn't beaut, not *really.* It was something else entirely.


He remained patient, self-possessed – so habitual had the mood become that he no longer remarked it. It was of no significance to him that perhaps weeks, even months, stretched ahead of him; evasions, disguise – even the lying-low of a hunted animal – nothing dismayed him. There was an accepted sense of duty, which sustained him much as a faith might have done, something evangelical. Malan had given the order, or sanctioned it at the least. So van Vuuren had said. *QED* – Malan had murdered Margarethe in trying to remove him. Malan would honour the debt he had incurred.

Even the surveillance no longer niggled, and hadn't become mere routine. He left his car parked where it was all day, only leaving the car park when Malan left MLC. He returned to the exact place early each morning, so that the vehicle occupied the same position on the same floor of the multistorey car park – overlooking Malan's suite of offices. Overlooking, too, the adjoining executive car park for the MLC building, where he could remain aware of the movements of Malan's long, cream-coloured Mercedes and its driver. Eventually, he would have to hire another car. It was the best he could maintain without drawing attention to himself, to that *white extremist responsible for the kidnapping and death of Piet van Vuuren, respected senior executive, loving husband and . . .* blah, blah, blah. He was dedicated to this one thing and it would be accomplished. The police were looking for him, old pictures and more recent but bearded pictures of him had been shown, his background had been slandered and his history curried and spiced by interviews with people like Bright. Dangerous psychopath, outraged and demented sympathizer with black violence . . . fifty other darkened images of him. He knew he could avoid the police if he was careful enough. And, if he was patient enough, he could kill Malan.

He rested his elbows on the rough, grey concrete sill of the car park, his small binoculars sufficient to give him the assurance of movement in Malan's office. He caught glimpses of the man's heavy frame at his desk or moving about his office in shirtsleeves, through the slits of the vertical venetian blinds. Moving the glasses, he checked the executive car park. The driver was washing the Mercedes, soaping its bonnet as gently as he might have done a child's back, after the dust of Malan's drive to the Wanderers Club and his return after nine holes of golf with two senior government advisers and the chairman of Anglo.

He swung the binoculars back to the office suite. Malan was seated on the edge of his huge desk, papers in one hand, admonishing or instructing a seated trio of senior subordinates. The subject of their conversation was irrelevant, just as it was of no consequence that security men had prevented Anderson from approaching anywhere near the golfers that morning. He required

317

knowledge only of a physical body – where it went, how it travelled, where it came to rest, and when it might be left alone, isolated. When he knew all those things he would be in the position he wanted.

A moment later, Malan was left alone in his main office, after his secretary had cleared coffee cups and poured Malan more coffee from a percolator jug. He might, perhaps, kill from long range. The window might – at the least – deflect or slow any bullet sufficiently for it only to wound; unsatisfactory. Somewhere, at some moment, the physical frame, the vulnerable head – bending now over the desk, studying papers – would be devoid of caution and bodyguards . . . *just* for a moment. Then he would have *his* moment.

He poured himself tea from a vacuum flask into the cup-shaped screw top, then sipped it meditatively, or so it might have appeared. His mind was empty. Through the glass of the roof over the shopping mall, he saw the crowds of bright frocks and shirts drift like leaves. Beyond the MLC building, the day was wintrily hot, a pale sky without clouds. In the far distance, the slag heaps of spoil from the old mines, from the ancestry of Anglo and MLC. There was no sting to any of it now. He did not believe, as Aubrey evidently did, that Malan might move his operations out of South Africa. No one abandoned gold and diamonds, whatever else they acquired . . . only if the mines were nationalized.

Beyond the red-ochre, artificial hills, thin remnants of smoke hung in the distance, over Soweto. More township violence. Palls of smoke in the windless air, like the signals of encircling savages surrounding a white man's fortification. And probably only as real as a Western film. Zulu and ANC, AWB against the government, MLC and Anglo watching the price of their shares . . . even the vast, irresistible tide of genuine progress – none of it was of any significance. He finished his tea and flicked away the last drops from the cup before screwing it back on the flask. Then he placed it in the back of the car before resuming his surveillance of Malan's offices.

Blantyre had killed van Vuuren, or had him killed. Blaming himself was of secondary importance. Van Vuuren had talked. That much would have been evident from the bandaged, nail-less finger. It had been Blantyre in the car that had drawn up, in the increasing darkness of the dust storm. With two other men. Anderson pre-

318

sumed that the police patrol had, after all, been suspicious and had acted under orders not to alarm him. He had left van Vuuren to them, uncaring as to his fate, because he knew everything he needed to know. He had escaped by the back door, staggered through the wind and the blown sand to the dilapidated garage, started the car and driven violently towards the road, disappearing into the gloom of the storm which had swallowed the noise of his engine and discouraged and confused any pursuit. Side roads, the boundary of a golf course, the Reef, all half-seen, blurred by the dust outside the car. They had not been able to tail him. Eventually, he had found a cheap boarding house in the Hillbrow district, and gone to earth. And awoken to newspapers and radio and TV accusations and libels that were so exaggerated and urgent as to be laughable.

He had tracked the movements of the physical body that was Malan for the past two days . . . The afternoon sun was entering the man's office from another window, striped like the coat of a tiger by the venetian blinds. Malan sat in what seemed a hot, glaring dusk, his head bent over the papers on his desk. Then he looked up. His secretary's legs, then the grey trousers of a man's suit, which became the jacket and then the profile of an old man as the figure sat in the chair indicated by Malan, next to a glass coffee table. Anderson watched the old man, his shock dissipating almost immediately, with a detached, grim amusement. Observing life on another world, or from the strangest and most remote of habitats. Aubrey confronted Malan, who now perched on the edge of his desk. Aubrey and Malan . . . he had no interest in their business together. Aubrey would not tell Malan what he intended, of that he was certain. Therefore he could not come between them . . .

The light was behind Malan as he perched on the desk, discomfiting Aubrey, who had to squint to make out the man's features. The afternoon sun's striped shadows from the blinds fell across Malan's shoulders and thighs. Aubrey steeled himself to appear patient, relaxed, however difficult the assumption of calm. He cleared his throat and said:

'How is your father?'

'Not good. You should call on him – talk about old times,' Malan replied dismissively.

'Yes, I must,' Aubrey murmured.

319

The secretary brought coffee cups and a cafetière, smilingly poured for Aubrey, then left. His delicate demitasse rattled softly in its saucer as he lifted it from the table. He sipped like an anxious bird, deliberately remaining silent.

Malan brushed his right hand across his hair and said: 'You called, asking for a meeting. From London. I agreed. But I'm busy, Sir Kenneth –' Even his politeness was abrupt. 'What is it you want with me?'

'I see, from the newspapers and television at my hotel, that you have just, mm – lost a senior executive of the company.'

Malan laughed, then in the ensuing silence, Aubrey heard the air-conditioning's steady murmur. Malan shook his head. 'You wouldn't have had anything to do with that, of course,' he observed, leaning slightly forward on the edge of the desk, as if poised to attack. Then he rocked back, shaking his head and crossing one leg over the other, folding his arms across his broad chest.

'No, I would not,' Aubrey replied primly. He put down his tiny blue-and-gold cup and saucer.

'But you know – knew? – the man involved. He was working for you, I imagine.'

Aubrey flicked his hand. 'In a sort of unofficial capacity.'

Malan smiled. Through the windows across the room from Aubrey was a multistorey car park; beyond that the vast sky and the first heavy late afternoon shadows falling from high buildings on other office blocks.

'I understand, Sir Kenneth. What I don't understand is – why? Here? We played to some kind of draw, didn't we? In Venice. The game's over.' His smile was assured, even serene in a chiselled, sculpted way; the expression of some benevolent dictator in celebratory stone or bronze.

'I don't really think it is. Your old colleague Andrew Babbington may have destroyed the evidence, but there was much else that led us to Venice, and which implicates you. MLC, certainly. Matters that amount to considerable embarrassment, even outrage. In the present climate.'

'You want me to get out my cheque book now, man?' Malan replied scornfully. 'And you fill in the amount, right?'

'I am not blackmailing you, Malan.'

'Not yet.' He sighed, arms still folded. 'Go on. *Embarrassment*, you said.'

'We have a deal of proof regarding the network of companies, previous shipments, funding, takeovers – that kind of thing.'

'From here, it looks like good business.'

'Would such *good business* include nerve gas, Malan? I ask not merely from curiosity, you understand.'

Malan appeared genuinely perplexed, his brow creasing, then smoothing into jocular disbelief.

'I don't understand. Explain.'

'Your much regretted late senior executive had begun a sideline to your mutual interests in eastern Europe and the UK. Van Vuuren had arranged – am I telling you much that is new? – had *arranged* various smallish shipments of arms which followed the same route through Dumas Electroniques and then to Namibia as did the material so urgently sought by MLC and the Soviet Union –' Malan was shaking his head, but his eyes were bright with attention. '– I am not certain how many such shipments there were. The latest of them contained nerve gas, in some quantity. Of that I *am* certain.'

'Nerve gas – why?'

'I presume he intended supplying it to extremist white organizations here. As he did the small arms. I am here to find out *who* the intended recipient is, and *where* its destination is.'

'Where is it now? No, I can't believe you. It's an easy deception to foist on a dead man.'

'There I agree with you.'

'This is from the crazy man who wandered out of the Bush, isn't it?'

The intercom buzzed. Malan snapped down the switch and growled into the machine. Then he looked up again as Aubrey shook his head.

'Not entirely. Agreed, van Vuuren confessed as much to him –'

'Before he killed him.'

'He assures me that van Vuuren was alive when he left.'

'Robin Blantyre assured *me* that he was dead. After being tortured.'

'Ah, yes. I'm afraid that was likely. But I believe that *crazy man*, as you call him. Which leaves Blantyre, who at this moment is –?'

Malan was about to speak, then shook his head, and said, 'I know where Blantyre is.' It was evident that he believed what Aubrey said, and yet was disconcerted; like a man moving boxes which contained stolen goods and finding a decayed, skeletal body behind them, evidence of a viler, unacceptable villainy.

'Good. I'm glad you do. I believe that Blantyre has to be involved – though there I must in part take the word of the crazy man.' Aubrey smiled thinly as Malan slipped from the desk and half-crossed the room to him. His folded arms and stance now seemed less assured. 'The fact remains, I have come to make a bargain with you.'

'On the basis of blackmail?' Malan said. Aubrey merely shrugged and stirred the brown sugar in the delicate bowl with the silver spoon. 'I don't think so, Sir Kenneth.'

'Hear me out.' Aubrey did not look up. 'I have no doubt that you believe yourself immune from my small stings. You assume that I am at the end of my career, and probably at the limit of other people's indulgence. You may, in that assumption, be correct.' He looked up. 'But I can make a deal of trouble for you – with your government and the ANC, if not in the UK. That much I can promise you. Self-driven, if necessary, by more personal motives. You understand me? It is all in the past now, my niece's unfortunate death, but I have never ceased to hold you responsible in some important way.' He cleared his throat of memory. 'I am as much a crazy man as the man from the Bush. I may become reckless. Unless you agree to help me.'

Malan was silent for some time, standing at the windows as if contemplating the architecture of the car park and the city beyond. Then he said, without turning: 'You might – *just might* – be troublesome.'

'Were there to be some *atrocity*, some use made of this nerve agent – and we both know there are men mad enough in any country to use it, perhaps especially here – then I could certainly implicate MLC, van Vuuren, probably Blantyre – and, thus, by a causal chain, yourself. I would do that, I assure you.'

Malan whirled round, moving lightly, almost boxer-like, towards Aubrey; his face gratified by Aubrey's tiny flinch. 'Christ, man, you must hate me,' he announced, shaking his head, hands thrust into his pockets. 'You really must hate me. I had nothing to *do* with your niece's death.' Then he straightened. 'No, it's not just that, is it? Even if you wanted it to be. It's something else – you want, what? Things to be *right*? Above board, straight? You're out of your depth, Aubrey. Even Babbington, who went to the same kind of school and belonged to the same kind of clubs, knows it doesn't work like that!'

'I can't change the world, Malan. I realize that –' He smiled. '– with some reluctance, I accept it. But I will *not* ignore this!'

Malan raised his hands, palms outward, in front of his chest. 'All right, all right, Aubrey. I knew nothing of this. What is it you want, in exchange for your silence, your lack of interest? You'll die soon, anyway, just like my father. Make the air a little less choked with moral exhaust.'

Aubrey shivered. 'I dare say. But however much you intend abandoning this country –'

'Is that what you think, man?' Malan scoffed. 'All you've seen or guessed is *insurance*, nothing more or less. I work with the Russians because it suits, as it always has done. So *if* the kaffirs nationalize the mines, freeze the assets, *I* won't choke to death? *Now* do you understand, *royneek*?' He slumped into the opposite chair with a shrug, and added: 'What do you want me to do?'

'It is quite simple. I need your assistance in stopping that shipment reaching the Republic and being distributed. I need to know to whom, and to where.'

'From where?'

It was Aubrey's turn to shrug. 'I guess at Walvis Bay, but I am not certain of that.'

'I'll check. It left Venice when?'

'When you did – when Babbington did.'

'OK. Who's it intended for?'

'Again, I'm uncertain. The AWB – people closely connected with van Vuuren, at any event.'

'Piet was a fool – and disloyal. I'm no longer angry your man killed him.'

'Or whoever.'

Malan glared at him, then scribbled something on a pad he had dragged from the table onto his knee. 'Give me the rest of the day, and tonight,' he said. 'I'll call you tomorrow. Which hotel – the Carlton?' Aubrey nodded. 'OK.' He stood up quickly. 'I think that takes care of our business, Aubrey. I'll do this for you because you can apply pressure – *this* time. Do anything else, overstep this request, and I'll do you harm. Do we understand each other?'

'We do. I think well enough not to shake hands, don't you? Thank you, Malan. I'm grateful for your time.'

He collected his stick and allowed himself to be walked to the door. Malan's frame loomed beside him.

'You stay out of *everything* else, Aubrey. Understand?'

'Agreed. I will be kept out of much – as for the remainder, I will not embarrass you to your government, providing this business is satisfactorily concluded. Goodbye, Malan.'

The door closed on Malan's unsmiling features, his eyes hard with anger and contempt. Malan was barely in control of himself, but Aubrey realized that he was in no sense in control of Malan. But, there had been no other way, none whatsoever. For himself, he had made a devil's bargain indeed! Necessity was certainly not the parent of probity.

He smiled at Malan's principal secretary, the young woman who had brought his coffee, as he passed her desk.


Babbington slid into the rear seat of the Mercedes beside Malan, his jacket over his arm, his tie loose. Together, they completely occupied the rear seat, almost touching after Malan had folded up the armrest. The airport lights glowed in the cool of midnight. There was a bitterly amusing irony in the multiplicity of 747s from a great many of the world's airlines. *Welcome to South Africa* – moral smallpox has been eradicated. The big jets brought planeloads of businessmen every day. Even Russian businessmen, though Babbington could hardly be said to qualify – especially as he appeared now, unkempt and tired and angry with more than the irritation of aircraft incarceration.

'Good flight?' Malan murmured. They had hardly shaken hands.

Babbington glowered in the dusky interior of the car, his eyes preternaturally bright, as if he were drugged. 'What?' he snapped.

'Doesn't matter.'

The limousine glided towards the airport exit, passed through the perimeter and then, ahead of them, Johannesburg glowed as if set on fire. The city's lights overwhelmed those of Alexandra township. The ranks of hostels for migrant male workers were all but dark.

They'd even begun pulling them down, rebuilding *family* homes. They said de Villiers had been outraged when he'd made his first visit to Alexandra, rounding on his staff and accompanying ministers *in front of kaffirs* and berating them. Aubrey and the nerve gas . . . there was some point to van Vuuren's lunacy. At least it was understandable.

'He came to see me this afternoon.'

'Aubrey?' There it was, the Englishman's habitual shock at a world not behaving according to his precepts. 'Why?'

'To ask for my help.' Malan grinned.

'Help? To destroy yourself. He gave you a revolver and told you to do the decent thing, I presume?' The sarcasm was cool, recovered, as if Babbington had transmuted from some travelling persona that was less assured.

'Not quite. Something else. There was another consignment, one I didn't know about, just as you didn't – ' Babbington's stare was suspicious. The Mercedes moved smoothly down the outside lane of the motorway towards Gillooly's Interchange. 'Nerve gas,' Malan announced. 'One of my people, trying to supply some of his friends, so Aubrey told me.'

'And you knew *nothing* of this?' Babbington asked accusingly.

'Should I have? The shipment came from Czechoslovakia or somewhere. Van Vuuren – '

'What have you done with him?'

'Van Vuuren's dead.' Babbington nodded and Malan added no details. Instead, he remarked: 'Aubrey wants to trace the shipment. That's why he's here – why he asked to see me and why I informed you he was coming.'

Babbington rubbed his chin. The beard rasped.

'I see nothing to concern us in this nerve gas matter. I will find out, however. People *I* use must be involved. It is, of course, typical of Aubrey, to come haring out here in pursuit of it! That man's impossibly grand sense that he is the moral arbiter of international affairs never ceases to amaze.'

'He's just an old man.'

'People have underestimated him on such grounds before. His appearance *is* deceptive.' Babbington's face was grim with admission.

'He's here,' Malan remarked impatiently. 'That's all that matters

– apart from the method. I've stalled him until tomorrow. Then I can spin him any line we wish. That *is* why you've come?'

Babbington appeared challenged, even insulted. Then he nodded and smoothed his creased jacket on his lap like a pet animal. He was nodding at some inward satisfaction. Then he said: 'Yes. It was necessary before – vital now. I am – *charged* with ridding ourselves of that odious little man!' The contempt did not quite efface the anger at being the recipient of a direct order – some kind of *field agent*, his lips almost expressed. Babbington's fury amused Malan. He knew Aubrey's suite number, had people watching him, *knew* the man was alone and had made no effort to contact any South African intelligence officer or politician, however sympathetic they might have been to his story. The old man actually believed, in the blindness of his rectitude and self-esteem, that Malan could be bent to his will, would actually assist him in response to his threats. His mistake, then.

After the interchange's clusters of high, overhanging lights, the motorway looked down on neat suburbs and the oddly-symmetrical dark shapes of golf courses and parks. The city had brightened ahead, vinelike lights climbing into the night. Malan considered mentioning van Vuuren's death once more, then remained silent. The crazy man from the Bush was of little or no account. There had been no contact between Aubrey and Anderson, or whatever his name was. He must have been slaked by van Vuuren's murder. Traffic thickened, coming away from the city. Headlights glow-wormed along quiet suburban streets on either side of the motorway. The Reef was invisible in the night. A detached glow, like a source of radiation, burned away to the south. Soweto.

'You'll want my people's help. Tell me tomorrow what you need,' Malan said. 'You won't be using your people, I assume.' Babbington shook his head. 'Better if you implicate me in everything, uh?' Malan smiled, then shrugged. 'I don't mind, Andrew. Just assure me that Aubrey makes a full stop, not just a comma, will you?'

Babbington's right hand formed a fist in a spasmlike movement. He opened it slowly, as if expecting the moth he might have caught to be dead. 'I am in receipt of assurances. From the London Rezident. Aubrey's powers of investigation, the scope of the enquiry, have both been drastically curtailed, from all the available evidence.' Again, he worried at his beard, as if it were no more than

326

stage make-up, a disguise. 'People like Longmead, people in the Cabinet, don't want to rock the boat here, *nor* do they wish even the slightest breath of scandal to touch David Reid. Both are powerful considerations, of far greater import than Aubrey and his theories. Without Aubrey, it will all dribble away into the sand.'

Malan nodded, as if he had just achieved possession of a potential fortune. 'Good. Right, man – we'll get you home, you can take a shower and have a sleep, then we'll decide what to do with Sir Kenneth.' He chuckled.

'It must be accidental.'

'Accidents are easy to arrange, uh, Andrew? An old man, alone in a strange city – not too much of a challenge for you and me.' His laughter was full and genuine, even infectious.

He struggled awake, clumsily putting on his spectacles and switching on the bedside lamp. The digital clock proclaimed two in the morning. He felt drugged with jet lag. The nightcap whisky was salty on his palate. Levering himself into a sitting position in the bed, he snatched up the telephone.

'Kenneth – Richard.'

'Richard – what – where are you, *here*? My dear fellow –'

'Kenneth, I know your instantaneous charm of old. Just listen to me.'

Aubrey swallowed and rubbed his eyes beneath his spectacles, pushing them up almost to meet the strands of hair that had invested his forehead. He frowned. The room was quiet beyond the light's spillage.

'Yes, Richard. But we *must* talk – meet.'

'I don't think so, Kenneth. You'd try to dissuade me. And you should not be the one to talk of putting heads into lions' mouths, coming here alone.'

Anderson sounded tired but detached.

'Richard, I can only *understand*, not disapprove. But, your effort concerns me, your safety.' He hunched over the receiver, as if he were on the point of whispering. 'I have come to an understanding with Malan. I must stop that consignment reaching the Republic, Richard. Your help was invaluable –'

'You don't want harm to come to Malan until your little job's all done, eh?'

'No, not that. Just that there are *other* ways!'

'You think so? Kenneth, I rang simply to warn you. I followed Malan's car to the airport this evening – midnight, to be precise. Not long ago I got back. He collected someone and took him out to the estate. Andrew Babbington. I recognized him.'

'What?' Aubrey whispered.

'Andrew Babbington is here in Johannesburg, in Malan's company. I wouldn't say it boded well for your little plan, would you, Kenneth? And you *alone*. Be careful, Kenneth. I don't really think you understand the kind of people you're dealing with. I'm sorry I can't help further. I have my own priorities. Goodnight, Kenneth – sleep well.'


The noise, whatever it was, woke him from his doze, making him flail his arms inside the quilted blanket he had wrapped around his body against the chill of the night. It was still dark, only a pencil line of light on the horizon, sketching the distant escarpment. He struggled his way out of the blanket, cursing, the sand clinging to his damp, warm palms. He'd fallen bloody *asleep* for Christ's sake!

He rolled onto his stomach and wriggled to comfort on the lip of the dune, the binoculars extricated from the folds of the quilt. He shivered. It was bloody cold at night, and this was bloody *Africa*! Tropic of Capricorn right overhead . . .

Through the infra-red binoculars, he saw the movements in the fenced compound as the shifting of solid grey ghosts and bulks. Even the exhaust fumes writhed greyly, like windblown curtains. Two container trucks . . . two 4WDs, one a scout car, the other a *bakkie*, pick-up truck. He counted the men. Two to each cab – thank Christ, they might stop, then, once in a bloody while. He felt warmer, encouraging his anger, his cursing. Four men in the *bakkie* – must carry the supplies, that – and two men in the scout car. Ten. Then he saw two more men – he could even see the rifles they carried – climb into the rear of the pick-up. All of them wore bush shirts and shorts or khaki trousers, and floppy bush hats. Twelve good men and true, then.

The gates of the compound were opened and the leading XR 311 scout car – that must be Blantyre, it was the set of his body and head – passed through and out onto the gravel road. Its headlights swung – *east*. The *bakkie* followed – call it a ute, mate, and I'll know what you're on about – then the first of the container lorries.

Hyde scrambled to his feet, folding the quilt awkwardly beneath one arm, the glasses slung around his neck and the automatic rifle in his right hand. He scrabbled down the slope of the dune, wading with big, balancing strides until he reached level ground. He'd moved the Land Rover closer, but very quietly and carefully, during the small rush-hour of departures by the MLC staff, just before dusk. He began running, carefully dodging the pebbles and small rocks scattered across the gravelly sand. Then he found the shallow depression and the vehicle, which nudged over the lip as if curious as to his whereabouts. He threw the quilt in the back, then listened in the silence . . . not quite. The noise of retreating engines and the rumble of heavy vehicles, like the sound of a distant storm.

Twelve good men and true – Jesus wept. He started the Land Rover's engine, slipped into four-wheel drive and lurched out of the shallow depression, the sand churning beneath the tyres, the vehicle emerging like something from a swamp in a very cheap movie. Then it levelled and he accelerated gently towards the gravel road, without headlights. The escarpment along the horizon was tinged with reddish gold and the lip of the dune was already ochre in colour. A tall radio mast rose silverly into the lightening sky above the MLC buildings.

He bounced onto the road and turned the Land Rover eastwards. The dust from the convoy hung ahead of him like a pillar of cloud. He glanced at the dashboard clock. Six-ten. It would take them – with regular stops, please God – two days to reach the South African border, whichever route they took. Once they crossed it, action against them would become suicidal at best. It had to happen in the next two days, in Namibia, in the silence and emptiness. Twelve men . . . versus the mighty – *him*. Jesus –

# to be safely thus

Around mid-morning, they had passed through some place called Solitaire that was no more than a street of shops, one hotel and a couple of bars. Its few inhabitants were dressed in working clothes or print frocks and scattered amid a few weary cars; the black faces had far outnumbered the white. Then the isolated, cramped little place had settled invisibly into the dust behind him, the spike of its German church thrust up out of his dust trail, making him shiver. Solitaire. This was Blantyre's country and he was being drawn farther and farther down a narrowing tunnel in the man's wake.

Then, around one in the afternoon, the convoy was no longer ahead of him and he had to slow suddenly and slip off the road onto a dirt track that skirted the village of Maltahöhe. The two container trucks and their escort had halted at the petrol station. Then he lost sight of them as he passed behind a string of low houses. A black gardener looked up in surprise and some chickens stirred nervously on a greener patch of dust.

Corrugated roofs flashed in the sun. White, red-roofed houses, a wooden German church, the white blur of goats – until eventually he halted in the shade of a dusty, spreading acacia, its lower bark protected from grazing animals and the depredations of dogs by a leaning, rusty iron railing. The square was small and quiet, as if the centre of the tiny town had moved a few hundred yards away, to the wider square ahead of him around which a small supermarket, a new, low hotel and a few shops had gathered.

The dust settled on his clothes. A bar winked at him from the corner of the forgotten square, constricting his dry throat. People drifted near the shops, their colours mingling. A white man engaged in conversation with two black men and a willowy young black woman under a shadowy awning. The mannequins in the window were as still and posed as the people on the pavement. A woman's face peered from the side of ornate net curtains behind a shabby wooden fence as he swilled water from a plastic bottle and then rubbed his lips with the back of his hand.

He had waited all morning, as he trailed behind their dust signals, for some sight or sense of a place where he might halt their progress. As they had climbed gently up the escarpment onto the plateau, everywhere had been flat and open. There had been nowhere he could pull the landscape over them like a net. Certainly, it couldn't be done here, in Maltahöhe, which sat on the plateau like a sullen, abandoned member of a wagon train that had ventured farther inland.

He glanced round. The old white face had removed itself from the window of the low bungalow and the net curtain had fallen back into place. A dog relieved itself against the rear, nearside tyre. The heat settled as certain as the dust. He unfolded the map on his knee with a quivering hand. Reaction from gripping the wheel . . . except that he knew better. It was reaction to Blantyre, as if the man had been seated beside him throughout the morning, not up ahead and invisible in the dust cloud. He had been *there* – every memory of him. Hereford, the Brecon Beacons, even Oman for one short tour of duty. Blantyre, who had been more efficient, more ruthless, more competent during their mutual training. More of a bastard . . . perhaps because he didn't have two ageing aunts in the East End who were quietly appalled at the changes being wrought in their nephew by SAS training. The nephew who had joined the army from an undistinguished progress through a certainly undistinguished state school. Blantyre had attended the best school in Salisbury – Rhodesia. To where he had eventually returned, to enlist in the Selous Scouts. Moving, after Rhodesia became Zimbabwe, to Namibia. Hyde stared at his knuckles as they gripped the steering wheel. Blantyre, the world's biggest bastard; his head prefect, his tormentor, who had despised more than anything else the indifference Hyde had always displayed towards him.

Not now, though . . .

He looked down at the map on his dusty thighs, and flicked open the neatly labelled album of prints that rested on the passenger seat. RAF enlargements, tourist snapshots, colour photocopies culled from coffee-table books, all so hurriedly assembled that his first opportunity to study them had been aboard the Hercules. His forefinger traced along the road they had travelled that morning, the C14. If Blantyre chose to stay on it, then follow the C13, he would head directly south through the Schwarzrand range of hills and then the Rooirand. He flicked the album's polythene-folder pages. There was an airport at Aus, which meant that relief could be flown in, reinforcements. But, after Aus, the Namib opened out again, inland of the diamond mining area at Lüderitz – from which MLC could reinforce Blantyre. Anyway, the desert was far too open for a successful ambush.

His finger followed the major road, the B1, east. Better going – more flat land. More airports. The landscape conspired with Blantyre. MLC was everywhere in Namibia, as close as radio contact and an hour's flying could make them.

He rubbed his arms. *Stop them*, Aubrey had said, as if it was a matter of traffic and nothing more. *Cause a road block, perhaps . . . ? I leave it to you, Patrick.* Only because, you old bugger, you couldn't think of any way of doing it. Now, the old man was fiddling in Johannesburg while Hyde burned! His *Good luck* and nervous handshake had been furtive and quick. His manner had been strange, though. As if he were looking over Hyde's shoulder all the time, at something or someone else. If he didn't watch himself, the old bugger'd be as much in the shit as he was! The old white face was back at the window of the bungalow, wrinkled like the surface of a moon. The net curtain was hitched up like a long, Victorian petticoat. Hyde smiled and the old woman flicked out of sight. *You wouldn't want to see the rest of the story anyway, darling.*

He would have to scout ahead of them, just as soon as he was certain which road they were taking. After that, they could be left for hours, heading in one, unchanging direction. He rubbed his stubbled chin and pulled his bush hat lower over his eyes. All he had to do was find one ambush point along the four hundred miles that remained to the border with South Africa. He idly flicked through the album of photographs, shaking his head again and again as he checked the picture with the map on his knee – looking up at the noise of an aircraft. A small Cessna, red and white, floated towards Maltahöhe's landing strip.

As he looked down, Blantyre's 4WD, then the rest of the small column, passed across the main square ahead of him. Heading *east*, towards Mariental. He switched on the engine. The face appeared again at the window and he waved at it. It paused before removing itself, as if it might break out of the egg of its routine and return the gesture. He let out the clutch. The dust of the convoy was beginning to settle as he reached the main square. A few miles along the road, there was a track that the container trucks couldn't use but he could in the Land Rover. It cut like a hypotenuse across flattish escarpment to join the B1 forty miles south of Mariental. He could scout down as far as Keetmanshoop before dark, if he got a move on.

He turned left across the main square. The convoy's dust column rose ahead of him, beyond the town.


It was a harsh, arid place now slipping quickly into evening, and was sparsely littered with karakul sheep and listing fences. Hyde rubbed his forehead. His skin was dry and gritty with dust, his lips powdery and cracked. Inwardly, he was enraged. There was nowhere – *nowhere* . . . even a leopard couldn't have ambushed its prey with any certainty out here. He had driven the main road south through Namaland, passing a scattered succession of sheep stations, tiny villages and outposts, the open country spreading depressingly out around him for most of the journey. Sheep, the occasional herdsman in a woolly hat, the odd vehicle or three. The road followed the easiest land and the railway ran beside it for most of its length. He had pressed on to Keetmanshoop, deeply frustrated and angry.

He looked down now from a rocky outcrop towards the main road, as the sun's red disc was swallowed by the ridged, toothed horizon and the open, scrubbily-grassed landscape darkened. Sheep drifted away towards shelter and the first jackal was snouting through clumps of stiff grass only hundreds of yards away. What might be a dust column wavered in the distance, thrown up by more than one vehicle. If Blantyre had maintained the morning's pace, it would be them. The rocks around him were reddened by the sun's last touch before it dropped into the horizon's grasp and darkness pounced on the landscape. He could make out the pin-pricks of headlights approaching along the dusty snake of the road. His throat constricted. In one day, they'd already travelled more than four hundred miles. The first big, soft stars bloomed overhead and the thin moon, now visible, was already high. The sky was blue-towards-black.

The vehicles were already as big as toys as a slight cool breeze sprang up. The headlights were foggy inside the dust cloud thrown up by the convoy. They would make their overnight stop – please God – in Keetmanshoop or somewhere close by. If they didn't, then he'd need the pills just to stay awake – just to keep going.

He slipped the strap of the Nova night-vision goggles over his head, adjusting the eye-pieces to comfort. The goggles fitted like a diver's face mask, but they were heavy. They made neck muscles ache with the effort of keeping the head upright against the weight of the single lens barrel that jutted out like the horn of a unicorn. He switched the goggles on, and immediately the fog of the dust cloud seemed to clear, so that he could see tiny, ghostly figures in the leading vehicle and obscure shapes behind the windscreen of the leading truck. Even the figures in the fourth vehicle were visible, small black dots of heads. Twelve good men and true. He removed the goggles and placed them on the passenger seat, then started the engine. There had been one scouting jackal, a grey, swift shape, near the road and another closer to the hillock on which he was concealed. He let out the clutch and the Land Rover bounced down the slope. He replaced the goggles – he was getting tired, forgetting simple things. Clumps of grass, tussocky bushes and thorny scrub, the occasional leaning aloe. A hunting bird rushed whitely across his path and disappeared into bushes with the vigour of attack. Then he bumped onto the road and turned towards Keetmanshoop in the wake of the convoy.

He had to do something tonight, whether they stopped or not. It meant declaring his presence, unless he could make any action of his look like an accident. Disabling one of the vehicles, perhaps . . . ?

He drove beneath stunted acacias on either side of the road. They thrust up from the ground like wind-flattened, small clouds on thin poles. The lights of the convoy were sharp amid the aura of the town's lights, which glowed like the heat from a fire. He glimpsed the sliding shape of something that might have been a leopard beside the road, then it vanished with a gleam of eyes. Then the quiver trees replaced the acacias, strange low aloes with pineapple-like bark and tufted with leaves that jutted like starfish spines. He realized he was overtaking the convoy and slowed to a crawl. The kokerbooms – quiver trees – crowded the road threateningly, and they seemed ever thicker as he halted at the side road where the convoy's lights had turned off into the forest. It had to be their overnight camp, there was nothing on the map except a farm and a few scattered homesteads. Blantyre was taking no chance of drinking or indiscretion in Keetmanshoop.

Hyde waited until the glow of the headlights diminished into meteor-like flickerings. He could make out the jutting debris of boulders, as if some great stone temple had collapsed and the aloes had slowly encroached onto consecrated ground. Off the track, there'd be little chance of making progress even in the Land Rover.

Then the lights seemed to halt and gather together. They must have found a clearing they could use to set up camp. He accelerated and drove carefully along the main road, looking for –

A shallow, long ditch that dipped away from the road and from which the trees seemed to have drawn back. He switched on the headlights as the Land Rover bumped off the tarred road. It lurched like a drunk over rocks he could not avoid, then the aloes began to close overhead once more. Eventually, he drew to a halt and pulled on the handbrake, switching off the engine. The silence rushed in against his ears like the pressure from an explosion. Then he heard something die in the darkness away to his left, its surprise choked off by the asphyxiating bite of a big cat. Perhaps it was the leopard he had seen beside the road. He shivered and looked up. The sky was pearl-grey as silk and the stars shone through the cloth like small tears. His eye sockets ached from the pressure of the goggles and he rubbed his stiff neck. Might just save your life . . . Who'd said that, Aubrey or the armourer? He stepped out of the Land Rover onto a rock as big and smooth as a hippo, standing with his hands on his hips. He could make out no source of light in the direction he knew Blantyre to be – trees too close together, or some rocky outcrop masking them from him.

An accident, then.

You'll be bloody lucky to convince Blantyre of *that*, sport. He jumped down from the rock into tussocky grass, overbalancing and steadying himself against the door of the Land Rover. The trees were little more than twenty feet high, their bark as rough as the skin of a tropical fruit. He slapped his hand softly against one of the

335

trunks, pondering. By the time they'd set up camp and eaten, it would be hours before they relaxed into sleep and routine. He reached into the vehicle for a water bottle, drank from it, then ate chocolate. Cold beans later, even some compressed cheese and hard biscuits. No time to risk a fire and some soup.

When he had finished eating the chocolate, he climbed into the Land Rover and fished a second sweater out of one of the bags, drawing it clumsily on over the goggles. Then, irritated with their weight and pressure, he removed them. The manufacturer liked them but most of the soldiers who used them didn't. Removing them because of discomfort had killed quite a few who'd tried to rely on their own unassisted night vision. He rubbed his eye sockets. The African night pressed close around him and he thought of the leopard. It would be eating now, but it was still difficult to ignore. Two hours. He'd try to rest, and it would give them time to cook whatever they –

He heard a shot. Whatever they'd just killed, he told himself, calming the ragged nerves that had twitched at the noise of the rifle. Settle down, relax . . .

He jerked awake and at once looked at his watch and listened to the silence of the night. More than two hours. He'd dozed, even slept soundly for a time. He massaged his cold arms and thighs, yawned and rubbed his eyes. Then he got down from the Land Rover and drew the Heckler & Koch G3 rifle from the rear of the vehicle, weighing it in his hands for a moment. Nice lot of plastic parts, it didn't make much noise in contact with other surfaces. Then he checked the pistol and slipped it into his belt. Then the spare clips of ammunition. The VP 70 was half-plastic, too – clever buggers, the Krauts. He slung the rifle across his chest, its butt folded beneath the barrel. Then he slipped his arms through the straps of a small pack and adjusted its weight on his hips and shoulders.

He began walking in the direction of Blantyre's camp, orientated by the glow of a passing vehicle's headlights on the main road. The stars were like great damp eyes in the darkness. Something small skittered near his feet through the scrub, then careered away. A shrew?

The camp was, indeed, in a small clearing. He reached it after twenty careful minutes of walking, coming first upon their casual, incautious noises and conversation. Then the glow he had seen ahead hardened into the illumination of lanterns. He skirted the clearing until he was down-breeze of it. He climbed a knoll of crumbly rock which overlooked their camp and lay down on his stomach.

A man was bent into the bonnet of the pick-up truck, the nearest vehicle. He heard the clatter and scrape of tools against engine parts, and the scratch of utensils against tin plates and cups. The man being swallowed by the truck was whistling, unworried. There was no way the vehicle wouldn't be able to continue in the morning. Hyde dragged the goggles over his head and the bright firelight and lamplight greyed once more, becoming detached and strange. The two container lorries were turned towards one another like large cats sleeping at either side of a fire. Beside the remaining vehicle, he saw four people gathered, Blantyre the tallest of them. On the bonnet of the scout car, a map lay spread like a tablecloth. At the edge of the clearing, the single man on patrol seemed to leer envyingly into the grey firelight, which someone else fussed around, cooking meat Hyde could smell.

He swung his head ponderously like a much larger creature because of the nightsight, back towards Blantyre at the 4WD, greedy for a glimpse of the sheet of paper that was tapped so insistently. They gesticulated and talked . . . and evidently agreed. The route for the following day, their rendezvous in the Republic – which road? If he could only . . .

The smell of roasting buck over the roaring fire, the burning of its fat as its carcase hung from a spit, churned at his stomach. The assured noises of the camp nibbled at his confidence like a wearing, repeated question. If he could risk – take one look at the map . . . that Blantyre now folded away as he grasped a bottle of beer from a corporal and grinned. The cook was using a long, glinting knife on the buck's flesh, and there was impatience even from the patrolling sentry. The mechanic had emerged from the jaws of the small truck with a positive signal and vociferation. There was an impregnability about the place, despite his eyrie above it. He'd try to disable the scout car . . . or at least get at the map. Then he'd know what Blantyre intended. He watched them settle into easier routines, into harmlessness. He shrugged himself to greater comfort, one hand supporting the bulk of the Nova sight, the rifle placed noiselessly

337

at his side, the pistol in the small of his back, his thighs and knees less conscious of the rock on which he lay. The perimeter guard was waved towards the bright fire and the buck's carcase diminished with the flashing and cutting of the long knife. The truck's bonnet was slammed shut and the mechanic wiped jelly over his hands, laving them, before joining the others around the fire.

Shit, two of them were placing about the camp's perimeter, at each imagined corner of the clearing, what might have been wheeled stands for hi-fi speakers, or skeletal, closed camera tripods. Leads snaked away from them towards one of the tents. Blantyre watched the two men setting up the microwave fence with minimal interest. British manufacture. He recognized it. The invisible fence between the scattered stands with their letter-box-like shutters at the top would be two and a half metres high and the same in width. In the tent, the leads would be connected to a control unit and an audible alarm. His head flicked between the stands. Tight as a fucking drum, impenetrable. It was as if the scene around the fire had become a framed picture beyond a security cord, priceless and unapproachable. The two container trucks, the scout car and the pick-up truck were contained within a mushroom circle, protected by the fucking fairies! Blantyre's laughter over the beer and the meat irritated him further.

Shorrock's — ballocks. He'd used that bloody equipment time and again — light, portable, mobile, effective. He'd even had his and Ros' flats secured by Shorrock alarm systems. He'd paid the buggers money and now they'd sold this fucking set-up to Blantyre, keeping him out! He took off the goggles and wiped his sweating face, trying to calm himself. One needed to be a fucking monkey to jump over that. Eight feet high, eight feet thick, and invisible. But he *needed* that bloody map! The conversation occasionally burst out in laughter or mockery. Behind him in the trees, something moved stealthily away. He heard the rustle of grass as either it or its intended prey accelerated. One of the men in the clearing, hearing the noise, looked up, then shook his head, returning to the buck and potatoes.

A slender, twisted aloe, like a young girl with a limp, dragged itself out over the clearing, approaching a large quiver tree like a supplicant. Need to be a bloody monkey, his thoughts repeated. Would it bear his weight . . . ? He judged the distances, the stoop and halt of the smaller tree, the upright sturdiness of the larger. It

338

was the only possibility. Getting out would be – well, they'd know by then, wouldn't they? It wouldn't matter, *afterwards*. He rolled silently onto his back, staring at the slim trunk of the bent, crippled aloe – winked at it. You're all I've got. Below him, in the clearing, the noise of companionship and safety continued unabated. He had to wait, wait . . .

He jerked awake, aware he must not move, then squinted at his watch, his arm held close to his eyes. Just after two in the morning.

He rolled stiffly onto his stomach, ignoring the companionable aloe for the moment, looking down into the clearing, which brightened as he dragged on the goggles. Grey ash where the fire had been, grey shapes of the tents, grey shapes of sleeping men, two of them out in the open near the trucks. And the damnable little stands of the microwave fence, dotted about as if no more than lumber to be thrown away. He rubbed his arms cautiously, the night's chill deep in his flesh and bones. He sat upright, facing the clearing, rubbing his cold legs into suppleness as he stared at the bent aloe. Then he checked down in the clearing – a patch of grey, footprinted sand to cushion his landing, muffle any noise. Blantyre was in the tent with the control unit of the microwave fence, the rest of them outside or scattered in two other tents. He listened, heard the noise of something splashing, then one of them came sleepily back into view from the bushes, zipping his flies. Hyde watched him return to the tent, where his snoring began almost at once. They'd be breakfasting and leaving before dawn.

He picked the rifle up carefully and drew its strap over his head, the butt retracted. It nuzzled against his chest. He checked the spare clip, then the pistol, finally the knapsack, tightening the straps further. Then he approached the aloe, hands reaching for it, feet moving softly across the rock of the outcrop. The roots of the tree thrust down into a cleft in the rock. He tested its strength. Slowly, he began sliding himself up the trunk, across the gritty, knobbled bark. The tree shivered at his weight and movement. Gradually, gently, it bowed towards the invisible fence as he eased forward, out over the sand. He was sweating profusely and blinking the moisture from his eyes. He inched forward again, straddling the tree, pushing with his hands and scraped knees. Estimating – head back and forth, still wearing the goggles – the line of the invisible beams. The tree became more suppliant, bending into a cower. The

339

closest receiver was fifty metres from its companion transmitter, and the tree was bowing and fucking scraping like a menial just over the bloody fence –! His hands were slippery on the rough bark, his knees trembling. The tree quivered with his exertions and panic and its wood began to groan – monkey, all fours, poised –

He thrust out, twisting in the dark air, managing to land on his feet. His whole frame and mind were hunched and tense against the noise of the alarm as he curled to one side in a parachute landing, and rolled, his hands cushioning the goggles. The two black stands glowered silently at one another, *behind* him –

– *inside*. His chest pumped but he held his breath, staring up at the tree as it shuddered above him. He grinned. He rolled onto his stomach, shivery with adrenalin at the slight noise of someone stirring on a camp bed. The tents remained dark, their flaps closed. The two in sleeping bags near the trucks remained oblivious, unmoving. The starlight and the sheen from the paring of moon seemed to fall tiredly into the clearing. Hyde got to his feet in a crouch, then skittered like an elephant shrew towards the scout car. The map first, then any damage he might disguisedly do to that vehicle or the truck.

He moved across the clearing, spinning occasionally on his heel, then obliterating the professional marks, watching the tents, the vehicles, the sleeping bags. Somewhere in the trees, a monkey grumbled in its sleep. More distantly, the bark of a wild dog or jackal. The sounds flowed into the clearing more coldly and sharply than the starlight. He reached the XR 311 scout car. Blantyre had put the map back in the glove compartment. Gingerly, he touched the door handle, paused, then opened the passenger door.

Through the goggles, the map, as he carefully unfolded it, seemed distant, featureless. Then he saw the snail track drawn from Keetmanshoop, south and then southwest, tomorrow's route. His breath caught. They were going the way he wanted. It was the only likely place, the only terrain suitable for an ambush that would immobilize them and cut them off from outside help. He breathed out gratefully. He stowed the map inside his shirt. It had to be the scout car then, to cover the missing map –

He heard the tiny noise of metal moving against metal. He whirled around, seeing the man and beyond him one of the sleeping bags, opened. The man was holding an R5 rifle at his hip and

340

grinning as if he found the froglike mask of the goggles disarmingly amusing. Hyde fired twice, the pistol in his right hand, the map still held in his left. The silencer made the faintest of noises. He ran, pouncing on the slumping body and catching the man's weight against him, trapping the loosely-held rifle under his armpit. Immediately, he squeezed the trigger of the rifle, certain the angle was correct for the scene behind him. The magazine, an automatic, emptied immediately with a terrifying noise. The goggles were steamed up with his effort and the rifle's barrel was hot against his side and arm. Then he dropped the body and ran, until he was thrust forward by the explosion behind him. He felt the heat from the scout car's exploding petrol tank on his back and shoulders.

He hardly heard the alarm he triggered as he blundered through the beams of the fence, or the voices that rose in surprise and panic above the crackle and roar of the flames.


Malan snapped angrily: 'He believes me because I've told him the *truth*! Those bastards in that junkyard are waiting for Blantyre and what he has to deliver.' The statement amounted to a confession – of Blantyre's working *independently*, of having conceived and executed this business with the Czech nerve gas. An admission to Babbington of all people! 'They've been promised nerve gas,' he continued with an effort at calm. 'For a great deal of money. I found them because Aubrey would not have believed anything but the truth . . .' He scowled, then continued, 'There are bound to be consequences if you kill Aubrey now – *here*.'

Babbington spread his hands in a mockery of benediction.

'It cannot be any other way, Paulus,' he murmured. 'We have come this far. There's no other solution.' He sipped at the whisky he had held like the Host as he spread his arms in blessing and certainty.

'Aubrey's not some nameless black from Alexandra. People will interest themselves in his death. My government –' The contempt was undisguised. '– will interest itself.' He turned away momentarily from Babbington's implacable confidence, then snapped his head round and said: '*Your* masters want him dead – the ears of the bull, right, man? But why not wait and see? He might lose interest, be sidetracked or called home, for all I know!'

'No, Paulus, I'm afraid not. Our safety depends on Aubrey's over-due demise. It has to be done and done quickly. Tomorrow night, for certain.'

Malan turned from the drinks cabinet on the far side of the spacious, lamplit room to find the same pretence of utter confidence on Babbington's features, daring him to dissent. And the hatred of Aubrey, the greed for it to be done, glittered in his eyes. Malan detested his subordination to the Englishman.

'I don't work for the KGB!' he snapped.

'*Your* interests are as well served by his death as are mine – and the people I represent. Stop wriggling under the inevitable, Paulus.' Babbington smiled loftily.

Malan slumped back into his armchair. Eventually, his features stilled from their vigorous mastication of his anger and he mur-mured: 'Very well, Andrew. All *right*.'

Why was he now reluctant? He saw, for God's sake, just as clearly as Babbington did, the necessity of Aubrey's death. He would enjoy it as Babbington did, but then it wasn't personal. Was it?

It was like some kaffir curse put on another black, he admitted reluctantly. Aubrey's niece, his own father, the connections between himself and Aubrey. There was a sense of it going wrong, of not working out . . .

He was aware of Babbington's studious gaze, his intent scrutiny. Fuck Babbington. He hardly needed the continuing links with the KGB. They'd be coming to him in twelve months, desperate to unload vast amounts of diamonds on the market for hard currency. He could afford to wait . . . except that he couldn't. Aubrey was getting closer and closer. He looked up, to find Babbington still studying him. Then the Englishman smiled.

'I mean to have it done, Paulus.' He looked at his empty glass. 'I mean to have that infernal, interfering old man dead – and I intend to be there to see it done.' He yawned through his cold smile. 'Past my bedtime, I'm afraid. I'm not certain I shall sleep, but I think I had best try.' He stood up and stretched luxuriously. 'You'll see those people first thing, Paulus – just to make certain?'

Malan looked up angrily, then merely murmured: 'Yes, I'll see to all the *arrangements*. Stage-manage the last little act of your overlong drama, Andrew.'

'Thank you, Paulus – thank you.' His sigh of satisfaction was stomach-turning. 'Good night, then.'

When he had closed the door behind him, Malan sat on, unable to calm himself, unable even to adopt a pretence of relaxation. He almost gagged on his drink as he swallowed it.

What he hated was being *subject* to Babbington, having to obey him, to fulfil another's priorities, not his own. Even if it was inevitable, and altogether better, that Aubrey died tomorrow night . . .


He drew to a halt near the outskirts of Alexandra. He was aware of the former bachelor township just beyond the ragged horizon of spoil-heaps from the mines. Its history pressed against the windows of the car like a wild crowd bent on mischief. He stared across the road at the scrapyard and its heaped cars, still retaining on his retinae the image of Malan's red Porsche turning through the rickety corrugated metal gates a few moments earlier.

Anderson rubbed his cheeks and yawned. Lights still glowed in a grubby halo around the township. He had been surprised from a doze as Malan's car had turned out of the electronic gates of his estate. It had been difficult to keep up with him, easy to keep him in sight in the necessarily red sports car. Then the Porsche had slewed aside from this winding road in a decaying suburb into the scrapyard outside which Anderson had drawn to a shocked halt. *De Vries* was the name daubed untidily in black paint on the corrugated gates. The name meant nothing to Anderson.

He pulled forward perhaps three hundred yards, from his position opposite the gates, onto a grubby, weed-strewn patch of concrete that masqueraded as a car park and warned against black customers. The bungalow motel behind its car park wished to remain in the past. He opened the door and got out. The early morning was cool, fresh, and he felt his curiosity come awake like hunger. On the faint breeze, he smelt frying bacon, and his stomach protested. The distant factories and mines, on which everything depended, belched smoke and dust into the lightening sky. He opened the boot and took out his pistol and the directional microphone. Blacks moved along the pavement or tottered in the road itself, either going to work or away from *shibeens*, with irremovable grace.

The place was flat, seedy, and the scrapyard's heaped contours of wrecked or old cars and trucks provided its immediate horizon. He crossed the road and looked through the gates. There was no sign of Malan's Porsche. He moved inside, adrenalin itching in his stomach, his body expressing the aches gathered during his night's uncomfortable sleep. He was met by cranes, crushers, great suspended grabs – like the little cranes in glass boxes in amusement arcades from his childhood holidays in Bournemouth or Weston-super-Mare. Tiny cranes whose grabs were suspended over chocolate bars and trinkets. Money in the slot, turn the wheel furiously, guide the crane before the time the pennies had bought ran out ... Now, these grabs that hung poised over last year's models, eager to seize and deliver them to the crusher, might catch him Malan, a far greater prize. He moved with exaggerated care around and through anthills of rusted metal, the long microphone dibbing ahead of his steps like an extravagant gardening tool –

– to find, after avoiding the few blacks and even fewer whites who worked in the scrapyard, Malan and two other men paused on the steps of a leaning, dishevelled caravan which seemed parked against a portable lavatory. Which he could scent on the morning air. The two men were caricatures; stubbled, potbellied, thick-necked. Anderson rested his elbow on the dented wing of a red, rusting Ford and adjusted the focus of the heavy telephoto lens attached to the camera. Malan and the two men jumped into close-up. He snapped the photographs, concentrating on the other two but always including Malan in profile in the shots, as if concerned merely with composition.

Why not kill him now? But he knew the answer. He wanted to survive. He was almost ashamed to admit it. Despite Margarethe and his grief, he didn't really want to *die* in the process of killing Malan.

Malan was gesticulating angrily at the other two, causing Anderson to raise the directional mike quickly and steady it on the bonnet of the Ford, thrusting it towards the dilapidated caravan. He fitted the earpiece of the mike and heard: 'I'm bringing the Englishman here tonight – I want it finished then. My people will take care of it.' Malan was using his hand in chopping, assertive motions. '– no problem.' The muttering of the Afrikaaner was masked to the microphone, but seemed to be conciliatory at the mention of reward. He gestured Malan inside the hut and they went in

344

together, closing the door behind them.

Anderson, cursing, could see them moving excitedly to and fro like insects behind glass, but the murmur of their voices was drowned by the upstart of a crane and the hoisting of the first of the day's ruined cars into the sunlight, so that it gleamed and shone before being dropped into the crusher, whose eating noises made him lower the microphone as he realized that Aubrey must be the subject of their conversation. Malan moved into view inside the hut, smiling, his arms moving in decisive gestures. It was a set-up. They intended Aubrey's death, Malan and Babbington. A disposal job, Aubrey ending up in the scrapyard. He glanced around him, at the cars and tyres and other metal piled like termite mounds of disposable technology.

Then, Malan emerged from the hut and stood posed on its steps as if for assassination. Anderson realized he could kill Malan that night *and* have a margin for escape.

He allowed Malan to move down the steps and reach his car with a luxury of confidence. He knew now, and that was all that mattered. The metal around him began to warm with the slanting rays of the sun, and the dust and smog over the city started to dissipate. It was the nearest to a good dawn since Margarethe's death. Malan smoothed the Porsche away from the noisome hut, down another channel between the great, untidy flexed muscles of the car-heaps. The crusher continued to chew as another mangled car was dropped into its throat. He shivered as he thought that someone must have died in that, the wreckage was so maimed and twisted. Then he regained confidence as he remembered that Malan was walking into a trap. Not Aubrey – Malan. If Aubrey had to be the tethered goat, then so be it. He owed Aubrey almost nothing. If he hadn't remembered Aubrey when he'd discovered the crashed Dakota, then she would not now be dead.

He moved cautiously down one of the alleyways between the walls of dead cars, the mike trailing like a spade in the hands of a weary gardener, the camera around his neck. A black man near the main gate alarmed him, but was intent upon worrying something that glowed dully like copper from the middle of a hive of broken cars. Above him, the sky was cleanly blue. He scuttled towards his car, the dust from Malan's Porsche already settled on the road. He threw the mike and the camera carelessly into the boot. He needn't

345

even follow Malan. The time between now and tonight mattered nothing. He started the engine and turned the car. He could go back to the cheap boarding house and the lumpy mattress and sleep. He'd put on the travelling alarm clock as if he needed to wake simply to go to work . . . which is what it would be, just a job, the *last* job.

The road bustled with drivers heading for city work. An accident, a car mangled and scorched beneath the cab of a lorry, hardly disturbed his mood. Two more fragments of the newest heap in the scrapyard where, that night, Malan would become his victim, where he would fall backwards with a little hole in his forehead before his mouth opened in shock and final exhalation. It would do – it would do very well.

The city gathered about him, straggly suburbs eventually becoming more dense, clotted. Not wealthy, just small front lawns or apartment buildings and old, decayed bungalows. Almost a shabby gentility in places. The golf courses and the parks and the white, stuccoed houses were masked by grubby lines of houses, like washing taken in from the wealthier areas, as he moved closer to the centre of Johannesburg. Neat estates became leaning, crowded boarding houses and twisting, mean-faced streets. Hillbrow. Translation into the dialect of tourists, hitchhikers and migrant workers of sallow complexion – cheap lodgings.

He turned into a narrow, curving street where old cars jostled each other in the gutters and the stained pavements fronted tall, narrow houses with pinched expressions, undernourished and deprived of sunlight. The boarding house at which he was registered under another name was on the left, where he looked for a parking space –

– and found police cars, their occupants spilt onto the pavement and into the road. Blue lights whirled slowly, hypnotically above the cars. Guns. Outside *his* boarding house, cutting it off. The main street of lodging houses, snack bars, dosshouses and shops leered at him, as if it had planned this shock.

Malan's power and influence. They'd found him.


Hyde had had to wait outside Holoog, to be certain that they stuck to the route sketched on the stolen map. Then, once they were on the winding, climbing road through the hills towards the Fish River Canyon, he had scuttled ahead of them in the Land Rover, giving himself perhaps an hour before the container trucks and the now cramped pick-up truck arrived . . . just *here*.

The winter afternoon weighed on his shoulders and stuck his sweat-stained shirt to his damp torso. He had hidden the Land Rover almost a mile from the canyon, forcing it up a narrow track further along the road, which wound through the maze of hills that lay to the southwest of the canyon. Then he had scrambled and urged himself back here, to *this* spot. Where he could ambush them, could pull rock and earth down in front of them and behind, boxing them in, with no escape except on foot.

He looked down from the road to the bottom of Fish River Canyon. A few scattered water holes, nothing more in the dry season. The river only ran in spate during the wet season – if the rains came. There were a few buck, some zebra and a couple of baboons scattered around the nearest and largest of the water holes. The canyon snaked out of sight within a couple of miles in either direction, twisting its way through a tumbled, mountainous land-scape. He looked up. Hills and flat-topped plateaus stretched away in every direction, blue and hazed in the afternoon. The whole landscape was fingered with canyons and narrow valleys, and was dry and empty, red-brown or flint-blue under the sun. A mountain desert in Namibia, no more than forty miles from the border with South Africa – the last place and the only place he could hope to stop them. Here, on this narrow dusty strip of road, he could do it.

Here the road dropped below the lip of the canyon for a distance of some miles, sagging like a rope bridge suspended alongside the cliff face. Rock overhung the road, rock that could be blown down in a landslide.

One of the two overhangs he had selected was hidden from the other by a bend in the road. Which meant he would have to be somewhere in the middle, concealed by no more than rubble beside the road, and he would have to be quick and certain. He looked at his watch after staring up at the sun. Their speed along this stretch of the road – for the last ten miles or so – would be about twenty-five. He had three or four minutes. He sensed the ground beneath his feet. Nothing yet, no quiver of the approaching weight of the two container trucks.

And, once he'd declared his hand, they'd try to reverse out of the trap, back towards – *you*, sport, standing in the middle of the road like a fucking lemon. He glanced back the way he had come, but there were other twists in the road that hid their approach. No column of dust, not yet.

He rubbed his hands through his hair, his temperature jumping as if he had been pricked by a needle. He moved to the side of the road and knelt beside the two fibreboard boxes he had brought from the Land Rover. Twenty-five kilos, combined weight. His arms ached as much from hurry and tension as from the effort of carrying them. The ground beneath his foot and bent knee seemed to quiver, as if warning of an imminent earthquake. It was them.

He fumbled open one of the boxes and withdrew a short tube, laying it on the ground beside him. The dust trembled underneath his fingertips as he did so and sweat broke out on his forehead. He removed the second tube from the box and then opened another one, laying two more tubes on the ground, then four closed-finned rockets beside them. Feverishly, bent over his work as if secretive, he loaded each of the tubes with a rocket, after first extending the inner tube of each launcher and hearing the cocking mechanism operate – he just heard the last as the noise of approaching heavy vehicles grinding against their brakes seemed to rush over him.

He checked the sight on one of the tubes, and then flung himself flat against the shaking earth, behind the shelter of a scrubby little thorn bush and a litter of small boulders as the noise of the two trucks became deafening. The ground shuddered against his body. He thrust his hands over his ears as the dust rolled over him and then a vast shadow cut off the sunlight. He glanced sideways and saw –

– a small, old green car, overawed by the dust from the first of the trucks. A white-haired man drove, with a white-haired woman in the passenger seat, travelling at twenty miles an hour, their faces agape with the view and the drop to the right. Then the first truck passed, then the second, its shadow cold. He glanced up again, and imagined Blantyre in the pick-up as it passed. He sprang to his feet in the swirling dust and, gripping a tube, ran out into the road after the convoy. Shit, why did those two silly old buggers have to be there just *now*? They'd have to be trapped, that was all, have to be . . . maybe the old green car wouldn't be buried –

He felt exposed by the settling dust and raised the tube to his shoulder, pressing the rocket launcher's crude, effective sight to his eye. He saw nothing but dust for a moment, then the stadia lines and crosses enclosed the shadowy bulk of the pick-up truck. He raised the tube slowly, his hand cupped over the trigger bar, the safety handle pushed to the armed position. He glimpsed the green car for an instant before he focused on the overhang. Range, two-fifty metres. Target stationary.

He squeezed the trigger bar. There was the slightest jolt. He sensed the six spring-loaded fins snap out from the missile, then saw the small jet of flame from the motor before he lost sight of the tiny, inadequate projectile. Then he saw the impact, detonation and explosion, and the burst of rock and debris from the overhang. He snatched up the second tube, discarding the first, armed it, sighted, paused. The rock was falling out of a cloud of dust, like the collapse of slums being pulled down. It was almost as if he antici-pated a bathroom's weary wallpaper to be exposed rather than raw rock. He fired the second missile. The green car, for Christ's sake – poor old buggers –

He heard the noise of violent braking, he even heard voices, coming out of the slow roar of the landslide. Then the second explosion obscured everything in more dust, the noise recoiling from the walls of the canyon. The dust rolled along the road towards him like a sea fog coming inland. Perhaps the green car had slipped through –

He lurched to the side of the road as if nauseous and picked up the third and fourth tubes. The noise of the explosions seemed to growl back from the landscape. He saw brown hills and blue mesas for a moment before the dust enveloped him. Then he heard the screech of reversing tyres. He ran back along the road towards the second overhang. It might not be enough. He couldn't know how much of each landslide would fall off the road and into the canyon. He came blunderingly out of the dust cloud into the blinding sun-light. Tyres squealed and shifted and there were shouts behind him. He passed beneath the overhang, turned and paused to breathe deeply. His throat was thick with dust. Then he sighted the tube and fired. Flame, fins, diminishment – explosion. Rocks grumbled, even squealed in protest as they began to tumble. Then the pick-up truck reversed out of the dust and he saw wild faces watching the

349

road and the drop beside it – before they saw him. At once, there was yelling and the movement of the black sticks of rifles.

He ducked onto one knee and fired again into the maelstrom of dust and rock tumbling down the cliff face. He did not see the flame of the explosion, but heard the detonation. The rock face slithered viscously like mud onto the road between himself and the truck. One shot whined harmlessly near him.

Hyde heard cries and the roar of an engine accelerating away from the landslide. Then he turned and ran ahead of the rolling cloud of dust. He reached the narrow, slitlike crevice that ate into the cliff face and wound jaggedly to its top. Get up there, look down on them, check the damage. Green car, two old people . . .

As he began climbing, feet and back braced against rock, sweat bathing his body and dust choking his throat and nostrils, he saw the landscape open out beyond the rolling dust. The G3 rifle clinked against the rocks. He'd begun it now – not with the murder of two civilians, please . . . but begun it he had. The canyon was a deep, twisting scratch in the arid land which tumbled and jutted away from him in every direction, hills and plateaus empty and barren under the afternoon sun.

He pushed himself higher up the crevice, his muscles quivering with effort.

Green car. Poor old buggers.

# dare me to the desert

The lift climbed the floors of the car park with asthmatic, shuddering difficulty. The graffiti of hatred and inconsequence jostled against each other on the metallic walls. Anderson glanced down at the briefcase he carried, containing the rifle, the nightsight, the spare ammunition and clothing, and felt himself settled by it. It had been easy to drive past the boarding house in Hillbrow, ignoring the police cars and the small crowd of loungers and gawpers on the opposite pavement. Easy, too, to return to the car, almost easy to eat breakfast . . . by lunchtime, it was different, extending his nerves to breaking, because they were ever more intent in their search. The midday editions of the evening papers all carried his picture. He had spent much of the afternoon checking and rechecking that he was not being tailed, that he could survive without being immediately recognized.

The lift jolted and Anderson's temperature jumped like an insect, feeding on his anxieties. It *was* closing in, like this scarred metal box of a lift. Malan had gone to see Aubrey at the Carlton, no doubt confirming the arrangements for the set-up! That night they would get rid of the inquisitive old man. He rubbed the arm that carried the briefcase with his free hand. The lift dragged to a halt and the door opened. He stepped out into the shadowy air-raid shelter of the car park.

He had to use Aubrey. But the old man had his own reasons for being there. Only his ignorance would be *used*. His quiet footsteps echoed above the hum of the city's traffic. The hot afternoon sun hardly intruded, except to emphasize shadow. He had his reservations, but Aubrey's death would hardly weigh, after all, beside Margarethe's . . .

He noted slabbed glimpses of hard afternoon light beginning to mellow towards evening, and rainbow pools of oil and petrol, the

351

scent of fuel. Far below, impatient tyres screeched, turning a sharp corner from one floor to another. He'd remain here, watching Malan's office, until the man left for home or for the Carlton to collect Aubrey.

A memory of the old man's impatient, irresistible moral outrage caused him to stumble. He righted himself and shook his head. That was then, this is now, he told himself. He spotted the boot of the car jutting out near the end of the row of vehicles, and began to hurry towards it.

He opened the boot to place the briefcase inside and take out the binoculars. One small suitcase, a second handgun, night-vision binoculars – all he needed. The sun began to slant into the upper floor of the car park, spilling across the scarred bonnet of the car, its dusty paintwork –

Hand poised to slam the boot, hand making prints on the paint-work . . . just like the hand that had made an impression on the edge of the bonnet, which was normally tightly closed, but there was another smudgy print near the first, as if two hands had closed the bonnet very carefully. The sun exposed the intrusion. His hand quivered on the boot lid, still holding it aloft, his fingertips sweaty, his brow prickling with damp. Smell of petrol, sharp as a winter morning's exhaust fumes. His stomach churned as the bonnet threatened to bulge like a frog, explode –

Carefully, with a huge effort of will, he lowered the lid of the boot until it touched the knuckles of his other hand. He let it rest on its hinges and moved carefully towards the front of the car. The smudged signals of interference vanished until he bent, cocking his head sideways, and caught them again. Two thin-gloved hands closing the bonnet . . . after –

He knelt on the stained concrete and peered beneath the car. Sump, gearbox, exhaust . . . and a cancerous tumour sprouting wires. Trembler trigger or mercury switch – or radio-controlled. He bolted upright, staring wildly around him. No one. Sure? Again, his eyes swept the car park floor. No one. He was sweating pro-fusely. He wiped savagely at his face, shuddering with anxiety.

He opened the boot carefully, and took out the briefcase as the first silenced bullet sprang with a wasplike noise off the boot lid. Pistol, low velocity, only denting the metal. He jerked round but his hand did not forget to lower the boot lid carefully as he ducked beside the car, crouching against the rear wheel, his knee in a pool of damp, grubby oil. A second shot shattered the rear window above his head, showering his hair and neck with fragments. He was shudderingly aware that he was on the same level as the bomb, that any impact might trigger it. Oh, Christ ... A third shot – from where? *Where?* he wanted to scream. No muzzle flash from a silenced gun. The third bullet broke into the car next to his, frosting both the side window and windscreen. How many? He bent forward and drew the briefcase towards him, and the concrete puffed up dust near his hand. One gunman? The bullets seemed to be coming from the same direction. Silence, except for tyres moving on a lower floor and the hum of the traffic, the occasional impatient horn.

He slid behind the nearest car, moving closer to the gunman, squeezing his crouched body between the bumper and the concrete sill of the car park wall. Then a second car, then a third – flinching at a shot whining away off the roof of his car. The briefcase clutched to his chest, he eased past another radiator – Volvo grille and badge. The pistol in the small of his back, under his jacket, scraped silently along the concrete wall, over which seeped the noises of Johannesburg's indifferent afternoon. He wiped his forehead and eyes –

– footsteps, scuttling like rat noises in a cellar. He raised his head above the parapet of a BMW and glimpsed a shadowy figure, arm clutching a blunt little shape, other hand pressing something against an indistinguishable face. Calling for help. Unconsciously, he drew the pistol from his belt, slipped off the safety and a round into the chamber. The bulk of an American limousine hid the man for a moment, then he was a stronger shadow jutting above the curve of the Cadillac's roofline, just for ... elbows resting on the BMW's roof, gun extended, finger squeezing twice. Spit of bullets onto concrete, the kick of the gun – the jerk of the struck head and shoulders and the skitter of the dropped handgun across the concrete. The screech of tyres shut out all other noise, even that of his breathing as he ran for the exit door and the stairs.


He threw himself down at the top of the crevice, elbows jarring as he raised the glasses to his eyes. The lenses clouded for a moment, then cleared. The speck of green at the periphery of the binoculars' vision drew him with a surge of relief and he focused on the old car and the older couple doddering out of it, dazed at the sight of the collapsed cliffside behind them. Christ, they'd escaped, thank God. The old man and woman clung together as if amid the wreckage of their home. His thin, shaking hand kept patting her shoulder and cheek. It was strangely affecting, so that he flicked the glasses aside —

– to see Blantyre, arms waving, pointing. Hyde's shirt began drying on his back, stuck unwelcomely to it. The cab of the leading truck was crushed inwards, like a beer can that had been closed in an angry fist, but the container itself, thank Christ, was intact, merely scarred and dented by the falling rocks. Two men were trying to open the door, flinching against any escape of the cargo, goaded by Blantyre's yelled instructions. The door wouldn't open. His heart continued to thud against the rock on which he lay prone. The road ahead of them was completely blocked with tons of rock and debris above which dust seemed reluctant to settle. He swung the glasses hesitantly past Blantyre's angry bulk and the rest of his troops, one of whom seemed to be nursing an arm, towards the other fallen outcrop. Much of it had spilled over the canyon, down towards the dry river . . . but a great, dull mound of rocks lay across the road, perhaps twenty feet high. Impenetrable. Both ways out were blocked, they were in the box. Thank Christ . . .

Blantyre had glasses up to his eyes now and was scanning each broken outcrop in turn. He must be able to smell the explosives even through the amount of dust in the air. He'd know – and know who. Even if they had persuaded themselves that SWAPO remnants or bandits had killed the patrolling guard and destroyed the scout car. Blantyre's mind must already be forming the name and the accompanying expletives, and before long he'd react —

– waving at the clifftop, and yelling. Hyde shuffled, as if flinching, a yard farther from the edge. One of them, the driver of the second truck by the look of it, was gesticulating as he argued with Blantyre, whose face was suffused with rage. Then he calmed, his shoulders relaxing, his head beginning to nod, as the driver pointed beyond the fallen outcrop that blocked their route.

Blantyre ordered them around him and began gesturing at the wall of rock. Then he hurried towards it. Hyde shifted the glasses and caught the speck of green that was the old couple's car. She was holding the top of a Thermos flask in both hands, sipping at something that smoked hotly. He was holding her upper arms and talking to her with slow gestures of his head . . . Christ. Witnesses. Blantyre was scrabbling up the slope of fallen rock, dust billowing around him. Two others, with Uzis or something else blunt and dangerous slung across their backs, were climbing in his wake. The old woman went on sipping obliviously. The hot drink evidently calmed her. They stood close together, *were* together. Blantyre had scrambled to the top of the mound, then paused. The other two joined him, and there was instant gesticulation at the two elderly people. Witnesses, that was all they were, to be eliminated. He saw in the faces of the two old people a growing sense of concern at what might have happened to the convoy which had been behind them in their cautious progress . . . so that they turned, as Blantyre's two companions levelled their sub-machine guns.

Oh, you bastard . . . It was futile to call out. They could not escape their execution. Hyde bit his bottom lip as his body flinched against the noise of the two Uzis. He watched the two slowly collapsing bodies. They fell apart as they would never have wished, one to either side of a scattering of small boulders. Blantyre immediately clambered over the lip of the rubble and raised dust as he slid invisibly down the other side. Hyde's reaction was instinctive, even stupid. He raised the rifle, butt extended against his shoulder – round carried in the chamber. He fiddled quickly with the adjustments to the telescopic sight. A sweat-streaked back enlarged, became clear – and he fired. Then he transferred his aim to the other man. Blantyre came back into vision as he reached the bottom of the mound and glanced back at the noise of the first shot. Hyde fired again, then a third time because his finger had jumped on the trigger rather than squeezed. The second sweat-stained shirt slumped against the rocks as if exhausted. Two dead, for those two.

Blantyre had already ducked away from the suspected line of fire towards a scatter of boulders, leaving the two old bodies. It was somehow obscene that the old woman's skirt had ridden above her narrow thighs when she fell and their outstretched arms had no hope of reaching each other. They were lying only yards from the green car. The cliff above Blantyre's hiding place was bathed in late afternoon sunlight.

On this side of the trap, men scurried for cover like ants. He had

355

invaded their nest. He fired three shots, cartridges puffing out of the right cheek of the rifle, and then the scene went silent. Lack of movement, stillness. They were all, suddenly, hidden from him.

And now it began. *Keeping* them here, in the trap. The silence pressed against his ears, drumming. The two old bodies on the road, the two bodies on the rubble mound like dirty clothes drying in the sun. He had to keep them *all* here . . .

His rain forest had gone, his natural habitat of anonymity had been razed. Every evening newspaper carried pictures of him with banner headlines in thick black type, blazoning his fictitious crimes. In a paranoid moment in a paranoid country, he had become a right-wing terrorist plotting to overthrow the government and the process of peaceful change. He had murdered an unarmed police-man who had been keeping his car under surveillance. There was even to be an enquiry as to why defenceless police officers were forced to risk their lives to confront men as dangerous and mad as he. His face was everywhere; he could not risk confronting anyone – car rental firms, cheap lodging-house clerks, waitresses in dingy cafés . . . He was the last lion on a scorched veldt, exposed to the hunt.

Anderson leaned against the warm brick of an alley wall, the lights from one of the city's main thoroughfares leaking into it. Car headlights and the flicking spray of red or blue from police patrols flashed frequently into the darkness. Somewhere farther along the alley, a black man had discovered oblivion in a bottle and was snoring. Occasionally, there was noise of a radio or a quarrel, laugh-ter passing the end of the alley where a restaurant's rubbish attracted thin cats with its smell. His whole body quivered in a spasm as one of the cats knocked off a dustbin lid and it rolled along the alley like a grenade. He wiped his sheened face, feeling on his skin the shiver of his fingers. Christ . . . oh, *Christ*! The briefcase was at his feet, the small of his back was numb where the gun had been pressed between cloth and brick. There was no way of going on and little or no possibility of getting out. He stared at his hands in the splashed light of a passing car. There was nothing he could do, not now. He could never get to Malan and survive. He would be lucky to get out of Jo'burg alive.

Because your bottle's gone, old boy. His courage, determination, whatever name you gave it, had slipped away. He couldn't find revenge any longer, nor even hatred. Their superiority was too evident, too omnipresent as he had skirted a newspaper stand or lighted shop window; too evident each time a patrol car or a policeman on foot passed him. Finally, having fled into this drunk-inhabited, cat-roamed alley at the siren of yet another patrol car, he had surrendered to his body's spasms and vomited with fear. He could smell that, too, mingled with the alleyway's other scents.

All he could do, he admitted – if he could get up the nerve to move at all – was to call Aubrey. At least warn him what Malan had planned for him. Sign off, bow out with a little face-saving gesture. He pressed the face of his watch close to his eye. Nine-twenty or thereabouts. The night enlarged, extended, making him shiver . . .

It was nine-forty before he had pushed his way along the wall to the end of the alley. One of the cats had inspected his shoes because he must have stepped in something fleshy and enticing. The lights made him flinch, the people passing possessed loud, accusing voices. A patrol car forced him into a runner's crouch for a long moment. Eventually, he straightened, back pressed against familiar brick, hands spread so that his palms were comfortingly gritty with brick dust. If he waited until the streets emptied, Aubrey would be dead for certain –

The telephone booth was perhaps fifty yards along the well-lighted, crowded street. Nine forty-five. A blue-shirted police back, a streak of sweat darkening the uniform in a ragged stripe from neck to waist. Hands on hips, the armed policeman was no more than six or eight yards beyond the telephone booth – which was empty. He touched the handle of the briefcase with numb fingers, then picked it up, wiped his forehead brusquely, and stepped out of the alley into the drifting crowd, allowing himself to be shunted towards the telephone and the oblivious policeman. Thirty yards, then twenty, the scene joggling in his vision. He gripped the briefcase unfeelingly. A minute, no more, just enough time to blurt out, *They're going to kill you tonight, don't go anywhere with Malan* – then he could try to get out of the city, out of the country, find some desolate border crossing into Botswana or even Namibia.

A black lifted the telephone off its hook and began dialling.

Anderson halted and the crowd jostled before parting around him. The policeman scanned the street and the pavement and Anderson bolted against a shop window, staring unseeingly at trinkets and watches behind a heavy grille. When he glanced round at the telephone booth, the black was gesticulating, arguing with whoever he had called. Time ran as slowly as the beads of cold sweat down Anderson's sides. The black man continued to bellow silently into the receiver. A patrol car passed . . . slowed, then drew across to the pavement and the relaxed policeman. Its headlights remained on, as if looking for Anderson. The black left the phone booth, throwing aside a cigarette butt before moving angrily away. The policeman was leaning into the patrol car, then he emerged, nodding and grinning. A smell of frying onions. The policeman nudged his way to the front of the small queue at the vendor's cart and returned to the patrol car with two dull buns around fat, shining sausages and one polystyrene cup. He handed the food and drink into the car . . . which slid casually out into the traffic. Anderson darted to the booth and dialled the Carlton Hotel. The policeman had drifted back to the vendor and planted himself once more at the head of the queue.

'Sir Kenneth Aubrey,' he blurted. 'Quickly!' The heat of tension mounted in his frame, burned on his cheeks and forehead. He glanced at the policeman, his mouth blocked with some kind of burger. The stench of frying onions was utterly nauseating. His fist punched harmlessly at the directory on its chain. Come on –

'Yes?' he heard. There was a palpable tension in Aubrey's voice.

'Kenneth – Richard.'

'Richard – please listen to me. I've seen the news, you must *not* –'

'What – not do anything to upset your plans, Kenneth?' His anger was delaying him. 'Christ, do you realize Malan's about to have you killed?' He heard his own breathing and smelt onions and petrol fumes. He felt sick.

'Richard, you must be careful, you're in considerable –'

'Christ, don't tell me, Kenneth!' A car drew up, a small BMW, and the driver got out almost close enough to nudge against the glass of the booth. He strolled to the vending cart, passing the chewing, bovine policeman. 'I'm in danger *now*! This minute. But you can't go with –'

'I have to, Richard. I don't yet know what I need to. Thank you, however.'

'I'm getting out, Kenneth. Before they get *me* –'

The keys were in the BMW's ignition. The policeman had finished chewing and was being asked directions. The driver was still behind one other in the queue, casually smoking.

He slapped the receiver back onto its hook and picked up the brief-case. It was a sign, a gift. Before the number could be circulated and watched for, he'd be beyond the city's outskirts and into the night. On a road out of the country, the damned *fucking* country! He threw the briefcase into the rear of the car as he glanced at the driver, who was studying two young women. The policeman's arm was gesticul-ating at some destination streets away. Anderson started the engine, slipped the car into gear and skidded out with a screech of tyres into the street's traffic. In the driving mirror, the owner of the car only slowly became aware. He swung north onto a narrower street that would take him towards the nearest motorway.

He was getting out.


Aubrey slowly put down the disconnected telephone, then straight-ened in his chair and sighed. He shivered as if a chill breeze had penetrated the warm sitting room of his suite – which itself seemed to diminish, as if he were suddenly outside it, looking at a photo-graph of its furniture and carpet and drapes. He sighed again and clutched his thighs with his fingers. He felt a sharp concern for Anderson . . . and perhaps regret that matters could not be settled in the way that Richard would have wished, by a quick strike, an execution. He knew it to be wrong – and shortsighted, of course. *He*, Aubrey, had to know, to discover more before Malan could be consigned to the flames of whatever hell he admitted. That was paramount. Malan would offer him real people, real conspiracies, as the price of silencing him.

He puffed out his cheeks and exhaled, then rose and poured himself a small whisky, returning with it to one of the suite's ample sofas. Ten o'clock. Malan had called an hour before, arranging to collect him at twelve. He had been circumspect and devious, but he *had* located the destination of Blantyre's cargo of nerve gas, however he had arranged matters since. Malan himself would put those people to the sword – but it was essential that Aubrey play his part as innocent seeker-after-truth and victim.

He sipped at the glass and his fingers quivered it against his dentures. He adjusted the half plate, a mirror caught his action dimly on the other side of the sitting room. He shook his head at himself. Why not walk away? He couldn't. He thought of the Prime Minister he had served for so long going out in her own blaze of immolation; of her deep and genuine rage against circumstance. The man who succeeded her was *not half the man she was,* as a tabloid had recently claimed. And he could acknowledge that, despite her abiding distrust of him. His rage was similar, one of entire rectitude. He had to *ensure* that this business was stopped. He glanced across at the drawer of the desk where the pistol lay. He hardly knew how to use it, such a modern weapon. Malan had been responsible for so many deaths – Kathryn, his niece, in California all those months ago, Michael Davies, whose company had been the conduit for the smuggled high technology, and Terry Chambers, who was knifed to death in a quiet Midlands street. It had poetic, *just* symmetry, at least.

He rubbed his creased forehead and stared into the whisky glass. Such memories seemed to hurt and tire these days – that was part of the problem. When Paulus Malan came for him, he would get into the car – to be taken wherever, like a seeker after knowledge and a lamb to the slaughter.

Thus resolved, he nodded to himself and rose to replenish the whisky in his glass. He poured the drink from the bottle of malt. The neck clinked against the tumbler. He knew that Babbington was on a course of action that must result in the death of one or both of them. Here, or in London, or at the cottage in Oxfordshire, even in a street or field somewhere, Babbington would have him killed. He swallowed the whisky calmly and dedicatedly. It might as well be here, in Johannesburg – tonight.

He touched the drawer and pulled it out, exposing the gun. Be *damned* to you, Andrew Babbington – and to you, Paulus Malan.

He finished the whisky. What was the bloodstream's capacity to absorb alcohol, for someone hoping to kill a man at close range? He shook his head. Better not risk another drink . . .

\*

Had it been childhood, they would have made coyote or whip-poorwill calls and would have been Apaches or Comanches, as they moved in the rocks and amid the stiff, rattling vegetation. They would have been his friends from other dusty frame houses along the barren street of the suburb where he had spent the years before his mother died. Hyde shrugged. It wasn't any old game – but it was *the* old game, the wild hunt, the one he had played most of his adult life.

At the latest count, there were six of them. He could never be certain, of course, because they were scattered in their search for him. But there were four dead or wounded . . . the bloke he'd killed beside the scout car, two on the scree slope from his landslide, at least one injured when the cliff had fallen on the cab of the leading truck. That left eight in total, and two of those were guarding the stranded vehicles. Six out looking for him – once he had been forced by their fire and their attempt to outflank him to retreat from the lip of the canyon, back into the hilly country southeast of the river.

But the passage of time had adjusted the odds and even two of them would be an army if they kept out of sight and were certain their opponent was alone. And they were aware that he had begun to hoard his ammunition, that they were safe if they kept out of sight. Safer still, after nightfall. They only existed for Hyde as occasional calls, or in brief skirmishes with no outcome . . . as he had gradually retreated from the canyon, along dry gullies, up crevices in steep hillsides, across plateaus, drawing them after him. Now, it was eleven at night and the moon was thin, like a nail paring, low over the silent landscape. It stretched away from his vantage point towards the canyon, lumped and bald and ravined, a maze in which he had not yet lost them – or killed any more of them, either.

He listened intently, disregarding the occasional calls of harmless, night-hunting creatures that moved among the hills. Someone -- it was human by its clumsiness and the slow progress it was making – was climbing up the gully he had used himself to reach this ledge. He heard small explosions of breath and the scrape of metal on rock. He leaned out and looked over the lip of the ledge, but could see no glint of weaponry in the weak moonlight. The man was thirty feet away at most, and coming closer.

His Land Rover was still hidden in the gully he'd found a mile from the road. He had led them away from it, circuitously and slowly, but always away. He had with him food and water, an emergency kit. And it wasn't going to be long or drawn-out, not unless he could keep them distracted and scattered and away from the road. As soon as they managed to kill him, they'd return to the guarded vehicles and summon assistance to get the nerve gas out.

He touched the barrel of the G3 rifle at his side as he might have done a child's comforter, once more hearing the scratch of metal on rock. Then came an involuntary, breathed curse. The climber did not know he was there. Hyde grinned. Soon will, mate – soon will. He knew they would have to eliminate him that night. Blantyre wouldn't want to risk the morning and the chance of more traffic on the road, the report of the landslide, other people taking an interest in the vehicles and their cargo.

The goggles hung unused around his neck. From time to time, he had glimpsed their shapes, less ghostly than those of zebra and occasional monkeys on the lower slopes of the canyon floor. But never for long enough to *load-aim-fire*. He hadn't seen Blantyre, not once. He'd only heard his voice shouting in the darkness, taunting him.

He strained to listen. A careful footstep, the slither of dry fingers seeking purchase, the creak of muscles hoisting a man's weight to a higher perch. Hyde withdrew the knife from the sheath strapped beneath his arm. Its blade was darkened. He raised himself slightly on his haunches, seeking an aggressive balance. He could hear each breath now as the man moved upwards unaware of him.

'Come on, Hyde!' the loudhailer bellowed, distorting Blantyre's mockery. 'You can't take all of us on. You haven't got a hope, man!'

The still darkness boomed with Blantyre's voice, to the left somewhere, perhaps four or five hundred feet away. Hyde leaned out from his perch, but could still discern nothing, could still hear nothing now, until Blantyre's noise erupted again, breaking like another wave as the echoes ebbed: 'You crazy bastard – you can't stop it, Hyde! You were *never* good enough!'

Hyde's hands twitched as they held the knife. Where was the bugger climbing up towards him? He couldn't hear *anything* – had he paused?

'Before midnight, Hyde – before the midnight hour, you'll be falling down here somewhere! We'll look for the body in the morning –!'

Hyde opened his lips, as if to shout back. *Where was the* –? An arm snapped closed like a jaw across his throat, pulling his head back. A broad hand clamped on his right wrist even in the instant that he reacted by raising the knife. The arm across his windpipe tightened and his vision flashed with lights. He was unable to breathe.

'Quick, Dirk – *here*, man!' his attacker grunted like a huge animal.

The climber was scrambling noisily the last few yards up the dry gully like a startled goat. There was a silence outside the small, rocky perch, as if the others were listening in the darkness for the scuffling noises of the kill. Hyde was dragged backwards on his haunches as the man pressed his weight down on him and tightened his grip. The hand holding the knife was becoming numb. His left hand clawed behind his head, gripping the man's shirt, his skin, shoulder, face – not hurting the man. Lights flashed and the climber came out of them, heaving himself over the lip of Hyde's perch as if to fall heavily on him.

After an attempt to thrash his body free, Hyde relaxed suddenly. His weight slumped, surprising the man behind him for a moment, halting the climber's rush at him. The grip on his wrist did not slacken for an instant. He allowed his hand to relax. White teeth flashed in a black-streaked face. Hyde's left hand flopped feebly at his side. He felt a rock under his left hand as the arm across his throat started to slacken, then it tightened again. He tried not to struggle. The climber was drawing his knife slowly, enjoying the strength of his companion, the ease with which Hyde was being asphyxiated. The sharp-edged rock was in his hand, but his throat ached and he was beginning to black out. The man choking him was breathing angrily against his cheek and temple. Head just *there* –? In his oblivion, the climber seemed to swim away from him as if falling backwards from the cliff, the arm across his throat was simply a numbness, his right hand holding the knife was numb, too. He thought he still held the knife but could not be certain . . . the rock was in his left hand – *head*? He screamed at himself. He couldn't feel his legs any longer, or see the warm stars, if they were anywhere in the same blackness as himself.

He moved his left arm as slowly as if he were merely flexing the muscles after sleep, and clashed the rock against the man's elbow – whose scream of pain was a drawn-out, electronic version of a human cry. The numbness around his throat, which seemed to have spread to his cheeks and temples, eased. The climber moved a half-step back in surprised slow motion. Hyde's hand retained control of the rock and flung it upwards again, to where the man's head breathed and salivated against his temple. The noise of contact was subterranean, then the man fell away and Hyde collapsed on top of him, his legs buckled under him. His right arm was still numb as the climber came towards him, cursing loudly. The man blundered forward onto Hyde's knife, which impaled him. Blood spurted from his stomach into Hyde's eyes. He dropped the knife because his still-numb arm could not support the man's sudden weight. The climber fell aside, his face dropping below the level of Hyde's eyes, then away altogether as Hyde rolled aside from the thrashings of the man beneath him. His left hand raised the rock twice and smashed downwards, breaking the dimly seen face.

He was not aware of dropping the rock or of collecting the knife and wiping it on the dead man's shirt. He slumped to one side, as if himself wounded.

He heard Blantyre's distorted demands for information billowing towards him from somewhere hundreds of feet away. He massaged his throat and tried to breathe so shallowly that it would not feel like swallowing sharp crystals of ice. The climber was dead, the other man's body heaved with tormented breathing. Blantyre's orders continued, more concentrated and urgent than before. Answering calls, as if they were an enlivened and blood-smelling pack of wild dogs. He raised himself to look. Torches flashed around and below him as they attempted to converge.

Out of the blur of sight and reason, he heard an R/T, which terrified him until he realized it must be in one of their pockets, close to him. *If you can't locate the bastard, find his vehicle . . .* a repeated message.

Hyde sheathed the knife, checked the pistol and the G3, and dizzily stood up, leaning against the rocks for support. Torches flicked in their eagerness, he could hear noises of ascent and clambering down, of running. He stepped forward and looked over the ledge, down the dry gully. Nothing there. Hefting his pack for comfort, shaking his head to clear his vision, he began to descend the gully.


Hyde worked his way carefully along the old, dry watercourse, avoiding contact with the jagged, stiff bushes and stunted trees that littered the sandy gully. His footprints were broken by rocks and pebbles. Blantyre's people were well behind him now, as far as he could determine, slowed by the shock of another of their number dead and a second incapacitated. The paring of moon had risen higher in the sky, loitering like a narrow spectator. The temperature had dropped, but he felt hot with exertion and the necessity of silence and stealth. It was a little after midnight, and he was still alive. Blantyre had stopped employing the loudhailer. Hyde needed more food, water, ammunition. He intended to survive.

Something, probably a scorpion, crackled like a blown dead leaf across a small rock near his feet. It disappeared into the darkness and he moved on, ducking beneath the stiff, sticklike arms of a weathered bush that jutted out from the bank of the dry gully. He was a mile from the canyon itself. And holding them. Blantyre and what? Five others now ... He had to hold them until Aubrey turned the hunt on Blantyre.

He could now make out the bulk of the Land Rover beneath a lolling tree in a narrow jaw of the gully. He squatted on a rock, watching, listening. Aubrey needed to achieve *control* over Malan, then arrange assistance. He forbade himself to sniff disdainfully. He listened to the night's distant noises – the disturbed or dreaming animals, the sudden creak of rocks, the scuttle of large insects – and declared them harmless. He hunched in the barely-moonlit dark, the rifle between his knees, the pack light against his shoulders and the pistol at the base of his spine. The Land Rover was safe ... he could wait another minute or two. Then he slouched, half-bent, along the distance that separated him from the vehicle. His hand touched metal and he rose into a taller crouch over the Land Rover, at once beginning his harvest of water, a pack of chocolate, an ammunition clip, then a second, his hands playing as cleverly as those of a blind pianist, by familiarity. He opened packets, compartments, zipped-shut packs; the zips sounded like tears in the night, startling him each time. His hands thrust his supplies into his pack like the paws of a greedy squirrel –

The windscreen crazed an inch from his hand, which jerked away, his body dropping beside the vehicle. Another silenced bullet careened off the bonnet, making him leap with tension.

He heard a voice summoning others by R/T. He hurriedly slipped his arms through the straps of the backpack, his breathing hard, preparatory. He rested his weight against the panel of the Land Rover. Another shot struck, thudding like a blow and burying itself somewhere in the upholstery. Then the silence flowed back, and Hyde flung himself to his feet and away along the gully. He was cuffed from behind by the first ripple of disturbed air, then lifted and flung forward by the wave of the detonation. As his hands clamped over his ears and the ground lit up to receive the impact of his body, he heard the explosion of a grenade, then the second, immediate detonation of the petrol tank. The rocks flared red as if dyed, and the ground quivered climactically beneath his body – then he scrabbled away from the light, his shadow dancing like that of a hunchback. Shots whined, the noise of the rifle now evident, the silencer removed for greater muzzle velocity.

Hyde dropped exhausted behind a rock, dimly hearing the first delighted cries from others, and the gradual decline into disappointment and recrimination. Then he heard only his own pulse, thudding in his ears. He rolled onto his stomach and then got to his haunches, then to a crouch. They'd have night-vision goggles, at least nightsights. He was hidden by a jutting rock around which the ancient stream must have run. He scrabbled away from the place, farther up the gully, back the way he had entered it in the Land Rover – whose fire was burning down now, the air chilly again and darkening. He continued like some apelike ancestor, almost on all fours, scrambling towards evolution and two legs.

He straightened eventually, his back aching, the unbalanced weight of the pack against his neck dropping away to settle on his hips. He climbed quickly out of the gully, onto the edge of a mesa – which seemed no more than a vantage to look at rising, craggy hills stretching away. The canyon was – that way. A light flashed briefly some hundreds of yards away, then flicked off at a snarled command. He couldn't see their shapes against the stars or the dismal, impoverished moon. He scrabbled silently across the mesa until he reached its edge. Gently, as if getting into a too-hot bath, he lowered himself over the edge, feet testing for firm purchase, then began to slide slowly, *gently*, down the steep slope towards inky shadows, using his feet as brakes.

His feet touched bottom. He stood up, and saw himself in a sharp knife-cut of a ravine, one that sloped in the direction of the canyon. If he followed it down, he might find the narrow track that led back to the road. The floor of the Fish River Canyon would be safer now, filled with scrub, water holes, vegetation, caves. Up here, he felt exposed. He patted his equipment again. Pack, gun, pistol – he thrust that back into his belt, it had begun to work loose . . . knife. Goggles –

No . . . He'd dropped them somewhere – farther up the slope? He looked wildly upwards. No, he hadn't had them when the Land Rover exploded, had just forgotten about them. Damn – fuck it. He adjusted the pack, making at once for the steep twist of the gully. As he started down it, he heard distant voices.

They seemed to be shouting, giving and taking orders. He stumbled in his haste, rolling over, scraping hands and bare knees and then his side against rocks, bouncing on pebbles and sharp, small stones, trying to grip hold of some rock that wouldn't move after filling his fingernails with dirt –

Halted, breathless, skewed almost upside down, legs above his head, hand holding onto a rock, the rubble sliding and puffing past him and rattling on down the gully. The stars joggled above and the moon swayed like a drunk. His breathing bellowed –

– above a scrabbling noise too delicate for the stones that had been disturbed by his fall. The rifle, butt folded, was in his right hand, saved from loss. His left hand held the edge of a creased rock, halting him. He raised the rifle butt –

– the hunting scorpion was too quick. He had disturbed and angered it. He saw its twin stings protruding from the black bud at the end of its tail, raised in an arch above its back, its claws ceasing to click and knit on the rock as it steadied itself to strike. As he moved the scorpion struck, its sting burying itself in his left forearm. He crushed the life from it with the rifle's blow, hurting his knuckles against rock as the barrel cracked the scorpion open. His left arm was immediately on fire.

\*

367

Aubrey glanced surreptitiously at his watch. The leaning, crane-like lights of the motorway heading towards the northern suburbs winked at the watch's face. Twelve-thirty. He let his wrist fall casually away so that his hand rested on the edge of the cream leather seat of the long Mercedes limousine. Malan's physical bulk and intent loomed against his nerveless side, even though the man looked unconcernedly out of his own window. The driver's neck, just in front of Aubrey, was slim and clean-shaven. Both he and Malan seemed as unconcerned as if they were transporting livestock across the Channel to some European abattoir.

Aubrey calmed the nervous little twitch of his fingers against the seat's leather. Oh, yes – Malan certainly *was* offering him some right-wing extremists who actually were involved with van Vuuren and Blantyre and the nerve agent shipment. After all, he'd had to find them simply so that they did not exist outside his gravitational pull. Unknown, they were dangerous, and could cause him embarrassment with the de Villiers government. Now, he could offer them up patriotically at a moment's notice, or use them to his advantage. For he certainly did not intend that Aubrey should expose them.

The dark blotches of unlit parks and golf courses flashed by, surrounded by rows of streetlights which semaphored the presence of neat, orderly suburbs. Ahead, beyond the motorway lights, the darkness spread more widely. He felt, in the circumstances, rather calm; surprising himself. The suburbs slipped aside like a stage curtain and the darkness spread as the lights tried more unsuccessfully to signal to each other. A moment later, the Mercedes purred away from the comfort of traffic, down onto a sliproad, then at once onto a wide, sparsely-lit avenue lined by small factory units and dim housing. A few moving cars, some others parked, the occasional pedestrian; some dogs. He settled his shoulders to disguise a shiver of anticipation.

'These people –' he began, clearing his throat. Malan's head twitched towards him, his eyes gleaming. 'These people, Malan – they will believe my cover?'

Malan grinned and nodded. 'You worry too much. They're not very smart. They'll think you're the money man. You look like a shrivelled accountant, after all.' His grin broadened and Aubrey attempted to respond to it.

'And afterwards? After I – *we*'re certain of them?'

'We drive quietly away and you can talk to who you like.' The streets around them became shabbier and darker, people flitting out of the shadows between the sparse streetlights. 'I've given you two names. They'll listen quickly and they'll understand. You won't have any problems.' He sighed. 'Satisfied?' Then he seemed to remember his lines in a play in which he had lost interest, and added: 'This clears our debt, our *account*?'

Aubrey nodded. 'Agreed. It is all I can do, or wish to do. Anything else would now be beyond me.' His hand flapped loosely, like that of an invalid speaking from his bed. 'I shall leave you to your own devices, if you give me these people.'

'Your man may not finish off Robin Blantyre,' Malan observed. 'Probably won't, in fact. Robin's a hard man.'

'What?' Aubrey asked dispassionately.

Malan grinned, and seemed to relax. 'Oh, I know where Blantyre is – and that's where you've sent your wild dog, Hyde. Otherwise, he'd be here, watching your back. After Venice. He killed the girl, Valentina, I heard?'

'That – is true.' Aubrey rubbed his chin. 'Yes,' he murmured. '*I* shall stop Blantyre. With your assistance tonight, of course.' He smiled. 'Even though you wish your contribution to remain anonymous, like all the best charitable donations.'

Malan turned away. Aubrey, too, resorted once more to gazing out of the tinted window that made the few lights even more distant and small. He could just make out a handful of stars overhead.

He did not need to steel himself further. He had entered the situation and had heard the key turn in the lock behind him. He could not withdraw. It was simply a matter of keeping his nerve, remaining calm. How he might escape was unclear, but he had the gun, of which he believed Malan remained unaware. The car passed a telephone kiosk. There would be telephones. He had not rung the embassy or any of the few people he vaguely knew in South African Intelligence. Any contact would have only invited restraint, complications. If necessary, he would come away as he arrived, with Malan as his companion, at the point of a gun.

Malan, of course, was right. It might prove impossible for Patrick

369

to remain alive, let alone prevent the nerve agent from reaching Johannesburg. Malan assured him it had not yet arrived. That, at least, he believed. Malan could be ruined by news of its smuggling, its *purchase* by employees of MLC. No, there was still time, providing he – and Hyde, but mostly it seemed to devolve upon himself – could remain alive.

The Mercedes hurried off an ill-lit street of low houses, empty lots and factory units, through gates of corrugated tin, into –

Startled, he saw in the darkness, outlined by the glow from Alexandra township, the car's headlights reflected from buckled metal. Bumpers, bonnets, hubcaps, boots. Cars were heaped upon one another as if to simulate the orgy of a million frogs or crabs. He shivered and Malan's laugh at his discomfiture was hard. Then the South African opened the door of the limousine. Aubrey, too, got out. The night was cool, windless, the stars glittering above the slag heaps and temples of broken vehicles. He shuddered. It was too easy to imagine how many lives had ended or been ruined or distorted inside the crumpled metal boxes.

'This way,' Malan announced, steering him by the elbow.

Ahead of them, light showed grubbily in slitted lines and scratches around something which, as his eyes became accustomed, appeared to be a low caravan.

'Yes,' he murmured. 'Very well.'

The driver remained beside the car, his cap pushed back on his head. The scrapyard was silent. A crane loomed over the city of wrecks like a long-necked vulture. Aubrey cleared his throat and his hand involuntarily gripped the gun in his coat pocket.

How many of them would there be?

Too many, he suspected, for one old man.

# SIXTEEN

# the blanket of the dark

Anderson raised his body from a stiff, awkward crouch, his fingers crooked on the sill of one window of the lopsided caravan, and squinted into the dim, shadowy interior. There were rough mugs on a stained, narrow table, greasy cushions, abandoned clothing. Crockery lolled unwashed at the edges of the metal sink.

Why in God's name had he come *back* here? There had been no sign from heaven, no pointing finger instructing him that he couldn't leave Kenneth Aubrey to his fate . . . just the old man's face and resolution, pricking at him. So that, eventually, he had had to turn back, far along the northbound road and against every conscious thought or wish . . .

Because *her* face had been against the windscreen, not just that of Aubrey, as if she were trying to break into the car. He had slewed the BMW violently, as if avoiding a child caught suddenly in the headlights, and had sat for a long time at the side of the road, his face in his hands, his whole body shaking and reluctant. Revolting against what he knew must be done . . . Until he had admitted it, and turned in the road and headed back towards Johannesburg.

As his eyes probed the caravan's interior, he eventually realized that a foot was jutting out from behind the lumpy armchair drawn close to the table. Then he saw that the other foot – leg – was sprawled towards the kitchen sink. The rest of the body was hidden by the chair. There was no sign of any other body. Those who had been here to meet Malan's people had probably been thrown into wrecks, ready to be given to the crusher. Then a harder light was switched on inside the caravan and he ducked out of sight, his breathing suddenly loud and hoarse.

He realized he was illuminated by the greasy light. Malan's people were waiting for Aubrey – one of them was inside now. They'd killed already, and would have been warned to watch out for him, for anyone.

Headlights flashed along the road outside the scrapyard, then glared their way into it. Aubrey, being brought to the slaughter by Malan. He heard the big engine slow to a halt some distance away, crouching into himself as much as possible, his back against the caravan's peeling paint, his arms wrapped around his knees with the rifle resting across his forearms. Then he heard only silence –

– into which dropped the separate pebbles of a car door closing, a brief murmur of voices, then footsteps. He drew the nightsight from his windcheater and crept silently towards the corner of the caravan. Then he raised the sight to his eye and focused it. Two figures came into focus, one tall and bulky, the other more hesitant in its movements, with a walking stick. They were moving side by side down an aisle of wrecked cars. Aubrey's breath was visible around him. He flicked the tube of the nightsight rapidly over the cathedral of broken vehicles, until –

*There.* One of them, dressed in black, face smudged with shoe polish, his stained hand gripping the barrel of a rifle as if he might turn it into a club. Anderson felt the adrenalin course through him like old, familiar music. The cold, urban landscape pressed against him like a place he knew well, his hunting ground. *There.* The back-up man, moving with utmost purpose and quiet into a position to cover the flank of the caravan. Neither man was ready to fire. Evidently, Aubrey was to be gloated over, was to meet the man who had turned on the light inside the caravan . . . before he was murdered. He wanted to confirm his suspicions, but remained still, watching Malan and Aubrey slowly approach. He heard the creaks of settling metal, their footsteps, the whisper of the bottled gas supply beneath the caravan. Carefully, he slipped the first round into the breech of the sniper's rifle, unfolding the butt so that it came easily and at once against his shoulder like the reassurance of a friend. He fitted the nightsight and adjusted its focus on the first gunman, whose head peered from between the crushed radiator grille of a Japanese car and the open-mouthed boot of a rusting Citroën. The clouding of excitement cleared from the lens, and he refined the focus. Then he transferred the sight of Aubrey's face, adjusting into focus his grim features, carved and stony. Malan was

372

beside him, his face inexpressive. His finger tightened involuntarily on the trigger, now, *now* –

He forced himself to ease the trigger back and slacken his grip on the rifle. Not yet, not until you can ensure your escape, and perhaps Kenneth's . . . His hands were shaking. Aubrey and Malan were murmuring together as they reached the caravan. Margarethe's face intruded for a moment, but it was distant and lifeless and had no business in this place with him in his present mood. Later, later . . .

Tears, unexpectedly, dripped into his throat because he could not noisily sniff them away. *Later*, he snapped angrily at himself.

He heard movement inside the caravan, in anticipation of Aubrey's arrival. He lurched to his feet and scuttled bent double to the window, peering inside. He recognized at once a bearded profile, as he also recognized the gleam of light on a pistol. Jesus, they weren't going to savour killing Aubrey, they were just going to do it now.

The pistol moved upwards, to point at the door of the caravan, waiting for it to be opened.


As Malan held his elbow, as if assisting him to cross a busy street, Aubrey sensed his alertness. Aubrey puffed smoky air like an impatient little steam-engine. Malan's feral attentiveness trembled through the old man's arm.

'What is it?' Aubrey murmured.

'I thought I heard something. Just wait a moment.'

Aubrey had seen an outlined shadow appear inside the caravan, just before the main light had come on. The whole caravan listed like a boat going down in the dark. He suppressed a shiver of anticipation. The night was windless but the scrapyard creaked around him like condemned tenement blocks in a gale. Eerie, the noises of old vehicles, as if murmuring their separate demises.

'What is it, Malan?' he repeated with some impatience.

'I'm just looking after your health, Sir Kenneth.' There was confidence in the man's voice again, a belief that everything was in place, a trap poised to snap shut.

'Shall we go in? Someone awaits us.' He quailed as Malan removed his hand. It had to be his oldest enemy. Babbington. Dear Andrew, his personal Alberich, consumed by unenacted revenges.

As *yet* unenacted. He gripped the butt of the pistol more firmly in his coat pocket. Given the opportunity, he *could* kill Andrew Babbington, as easily as Babbington could dispense with him.

'Yes,' he murmured.

The scurrying of something that might have been a rat delayed his reply.

'Let's go in, then.'

Aubrey squared his shoulders and stepped onto the creaking steps of the caravan. He must now continue this charade, though he expected to learn nothing more. There was the startling noise of breaking glass and he stumbled back from the steps. He heard a voice that he recognized as Anderson's bellow out: 'Kenneth, it's a trap! Watch yourself!' Then: 'Babbington, stay where you are or I'll kill you now!' Finally, even louder: 'Kill the old man and Malan dies – do you hear me? Babbington, *stay where you are –!*'

*You never fucking die of a scorpion sting*, it says so in the rules – Oh, *Christ*, this *hurts*!

Hyde lowered his arm once more into the water that seeped down one wall of the cave before trickling along the narrow channel beside which he lay stretched out, exhausted. The noise of the water made the cave seem larger, hollower than it was. The low night temperature had no effect on the burning pain in his stiff, swollen arm. The aspirin he had taken against an insistent sense of survival had had no effect, either. He had no anti-venom because *some bastard forgot to pack it!* You don't die of scorpion stings, not unless you're a baby or a heart case aged three hundred . . . it just seemed like it!

*Try to rest the affected area*, the book said. He'd applied a pressure bandage to slow the spread of the venom, and had doused the arm in cold water. There were no other remedies available. Not even lying still. He flicked on the thin beam of the torch, then immediately switched it off. Best not to look at the swollen, almost immovable limb. He felt nauseous, close to fever. He lay on his back, staring at the invisible roof of the cave. That the scorpion had cracked like thin ice beneath the blow from the rifle was of no consolation. Damn, fucking scorpion.

He flicked on the torch once more, then returned himself to the darkness. Something whirred away like a windblown leaf – a bat, probably.

He shouldn't have tried to reach the road . . . shouldn't have climbed down to the floor of the Fish River Canyon, abseiling with his one good arm, spinning like a top, feeling sick and wanting to bellow with pain and effort. The venom had been pumped round his system by his exertions – but the only other choice was to wait for Blantyre and his people, who were even more poisonous than the scorpion. He was – whatever shape he was in – still alive. He stifled a groan of pain as he attempted to move his arm. Then he lay back again, letting his arm rest in the trickling water it could barely feel. The water was brackish, salty. He couldn't drink it, but it had, initially, cooled his face and forehead. And his arm, for a few moments. Now, it was burning again like a small, intense bonfire. He couldn't stop shivering.

He flicked on the torch and looked at his watch. Almost one in the morning. He switched off the beam, and the bat rustled and chittered back to its roost above his head. He knew he'd have to move soon.

It was as if the scorpion sting had been an electrical shock, goading him into frenzied activity. He had blundered away into the darkness, hearing their cries of surprise and puzzlement clear on the night air. He'd struggled in a maze of gullies and ravines and eventually found the track and made better time down to the road, half a mile from the landslide. He was terrified contemplating his only means of escape, down the canyon wall to the riverbed. It had taken him a long, nauseous time. His swollen arm was just able to grip the rope and let it slide through stiff, lumpy fingers up to the good hand, which had had to take all his weight, as he eased himself down the canyon wall.

Eventually, exhausted, he had reached a litter of boulders and the rope had come tumbling about him like the coils of a python. He had rested for a few minutes, then moved out across the canyon. Up on the road, he had seen the faint glow of a fire from the vicinity of the two container trucks.

Then he had scouted along the canyon until he knew he must rest or collapse, and had found this bat-invaded cold darkness and the noise of dribbling water. And isolation . . .

He forced himself to sit up. His head whirled and in his vision small, separate lights flashed like fireflies. He held his brow with his right hand, draping his left arm into the water once again. You're not going to get any better, sport, so get used to it. Blantyre, of course, had the perfect antidote, though unacceptable. He got painfully to his knees and heard, above his dry retching, the distressed bats whirr and click and rustle like old umbrellas being opened. Using the G3 as a stick, he levered himself to his feet and turned dizzily around to face the dim starlight seeping from the entrance. Something skittered across the rocky floor, then was muffled by its passage across sand. Scorpions, like lightning, never strike twice.

He hauled himself towards the opening of the cave. The pack was heavy on his back and the strap over his left shoulder bit into swollen flesh. He slipped the rifle into a sub-machine gun position against his hip, the strap over his right shoulder. He saw torches, hundreds of yards away, creeping down the cliff face on the other side of the canyon. Tiny lights, insubstantial and wavering. Either they'd found the marks of his descent or were still working on supposition. Either way, they were right.

Eventually, he made out six separate lights bobbing and wobbling down the cliff. Above them, the headlights of one of the trucks spilt over the lip of the canyon like poured silver. Hyde leaned heavily against the curve of the cave mouth, the rock pressing into his side and back, his arm jutting out as if held by a plaster cast. The rifle now hung in his right hand like shopping and the pack at his back was heavier than ever.

It wasn't that he couldn't respond – not physically, anyway. He could do that. There was plenty of rock to steady himself against. The sliver of moon shone in a gap of water out in the middle of the canyon. He shook his head carefully, but could not avoid the dizzy nausea. He was shivering continually now. It wasn't even that – he could manage to still the shakes for long enough to kill one or two of them . . . It was *beginning* it. All field agents demanded to go into the final phase of any operation fit and well, no more than weary or strung-out. *Not* with scorpion stings or bullet wounds. The moon slipped across the pool of water to which cats and their prey would be drawn at dawn – as to other pools dotted along the canyon's umbilical extent. In the morning, too, there would be traffic up on the road. Investigation, assistance –

– not for *you*. Blantyre's advantage entirely. He was sweating violently. The small lights on the opposite cliff danced in and out of focus. The first man had reached the canyon floor and his light was extinguished. Blantyre would be second or third in the descent, just in case Hyde was still *compos*. Six against one. He glared blearily at his swollen, hanging arm. He dreaded beginning it: the *Finale*. Once he announced with a rifle shot that he was fit enough to kill or wound, it wouldn't stop until they had him or he had finished them, *all* of them. He felt sick at the prospect and hung his head, the floor beginning to turn under him like the earth's rotation. Then he sniffed, the noise seeming to carry. He raised the rifle against his side and checked the nightsight. As he unfolded the stock with one hand, the muzzle scraped against rock. Then he moved, feeling a screech of pain and the sweat of effort, using his right hand to lift the left limb into position, to take the weight of the rifle in the inflamed hand. He watched his hand close around the forward grip as slowly as a crustacean making an attack on an immobile prey. It had to be a tight enough grip. He adjusted the nightsight. Light sprang into the circle of the sight, flaring grey. Amid its pale, dead glow was a figure shunting itself down the cliff in little repeated bounces. His brow was wet and he blinked furiously. His arm was on fire and the fingers of his left hand were entirely numb. He squeezed the trigger as much because his arm *had* to be moved, as for any reason. Almost at once, the figure amid the grey light seemed to shudder against the cliff, then fall dreamlike out into the air, which let him fall.

It had begun, then. He heard their alarm, their orders and sudden, fierce application. He shivered aside from the cave mouth, sliding into shadow.


Babbington had turned in the doorway, enraged, and glared back towards the shattered window as Anderson was shouting. But something had halted his first quick step, made him thrust his hands into his pockets and strive for calm and calculation. He heard Aubrey's voice, which stung him like a lash, his shoulders twitching at the sound.

'Richard? *Richard!*' with the greatest relief.

'Babbington!' he heard Malan bark, then some muffled curse. He had to get to the other side of the caravan – and be picked off like a fly?

'Kenneth, there are two snipers somewhere –!' Anderson shouted. 'Be careful!'

Babbington stared into the muzzle of the rifle that was poked through the broken window as if failing to recognize it and seeing some other, closer enemy on the frayed strip of carpet in front of his feet. His pockets worked like glove puppets over his knuckles. Then he heard: 'I'm all right, Richard – warn them, Malan – warn them!'

Babbington shuffled, as if distracted, towards the rifle muzzle and the shattered window, his breath smoking in the caravan's suddenly reduced temperature. Anderson glared at him, nudging the rifle in threatening gestures.

'Stand *there*!' he snapped. 'Just there, and turn around and face the door.'

Babbington seemed like a child, the rage of disappointment and the sense of having been cheated so evident on his distorted features. His handsomeness declined into cunning, wizened frustration. Then he turned reluctantly to present his back to Anderson.

Aubrey called: 'Richard, what now?' in a confused, lost voice.

Anderson grimaced. 'I've got Babbington covered, Kenneth. You and Malan get inside. Come forward, but be careful.'

Anderson's hand reached along the rusty flank of the caravan and touched the handle of the door on that side. He waited until the door on Aubrey's side clicked open and he could see Malan's bulk lumbering into the interior, Babbington cautiously making way for him – waited until Aubrey's smaller frame made the caravan even more cramped and the door shut behind him. Then he opened the door on his side and darted inside, shutting it quickly and noisily behind him.

Aubrey's face gleamed palely like a puzzled moon. Malan glowered at him. Babbington's hatred was undiminished. Anderson listened. They hadn't risked firing even one shot, whether or not they had him in their sights. A bullet could enter the flimsy tin wall of the caravan and kill – anyone; the bullet could even pass right through the wallet that would pay them for the job. Bad for business . . . He grinned, surprising himself. Outside, one of them called to the other, but he could not make out the words. What he really

378

heard was his own breathing and pulse rate, and almost a noise of tension between the three men at whom he pointed the rifle, their mutual hatred and mistrust rubbing like the friction of metal on metal.

He levelled the rifle on Malan. He'd be the first to die, anyway, just in case there was no time for a second shot. If the two outside adopted an independent assessment of the situation, decided on taking a risk or got close enough to distinguish their legitimate targets, he'd have to ensure that Malan was going into the dark. That much was certain.

'Hello, Kenneth,' he announced softly. Then he added, with a mocking nod: 'Shall we all sit down, gentlemen?'

He stood between two bunk beds, facing the three of them, who were grouped as tightly as guilty schoolboys around the narrow table. He saw the legs of the dead man sticking out from behind the chair, in which Malan sat unconcernedly.

'Kenneth, up here, please,' he ordered. 'Stay out of the firing line.'

Aubrey sidled with exaggerated caution to Anderson's end of the caravan and sat down, at a nod from him, on one of the bunk beds. Babbington perched himself with massive reluctance on the edge of a hard chair beside the table, his right hand at once fiddling and twitching amid sugar grains and the untidy pages of a tabloid newspaper. He glanced at Aubrey, who smiled loose-toothed in gratitude.

'Good,' Anderson said, then he flicked the switch and doused the caravan's lights. At once, there was a jackal-like response from outside. Inside, Anderson heard their collective breathing like the noise of wolves as yet curious, undecided. But hungry. He heard Babbington's chair scrape, then said, 'I can see both of you. Don't provide me with an excuse so soon.' His calm was studiedly chilling amid the claustrophobia of the confined space and their pressing rage.

Aubrey murmured: 'Thank you, Richard.' His relief was deep.

'Not for you,' he replied, so that Malan could understand his meaning. Then he added: 'I came back for Malan. It's him I want.'

The caravan was lighter now. The glow from the surrounding streets and from the township seeped through the smashed window. Babbington's haughty profile was more that of a woman in deep hauteur, excepting the beard. Malan slouched harmlessly and cunningly in the armchair, his face turned to Anderson, who lowered himself onto the other unmade bed opposite Aubrey, their knees almost touching. He patted Aubrey's arm with his left hand, holding the rifle against his right side, pointed always at Malan. Except, he decided, he would nudge it occasionally towards Babbington, whom he failed to understand; the man was from Aubrey's drama, not his own, but it might prove fatal to ignore him. So he calmly said, 'I know you're armed, Sir Andrew. Put the pistol on the floor, please.'

Babbington growled, then withdrew the gun from his coat and lowered it by the butt to the floor, kicking it away before commanded to do so. We all know the routines, Anderson thought with a smile. Even Malan, probably. Gradually, the caravan's occupants became more firmly pencilled by the growth of his night vision. The tension was as palpable as the condensation on the metal walls.

How should he finish it, since he wanted to survive? Malan *had* to be killed – he couldn't settle for less. Aubrey's breathing was shallow beside him. There were two marksmen outside, with nightsights and sniper's rifles. He suppressed a shiver. But the nightsights couldn't penetrate. All they would be able to see, through the broken window, was Malan . . . it would take them some time to convince themselves that he and Aubrey were just where they were, at the other end of the caravan.

Then Malan ventured, sarcastically: 'This is cosy. But what now?'

His words seemed to release Babbington's furious concentration on Aubrey, and he growled: 'What went *wrong*? What the hell went wrong?' The chair creaked as he leant heavily forward. Anderson tensed himself.

'Nothing,' Malan replied sullenly. Then he looked towards Anderson. 'Just a wild card. The unexpected.'

Babbington's arm pointed stiffly at Anderson. '*He* should have been found and disposed of *days* ago! I warned you of the man's past for God's sake – what he might do.'

'I know that. He wasn't taken care of. That's all.'

Babbington was staring at him and Aubrey now, and the old man's hand quivered on Anderson's arm. He felt, depressingly, like the relative of a very old person on whom the duty of visits and care had devolved.

'Well, Anderson, what now?' Malan growled.

'It's called a stand-off. The problem is simple – how to kill you and still get out alive.' Malan's face was composed entirely of lines and planes, dull surfaces amid which his eyes glittered.

'Impossible.' Babbington placed his hands flat on the stained table as if he had declared a winning hand. 'Malan's car is too far away for either of you to get to it unhurt, Anderson.'

'Perhaps we should telephone the driver?'

'You'd still have little chance of surviving.'

Babbington was studying him as if attempting to match his features to those in some old, sepiaed photograph. His body was stiff as he suppressed the evidence of a disease-like rage. The hairs on Anderson's neck and arms tickled with nerves. Malan was more obviously angry, like a wild animal behind bars.

'Therefore, what shall we do to amuse ourselves, in these temporary circumstances?' Babbington taunted.

'Now you can't kill Aubrey?'

'I shouldn't be too certain of that, were I you.'

The patently assumed drawl infuriated Anderson. It reminded him of past debriefings, all of which he had exorcised for so many years. And made him more alert to the prowling marksmen outside, who must by now be in debate, frustrated by the constant shadowy reappearances of Malan and Babbington. Soon, they might decide it would be worth their while to place a few shots into *his* end of the caravan. He glanced sideways at Aubrey.

The old man appeared to be watching Babbington with the stillness of a cat, with an infinite patience that bore the appearance of sorrow. He did not seem to be fearful on his own or anyone else's account; so still was he, he seemed the result of taxidermy. Then his old eyes blinked once behind his spectacles, slow as those of a fish.

Malan stirred again, snorting and impatient as the captured animal he was. 'All right, Anderson – what do you want? What happened to your woman – I'm sorry it happened. Now – how *much*?'

'Your apology is *not* accepted,' Anderson replied through clenched teeth. Then: 'My *wife*, by the way.'

Malan was silent, but remained urgently alert for possible activity outside. Babbington appeared unconcerned, as if recognizing that Anderson was no more than a minimal, transitory interruption of his own strategy. He continued to glower towards Aubrey, the author of all his woes. Given the slightest opportunity, Babbington would try to kill the old man.

Anderson leaned towards Aubrey and whispered: 'Are you armed?' Aubrey nodded. 'You can kill either of them if necessary?' After some hesitation, Aubrey nodded again. 'OK. You may have to. Babbington won't let you go without some attempt.'

'I understand, Richard. He and I understand each other perfectly.' Then he cleared his throat and, raising his voice, said: 'I take it, Malan, that our dead friend was one of those expecting the shipment of nerve gas.'

'What? Yes, he was – there are a couple more of them out there in the dark, prematurely deceased. They were real enough. You might not have come otherwise.' He grinned.

'Then you've satisfactorily cleared up this end of the business, saving your government both time and money. Thank you, on their behalf and mine.'

'A pleasure, man.'

Aubrey leaned towards Anderson. 'Richard, I need Malan alive,' he whispered.

'No,' Anderson replied with utter conviction, shaking his head.

Aubrey sat back, studying Anderson – the motive force trapped inside the box of the caravan – and admitted that the man was approaching the point where he might well sacrifice his own life to ensure Malan's death. It was the confinement, the claustrophobia, that was affecting him. Affecting himself, too. It would be easier, now, to shoot Babbington, should the man make any slight, suspicious move. And Andrew had long reached the same conclusion. His pistol lay on the floor, closer to Aubrey than to himself, but there was no real safety in mere distance. Babbington would risk anything to ensure he killed his oldest enemy. *Any* action, so long as it brought about Aubrey's death.

He sat back, recognizing that he could hope to persuade neither Babbington nor Anderson. But he had to engineer something which allowed him to remove himself from this situation and get assistance to Hyde. He was the only one in the caravan with any shred of rationality left. He did not hate Babbington, after all, he merely despised him. He did not need any of them dead as the fulfilment of his purpose. Which only made him impotent, unable to prevent –

What was already beginning to happen. He sensed, then heard, a slight, ratlike noise outside the caravan. It alerted Anderson, even before the other two appeared to become aware. He realized, from Anderson's reaction as Malan was stung into hopeful awareness, that events could no longer be prevented. Anderson hesitated for only an instant, then fired at the window where, momentarily, there had been a dim shadow. Malan continued to his feet and blundered like a bull towards and through the door, even as Aubrey was still raising his hands in supplication, like a child attempting to prevent the tide from demolishing his sandcastle.

Babbington hunched down as Anderson turned the rifle on Malan's disappearing bulk. Malan was bellowing something into the night about his identity and *not shooting* as Anderson fired again, the noise deafening in the cramped space. Aubrey expected Malan to lurch sideways, or be thrust forward, then he realized that Anderson had not fired at his quarry, but down at the floor. He was dazzled by the muzzle flash and by the time he could see through the dancing lights, he saw Babbington scrabbling near his feet. His body straightened slowly, as if the man felt tired after vigorous exercise and chose to lie, straightened and quiet.

The black rectangle of the doorway was empty, and Aubrey heard above the reverberations of a third shot, and the partial deafness it induced, the clump of running footsteps and the cry from Malan of: 'Kill him, kill him!'

Aubrey looked up at Anderson, who hesitated for no more than a moment to glance at Babbington's prone form, before bundling himself through the caravan's rear door. It slammed behind him, and Aubrey heard two shots.

He slipped from the bed into a sitting position on the floor, dragging the thin mattress down beside him as inadequate protection. More protection was to be had from the fact that Malan and Anderson were both outside, and the gunmen were concerning themselves with them. He heard further shots from outside, close upon more running footsteps. He reached forward as if towards a wounded wild animal and felt for the pulse in Babbington's neck. Faintly there. He got slowly to his knees and turned Babbington's heavy frame, so that his pain-clenched features stared up at the

383

low, grubby ceiling. Then, breathing heavily, Aubrey crawled with the utmost caution towards the still-open door of the caravan and squinted into the chilly night's dull glow.

In the dipped headlights of the distant Mercedes, he saw an enlarged shadow that was Malan fleeing towards the limousine. There was something awkward and wounded about his shuffling, hunchback gait. There was a body, too small to be that of Anderson, lying fifty yards away. The doors of the Mercedes were open and the driver crouched behind one of them, probably armed. There was no sign of Richard.

Malan reached the car and flung himself desperately into the rear of it. The driver at once got in and slammed the doors, reversing wildly towards the gate in a flurry of dust that looked frosty in the headlights. The limousine skidded through the gates and turned violently before accelerating out of sight towards the city.

Almost at once, a smaller car squealed into view, following Malan. Aubrey had heard shots muffled by the noise of the Mercedes' engine. He strained to see . . . yes, something once human was lying near the gates. It had fallen away from the second car after a desperate attempt to hold on. It did not move.

He knew that Malan was finished. Anderson had killed both marksmen, and would not now let go. The shark had tasted blood, and was moving in for the kill. It might take hours, even days – no longer than a few days – but he knew with utter certainty that Anderson would kill Malan. Settle *both* their accounts. *Nothing*, not even Babbington's dying, was more certain.

Which, he realized lightheadedly, rendered him safe. Bereft of proof, but safe.

He looked down, sighing before he crawled back towards Babbington's heaving chest. His face was twisted with the growing fear of the nature of his wound, from a high-powered rifle, at close range. The bullet was probably buried six inches in the dirt beneath the caravan. It had passed through Babbington's middle. His frame was already rigored long before the heart and mind accepted the fact. He sat beside him.

There was spittle on Babbington's beard, bright as tears. Blood glistened on his coat and shirt. He was bleeding to death and it was pointless to try to staunch the bleeding. The effort would be no more than cosmetic – and it was a gesture he had no intention of making. Instead, he and the dying man seemed mutually exhausted.

The two of them were alone in the vast scrapyard. Then Babbington groaned, the sound seeming much more like a quiet scream of protest, not so much at his end but at business left unfinished. Aubrey stared at the ceiling, as if embarrassed, as Babbington gargled blood.

*Consummatum est* – it is finished.

Eventually, Babbington's liquid throat was quiet again, and the eerie creaks of the scrapyard once more intruded. Aubrey's breath smoked, but he did not feel the cold. Babbington's intermittent puffs of clouded breath were like vain attempts to strike a spark as he went headlong into the dark. The noise of cars in flight and pursuit had long faded, sounds from a distant past.

Then the ugly, wet noises in Babbington's throat became more desperate. Aubrey looked down. Andrew's eyes glared like those of some enraged revenant, a corpse not yet dead. His lips worked mutely, his voice spluttering like a mechanism that refused to start. Then, most strangely, as if surrendering to his fate, his clawed fingers reached out and touched Aubrey's sleeve. Aubrey watched the hand crawl down the cloth of his coat, then attempt to grasp his hand. He opened his fingers and gripped Babbington's hand. The gesture was little enough, after all. Babbington was all but dead. It was hardly forgiveness . . . just *company*, for a brief moment. He shook his head at the vivid image of the darkness above which Babbington was poised.

Gradually, Babbington's features lost their expression of baffled malevolence and growing terror. They relaxed not into peace or resignation, but into familiarity. Strange meeting, he thought, after so long a time. *It seemed that out of battle I escaped* . . . Their feud, and the war in which they had so vigorously engaged, were both over, at least for them. *Piteous recognition* . . . He looked down at Babbington's ghostly, bearded features. He had never particularly warmed to Wilfred Owen, but now the lines of one of his poems came unbidden and freshly out of the back of his head. *Wisdom was mine, and I had mastery* . . . He must once have had to learn it as an imposition, set by a prefect somewhat like Babbington, the eternal Head of House – and gone to the bad, like so many of them had. *I am the enemy you killed* . . . No, he felt nothing for the man, no pity or sorrow, not even a small regret such as towards a stranger whose name one had heard or read.

He tightened his grip on Babbington's hand, aware that the man's ruined chest still fluttered after breath – a few minutes now, at most. He was *not* holding the hand of some *alter ego*, he refused such identification between the two of them; he was just holding the hand of someone whose history might have been identical, but had not been because of vanity and appetite – and treason.

He felt very tired, but continued to hold the man's hand, until the end. *Let us sleep now* . . .

He sensed the moment when Babbington's muscles relaxed and his hand became heavier. Nevertheless, Aubrey did not release his grip, instead he continued to listen to the creaking silence outside, indulging a sense of completion and an almost fey, detached mood. Even Patrick Hyde's fate failed to concern him.


Hyde sat cross-legged amid the stiff, rustling reeds that surrounded a small water hole, hugging his wounded arm across his chest with his good hand. They were less than a mile behind him now, following his progress like a drift net, confident that he was ahead of them. They checked out each cave, each water hole . . . Blantyre would have found the signs, long ago, of his frequent halts, his numerous falls and stumblings. And he would know that he was wounded.

They'd overtake him long before dawn . . . what time was it? He shook his hanging head. Not worth the eyestrain. It wasn't important. They'd have him before it got light, and that was all that mattered.

He shuddered with shock at the explosion behind him. He turned and saw the afterglow, and heard the slow growl of falling rock. Someone had thrown a grenade or fired a rocket into one of the caves. In the starlight, he saw the dust puff out less than half a mile behind him.

If he was remembering the map accurately, the canyon ahead of him twisted like a wounded snake, again and again, narrowing, too. He probably wouldn't get that far. And he couldn't climb out, not with his immobilized arm and as dizzy as he was. There were tracks up to the clifftop, but he'd be more than lucky to find one in the dark. He just had to try to keep ahead of them.

Why? At dawn, if he lived that long, there'd be at least one helicopter, maybe more. Blantyre would organize people he could trust and get them up from Oranjemund or from inside the Republic. And, if Aubrey hadn't got Malan by the balls, then even *he* might think it worth a cover-up – after all, he had only to eliminate one wounded soldier and a nosey old man.

He rubbed his face. The next twist of the canyon would hide him from them for a while. Even though reluctance seized him like nausea, he knew it was time to attempt some kind of ambush. He touched his arm. No way, son, no fucking way . . . He got wearily to his feet, using the rifle to lever himself upright. There was no one outlined against the dying fire of scrubby bushes and there were no noises of R/T communication. Five of them still fit and well, and goaded on by Blantyre. Hyde struggled off in a caricature of rapid movement that Hollywood might associate with a hunchback and call characterization.

He'd seen headlights moving along the road up on the cliff perhaps an hour earlier. They'd ducked out of sight in a twist of the canyon long before reaching the landslide. Now, the driver and whoever else were probably camped beside the mound of fallen rocks, perhaps even sharing food and laughter with those Blantyre had left on guard. No help for *him*, whoever they were.

He turned the twist in the riverbed and the cliffs seemed to crowd mockingly above him. He huddled against a large boulder, his head spinning. He pressed the rifle against his cheek to cool himself, but the barrel was hot from his feverish grip. Gradually, the stars slowed once more and his breathing calmed. The dotted water holes gleamed blackly like a wet, tarred road in the starlight as they skulked behind beds of reeds or low, stunted bushes. Otherwise, the landscape was bouldered and pebbly and hollowed with low, narrow caves like the one in which he had hidden.

Wise to that halt, they'd already grenaded or rocketed three caves during the night. Each of the caves he had passed had tempted him, but he *wasn't that far gone*. At the slightest noise or suspicion, they'd blown caves apart . . . liking the destruction, the noise and light feeding something.

Slowly, carefully, he eased himself back into the rocks, his feet scrabbling heels-first up the slightest of inclines until he was twenty

387

feet or more above the riverbed. Only during a flood would the river reach the rocks around and behind him. The place was desiccated, lunar.

Blantyre liked inflicting fear and pain. There had always been a few of them in SAS, more in the Selous Scouts and the Rhodesian SAS. And the SADF. Blantyre had followed a trail of certainties, a trek down through southern Africa, always looking for another border, another incursion, another set of niggers becoming uppity and being armed by the East Germans and the KGB. Christ, what a terrible *redundancy* had faced him until he'd signed up with MLC!

The anger and contempt cleared his thoughts and enabled him to concentrate, so that he could squint into the nightscope on the G3 without feeling woozy. There was nothing coming, yet. He unscrewed the top of a water bottle and swilled the tepid liquid in his mouth – don't drink from the water holes until you have to, leopards and zebra might have pissed in them . . . The guide books didn't quite put it like that. He screwed back the top. Not much wider than a quarter of a mile here, a narrow waist of canyon between two hips of rock. Yes, Blantyre had trekked all the way, following the Promised Land of violence and destruction, from Hereford and the Brecon Beacons and Oman and a few other places, down through Rhodesia and South Africa to –

– here. A figure appeared in the nightscope, stalking in a crouch and moving with expert speed, ducking quickly behind the nearest available cover so that the grey ghost of a bush masked his grey shadow. Then came a second man slightly more upright.

He fired. The shadow's arms went greyly up and then it tumbled back and out of sight behind the dust thrown up by a pebbly slope. He heard their voices exclaim and protest, and then knew he had made a mistake as the first rocket burst behind him, an instant after he had seen the small spit of flame. The stovelike pipe slung over the man's shoulder had hardly registered until then. Rock screeched, then roared outwards above his head. He pressed back, feet scrabbling, his arm shrieking again as his fingers clawed backwards.

The starlight disappeared in rock fragments, boulders and dust, which were flung away from him by the narrow jut of rock under which he sheltered. The rocks bounced away, terrifyingly enlarged in the lens of panic. The dust choked him, caught at his throat, made him cough. They'd come in concertedly and quickly now, like a hunting dog pack. He edged his way beneath the overhang. The dust was thinning. Movement made night-time shadows easier to see in the sniperscopes. *Four* of them. The barrel rested like a hot blade on his injured arm as he shuffled the rifle to some kind of readiness, ducking behind another clutter of boulders, gagging on, then swallowing, the gritty dust.

Wait for them.

'Where is he? Can you see him, Pik? *You*, Danie?'

'The bastard's killed Danie!' someone yelled back.

'Shut up, you cretin!' Blantyre shouted. No R/Ts now.

Hyde's arm ached beneath the impossible weight of the rifle barrel and he gritted his teeth against the pain. He even forced the numb, swollen arm to raise itself until the barrel could rest on top of the boulder and he could lever himself into something like a firing position. His head, with great luck, would look like a jut of rock through a nightsight – until he fired. He squinted into his own 'scope.

'Give the bastard another!' Blantyre yelled, and there was almost at once an obedient spit of flame, then the cliff erupted again, the rocks splitting and tumbling thirty yards or more to his left. He ducked, terrified, as a huge boulder flung itself towards him, then bounced over his hiding place, careering towards the nearest water hole, where it startled invisible animals. The dust pall dragged itself towards their positions, and the noise reverberated. The slight scrape of his rifle on the rock would be noticed –

He fired at the bush, twice. A cry, and the stretching of a shadowy leg. Hurt, not killed.

'Pik?'

'The bugger's shot me!'

'Keep your fucking voice down or he'll *kill* you!'

That was from behind that rock there – shoulder, head for an instant? Hyde fired again, saw rock splinters fly up and something move quicker than an animal. He fired twice more, then the returned fire drove him behind the rock. Three fit, one wounded. He turned awkwardly, studying the terrain. There were enough littered boulders, if he was quick, to afford him enough cover, were he fit and in control. He slung the rifle's strap around his neck, holding it against his chest with the injured arm. The pressure was appalling. He shook his head, and blundered towards the nearest cover, paused, then moved again. Bullets skipped behind him like flung stones, rock slivers grazed and slit his legs and back – *cover*! He fell rather than stretched behind it, gasping for breath, his arm aflame and his chest heaving.

'Did you get the bastard?'

'Might have winged him, Colonel.'

No you bloody didn't . . .

'Not good enough!' he heard Blantyre cry. 'Get up there and take a look!'

'Look your-fucking-self – sir!'

'Vermaak, either get up there or *I'll* finish you off!'

Come on, Vermaak. Come and have a look. You can make it across forty yards of open country against an injured man with good night vision – come on . . . Was that effort in Blantyre's voice, a shortness of breath more to do with pain than anger? Too much to hope for, that he'd slowed the bastard down, even caused him grievous bodily. Hyde shook his head. Bastards like Blantyre never died that easily. Enough people had got the shitty end of the stick already, trying to kill him. Come on, Vermaak, follow the officer's order – *there*!

He fired a ten-round burst, then returned the G3 to single shot, moving the fire lever back into position. Then he fumbled a new, twenty-round magazine from a pocket and clipped it onto the rifle. One up the spout, ready to go again – not knowing whether he'd hit Vermaak or not.

'Vermaak?'

'Yes, Colonel – go your-fucking-self, sir!'

He'd missed. Shit.

Blantyre suddenly scrabbled from cover towards the bush that had masked the man with the rocket launcher. Hyde fired once before ducking down from their returned fire. Had Blantyre been carrying one shoulder higher than the other, as if protecting it? He couldn't be certain. Hyde raised his head again, very slowly, and squinted through the nightsight. There was activity behind the bush, the bodies of Blantyre and Pik hotter than the bush, but indistinct. He didn't have another magazine to waste on a burst of automatic fire. Two shots flicked off the rock near his face and he ducked out of sight.

He rose, fired once towards the bush, then dropped down. More shots skittered off the rock. They've got you pinpointed. *Move –*

He scuttled in a crouch to his right, where he would be well covered by rocks – and where they would expect him to move, in the direction he had always taken – go *left*! Left, you stupid sod, *left*!

He scrambled back to the rock that had hidden him and then beyond it, back through the litter of newly fallen rock. Sweat bathed his body and his arm thudded with the impact of his racing blood. The explosion seemed overhead, then, as he stumbled and half-turned, he saw the hiding place he would have chosen disappear in rubble and dust. Bastard. Blantyre had almost been right. He'd have buried Hyde, for certain. He got to his feet and moved again, picking his way across the new scree slope, using the cover of boulders and the enveloping dust. They'd hesitate now, for a few seconds at least, confident that there was no hurry, that he was under half a ton of rock.

The rifle scraped against a boulder as he lost his balance on loose rock. There were shots immediately, and he returned fire because there was one solid shadow that was too clear to miss. Then he ran again, the noise of his movements amid the tumbled boulders hardly audible above the sound of his heart and lungs. His injured arm was detached from him, its pumping ache as he blundered along happening to someone else. He ran, off-balance, down a shallow, rippling slope of pebbles towards the riverbed, the canyon suddenly seeming to enlarge and spread out around him. His arms flailed, his feet were noisy, the slope rumbled and muttered behind him. Then he turned suddenly, when he could no longer bear the tension of anticipating their fire.

He flicked the rifle to automatic and emptied the magazine in a fraction of a second. The noise was deafening as he fired up the slope at the starlit shapes giving chase. Then, without waiting and dropping the now-useless rifle, he fled on down the slope, dodging and weaving as if running with a ball in some lunatic sport. There was silence behind him, but his skin slowly stretched tighter and tighter across his shoulder blades like drying leather as he waited for their first shot. His feet stumbled again, clumping like those of a heavy child learning to walk, legs threatening to give way. He clutched his injured arm against his chest with his other hand, his shoulders hunched, as if he carried some weighty treasure he refused to drop.

Still silence – then he thought he heard a rocket burst harmlessly a long way behind – if it had, then someone was still alive. But he heard only the one detonation, and that might have been illusory. Then he fell as if hit, his injured arm stretched out in front of him and finding an element that moved aside, that splashed back to wet his face and neck. Things rustled and scraped against his stubbled face. Reeds. Water. He scrabbled into the reeds and they bent obsequiously, masking him. He dimly realized his arm was in water, and his body was quivering against spoored and printed earth. Water hole, he thought as he blacked out, the adrenalin failing like a light going out.

Behind you . . . They're still behind you, still *there* . . .

The realization was not sufficient to keep him conscious. He sensed himself curling into a ball, cradling his injured arm, as the blackness he welcomed engulfed him.


He was curled foetally, he realized, as he opened his eyes. He even remembered that that was how he had surrendered to unconsciousness. He saw the big male leopard fifteen yards away, in the reeds, lying with its front paws extended like a harmless domestic cat. Around him – he suppressed a shiver – were its prints, and he could almost sense its big, rough tongue on his skin. There was a smug certainty on the leopard's streaked and blotched facial fur. It was very big . . . about a hundred and thirty pounds. Hyde realized that it was almost dawn, that the landscape was grey now, no longer dark, and the sky was empty of stars, dotted instead with high clouds already pinking with the rising sun. He forced himself not to move, clenching his arms into his body, clenching his watery bowels.

Oh, Christ, has the fucking thing killed? Has it eaten?

He knew it hadn't. Leopards were night-hunters when they could afford to be, secretive, lone. It wouldn't be waiting now if its belly was full. If it had already killed, it would have dragged off its prey to whatever cave it lived in. It was still waiting for a meal. Oh, Christ –

The leopard was watching him with lordly indifference. It was waiting for the first buck, even monkey, to come to the water. Prey that moved, evoked curiosity and hunger. Had it been starving, it might have eaten him as he'd slept . . . Oh, Jesus, keep your fucking imagination under control! Perhaps it had been the defensive, harmless crouch in which the leopard had found him that had disarmed it – in which he still lay, terrified into immobility.

He swallowed drily, with the utmost care. He was too weary to move, too unnerved to even twitch. He was certain that any move would be the last, fatal one. The pistol still nestled in the small of his back – he could shoot the leopard. If he was quick enough. One shot was all that he would be allowed. He didn't feel capable, not yet. It was easier to remain still, breathing shallowly, accustoming himself to the leopard's proximity.

And he would have to hit it in an eye, or straight through the heart, or it would bully through the impact of the bullet as if shrugging off insects . . .

The leopard's ear flicked, not against the first of the day's flies, but attentively. No one as shagged-out as you, as slow to react, takes on a big male leopard at fifteen paces. Its ears were now twitching attentively. Zebra, buck or monkey – something was moving towards the water hole. Hyde could hear nothing. The leopard's ears strained back, exactly locating the source of the sounds. Hyde kept his arms still, his hands pressed together between his thighs. Now that the big cat was alert, he knew that soon the scent of his fear would distract the leopard away from its anticipated prey towards himself.

Then he would have to be quick and certain enough to kill it with one shot. He had to reach behind him, draw the VP 70, chamber a round, sit up, aim and fire – Christ, he'd never do it, not one-handed.

He could smell his fear now, sour and rank. The leopard's staring eyes watched him intently, even though its ears were still alert to pick up the noises of the approaching animal – the *other* prey. Oh, dear Jesus –! Somewhere out there, however many of them were still alive were looking for him. They'd find the bloody bones, or rags of flesh and clothing, the marks of his being dragged off . . .

Then he, too, heard the noise of an animal blundering incautiously through the reeds surrounding the water hole. The leopard tensed, a slight alteration of shape and readiness. It released

393

his own tension – which immediately began to build again. The bloody animal would hear his heartbeat if it got any louder. Best bloody shot of your life, sport, the very best –

An upright human form blundered through the reeds to the water's edge. Blantyre grinned with immense, pained satisfaction as he saw Hyde's body curled by the pool. There was a slow, awkward but inexorable movement of the pistol from his side to an extended, one-handed aim. Hyde could see a big dark stain of blood on his bush shirt – on almost the whole shirt. The gun quivered and Blantyre seemed about to lose his balance. He tottered slightly –

– before the leopard, excited out of caution by the smell of blood, knocked Blantyre off his feet as it sprang on him. The pistol discharged into the air and then Blantyre screamed, high and loud like an animal caught in a mantrap. Then his screams were drowned by the snarling roars of the leopard. The reeds, which masked both bodies, thrashed and swayed with the throes of something that was not a contest. Blantyre was half again as big and heavy as the leopard, but the animal had known he was wounded.

Hyde heard one last scream as he got to his knees and stumbled away. Then he glanced briefly back. What remained of Blantyre was striped and stained with blood. He was dead now. The leopard was beginning with the stomach, since the man had no fur to be fastidiously picked off before it ate. The leopard was oblivious to Hyde, its facial fur deeply dyed with Blantyre's blood.

Hyde walked carefully, slowly away from the water hole, holding his wounded arm against his chest, the pistol in his right hand. There was no one else in sight on the floor of the canyon. The others must be dead – or wounded. Only Blantyre had come after him, determined to finish him. The leopard would spend most of the morning dragging the bastard to its cave or up a tree. Jesus Christ –

He retched drily, then moved on, his throat sore, his arm throbbing and woodenly stiff, hugely swollen. But the pain was diminishing, very slowly. All he had to do was find a path up to the road and wait. He stood, right hand still holding the pistol and pressed to his forehead to shield his eyes from the first glimpse of sun. He saw a path less than a quarter of a mile away, like a pale parting in reddish hair, wavering up to the cliff road. The canyon was silent. A single vulture circled on the earliest thermal.

At the top of the path, he saw a parked 4WD. And the flash of the first sunlight on field glasses and chrome. A vehicle and two people, distant and small as toys. The smaller of the two – a woman? – pointed towards him, then he saw her tiny, matchstick arm raised in a greeting. He waved wearily back. *Civilians*. Tourists. He waved again. Now, there was no hurry, no urgency at all.

He sat down on a rock as the dawn slid down the opposite wall of the canyon, golden and clean. Glad morning.

# POSTLUDE

'Since he means to come to a door he will come to a door,
Although so compromised of aim and rate
He may fumble wide of the knob a yard or more,
And to those concerned he may seem a little late.'

Robert Frost: *Willful Homing*

Dear Prime Minister,

It is with the utmost regret that I tender my resignation as Chairman of the Joint Intelligence Committee. Reluctantly, I feel the time has come for younger minds and hands to take up such arduous tasks as an uncertain future might place before our country.

I wish to thank you most warmly for your support and trust during our too-brief acquaintance.

Yours most sincerely,

*Kenneth Aubrey*

56

# Dark Watch

# Dark Watch

CLIVE CUSSLER
*with* JACK DU BRUL

A NOVEL FROM
THE OREGON® FILES

MICHAEL JOSEPH
*an imprint of*
PENGUIN BOOKS

MICHAEL JOSEPH

Published by the Penguin Group
Penguin Books Ltd, 80 Strand, London WC2R ORL, England
Penguin Group (USA) Inc., 375 Hudson Street, New York, New York 10014, USA
Penguin Group (Canada), 90 Eglinton Avenue East, Suite 700, Toronto, Ontario, Canada M4P 2Y3
(a division of Pearson Penguin Canada Inc.)
Penguin Ireland, 25 St Stephen's Green, Dublin 2, Ireland (a division of Penguin Books Ltd)
Penguin Group (Australia), 250 Camberwell Road,
Camberwell, Victoria 3124, Australia (a division of Pearson Australia Group Pty Ltd)
Penguin Books India Pvt Ltd, 11 Community Centre,
Panchsheel Park, New Delhi – 110 017, India
Penguin Group (NZ), 67 Apollo Drive, Mairangi Bay, Auckland 1310, New Zealand
(a division of Pearson New Zealand Ltd)
Penguin Books (South Africa) (Pty) Ltd, 24 Sturdee Avenue,
Rosebank, Johannesburg 2196, South Africa

Penguin Books Ltd, Registered Offices: 80 Strand, London WC2R ORL, England

www.penguin.com

First published in the United States of America by The Berkley Publishing Group
a member of Penguin Group (USA), Inc 2005
First published in Great Britain by Michael Joseph 2007

1

Copyright © Sandecker, RLLLP, 2005

Printed in Great Britain by Clays Ltd, St Ives plc

A CIP catalogue record for this book is available from the British Library

ISBN: 978-0-718-14799-0

# I

The aging Dassault Falcon executive jet drifted smoothly from the sky and touched down at the Sunan International Airfield, twelve miles north of Pyongyang. The MiG that had flown a tight escort from the moment the aircraft entered North Korea's airspace peeled off – twin cones of flame from her engines cutting the night. A truck was sent to lead the Falcon to its hardstand, and in its bed stood a machine gunner who never took his aim off the cockpit windows. The plane taxied to an open expanse of concrete at the far side of the airport complex, and even before its wheels were chocked a squad of fully armed troops had formed a perimeter around it – their AK-47s held ready for the slightest provocation. All this despite the fact that the passengers on board were invited dignitaries and important clients of the reclusive Communist country.

Several minutes after the engines spooled to silence, the passenger door cracked open. The pair of guards positioned closest shifted in anticipation. Then the door was lowered, showing the integrated steps that formed its internal side. A man wearing an olive uniform with a flat cap stood at the doorway. His features were harsh and uncompromising, with near-black eyes and a hooked nose. His skin was the color of weak tea. He stroked a finger along his dense black mustache and cast an unimpressed eye at the ring of soldiers before stepping lightly from the aircraft. He was followed by two more hatchet-faced men, one wearing traditional

Middle Eastern robes and a headscarf, the other in an expensive suit.

A trio of North Korean officers marched through the cordon and approached. The highest ranking officer gave a formal greeting and waited for another, a translator, to render his words into Arabic.

'General Kim Don Il welcomes you to the Democratic People's Republic of Korea, Colonel Hourani, and hopes you had an enjoyable flight from Damascus.'

Colonel Hazni Hourani, the deputy head of Syria's strategic rocket forces, bowed his head in acknowledgment. 'Thank the general for meeting us personally at this late hour. Tell him our flight was indeed enjoyable since we flew over Afghanistan and were able to dump the contents of the aircraft's septic system on the American occupiers.'

The Koreans shared a round of laughter once they heard the translation. Hourani continued, speaking to the translator directly, 'I applaud the skill in which you use our language, but I think our dealings would go smoother if we spoke in English.' Hourani switched to that language. 'I understand, General Kim, that we both speak the language of our common enemy.'

The general blinked. 'Yes, I find it gives me an advantage over the imperialists to know their ways better than they know mine,' he replied. 'I also speak some Japanese,' he added, trying to impress.

'And I some Hebrew,' Hourani answered quickly, playing the game of one-upmanship.

'It seems we are both dedicated to our countries and our cause.'

'The destruction of America.'

'The destruction of America,' General Kim echoed,

sensing in the Arab's intense stare that the same fires burned in his belly, too.

'For too long they have pushed their influence into all corners of the globe. They are slowly smothering the planet by first sending in soldiers and then poisoning the people with their decadence.'

'They have troops on your borders as well as mine. But they fear attacking my country, for they know our retribution would be swift and final.'

'And soon,' Hourani said with an oily smile, 'they will fear *our* retribution as well. With your help, of course.'

Kim's smile matched that of the Syrian. These two men, from different sides of the globe, were kindred spirits, devout haters of all things Western. They were defined by this hate, shaped and molded through years of indoctrination. It didn't matter that one worshiped a bent view of a noble religion and the other a warped faith in the infallibility of the state, the results were the same. They saw beauty in savagery and found inspiration in chaos.

'We have arranged transportation for your delegation to the Munch'on Naval Base near Wosan on the eastern coast,' General Kim told Hourani. 'Will your pilots need accommodations in Pyongyang?'

'That is most generous, General.' Hourani stroked his mustache again. 'But the aircraft is needed back in Damascus as soon as possible. One of the pilots slept most of the way here so he can fly back to Syria. If you could arrange for refueling, I would like them to leave immediately.'

'As you wish.' General Kim spoke to a subaltern, who passed the order to the head of the security detail. As Hourani's two assistants finished unloading their luggage, a fuel tanker arrived and workers began to unreel the hose.

The car was a Chinese-made limousine with at least two hundred thousand miles on the odometer. The seats sagged deep enough to almost swallow the slightly built North Korean general, and the interior reeked of cigarettes and pickled cabbage. The Kumgang Mountain highway linking Pyongyang with Wosan was one of the best in the nation, yet it taxed the limo's suspension to the breaking point as the vehicle ground its way around tight switchbacks and along precarious gorges. There were few guardrails along the highway, and the car's headlamps were little more than dim flashlights. Without the moon's cool glow the drive would have been impossible.

'A couple of years ago,' Kim said as they ascended higher into the mountains that ran like a spine down the length of the country, 'we gave permission for a company in the south to arrange tourist trips into these mountains. Some consider them sacred. We demanded they build the roads and trails as well as the restaurants and the hotels. They even had to construct their own port facility to dock their cruise ships. For a while the company had many people making the trip, but they had to charge five hundred dollars per passenger to recoup their investment. The pool of nostalgia seekers turned out to be a small one, and business quickly dropped off – especially after we posted guards along the routes and harassed the tourists any way we could. They no longer come here, but they are still paying us the one billion dollars they guaranteed our government.'

This elicited a smile from Colonel Hourani, the only Syrian who spoke English.

'The best part,' Kim went on, 'is that their hotel is now an army barracks, and their port is the home to a Najin-class Corvette.'

4

This time Hourani laughed aloud.

Two hours after leaving the airfield, the limousine finally descended the Kumgang Mountains and crossed the coastal plane, swinging around to the north of Wosan, and arrived at the outer perimeter fence for the Munch'on Naval Base.

Guards saluted the limo through the gate, and the car crawled across the facility, passing several impressive maintenance buildings and over a half mile of wharf space. Four sleek gray patrol craft were tied to the quay, and a single destroyer lay at anchor in the mile-square inner harbor, white smoke from its stack coiling into the night. The driver swung around a rail-mounted derrick and parked alongside a four-hundred-foot cargo ship at the end of the wharf.

'The *Asia Star*,' General Kim announced.

Colonel Hourani checked his watch. It was one in the morning. 'And when do we sail?'

'The tides are mild here in Yonghung-man Bay so you can leave anytime. The ship is loaded, fueled, and provisioned.'

Hourani turned to one of his men and asked in Arabic, 'What do you think?' He listened to the long reply, nodding several times, then turned back to the general, who sat opposite him in the limo. 'Assad Muhammad is our technical expert on the Nodong-1 missile. He would like to take a look at them before we depart.'

Kim's expression didn't change, but it was clear he didn't like the idea of a delay. 'Surely you can accomplish your inspection at sea. I assure you that all ten missiles your country has purchased are aboard.'

'I'm afraid Assad does not do well on boats. He would prefer to inspect the missiles now, because he will likely spend the voyage in his cabin.'

'Odd that you would have such a man accompany the rockets back to Syria,' Kim said coolly.

Hourani's eyes tightened. His country was paying nearly a hundred fifty million sorely needed dollars for the medium-range strategic missiles. Kim had no right to question him. 'He is here because he knows the rockets. He worked with the Iranians when they purchased their Nodongs from you. That he has trouble on the sea is not your concern. He will inspect all ten, and we will sail at first light.'

General Kim was under orders to stay with the Syrians until the ship departed. He'd told his wife he wouldn't return to Pyongyang until morning, but by remaining with the Middle Easterners, he would forfeit several hours with his latest mistress. He sighed at the sacrifices he made for the state. 'Very well, Colonel. I will have the harbor master informed that the *Asia Star* won't leave until first light. Why don't we get on board? I will show you to your cabins so you can stow your luggage, then Mr Muhammad can inspect your new toys.'

The driver opened the rear door, and as Kim slid over to exit, Colonel Hourani placed a hand on his uniformed sleeve. Their eyes met. 'Thank you, General.'

Kim's smile was genuine. Despite their cultural differences and the inherent suspicion and secrecy surrounding this mission, he felt he really did like the colonel. 'It is no problem.'

The three Syrians each had their own cabins, but only a minute after being shown their accommodations, they met in the one occupied by Colonel Hourani. Assad Muhammad sat on the bunk with a briefcase beside him while Hourani placed himself at the desk below the room's single porthole. The oldest of the trio, Professor Walid Khalidi, leaned

6

against a bulkhead, his arms crossed over his chest. Hourani then did a very strange thing. He touched the corner of his eye and shook his head, then pointed at his ear and nodded in the affirmative. He indicated the ceiling-mounted light fixture in the center of the cabin and the cheap brass-plated lamp attached to the desk.

'How long do you think the inspection should take, Assad?' he then asked.

Assad Mohammed had taken a miniature tape recorder from his suit jacket and hit Play. A digitally altered voice, actually that of Hourani himself, since he was the only member of the team who spoke Arabic, replied, 'I think no more than a few hours. The most time-consuming part is simply removing inspection covers. Testing the circuits is simple.'

By this time Hourani had also drawn a recorder from an inside jacket pocket and set it on the desk. As soon as Assad finished speaking, he, too, hit the Play button, and the conversation continued as the men remained silent. At a predetermined moment in the script, Walid Khalidi added his own recorder to the ruse. Once the three recorders playing altered versions of Hourani's voice were working, the trio of 'Syrians' moved silently to the far corner of the cabin.

'Only two bugs,' Max Hanley mused quietly. 'The Koreans really do trust their Syrian customers.'

Juan Cabrillo, the chairman of the Corporation and the captain of the merchant ship *Oregon*, tore the fake mustache from his upper lip. The skin beneath was lighter than the layers of self-tanning cream he'd used to darken his complexion. 'Remind me to tell Kevin in the Magic Shop that his appliance glue is worthless.' He had a bottle of the suspect glue and reapplied a line to the back of the mustache.

'You looked like Snidely Whiplash trying to keep that thing in place.' This from Hali Kasim, the third-generation Lebanese-American who'd been newly promoted as the *Oregon*'s Security and Surveillance director. He was the only member of her crew who didn't need makeup and latex inserts to pass as Middle Eastern. The only problem was he didn't speak enough Arabic to order a meal in a restaurant.

'Just be thankful the Koreans left their translator at the airport,' Cabrillo said mildly. 'You mangled the little soliloquy you'd memorized and delivered during the car ride. Your proposed examination of the missiles sounded more proctologic than scientific.'

'Sorry, boss,' Kasim said, 'I never had an ear for languages, and no matter how much I practice, it still sounds like gobbledygook to me.'

'To any Arabic speakers, too,' Juan Cabrillo teased.

'How are we on time?' Max Hanley asked. Hanley was the Corporation's president and was in charge of all their ship's operations, especially her gleaming magnetohydrodynamic engines. While Cabrillo negotiated the contracts the Corporation took on and was responsible for a great deal of their planning, it fell on Max's capable shoulders to make sure the *Oregon* and her crew were up to the task. While the crew of the *Oregon* were technically mercenaries, they maintained a corporate structure for their outfit. Apart from his duties as the ship's chief engineer, Hanley handled day-to-day administration and acted as the company's human resources director.

Under his robes and head scarf, Hanley was a little taller than average, with a slight paunch. His eyes were an alert brown, and what little hair remained atop his reddened skull was auburn. He had been with Juan since the day the Corporation was founded, and Cabrillo believed that without his number two, he would have gone out of business years ago.

'We have to assume Tiny Gunderson got the Dassault airborne as soon as he could. He's probably in Seoul by now,' Chairman Cabrillo said. 'Eddie Seng has had two weeks to get into position, so if he's not alongside this scow in the submersible now, he never will be. He won't surface until we hit the water, and by then it'll be too late to abort. Since the Koreans didn't mention capturing a minisub in the harbor, we can assume he's ready.'

'So once we plant the device?'

'We have fifteen minutes to rendezvous with Eddie and get clear.'

'This is gonna hurt,' Hali remarked grimly.

Cabrillo's eyes hardened. 'Them more than us.'

This contract, like many the Corporation accepted, had come through back channels from the United States government. While the Corporation was a for-profit enterprise, the men and women who served on the *Oregon* were for the most part ex-U.S. military and tended to take jobs that benefited the United States and her allies, or at the very least, didn't harm American interests.

With no end in sight in the war on terror, there was a never-ending string of contracts for a team like the one Cabrillo had assembled – black ops specialists without the constraint of the Geneva Convention or congressional oversight. That wasn't to say the crew were a bunch of cutthroat pirates who took no prisoners. They were deeply conscientious about what they did but understood that the lines of conflict had blurred in the twenty-first century.

This mission was a perfect example.

North Korea had every right to sell ten single-stage tactical missiles to Syria, and the United States would have begrudgingly let the sale proceed. However, intelligence intercepts had determined the real Colonel Hazni Hourani planned on diverting the *Asia Star* so that two of the Nodongs and a pair of mobile launchers could be off-loaded in Somalia and given to Al-Qaeda, who would launch them hours later at targets in Saudi Arabia, notably the holy cities of Mecca and Medina, in a twisted plot to oust the Saudi royal family. It also appeared, but couldn't be verified, that Hourani was acting with the tacit approval of the Syrian government.

The United States could send a warship to intercept the *Asia Star* in Somalia; however, the vessel's captain would only have to claim that they were diverted for repairs, and the ten missiles would end up in Damascus. The better alternative was to sink the *Star* en route, but if the truth came out, there would be an international outcry and swift retaliation from terrorist cells controlled by Damascus. It was Langston Overholt IV, a high-ranking official in the CIA, who came up with the best alternative: using the Corporation.

Cabrillo had been given just four weeks to plan how to get rid of the problem as quietly and with as little exposure as possible. Cabrillo had intuitively known that the best way to prevent the missiles from reaching their customers, be they legitimate or otherwise, was to stop them from ever leaving North Korea.

Once the *Oregon* was in position off Yonghung-man Bay, Cabrillo, Hanley, and Hali Kasim headed to Bagram

Airbase outside of Kabul, Afghanistan, in a Dassault Falcon identical to the one used by Colonel Hourani.

CIA assets on the ground in Damascus confirmed the flight time for Hourani's trip to Pyongyang, and a dedicated AWACS had tracked the corporate jet as it flew halfway around the world. Once it entered Afghan airspace, an F-22 Raptor stealth fighter that had been flown expressly to the theater for the mission had taken off from Bagram. The Corporation's own Falcon had left a moment later, heading south, away from the Syrians. While the U.S. controlled all of the radar facilities capable of monitoring what was about to happen, it was imperative that there be no evidence of the switch.

In one of the few zones where radar coverage was nonexistent, Tiny Gunderson, the Corporation's chief pilot, began to turn back north. Only this time the Dassault Falcon wasn't alone. She'd been joined by a B-2 stealth bomber from Whiteman Air Force Base in Missouri. Because the bomber was larger than the Falcon, yet undetectable by radar, Tiny kept his aircraft fifty feet above the flying wing. No ground-based radar on earth could track a B-2, and by shielding the Falcon, the Corporation's jet remained hidden as they began to close on Hourani's plane.

At forty thousand feet, the Syrian Falcon jet was at her maximum ceiling, while the Raptor fast approaching her could have made the intercept four miles farther into the sky. The timing was critical. When the B-2 was a mere half mile behind Hourani's aircraft, the Raptor opened her weapons bay and unleashed a pair of AIM-120C AMRAAM missiles.

Had the Syrian jet carried threat radar, the missiles would have appeared out of nowhere. As it was, the older

French-built aircraft didn't have such a system, so the two missiles impacted the Garrett TFE-731 turbofans without the slightest warning. Even as the Dassault exploded in midair, the pilot of the B-2 dove away from Tiny Gunderson's Falcon. At that altitude anyone on the ground who saw the brief fireball would have assumed it was a shooting star. And anyone watching a radar screen would have noticed the Syrian aircraft suddenly vanish for an instant, then reappear a half mile to the west before continuing on normally. They might have guessed their system had glitched, if they gave the incident any thought at all.

Now that Cabrillo, Hanley, and Kasim were safely aboard the *Asia Star*, all that remained was to plant the bomb, avoid detection getting off the ship, rendezvous with Eddie Seng in the minisub, slip out of the best-protected harbor in North Korea, and reach the *Oregon* before anyone realized the *Star* had been sabotaged.

Not a typical day for members of the Corporation. But not all that atypical either.

# 2

A scream woke Victoria Ballinger.

It also saved her life.

Tory was the only female aboard the Royal Geographic Society's research ship *Avalon*, after her cabin mate was transported to a hospital in Japan for acute appendicitis a week ago. Having a cabin to herself also contributed to her salvation.

The ship had been at sea for a month, part of a co-ordinated international effort to fully map the currents of the Sea of Japan, an area little understood because Japan and Korea fiercely protected their fishing rights and felt any cooperation could jeopardize them.

Unlike her roommate, who'd brought suitcases loaded with clothes and personal items, Tory lived a spartan existence aboard ship. Other than her bedding and a week's worth of jeans and rugby shirts, her cabin was empty.

The scream came from the passageway outside her door, a male cry of agony that snapped her awake. Even as her vision cleared of sleep, she heard muted gunfire. Her senses sharpened, and she heard more automatic weapons fire, more shouts, and more screams.

Everyone on the *Avalon* had been warned that a band of modern-day pirates were preying on ships in the Sea of Japan. They'd attacked four vessels in the past two months, scuttling the merchantmen and leaving any crewmen alive to make their own escape on lifeboats. To date only 15 out of

172 had survived the attacks. Just yesterday they were told that a container ship had simply vanished without a trace. Because of the pirate threat, an arms locker had been placed on the bridge, but the pair of shotguns and the single pistol were no match for the assault rifles cutting through the group of scientists and professional mariners.

The fight-or-flight instinct kicked in, and Tory quickly got to her feet. She wasted two precious seconds making a choice she didn't have. There was no place for her to go. The pirates were somewhere in the corridor outside her cabin, shooting into the rooms, from the sound of it. She'd be gunned down the moment she opened her door. She could not flee, and there was nothing in her room to use as a weapon.

The light of a full moon shining through the porthole fell on the stripped bed opposite Tory's and gave her inspiration. She whipped the blankets and sheets from her bed and bundled them under the frame. Then she pulled her clothes from her locker, making sure to leave its door open, just like her absent roommate's. She didn't think she had the time to empty the bathroom of toiletries. She crawled under the bed, pressing into the deepest corner, and packed her clothes around her body.

She fought to hold her breathing steady as the first wave of panic nibbled at the edge of her mind. Tears leaked from the corners of her blue eyes. She stifled a sob just as her cabin door was thrown open. She saw a flashlight beam slice the room, tracking first across Judy's empty mattress before sweeping her own, pausing for a second on the pair of barren lockers.

The pirate's feet became visible. He wore black combat boots, and she could make out that the cuffs of his black trousers had been stuffed into them. The pirate crossed to the tiny bathroom, sweeping it with his flashlight. She heard the shower curtain ripple as he checked behind it. He either didn't see Tory's soap, shampoo, and conditioner or didn't think they were important. He slammed the cabin door on his way out, apparently satisfied it was vacant.

Tory remained motionless as the sounds of the struggle faded down the hallway. There were only thirty people on the ship. Most of them were asleep in their cabins because at night the engine room ran on automatic, and only two stood watch on the bridge. Because her cabin was one of the last on the corridor, she was certain that the pirates were about finished with the crew.

The crew. Her friends.

If she wanted to get out of this alive, she couldn't let that thought seep any deeper into her brain. How long would they take to loot the vessel? There was little of value to pirates. All of their expensive equipment, their scientific gear, was too large to steal. The underwater probes were worthless to anyone outside the scientific community. There were a few televisions and some computers, but it hardly seemed worth the effort to take them.

Still, Tory figured the pirates would need a half hour to scavenge the 130-foot *Avalon* before opening the sea cocks and sending her to the bottom. She counted out the minutes by the luminous dots on the men's Rolex she wore, allowing herself to fall into the tiny galaxy of phosphorescent points in order to keep from panicking.

Only fifteen minutes passed before she felt the ship's motion change. The night was calm, and the *Avalon* rolled with the gentle swells, a normally comforting motion that lulled her to sleep each night. Tory began to sense the ship's sway had changed, slowed – as though she'd become heavier.

The pirates had already opened the sea cocks. They were already sinking the research vessel. She tried to see the logic in their action, but it didn't make sense. They couldn't possibly have ransacked the ship so quickly. They were scuttling the *Avalon* without even robbing her!

She couldn't wait. Tory slithered out from under her bed and bolted for the porthole. On the horizon she could see what at first appeared to be a low island, but she realized it was a huge ship of some kind. There was another smaller vessel near it. It looked as though the two were going to collide, but it had to be a trick of the moonlight. In the foreground she made out the stern and wake of a large inflatable craft. The sound of its outboard engines faded as it raced from the stricken oceanography ship. She imagined the pirates aboard it and felt her anger flare.

Tory whirled away from the porthole and bolted from her cabin. There were no bodies in the passageway, but the deck was littered with spent shell casings, and the air had a raw, chemical stench. She tried not to look at the blood spattered against the long wall. From her orientation when first coming aboard, Tory knew there were survival suits in the Zodiac life raft near the *Avalon*'s bow, so she didn't care that she wore only a long T-shirt. Her bare feet slapped against the metal decking as she ran with one arm clamped over her chest to keep her unsupported breasts from bouncing.

She climbed a set of stairs to the main deck. At the end of another corridor was the door leading to the outside. Between her and the exterior hatch was a body. Tory whimpered as she approached. The man lay facedown, a shiny slick of blood dampening his dark shirt and drizzling

16

onto the deck. She recognized his shape. It was the second engineer, a high-spirited Geordie, whose flirtations she had begun to encourage. She couldn't bring herself to touch him. The volume of blood told her everything she needed to know. She kept herself pressed to the cold corridor wall as she stepped past the corpse. When she reached the end of the hallway, she looked out the hatch's small window, straining to see if anyone remained on the dim foredeck. She saw nothing and cautiously turned the handle. It wouldn't budge. She tightened her grip and tried again, pressing all her weight against the jammed mechanism, but it remained frozen.

Tory kept calm. She told herself that there were four other ways out of the superstructure and that she could always smash the glass in the bridge if the wing doors were also sealed. She first examined the other doors on the main deck before climbing another set of steps to the bridge. She knew she would get out of this, but as she approached the door leading to the command deck, a deep dread welled up. Although they'd killed the entire crew, the pirates had taken the time to seal the ship like a coffin. They wouldn't have left such an obvious means of escape. Her long fingers trembled when she touched the knob. It turned.

Tory pushed against the solid steel door, but it wouldn't open. It didn't even creak. There were no large windows she could crawl through, no porthole big enough for her to wiggle out. She was trapped, and that realization destroyed any composure she'd been able to maintain. She threw her body at the door, slamming her shoulder into it again and again until her arm was bruised down to her elbow. She screamed until her throat was raw, then fell back against the door and allowed herself to slide to the deck. She sobbed into her hands, her dark hair falling around her face.

The *Avalon* shifted suddenly, and the lights flickered. The water pouring into her lower compartments had found someplace new to flood. The shudder sent a jolt through Tory. She wasn't dead yet, and if she could stop the ship from sinking, she'd have the time to figure a way out. She'd seen a cutting torch in one of the workshops. If she could find it she would burn her way out.

Now as energized as she was in those first desperate seconds when she heard the scream – she was certain now it had been Dr Halverson, a genteel oceanographer nearing seventy – Tory launched herself from the floor and ran back the way she'd come. She passed through the crew's accommodation block and reached a set of stairs that descended into the engineering spaces. She felt the first cold rush of air as she reached the bottom landing. The sound of flooding was like the roar of a waterfall.

She stood in a small antechamber with a single watertight door leading into the engine room. She put her hand to the metal. It was still warm from the big diesels. But when she placed her hand low down, next to the bottom jamb, the steel was icy to the touch. She'd never been to the engine room and didn't know its layout. Still, she had to try.

'Here we go.' Her voice quavered as she undogged the hatch.

Water gushed across her bare feet, and in seconds she was standing knee-deep, with the level rising perceptibly. An open set of steps led down to the floor of the well-lit engine room. Beyond the tangle of pipes, ducts, and conduits, Tory could see that the giant motors, each the size of a minivan, were already half-submerged. Water sloshed against a generator housing.

She stepped over the coaming and started down. She gasped when the water reached her chest. It was probably sixty-five degrees, but she began to shiver. At the bottom step she had to get on her toes to keep her head above the flood. Half walking, half swimming, she struck out across the cavernous space with a vague plan to find how the water was entering the ship.

As the *Avalon* continued to sink on a more or less even keel, she still pitched with the waves. That slight motion made it impossible for Tory to feel currents in the water and pinpoint where they were strongest, where she guessed open pipes led to the sea. The water in the flooded engine room seethed like a boiling cauldron. In just a few minutes of frantic searching, her toes lost their tenuous grip with the deck plating. Tory swam fruitlessly for a minute more. There was nothing she could do. Even if she found the sea cocks, she had no idea how they operated.

The lights flickered again, and when they came back on, they were only half as bright. It was the signal for her to leave. She'd never find her way out of the labyrinth-like space in the dark. She cut smooth strokes through the water and swam directly into the antechamber. Getting to her feet, she found the water had risen to the level of her waist. It took all her strength to close the door. She prayed that once it was sealed the ship might remain buoyant enough to stay afloat until another ship passed by.

Cold and shivering, Tory climbed back to the second deck and padded to her cabin. She toweled off in the bathroom, bound her shoulder-length hair in a ponytail, and threw on her warmest clothes. The air was markedly chilly. She hadn't noticed, but somewhere in the engine room she'd cut the corner of her mouth. She wiped the watery trickle of blood from her lip. Under normal circumstances, the sharp planes and angles of her face were arresting, especially with her startlingly blue eyes. Looking at her reflection in the mirror above the sink, what Tory saw was the haunted look of someone on the way to the gallows.

She turned away quickly and went to the porthole. She could no longer see the moon or even its milky glow, nor could she see the pirates' boat or the big ships she'd glimpsed on the horizon. The night had gone completely black, yet she would not turn away from her only window to the outside.

Maybe if she got some grease or cooking fat she could lube her body and squeeze through the porthole. She thought the windows in the mess hall upstairs were a little bigger. It was worth a shot. She was about to turn away when something dark flashed by outside. She peered closer, her eyes watering with the strain.

She thought she saw it again, maybe ten feet from the ship. A bird? It moved like one, but she wasn't sure. And then it loomed in front of her, taking up the entire porthole. Tory stumbled back with a scream. Outside her cabin, a large gray fish stared at her with its mouth agape, water pumping through its gills. The giant sea perch watched her with its yellow eyes for a moment longer, attracted to the light in the cabin, before finning away into the depths.

What Tory Ballinger couldn't see from her cabin low in the hull was that the deck of the research ship *Avalon* was already awash. Waves lapped at the stern and bow cargo hatches. In a few minutes the water would climb the bridge, swamping the ship so her stern-mounted crane would stick from the sea like a spindly arm clawing for rescue. A few minutes after that, the ocean would close around the top of her single funnel, and the *Avalon* would begin her plunge toward the sea floor nearly two miles down.

# 3

When a pair of North Korean agents from the brutal State Safety & Security Agency came to fetch their Syrian clients, two were quietly reading their Korans while the third studied spec sheets for the Nodong missile. A guard made a gesture for the trio to follow that also showed off a pistol in a shoulder holster. Cabrillo and Hali Kasim tucked away their Korans while Hanley slipped the schematics back into his bulky briefcase and thumbed the locks.

They threaded their way through the *Asia Star*, a Panamanian-registered bulk carrier converted to the container trade. While worn, the interior spaces were well maintained, and the bulkheads were glossy with new paint. The ship also appeared deserted except for the pair of spies on escort duty.

At a hatchway below the main deck, one of the guards undogged a hatch. Beyond loomed a darkened steel cavern that smelled faintly of bilgewater and old metal. The man snapped on banks of overhead lights, and the fluorescent glow revealed the ten Nodong missiles settled into special cradles, their outlines blurred by thick plastic sheeting. Each missile was sixty-two feet in length and four feet in diameter and weighed fifteen tons when loaded with liquid fuel. Based on the venerable Russian Scud-D, the Nodong could carry a one-ton payload nearly six hundred miles.

In the dank hold of the freighter, the shrouded rockets didn't lose any of their aura of menace or death. And knowing what was planned for two of these missiles deepened the resolve of the Corporation members.

The three men descended a set of metal stairs to the cargo hold's floor. Max Hanley, in the guise of the missile expert, stepped boldly to the first rocket. He barked at the government minders holding back at the hatchway and indicated that he wanted the plastic removed from the Nodongs.

General Kim arrived just as Max had removed an access panel from the first missile and was bent over the opening with a circuit tester. 'I see you couldn't wait to inspect your newest weapons.'

'They are formidable,' Cabrillo replied for lack of anything else to say.

'Our experts have greatly improved on the old Soviet design, and the warheads are much more powerful.'

'Which two are to be offloaded in Somalia?'

The North Korean repeated the question to one of the guards, who pointed out a pair of the rockets near the back of the hold. 'Those two under the red plastic. Because of the primitive facilities available in Mogadishu, the warheads have already been mounted. Fuel for those two can be loaded from the tanks in the forward hold in order to meet the tight schedule for firing, provided you don't add the corrosive mixture too soon. Three days from Somalia is soon enough.'

'I think one day is safer,' Juan countered. He knew that Kim's statement had been a test of his knowledge of the missiles. Loading the liquid fuel three days before launch would cause it to dissolve the rocket's thin aluminum tanks and likely blow the *Asia Star* out of the water.

'Where is my head? Forgive me. Any more than one day

would be disastrous.' There was little warmth in Kim's apology.

Silently, Cabrillo hoped the general would remain on board when the missiles blew. Max Hanley called him over to see something within the Nodong's electronic brain. Hali Kasim stood at his other shoulder and for fifteen minutes the three men mutely stared into the tangle of wires and circuits. As they'd intended, they could hear Kim impatiently shifting his weight from foot to foot and muttering to himself. 'Is there something the matter?' he finally asked.

'No, all seems in order,' Cabrillo answered without turning.

They played the game again for another fifteen minutes. Occasionally Max would consult a detail from the plans he carried, but other than that, the men remained as statues.

'Is this really necessary, Colonel Hourani?' Kim asked with ill-disguised impatience.

Cabrillo ran a finger along his false mustache to make sure it was in place before turning. 'I am sorry, General. Mr Muhammad and Professor Khalidi are very thorough, although I believe once they satisfy themselves that the first missile is in working order, they will be quicker with the others.'

Kim shot a look at his watch. 'I can take this opportunity to attend to some paperwork in the captain's cabin. Why don't you find me when you have completed your inspection. These men will remain with you, should you need anything.'

Juan suppressed a grin. 'As you wish, General Kim.'

The three members of the Corporation moved on to the second missile ten minutes later. The two guards had sat themselves on the stairs overlooking the hold. One smoked a continuous chain of cigarettes while the other watched the Arabs without seeming to blink. Both kept their suit jackets opened enough to reach their weapons. Kim might have grown bored with the operation, but the pair of secret policemen maintained their vigilance.

There was no set time to rendezvous with Eddie Seng. If everything had gone according to plan, he would have the minisub positioned a short way from the *Star*'s stern, close enough for the craft's sophisticated passive sonar to detect the sound of the three men hitting the water. The time constraint Juan felt came from his desire to get the *Oregon* as far into international waters as he could before first light.

Dawn was three hours away. He calculated the time it would take to board the minisub, make their escape from Yonghung-man Bay, and link up with the *Oregon*. From that point on, it would depend on the ship's magnetohydrodynamic engines, in which Cabrillo placed his full trust. The technology of using free electrons extracted from seawater to power the vessel was still in its experimental stages, but in the two years since taking delivery, the complex system of cryo-cooled magnets that generated power to feed pumps for her four pulse aqua jets had never let him down.

It was time. Cabrillo felt a slight twinge in his stomach, not fear exactly but a tension brought on by his old nemesis, Murphy's Law. It was almost a religion to him. He was a superb tactician and strategist, as well as a master planner, but he also recognized the vagaries of chance, an obstacle that can never be overcome entirely. The operation had gone smoothly to this point, which only increased the possibility of something fouling now.

He had no doubt they could maintain their ruse until the

ship reached Somalia, where they could easily escape. But that would mean failure, another of Cabrillo's old adversaries, one he hated even more than Mr Murphy's famous precept. But he knew that once they committed, there would be no turning back. If the dice fell the wrong way, he and Max and Hali would die. Eddie Seng might stand a chance to escape, but it wasn't likely. However, if Lady Luck held, in a couple of hours ten million dollars would appear in the Corporation's Cayman Island account courtesy of Uncle Sam's black budget.

Cabrillo tapped his watch, their prearranged signal, and suddenly the anxiety vanished. Juan went on automatic, relying on skills first learned in the ROTC, then honed at the CIA's training facility in rural Virginia before being perfected by fifteen years in the field.

Hali shifted his position slightly, blocking the guards' view of Hanley as Max snapped a hidden set of locks in his case. Juan turned from the missile, caught the eye of the guard with the nicotine addiction, and made a universal gesture of wanting to borrow one of his cigarettes. He started across the hold as the North Korean pulled a nearly depleted pack from his coat.

Out of view of the distracted guards, Max Hanley eased the bomb from the false bottom of his valise. The explosive device was smaller than a compact disc case, a marvel of miniaturization that packed the detonative force of a claymore mine.

Five feet from the staircase, the smoker got to his feet and descended to the deck level. Juan had banked on the man remaining seated next to his partner. Damn Murphy. He accepted the proffered cigarette and held it for the guard to light with his prized Zippo.

26

Juan took a measured drag, held the smoke in his mouth for a second, then exploded in a wrenching cough, as if the tobacco was harsher than he'd anticipated. The guard chuckled at Cabrillo's discomfort and flicked his attention to his partner to make a comment.

He never saw that Cabrillo's coughing fit had allowed him to torque his body like a coiled spring so when Juan threw the punch, it contained every ounce of strength in his six-foot-one-inch frame. The blow landed on the point of the guard's jaw and corkscrewed him to the deck as though he'd been shot. Juan couldn't believe the reflexes of the second guard. He'd anticipated at least two seconds for him to even realize what was happening.

Instead, the man was already up at the top of the short flight of steps and was just reaching into his shoulder holster when Cabrillo dove for him. Juan jumped for the stairs, reaching for the man's ankles. The automatic's barrel had just cleared the holster when Cabrillo's hands closed around the Korean's shins. Cabrillo fell heavily onto the steel steps, gashing his chin on a sharp edge, but his momentum pulled the North Korean off balance, sending him tumbling backward. The gun clattered onto the upper landing.

Cabrillo scrambled to his feet, blood running from his chin, adrenaline surging in his veins. Even if the Korean couldn't aim the pistol, the sound of a single shot would alert Kim and call an army of security guards to the vessel. Behind the grappling men, Max Hanley had raced to the missile destined to blast the holy city of Mecca. He had to set the bomb close enough to the warhead to cause a sympathetic detonation. Hali Kasim pulled a stiletto hidden in the binding of his Koran and ran for the stairs, knowing the fight would be over before reaching his boss, but making the effort nevertheless.

Juan tried to smash his elbow into the Korean's groin as he clawed his way up the stairs. The blow missed as the lithe guard twisted, and he felt his right arm go numb from the elbow down as it smashed into the deck plate. He cursed and managed to grab the man's right wrist just before his fingers curled around the gun. Even with his superior size and strength, Cabrillo was in an awkward position, and he felt the Korean draw closer to the weapon.

Hali was ten feet from the steps when the guard made a lunge for the pistol. Juan allowed himself to be thrown with the man's desperate grab, and his useless right arm arced like a pendulum into the side of the Korean's head, stunning him for a moment. The guard shook off the blow and kicked at Juan's right leg, slamming it against a railing. What sounded like the crack of broken bone echoed over the labored breathing of the combatants. The guard was sure the Syrian was finished and turned his attention back to getting the weapon. But Cabrillo wasn't even fazed. As the Korean grabbed the barrel of his pistol, Juan grasped his wrist and smashed it repeatedly against the deck. On the third blow the automatic flew from his grip and bounced down the steps. Hali scooped it up, mounted the stairs three at a time, and clipped the guard on the side of the head with the butt. The Korean's eyes fluttered, and he was out.

'You okay, boss?' Kasim asked, helping Cabrillo to his feet.

Max bounded up the stairs with the speed of a man half his age. 'Ask him later. Bomb's ticking, and we have fifteen minutes.'

Familiar with all manner of ships, the three men ran

unerringly to the main deck where they paused for just a moment to make sure there were no guards patrolling the area. They could see the sleek destroyer in the middle of the bay, her turret-mounted 100 mm guns trained on the outer harbor. There was no one on deck, so the three rushed to the railing and unceremoniously tossed themselves overboard.

The water was cold and tasted like kerosene soup. Max spat a mouthful as he slid his robe over his head. Beneath it he wore a pair of swim trunks and a tight thermal top. Juan struggled out of his boots but left his uniform on. He'd grown up in the surf of Southern California and was as comfortable in the water as on dry land. Hali, the youngest of the assault team, shed his jacket and kicked off his brogans, forcing them under the black surface. They swam silently to the ship's fantail and ducked under her curved hull so as not to be spotted from above.

There was a balance between speed and stealth. Eddie could have kept the thirty-two-foot Discovery 1000 submerged, and the men could have cycled through the airlock, a time-consuming process even in the best circumstance. Juan had decided that Eddie should broach the sub so the men could climb through her topside hatch. They would be visible for no more than thirty seconds, and surfacing near the acoustical clutter of waves striking the *Asia Star*'s idle prop and rudder would mask any sounds from Korean detection gear.

The wait was no more than a minute before bubbles erupted directly astern of the *Asia Star*. They were in motion even before the minisub's flat upperworks broke through the waves. Hali reached the sub first and swung himself aboard. He was working the hatch cover as water sluiced off the sub's matte-black hull. The seal broke with an audible hiss, and he threw himself down into the dark confines of the sub, followed closely by Max and Juan. Cabrillo and Max had the hatch resealed an instant later, working by feel more than sight, since the only light in the Discovery 1000 came from the faint glow of electronics in the forward cockpit.

Juan hit a switch midway up a bulkhead, and a pair of red blackout lights snapped on. The Discovery wasn't designed to dive much below a hundred feet and could operate for no more than twenty-four hours without recharging and replacing the $CO_2$ filters. For this mission her seating for eight had been removed to make room for racks of batteries, bulky industrial boxes joined with a snaking nest of wiring conduits. Crates of filters were crammed in the other available spaces as well as provisions for Eddie Seng. A chemical toilet sat amid a clutter of empty food cartons. The air was heavy with humidity and carried a locker room funk.

Eddie had been alone on the sub since launching off the *Oregon* fifteen days earlier. With the harbor ringed with underwater listening stations and routinely swept with active sonar, it had taken that long for Seng to drift into the heavily defended port. He had grounded the sub during the slight ebb tide and allowed her to drift when the tidal surge washed into the harbor, only chancing to run the electric motors under the cover of an inbound ship or patrol boat. There was no other way to get the sub into the naval base without being detected.

While there were other sub drivers among the *Oregon* crew, as director of Shore Operations, Eddie wouldn't let anyone else take the risk. Seng was another veteran of the CIA, although Juan hadn't known him when they were in the Agency. He'd spent most of his career working the Middle East, while Eddie had been attached to the American embassy in Beijing running several successful spy networks. Budget and policy shifts following September 11 had seen him transferred to a stateside desk. Still hungry for what he called 'the teeth of the trade,' Seng had joined the Corporation and quickly established himself as an indispensable member.

Cabrillo crawled over batteries and empty crates and slid into the copilot's seat to Eddie's right. Eddie's black hair was lank from going so long without washing, and stubble marred his otherwise sharp features. The emotional and physical strain of the past two weeks had dimmed his normally bright eyes.

'Hiya, boss.' Seng grinned. Nothing could diminish his easygoing charm. 'Welcome aboard.'

'Thanks,' Juan said, noting that the sub had already descended to thirty feet. 'The clock's ticking, so set a course out of the harbor and punch it. We've got eleven minutes.'

The Discovery's motors ramped up, and the single prop bit into the water. There was nothing they could do about the noise. They had to get as far from the *Asia Star* as possible, because water does not compress, making the coming shock wave doubly brutal.

Cabrillo kept his eyes on the sub's sonar, and only a minute after they began pulling away from the doomed freighter there was contact. 'Mr Murphy's rearing his ugly head.'

'What do you have?' Hanley stood just behind Juan and leaned over his shoulder.

The computer analyzed the acoustical signal, and Cabrillo read the grim facts. 'Sinpo-class patrol boat. Crew of twelve. Armed with a pair of 37 mm autocannons and tilt racks for depth charges. Top speed is forty knots, and our contact is already churning twenty and headed straight for us.'

Eddie turned to Juan. 'It's routine. They've been doing this ever since I entered the harbor. Every couple of hours a single patrol boat races along the dock. I think they're searching for sailors trying to jump ship.'

'If he maintains his course, he's going to pass right over us.'

'Does that class of boats carry sonar?' Max asked.

Juan checked the computer again. 'Doesn't say.'

'What do you want me to do?' Eddie's voice remained calm and professional. 'Keep running, or settle onto the bottom and let him pass?'

Cabrillo checked his watch again. They'd traveled little more than a quarter mile. Too close. 'Keep going. If he hears us or detects our wake, he's going to have to slow and turn back to try to find us again. We only need six minutes.'

A moment later the four men inside the minisub could hear the thrash of the patrol boat's props through the water, an angry sound that rose in pitch as the craft drew closer. As it roared overhead the din filled the hull, and the men waited expectantly to hear if it would come back for another pass. The moment stretched as time turned elastic. Max and Hali let out their breaths as the patrol boat continued on. Cabrillo kept his eyes glued to the sonar screen.

'They're turning,' he remarked a second later. 'Coming back for another look. Hali, check the radio, see if he's transmitting.' Hali Kasim headed the *Oregon*'s communications division and could play radios like a concert pianist.

The communications suite aboard the *Oregon* was sophisticated enough to scan and record a thousand frequencies per second and had a language program that could translate fast enough for an operator to hold a conversation close enough to real time to fool most listeners. With the Discovery 1000's limited electronics they would be lucky just to pick up a broadcast, and since none of the men spoke Korean, they wouldn't know if the patrol craft was asking permission to depth charge or commenting on the weather.

'I'm not getting anything,' Kasim answered after a few moments.

The North Korean patrol boat crossed over the minisub again, and the men heard her engines throttle back.

'They're pacing us,' Eddie said.

The powerful sonar picked up a pair of splashes too small to be depth charges. Juan knew immediately what was about to happen. 'Brace yourselves!'

The grenades were knockoffs of the Soviet RGD-5, and while they only contained four ounces of high explosives, the water amplified their explosive power. The two grenades went off nearly simultaneously just yards behind the Discovery. The sub pitched up by the stern, knocking Hali Kasim against a bank of batteries. Eddie fought to bring her nose up as the murky bottom suddenly loomed outside the large acrylic view port. With their ears ringing, no one heard a second pair of grenades hit the water. They blew just above the minisub, slamming her into the mud just as Eddie got her on an even keel. Billows of silt exploded around the Discovery, cutting visibility to zero. Electricity arced and snapped from a loose connection in dazzlingly bright flashes that temporarily blinded the men.

Eddie quickly powered down the sub to give Max a chance to fix the connection. By the glow of a miniature flashlight clamped between his teeth, the engineer worked to bypass the affected row of batteries, but the damage had been done. The flashes of electricity could be seen from the surface through the sub's portholes and looked like an eerie blue glow from the depths.

'They've got us now,' Hali said. 'They're transmitting something. Just a short message, but I think the jig is up.'

'How's it coming, Max?' Cabrillo inquired with no more concern than if he were asking when coffee would be ready.

'Just a few more seconds.'

'Anything from shore yet, Hali?'

'Negative. The brass must be mulling over the report from the patrol boat.'

'Got it,' Max announced. 'Eddie, turn her back on.'

Eddie Seng hit a button, and the display screens lit with their muted glimmer.

'Okay, Eddie, emergency blow. Bring us to the surface.'

'The patrol boat's right above us, boss.'

Cabrillo's response was a dark smile.

'There goes our warranty,' Eddie muttered, then blew ballast from the Discovery's tanks with compressed air. The little sub seemed to launch itself from the bottom. He watched the depth gauge and called out the numbers. When he said there were only five feet of water over the Disco's top deck, all four men instinctively ducked lower in their seats.

The steel hull slammed into the underside of the North Korean craft with a deafening screech. The sub was several tons lighter than the patrol boat, but her upward momentum tipped the Koreans until their starboard rail was in the water. One crewman had his legs crushed when he was pitched over the side by a rolling fuel drum. Juan reached across Eddie and punched the command for a crash dive before the upper deck broke the surface.

34

High-speed pumps filled the ballast tanks in under fifteen seconds, and the Discovery dropped like a stone.

'That ought to keep 'em busy for a few minutes,' Max said.

'We only need a few. Okay everyone, get your earphones on and strap in.'

The men donned bulky headsets that they jacked into a piece of electronics specially installed for the mission. Built by Sound Answers, the experimental noise-canceling device took in sound waves, evaluated their frequency and amplitude, and played back the exact opposite sound, nullifying 99 percent of the decibels. Such devices, once perfected and miniaturized, would soon make it possible for silent vacuum cleaners and end the anxiety of listening to a dentist's drill.

Aboard the *Asia Star* one of the North Korean spies sent to guard the Syrians had come to. He wasted precious seconds checking on his partner. The lump where he'd been clipped with the pistol was as tight as a drum. The man wouldn't awaken. The guard knew his duty. He ran from the hold, shouting at the top of his lungs, ignoring the pain it caused in his head. He ran up to the main deck, checking doors along the corridor behind the bridge until he found the captain's. He considered knocking, but what he had to report was too important. He burst through the door. General Kim was on the telephone.

'And then what will you do to my little lotus?' Kim snapped to his feet when the door crashed against the cabin wall. He roared, 'What is the meaning of this?'

'General,' the guard panted. 'The Syrians, they attacked us. I did not see them in the hold. I think they might be trying to escape.'

'Escape? Escape what?' Kim no sooner asked those questions when he realized the answer. He cut the connection to his mistress, pounding on the Reset lever to alert the shore operator. 'Come on, you damned thing,' he cursed, then addressed the guard. 'They weren't Syrians; they were American saboteurs. Search the hold for a bomb.'

Finally a voice sounded in the telephone. Kim knew that even if he died, getting a warning out would make sure the Americans would pay for their treachery. 'This is General Kim aboard the *Asia Star*—'

At the back corner of the hold, Max's bomb wound down to zero.

The bomb blast tore through the missile where it had been hidden and an instant later caused a secondary explosion of the warhead. Overpressure built inside the hold until the four-ton hatches blew into the night sky as though a volcano had erupted. The *Star*'s old hull plates split at their welds like peels from an orange as the tons of rocket fuel stored in her forward hold detonated.

The ship disintegrated.

A seven-hundred-foot wedge of the concrete dock shattered, and chunks of it were thrown miles inland. The two massive loading cranes along the wharf toppled into the water, and every window along the harbor was blown to pieces. Then the shock wave spread. Warehouses were blown flat for a quarter mile, and those farther away were stripped of their siding so only their skeletal steel frames remained upright. The concussion stripped the first six feet of water from the bay and piled it into a wave that slammed the destroyer lying at anchor, breaking her keel and capsizing her so fast that none of her harbor watch had time to react.

Night turned to day as the fireball climbed to eleven hundred feet, and sheets of rocket fuel fell like burning rain, setting fires all around the navy yard, while bits of the *Asia Star*'s hull scythed through the base like shrapnel, leveling buildings and wrecking vehicles.

The concussion plucked the floundering patrol boat from the sea and sent it tumbling across the surface of the bay, rolling it like a log down a mountainside. With each revolution more of her upperworks tore free. First it was her fore gun mounts, then the pair of .50 calibers at her stern, and finally her small cabin came apart, leaving just her hull to barrel roll atop the waves.

The noise dampener did its job, but still the concussion wave rang through the Discovery 1000 as though she was a bell. The whole hull shook as the shock wave passed over and the plucky little sub lurched forward, then ebbed violently, straining the safety straps and scattering loose equipment from storage bins. Eardrums were brutally assaulted by the blast, and had it not been for the counter-frequencies channeled into the headsets, the four men would have been permanently deafened.

As it was, Cabrillo had to shout at the top of his lungs to inquire about his men. Eddie and Hali were unscathed, but Max had taken a bump on the head from a falling battery. The skin hadn't broken, and he hadn't been knocked out. He'd suffer a headache for a while, and it would take days for the knot already forming to subside.

'All right, Eddie, take us home.'

The minisub slipped out of the harbor undetected and was two miles from the coast before they picked up helicopters thundering toward Wonsan. The choppers were flying too high and too fast to be ASW (antisubmarine warfare) birds. They were most likely rescue helos ferrying medical supplies and personnel to the devastated base.

Like all other coastal nations on earth, North Korea was afforded twelve miles of ocean as sovereign territory. Just to play it safe, Juan Cabrillo had scheduled the rendezvous for twenty miles out, a long slog in the reeking confines of the Discovery that took nearly three hours longer than planned. The Discovery had to stay deep as dawn approached in case the North Koreans did send out aerial reconnaissance.

At last they came to the spot of ocean, and Eddie eased the craft up from eighty feet where she'd remained hidden. The underside of the *Oregon*'s hull was coated with red antifouling paint and loomed over the small sub. Juan noted with pride that the hull was clear of barnacles and looked as new as the day he'd taken possession of her. In order to take advantage of the tremendous power generated by her revolutionary engines, the *Oregon* utilized an MDV design as perfected by high-speed European express ferries. Her monohull, deep V arrangement allowed her to knife through the seas at unheard-of speeds. To maintain stability she sported several retractable T-foils and fins, undersea wings that kept her planing smoothly at up to forty knots. Beyond that speed the wings produced too much drag. They were drawn back to the hull, and the crew had to strap themselves in like offshore hydroplane racers.

Eddie grabbed a device the size and shape of a garage door remote, pointed it up at the *Oregon*, and pressed the single button.

Splitting at the keel, a pair of eighty-foot-long doors hinged downward. Bright light from inside the ship filtered through the water and bathed the underside of the ship in a green glow. Eddie nudged the thrusters and adjusted the ballast, centering the Discovery in the opening. He held station just below the hull as two men in scuba gear jumped from inside the ship and attached lift cables to hardpoints fore and aft. The minisub and its larger sister, a Nomad 1000 also kept aboard the *Oregon*, could surface directly into the moon pool, but the maneuver was risky and used only in emergencies.

The frogman swam in front of the view port and gave Eddie and Juan a wave, then slashed his hand across his neck. Eddie killed the motors. A second later the sub lurched, then began to rise smoothly into the flooded moon pool. As it cleared the surface, Seng opened valves so the ballast tanks could drain.

Juan spotted Julia Huxley, the *Oregon*'s medical officer, standing at the edge of the pool with a pair of orderlies. He shot her a thumbs-up, and her concerned frown turned into a smile. She'd joined the Corporation after a career in the navy, finishing with a four-year stint as the chief medical officer at San Diego Naval Base. Under her lab coat, the five-foot-three-inch Julia was curvaceous without running to fat. He rarely saw her dark hair out of a ponytail, and the only makeup she used was to highlight her soft, dark eyes.

The overhead crane lowered the sub onto a cradle, and a workman clambered on top to crank open the outer hatch. When it finally released, the crew inside heard him gasp. 'Whoa.'

'Try being sealed inside for two weeks,' Eddie called, pulling himself from his seat. He'd already unzipped the front of his jumpsuit in preparation for his first shower in fifteen days. His chest and stomach were so lean that individual muscle fibers were visible. Eddie was built like famed martial artist Bruce Lee, and like Lee was a master in several Eastern fighting techniques.

Juan allowed his men to precede him out, but as soon as he'd taken his first deep breaths he called to a sailor nearby, 'Get these doors closed, and contact Eric in the control room. Have him set a course due east, say twenty knots. As long as the threat board remains green, there's no need to draw attention to ourselves by opening her up.' Eric Stone was a control room operator, the ship's best, and the only man Juan wanted at the helm during critical operations.

'Aye, sir.'

When the doors were closed, pumps came online to drain the moon pool, and workers laid decking grilles over the hole. Technicians were already assessing the damage caused when the Discovery rammed the patrol boat, while others were bringing gallon jugs of bleach to sanitize the interior.

Julia approached Juan when he came down the ladder from the top of the minisub. 'We heard the explosion out here, so I don't need to ask how it went.'

'You don't sound too happy about it.' Juan stripped off his Colonel Hourani uniform coat.

'Just bored, Mr Chairman. Other than a few strained muscles, I haven't had much to do in months.'

Juan smiled. 'I thought that was a good thing for a doctor.'

'For a doctor, yes; for an employee, it's dullsville.'

'Come on, Julia, you know us. Give it a few days or a week, and we'll get into some sort of trouble.'

Cabrillo would soon regret those words. In just ninety-six hours, Dr Julia Huxley was going to be literally up to her elbows in work.

# 4

'Come,' Cabrillo called at the sharp knock on his cabin's door.

The *Oregon* was safely beyond the range of all but North Korea's best fighter jets and, according to intercepted communications, it seemed unlikely any would be scrambled before the vessel was outside their range, too. He had allowed himself an hour-long soak in the copper Jacuzzi tub in the adjoining bathroom and was just finishing getting dressed. Not one to stand on formalities aboard ship, he wore cotton trousers and an open-neck shirt.

Unlike his Colonel Hourani disguise, and despite his Hispanic name and background, Juan Cabrillo's eyes were blue, and his spiky hair was white-blond from a youth spent in the sun and surf. His features, too, looked more Anglo than Latin, with an aristocratic nose and a mouth forever poised at a smile from some joke only he knew. But there was a hard edge to Cabrillo, one formed over years of facing danger. While he masked it well, people meeting him for the first time could still detect an intangible quality that commanded immediate respect.

Linda Ross, the Corporation's newly promoted vice president of Operations, stepped through the door, a clipboard held against her chest. Linda was another navy veteran, having spent time as an intelligence officer aboard an Aegis cruiser followed by a stint at the Pentagon. Trim and athletic, Linda possessed a soft-spoken demeanor and a razor-sharp mind. When Richard Truitt, the Corporation's former VP, unexpectedly resigned after the Sacred Stone affair, Cabrillo and Hanley knew that Linda was the only one who could fill Dick's shoes.

She paused at the door, mesmerized by the sight of Juan adjusting his prosthetic right leg and rolling down his pants cuff. He slid into a pair of Italian moccasin-style boat shoes. It wasn't that she wasn't aware of the fake limb, but it was always a shock to see it, since Cabrillo never seemed bothered that he was missing a leg below the knee.

Cabrillo spoke without looking up. 'On the *Asia Star,* a North Korean guard smashed the leg against a railing and cracked the plastic. He was sure surprised when I kept fighting with what he assumed was a broken shin.'

'You just proved North Korean propaganda,' Linda said with a low chuckle.

'How's that?'

'That we Americans are just robots of our imperialist government.'

They shared a laugh. 'So what's been happening since we left for Afghanistan?' he asked.

'Do you recall Hiroshi Katsui?'

It took Cabrillo a moment to place the name. 'Hiro? God, I haven't thought about him since UCLA. His father was the first billionaire I ever met. Big shipping family. Hiro was the only guy on campus with a Lamborghini. I will give him this, though; the wealth never went to his head. He was real down to earth and generous to a fault.'

'Through some cutouts he approached us representing a consortium of shipping owners in these waters. In the past ten months or so, piracy has been on the rise from the Sea of Japan all the way down to the South China Sea.'

42

'That's a problem usually confined to coastal waters and the Strait of Malacca,' Cabrillo interrupted.

'Where natives in small boats attack yachts or board freighters to make off with whatever they can handle,' Linda agreed. 'It's a billion dollar a year enterprise and growing every year. But what's happening around Malaysia and Indonesia is nothing more than thugs mugging old ladies on darkened streets compared to what's been happening farther to the north.'

Cabrillo crossed to his desk and removed a cheroot from an inlaid box. He listened to Ross as he prepared the fine-leafed Cuban cigar and lit it with a gold and onyx Dunhill.

'What your friend Hiro is reporting sounds more like the bad old days of the mob hijacking trucks at Kennedy Airport. The pirates are well-armed, well-trained, and highly motivated. They are also as brutal as hell. Four ships have vanished completely. No sign of the crew at all. The most recent was a tanker owned by your friend's company, the *Toya Maru*. Several others have been hit with significant, and I might add unnecessary, loss of life since none of the crew reported putting up any resistance.'

'What are the pirates taking?'

'Sometimes the ship's payroll.' It was customary for cargo ships to carry enough cash to pay their crews at the end of a voyage in case some men didn't wish to continue on. To Cabrillo this sounded like overkill for fifteen or twenty thousand dollars. 'Other times they take shipping containers, transferring them to their own vessels, which, from the sketchy descriptions, sound like converted fishing trawlers mounted with cranes. And like I said, sometimes entire ships just disappear.'

Juan let that sink in, watching jets of smoke bloom against the teak coffered ceiling where he blew them. 'And Hiro and his consortium want us to put a stop to it?'

Linda glanced at her clipboard. 'His words are, "Make them pay like a quarterback facing the Raiders defense."'

Cabrillo smiled, recalling Hiro's fondness for American football and especially for the Raiders when they played in L.A. Then his smile faded. Because of the Corporation's structure, each crew member was an owner, their percentages determined by their rank and years of service. Dick Truitt's unexpected retirement had put a dent in the Corporation's cash reserves. The timing couldn't have been worse, because the Corporation was heavily invested in a real estate deal in Rio de Janeiro that wouldn't show a return for another two months. He could bail out of the deal now, but the expected profits were too great to ignore. The just-finished job for Langston Overholt would cover what Dick was entitled to, but that left Cabrillo in a bit of a cash crunch to keep up with payments on the *Oregon,* insurance for his people, and all the other myriad expenses that any company must meet month to month. Just because they operated outside the law didn't mean he could avoid the financial realities of a capitalistic world.

'What are they offering?'

Linda consulted her clipboard once again. 'One hundred thousand a week for a minimum of eight weeks and a maximum of sixteen, plus a million dollars for each pirate ship we destroy.'

Cabrillo's frown deepened. The pay structure would cover expenses, barely. What bothered him was that by agreeing, he was stuck for two months and would be unable to take off if something more lucrative should arise. But it did buy him the time he needed before his Brazilian investment paid out, and once that was in, the Corporation would be deep into the black once again. Also, Juan held every mariner's contempt for piracy and would like nothing more than to help put an end to the scourge of the sea.

From reports he'd read, he knew that modern-day pirates bore no resemblance to the swashbuckling legends of old. There were no more bearded captains with eye patches and parrots on their shoulders. Today's pirates, at least the ones he'd read about operating in the Straits of Malacca, were usually poor fishermen armed with whatever they could scrounge. They attacked at night and vanished just as quickly, taking whatever they could carry in their dugouts and pirogues. There had been murders, surely, but nothing on the scale Linda described.

Juan had always harbored a fear that one day a leader would come along to organize pirates the way Lucky Luciano had formed Murder Inc., turning a ragtag band of criminals into a well-oiled machine. Had that day come? Had a mastermind entered the picture, convincing others that by organizing they could double or triple their profits, and elevated piracy to an act as deadly as terrorism? It certainly wasn't inconceivable. And as he sat at his desk, Cabrillo wondered if the two weren't linked. In the years since 9/11, terrorist funding had dried up over much of the world. It was possible, no, he thought, it was likely that groups like Al-Qaeda would turn to piracy and other illegal enterprises to fill their war chests once again.

That link cinched it for him. It was true that Cabrillo and his crew did a great deal of covert work for the U.S. government. This would be one of those times that a private sector operation would also benefit American interests and save

45

Uncle Sam from picking up the tab. He turned his gaze back to his VP of Operations. 'Did he say how many pirate ships they suspect are operating out there?'

'There are no firm numbers, but they're believed to have at least four converted trawlers because of distances and the timing of some of the attacks.'

That would translate into four million dollars. It sounded like a great deal of money, but Cabrillo knew well just how quickly the Corporation could eat up that sum. If they'd done structural damage to the Disco minisub, a replacement would set them back two million dollars. He considered the proposal for another moment. 'Contact Hiroshi, tell him we'll take on the contract with two provisions. Number one is that the bonus for each ship sunk is two million and that we reserve the right to sever the contract at our discretion with one day's notice.' A single ship-to-ship missile from the *Oregon*'s launcher cost just under a million dollars. 'Then get in touch with Overholt at Langley and tell him what we're up to and let him know I'll have a detailed after-action report to him in a couple of days.'

'What about Eddie Seng?' Eddie had been promised two weeks' vacation for having to endure the same amount of time locked in the minisub.

Cabrillo flicked on the plasma monitor on his desk and moused through a few screens before finding the one that showed the *Oregon*'s location. He calculated distances and the range of the Robinson R-44 helicopter stowed in a concealed hangar under an aft hatch. 'We can fly him to Seoul sometime tomorrow. He can catch a commercial flight from there.'

'That's not the problem. He told Julia that he doesn't want to leave.'

Juan wasn't surprised. 'You can lead a man to vacation; you can't make him relax.'

'I'm just concerned that he's pushing himself too far. He's been through hell since we cut him loose two weeks ago.'

As chairman, Juan Cabrillo was the only member of the Corporation to know every detail of his crew's files. He wondered if he'd be breaking a confidence by telling Linda how back in his CIA days Eddie had spent two months under double cover, first as a Taiwanese traitor eager to sell the Red Chinese information about Taiwan's military disposition along the Formosa Strait and then as a counterspy with the ultimate goal of discrediting the group of Chinese generals who had bought his information. He'd pulled off the coup brilliantly, and four of China's best battlefield commanders were transferred to an outpost in the Gobi Desert while the government wasted millions of dollars building fortifications for an invasion that would never come. It had been his last mission before his transfer to Washington. Juan left the story untold and merely said, 'If Eddie wants to stay on board, I'm not going to argue with him.'

'Okay.'

'Did Hiro provide details of the attacks?'

'His communiqué said that he'd transmit them if we took the assignment.'

'As soon as they arrive get Mark Murphy and Eric Stone working on a computer model of where the pirates are likely to strike next and have them come up with a cover story to make us sound like a juicy target.' Young Murph was the *Oregon*'s weapons specialist and a dogged researcher with an uncanny eye for pattern recognition.

Linda made notes on her clipboard. 'Anything else?'

'That should do it. Once Mark and Eric have their position, set a course and get under way.'

Cabrillo finished his cigar while working on his report to Langston Overholt, deciding to get it over with now rather than prolong the tedium. As the cheroot burned down to a stub, he dumped the report into an encryption program as powerful as those used by the NSA and e-mailed it to his old friend at CIA headquarters. Still buzzing with adrenaline and despite lunch being served in the main dining room, he decided to take a tour of the ship.

From her gleaming engine room where the magneto-hydrodynamic engines purred to her high-tech operations center located below the bridge where just about every wall was covered in plasma screens, and through her multiple weapons bays, Magic Shop, armory, hangar, and the lavish crew accommodation areas, he skulked his ship, greeting crewmen as he roamed. He visited the stainless steel galley where a team of Cordon Bleu chefs prepared meals fit for the finest restaurants of New York or Paris. He looked in on the spa with its ranks of exercise machines and free weights as well as the popular saunas. He laid a hand on one of the four black Sun/Microsystem supercomputers, sensing its raw power and knowing no problem was too complex for it and its operators.

He was fully aware that every detail, each inch of wiring and ductwork, her deck layout, and even her interior color scheme had been born in his mind and transformed into steel and plastic and wood on his order. The *Oregon* was both his castle and his refuge.

But what gave him the most pride was the moment he stepped out onto the deck. For it was outside that the *Oregon* showed off what made her the greatest espionage platform ever devised. The Russians had been too slavish at disguising spy ships as trawlers, making them somewhat a cliché whenever they arrived off a coastline. The U.S. Navy made use of undetectable submarines for their spy operations, an impossible option for what Cabrillo and his crew did. No, the Corporation needed anonymity at the very least or outright ridicule at best.

For that reason from the outside the MV *Oregon* looked like a derelict on borrowed time from the breaker's yard.

Juan had entered the ship's bridge using the elevator in the operations center located just below the main deck. From there he'd stepped out onto the starboard wing bridge and surveyed his ship. The *Oregon* was 560 feet long, 75 wide, and had a gross tonnage of 11,585. Her superstructure stood a little aft of amidships, so she carried three cargo cranes fore and a pair of them aft. The cranes were rusted wrecks festooned with frayed cables, and two of them actually worked. The deck was a scabrous patchwork of rust and various colors of marine paint. Her rails sagged dangerously in places, and several of her cargo hatches appeared sprung. Oil had leaked from drums stowed along the front of the wheelhouse into a gooey slick, and rusted husks of machinery lay scattered about, everything from broken winches to a bicycle with no tires. Looking along the outer hull, Cabrillo saw smears of rust below every scupper, and steel plates that had been welded as if to cover cracks. The hull's main color was a turbid green, but there were splashes of brown, black, and midnight blue.

He threw his customary one-fingered salute at the Iranian flag on the stern jackstaff before glancing around the bridge. The once-polished deck was scarred and littered with cigarette burns. The windows were coated with equal mixtures of grime and salt, while her consoles were coated in dust. The brass of the engine telegraph was so tarnished it looked black and was missing one indicator needle. Some of her electronics, such as her navigation aids, were old enough to be museum displays. Behind the bridge was a chart room littered with poorly folded maps and a radio with no more than a few miles' range.

The crew's accommodations in the superstructure were also in disarray. Not a bed was made in any of the cabins, and not a single piece of crockery or silverware matched in the filthy galley. Cabrillo was especially proud of the captain's cabin. The room reeked of cheap cigarettes and was decorated with tacky velvet paintings of sad-faced clowns with liquid, mournful eyes. In the desk was a bottle of South American Scotch laced with syrup of ipecac and two glasses that had never been cleaned. The adjoining bathroom was dirtier than a men's room in a West Texas roadhouse.

All this detail was designed to encourage inspectors, harbor officials, and pilots to get off the *Oregon* as quickly as possible and ask the fewest questions. The record for the shortest stay so far went to a customs inspector in Cape Town who refused to even step foot on the ship's wobbly gangway. The wheel and the engine telegraph could, with computer assistance, maneuver the ship and operate her engines. This was for the benefit of harbor pilots and those who guided the freighter on her trips through the Panama Canal, but the vessel was actually run from a digitized workstation in the state-of-the-art operations center.

It was her dilapidated condition that allowed the *Oregon* to enter any port in the world without drawing attention. She was quickly overlooked as just another tramp steamer slowly rusting away as ocean commerce turned to containerization. Anyone who knew ships could tell that her owners had pretty much written off their vessel and no longer replaced worn-out machinery or even sprang for a few gallons of paint. And when the need arose, her crew could appear as decrepit as their ship.

A noise disturbed Cabrillo's inspection. Max Hanley rode up the elevator from the op center and joined him on the wing bridge. Max had scrubbed the makeup from his face, revealing a florid complexion and a bulbous nose. He wore coveralls, and Juan suspected he'd gone straight from a shower to inspect his engines. The wind danced through Hanley's sparse auburn hair as the two enjoyed a companionable silence.

'Thinking about Truitt?' Max finally asked. Juan hadn't spoken much of their partner's retirement.

Juan turned so his back was to the sea and rested both elbows against the fore rail. He had to squint against the bright glare reflecting off the waves. 'I was just walking around, touring the ship,' he said after a moment, 'feeling mighty pleased with what we've accomplished.'

'But?'

'But the *Oregon* is a means to an end. Dick knew that, and for a few years I thought he believed in it the way you and I do.'

'And now you're doubting that, and doubting Dick Truitt, because he pulled stakes and hit the road.'

'I thought so at first, but now I think I'm doubting myself and our mission.'

Max slowly filled a pipe and lit it, shielding his match from the wind as he considered his friend's response. 'I'll tell you what I think is going on. We've been working for a few years now, squirreling away money with each assignment. We all knew there was a pot of gold at the end of the rainbow, only now with Dick's retirement we both got to see just how big it was. He's cashing out to the tune of forty-five million dollars, tax free. I'm worth even more than that, and you've accumulated even more than me. It's hard to ignore that kind of money when you're putting your butt on the line for an ideal and a paycheck.'

Juan said, 'A big paycheck.'

Max conceded the point. 'True. Let me ask you, when you were doing duty for the CIA, twisting in the wind in places like Amman and Nicaragua, did you do it for a measly GS-17 salary and a government pension?'

'No,' Cabrillo said sincerely. 'I would have done it for free.'

'Then why feel guilty that we're making good money now, doing what you used to do for a pittance and having the power to turn down operations we don't feel right about? You couldn't do that working for Langley or when the pressure came down from the Pentagon E-ring. They said jump, and you landed in the shit.' The outermost ring of the Defense Department building was the home to all the top brass and their civilian overseers.

Cabrillo opened his mouth to reply, but Max continued speaking. 'Actually seeing that we've got enough money to retire to a private island someplace and live the good life has made you understand just how much we risk every day. You and I have always put our lives on the line. It's what makes us who we are. Only now we both know our lives are worth a little more than we thought.'

'And our mission?'

'You have to ask? We're the last line of defense, my boy. We agree to the jobs Langley and the E-ringers need done but can't touch. The gloves have come off in the twenty-first century, and we've become the iron fist.'

Cabrillo absorbed the words before asking with a smirk, 'When did you become such a poet?'

Hanley grinned as if he'd been caught. 'That actually just sort of came out. Sounded damn impressive, if you ask me.' He turned serious once again. 'Listen, Juan, what we do is important, and I for one am not going to feel guilty because we're getting rich doing it. There's no shame in profit, only in failure.

'And as for doubting Dick Truitt, you can forget about it. Dick put a lot of sweat and blood into the Corporation. He was there at the beginning and believed just as strongly as you and I. But he'd reached his limit. He'd had enough. Him leaving wasn't about the money; it was about Dick listening to that little voice inside his head that we all have, and it was saying he'd run his course with us. You can best believe, though, that Dick Truitt hasn't given up the fight. I wouldn't be surprised if he poured his money and expertise into a security company or intelligence think tank. I bet –'

Max stopped in midsentence. He'd noticed the spark in Cabrillo's eye and the crooked, almost piratical smile that played along his lips. As always, Juan Cabrillo had been one step head of his corporate president. Juan had been testing Max, getting a sense of how he felt about Truitt's leaving. Cabrillo had never doubted his mission or himself, but this was a pivotal time for the Corporation, and Juan needed to make certain Hanley was still 100 percent behind their goals. Juan had set the trap perfectly by acting unsure, and Max had wandered blindly in. This was why no one played poker with the chairman.

'You're a crafty one.' Max said with a throaty chuckle.

Just then, a high-pitched hiss sounded from the *Oregon*'s water line. They peered over the rail. Special tanks along her outer hull were filling with seawater to ballast down the tramp freighter and make her look like her holds were full. Juan looked along her wake line and detected a subtle change in course. The long line of white on the otherwise empty sea arced ever so slightly to the east.

'Murph and Stone must have found the spot of ocean for us to play staked goat,' Max said offhandedly and checked the time on an old pocket watch looped with a chain to his coveralls.

Cabrillo thought about the awesome arsenal of weapons secreted about the *Oregon* and the men and women trained to use them. 'Staked tiger, my old friend, staked tiger.'

A day later the *Oregon* reached the grid that Mark Murphy and Eric Stone had calculated would be the most likely to attract the pirates. Hiro Katsui had agreed to Cabrillo's negotiations, replying, 'It takes a pirate to catch a pirate. Good hunting.' And he had transmitted everything his consortium had on the recent attacks. Murphy and Stone had dissected the information, finding commonalties in the attacks overlooked until now. They cross-referenced weather, the phases of the moon, size of the ships, cargo manifests, crew numbers, and a dozen other factors to find a spot in the Sea of Japan where it was most likely the pirates would attack the *Oregon*.

A legend had been created concerning the ship and her cargo and was hacked into various databases in case that was how the pirates found their marks. The ship was purportedly carrying a mixed cargo of timber and electronics from Pusan to Nigata, Japan, but what made her a tempting target was the presence of a passenger on her manifest, an eccentric American author who wrote while tramping around the globe on cargo ships.

Richard Hildebrand was a real person, and his fondness for working at sea was well documented in the media. He was currently working on his next best seller aboard a supertanker deadheading back to the Persian Gulf from Rotterdam, a detail the Corporation doubted the pirates would verify. Between book royalties and the price his books commanded in Hollywood, Hildebrand was one of the wealthiest writers in the world and ripe for kidnapping. While the pirates had yet to attempt such an act, Murph and Stone, with Juan agreeing, believed snatching Hildebrand was a logical escalation of their criminal activities.

In case they wouldn't risk ransoming a hostage, Murph and Stone had also listed the *Oregon*'s complement at fifty-seven, large by the standards of modern merchantmen, and to the pirates she'd be a tempting target because of the correspondingly large payroll in the ship's safe.

The sunset's palette of reds and rose and purple had been made even more spectacular by the volcanic ash pumped into the atmosphere by an erupting volcano far to the north on the Kamchatka Peninsula. Now the bloodred moon cast a hellish reflection off the calm sea while the stars had dimmed to pricks. The crew was at battle stations. Julia Huxley and her staff were ready in the medical bay to treat anything from a wood sliver to multiple gunshot wounds. The ship's armaments were primed and ready in their concealed redoubts. Like the German K-boats of World

War One, plates along each side of the *Oregon*'s hull could be lowered to reveal 120 mm cannons utilizing the same fire control and ranging system as found on the M-1A1 Abrams tank. She also carried three 20 mm radar-controlled multibarrel Gatling guns. Each weapon could pump out three thousand rounds per minute. While primarily an antimissile system, the Gatlings could also take out aircraft, and a barrage against the waterline of an unarmored ship would punch enough holes in its hull to send it to the bottom.

The *Oregon* also sported concealed machine guns on her decks with thermal and IR sights. Gunners with video displays controlled these remotely from the operations center. One of her forward hatches could be blown off to launch four Exocet ship-to-ship missiles, and another hatch hid a pair of Russian-made land-attack cruise missiles. Although Langston Overholt at the CIA had paved the way for the Corporation to acquire some American military hardware, he'd drawn the line at missiles, thus forcing Juan to search elsewhere. Overholt had also vetoed the Corporation from getting Mark-48 ADCAP torpedoes. No other nation on earth used them, so they could be too easily traced back to the United States. The fish in the pair of forward-facing tubes had also been bought with hard currency from the same corrupt Russian admiral who'd procured the cruise missiles and supplied the end user certificates for the French Exocets.

It was nearly midnight when Juan entered the operations center. He regarded his people under the red glow of battle lights and the muted shine from their display screens.

Mark Murphy and Eric Stone occupied the workstations closest to the forward bulkhead. Stone had come to the Corporation from the navy, while Murphy had never spent time in the military. The young prodigy had earned a Ph.D. by the time he was twenty and joined the Corporation straight from private industry, where he'd designed weapons systems. Juan had been suspicious of him at first, fearing he lacked the mettle to cut it as a mercenary. In truth, his fear was that Murphy would turn out to be a psychopath who thrived on killing, but a battery of tests and psychological profiles showed that Murphy would have excelled in the military, provided the people around him were on the same intellectual level. Because Juan recruited only the best and brightest, Murph had settled in perfectly, even if no one else shared his joy of punk rock and skateboarding.

Behind and off to the sides of their stations were Hali Kasim monitoring the communications gear and Linda Ross on the radar and the waterfall sonar display. Along the back wall of the op center were stations for the remote deck guns, as well as fire and damage control coordinators. The rest of the crew had their positions, some suited up to fight fires, others to act as corpsmen, and still others who made sure the rapacious guns had enough ammo. Eddie Seng was in charge of the tactical troops on deck, ready to repel boarders. Juan could hear Max on a comm link from the engine room talking to Eric, announcing that the ship's propulsion system was green across the board.

What had brought everyone to battle stations was an announcement from Linda that a contact thirty miles from the *Oregon* had suddenly changed course and was heading for the ship. In the world of maritime operations, efficiency was the name of the game. A deviation of a degree or two could add hundreds of miles to a journey and thus cost more money. Unless there was an emergency, and with the radios quiet there wasn't, the approaching vessel was up to something. And because they'd been warned what to expect, the crew of the *Oregon* knew what was coming.

Cabrillo took his command station in the middle of the room and surveyed the high-tech equipment around him. He believed when he'd designed the op center he'd been subconsciously influenced by the bridge on the old TV show *Star Trek,* right down to the large flat-screen monitor above Stone's and Murph's heads. But it wasn't the weapons or the sensors or the computers that made the *Oregon* such a formidable opponent. It was the people in this room and those supporting them throughout the ship. That had been Juan's greatest accomplishment, not the steel and electronics and guns, but assembling the finest crew he'd ever had the pleasure of knowing.

'Sit rep,' he called, turning on the computer screens near his centrally placed chair. The Kirk Seat, as Murph called it.

'Contact bearing oh-seventeen degrees and closing at twenty knots. Range is twenty-one miles.' Linda Ross answered without looking up from her screen. Like the others, she was dressed in black battle fatigues, a SIG Sauer pistol belted around her waist.

'What do you make of her?'

'Approximate size is seventy feet, and I can tell she has a single screw. She'd been running at four knots, as though she were trolling, before turning on us. It sounds like one of the fishing boats the pirates are using.'

'Anything on the radios, Hali?'

'Nothing from the target, Chairman. I've got regular chatter from a pair of bulk carriers well outside our grid.'

Juan dialed in the *Oregon*'s hangar bay. 'This is Cabrillo. I want the pilot suited and the Robinson on five-minute alert for takeoff.' He then punched up the shipwide channel.

'This is the chairman speaking. We have a target closing in that looks like the real thing. It's unlikely that the men aboard her are very high on the food chain, so we need prisoners not corpses if we're to cut off the head of the organization. Don't, I repeat: Do not take unnecessary risks, but if it's a choice between a kill or a capture, try to take them alive. Good luck to all.'

His eyes swept the room once again. There was neither grim fatalism nor any expectant gleams in the faces around him. The next move belonged to the pirates, and the crew waited with cool efficiency.

'Conn, slow us to eight knots. Let's make us too tempting to ignore, but have the ballast pumps ready in case we have to lighten up and run.'

'Aye.'

'Range?'

'Ten miles,' Linda answered crisply, then her voice took on an odd tone. 'What the . . . ?'

'What have you got?'

'Damn! Sonar contact directly below the ship, depth seventy feet.' She looked up from her display, catching Juan's eye. 'They have a submarine.'

## 5

The op center crew had no time to digest her words before Mark Murphy at the weapons control announced, 'I have a missile launch from the trawler. Time to impact forty-seven seconds. Gatlings are coming online.'

The tactical situation had spiraled out of control in only a few seconds, leaving Cabrillo little time to react. He relied on his mind and not the expensive equipment around him to visualize the battle and seek a solution. 'Hold your fire for my signal. Conn, pump us dry and prepare for full power. Wepps, be ready to launch countermeasures and depth charges. Sonar, what's the sub doing?'

'She's seems dead in the water, no propulsion and no indication she's going to fire.'

'Time to impact?'

'Thirty-one seconds.'

Cabrillo waited, feeling how the *Oregon* rode differently as the waist ballast tanks drained. At maximum speed the magnetohydrodynamic engines could move the ship her full length in just a couple of seconds. Even if his plan didn't work, the freighter wouldn't be where the missile thought it would.

'Sonar?'

'If anything, I'm getting the sound of escaping air, but the sub isn't submerging.'

That cinched it for him. The sub wasn't a threat, yet. Cabrillo wanted to blow the missile as close to the *Oregon* as possible to make the pirates think they'd scored a hit. 'Okay, Wepps, when the missile is ten seconds out, smoke it with the Gatling. Conn, ballast us back down, but be ready on those throttles.'

Mark Murphy, also wearing dark fatigues but over a black T-shirt with the saying 'Never Mind the Bollocks We Are the Sex Pistols,' brought up an external camera on the main screen. From out of the darkness a streaking corona of light raced for the *Oregon* a few dozen feet off the surface of the sea. The rate of closure was astronomical – at least a thousand miles per hour. The missile appeared to have been fired at an oblique angle so it would impact on the *Oregon*'s stern. The pirates' intention was to take out their victim's steering gear and propellers and leave them unable to run. Not a bad plan if they wanted to kidnap a hostage or plunder the ship's safe.

With eleven seconds to go, Mark released the trigger safety on the Gatling gun. It was as though the weapon was eager to prove itself, like a police dog held back on its leash while its master was being mauled. The electronic brain, slaved to a dedicated radar system, found the missile in a microsecond, calculated trajectory, windage, humidity, and a hundred other factors.

The plate hiding the gun emplacement had automatically lowered when the master radar had first detected the missile launch. The autocannon adjusted its aim slightly as electric motors spooled up the six rotating barrels. The instant the computers and radar agreed it had a target, foot-long twenty-millimeter depleted uranium shells fed into the breach at three thousand rounds per minute.

The Gatling sounded like an industrial buzz saw as it cranked out a five-second burst. Forty yards from the ship

61

the missile hit the wall of slugs. The explosion rained fire onto the sea, illuminating the side of the *Oregon* as though it had been caught in a miniature sunrise. Pieces of the rocket fell, carving trenches into the ocean, and a few smaller ones even rained against the ship's hull.

'Conn, all stop, steer ninety-seven. Hali, give it a few seconds, then send a mayday on the emergency frequencies, but keep the power setting low so only our friends out there hear us.' Cabrillo dialed the engine room. 'Max, lay a small smoke screen. Make us look like we took damage.'

'They'll think they hit us and the ship's dead in the water,' Eric Stone said with admiration. 'You're going to sucker them all the way in.'

'That's the plan,' Juan agreed. 'Sonar, anything on that sub?'

'Negative. We've now put her a mile astern. I can't hear any machinery noises or anything else but a slow air leak.'

'Did you get her dimensions?'

'Yes, and they're odd. She's a hundred and thirty feet long and nearly thirty-five wide. Short and squat by conventional standards.'

Juan considered a possibility. 'A North Korean minisub that somehow followed us here?'

'The computer couldn't find a match, but it's not likely. We're four hundred miles from the Korean Peninsula, and I get the sense that sub's been sitting here for a while. No way they could have beat us.'

Cabrillo didn't doubt Linda's assessment. 'Okay, keep an eye on her. For now our priority is the pirates' trawler. We'll come back to investigate later.' Across the room Hali Kasim was calling out his mayday and giving an Academy Award-winning performance.

'Motor vessel *Oregon,* this is the trawler *Kra IV,* what is the nature of your mayday?' The voice over the radio was scratchy, and the output was weak, as though the pirate was transmitting at low power. No one could place his accent.

'*Kra IV,* this is the *Oregon,* we appear to have had an explosion in our steering gear. Helm is not responding, and we're adrift.'

'*Oregon, Kra.* We are six miles away and closing at maximum speed.'

'I bet you are,' Hali muttered under his breath before keying the mike. 'Thanks be to Allah you are here. We will lower our boarding stairs on the starboard side. Please bring all the firefighting equipment you have.'

'*Kra* acknowledges. Out.'

Juan switched frequencies to the tactical radios carried by Seng and his handpicked team. 'Eddie, can you hear me?'

'Five by five, Chairman.' Eddie waited with his five men in a passageway in the deserted superstructure. The soldiers wore Kevlar armor over black fatigues, and all had third-generation night vision visors. Each carried sound-suppressed MP-5 machine pistols and SIG Sauer automatics. Their ammo was short loaded in the armory, meaning it had a reduced powder charge. It was powerful enough to put down a man but wouldn't overpenetrate and potentially cause a friendly fire incident in the confines of the ship. From combat harnesses hung flash-bang grenades and enough spare magazines for a ten-minute firefight.

Only Eddie Seng wore civilian clothes and sported a bulky rain slicker that disguised two bulletproof vests. He was the point man, charged with meeting the pirates as they came up the stairs now lowering to the sea. His was the most dangerous job. He had to lure as many pirates as possible onto the ship for his team, mostly SEAL veterans, to take out. He carried a single pistol in a slim rig at the small of his back. The vests were to buy him a few seconds if the pirates came up with guns blazing.

'What have we got?' Seng asked.

'Trawler calling itself the *Kra IV* coming up the starboard stairs to lend firefighting support,' Cabrillo answered. 'If I were them, I'd send over at least nine men. Two for the bridge, two for the engine room, four for flexible duty, plus one leader.'

'We said the *Oregon*'s sailing with a complement of fifty something,' Eddie countered. 'They'll send at least a dozen.'

'Good point. Do you have enough men?'

'Roger, as long as the deck machine guns can take out the cannon fodder while we concentrate on capturing officers.'

'Sounds good,' Cabrillo responded. 'Call me when you have visual.' The ops team watched the trawler approach the *Oregon* through low-light cameras mounted high atop a deck crane. The *Kra IV* matched the description given by the few survivors of pirate attacks. She was seventy-three feet long and beamy, with a blunt bow and an open aft deck. She sported a tall A-frame derrick over her fantail, and they could see a single cargo container lashed just aft of her pilot-house. The distortion of the night optics couldn't prevent the crew from seeing that the trawler was well-worn. Her machinery looked as dilapidated as that aboard the *Oregon,* and Juan decided the pirates used the same ruse the Corporation utilized to lull their adversaries.

'Target is twenty yards to starboard,' Eddie radioed. 'I can see a dozen or so men on her deck. They're dressed mostly in shorts or jeans. A few are wearing foul weather gear. They look like they're carrying equipment, but I bet it's cover for weapons.'

'Acknowledged.' Cabrillo called down to the engine room to tell Max to cut the smoke screen. With their forward speed down to almost zero, the thick smog blew across the decks and would make visual identification difficult for Seng, as well as the operators of the remote machine guns.

Eddie watched one of the 'fishermen' raise a bullhorn to his mouth and hail the *Oregon*. He stepped from the shadows and took a position at the head of the gangway stairs. A bead of sweat trickled down his rib cage. 'Are we glad to see you,' he called back with the right tinge of fear and relief. He noted that the curtain of smoke began to thin. 'I think we have contained the fire but don't know what damage we've sustained.'

'We will offer any assistance we can,' the pirate replied. Eddie could hear the mocking tone in his voice through his accent.

As the two boats came together, deckhands on the *Kra IV* secured their ship to the gangway, and two of the pirates started up the stairs. If the first shot was to come, now was the time. Eddie tensed, his pistol out of its holster but held out of view.

Several things happened in the space of the next few seconds. Unseen searchlights on the trawler snapped on, bathing the side of the *Oregon* in stark white light and over-loading most of the crew's night vision capabilities. Just short of the deck, the leading pirate raised an automatic and put two quick rounds into Eddie's chest and motioned to his companions. They charged up the gangway, shouting incoherent challenges as another dozen men rushed from the *Kra*'s pilothouse.

Eddie felt as though he'd been hit in the chest with a sledgehammer. He staggered back, his body numb. He heard more than felt his pistol fall from his deadened fingers.

Four of the pirates had gained the deck by the time Eddie's men reacted. Two of them were cut down in the first burst of gunfire from their concealed positions, but five more reached the *Oregon* to take their place. That they were meeting resistance sent the boarding party into a frenzy. They came on like berserkers eager for battle. In another few seconds the odds were five to one against the Corporation fighters and lengthening with every tick of the clock. Red beams from laser sights crisscrossed in the smoke as the firefight turned into a frenzy.

As soon as the screens in the op center whited out under the luminous onslaught of the arc lamps, Cabrillo understood the pirates' strategy. It had been called shock and awe during the second Gulf War – overwhelm your enemy in the first few moments of battle by creating the maximum confusion. An untrained crew on a merchant vessel would be so paralyzed by the lights, the screams, and the sheer number of men storming their ship that they wouldn't even get off a mayday.

And while the tactic was designed to defeat an unarmed crew, it also happened to negate the Corporation's advantage. The night vision gear was worthless, and there was still too much smoke blanketing the deck to use regular sights. The infrared system couldn't discern friend from foe, so for the moment the remote gunners were useless.

Cabrillo launched himself from his chair, snatching a pair of night vision goggles and a machine pistol from the rack along the aft bulkhead. He was in the elevator before anyone knew he'd moved.

'Lock down the elevator when I reach the bridge,' he called as the hydraulic lift whisked him five stories to the bridge.

Even from high above the deck, the sound of the gun battle was ferocious. The former SEALs were making a good show for themselves, but it was only a matter of time. Cabrillo raced out along the wing bridge, taking a second to peer down. At least twenty pirates had taken defensive positions all around the forward deck and poured blistering fire into the superstructure. He spotted a figure slowly crawling away from the head of the gangway. He had his weapon up and his finger an ounce away from firing when he recognized Eddie's rain jacket. His gaze swept the pirates again just as one popped up from behind a winch, taking aim at Seng with an AK-47.

Cabrillo swung his weapon and put a bullet through the pirate's face, adjusted slightly, and dropped another with a double tap to the chest. He ducked behind the solid curtain rail as bullets whizzed by like angry hornets and sparked against the steel. He clicked the selector on the MP-5 to auto, raised it over the railing, and let loose with a long barrage, hosing the deck with fifteen rounds. In the seconds-long pause in counterfire, he got to his feet, flipped the selector back to single, and took aim at the searchlights aboard the trawler.

His heart was beating like a trip-hammer, so the first two rounds missed. He took a steadying breath, let half out, and fired twice more. The pair of lights exploded in a shower of glass, and darkness descended once again.

Almost immediately he heard the staccato bark of the hidden .30 calibers and the pinging rain of spent brass ejected onto the deck. The remote gunners were back online.

Cabrillo's machine pistol had a spare magazine taped to the one in the receiver. He changed them over, settled the goggles over his head, and got to work. In the eerie green cast of the night vision device, muzzle flashes looked like fireflies while men appeared like radiant ghosts. He dedicated himself to be Eddie Seng's guardian angel.

Eddie was still pinned in the open, and judging at how slowly he was moving, Juan knew he'd been hit. There was no trail of blood, so it was likely the vests had saved his life; however, Juan had taken a hit once through a vest and knew it would be hours before Eddie could even catch his breath. It took several agonizing minutes for Eddie to reach the hatchway into the superstructure, where a pair of hands hauled him to safety.

Through the cordite smoke drifting like a dense English fog, Cabrillo identified potential targets and fired with mechanical efficiency. Until the crew gained the upper hand in the battle, he couldn't worry about taking prisoners.

Blood ran thick across the deck as bodies piled up, but fire from the SEALs had withered to an occasional desultory burst. They'd taken losses. Cabrillo spotted two pirates dashing forward, moving from a hatch cover where they'd hidden to the base of one of the cranes. One pulled something from the knapsack worn by his partner. Juan recognized the satchel charge and cut them down before they had time to arm the device. Another tried to race for the superstructure. As Cabrillo swung to fire, one of the remote machine guns turned on its gimble. The sustained burst cut the man nearly in half.

That seemed to break the back of the pirate horde. The ten or so survivors ran for the gangway just as the big diesel on the *Kra* bellowed out of idle. They ran into devastating fire from the superstructure. By holding back, Eddie's men had fooled the pirates into thinking their avenue of escape was clear. Two dropped to the deck, their corpses skidding in their own blood.

The *Kra* began to pull away, abandoning their boarding party. Cabrillo stitched the trawler's deck, but there were no targets. The lines securing the gangway to the fishing boat were still secure, so it was slowly torn from its mounts. Two pirates were halfway down it when the *Kra* began to move. The gangway stretched like a bridge from one ship to the other until the ropes on the *Kra* parted under the strain. The eighteen-hundred-pound set of stairs twisted, then pulled free from the *Oregon,* dumping the men into the sea, then crushing them when they surfaced.

The *Kra* changed angle slightly, narrowing the gap to give their men on the *Oregon* a chance to jump for it. Eric Stone at the helmsman's station in the op center recognized the maneuver and turned the *Oregon* to port and gave her some speed just as the remaining pirates leapt for the rails. One landed on the *Kra*'s main winch. High above on the wing bridge, Cabrillo heard bones shatter and saw his body tumble to the trawler's deck. A second gunman smashed into the *Kra*'s hull, fell into the water, and never resurfaced. The remaining six landed in the narrow space between the two ships.

Juan didn't know if the helmsman on the fishing boat didn't see what had happened or just didn't care. He continued to turn into the *Oregon*. Eric Stone hit the bow thruster in an attempt to shove the *Kra* aside, but the prop's athwartships tunnel was well forward of the trawler, and its powerful wash merely rippled the waves.

The two hulls came together in a grinding crash of steel,

smearing the men struggling in the water, turning flesh and bone into a pink paste that washed away when the ships separated.

Juan fetched a walkie-talkie from a drawer at the back of the wheelhouse. 'Wepps, Cabrillo. As soon as you have a sight picture, hole her at the waterline. Let the sons of bitches know they aren't going anywhere.'

'Roger,' Mark Murphy replied.

As the distance between the two vessels grew, Cabrillo saw a deckhand aboard the *Kra* attach the cable from the A-frame derrick to lines already secured to the shipping container sitting aft of the wheelhouse. The chairman squeezed off a few rounds from his H&K, but hitting a target that's bobbing with the swells from an unstable platform was next to impossible. The man didn't even look up from his task as bullets ricocheted around him. An unseen winchman cranked up the derrick. Because the A-frame angled out over the trawler's stern, the large container was dragged across the *Kra*'s deck, leaving deep scars in the wood planking. The bottom edge caught on a bollard, but the winch drum continued to revolve. The container teetered for a moment before flipping on its side with an echoing clang. When it was finally under the crane, it was hauled into the air and swung free over the transom. The winchman released the brake, and the container smashed into the sea, bobbed for a moment, then began to fill with water.

Cable stripped away from the freewheeling winch drum as the *Kra* continued to increase the distance. Whatever contraband the trawler was carrying was doubtlessly in the container, and Cabrillo felt if they were quick enough, they could disable the fishing boat and tie on to the unspooling line before it vanished forever.

As if reading his thoughts, Mark Murphy loosened a one-second burst from the Gatling gun hidden in the *Oregon*'s bow. Fifty depleted uranium slugs punched into the *Kra* at the waterline just fore of the pilothouse at a spot Murph assumed was clear of hitting her fuel tanks.

The tanks were well aft of the gaping hole, but the rounds impacted the pirates' weapons cache. The first explosion was relatively small and contained. Only a lashing tongue of fire belched from the gash cut into the hull by the Gatling. The second blast punched through to the deck and blew out an eight-by-eight section of hull. Fire and smoke rolled from the trawler as she heeled over like she'd just fired a broadside of cannons. Cabrillo watched helplessly as more explosions ripped apart the fishing boat. It looked as though she'd been rigged to blow by Hollywood effects masters. The pilothouse vanished in a splintering pall of flame, and then her aft deck erupted when her main tanks detonated, slamming her stern so deeply into the water that her bow lifted clear. Shrapnel and debris peppered the side of the *Oregon,* forcing Cabrillo to duck behind the rail. The trawler's stern winch flew right over the freighter's rear deck, trailing cable that looked like gossamer in the moonlight. The *Kra*'s keel split where the explosions had weakened it. The smoking bow settled back on the water as the stern sank from view, and then the fore section lifted free again before it, too, was dragged under the waves.

The entire sequence of events, from the first impact of 20 mm rounds to the final hissing plunge, took nineteen seconds.

Juan got back to his feet, wiping a smear of blood from where a piece of hot steel had nicked the back of his hand. A wide circle of smoking flotsam coated the sea, no piece larger than a garbage can lid. The quiet roar of oily fires burning on the swells was the only sound once the concussion waves dissipated across the uncaring waters. There were no moans from the injured, no cries from the stranded. No one had survived the conflagration.

He remained rooted for ten seconds, perhaps for as long as thirty, before he realized there was hope of salvaging what had turned into a debacle. The cable securing the pirate's container lay across the *Oregon*'s deck, slowly slipping into the ocean as the weight of the container pulled it down.

'Deck party to the aft deck for cargo detail,' he barked into the radio. 'Security to the foredeck. Check for survivors.'

He raced through the deserted superstructure, taking stairs four at a time in a race to the aft deck. He burst from a hatchway just as a team of deckhands reached the slithering cable. Because the winch spool had unwound as it sank on the far side of the ship, there was little counterweight to the rapidly sinking container. The cable rasped across the deck, and smoke from blistering paint coiled into the air.

Juan grabbed a length of chain from a pile left haphazardly at the base of a derrick. He looped it several times around the cable where it rose over the rail, then snapped the links into the hook of a small cargo winch. While the winch looked as though it hadn't worked in years, its two-cylinder engine fired at the press of a button. He threw the lever to draw on the hook, and the chain tightened around the cable. The friction of steel against steel created an acrid stench as the links clenched further. The cable slowed enough for the deckhands to create a loop long enough for them to wrestle over a capstan. The cable came taut, vibrating with the strain, but it held.

It took several more minutes for them to rig a more secure system to hold the cable steady and attach it to the one operational crane on the *Oregon*'s aft deck. Eddie Seng and Linda Ross joined him just as they started to haul up the container. Seng was pale and walked with a slight stoop, a hand pressed to his chest where he'd taken the two shots.

'How're you doing?' Cabrillo asked.

'It only hurts when I laugh,' Eddie said gamely.

'Then let me tell you the one about the hooker who walks into a bar with a parrot and a roll of quarters.'

Eddie held out a hand and groaned. 'Please don't.'

Juan turned serious. 'How bad was it back there?'

'Believe it or not, I'm the worst of the injured. My boys suffered a grand total of one concussion and a single flesh wound among them.'

'And the pirates?'

'Thirteen dead and two injured,' Linda answered. 'Julia doesn't think either's gonna last an hour.'

'Damn.' They might get something from forensic autopsies, the ages and ethnicities of the pirates for example, but nothing to lead them to who was behind the attack.

'Clear the rail,' a deckhand shouted.

The trio stepped away from the ship's side as the container was lifted from the sea. Water poured from its top and jetted from holes drilled along its sides. The twenty-foot container swung over the rail, and the crane operator settled it onto the deck as though it was as fragile as an egg. Juan was handed a pair of bolt cutters, which he used to shear the padlock securing the doors. Everyone crowded around, each with their own private thoughts about what they'd find inside. It was inevitable that some believed the pirates' trove would contain gold and precious gems, as though this was the eighteenth century.

Cabrillo held no such illusions, but he wasn't prepared for what spilled from the container when he unlatched the doors. A crewman retched when he realized what he was seeing, and even Juan had to clench his jaws as acid surged up his throat. Borne by several tons of water still trapped inside the steel box, a tangle of thirty naked bodies tumbled onto the deck of the *Oregon*.

# 6

The chateau sat in a valley near the base of Mount Pilatus just south of Lucerne and only a short train ride from Zurich. Although the forty-room mansion looked as if it had dominated the landscape for generations, it had been constructed only five years earlier. With traditional steeply pitched slate roofs and countless gables and chimneys, the structure was storybook beautiful. The circular drive curved around an enormous marble fountain decorated with a dozen nymphs who poured water into the clear pool from filigreed urns.

Around the main house were several stone outbuildings to make the estate look like it had once been a working farm. In the surrounding alpine meadows, brown Jersey cows sporting bronze bells kept the fields trimmed and fertilized.

Seven dark limousines were ranked in a parking annex next to the garage, and behind it lay an enclosed field where a pair of Aerospatiale Gazelle helicopters sat, their pilots drinking thermos coffee in the cockpit of one of the executive choppers.

The summit meeting of European finance ministers in Zurich drew little media attention, since nothing much was expected of the gathering. However, it provided an excuse for the men meeting at the chateau to be in the same city at the same time. They met in the mansion's great hall, a lofty two-story room paneled in oak and decorated with boar and stag heads and large Swiss horns crossed over the walk-in fireplace.

As Switzerland is one of the world's great banking centers, it was little wonder that with one exception the fifteen men represented some of the largest banking concerns in Europe and America.

At the head of the table sat Bernhard Volkmann. Raised Catholic in a strict household run by his banker father, Volkmann had forsaken his religion early in life for another, that of wealth. Currency had become his god, cash his Eucharist. He was a high priest in the world of finance, respected for his dedication and a little feared for his uncanny instincts. Every action of every day went toward the accumulation of more money, for his bank and for himself. Volkmann had a wife because it was expected of him and three children because he'd allowed himself to sleep with her on a half-dozen occasions. He considered them a necessary distraction from his professional life but could not recall any of their birthdays or the last time he'd even seen his youngest, a twenty-year-old student he believed was at the Sorbonne.

Volkmann arrived at his office on Zurich's Bahnhof-strasse at six each morning and left at eight each night. This routine varied begrudgingly on Sundays and holidays when he would work out of his home for at least twelve hours a day. Volkmann neither drank nor smoked and would be no more likely to enter a casino than a Muslim would become a swineherd. At sixty, he was paunchy and almost uniformly gray. His skin was the same washed-out shade as his hair, and behind his glasses his eyes were the murky color of dish-water. He even took to wearing gray suits, and though his shirts were white, they invariably took on his gray cast.

76

Those who worked for him had never seen Volkmann smile, much less laugh, and only a severe financial upheaval would elicit a slight downward tug at the corners of his mouth.

Around him were similarly severe men whose dedication to money was no less intense. They were presidents of banks whose decisions affected billions of dollars and millions of lives. And today they were gathered because the very foundation of the world's economy was about to crumble.

On the table in front of Bern Volkmann a simple black cloth covered a small rectangular object. When the men were settled around the table, water poured, and attendants withdrawn, Volkmann reached out and pulled away the cloth.

The bankers and their guest were among a handful of people in the world who wouldn't noticeably react to the object on the table. Yet Volkmann saw that even these seasoned professionals couldn't mask all emotion. A few drew shallow breaths, one contemplatively stroked his chin. Another's eyes widened for an instant, then the person glanced around as if he'd given a tell in a poker game. The six billion other people on the planet would have gasped in wonder and rushed to touch the object as their minds filled with possibilities.

The trapezoidal bar weighed twenty-seven pounds and was known as a London Good Delivery. Its facets radiated a warm buttery yellow, and it possessed an almost oily sheen in the subtle lighting of the great hall. Refined to 99.9 percent, the ingot of pure gold was worth approximately one hundred sixty thousand dollars.

'Gentlemen, we have a crisis,' Volkmann began in accentless English. He spoke crisply, enunciating every word so there could be no confusion or misinterpretation. 'As you are all aware, the world will run out of gold very shortly. In fact, demand far outstrips supply for a very simple reason. Some of you became greedy.

'Starting more than a decade ago many of you approached your country's central banks with a proposition that at the time seemed profitable for everyone concerned. You, as bankers, would borrow the gold held on deposit with the promise to repay at one-quarter percent interest. The gold, as it sat in vaults in New York, Paris, London, and elsewhere, had no value so long as it was kept out of circulation. By paying a quarter point you would make the gold work for the central banks as it never had in the past.

'Had it ended there, we would not be facing a crisis. But it did not end. You turned around and either sold the gold on the open market or used the value of your holdings as leverage and collateral for other ventures. In essence you pledged or sold a commodity you had only the right to borrow. The central banks gave tacit approval to this action yet maintained the right to recall the gold at any time. Had this scheme taken place in only one country or on a small scale, there would remain enough surplus gold on the market to cover such a call.

'However, your greed got the best of you all. As it stands today, twelve thousand tons of gold valued at one trillion euros is on the books of central banks but is, in fact, on the fingers and around the necks of women all over the world. In a word, gentlemen, it is beyond redemption.

'Several central banks are aware of the situation and continue to accept their quarter percent on the gold's value, but some are asking for the gold's return. Two years ago the French national bank announced they were going to sell some of their reserves. We got together to finance the purchase of enough gold to replenish their treasury so the sale could go through. As you recall, the price of gold rose fifty euros in just a few weeks when traders realized such buying was taking place. The French then sold their gold, and the price stabilized once again. Our scramble to cover the call cost us nearly a billion euros. We told our stockholders it was a one-time charge-off, but in truth it is a charge-off we will face any time a central bank calls in their assets.'

'Bern, we don't need a history lesson,' a New York banker said testily. 'If you look around you'll see there's a few familiar faces missing because they were canned by their boards of directors.'

'Being "canned by their boards" as you put it, Mr Hershel, is now the least of our worries.' Volkmann gave the American a stare that silenced any follow-up rejoinder.

'Banking is a business of trust,' he continued. 'A worker cashes his paycheck, spends what money he needs to survive, and trusts a bank to hold the rest. What happens to it afterward is frankly beyond his understanding or threshold of interest. He has done his job of converting labor to capital and trusts us to do our job of maximizing that capital. We lend it to entrepreneurs who build new businesses to employ more workers to transform more labor into more capital in a system that has worked well for centuries.

'But what happens when that trust is abused? Surely there have been banking scandals in the past; however, what we now face is a crisis of confidence of unprecedented proportions. The store of capital that governments use to assure their people of the country's strength, their gold reserves, has been sold off for what is in essence an IOU that can no longer be paid. We cannot honor our promise to the central banks. Even if we had the money to buy the gold to return to the central banks, there isn't enough of it in the world to cover what we owe.'

'Production can be increased to buy us the time to fill a call order.' This from an Englishman in a Savile Row suit.

'It can't.' The answer was short and blunt, like the person who gave it. He, too, had an accent, somewhat British in nature but with a Colonial twang.

'Mr Bryce, would you care to explain.'

Bryce stood. Unlike the others, he had tanned, weathered skin, and his blue eyes were hidden behind a permanent squint. His hands were large, with swollen knuckles. He was someone who'd worked to obtain his wealth, toiled in ways the bankers could never understand.

'I've been chosen to represent South Africa's mining concerns here,' Bryce said. 'Mr Volkmann told me what we were to discuss, so I talked with my people beforehand to give you accurate information. Last year South Africa produced about thirty-four hundred tons of gold at a cost of around two hundred and eighty dollars an ounce. This year we project the same tonnage but at a price of three hundred and eighteen dollars an ounce. Labor costs have risen since the end of apartheid because of the power of the trade unions, and we're under heavy pressure to sign a new contract that's even more generous.'

'Don't give in to them,' the president of Holland's biggest bank interjected.

Bryce shot him a look. 'Hard rock mining isn't assembly line work. It takes years of training to become proficient. A strike now would cripple us all, and the unions know it.

They see gold trading near five hundred an ounce and know the mines aren't losing money.'

'Can you increase production?' another at the table asked.

'Our mines are two miles deep now. Every level we sink farther is a geometric increase in cost. It's like building a skyscraper. To make it taller you can't simply add a floor to the top. You must first reinforce the foundation and the structure. You must make sure the elevators can reach and that your water and sewer lines can take the additional capacity. Adding a floor to the top, architects say, costs as much and is as difficult as slipping a new floor under an existing building. Every new level we dig in our deepest mines costs two to three times as much to excavate as the one above it. We could get the gold, sure, but the expense far outweighs the profit.'

'Then we need to find alternative sources of bullion. Russia perhaps? Canada? The United States?'

'Not enough capacity to make a dent in the shortfall,' Volkmann answered. 'Also, environmental protections in North America add a thirty to forty dollar premium per ounce.'

'What about exploration? We develop new mines, maybe bring order to the chaotic gold mines of Brazil so they can increase production.'

'Even with the latest equipment and management, the veins in Brazil aren't big enough to fill an armored car in a year,' Bryce replied. 'And as for exploration, there are gold reefs out there. We even know where some of them are. It would take years just to cut through the bureaucracy to stake claims, and then you'd need to invest billions of dollars to bring any of them up to the production levels you gentlemen require.'

'Then the solution is simple,' a Frenchman said into the short silence following Bryce's gloomy assessment. 'We must convince the central banks to never call in their reserves. Perhaps we could promise them a greater interest rate to ensure their cooperation.'

'That's just a temporary fix,' said another New Yorker. 'We can't run from our obligation forever.'

'But if we have time to refill the central banks' coffers, we can maintain price stability and avoid what happened when my country announced their sale.'

'And when the *Wall Street Journal* breaks this story,' the New Yorker countered, 'what then? People are going to demand to see the gold their government promised them existed. Joe Six-Pack thinks there's a vault at Fort Knox brimming with the stuff. He's not going to be too happy when he learns it's empty except for a bunch of worthless promissory notes. He's going to panic because his government lied about the one thing it never had in the past, the surety of the greenback.'

'Which is precisely why I said earlier this is a crisis of unprecedented proportions,' Volkmann said. 'We have removed the foundation of the capitalist system, and as soon as the public learns of this, it is going to crash down like a card house.'

The Swiss banker paused, scanning the room. He saw that he had their attention, and he could tell by the dour expressions that some of them already anticipated what he was about to say, even if they didn't know the specifics. He sipped from a glass of water before continuing. 'For the past six years Germany has embarked on a series of failed economic policies. The result has transformed the country from Europe's industrial engine into something akin to a welfare state. Productivity is down, unemployment is at the ceiling allowed by the EU, and shortly the government will face the likelihood that it will default on their overly generous pensions. In a word, Germany is about to go bankrupt. I learned two weeks ago that they are going to sell all of their gold stock.'

The collective gasp was the sound of men realizing they were facing the abyss.

'That is six thousand tons, gentlemen – or roughly two years' worth of South Africa's production. As it stands there are only two thousand tons on reserve in Berlin and Bonn. We have to make up a four-thousand-ton shortfall.'

'How soon?' the Frenchman asked, having lost his earlier bluster.

'I'm not certain,' Volkmann replied. 'In order to keep prices stable I suspect it will be over some time.'

'But not enough,' the New Yorker muttered.

'And keep in mind,' Volkmann went on doggedly, piling disaster on top of disaster, 'if commodity traders realize the bind our banks are in, they will gouge us, and prices might double or even triple.'

'We are ruined,' the banker from Holland cried. 'All of us. Even if the Germans accepted currency, we could not repay. The money we made selling the gold has already been lent to others. We would have to recall loans, all of our loans. It would ruin the Dutch economy.'

'Not just yours,' the banker named Hershel said. 'We bought and sold twenty billion dollars' worth of German bullion, and a good chunk of that evaporated during the dot-com implosion. We would have to deplete our savings-holders' accounts to pay it back. There would be runs on banks all over the United States. It would be the Great Depression all over again.'

A despondent silence enveloped the room as they considered those words. These men were too young to recall the Depression that enveloped the world in the 1920s and '30s, but they'd heard firsthand accounts from grandparents and other relatives. But this time would be much worse, because the global economy was so interconnected. A few even thought beyond their own losses and those of their home countries. With nations struggling to provide for their own people, international aid would end. How many people in developing nations would die because the men at this table had sold borrowed gold in order to fatten their profit ledgers?

Suddenly the sleek corporate high rollers were as gray as Bernhard Volkmann.

'Is there any way to dissuade the Germans?' one asked after a few moments.

'We can try,' another answered, 'but they have to look after their own interests. They need their gold back, or they'll face insolvency and possible rioting, maybe insurrection.'

Volkmann allowed the conversation to continue for a few minutes on its own as the bankers bandied ideas of how to save themselves, their banks, and the world. In the end they had no answers. It was as the talk died down to silence once again that he asked the South African mine representative, Bryce, to leave the room.

When the door closed behind him, the bankers gave their undivided attention to Volkmann. He remained silent until someone finally asked the question they all prayed he could answer.

'Did you call us here because you have a solution?' asked the English CEO of the world's sixth-largest bank.

'Yes,' Volkmann replied simply and almost felt their relieved sighs on his skin. He tapped a text message on his PDA and a moment later the great hall's doors swung open again. The man who entered strode in with a sense of confidence that the bankers would never admit they only possessed as a front, camouflage to hide their insecurities. He moved loose-limbed and with his head high. He was their age, early fifties, perhaps a little younger. It was hard to tell. His face was unlined, but his eyes seemed old and his bristle-cut hair was more silver than brown. Unlike the bankers, he didn't have the self-satisfied smugness of entitlement, the sense of superiority that came with the illusion of wealth and power. He was simply a presence, an undeniable force that had entered their meeting and seemed the center without having to utter a word.

'Gentlemen,' Volkmann said as the stranger took a seat next to the Swiss. 'This is Anton Savich, formerly of the Soviet Bureau of Natural Resources. He is now a private consultant.'

No one said a word or made a move. None could fathom the presence of a former Russian functionary.

'I've known something like this was coming for some time and secretly made plans,' Volkmann continued. 'There can be no argument about what I propose, nor any dissent. This is our only option, and when I am finished, each of you will agree to it without reservation. Mr Savich will outline the particulars.'

Without getting to his feet, speaking casually with an arm draped over the back of his chair, Anton Savich told them how he was going to save their banks. It took ten uninterrupted minutes and left the faces of the other men with a mixture of shock, anger, and outright revulsion. The Dutch banker looked like he was going to be physically ill. Even the tough New Yorkers, one of whom Volkmann knew had fought in Vietnam, had gone ashen.

'There is no other way, gentlemen,' Bern Volkmann said. No one could actually agree orally. Volkmann passed his gaze from man to man, meeting their eyes, and knew he had their assent when they either looked away or gave an almost imperceptible nod. The last was the Dutchman. He gave a weak moan at the thought of what he was agreeing to and dipped his eyes.

'I will make the arrangements,' Volkmann concluded. 'We need never meet like this again.'

The New Yorker who'd spoken of Fort Knox said, 'Oh, I'm sure we will. In hell.'

Cabrillo crossed himself.

The victims were of all ages, though they were pre-dominantly in their twenties, from what he could tell. Some had been dead for quite some time. Their bodies were black with lividity, and several were bloated with internal gas. Others had apparently drowned when the pirates dumped the container over the side of the fishing boat. They appeared sickly pale under the deck lights. It was hard to tell in the jumble of limbs, but it looked as though there were more men than women. The one thing they all had in common, other than their gruesome deaths, was that every one of them was Chinese.

'Snakeheads.' Cabrillo spat with disgust, looking out to where an oil slick still burned on the dark ocean.

Eager to seek work outside China, peasants and even moderately well-to-do workers paid upwards of thirty thou-sand dollars to be smuggled out of the country. Of course, even a wealthy Chinese couldn't come up with that kind of cash, so a system was put in place whereby the illegal immigrant would work for the gangs who smuggled them, paying off the debt by toiling in sweatshops or restaurants in every city from New York to New Delhi. The women were generally prostituted in 'massage parlors' that sprang up even in small towns across America and Canada. They labored for years, living in overcrowded apartments owned by the gangs, until the entire debt was repaid. If they tried to run away, their families back in China would be tortured or killed.

In this way more than a million Chinese a year left one bitter, dead-end existence for another, all believing the promise that things would improve if only they worked harder.

The immigrants had a name for their journey to a new life. It was called riding the snake, and those who ran the gangs were called snakeheads.

Cabrillo and his crew had intercepted a shipload of illegals most likely on their way to Japan, or the pirates had hijacked such a boat and were planning on selling the laborers back to the gang or to some third party. Either way, they had stumbled onto a human trafficking ring. Past his horror at what lay on the deck of his ship, beyond the grief that built behind his eyes, Juan Cabrillo felt a spark of anger flare in his chest. He nurtured it, fanning it with hate until it roared and threatened to consume him.

He turned to Linda Ross, his eyes glacial hard. 'Get Dr Huxley up here as soon as she's able. There's nothing she can do for these poor people, but autopsies might shed some light on what happened.' He motioned to the deckhands. 'As soon as orderlies empty the container, check it for any kind of ID numbers, then heave it over the side.'

'Are you okay, Juan?' Linda asked with concern.

'No. I'm pissed,' he said as he strode away. 'And I still have a submarine to deal with.'

He took his seat in the operations center. Word had already spread, and the mood was subdued. Mark Murphy was running systems checks on the shipboard weapons in case they were needed again, while Eric Stone sat quietly at the helm station awaiting orders.

'Mr Murphy,' Cabrillo called sharply.

Mark turned in his seat, a grave look on his face. It had been his shot that blew up the *Kra* and ruined any chance of interrogating prisoners. 'Yes, sir?'

The chairman's voice softened. 'Don't blame yourself. I would have plugged her in the same place. We're in this for the long haul. There'll be others.'

'Yes, sir. Thank you.'

'Mr Stone, make your speed thirty knots and put us over that submarine.'

'Aye, sir.'

Linda was still on deck, helping Julia and her medical team. Juan monitored the passive sonar array and called course and speed corrections to Stone until they had the *Oregon* directly over the mysterious sub. It had settled to seventy-five feet in the half hour since they'd first detected it. He washed the acoustical signal through the computer, filtering out extraneous sounds, until all he heard was the slow escape of air from the craft. He couldn't tell if the sub was just playing dead or if it was having a problem. But if there were some sort of emergency, surely he'd hear alarm Klaxons and crewmen working within the pressure hull. Even without the sophisticated listening devices, the sound of metal banging on metal would carry right through to the *Oregon*. Yet all that came through was the burbling hiss of the slowly sinking sub.

Juan pulled up a chart of the region on the computer. There were nearly two miles of water under the keel. It would be days before the sub hit bottom, although by then she would have long since collapsed after passing her crush depth.

He went back to his own seat and called down to the

moon pool, 'Dive master, this is Cabrillo. Open the hull doors and prepare an ROV for a shallow-water recon. Also have two divers standing by and lay out some gear for me.'

Fifteen minutes later Cabrillo stood behind the ROV's pilot wearing an orange wet suit. His goggles were strapped around his left arm. There was no need for him to dive on the sub but for his own desire to feel the freshening calm of the ocean's embrace. His shoulders and neck ached from tension and rage.

The underwater probe was a small, torpedo-shaped craft with three variable-pitch propellers along its axis for propulsion and maneuverability. In its domed nose was a high-resolution video camera, and mounted on its back were enough lights to illuminate a ten-foot swath in even the murkiest water. The craft had just been launched, and two workers made sure its unspooling tether ran free from the ship.

The huge doors that were opened to the sea allowed a chill to creep into the cavernous amidships hold while underwater lights attached to the hull cast a wavering green reflection along the bulkheads. The big Nomad 1000 submersible loomed over the pool like an airship, ready just in case they needed her powerful manipulator arm.

'Passing fifty feet,' the operator announced, his attention fixed on the screen showing a live feed from the ROV's camera. All it revealed was blackness. His fingers rested on a pair of joysticks that controlled the probe.

'Sixty feet.'

'There.' Cabrillo pointed.

From out of the gloom came the faintest trace of an outline. It was murky and indistinct at first but resolved itself as the ROV approached. The probe had come upon the sub from the stern. It was her bronze propeller that glinted in the powerful lights. Then they could discern her rudder. It looked like no sub Juan had ever seen.

'Bring us up five feet and forward another ten.'

The operator followed his orders, and the prop slid under the camera's view. They could see steel hull plates, but these weren't in the cigar shape of a typical submarine. Linda had said the craft was odd when she'd hit it with active sonar to check its shape.

Suddenly they could see the word HAM painted in white against the black hull.

'Back us off,' Cabrillo said.

The little undersea robot eased in reverse, and the word expanded into gibberish. UTHAMPTO.

'What the hell is an Uthampto?' one of the divers asked.

'Not what,' Juan replied. 'Where. Southampton, England.'

And as he spoke, the full name of the vessel's home port came into view as well as her name: *Avalon*. And she wasn't a sub at all.

'Do you think this is the ship where the pirates pulled the refugees?'

'I doubt it.' Cabrillo stared at the screen as the probe sailed over the ship's stern rail and across her aft deck. A few fish swam amid the tangle of gear. 'But I'm sure she was one of their victims. I bet she was attacked just before we got into radar range.' He called up to the bridge to have Mark Murphy run a check on the British-flagged ship.

'Wouldn't we have heard an SOS?' the diver asked.

'Not if the pirates jammed them or boarded using some trick that allowed them to take out her radios before a warning could be sent.'

'Chairman, it's Murph. The *Avalon* belongs to the Royal Geographic Society. Launched in 1982, she's a hundred and thirty feet long, displaces –'

Cabrillo cut him off. 'When was she last heard from?'

'According to a press release from the RGS, all contact was lost with her four days ago. American search and rescue units out of Okinawa didn't find a thing.'

'That doesn't make any sense,' Juan said for his benefit and not for those around him. He puzzled aloud. 'If she was boarded and the pirates cut communications, the SAR crews should have spotted her in no time.'

'Not if they sank her right away,' the ROV pilot answered.

'There's no way she would have sunk only seventy-five feet in four days.' Cabrillo paused. 'Unless ... unless someone managed to stop her from taking on more water.'

'She'd still keep sinking,' the diver said. 'If she'd lost enough buoyancy to sink this far, she'd have lost enough to keep going down.'

Cabrillo regarded the man. 'Good point, unless she became trapped in a halocline, a band of highly saline water. Salt water is more dense than fresh, so an equal volume displaces more weight. The ocean is layered like a cake with striations of water with differing salt levels and temperatures. It's possible the *Avalon* sank into a layer of superdense water that's maintaining her equilibrium for the time being.' He was aware that the ship was still taking on water, so eventually she would slip through the band of water, then plunge like a stone.

The men watched in silence as the probe glided over the sunken vessel. There were no outward signs of a struggle, no bullet holes or evidence of explosion. It was as though

92

she'd just slid beneath the waves without a fight. Once the probe reached the *Avalon*'s bow, Cabrillo had the pilot swing her along the superstructure and see if they could peer into any of the windows.

'Do you think anyone's still alive on her?' the diver suddenly blurted.

Juan had already considered and discarded the idea. He'd seen firsthand how savage the pirates were and knew they wouldn't have left behind any witnesses, even on a scuttled ship. Further proof was the derelict's silence. If he'd been trapped on a sunken vessel, he would have done something to attract attention, no matter how futile. He would have banged on the hull with a wrench until he could no longer move his arms. Then he would have shouted until his dying breath. No, he was certain no one was left alive aboard the *Avalon*.

The ROV swept back across the *Avalon*'s deck, heading for the bridge. In the tight cone of light they could see the big windows had all been smashed, either by the pirates or when the research vessel slipped into the sea. The pilot eased the probe through one of the empty window frames, mindful that the armored tether could easily tangle. The ceiling looked like a shimmering wall of liquid mercury. It was an air pocket fed by a string of bubbles leaking up from a small hole in the floor.

There was ample evidence of the attack on the bridge. Stitched lines of bullet holes crisscrossed the room, and brass shells littered the deck. A pile of what looked to be rags or a tarp in one corner revealed itself to be a body. Tiny fish darted at the tendrils of blood still leaking from the numerous wounds. The pilot tried to maneuver so they could see the dead man's face and maybe make an ID, but the little probe didn't have the power to roll what had once been a large man.

'See if you can find a way to access the rest of the superstructure,' Cabrillo ordered.

The pilot tried, but they found the door at the rear of the bridge jammed with a metal bar across the latches.

'Never mind. Back us out and check the portholes. Maybe we can see inside her.'

The probe ran first down the *Avalon*'s port side, pausing at each porthole, but they couldn't see anything within the hull. Inside was stygian black. The operator swung around her stern and started up the starboard. The light cast a perfect circle along the black hull, and each round window glittered like a jewel. The instant it shone into one of the cabins there came the sharp sound of metal banging against metal. It was a frantic, staccato tattoo. The men monitoring the screen recoiled as a pale face suddenly appeared at the window. It was a woman. Her eyes were huge with fear, and her mouth moved as she shouted a scream they could not hear.

'Dear God! She's alive.'

Cabrillo had already moved to a bench seat and was snugging the straps of his twin air tanks over his shoulders. Next came the buoyancy compensator that looped around his neck. He struggled to his feet to cinch a weight belt around his waist. The two other divers were quickly following suit. He snatched up a pair of swim fins and a powerful flashlight.

'Alert Huxley,' he said as he waddled to the moon pool, burdened by sixty pounds of gear. He adjusted his mask, checked his airflow, and fell back into the water.

As he dropped through a curtain of bubbles, Cabrillo slid his feet into the fins, then purged some water that had seeped in around his mask. The water wasn't that cold, and his body heat quickly warmed the thin layer trapped inside his wet suit. He waited just long enough for the two other divers to hit the water before dumping air from his BC and dropping into the darkness, one hand on the probe's tether as a guide.

How had she survived? he wondered. Judging by the damage fish had done to the corpse on the bridge, the pirates had scuttled the *Avalon* shortly after taking her. Was there that much air trapped inside her hull? Obviously, the answer was yes. The question was if it would last until they could get her out.

Below him he saw the corona of light from the probe and shadowy details of the research ship. Air spilled from at least a dozen spots around her hull, as though she were bleeding. Juan felt a superstitious chill down his spine. The *Avalon* had become a ghost ship, but unlike the *Flying Dutchman,* she'd been cursed to sail through the darkness below the seas, a forlorn wanderer on borrowed time.

When he reached the main deck, Juan checked the depth gauge on his dive computer. He was down to eighty-three feet. The *Avalon* was sinking faster. Her borrowed time was running out.

He finned down to where the ROV hovered motionless outside the porthole where they'd spied the survivor. When he peered in through the small, round window, the trapped woman jumped back in fright. She quickly came forward again so an inch of water and a thick pane of glass separated their faces. If Juan didn't come up with something quick, the gulf would remain insurmountable.

She wore two jackets and several sweaters. Her hair was covered in a wool watchman's cap. The air inside the ship would be the same temperature as the water. A quick check told him fifty-one degrees. Her eyes were bright blue, and now that he'd arrived, they had lost their edge of madness. As desperate as she was, she still retained some semblance of humor, because she tapped her watch as if to say, *About time*. Juan admired her courage.

Then he took in the subtle details and noticed her lips were blue and her face an unnatural white. Her body quivered with uncontrollable paroxysms. He looked deeper into the cabin. Water completely covered the small room up to the level of the bed frames. One mattress floated free while the woman kept the other anchored with her weight. Yet even her refuge hadn't remained dry, and neither had her clothes. With her kneeling on the mattress, her weight formed a depression that pooled with seawater. No doubt her feet were soaked as well. Unable to know how long she'd been in this condition, he was certain she'd be hypothermic soon.

Juan removed his regulator and mouthed, 'Are you all right?' The seawater against his lips was bitterly salty, confirming his earlier supposition about how the *Avalon* had delayed her plunge to the bottom.

She gave him a flat stare as if to say he was nuts to ask, given the circumstances, then nodded to tell him she wasn't injured. He pointed at her and held up a finger, then pointed to other places on the ship, holding up more fingers. It took her a moment to realize he was asking if there were others with her. She shook her head sadly. Then she held up a finger and disappeared for a moment. When she returned she had a pad of paper and a black marker. Her hand shook so much her writing was barely legible. 'I'm the only one. Can you get me out?'

Juan nodded that he could, although he had no idea how. They could attach lines from the *Oregon*'s cranes to the research vessel and try to haul her to the surface, only the cranes had nowhere near the power to deadlift a sinking ship, and if they got the balance wrong, she could tilt and fill even faster than she was now. However, it would be worth getting some lines down to the *Avalon* so they could at least stabilize her for the time being.

The other divers reached Juan. He wrote out instructions on a slate one of them carried and sent the man back to the *Oregon*. He turned back to the trapped woman and winked. She wrote something on her pad and held it to the glass. 'Who are you?'

He wrote out his name. She flashed him a look of frustration and wrote 'Are you with the navy?'

Uh-oh. How could he explain their presence? He wrote back that he headed a private security company hired to bring the pirates to justice. She seemed satisfied. He asked her to describe where water hadn't yet flooded the *Avalon*. She wrote that the bridge deck was flooded and the bilge and engine room. Water had been climbing her deck for the past twelve hours. He asked if there were any exterior doors that he could open that would only flood a small room, an antechamber of some sort that could be isolated from the rest of the ship.

She wrote that she wasn't sure, then fell back onto the bed. Water welled up through the mattress around her backside and shoulders. The woman didn't seem to notice or no longer had the strength to do anything about it. Juan pounded the butt of his dive light against the hull to rouse her. She opened her eyes but barely registered his presence. She was slipping away. He pounded his light again, and the woman crawled to the porthole once more. Her eyes were glassy, and her jaw chattered like she was holding the business end of a jackhammer. He couldn't get her out without her help, and she was maybe five minutes away from unconsciousness.

'What is your name?' he wrote.

She stared at the words for a moment then mouthed something Juan couldn't understand. He shook his writing slab to remind her how they were communicating. It took her twenty seconds of intense concentration to write 'Tory.'

'Tory, you must stay awake!!! You sleep, you die. Is there a small room you can seal that has an exterior door?' He was afraid she was too far gone to understand the question, but her shoulders suddenly straightened, and she managed to clamp her jaw tight. She nodded and began to write. It took four minutes by Cabrillo's stainless Concord chronograph because she had to erase many of the words and start over.

She finally held her notebook to the porthole. The letters looked like a child's first attempt. She had written, 'Tne att port doon one dek op opons to a stoinwll thot can be sealecl.' It took Juan another precious minute to decipher the illegible scrawl. 'The aft port door one deck up opens to a stairwell that can be sealed.'

'You must go there and seal yourself in. Do not leave, no matter what. Trust me.'

Tory nodded and heaved herself off the bed. As she stood in the knee-deep water, agony etched itself across her features. Juan could almost feel the icy fingers of cold cramping her muscles and sending jolts to her brain. She lurched across the room, lost her balance, nearly caught herself against a bulkhead, then fell heavily. If he could have

98

squeezed through the porthole, Juan would have done so and gathered her up in his arms. As it was, he hung helplessly in the water as Tory slowly dragged herself to her feet. She was drenched. She staggered to the door without a backward glance, moving stiff-limbed like a zombie in a horror movie.

As soon as she was out of sight, Juan swam up to find the door she'd described. As he cleared the rail he saw four other divers working to attach a cable sling to the *Avalon*'s stern bollards. They had set up big underwater lights and worked efficiently in their glare. He imagined a team doing the same fore. The ship had now settled to a hundred feet. Even if the cranes couldn't lift the research vessel, having her secured to the *Oregon* would prevent her from sinking any deeper for a while.

But depth wasn't the problem. Tory's endurance was.

Unbeknownst to Cabrillo and his crew, the *Avalon* had large holds both fore and aft that stretched from her bilge to her main deck and almost the entire breadth of the ship. So far, they had remained dry, thanks to tightly dogged hatches and servo-controlled louvers on the ventilation system that sealed it nearly airtight. It was their buoyancy that aided in keeping the survey ship from free-falling into the depths. While Juan was scrutinizing the door, one of the tightly closed vents began to buckle under the increasing pressure of water that was bottled within the ventilation ducts behind it. A flat jet of water sprayed from a gap between two of the louvers. It fell in a fine mist almost all the way across the hold. The slit between the louver's metal fins was tiny, and only a few gallons per minute entered the hold – but every second saw the gap widening, and it was only a matter of time before the louver failed entirely, and a three-foot-square column of water roared into the hold.

The door, Juan noted, was a solid slab hinged from the outside. He could turn the handle freely once he'd removed a steel clamp that had been locked to prevent anyone from escaping during the initial raid. Only the pressure of the surrounding water kept him from drawing it open. To do that he needed to equalize the pressure on both sides. And to do that, he had to flood the antechamber on the other side with Tory trapped inside. It was a straightforward concept, and while Tory was in for the fright of her life as the room filled with water, Juan would have her out and breathing off a spare scuba tank before she was in any real danger.

He motioned over one of his divers and wrote what he needed on his slab. This man wore a full helmet with an integrated communications system that allowed him to talk with the dive master aboard the *Oregon*. Juan tapped the beat of 'Shave and a Haircut' on the door while he waited for both Tory and his delivery from the ship. Waiting for either was interminable, but when the basket of tools and dive equipment was lowered from above and Tory still hadn't arrived, Juan began to fear the worst.

Being trapped anywhere with the bodies of her friends littering the hallways was bad enough. Adding to the psychological stress was the fact that her prison was a hundred feet underwater and continuing to sink. It was amazing Tory hadn't gone catatonic days ago. She was frightened, near hypothermic, and now soaking wet. Did she have it in her to reach the antechamber and remember to seal the room from the rest of the ship?

Cabrillo had his doubts. But there was no other way. Her cabin door would have burst and flooded the ship had they cut their way into the room. She would have drowned long before they could have made a hole big enough to even pass her a regulator. No, he thought, this was the only plan that could work.

He tapped his rhythm against the steel with his light again and again. Then he thought he heard something from within the ship. He tapped again, 'Shave and a Haircut,' pulled off his hood, and pressed his ear against the door.

There. The unmistakable reply. Tap tap. *Two bits*. She'd made it.

He reached into the basket of tools he'd requested from the *Oregon*. First, he checked that the spare scuba tanks were ready. Next came the drill, which fed off two compressed air cylinders slung under the wire-mesh cage and attached by a long hose. The tip was specially hardened and at the RPMs generated by the air tanks would cut through the door in seconds. Cabrillo looked around. The divers at the stern must have finished securing the cable sling to the *Avalon*. A pair of them went to help those working at the bow while another two came over to help him.

Cabrillo braced his back against the heavy basket, pressed the drill bit near the bottom of the door, and pulled the trigger. The piercing whine was like actually standing on a tooth while a dentist went after a particularly nasty cavity. It drove spikes through his ears that met in the middle in a blinding point of pain. He ignored it and watched silver slivers of metal curl away from the drill point. In just a few seconds the tip bored through, and Juan carefully removed the drill from the hole. Water and bits of the shavings were sucked into the ship. He didn't know the size of the antechamber and couldn't guess how long it would take to fill, so all he could do was wait until the pressure had equalized enough for him to open the door.

He used a metal pry bar to tap at Tory and tell her he was with her. Her reply came instantly and angrily. She hadn't expected that this was how she'd be rescued.

After four minutes, Juan pulled at the door with the pry bar, but it remained sealed tight, so he drilled two more holes and tried again every minute afterward with the same result. He was about to drill a few more to hurry the operation when something happened.

A sudden gush of bubbles exploded from someplace ahead of the superstructure. The louver in the fore hold had given way, and thousands of gallons a minute poured into the derelict. The quick rise in pressure had popped an inspection hatch on the main cargo hatch. The six divers working at the bow appeared from over the *Avalon*'s squat funnel, fighting their way through the maelstrom of bubbles and surging water. One of them made a cutting gesture across his throat as soon as he was within the circle of light cast by the undersea lamps. They hadn't completed securing the forward sling.

In moments the *Avalon* began to drop by the head. And then she started to roll to port. The divers had managed to secure only the starboard side of the sling. The *Avalon* was held to the *Oregon* by three cables, two aft and one forward. For a few moments the ship appeared to stabilize, but her off-kilter angle allowed water to enter from other places. The crane operators on the *Oregon,* no doubt supervised by Max, gamely tried to hold the ship steady for as long as they could, but it was a losing battle.

Cabrillo had floated free from the deck in those first frantic seconds but quickly dropped back to the door. The basket of tools had slid all the way to the scupper. He motioned for one of his men to retrieve it while he hauled on the unyielding hatch.

Tory would have been tossed around inside the antechamber when the ship torqued over, and her new angle meant she'd have to tread water until he could get the door open. It was a race against the clock, and time had just accelerated.

The cable sling at the bow was looped to one of the ship's mushroom-shaped cast-steel bollards. The free end was caught in a jet of air bubbles and danced around the rigging holding the *Avalon*'s forward mast. Because of the uneven load, the cable pulled at the top of the bollard and started to slip off. The steel strands rasped as they were drawn over the top of the bollard, a pitiable cry like a mountain climber at the moment his grip slips from a rock face.

With water gushing into the forward hold, the cable remained taut for a few seconds more before sliding off the bollard. The *Avalon*'s bow plummeted, tilting the ship through ninety degrees until she dangled nose down from the straining crane aboard the *Oregon,* her knife-edged prow pointing into the abyss. Rated for sixty tons, the crane was probably fighting to hold three times that weight, and every second increased the strain.

Because of water resistance, the ninety-degree rotation had taken a few seconds, long enough for Juan to clutch the door as the deck became a wall and the aft bulkhead became the floor. Then there came a scraping sound, one that tore through the water and seemed to come from every direction. Juan frantically looked around for the source. The light towers his crew had erected were still tumbling across the deck, creating a nightmare effect of glare and blackness.

The sound grew louder. Juan glanced up to see a lifeboat that had pulled free from its davits hurtling down the length of the ship. He dove to the side as it raced past, its momentum pulling at him like a whirlpool. The davit cables trailing the lifeboat were a thick tangle of inch-thick rope that caught him just as he looked back to see if his people had avoided the speeding projectile. The knot of rope slammed into the back of his head, tearing off his face mask.

He fought the pain and disorientation, groping for the mask as it swirled in the back eddies. He opened his eyes, the sting of salt worse than any he'd ever felt. But there, just beyond his fingers, the orange mask was slipping into the depths. He grabbed it, snapped it back over his face, purging it by tilting his head and allowing air from his regulator to expel the water. He swam back to the door, checking his wrist computer. The *Avalon* was sinking at ten feet a minute and accelerating. He knew Max would run out every foot of cable on the *Oregon* to slow her descent, but there were limits to how deep they could breathe off compressed air.

The other diver had been thrown violently when the ship upended. It took him a few moments to clear his head and find the tool chest where it had lodged against the rail near the ship's jack staff. He didn't bother with the drill and instead concentrated on taking the spare air tank and a dive bag up to the chairman.

Together they heaved against the door with the pry bar. A curtain of bubbles exploded around the seam for a second. They'd managed to open it a crack, but pressure slammed it closed again. They pulled harder. Juan felt as though the muscles of his back were being stripped from his bones, and black stars exploded behind his tightly closed eyes. Just as he was about to stop and shift to a new position, the door swung open, instantly flooding the last of the interior space.

The powerful lights they'd set on the aft deck had either smashed themselves to pieces or were lost over the fantail, so all he had was his trusty dive light. He swung the beam around the antechamber. The space was cramped, painted a drab white. A set of metal stairs dropped to a solid-looking hatch that had once led to the bridge deck. Another door to the right that gave access to the interior of the main deck had also been secured. Then he saw Tory, a dark drifting shape of sodden clothes and loose limbs. Her hair fanned around her head like an anemone on a tropical reef.

In two swift kicks Juan was at her side. He slid his regulator past her slack lips and upped the airflow, trying to force the precious gas into her lungs. The other diver joined him and ripped open his dive bag. As fast as he could work, he plucked fistfuls of chemical warming packs from the bag, shook them violently to start the reaction, and stuffed them under Tory's clothes. They had several decompression stops to make on their ascent, and this was the only way Juan could think of to protect her from the biting cold.

He took back his regulator to take a quick breath before again feeding it to Tory. A third diver joined them. A knot was forming on her head from where she'd struck it against something, most likely when the ship rotated, and a fine feather of blood stained the water around the welt. He had the spare tanks and a dive helmet. Juan placed it over Tory's head and gave her sternum a sharp rap. Tory coughed into the helmet, a small amount of water pooling around her neck. Her eyes fluttered open, and she retched again. Juan used his regulator to purge the water from her helmet and kept his eyes locked on hers as she slowly came back. He knew she was going to be okay when she realized a stranger had his hand down her pants.

Other divers appeared. They guided Tory and Juan out of the room. One checked Cabrillo's tanks. He'd been down the longest and working the hardest. He was okay for now but would need fresh tanks during the decompression. Once they had swum far enough from the dangling survey ship, one of the men sent word to the *Oregon* that they could release the doomed vessel. A moment later, her slow downward plunge turned into a runaway plummet, and the *Avalon* slipped from view. The severed ends of cable trailed behind her like steel tentacles.

The team ascended in a tight group centered around Tory and Juan. The dive master shaved as much time as he dared from their stops, but it was still ten minutes before the freshest divers could guide Tory up into the moon pool and another fifteen before Juan and the others allowed deckhands to drag them onto the metal deck plating.

Juan stripped off his mask and dive hood, taking great gulps of air. The moon pool smelled of machinery oil and metal but tasted as sweet as a clear mountain morning. Max appeared at Juan's side, handing over a mug of steaming coffee. 'Sorry, old friend, no booze until all the nitrogen has dissolved out of your blood.'

Cabrillo was about to tell Hanley he would risk it for the worst case of bends in history, but he tasted the coffee and savored the sting of Scotch Max had laced it with.

He let Max help him out of his gear. Then he tried to get to his feet. 'How is she?' he asked, his voice weak and thin from the cold.

Max put a restraining hand on his shoulder. 'She's with

Julia. We'll know for sure soon, but I think she's going to be okay.'

Juan sagged back against an equipment rack with a tired and satisfied smile. At least they'd snatched one of the pirates' victims from certain death. Then he noticed several deckhands eating premium ice cream from pint containers. He knew why. Julia needed room in the big freezer for the victims they were too late to save.

# 8

Consciousness slowly congealed for Tory Ballinger through the haze of pain. She first became aware that every inch of her body ached, but it was a shin and her head where the agony appeared centered. The rest was low-grade throbbing. She levered open her eyes, blinking rapidly to clear them of sleep. Above her a fluorescent light shone with indifferent intensity. More light streamed through a nearby porthole. Three people were leaning over her. She didn't recognize them but somehow knew they were not a threat. The woman wore a doctor's white coat, and her dark eyes were filled with compassion and competence. One of the men was older, early sixties, and looked kindly. His features were weathered, and his bald head was blotchy, as though he'd spent a great deal of time outdoors. The unlit pipe at the corner of his mouth reminded her of her grandfather, Seamus. It was the second man who held her attention. The lines etched into the corners of his eyes and along his wide mouth weren't the inevitable effects of age. They had been chiseled into his skin by hard-won experience. They were the marks of someone who had struggled with life, someone who treated it as a day-to-day battle. Then she noted his eyes, blue and bottomless, with just a hint of humor, and she knew he won more of life's battles than he lost.

She felt as though she knew the man or should know who he was. He wasn't an actor. Perhaps he was one of those billionaire adventurers who flew hot-air balloons around the world or paid to be launched into space. He certainly had that roguish presence about him, a confidence borne out by a history of success.

'Welcome back,' the female doctor said. She was American. 'How do you feel?'

Tory tried to speak and managed only a hoarse croak. The older gentleman produced a cup and tenderly held the straw to her lips. The water soaked into her tongue like the first rain on a desert. She sucked greedily, relishing at how the liquid sluiced away the sticky coating in her mouth.

'I think –' Tory began but started to cough. When she was finished, she cleared her throat. 'I think I'm okay. Just cold.'

For the first time she realized she was under a mound of blankets, and the one closest to her body was electrically warmed. It made her skin prick.

'When you were brought here, your core temperature was about two degrees colder than the charts say you can survive. You're very lucky.'

Tory looked around.

'This is a shipboard infirmary,' the doctor answered her unasked question. 'My name is Julia Huxley. This is Max Hanley and our captain, Juan Cabrillo.' Again Tory felt she knew the man. His name seemed so familiar. 'It was the captain who rescued you.'

'Rescued?'

'Do you remember what happened?' the man named Hanley asked.

Tory thought hard. 'There was an attack. I was asleep. I heard gunfire. That's what woke me. I remember hiding in my cabin. Then I . . .' She lapsed into frustrated silence.

'It's okay,' Captain Cabrillo said. 'Take your time. You've been through a hell of an experience.'

'I remember wandering around the ship after the attack.' Tory suddenly buried her face in her hands, sobbing. The captain placed a hand on her shoulder. It steadied her. 'Bodies. I remember seeing bodies. The whole crew was dead. I don't recall anything after that.'

'It's not surprising,' Dr Huxley said. 'The mind has defensive mechanisms that act to protect us from trauma.'

The captain spoke. 'After your ship was attacked, the pirates scuttled it. We happened along before it sank too deeply for us to rescue you.'

'It was a near thing,' Max Hanley added. 'A couple of days had passed since the attack. Your vessel was held steady in a highly saline band of water.'

'Days?' Tory exclaimed.

'Think of yourself as Jonah,' Juan Cabrillo said with a warm smile. 'Only we had to rescue you from the whale's belly.'

Tory's eyes widened. 'I remember you now! I saw you in my porthole. You swam down to get me.'

Cabrillo made a self-deprecating gesture as if to say it was no big deal.

'It was you who told me to go to the aft hatchway and close the watertight doors. And it must have been you who drilled holes into the hatch. I thought you were going to kill me, and I almost ran back to my cabin before I realized you had to equalize the pressure so you could get me out. That was the worst. The water level rising inch by inch. I climbed the steps up to the bridge deck to stay out of it for as long as I could, but then there was no place to go.'

She paused as if feeling the agony of the freezing water all over again. 'I waded in when it was already up to my chest. It took forever. God, I've never been so cold in my life. I'm surprised my teeth didn't shatter from chattering so hard.' She looked up at the trio standing around her bed. 'The next thing I knew was just now, waking up here.'

'Your ship began to sink much faster, and it tilted in the water as the bow section flooded. You must have been tossed against a railing or pipe and hit your head. When I finally got the door open, you weren't breathing, and you had a gash in your scalp.'

Tory touched for the spot on her head and felt a thick bandage.

'We've already contacted the Royal Geographic Society,' Cabrillo went on, 'and I'm sure they've told your family that you're okay. A charter helicopter is standing by in Japan to get you to a proper hospital as soon as we're in range. Are you sure you don't remember anything else about your attack? It's very important.'

Tory's face scrunched with concentration. 'No, I'm sorry, I don't.' She looked to Julia. 'I think you're right. My brain has blocked it all out.'

'Last night when you were brought aboard you spoke to the ship's third officer. Her name is Linda Ross. Do you remember talking to her?'

'No,' Tory replied a little testily. 'I must have been delirious.'

Cabrillo went on despite a warning glance from Julia. 'You told her your name and said you were a researcher. You went on to talk about the attack and said one of the pirates searched your cabin while you were hiding. You told Linda he wore a black uniform and black combat boots.'

'If you say so.'

'You also told her that you saw two other ships nearby. You said that you thought one of them was an island at first because it was so big. You described it as being perfectly rectangular. The other ship was smaller, and it appeared the two were going to collide.'

'If I don't remember being trapped on the *Avalon* for four days, I certainly don't remember what happened minutes after the attack. I'm sorry.' She turned to Julia. 'Doctor, I think I'd like to rest now.'

'Of course,' Julia said. 'My office is just outside your room. Call if you need anything.'

'Thank you.' Tory gave Juan an odd look. It passed quickly, and she said, 'And thank you for saving my life.'

He touched her shoulder again. 'You're very welcome.'

'Helluva looker,' Max remarked when he and Cabrillo were in the corridor outside the medical bay.

'Helluva liar,' Juan said.

'She's that, too.' Max tapped his pipe stem against his big teeth.

'Why, do you think?'

'That she's a good liar or that she lied to us at all?'

'Both.'

'Haven't a clue,' Max said. 'I'm just glad Linda had the foresight to debrief Miss Ballinger last night.'

'I wouldn't have thought of it,' Juan admitted.

'The shape you were in, I'm amazed you even found your cabin.'

'Linda said the way Tory described the ships and the pirates' uniforms made her think our passenger might have some military training.'

'Or she's a researcher, just as she and the Royal

Geographic Society claim, and she applies her scientific observation skills to everything she encounters.'

'Then why lie and say she doesn't remember what happened to her when she was trapped on the *Avalon*?' Juan's gaze turned somber. 'No one told her how long she was down there, and yet she knew exactly how many days. There's something more to her than she's letting on.'

'We can't force her to tell us, and we can't hold her. The chopper that the RGS chartered is going to be here in a few hours.'

Juan went on as if he hadn't heard Hanley's comment. 'And uniforms. She said her pirates wore black uniforms. The guys we tangled with last night wore mostly jeans, shorts, and T-shirts. None of this adds up.'

They entered the operations center. Linda Ross was the officer on duty. She was seated at the command station munching on a bagel sandwich. 'How'd it go?' she asked around a mouthful of food, realized the gaffe, and tried to cover her mouth with a napkin. 'Sorry,' she mumbled.

'Put yourself down for employee of the month,' Juan said. 'Talking to Tory last night was a stroke of genius. Today she claims she doesn't remember anything, not the ships, not the uniforms, not even how she passed the time after the *Avalon* sank. Which reminds me, she didn't get a good look at the moon pool, did she?'

'No, Julia was quick with a hot towel to wrap her face as soon as she was lifted from the water. She really didn't start talking until we were in medical and Hux had started to warm her up. She was still the color of a blue jay and shaking like a leaf, but she was pretty damned sure about what she saw. She made me repeat that the big ship had a rectangular silhouette. Now she doesn't recall any of it?'

'We're pretty sure she remembers all right, only she's not telling,' Max said.

'Why not?'

Juan checked a duty roster clipboard. 'That's the million dollar question. Answer it, and you'll get an employee parking spot.'

'Nice perk except my car's about ten thousand miles away at a garage in Richmond.' Linda turned serious. 'Like I told you when we spoke this morning, I got the sense that Tory was trying to brief me as though I were her case officer.'

Juan didn't question her assessment. With her background in naval intelligence, Linda had been in on many such debriefings and would recognize the situation. 'She wasn't sure if she was going to live, so she had to tell someone what she knew.'

Linda nodded. 'That's what it felt like.'

'And now she knows she's going to be okay, so she clams up. Sounds to me like Miss Ballinger is much more than a humble marine researcher.'

'Which would explain how she managed to survive her ordeal without losing her mind,' Max added.

Far from a simple operation to rid the Sea of Japan of piracy, Juan realized they were in the middle of something far larger. If Tory was to be believed, and there wasn't anything much more sincere than a deathbed confession, there were two sets of pirates in these waters: those that belonged to the ragtag band they'd engaged the night before and the men in the black uniforms who had assaulted the *Avalon*. Tory had told Linda they had been systematic and quick. That made them sound more like commandos than the undisciplined thugs who'd tried to overwhelm the *Oregon*. Then there were the mystery ships Tory spotted at the moment of her attack. He didn't know their role in all of this. And what of the hapless Chinese immigrants locked in the cargo container? Had they paid the ultimate price for being in the wrong place at the wrong time, or were they somehow involved?

He couldn't understand why Tory refused to cooperate. If she was as lucid during her rescue as he thought she was, then she'd remember what he'd written on the dive slate. He'd told her he was part of a security firm tasked to combat piracy. Did that agenda somehow interfere with whatever she was doing? It didn't seem likely, but how could he not consider it? None of it made sense.

He decided it was best that they get her off the *Oregon* as soon as possible so they could resume the hunt on their own. He had every confidence that his people would unravel this mystery and get to the bottom of what was really happening.

Mark Murphy wasn't on watch, but Cabrillo was glad to see him at the weapons station. Today he wore a concert shirt from a band called Puking Muses. Given Mark's taste in music, Juan wasn't surprised he'd never heard of them and was again thankful his cabin was nowhere near that of the young weapons specialist. Juan caught his eye. Murph took off his headphones, and even from across the room Cabrillo could hear his music, some techno-industrial sound played at a volume that could crack plaster.

'Up for a little research, Murph?'

'Sure thing. What have you got?'

'I'm looking for a ship that's large enough to be mistaken for an island and has a completely rectangular silhouette.'

'That it?' Murphy was clearly looking for something a little more to go on.

'It would have been in this area four days ago.'

Cabrillo misunderstood Murphy's disappointment. He wanted more of a challenge. 'So I'm looking for either a big container ship, a supertanker, or perhaps an aircraft carrier.'

'I doubt it's a carrier, but punch it into the search parameters anyway.'

Any station on the bridge had access to the *Oregon*'s mainframe computer, so Mark remained at his seat as he pulled up a maritime database for tracking shipping in the Sea of Japan. He remained hunched over his keyboard, his foot tapping the rhythm of the music pouring in over his headphones.

'What's the status on the chopper from Japan?'

'ETA is three hours,' Linda answered. Because there was so much traffic in the area – five ships were within the *Oregon*'s one hundred mile radar – they couldn't risk exposing themselves by fully exploiting her mammoth engines. The tramp steamer was only making twenty-two knots, delaying the rendezvous with the chartered helicopter.

'Okay, I'm going back to my cabin to inform Hiro Katsui that his consortium owes us two million bucks. Call me if Mark gets a hit or when the chopper's ten miles out.'

'Aye, Chairman.'

The screen saver had been pinging geometric shapes across the liquid crystal screen for an hour and a half as Juan sat at his desk, staring sightlessly at his computer. So far he had written exactly eleven words of his report to Hiro. Even discounting Tory's reticence, nothing fit the way Juan expected. Had a commando team attacked the *Avalon,* and if so, why? The most likely answer was to prevent the crew from seeing what was taking place on the other two ships.

Could Mark be right about an aircraft carrier, and this was a government operation?

The problem was the only naval force in the area that had any carriers was the United States. China wanted to buy an old Russian flattop, but as far as Juan knew, they were still negotiating, and there was no way pirates could have gotten their hands on one. He was sure it was some other type of vessel that Tory saw. He didn't discount the possibility that her ship was attacked by trained commandos, only he had no idea how they fit with the pirates Hiro had hired the Corporation to wipe out. Were they working together?

His intercom buzzed. 'Juan, it's Julia. Can you come down to my office?'

Thankful to escape the answerless questions swirling round and round in his head, he left his cabin and made his way down to medical.

He found her in the trauma bay, an equipment-packed room as modern as any level-one ER. The temperature was a cool sixty-five. A sheet-draped body lay on a gurney under brilliant lights. Julia wore green surgical scrubs. Her gloved hands were smeared with blood. Powerful ventilators prevented odors from building up inside the room, yet Juan could still sense the lingering smell of decay.

'One of the Chinese immigrants?' he asked, nodding at the shrouded form.

'No, one of the pirates. Want to take a look?'

Juan said nothing as Julia peeled back the sheet. Death never looked more ignoble, especially with the large sutured Y-incision Julia had cut to examine inside the chest and abdomen. The pirate was young, twenty at most, and skinny to the point of starvation. His hair was lank black, and his fingers and the bottoms of his feet were thickly callused.

The pair of sneakers he'd worn when boarding the *Oregon* were probably stolen during a previous raid and were the first he'd ever owned. There was a single neat bullet hole in the middle of his forehead, an obscene third eye that was puckered around the edges.

Cabrillo couldn't discount the brutality of what the pirates had done, but he also couldn't help feeling a little pity as well. He had no idea what circumstances drove the boy to crime, but he felt the kid should have been with his family, not laid out on a slab like a dissected specimen.

'So what have you learned?' he asked after Julia drew the sheet back over the corpse's head.

'This guy's dead.'

'Well, since you performed an autopsy, I assumed he would be.'

'What I mean is if he hadn't taken a shot to the skull, he would have died anyway, probably within the next few months.' She waved him over to a computer workstation. On the screen were spectrograph lines of a sample Julia had run. He had no idea what he was looking for. His puzzled expression prompted an explanation.

'Hair sample run through optical emission spectrometer.' The Corporation had bought the million-dollar piece of equipment not only for Julia's medical bay but also for analyzing trace evidence. It had been key a year earlier tracking a missing shipment of RDX explosives. 'During my exam,' Julia explained, 'I noticed some pretty significant symptomatology. For one, he was about to suffer complete renal failure. Also, he's anemic as hell; his gums are severely inflamed with late-stage gingivitis. I noted lesions all along his digestive tract and bloody crusts in both nostrils. It made me think of something, and the hair sample proved it.'

'What's that?'

'This guy had had long-term exposure to toxic levels of mercury.'

'Mercury?'

'Yep. Without treatment, the mercury, like other heavy metals, builds up in tissue and hair. It eventually shuts the body down, but not before causing madness as it deteriorates the brain. I bet if you recheck the video of the pirate attack, you'll see these guys fought with little regard for their own lives. The level of mercury contamination would have impaired this one's judgment to the point where he'd fight on, no matter what.'

'Some of them tried to escape,' Juan pointed out.

'Not all of them had such elevated or prolonged exposure.'

'What about the Chinese?'

'I only checked one for toxicity, and she came up clean.'

'But this guy's riddled with mercury?'

'You could fill a couple of thermometers off him. I checked two of his compatriots quickly and found the same thing. I bet they're all suffering to one degree or another.'

Juan ran a hand across his jaw. 'If we find the source of the mercury, we might find the pirates' lair.'

'Stands to reason,' Julia agreed, stripping off her gloves with a sharp snap. She removed her surgical cap and redid her ponytail with a well-practiced twist. 'You can get mercury poisoning by eating contaminated fish, but the risk's mostly to children and women who want to conceive. But with the levels I'm seeing here, I'd put my money on these guys basing themselves someplace close to a contaminated industrial site or an old mercury mine.'

'Any idea if there are such mines in this area?'

'Hey, my job's medical mysteries and patching you cutthroats back together,' Julia teased. 'You want geology lessons, call on someone else.'

'How about their ethnic background? That might help narrow the search.'

'Sorry. The fifteen pirates I have on ice are a veritable United Nations. This one looks Thai or Vietnamese. Three others are either Chinese or Korean, two Caucasians, the others are Indonesian, Filipino, and a mix of everything else.'

'Super,' Juan said acidly. 'We have the luck to run across a bunch of politically correct pirates who believe in diversity. Anything else?'

'That's it for now. I need a few more days to finish up everything.'

'How's your other patient?'

'Sleeping. Or at least pretending to so she doesn't have to talk to me. I get the feeling she wants off this tub ASAP.'

'Why am I not surprised? Thanks, Hux.'

Juan had only just gotten back to his cabin and ordered a lunch of steak and kidney pie when Mark Murphy knocked at his door. 'What do you have, Murph?'

'I think I found her.'

'Have a seat. So is it a bulk carrier of some kind or a container ship?'

'Neither.' Mark handed over a thin file. Inside was a single photograph and a half-page description.

Juan glanced at the picture and gave Murphy a questioning look. 'You sure?'

'She's on her way to Taiwan from Oratu, Japan, where she was used for a refit of a Panamanian tanker that threw a prop during a storm.'

Juan looked at the picture again. The vessel was 800 feet long and 240 feet wide. Just as Tory had described, the ship was completely rectangular, with no rake to her bow or stern and nothing protruding from her deck to alter her flat profile. Juan read what Mark had managed to learn about the odd craft. She was the fourth-largest floating drydock in the world. Built in Russia to service massive Oscar II–class submarines like the ill-fated *Kursk,* she had been sold to a German salvage firm a year ago but had then been sold again to an Indonesian shipping company who chartered it out like a service station wrecker.

Juan's pulse quickened.

Using a drydock to hijack an entire ship at sea was truly inspired but also frightening in scope and sophistication. His deep fear about a leader uniting pirates across the Pacific into a coherent group might well be the tip of the iceberg. With a drydock this size, they could snatch nearly any ship they wanted.

He pictured how they'd pull it off. First a team of pirates would need to board their intended target in order to subdue the crew. Then they would sail their captured ship to rendezvous with the drydock. Under the cover of night, and only when weather conditions were favorable, because it would be dicey work, the drydock would ballast down so the bottom of its open hold was lower than the keel of their stolen ship. Big winches at the stern of the drydock would then reel in the vessel. The bow doors would swing closed, ballast pumped out, and the tugs towing the drydock would continue on their way. Without a direct overflight, no one would ever know that inside the drydock was the booty of the most audacious pirate ring in history.

'Pretty slick, hey boss?'

'Yeah.'

'They come along and swallow up their victim.' Mark gave an animated pantomime of the action as he spoke. 'Haul it to their secret base. They'd have all the time in the world to offload the cargo before dismantling it. Rather than scavenge like hyenas, these guys are taking down their prey like lions.'

'Why dismantle the ship?' Cabrillo mused aloud. 'Why not make some changes to it, alter a few characteristics, paint a new name on her stern, and either sell her off or sail her for themselves?'

'I hadn't thought of that, but that makes even more sense.'

'So what do we know about the company that owns the drydock? Wait, what's it called?'

'The drydock?' Murphy asked and Cabrillo nodded. *'Maus.'*

'German for mouse. Cute. So, the company?'

'Occident and Orient Lines. O&O. They've been around for like a hundred years. Used to be publicly traded, but in the past decade most of the shares have been bought up by entity or entities unknown.'

'Shell companies?'

'So hollow even their names ring false. D Commercial Advisors LLC. Ajax Trading LLC. Equity Partners International LLC. Financial Assay –'

'LLC,' Juan finished for him. Then a thought struck. 'Wait. *Assay* is a mining term. Julia said the pirates were dying of mercury poisoning, and we both think they might be based near an abandoned mercury mine. I wonder if this Financial Assay owns mines in the region.'

'I haven't even started digging into the shell companies

yet. I thought you'd want to know about the drydock right away.'

'No, you're right, but you've got a lot more to research. I want to know who owns the *Maus* – not the corporate veil but the actual guy who holds the pink slip.'

'What are we going to do about the drydock? If what that British woman said is true, there might be a stolen ship in her hold and maybe some crew held hostage.'

'The most powerful tugs in the world can't tow a vessel the size of *Maus* at more than six or seven knots. How long do you think their head start's gonna last when we're pushing fifty?'

Murph grinned like a teenager given the keys to a Ferrari. He got up to leave.

Juan came to a quick decision. He knew at some point he was going to have to split his forces. The *Oregon* was a perfect platform for espionage operations, but he needed the flexibility of people on the ground with access to jet travel. He had no idea where this case was going to take him. Most likely Indonesia, if that was where O&O still kept an office, so now was the time to get assets en route.

'Do me a favor and find Eddie Seng. Tell him to pack up some gear. We'll be going international, so nothing that can't pass airport security. Have him pick two of his men. We're hitching a ride on Tory Ballinger's helicopter to go hunting hyenas and lions.'

'But where?'

Juan tapped Mark's report. 'Have an answer by the time we land in Japan.'

# 9

Anton Savich would have preferred meeting Shere Singh at his office in a downtown Jakarta high-rise, but the stubborn Sikh demanded they meet at the site of Singh's latest venture, across the Sunda Strait on Sumatra. Savich had developed a healthy fear of flying after crisscrossing the Soviet Union for years on Aeroflot and would have taken a ferry despite Indonesia's dismal maritime safety record but was saved when Singh offered him use of his company helicopter.

He looked out the yellowed Plexiglas at the strip of beach below the chopper that seemed to guard the jungle from the sea. It was a primeval landscape, and the villages that flashed under him looked as though they hadn't changed in generations. The wooden fishing boats clustered in secluded bays had likely been built by the grandfathers of the men who sailed them today. The land to his left was hidden by an impenetrable canopy of vegetation that had yet to fall to slash-and-burn farming or industrial timber cutting. To his right, the sea was clear blue and pristine. A double-masted schooner, a coastal freighter he assumed, cut through the light swells with her sails bellied taut by the trade winds. She looked as though she'd sailed out of the nineteenth century.

How could a people who had known such a paradise as the archipelago create a city like Jakarta with its eighteen million people, gridlocked traffic, crime, poverty, disease, and smog as thick and noxious as a World War One mustard gas attack? In their rush to modernize, the Indonesians had embraced the worst of what the West had to offer and then abandoned the best of their own culture. They'd created a patchwork of consumerism, corruption, and burgeoning religious fanaticism that teetered on the brink of collapse. Through contacts, Savich had learned that the United States had clandestinely stationed more than a thousand soldiers on the islands to help train local forces to fight the twenty-first-century war.

The pilot tapped Savich's arm and pointed ahead. He grudgingly looked away from the peaceful sailing ship and focused his attention on their destination. The complex was hidden in a bay by a rocky promontory, so all he could see was the flotilla of ships lying at anchor. Even from this distance and altitude he could tell they were derelicts, the steel husks of once-proud vessels that had outlived their usefulness. Several were wreathed in shimmering halos of their own spilled bunker fuel, like murdered corpses surrounded by their own blood and waste. One had lain so long here that her keel had succumbed to corrosion. Her bow and stern both pointed skyward with her crushed stack vised in between like a nut in a giant cracker. A quarter way to the horizon a line of oil containment boom cut a wide arc around the bay. There was an entrance gate manned by a pair of small tenders that could open the floating boom to allow the ship's entrance. No ships ever left the facility, at least by sea.

The chopper banked around the headland, and the Karamita Breakers Yard came into view. More ships of every size and description were moored within the bay like cattle in a chute headed for slaughter. A pair of super-tankers, each at least a thousand feet long, had been dragged up the sloping beach by a combination of tidal surges and huge winches. An army of men swarmed over the hulks, tips of glowing flame sparking whenever their cutting torches touched metal. A crane on wide crawler treads sat just at the surf line and plucked steel sections of hull as soon as they were sliced free. It swung them farther up the beach, where even more workers were ready to cut and beat the slabs into manageable chunks. Other teams of men ripped piping and electrical cables from within the ship's hull, eviscerating the supertanker as though they were dissecting a carcass for consumption

And in a sense they were. The smaller pieces of metal were transferred to railcars for the short journey northward to the Karamita Steel Works. There, the scrap was melted down and remilled into steel reinforcement bars for the never-ending construction boom going on in southern China. Behind the modern steel mill shimmered the artificial lake backed up behind Indonesia's largest hydroelectric plant, the engine that allowed for such heavy industry in an otherwise inhospitable jungle.

The once pristine sand that ringed the bay had turned into a black, tarry porridge that clung to the men's feet like clay. Beyond the oil boom the sea was reasonably protected, but inside the floating containment wall, the water was a toxic soup of oil, heavy metals, PCBs, and asbestos. Acres of land had been turned into storage yards littered with ships' boilers, mounds of lifeboats, an assortment of anchors, and hundreds of other items that could be resold on the open market. Behind the fenced lots rose dozens of drab dorm buildings little better than tenements. A squatters' camp of prostitutes, con men, and crooks had sprung up along the rail line to drain the workers of the few pennies a day they earned turning retired ships into scrap.

Savich noted that the forest behind the facility was slowly receding as thousands of workers cut the trees for their cooking fires. While the air was free of pollution because the mill ten miles north ran on hydro rather than coal or oil, an industrial pall hung over the breaker's yard, the miasma of its own corruption and filth.

But there was one modern element to the process, and this was doubtless what Shere Singh wanted Savich to see. On the far side of the tankers was a gleaming corrugated metal building nearly as large as the ships, with dozens of translucent panels on the tin roof to provide light within. Two-thirds of the eight-hundred-foot building was constructed out over the water on large pilings. Four sets of train tracks met the inland side, and as the chopper thundered over the facility Savich saw two pairs of small diesel engines haul a five-foot-long portion of a ship out of the building. He recognized the curve of the hull, the thick keel, and could see interior passages as though peering into a cutaway model. No, he thought, it reminded him of a slice taken from a loaf of bread. The cuts were straight, and the metal shone silvery in the tropical light. He couldn't fathom how something as large as a ship could be carved so perfectly.

The helicopter pad was several miles from the breaker's yard, protected from the din and smell by another promontory of naked rock. Around it were tended lawns and breezy bungalows for the supervisors, clerks, and skilled workers. An open jeep was waiting next to the landing zone, the driver standing by to help Savich with his luggage. The Russian had no desire to stay in Indonesia longer than necessary, so all he carried was a briefcase and a battered leather grip. The bulk of his luggage was in an airport locker.

He allowed the driver to put the bag in the back of the jeep but kept the calfskin case on his lap as they drove toward the breaker's yard.

It took a few moments for his hearing to return after an hour's flight in the helo, and when it did, his ears were assaulted by the racket of pneumatic cutting chisels, spadelike jackhammers, and the piercing throb of countless generators. The crane dropped a ten-ton slab of metal onto the beach with a dull thump, and seconds later men were hacking at it with sledgehammers and handheld electrical saws designed to cut steel. They wore little more than rags, and Savich could see their legs, chests, and arms were covered with dark scars from contact with hot, sharp metal. He saw more than one missing an eye, fingers, or part of a foot.

And then from the enclosed building came an unholy shriek that cut the air like a diamond being cleaved. It rose in pitch until Savich thought his head would shatter and continued on for a minute, then two. The driver offered him a pair of ear protectors, and he gratefully snugged them over his head. The noise was still there but low enough now that his eyes cleared of tears. To his amazement, the workers continued their tasks as though the screaming wasn't even there, and the driver seemed equally unfazed.

The jeep stopped outside the large warehouse structure just as the sound came to an abrupt end. Savich hadn't realized he'd held his breath. He let it out with a grateful whoosh and motioned to the driver if it was okay to remove the plastic and foam protectors. The Indonesian nodded.

'I am sorry,' he said formally in English. 'We are used to it.'

'What was that?' Savich asked.

'The ship saw,' he said and motioned Savich over to an exterior scaffold elevator that ran up the side of the ten-story building.

The driver handed Savich over to another worker. He was given a plastic hard hat with ear protectors that could be snapped into place. The worker slammed the elevator door closed, pressed a button, and waited patiently as the lift ascended the building. While not as impressive as the view flying in, Savich was amazed by the scale of Singh's operation. It looked as though the next ship to meet its fate after the rusting tankers had been rendered was a small white cruise ship that looked like a virgin bride amid a group of indigent hookers. A square hole had already been cut in her side, and a floating crane was transferring the vessel's desalinization unit to a waiting lighter.

The elevator reached the top, and the worker slid open two sets of doors. Savich recoiled at the stench of burned metal. When his eyes adjusted to the gloomy interior and he'd blinked away the effects of the fumes, he saw that the building was one huge open space with massive doors at both ends. Despite the size, it felt cramped because a large ship took up most of the volume. Or what was left of the ship.

The catwalk where they stood was almost directly in line with her bridge. Before being admitted into the shed, workers had cut away the ship's funnel and masts so she could fit inside. Nearly half the vessel had been lopped off, a neat line as though a giant guillotine had cut her clean. Large winches at the front of the building strained to drag the carcass up the inclined floor. Once in position, a mechanism on an overhead track lowered from the ceiling and tightened what looked like a large chain around the entire hull. Savich looked more closely. The chain was embedded with metal teeth like a flexible band saw.

'What do you think, my friend?' Savich's host called from the bridge of the derelict freighter.

Like all Sikhs, Shere Singh wore a long beard that covered the lower portion of his face that he tucked into his tightly wound turban. The hard hat perched precariously atop the white cloth looked like a child's toy helmet. His hair and beard were streaked with silver and discolored around his mouth from years of heavy smoking. His skin was nut brown and weathered, and he had intense, almost maniacal hazel eyes with a disconcerting tendency to stare unblinking. Singh was also at least six inches taller than Savich's five ten, with a barrel chest, shoulders as wide as a gallows' arm, and a heavy gut as solid as oak.

From a dossier provided by Bernhard Volkmann, Savich knew that the fifty-two-year-old Singh had raised himself up from a Lahore slum where from an early age he'd used his size and strength as tools of intimidation. He didn't have his first legitimate job until the age of twenty-six, when he purchased controlling interest in a Pakistani import-export company at the time the United States was funneling money into the region to counter the Soviet invasion of Afghanistan. Despite the conflict raging in that mountainous country, steady streams of opium smugglers still managed to get their product to Karachi, and Singh was more than willing to forward on their raw product to the heroin-producing centers in Amsterdam, Marseilles, and Rome.

Singh understood that American support guaranteed an Afghan win, so by the time the Taliban came into power and eradicated the opium trade, he had shifted his focus elsewhere. He diversified, using bribery to secure timber rights in Malaysia, Indonesia, and New Guinea. He bought a fleet of his own ships to haul the lumber. He sold private hunting rights to wealthy Chinese so they could harvest tigers on his land and have their bones ground into aphrodisiacs. Nearly every legitimate venture he embarked upon had an illegal angle to it. Four of the twelve apartment buildings one of his companies built in Taiwan collapsed during a mild earthquake because he'd ordered the use of substandard materials. So long as his wealth continued to increase, Shere Singh didn't care how or where he made his money.

No doubt, Savich thought as the Sikh stepped across to the catwalk, there was an illicit side to the Karamita Breakers Yard.

'Very impressive,' the Russian answered, looking at what the driver had called a ship saw and not bothering to meet Singh's reptilian gaze.

Singh lit a cigarette in front of a No Smoking sign. 'Only one like it in Asia,' he boasted. 'The trick to it is the teeth. Even carbon steel would wear out. The metal in the teeth was produced in Germany. Strongest in the world. We can cut ten ships before teeth need to be replaced. Have technician come from Hamburg to show us how. We call him dentist.' When Savich didn't laugh, Singh plowed on. 'You know, fix teeth. Dentist. Is very funny.'

Savich waved a hand to encompass the echoing shed. 'This must have been expensive.'

'You have no idea. But Indonesian government gave me tax credits if I modernize. Of course they don't think that I can fire a thousand workers because of this. Which is good thing. These monkeys are clumsy. Cost me a hundred thousand rupia to family every time some fool gets himself killed breaking ship. Fifteen die last week when a cutter didn't vent a bunker fuel tank and blew up a container ship in the bay.

'But now that I have the ship saw, government inspectors won't be around so much. I can start dumping all the asbestos we've stripped off ships back in ocean rather than haul to special dump. With the price of scrap ships down and the value of steel up, and a thousand Indonesian monkeys off my payroll, this will pay for itself in two years. So yes, expensive in short run. Profitable in long run.' Singh tried another smile. 'And I always say life is marathon.'

An alarm Klaxon sounded. Singh flipped the ear protectors down, and Savich just managed to get his into position when the eight-inch-wide saw blade began to rotate. It spooled up smoothly, rattling only when it ran around the two large sprocket gears near the ceiling. Like a boa constrictor squeezing its victim, hydraulic rams began to tighten the saw around the freighter five feet aft of the previous cut. When the chain reached its required speed, the rams choked back even farther, and the teeth bit into the ship's keel. The sound filled the metal shed, rebounding off the walls so it assaulted the two men on the catwalk from every direction. Water cannons on either side of the hull automatically tracked the toothed belt as it sliced the ship and kept the cuts lubricated and cool. Steel shavings and steam exploded from where the teeth ripped into the ship's keel, turning the metal red hot. The smoke coiling from the cut was dense and rank. Once through the solid keel, the saw shredded the much thinner hull plating like a chain saw cutting through rotted wood.

In just ten minutes the rotating chain had cut up to the main deck. Savich watched spellbound as the deck began to glow from the heat of the teeth cutting the metal, and then the chain emerged in an eruption of torn steel and cut through the freighter's railings as though they weren't there. A sophisticated braking system stopped the chain, and the entire mechanism retracted toward the ceiling. The dismembered section of hull had already been secured to a rolling crane that spanned the shed. The crane lifted the hull slice as the forward doors opened and the four small locomotives backed in to accept the load.

'They will lay the piece on its side out in the yard,' Singh explained. 'Men with hand cutters will chop it up to send to the steel plant. The only parts we can't cut with the saw are the ship's main diesels, but they are easy to remove once we cut our way into the engine room. By hand it takes two weeks to scrap a ship this size. We can do it in two days.'

'Very impressive,' Savich repeated.

Shere Singh led the Russian back toward the elevator. 'So what is it Volkmann sent you around the world to tell me?'

'We'll discuss it in your office.'

Fifteen minutes later they were seated in an office attached to the largest bungalow. Framed pictures of Singh's eleven children were arranged along one wall dominated by a studio portrait of his wife, a heavyset dowager of a woman with a bovine expression. Savich had declined a beer and drank bottled water instead. Singh drank through a bottle of Filipino San Miguel and was on his second by the time Savich had his briefcase opened.

'The consortium accepted everything Volkmann and I proposed,' Savich said. 'It's time to expand what we already started.'

The Sikh laughed. 'Was there any doubt?'

Savich ignored the sarcasm and slid across a file. 'These

are our projected needs for the next year. Can you fulfill them?'

Singh perched a pair of reading glasses on his large nose and scanned the list, mumbling the salient figures. 'An additional thousand immediately, two hundred a month first two months. Four hundred next two. Six hundred after that.' He looked across at the Russian. 'Why the increase?'

'Disease. By then we expect typhoid and cholera to run rampant.'

'Ah.'

Their discussion of specifics over the next several hours was Savich's way of making certain Singh fully understood the plan he and Volkmann had perfected since learning of the German central bank's intention to sell off their gold reserves. To his credit, or perhaps discredit, the Sikh had an inherent grasp of criminal enterprise and was even able to contribute a few inspired refinements.

Satisfied that everything on this end was handled, Savich said his good-byes two hours before sunset so as to have ample time to chopper back to Jakarta. There was no way he'd fly in the small helicopter after dark. He planned on staying in the city overnight before commencing the next leg of his journey, a roundabout odyssey of a half dozen flights to get him back to Russia. He wasn't looking forward to it.

Ten minutes after Savich left his office at the Karamita Breakers Yard, Shere Singh was on the phone to his son, Abhay. Because of the nature of his work, the senior Singh trusted only his sons to know the full scope of his business, which is why he had had six of them. His five daughters were merely a financial drain, one of whom hadn't yet married, meaning he still had her dowry to consider. She was the youngest and marginally his favorite, so he'd have to top the two million dollars he'd given the horse-faced Mamta.

'Father, we haven't heard from the *Kra IV* for two days,' Singh's eldest said after a brief exchange of pleasantries.

'Who is her captain?'

'On this voyage it was Mohamed Hattu.'

Singh was a reprehensible figure of a man, but that didn't mean he wasn't shrewd. He kept a tight rein on his enterprises and made it a point to know all his senior people. Hattu was a pirate of the old school who'd preyed on shipping in the Malacca Strait for twenty years before Singh made him an offer. He was audacious and reckless but also dogmatic about procedure. If he hadn't checked in for two days, something must have happened. And with that thought, Singh wrote off the *Kra IV,* her captain, and her crew of forty. 'There are others eager to take his place,' Shere Singh told his son. 'I will look into a replacement. However, alert your contacts to listen for any mention of a thwarted pirate attack. Whoever fought Mohamed Hattu and lived will want to tell the tale.'

'Yes, Father. I've thought of that. So far there have been no such reports.'

'On to other business. Anton Savich just left my office. The plan is in motion. I have his list of requirements. It's about what I anticipated.'

'On your order we've already begun to collect.'

'Yes, good. What about your men? Will they do what is necessary when the time is right?'

'Their loyalty is absolute. Savich and his European bankers will never know what hit them once we strike.'

The confidence in his son's voice sent a proud thrill

through Shere Singh. His boy was so much like him. He was sure that had Abhay not been born with wealth, he would have created his own fortune, clawing his way up like Shere had done in his youth.

'Good, my boy, good. They maneuvered themselves into a vulnerable position without even realizing it.'

'No, Father. You maneuvered them. You turned their fear and greed into action, and now it will consume them all.'

'No, Abhay, we don't want them destroyed. Remember always, you can continue to eat the fruit from a dying tree but not from one that is dead. Savich, Volkmann, and the others will suffer, but we will leave enough so we can feast on them for a long time to come.'

# IO

"You're going to wear a trail into the carpet,' Eddie Seng said from an overstuffed chair in the corner of the hotel room.

Juan Cabrillo remained silent as he paced to the plate glass window overlooking the dazzling lights of Tokyo's Ginza District. He paused there with his hands clasped behind his back, his broad shoulders rigid with tension. The *Oregon* was fast approaching the floating drydock named *Maus* and would be going into action soon. His place was on her bridge, not stuck in a hotel suite waiting for Mark Murphy to come up with something about the vessel's owners. He felt caged.

A driving rain blurred the view of the city from their thirtieth-floor room. It matched his mood.

Twenty-four hours had passed since stepping off the helicopter sent to fetch Victoria Ballinger. A representative from the Royal Geographic Society was on the windswept pad to meet the rented helo, a bearded man in a tan trench coat. From their body language it was clear to Juan that Tory and the representative had never met before. The man introduced himself as Richard Smith. While he thanked Juan for saving Tory, Cabrillo sensed he was reserved, almost wary. Tory was obviously grateful and gave Juan a kiss on the cheek as an orderly guided her to the private service ambulance Smith had arranged for her.

She had held up her hand just as she was about to be

placed into the ambulance, her blue eyes steady on Juan's. 'Last night I remembered something from the rescue,' she'd said.

*Uh-oh*, thought Cabrillo.

'When I was trapped in my cabin I asked if you were the navy, and you wrote back something about being a private security company. What was that all about?'

Smith was already settled on a jump seat in the back of the ambulance and had to lean out somewhat to hear the answer.

Juan paused, looking from her over to him, then back to Tory. 'I lied.'

'Excuse me?' She crossed her arms over her chest.

Cabrillo smiled. 'I said I lied. Had I told you I was the master of a rust-bucket freighter who happened to have fish-finding sonar and a few crewmen with scuba gear, would you have trusted me to get you out?'

Tory didn't speak for several long seconds, her gaze penetrating and doubting. She arched an eyebrow 'A fish finder?'

'The cook uses it when we're in port to catch dinner once in a while.'

'Then why was it on in the middle of the ocean?' Smith asked, his tone edged with accusation.

Juan kept his smile in place, playing the role. 'Just dumb luck, I guess. It went off when we passed over the *Avalon*. The watch stander happened to notice the dimensions of the target, realized we'd either discovered the biggest whale in history, or something wasn't right. I was called to the bridge and decided to turn about. The *Avalon* hadn't moved, so we discounted our monster whale theory. That's when I threw on my tanks and had a look.'

'I see.' Smith nodded. He wasn't entirely convinced, which made Juan even more certain that neither Tory nor the stiff Englishman were members of the Royal Geographic Society. His first thought was that they were Royal Navy and the *Avalon* was a spy ship, most likely in these waters monitoring North Korea or Russia's Pacific Fleet out of Vladivostok. But if that were the case, it meant the pirates were capable of approaching a modern combat vessel loaded with sophisticated electronics, taking out the crew in a lightning raid, and escaping undetected. Cabrillo just couldn't bring himself to believe that. Ex-Royal Navy then, perhaps using a ship belonging to the Society, but still out here on a mission of some kind.

'Then you must also thank the cook for me,' Tory said, nodding to the orderly to settle her in the ambulance.

Juan, Eddie, and the two former SEALs Eddie had selected were left on their own to arrange transportation. Rather than deal with hiring a car or finding a train station, they'd chartered the same helicopter that brought them from the *Oregon* to fly them to Tokyo, where Max Hanley had reserved a four-bedroom suite under one of the Corporation's front companies. And that is where they waited. The SEALs spent most of the time in the hotel's extensive fitness center, while Cabrillo paced the room, willing his cell phone to ring. Eddie took up guard duty, making sure his boss didn't damage the room out of frustration or boredom.

'They can bill me for a new rug,' Juan finally said without turning from the window.

'What about the ulcer you're giving yourself? I don't think Doc Huxley packed you any antacids.'

Cabrillo regarded Eddie. 'That's the pickled octopus I ate, not the stress.'

'Riiight.' Eddie returned to his English-language paper.

Cabrillo continued to stare out into the storm, his mind a million miles away. That wasn't entirely true. His mind was six hundred miles away, at his seat in the *Oregon*'s operations center. This wasn't the first time his ship had gone into battle without him, and it wasn't that he didn't trust his crew. He just felt a personal need to be part of the action as they went after the snakeheads.

*God,* he thought, *how old was I when I saw it?* He couldn't have been more than seven or eight. They were coming back from an aunt's house in San Diego. His dad was driving, of course, and Mom was in the other front seat: he remembered her shouting a warning to his dad about the traffic jam several seconds after he'd applied the brake. She'd immediately turned to check on him in the backseat. The quick deceleration hadn't even locked his seat belt, but she acted as though he had almost been launched through the windshield.

And for what seemed like forever, traffic inched along the highway. He remembered that for a while they were next to a car with a Saint Bernard in the backseat. It was the first time he'd seen one, and he'd been captivated by its size. To this day he still vowed that when he finally retired he'd own one of those huge dogs.

'Have you picked a name?' Eddie asked softly.

'Gus,' Juan answered automatically before realizing that he'd been telling the story out loud rather than in his head. He lapsed into an embarrassed silence.

'So what happened?' Seng prompted.

Juan knew he couldn't leave it there. His unconscious mind was telling him that this story had to come out. 'We finally approached the accident site. A car must have swerved and caused an eighteen-wheeler to jackknife. The trailer had detached and lay on its side, the rear doors facing the road. Only one police car had made it to the scene. The cop had already locked the truck's driver into his cruiser.

'One of the trailer's rear doors had popped open when it tipped, and the patrolman was helping the other victims of the crash. I have no idea how many, maybe a hundred Mexican workers had been in the trailer when it went over. Some were only slightly injured and helped the officer with the others. A few were better off and could walk from the wreckage. Others they had to drag. There were already two areas set aside. In one, women tended to the wounded. In the other, the bodies had been lined up in a straight row. My mother was very protective and told me not to look, but she said it softly as she stared at the carnage, unable to tear her eyes away. We passed the accident and soon were back up to speed.

'No one spoke for a few minutes. My mom was crying softly. I sat there not quite understanding what I'd seen, but I knew that people weren't supposed to be in the back of a semi. I remember my father's words when Mom finally stopped sobbing. "Juan," he said, "no matter what anyone tells you, there is evil in this world. And all it takes for it to triumph is for good people to do nothing."'

Juan's voice lost its soft tone as his mind returned to the present. 'When I was old enough, we talked about that day again. My parents explained how smugglers snuck people up from Mexico and how some never survived the journey. They told me the truck driver pleaded guilty to thirty-six counts of vehicular homicide and that he'd been killed in prison by a Latino gang.'

Eddie said, 'And when that cargo container was opened on deck and you saw those Chinese – ?'

'I was back on that hot interstate and felt just as powerless. That is, until I remembered my father's words.'

'What did he do for work, if you don't mind my asking?'

'An accountant, actually, but he had fought in Korea and believed there was nothing more evil on earth than Communism.'

'If he had as much influence on you as I think he did, you doubly want these guys – smugglers and Communists.'

'If it turns out that China's behind it, damn right.' Cabrillo gave Eddie an appraising look. 'I don't need to tell you about that. You were in their backyard for years.'

Eddie nodded gravely. 'I've seen firsthand evidence of entire villages being wiped off the map because someone spoke out against a local party official. The cities may be opening up to the West, but the countryside is ruled as ruthlessly as ever. It's the only way the central government can control a billion people. Keep them on edge, near starvation, and grateful for whatever handouts they get.'

'Something tells me,' Cabrillo said, 'that this isn't a Chinese operation.'

'It makes sense to me if it were,' Seng countered. 'They have a population crisis, and I'm not talking about overcrowding, though that is a problem. No, what China faces today and over the next twenty years or so is something far worse.'

'Worse than trying to feed a quarter of the world's population?' Juan asked skeptically.

'In fact it's a direct result of the one-child policy enacted in 1979. Today China's birthrate is 1.8 children per woman. The rate's even lower in the cities. For a sustainable population, a country needs a fertility rate of at least 2.1. Falling birthrates in the U.S. and Europe are mostly offset by immigration, so we're okay. But China is going to see their population ratios age dramatically in the next decades. There won't be enough workers to man the factories nor enough people to care for the elderly. Add to that the cultural bias against girls, select-sex abortion, and infanticide, and right now China has one hundred and eighteen boys under the age of ten for every one hundred girls.'

'So what's that going to do?'

'Unless a significant segment of the male population is gay or chooses celibacy, there are going to be about two hundred million men with no chance of having families of their own by 2025.'

Cabrillo followed through to the logical conclusion of Eddie's lecture. 'So you think they're shipping excess men overseas now?'

'It's a theory.'

'A plausible one,' the chairman agreed. 'And something I hadn't considered – the wholesale export of people.'

'About a million Chinese immigrate illegally a year,' Eddie told him, 'with the tacit approval of local governments, I might add. It's not much of a stretch for the leaders in Beijing to actually start their own program to get rid of what's already being called the "army of bachelors."' Eddie's voice turned bitter. 'Despite the propaganda spin over the last few years, China remains a brutal dictatorship. They invariably take the hard approach to any problem. They want to build a dam, they move thirty million people out of the way, show Western reporters the new towns they're building, but ultimately dump the population on collective farms.'

Juan let Eddie Seng's accusation hang in the air for a few seconds. He was well aware of how much Eddie hated the Beijing government. 'But there were only a few dozen people on the *Kra*,' he finally said.

'But what's on that ship Tory Ballinger saw?'

'You mean who?'

'Exactly.'

Juan's encrypted cell phone chimed. 'Cabrillo.'

'Juan, it's Max.'

'What's up?' He tried to sound nonchalant, but there was an edge to his voice.

'We're about twenty miles behind the *Maus*. We've already talked to them, establishing procedure for passing a drydock under tow. In about ten minutes we're going to launch an unmanned aerial drone with a low-light camera to take a peek into her open hold. I do have a boarding party standing by if we need to send over some Mark-one eyeballs.'

'Sounds good. What's the weather? It's raining here.'

'Fine. No moon at all. Seas are only a couple of feet, and the wind's light. Listen, the reason I called is we have some information for you.'

*About time*, Cabrillo thought but kept it to himself. 'Murph tracked down who owns the *Maus*?'

'No, he's still working on it. Julia came up with something during her autopsies of the Chinese folks we plucked from the container. I'm passing her off to you.'

'Thanks. E-mail the feeds from the UAV to my phone. I'd like to take a look at the *Maus* during the flyover.'

'You got it. Here's the doc.'

'Chairman, how's Tokyo?'

'It's all warm sushi and cold geishas.'

'I bet. I think I found something about our immigrants. They're all from the same village, a place called Lantan in Fujian Province. Most of them are part of the same extended family.'

'Did you do a DNA test?'

'No, I read the parts of a diary that hadn't been destroyed when the container went into the drink. A lot of the journal was illegible, but I scanned everything into the computer and let the translator take a crack at it. The guy who wrote it's last name was Xang. With him were two brothers, a bunch of cousins, and distant blood relatives. They had been promised work in Japan by a snakehead who called himself Yan Luo. Each of them had to pay this Yan Luo about five hundred dollars before leaving the village and would have to pay back about fifteen *thousand* once they reached a textile mill outside Tokyo.'

'Does he talk about the *Kra*? Was that the boat taking them to Japan?'

'He doesn't say, or that part of the journal was too damaged to read.'

'What else were you able to get?'

'Not much. He wrote about his dreams and how one day he would be able to afford bringing his girlfriend to Japan with him. Stuff like that.'

'What was the name of that town?'

'Lantan.'

'If we can't backtrack the *Kra* or the *Maus*, maybe we can backtrack the immigrants.' Cabrillo glanced at Eddie. His chief of Shore Operations had heard enough of the call to understand what was coming. It was in his eyes. 'I'll call you right back,' Cabrillo said to Julia and cut the connection.

'China, huh,' Eddie said with an air of the inevitable.

'I had a feeling it would come to this as soon as I saw them.'

'Can you do it?'

'You know my cover was blown just before I got out the last time. I've already been sentenced to death in absentia. I can name a dozen generals and party officials who would like nothing more than for me to step foot in China again. It's been a few years, but last I knew, my picture had been sent to every police department in the country, from Beijing and Shanghai to the smallest provincial outpost.'

'Can you do it?' Cabrillo repeated.

'My old network is long gone. I was hustled out of China fast after everything went down and couldn't get a warning out. I'm sure some of them were rolled up by the state police, which means the rest are compromised. I can't use any of them.'

He went silent. Cabrillo didn't ask a third time. He didn't need to.

'I've got a set of credentials in a safe-deposit box in L.A., one the CIA doesn't even know about. I had them made before Hong Kong was handed over to China in case I needed to get back in to help a couple of friends. They've since immigrated to Vancouver, so the identity is still viable. I'll contact my lawyer first thing tomorrow and have them sent by courier to Singapore. From there I can catch the Cathay flight to Beijing.'

'Shanghai,' Juan corrected. 'Julia said the village is in Fujian Province. If my geography is sound, the closest big city is Shanghai.'

'Oh, this gets better and better,' Eddie said as if his mission wouldn't be difficult enough.

'Why's that?'

'The people of Fujian have a dialect all their own. I don't speak it very well.'

'Then we'll call it off,' Juan decided. 'We'll just have to get some leads from the *Kra* or the *Maus*.'

'No,' Eddie said sharply. 'It might take you weeks to track these bastards through shipping records and corporate pyramids. If illegal immigrants somehow fit into the pirates' scheme, we need answers now. You and I both know that the ones dumped over the side of the *Kra* aren't the only ones who've been taken.'

Juan nodded, a curt, decisive gesture. 'All right. Make your arrangements.'

On the main display screen along the front wall of the operations center, the picture was a weirdly distorted view of the ocean, where the foam topping the low waves looked like green lightning forking across the black water. The camera's optics made the rhythmic pulse of the sea look like a beating heart. The image jerked slightly, and George Adams swore.

Adams was the pilot of the *Oregon*'s Robinson R-44 helicopter as well as the pair of matching UAVs, or unmanned aerial vehicles, that could be launched from an open space along the freighter's port rail. Although the U.S. military spent millions on their Predator drones, the Corporation's UAVs were commercially available remote-control airplanes fitted with low-light cameras. George could sit at a computer workstation inside the operations center and fly the model plane using a joystick within a fifteen-mile radius of the ship.

One of the few aboard the *Oregon* from the army, George 'Gomez' Adams had earned his reputation flying special ops teams into Bosnia, Afghanistan, and Iraq. Unmarried at forty, Adams cut the figure of a fighter pilot. He was dark-haired and dark-eyed, tall and lean with a charming cockiness that never failed to make him a center of attention with women. His good looks had been used in more than one past Corporation mission. He'd earned his nickname after one such mission when he seduced the mistress of a Peruvian drug trafficker who bore a striking resemblance to the television character Morticia Addams.

The telepresence given to Adams through the video link allowed him to see what was in front of and below the gimballed camera in the UAV's nose, but he couldn't feel the subtle updrafts or crosswinds that affected the five-foot-long airplane. He adjusted for the sudden gust that hit the plane and eased back on the stick to gain a bit more altitude.

'What's the range?' he asked Linda Ross, who was monitoring the radar picture.

'We're four miles astern the *Maus* and three miles to port.'

The UAV was too small to be seen by even the *Oregon*'s powerful search radar, but the massive drydock and the pair of tugs towing her showed crisp on her repeater screen.

Adams used a thumb control to pan the camera mounted in the model plane's nose. The ocean was still streaked with eerie green lines of sea foam, but a few miles ahead of the UAV a bright emerald slash cut the otherwise dark water.

'There,' someone called unnecessarily.

The glowing wedge was the *Maus*'s wake as she was hauled southward. Just ahead of her were bright, glowing points, searchlights mounted at the stern of the towboats to illuminate their ponderous charge. The thick hawsers securing the vessels looked as fine as gossamer from five thousand feet. There were a couple of less powerful lights along the side of the drydock, but her cavernous hold was completely dark.

'Okay, George. Take us in,' Max Hanley ordered from the command station. He then pressed a cell phone to his ear. 'You getting this, Chairman?'

'Kind of,' Juan Cabrillo said from his Tokyo suite. 'I can't make out much on this one-inch screen.'

'I'm going for a high pass first,' Adams said as he worked the joystick. 'If we don't get anything, I'll cut the engine and glide in for a closer look.' He took his eyes off his screen to glance at Hanley. 'If the engine doesn't refire, the UAV's a write-off.'

'I heard that,' Juan said. 'Tell George that we can't lose the element of surprise if we have to send over boarders. Tell him it's okay to ditch the drone.'

Max relayed the message, saying, 'George, Juan says that if you crash the UAV, it's coming out of your paycheck.'

'You tell him,' Adams said, fully concentrating on his screen once again, 'that I'll cut him a check as soon as Eddie pays for that submarine he banged up.'

George slowed the UAV to just above stall speed, but it still overtook the slow-moving caravan of ships. There was no chance the black airplane could be spotted from either the drydock or the tugboats; however, it was possible that an attentive crewman could hear the high whine of the UAV's engine. He kept the drone five hundred feet to the starboard side of the convoy and panned the camera as it flew down the eight-hundred-foot length of the drydock.

It looked more like a fortress than a vessel designed to travel across the ocean. Her sides were sheer vertical walls of steel, and there was only the barest hint of streamlining at her blunt bows. The pair of hundred-plus-foot tugs looked like toys compared to the behemoth in their charge.

Even as the pictures came in, Eric Stone and Mark Murphy were filtering the video through computer software to enhance the image. The pair of tech geeks cycled the feed to increase contrast and eliminate distortion caused by the UAV's engine vibration. By the time George had completed his run and peeled the drone away from the *Maus,* they had sharpened the raw data and played it back on the main screen.

'What the hell am I supposed to be looking at here?' Juan asked through the cell phone.

'Damn,' Max said, staring at the big plasma display. He held his cell phone in one hand and his unlit pipe in the other.

'What is it?'

'The lights along the *Maus*'s rail make it impossible to see into her hold. It's just a black hole in the middle of the ship. We need to make a run directly over her.'

'Coming around now,' Gomez Adams said, his body unconsciously leaning as the UAV swooped in a tight turn.

A few minutes later he had the drone lined up behind the drydock at two thousand feet. Rather than bleed off speed, he pressed the throttle to its stop, hurtling the tiny plane directly at the *Maus* on what he was sure would be a suicide run. The UAV's ignition system was temperamental at best, and a crewman usually had to hand crank the little propeller on deck prior to launch.

The bulk of the *Maus* filled the view screen as the drone bored in. George killed the engine when he was about a quarter mile out, and the picture lost its annoying jumpiness as the plane became a silent glider sliding out of the night sky. He checked the altimeter. The drone was at a thousand feet, and he deepened the angle of attack. It was now arrowing at the drydock like a Stuka dive bomber, but as silent as a wraith.

Eric and Murph double-checked that the recorders were burning the images onto disc just before the UAV crossed over the *Maus*'s vertical transom. Adams leveled the drone a hundred feet above the floating drydock and soared the little craft down the vessel's dark length, making sure the camera caught every detail of her murky hold.

Fifty feet from the bow, he heeled over the UAV, diving once again to gain airspeed. At an altitude of thirty feet he hit the starter toggle on his controls. The sea grew on the plasma screen monitor. When nothing happened, he calmly reset the toggle and tried again. The plastic prop turned once, but the engine refused to fire.

It was as though the plane accelerated in its final moments or perhaps the ocean reached up to pluck it from the sky. The team in the control room winced as the UAV augered in, and the screen went blank.

Adams got to his feet and cracked his knuckles. 'You know what they say: any landing you can walk away from is a good one.'

A few people groaned at the old joke as Murph put a replay of the aerial pass back on the screen.

'What did you see?' Cabrillo asked over the satellite link.

'Hold on a second, boss,' Max replied. 'It's coming up now.'

While the image was dark, Adams had done a superb job controlling both the UAV and its camera. The shot was steady and clear and not at all what they wanted to see. There was a cover of some type over the entire length of the drydock's hold. The cover wasn't solid, because sections of it rippled in the wind, but it completely blocked their view of anything the drydock might have been transporting.

'Well?' Juan's voice was insistent in Hanley's ear.

'We have to send over a recon team,' Hanley told the Chairman. 'They've got the entire hold covered with sections of dark cloth. We can't see diddly.'

Linda Ross was already at the control room's rear door. As the senior intelligence officer aboard the *Oregon,* it was her job to lead the team over to the *Maus.* She wore a black combat uniform and had slipped into the flak vest she'd had draped over her chair. Her fine, honey-blond hair was covered by a black watch cap.

Despite the determined set to her narrow jaw and the accoutrements of war, she still managed to look young and vulnerable. It didn't help that she had a high-pitched voice, not shrill but almost pubescent, and her cheeks were dusted with freckles. At thirty-seven, Linda was still carded at bars on her infrequent trips back to the States.

Although she had spent her naval career as an intelligence analyst, Linda was well practiced at the art of intelligence gathering, too. Because of her background, she usually spent less time on a particular covert mission than others simply because she knew exactly what information was needed. She could make quick assessments in the field, innately knowing what was crucial. For that she had more than earned the respect of the SEALs she was to lead.

'Tell Juan we'll be careful,' she said to Max and left to make her way down to a door at the waterline on the starboard side where they'd launch a Zodiac inflatable boat.

Three commandos were waiting for her in the aqua garage. They were similarly outfitted, and one handed Linda a combat harness. She checked that the silenced Glock she preferred was loaded. She liked that the pistol didn't have a safety that could be inadvertently activated on a quick draw. Because this was a reconnoiter, a sneak and peek, and they doubted there would be guards posted on a ship under tow, none of the team carried anything heavier than handguns, but these weapons were hot-loaded with mercury-tipped hollow points, a round packing enough kinetic energy to incapacitate with even a glancing blow. She settled the throat mike of her tactical radio next to her skin and secured the earpiece. She and the team did a quick test, making sure they could hear each other and Max in the op center.

The garage was lit by red battle lights, and in their glow Linda applied black camo paint to her face before slipping on tight no-shine gloves. The Zodiac was large enough for eight, powered by a big black outboard. Next to the four-stroke engine was a smaller battery-powered trolling motor that could silently propel the Zodiac at nearly ten knots. A few items they would need had been secured to the floorboards.

A cargo master checked each team member again before flashing the thumbs-up to Linda. She threw him a wink, and the deckhand doused the lights. A cable system opened the outer door, a ten-by-eight-foot section of hull plating just above the waterline. The hiss of the sea passing by filled the garage, and Linda could taste the salt in the air. While there was virtually no moon, the *Maus* stood out against the darkness, her forward sections lit by floodlights on the pair of tugs, and sodium arc lamps along her top deck cast her silhouette in strong relief.

The Zodiac pilot fired the engine with a press of a button, and with a pair of people along each side, the team shoved the inflatable down a Teflon-coated ramp and jumped aboard as soon as the craft hit water. They shot away from the *Oregon* in a burst of foam to escape the turbulent water running along the tramp steamer's flank before throttling back to eliminate their own wake.

The gap between the two ships seemed small when seen from the cameras mounted on the *Oregon*'s deck, but down in the trough of water between the vessels, the distance appeared enormous. The seas were light, and the inflatable rode the swells easily, gliding up the face, hanging for the barest moment before dropping back in a smooth rhythm. Even muffled, the outboard sounded loud in Linda's ears, though she knew that the craft was silent at full speed from a mile away.

Five minutes after launching from the *Oregon,* they had knifed through three-quarters of the way. The pilot cut the outboard and engaged the silent electric motor, taking a cue from Linda to circle around the stern of the *Maus* in order to find a suitably dark area to board.

The drydock was only making three knots, so they had little trouble passing behind the vessel and easing their way along her starboard side. The hull was a featureless wall of gray steel that stretched from stem to stern. The lights mounted high atop her rail washed down the plating, but amidships there was a patch of darkness where one of the bulbs was burned out. The pilot eased the Zodiac over, running right outside the wake zone next to the darkened section of hull. He had to constantly adjust the motor to keep the vessel stable in the choppy wash.

'Grapple,' Linda called over her throat mike.

One of the SEALs raised an odd weapon to his shoulder. It looked like an oversized rifle, but a hose ran from the pistol grip to a cylinder strapped to the floor of the Zodiac.

He activated a laser range finder slung under the ungainly rifle and pointed it skyward, centering his sights at a spot just above the *Maus*'s rail.

'Sixty-seven feet,' he whispered.

By the light of a small red-lensed flashlight, his partner dialed the number into a valve at the top of the cylinder. He tapped the shooter on the shoulder.

The man centered his breathing, feeling the gentle rise and fall of the Zodiac, and waited for the exact moment the craft reached the zenith of a wave. He eased the trigger.

A precise amount of compressed nitrogen exploded from the tank, launching a stubby rubber-coated arrow from the grappling gun. Behind the arrow trailed a millimeters-wide nanofiber line. At the apogee of flight, the arrow peeled apart to become a grappling hook. The hook cleared the rail by scant inches and fell silently to the deck.

Back in the Zodiac, the shooter pulled back on his weapon, dragging the hook high above so it locked around a rail stanchion. 'Secure.'

His partner unhooked the reel from the grappling gun and used a snap link to splice a nylon climbing rope to the nanofiber line. In smooth hand-over-hand motions, he hauled the line through a small pulley at the back of the grapple so the climbing rope rose into the night sky. It took barely thirty seconds for him to loop the rope around the pulley and recover the end. He secured one end of the rope to cargo straps at the bow of the Zodiac while the pilot did the same at the stern. Using sheer muscle power, the men pulled on the ropes, and the Zodiac lifted free of the water. They heaved again, and the little inflatable rose another foot. They did this three more times until there was no danger a wave would come along and capsize the craft. Had they left it bobbing in the wash while they were reconnoitering the *Maus,* the boat's rubber skin would have shredded against the drydock's steel hide.

All the lines were locked down, and one by one the team climbed the thick nylon rope, first making sure they had chambered rounds in their pistols. Linda climbed third in the stick, trusting the first team member would clear the rail under the cover of the number-two man. She heard the shooter call '*Clear*' through her miniature earpiece and looked up to see him slither between the metal railing.

She glanced down as she neared the top. The Zodiac pilot was right below her, and far down in the shadows she could see the inflatable snuggled up against the drydock like a seal pup nursing from its mother. The sea was a surging presence a littler farther down.

She accepted the hand from above and was dragged over the rail, thankful that the heavy flak vest protected her breasts. She doubted Doc Huxley with her 38-Ds could have done it.

The three of them formed a defensive perimeter around the rail until the last man clambered over. The shooter took a second to remove the grappling hook and secure the rope holding the Zodiac with a coupling device that could be disengaged once they were safely back on their boat.

The top deck of the *Maus* appeared deserted, though technically it wasn't a deck but a ten-foot-wide catwalk that circled the entire ship. Had huge sheets of stiff material not been drawn over the hold, the deck would have been like the parapet of an iron castle. Linda approached the protective covering. The material felt like woven plastic fibers. It had been pulled taut across the hold so it was stiff, like the canvas of a large tent. She pressed against it and felt no give.

One of the men had pulled a blued Gerber knife from a boot sheath and was about to cut the fabric. Linda held up a hand. Wordlessly, she pointed to the shooter and his partner and indicated they were to search the perimeter headed aft while she and the pilot would head forward. She pointed across the 240-foot hold to where she wanted to meet up.

Linda eased her Glock from its holster. There was too much light around the deck to use night vision gear but too little to see clearly. Fortunately, there didn't appear to be many places a sentry could hide on the catwalk. There were few ventilators or machinery housings to provide cover. Backed by the pilot, she stalked silently along the starboard rail, her pistol held steady near her waist while her eyes darted from shadow to shadow. Her breathing came easy and light, but she could feel her pulse in her throat and wondered briefly if her team could hear it through the tactical radio.

There was a structure near the bow, a blockhouse that probably housed the ballast and door controls. At first it appeared dark and deserted, but as they approached, Linda could see seams of light outlining several blacked-out windows. She pressed her back against the structure's cool metal, then cocked her head to place her ear to the steel. She couldn't make out words, or even the language, but she definitely heard voices inside. She heard four distinct voices, all male, and held up four fingers for the pilot. He nodded.

The pair of them eased past the blockhouse, keeping a wary eye on the single door. Just as they reached cover behind a massive ventilation hood, the door was thrown open, and a single man emerged into the night. Linda checked her watch. Two thirty. Time for a bihourly patrol. A second guard joined the first. Both wore black uniforms similar to the ones the Corporation team sported, but these men carried compact submachine guns on slings around their necks. Linda didn't recognize the model, though it didn't make any difference. She and her entire team were outgunned. The guards had the air of the military. Mercenaries, she guessed, hired by whoever headed the pirate ring. She also suspected that these men, or others like them, had been responsible for killing the crew of the *Avalon* and scuttling the research ship.

The first to emerge said something to his partner. To Linda it sounded like Russian or some other Slavic language. She wished Juan were here. He had an ear for languages. He spoke four fluently and understood enough of several others to at least get by.

Linda and her teammate ducked deeper into the shadow cast by the ventilator and let the guards pass. They moved at a brisk pace, their eyes following the beams of flashlights each carried in their left hand, leaving the right free for the wicked little machine pistols. They craned their necks over the rail every few feet to check the drydock's hull, then cast the beam out across the black expanse of material covering the hold. They seemed to miss nothing, so it was only a matter of time until they spotted the Zodiac dangling alongside the giant vessel.

Linda whispered into her throat mike once the guards had moved out of earshot, 'Team two, we have a pair of guards headed right for you.'

'Acknowledged.'

Linda's orders were to leave no evidence that she and her men had boarded the *Maus*. That wasn't going to happen.

She ran through some scenarios in her mind and decided there was only one way. She'd detected a whiff of cigarette smoke when the blockhouse door had opened. She could only hope that one of the guards on patrol was a smoker.

'There was a ballast tank vent thirty feet aft of where we hung the Zodiac,' she whispered to her team. 'We'll take them there.'

'Roger.'

'No guns.'

Rather than backtrack all the way around the bow, Linda and the Zodiac driver chanced walking across the covered hold. The material was so tight that their weight did nothing more than create shallow dimples around their shoes. She noted that the fabric was in twenty-foot-wide strips and had been tightly threaded together with wire through ready-made eyelets. A lot of thought and time had gone into hiding whatever lay in the *Maus*'s hold.

Once on the far side, she met up with the other team in the protection of the ventilator she'd seen earlier. These vents allowed air to escape from huge tanks along the length of her hull when the drydock ballasted down for a ship to be drawn inside. When it was time to raise the vessel, pumps someplace deep inside the drydock expelled the ballast water through nozzles dotted around the ship.

They tracked the guards' progression around the drydock by the beams of their lights. It seemed to take forever. Once they rounded the stern and started up the starboard side of the *Maus,* they were headed right for the ambush. They had nearly four hundred feet to cover. The team waited. Linda's mouth had gone dry, and she couldn't make her tongue work to moisten her lips.

She could smell the adrenaline as the guards drew nearer,

hers, her men's. The air seemed charged with it. They were within twenty feet when one stopped and patted his partner on the shoulder. The men spoke, shared a low chuckle, then one faced the railing and unbuttoned the fly of his uniform. He leaned over the rail to watch his arcing stream of urine.

It shouldn't have happened. They were on a moving vessel at sea. The wind of her passage should have blown the urine stream aft. But the drydock was only making a couple of knots, and she had a tailwind of eight to ten. To watch his drops fall away, he had to look toward the bow.

The guard rocked back in shock, nearly soaking himself. 'Nikoli!'

He'd spotted the Zodiac.

Linda and her team had less than two seconds before the alarm went up.

The guard named Nikoli didn't even bother looking over the rail. He doused his flashlight and started running across the fabric-covered hold, leaving his partner straining to empty his bladder. In an instant Nikoli was swallowed by darkness. This must have been the standard procedure. If one saw something, the other was to get away and radio the guardhouse.

'Take him,' Linda ordered without pointing to the guard at the railing. She sprinted off after Nikoli. A moment after running onto the tight fabric, she felt the vibration of the apparently Russian guard's footfalls ahead of her.

The stiff cloth flexed under the weight of her long strides, causing her knees to buckle with every pace. She was relying on this. At 108 pounds, plus the weight of her gear, she was still a good seventy pounds lighter than the guard. For him it would be like trying to run across a slack trampoline. She saw the glint of his machine pistol and the band of white skin below his hairline. Her Glock was in her hand.

The guard must have sensed her gaining. He had been struggling to draw a walkie-talkie from a hip holster. He forgot about the radio and began to turn so as to bring his weapon to bear. Linda slid flat, skidding across the fabric, her silenced pistol at full stretch. She fired as soon as she stopped.

The shot went wild, but the guard dropped flat. For a heartbeat he lay still. Linda raised herself and cycled through the clip as fast as she could pull the trigger. The distance was fifty feet. At a firing range she could put eleven of twelve shots in the center of a bull's-eye at this range. On the dark deck of a rogue ship she was lucky to connect with one bullet. The nine millimeter hit the guard on the top of his right shoulder and nearly took his arm off. The big Russian staggered to his feet, his arm dangling useless from his shoulder, blood shining like oil on his uniform. He had lost his gun but charged at Linda anyway.

With no time to reload, Linda got to her feet to meet his charge head-on. She tried to use his momentum to hip-throw him to the deck, but the guard got his good arm around her throat, and they both went sprawling. His knee had slammed into her chest when they fell, and Linda tried to reinflate her lungs, sucking oxygen while at the same time trying to get back on her feet.

Mortally wounded, Nikoli managed to lever himself upright, a four-inch knife in his left hand. Blood poured from his fingertips. He swiped at her with a clumsy under-hand thrust that Linda easily dodged. She tried to back away to give herself room and time to reload her Glock, but the Russian came at her with the determination of the damned.

Changing tack, Linda went on the offense and fired a

kick into the side of the guard's knee. She both heard and felt cartilage tear, and Nikoli went down. She rammed a fresh magazine into the butt of the Glock and racked the slide. Nikoli lay immobile as blood pooled around his mangled shoulder. Linda took a cautious pace forward.

'*Nyet, Specivo,*' the guard whispered when she came into his view.

She didn't move, realizing that his knife arm was under his body. He was still dangerous. She tightened her grip on the pistol. She should shoot him, but if she could get him back to the *Oregon* alive, they would have their first tangible lead.

'Show me the knife,' she ordered.

Nikoli seemed to understand. He cautiously dragged his left arm from under him. The movement drained the color from his face. Linda was four feet away, well out of range, and she'd put a bullet through his brain if he made to throw the blade. He held the knife out as if he was going to toss it at her feet. Then before she knew what was happening, he plunged the blade into the plastic fabric. Under tension, the tiny puncture split like a seismic fault, and the Russian vanished, plunging eighty feet to the bottom of the hold.

Linda had no time to react as the rip grew. Her weight caused the fabric to sag, and the next thing she knew, she was on her stomach, sliding headfirst toward the expanding hole.

Linda pressed her hands against the fabric, trying to find purchase, but her gloves could do little to slow her inexorable plunge. As her fingers reached the edge of the tear she frantically tried to grab the frayed edge. Her momentum was already too great, and a second later her head was over the hole, then her shoulders.

There wasn't even time to scream as her upper body slid through the rip and dangled high above the cargo hold of the drydock. Inside was pitch-dark, but she knew that she hung over an eighty-foot void. Her hips hit the edge of the tear, shifting her center of gravity. She was powerless as her body coiled under and her legs were lifted from the tough cloth covering.

Just as the top of her thighs slid over the precipice, strong hands wrapped around her ankles. For a precarious moment she continued to fall, and then she felt herself being drawn backward. She was plucked from the rent in the fabric and dragged back from the hole, not caring that the tough material scraped against the skin of her cheek.

Linda rolled onto her back and smiled into the face of the Zodiac driver. 'Jesus, thanks. For a second there I thought I was ...'

'For a second there you were.'

'The other guard?' Linda asked.

'Taken care of.'

'Okay, we only have another minute or two before these

guys are going to be missed.' Linda removed her combat harness as she spoke. She unclipped the suspenders from the belt, then reclipped them in a way to create an eight-foot-long rope of sorts. 'Team two, bring the body out here.'

'Roger.'

'Hand me your harness.' Linda worked this belt, too, doubling the length of her safety line.

She threaded an arm through a loop she had made, then secured a night vision monocle over her eyes. She averted her face from the perimeter floodlights to preserve her vision.

'Belay me,' Linda ordered once the other team arrived and lowered the dead guard to the deck. She noted two things. One was that someone had thought to close up his trousers and the other was that his neck was at an oblique angle to his body.

She crawled toward the elongated hole. Nikoli's knife had sliced next to a seam, the area of maximum tension, which was why it had torn open so easily. Originally she had planned to burn a hole in the fabric to dispose of the bodies, hoping the other guards would assume a hastily tossed cigarette was at fault. But this gash would serve her purpose just as well. The others aboard the *Maus* would guess their comrades had taken a shortcut across the hold and were swallowed when the cloth suddenly gave way.

Linda slithered closer to the rent, feeling the fabric sag under her weight but confident that her team could haul her back. As she neared the hole, she felt herself slide a little and instantly felt pressure under her arms as the men checked her descent. 'Okay, hold me here,' she said.

She lowered her head into the hold and snapped on a tiny flashlight.

Her first concern was Nikoli. Had he landed in such a way as to make his bullet wound noticeable, their covert inspection would be blown. Linda peered downward. Because of the two-dimensional quality of the low-light optics, she didn't experience the sense of vertigo she expected. Directly below her was a ship, a small tanker with its superstructure at the stern. She peered aft, seeing that they had cut off the ship's funnel and masts to make it fit under the tarpaulins. From this vantage she saw nothing to identify the vessel, no name or distinctive characteristics. But now they had their proof that they were dealing with hijackers as well as pirates.

She switched her goggles from low-light to infrared. Her vision went black with one glowing exception. A smear of light appeared at the ship's rail and continued down to the bottom of the hold where she saw a growing pool of bright color. She changed back to the night optics and trained her flashlight on the spot. It appeared that Nikoli had hit the freighter's rail when he fell, blood that had shown up as warmth on IR looked black now, and his body lay on the lowest deck, covered in gore. She doubted very much that anyone but a trained pathologist would notice the bullet wound amid the carnage the fall had caused.

Satisfied, Linda called for her men to drag her back.

'There's a tanker in the hold. They hacked off her funnel to make her fit. I put her length around four hundred feet.'

'Is there any way you can get her name?' Max asked from the op center.

'Negative. We have to clear out. Those guards are due back from their patrol about now.'

'Okay. We'll be ready for you.'

At a crouch the team ran back to where they had secured the Zodiac and climbed down the rope. The driver started the electric motor and was ready when the sniper released the rope. The inflatable smashed into the sea and immediately pulled away from the *Maus,* bobbing dangerously for a second before its speed evened out the ride.

Fifteen minutes later they approached the *Oregon* at twenty knots, the gasoline engine purring smoothly. The deckhand in the garage watched their approach through closed-circuit television and, as they drew nearer, he doused the red lights and opened the door just in time for the Zodiac to rocket up the ramp and come to a perfect stop. The doors were closing even before the pilot killed the engine.

Max Hanley was there to greet them. He handed his cell phone to Linda.

She peeled her watch cap from her head. 'Ross here.'

'Linda, it's Juan. What did you find?'

'She's hauling a midsized product tanker, Chairman. I couldn't tell her name.'

'Any sign of the crew?'

'No, sir. And since the hold was completely dark, my bet is they're either dead or on one of the tugboats.'

Neither needed to say that the second option wasn't likely.

'Okay, great job to all of you,' Cabrillo said. 'Put yourself down for an extra ration of grog.'

'Actually, I'm going to avail myself of a couple shots of the Louis XIII brandy you keep in your cabin.'

'That is to be enjoyed in a warm snifter, not shot down like cheap tequila.'

'I'll warm the shot glass,' Linda teased. 'Here's Max.' She

166

handed back the phone and left the garage for a long shower, and yes, a snifter or two of Juan's fifteen-hundred-dollar cognac.

'So what do you want us to do now?' Hanley asked.

'According to what Murph told me, the *Maus* is headed for Taiwan. Why don't you get ahead of her and wait to see if she enters port? If she does, I'll meet you there and we'll play it by ear.'

'And if she changes course and heads someplace else?'

'Stay with her.'

'You realize she's making about three knots. We could be shadowing her for a couple of weeks before she makes landfall.'

'I know. Can't be helped, old boy. Think of yourself as one of the cops following OJ on his low-speed chase along the L.A. freeways.'

'Low speed? Hell, lobsters migrate faster than that damn drydock.' Max turned serious. 'You do remember that the last ship taken from your Japanese friend's fleet was a tanker. The, ah . . .'

'*Toya Maru,*' Juan provided.

'Right. Stands to reason that's her in the *Maus*'s hold. Why not just contact the navy or Japan's coast guard?'

'Oh, I'm certain it's the *Toya Maru*. But this isn't about one ship, and I doubt anyone on those tugboats can tell us much. The pirates are playing this too smart. You mark my word: about a day out of Taipei they'll get orders to go someplace else. We take down the *Maus* now, we nab one vessel and a few low-level guys. We track her back to wherever they're going to scrap the *Toya* or disguise her so they can use her themselves, we'll have made a dent in their operation.'

'Sounds reasonable,' Max agreed. 'We'll play tortoise to their snail and see where this chase takes us.'

'I'm handing the phone over to Eddie. He has a list of things he's going to need for his insertion into China. You can send someone to act as courier when you pass through the Korea Strait. The Robinson has more than enough range to make it to Pusan. From there, the courier can take a commercial flight to Singapore and meet up with Eddie at the airport.'

'Hold on, let me get a pen. And some paper. And my reading glasses.'

Five hundred miles north of where the *Oregon* steamed near the *Maus*, another drydock, her sister ship in fact, was just clearing the La Perouse Strait separating the northern tip of Japan from the Sakhalin Islands and entering the frigid waters of the Sea of Okhotsk. She, being towed by more powerful tugs than the *Maus*, was making six knots despite the fact that the ship hidden inside her hold was considerably larger than the tanker Linda had seen.

The seas were building around the vessels, high, rolling waves that alternately tightened and slackened the long towlines so one moment they were submerged and the next they were as taut as steel bars, bursting with water wrung out by tension. The tugs turned into the seas, shouldering aside the waves as they plowed northward, meeting the ocean as a ship should, nimble and responsive to her vagaries. The drydock played no such game. She took the waves square into her bow so explosions of white froth were flung almost to her top deck. Then she would throw off the water, slowly, ponderously, as though the sea was merely a distraction.

Like the *Maus*, the drydock's holds were covered over,

but in this vessel's case, metal sheets had been laid over a steel framework and all the seams welded. The hold would have been virtually airtight except for several industrial ventilators mounted at the stern. These powerful machines drew in thousands of cubic feet of air per minute to circulate within the drydock's hold. The outgoing air was fed through banks of chemical filters to disguise the raw stench emanating from belowdecks, a smell that hadn't been found on the high seas for almost two hundred years.

Cabrillo was stuck in Tokyo until Mark Murphy came up with a lead, so he spent three days basically playing tourist in a city he'd never particularly enjoyed. He longed for the fresh air on an open sea, a horizon that seemed unreachable, and the peace that comes from standing on the fantail watching the wake curve into the distance. Instead he dealt with an impenetrable language, crowds that defied imagination, and constant staring by people who should be used to Westerners but acted as though they'd never seen one.

His feeling of impotence was further compounded by Eddie Seng's mission. Eddie had left days earlier, rendezvoused with the courier in Singapore, and had already gone on into China itself. He'd phoned the Oregon upon his arrival in Shanghai but then ditched the phone. While cell phones were ubiquitous in the cities, he was going deep into the countryside. Not only would there be no cellular service, but if he were caught with a phone, it would likely arouse suspicion. He would be completely on his own in a country that had already issued his death sentence until he'd learned the circumstances behind the villagers being aboard the *Kra*.

Cabrillo felt his phone vibrate in his jacket pocket. He slid it free and opened the line as he continued strolling the park surrounding the Imperial Palace, the only quiet location in the sprawling megalopolis. 'Cabrillo.'

'Juan, it's Max. Are you ready to put an end to your vacation?'

'Murph found something?' Cabrillo didn't bother to mask the delight in his voice.

'You got it. I'm putting him through, but I'm staying on.'

Juan found a deserted bench so he could give the conversation his full attention. He had a small pad and a Montblanc pen ready in case he needed to take notes.

'Hey, boss, how's it going?'

'Max tells me you have some information,' Cabrillo said, anxious to find a direction in which to hunt.

'It took a while, and I had to consult with Mike Halbert on quite a bit of it.' Halbert was a sometime consultant to the Corporation and also acted as their investment broker. He'd gone on a couple of missions aboard the *Oregon*, though usually he worked out of his New York apartment, a fiftieth-floor corner unit overlooking Central Park. Halbert was a whiz at the more arcane aspects of international finance, the shadowy world of front companies, tax havens, and derivatives, though right now, with the current sad state of the Corporation's financial situation, Halbert wasn't one of Juan's favorite people.

'So what do you have?' Cabrillo prompted.

'This might get a bit confusing, so bear with me.' Murph paused to study the notes on his computer screen. 'Okay, first what I had to do was find out who was behind all those dummy companies I told you owned the *Maus*. You remember, D Commercial Advisors, Equity Partners International, and all the rest. First off, it appears these companies were created strictly to buy the drydock. They don't have any other assets.'

'That's not uncommon,' Juan said. 'If there was ever an insurance claim against the vessel's owners, their only asset is the drydock itself.'

'That's what Halbert told me. None of these companies are based in the same place. One is Panamanian, another is headquartered in Nigeria, another is out of Dubai. I tried contacting D Commercial Advisors directly. They don't even have a phone number, so it's likely the headquarters are nothing more than a PO box with automatic forwarding to another address.'

'Is there any way to find out where their mail is sent on to?'

'Not without breaking into some Third World post office and having a look at their files.'

'We'll keep that option open,' Cabrillo said in all seriousness. 'Keep going.'

'Next, we checked the corporate structure of each company. These are public records and fortunately kept on a database. My hope was we would find the same names on the boards of each company.'

'You didn't think it was going to be that easy?' Juan chided.

'Well, I'd hoped. As you can imagine, no such luck. There was one common element, though. Of the seven companies that own the *Maus* and the forty people listed as directors of those companies, every one of them is Russian.'

'Russian? I thought they would be Chinese.'

'Nope, Russkies to a man. Which ties in with Linda's suspicion about the men guarding the *Maus* being from the land of the tsars. I have a search under way through Interpol right now. So far, I've already gotten hits on a few of these guys. They're members of the Russian mafia. No one highly placed, but they're definitely connected.'

'So this whole thing is a Russian enterprise,' Juan said, thinking aloud. 'I can see how they'd benefit from the hijackings, but what about the human trafficking? The snakeheads are well organized and entrenched in China. I can't see them allowing competition from the Russian mob.'

'I had an idea about that,' Max interjected. 'What if the snakeheads have a contract with the Russians? Could be they use Russian ships or allow the Chinese to use Russia as a conduit to get the illegals into western Europe.'

'That could be,' Juan agreed. 'They could use the port of Vladivostok. Dump the Chinese there, then send 'em across on the Trans-Siberian Railway. Once in Moscow or Saint Petersburg it's a simple matter of some forged documents, and they're on their way to Berlin, London, or New York. I've heard that customs police all over the world have closed a lot of the old back channels, so this could be their new route.'

Cabrillo was already thinking ahead. He didn't know many people in the cold water port city of Vladivostok, but he still had contacts in Saint Petersburg and Moscow. In fact, several of his old Cold War foes worked in private security for the new-generation capitalist oligarchs, and more than a few were wealthy oligarchs themselves.

'So I'm headed to Moscow,' Juan said.

'Not so fast, Chairman,' Mark countered. 'You might end up there, but there could be another way.'

'I'm listening.'

'I thought about how hard it would be to track down forty Russian gangsters and what leverage we could use to get them to talk. Mike Halbert and I talked about it at length, and we both came to the conclusion that the Russians probably don't have a clue what these companies do. It's likely that whoever set up D Commercial Advisors and Ajax Trading and the others paid the Russians a fee to use their names, and they know nothing beyond that.'

'You're talking a dummy board of directors for a dummy company.'

'Exactly. Complete deniability.'

'So where does that leave us?' Juan asked, slightly irritated that Murphy seemed to be leading him along.

'The guy who set up the companies.'

'Wait. Guy? You said guy?'

'Yup.'

'They screwed up,' Cabrillo exclaimed, irritation turning to excitement as he grasped what Murph had just said.

'Sure did, boss,' Mark agreed, a smile in his voice. 'Every one of the dummy companies had two things in common. They all own part of the *Maus*, actually on the documents it's called *Mice*, but I think it's a translation problem. And the other thing is they were all set up by the same lawyer in Zurich. Guy by the name of Rudolph Isphording.'

'Never heard of him.'

'No reason you should have, at least not until a few months ago.'

'What happened a few months ago?' Juan had suddenly become wary.

'Isphording was named as a star witness in the biggest financial scandal to hit Switzerland since it was discovered they had hoarded gold for the Nazis. He was caught up in a money laundering net, quickly saw the writing on the wall, and made a sweetheart deal with Swiss prosecutors. The scope of the investigation is expanding every day. A few bank presidents are under indictment, a couple of government ministers have tendered resignations, and now the investigators are looking into the Swiss representatives at the United Nations for potential bribe-taking. And there might be a link to the billions of dollars the late PLO chief Yasir Arafat hid away in Swiss banks that has yet to surface. It seems there's no limit to how high or far the scandal goes.'

'All because of this Isphording character?'

'He had a very long reach into some very dirty pockets.'

'If the PLO is involved, I'm surprised he hasn't been killed by now.'

Max Hanley spoke up with a low chuckle. 'He'll get a grateful hug by a suicide bomber only after the Palestinians find their money.'

'So where's Isphording now?'

'Under protective custody at Regensdorf prison outside Zurich. The only times he's been seen in the past five months is at special prosecutorial court sessions. He's driven to the courthouse in an armored van. The media aren't allowed anywhere near him, but one telephoto shot that might be him shows a figure in a flak vest with his face covered in what looks like bandages. Rumor circulating in the Swiss press is that he's undergoing plastic surgery during the proceedings and will be given a new identity after he's finished testifying.'

'An armored van?' Cabrillo asked, just to be sure.

'With a police escort. I said this was an alternative to tracking down forty Russians who may or may not know anything,' Mark replied. 'I didn't say it was an easier one.'

'Is he allowed visitors?' Juan asked, already thinking about what he could use as leverage over the attorney. Isphording was getting a great deal from the Swiss authorities. Why would he jeopardize that by talking to the Corporation about a handful of dummy companies he'd helped establish? Juan would have to get creative.

'Just one. His wife.'

That shot down his idea of trying to intimidate him in the prison's interview room. If they couldn't talk to him in jail, and he doubted Isphording would be allowed to speak to anyone in the courthouse, Juan saw his options as severely limited. He played a hundred different scenarios in his head and came up with nothing. Well, not nothing – but what sprang into his mind was one hell of a long shot.

'How sure are they about a PLO connection?' he asked.

'Reports are sketchy,' Mark said, 'but it fits with his pattern of corruption.'

'That'll have to be good enough. Even rumor can work to our advantage.'

'What's happening in that scheming mind of yours?' Hanley asked.

'I'm too embarrassed to tell you yet. It's that nuts. Are there any pictures of Isphording's wife?'

'Shouldn't be too hard to dig one up in newspaper archives.'

'Okay, get on it. I'm going to Zurich, get the lay of the land to see if my idea could even work. Where are you guys now?'

'We're in the East China Sea about two hundred miles north of Taiwan,' Max said.

'And the *Maus*?'

'Twenty miles ahead of us. We've determined this is the limit of her radar. We send up the UAV every twelve hours just to put some eyeballs on her and make sure nothing's changed. So far it's just a regular tow job. Nothing out of the ordinary.'

'Except the ship in her hold was stolen off the high seas.'

'Well yes, there is that.'

With the *Maus* only covering 150 miles a day, they were only a day and a half out from Taipei, although Juan was still convinced the vessel would change course and head someplace else. Taiwan was a modern democratic country and was too well-regulated for the pirates to use it as their base of operation. He was sure they'd continue on to Vietnam, the Philippines, or Indonesia.

That meant that if he was going to get to Rudolph Isphording, it would be without the *Oregon* as a base of operation. But he would need her unique capabilities if he was going to pull off what he'd been thinking. He calculated distances and times, factoring in the range of the Robinson R-44 in her protected hangar belowdecks. If he wanted to get equipment or personnel off the *Oregon,* he had a short window as the ship steamed past Taiwan in which to do it. Once she reached the South China Sea, they'd be too far from land to make any transfers. With a sinking feeling, he figured he had just two days after reaching Zurich to determine who and what he wanted off the *Oregon* before she was out of range.

They had needed three weeks to get everything set up to pull off the job in North Korea, and even then they had been rushed. And that caper was a piece of cake compared to what Cabrillo had in mind now.

# I 2

Eddie had always believed in the old adage that people made their own luck. That didn't mean he discounted the blind chance of someone winning a lottery or being involved in a freak accident. What he meant was that proper planning, attitude, and sharp wits were more than enough to over-come problems. You didn't need to be lucky to be success-ful. You just needed to work hard.

After the first two hours of lying in an irrigation ditch, he still maintained his beliefs. He hadn't had time to properly plan the mission, so it wasn't bad luck that brought him to this predicament. It was lack of preparation on his part. But now that he was into his fifth hour, and his shivering sent waves across the stream's surface, he cursed the gods for his bad luck.

His arrival in China had gone off without a hitch. Customs barely glanced at his papers and made only a desultory search of his bags. That hadn't come as much of a surprise, since he was traveling as a diplomat returning home from a year at the Australian embassy and was there-fore afforded special courtesy. The papers he'd planned to use while traveling in China were those of an unemployed office worker. He'd spent his first day in Shanghai just wandering the streets. He hadn't been in China for so long he needed to reacclimatize himself. He had to change his posture and walk – his was too brazen – and he needed to get used to the language again.

He'd learned Mandarin and English simultaneously from his parents living in New York's Chinatown, so he had no accent but rather a bland inflection that would sound foreign to a Chinese. He tuned into the conversations around him, relearning the accent he'd used when he'd been here with the CIA.

He couldn't believe the transformation in the years since he'd last been to China's largest city. The skyline was among the tallest in the world, with buildings and construction cranes crowding ever higher, and the pace of life was among the most frenetic. Everyone walking the sidewalks carried on excited conversations over ubiquitous cell phones. When night fell, the Shanghai streets were washed in enough neon to rival the Las Vegas Strip.

He vanished into society in incremental steps. After checking out of his hotel, he left his two suitcases behind a Dumpster that had just been emptied and wouldn't likely be moved for a few days, not that there was anything in the bags to incriminate him. The diplomatic papers had already been flushed in the hotel. Next, he bought off-the-rack clothes from a midpriced department store. The clerk thought nothing of a customer wearing an expensive Western suit buying clothes that didn't seem up to his standard. Wearing his new purchases, Eddie ditched his suit and bused out of the thriving downtown until finding an area of factories and drab apartment blocks. By this time, he'd gotten food stains on his shirt and had scuffed his shoes using a brick from a construction site.

He got a few looks from the poorer workers in their ill-fitting clothes, but for the most part no one paid him much attention. He wasn't one of them, but he didn't look like he was that much above them either. Again, the clerk at the clothing store where he bought two pairs of baggy pants, a couple of shirts, and a thin gray windbreaker assumed Eddie was a down-on-his-luck salaryman forced into the labor ranks. He bought shoes and a rucksack from another store and a few toiletry items from a third without raising an eyebrow.

By the time he arrived at the overland bus terminal for his trip to Fujian Province, on his third day without a proper shower, he was an anonymous worker returning to his village after failing to make it in the big city. The slow transformation not only ensured no one would remember him, it helped Eddie become the role. As he sat on a cold bench at the terminal, his eyes had the haunted look of failure and his body slouched under the weight of defeat. An old woman who'd struck up a conversation told him it was best he return to his family. The cities weren't for everybody, she'd said and told him she'd seen too many young people turn to drugs as an escape. Fortunately, her cataracts prevented her from seeing that Eddie wasn't as young as she assumed.

The trip had been uneventful, crowded onto a bus that belched great clouds of leaded gasoline fumes and stank of humanity. His trouble had started when he reached Lantan, the town where Xang and his family had begun a trip that ended with them murdered in a shipping container. Eddie had no way of knowing, again because he hadn't had time to prepare, that he'd arrived during regional elections. The army had set up a checkpoint in the town square, and everyone was required to pass through on their way to the polls.

Eddie had seen such elections before and knew that the townspeople had a choice among one candidate for each office up for election. Oftentimes the ballot was already checked, and the voter had to simply place it in the ballot box under the watchful eye of armed soldiers. This was China's version of a democratic concession to its people. Some high officials had come out from the provincial capital of Xiamen to watch the polling, and the military had even brought a tank, a massive Type 98 if Eddie's quick glimpse had been enough for an ID. He assumed it was a public relations ploy by the PLA, the People's Liberation Army, as well as a subtle reminder of where the ultimate power in China lay.

Although Lantan had a population of less than ten thousand, Eddie knew he'd attract attention. He didn't speak the local dialect all that well and didn't have a plausible reason for being in the isolated town if questioned by a curious soldier. Which was why he'd spent the past five hours under a bridge in an irrigation ditch just outside the town limits. He didn't plan on leaving his hiding place until the officials and military rolled on to the next target of their intimidation.

But once again the luck Eddie tried to make for himself had left him.

He'd been lost in his own world of cold and pain and didn't hear the voices until they were almost directly over-head.

'Just a little farther,' a male voice cajoled. 'I saw a spot when we entered town.'

'No, I want to go back.' It was a woman's voice, but young – maybe a teenager. She sounded frightened.

'No, it will be okay,' the male said. He had a cosmopolitan accent. Beijing or its environs. The girl sounded local.

'Please. My parents will wonder where I am. I have chores.'

'I said come on.' The man had lost all pretense of civility.

His voice was sharp, tinged with a manic, desperate edge.

They were on the bridge spanning the ditch, just a few feet over Eddie's head. A patter of dirt rained from the joints of the heavy wood decking. Their footfalls had become uneven. He could picture the couple in his mind. The girl was holding back, trying to slow them, as the man drew on her arm to the point of having to drag her.

Eddie gently pushed himself from the bank and sidled silently across the eight-foot ditch, listening as the man drew the girl across the structure. 'It will be fun,' he said. 'You'll like me.'

There was a dense copse of trees just beyond the village along the dirt road, a secluded spot that Eddie knew would soon become the scene of a rape. As the man and his victim gained the road, Eddie pulled himself up the embankment, exposing himself had there been a sharp-eyed observer in the nearby town. He shouldn't have even moved from his original spot. What was about to happen wasn't his concern, but he was about to make it so.

The man was a soldier, an AK-47 slung over his shoulder, his uniform clean compared to the dirty peasant clothes the girl wore. He had her by the arm, lifting her so her feet barely touched the ground in a frogmarch to the nearest trees, already in shadow as the sun set beyond a range of mountains to the west. She wore a skirt and simple blouse, long hair in a thick tail dangling between her narrow shoulders.

Eddie waited until they'd vanished into the woods. He peered back to the town. Electric lights were coming on in a few of the buildings, while outlying houses remained dark, their owners hoarding the candles they relied on for illumination. No one was looking in his direction, and the soldiers in the square appeared like they were making preparations to load the tank onto its special twenty-wheeled hauler.

He rose from the ditch and crossed the road, water streaming from his clothes. His feet were bare because he knew the cheap cloth and stitching would have dissolved after such a prolonged immersion. He merged into the forest, letting his sense of hearing guide him deeper into the woods. The girl was protesting, her voice pitched high before becoming suddenly muffled. The soldier must have a hand over her mouth, he thought, his feet silent amid the sparse ground cover.

He stopped at the base of a large pine. A flash of white had caught his attention. The girl's blouse. It lay on the forest floor. Eddie chanced a look around the thick trunk. The soldier had set his rifle on the ground next to where he'd pinned the girl. His upper body covered hers, but he could tell she was naked from the waist up. With one hand over her mouth, the solider used the other to pry the girl's skirts up to her hips. Her legs were thin and coltish, and they scissored in the air as they tried to throw off her attacker.

The soldier removed his hand from her mouth, but before she could cry out, he punched her across the jaw. Her head snapped to the side, and her body went still. Eddie had just moments, but there was no cover between him, the soldier, and his weapon.

He slid around the tree anyway, moving slowly at first. The human eye detects light and movement better at the periphery than straight ahead. He'd covered three of the ten paces to where the rape was about to take place when the soldier sensed Eddie's presence. Eddie burst into a run, his toes digging deep into the loamy soil like a sprinter's cleats.

Reacting fast, for he was already charged with adrenaline, the soldier twisted to grab up his rifle. He had the weapon by the grip, his fingers finding the safety in a well-practiced move. The assault rifle came up as he swung the barrel to his target. Even if he missed, the shot would be heard in the town and draw the attention of his comrades. The soldier must have known this because his finger tightened on the trigger before Eddie was in his sights.

Eddie launched himself, one arm arcing out wide to catch the barrel of the AK-47, the other knifing in with fingers extended into the soldier's windpipe. But he was too late; the soldier had applied the last bit of pressure to discharge the banana magazine. The gun didn't go off. Eddie's momentum ripped the soldier off the girl with such force her body rolled twice along the ground. Eddie ignored her as she cried out suddenly. The soldier lay atop Eddie when they stopped. Moving fast before the man could recover his senses, Eddie pressed the soldier's dead weight from his chest, used one arm to steady the man, and fired two swift strikes into the soldier's larynx. They lacked power, but hitting the same spot as his initial attack more than made up for it. The soldier's throat was crushed. He made a series of strangled gasps, then went limp.

Seng pushed the corpse aside without giving the would-be rapist a second thought. The girl lay curled on her side, clutching at her hand and moaning aloud. Eddie recovered her shirt and draped it over her. She clutched it around her frame as he gently turned her over. The punch hadn't dislocated her jaw, though she'd carry the bruise for a while. Her eyes were wide with fear and pain. He gently uncurled her hand. Her index finger was bent almost ninety degrees, and he understood why the AK hadn't gone off. She'd feigned her stupor rather than give her attacker the satisfaction of raping a conscious victim and at the last moment jammed her finger behind the rifle's trigger, preventing the bolt from releasing. She'd saved Eddie's life while saving herself from a crime most women believed was worse than death. Her finger had gotten broken when Eddie's charge had torn the weapon away.

'You are very brave,' he said soothingly.

'Who are you?' She sobbed through the pain and humiliation.

'I am no one. You haven't seen me, and this didn't happen. You broke your finger when you tripped walking back from the fields. Do you understand?' Her eyes darted to the figure of the dead soldier. He knew what she was silently asking. 'I will take care of him. You don't need to worry. No one will know. Now go back to your family and never speak of this day again.'

She turned her back to slip into her blouse. Enough buttons remained on the thin fabric to cover herself. She got to her feet, fighting the tears that welled at the corner of her eyes. It was pride, shame, agony. It was a face of China.

'Wait,' Eddie called before she vanished from the forest clearing. 'Do you know a family named Xang? Several of them rode the snake not long ago.'

At the mention of illegal immigration she stepped back protectively, ready to bolt. But she held firm, wanting to return something to the man who saved her. 'Yes, they live in town. They own a store that sells and repairs bicycles. The family live above. Do you have news of them?'

From the way she spoke he could tell she knew the family well. Perhaps she was the sweetheart Xang had written about. 'Yes,' he said, sickened by what he was going to tell her. 'They reached Japan, and they are all working. Now go!'

Startled by his last command, the girl vanished amid the trees. Eddie had perhaps done something far worse than the soldier just now. He'd given the girl hope.

He rifled the soldier's pockets for his identification and then pulled the dog tags from around his neck, settling the warm metal against his own chest. Using the sling from the AK-47 and the soldier's belt, he fashioned a rope and within ten minutes had the body wedged into the crotch of a twin oak tree twenty feet off the ground. Search parties looking for a deserter would take days to find the body, most likely drawn to it by the smell.

He used a branch to erase all tracks and traces of what had happened and made his way back to his hiding place under the bridge. The girl was probably back in town, most likely with her mother at the local healer's house having her finger set. Her problems were over. Eddie's had just begun.

The military presence in Lantan wouldn't leave until all the soldiers were accounted for. It looked as though they planned on staying the night, and it was doubtful the dead rapist would be missed till morning. His buddies would cover for him, assuming he'd found someone, either a professional or the proverbial farmer's daughter, whose legend of beauty and promiscuity were as popular in China as they were in America.

The trouble would start at the morning's roll call. When he didn't show up they'd search the town, then the surrounding farmland in ever widening circles. Eddie could no more abandon the mission than he could have left the girl, so that gave him until dawn to contact the snakeheads. And he no longer planned to interrogate them to learn what happened to Xang and the others. He now needed them to get him out of China.

He fingered the dog tags, knowing he had the perfect cover.

# 13

Anton Savich was relieved he had only one more flight to take to finally reach his destination. It had taken days to arrive at Elyzovo Airport outside Petropavlovsk-Kamchatskiy, the regional capital of the Kamchatka Peninsula on Russia's far east coast.

Petropavlovsk-Kamchatskiy, or PK, as it was commonly referred to, had been closed to the outside world until the collapse of the Soviet Union in 1990, and the ensuing years had brought little improvement. Nearly every building was made of concrete using ash from the 1945 eruption of the nearby Avachinsky volcano, so the city of a quarter million had a drab uniformity that went beyond its boxy Soviet architecture. Its streets hadn't been paved in decades, and its economy was in ruins because the military, which had once supported the city, had mostly withdrawn. Surrounded by towering snowcapped peaks at the head of beautiful Avacha Bay, PK was a dismal stain of a place where residents stayed only because they lacked the initiative to move.

The entire Kamchatka Peninsula had once been controlled by the Soviet military. Sophisticated radar stations dotted the rugged landscape to watch for incoming American ICBMs. There were several air force bases for intercepting American bombers, and it was the home of the Pacific Submarine Fleet. Kamchatka was also the designated landing site for Soviet ballistic missiles test-fired from the west. Today the subs of the Pacific Fleet rusted away at the

Rybachi Naval Base in the southern reach of Avacha Bay; several were so badly deteriorated that they'd sunk at their moorings, their tubes still loaded with torpedoes and their nuclear reactors still fueled. The radar stations had been abandoned, and planes remained grounded at the air bases for lack of parts and aviation gas. In the wake of the military withdrawal, countless sites had been left so polluted that even brief exposure would cause severe illness.

It wasn't the military presence that had first drawn Anton Savich to Kamchatka more than two decades ago. It was the geology. Kamchatka had risen from the sea two and a half million years ago, first as a volcanic archipelago like Alaska's Aleutian Islands. The sea quickly wore these mountains flat, but the land rose again, driven by endless reserves of molten rock from deep underground. Kamchatka was an arc within the Ring of Fire, a circle of volcanoes and earthquake zones that mark the boundaries of the vast Pacific tectonic plate. Twenty-nine of the more than 150 volcanic peaks on the peninsula were active, most notably Karymsky, which had been erupting continuously since 1996, and now an unnamed volcano in the center of the peninsula had started belching plumes of ash and steam.

Driven by economic necessity in the 1980s, the Soviet Union initiated a program of exploration and exploitation. To face Reagan's unprecedented military buildup, the Soviets scrambled to find the raw materials to feed the growing demand of their own military-industrial complex. These were the last salvos of the Cold War, fought not with bullets and bombs but with factories and resources. It was a fight the Soviet Union ultimately lost, but huge reserves of minerals such as coal, iron ore, and uranium were discovered in the process.

Anton Savich had been a young field researcher for the Bureau of Natural Resources, the agency tasked by the Central Committee to find all the wealth buried within the Soviet borders. He had come to prospect the Kamchatka Peninsula in 1986 with two other field men under the guidance of a geology professor from Moscow University, Akademik Yuri Strakhov.

The team spent four months scouring the peninsula from helicopters and all-terrain vehicles provided by the Red Army. Because of the active geology, it was felt there might be diamonds on Kamchatka, although they found no trace minerals to back Moscow's belief. What they found instead was just as valuable.

Savich recalled the days they'd camped at the foot of the reef, chipping samples by day and imagining the possibilities at night. They speculated as though what they found belonged to them, but of course it didn't. In likelihood they would receive commendations for their find, and maybe vouchers for larger apartments.

He wasn't sure who suggested it first; perhaps it was Savich himself, though it didn't really matter. Somehow the idea came up, mentioned as a joke at first for sure, but soon they discussed it in earnest. The rain had finally stopped that night, Savich remembered, which was unusual. They passed a bottle of vodka, which wasn't unusual. You couldn't get decent toilet paper in Moscow, but the state could keep you well-stocked in liquor five hundred kilometers from the nearest town.

Why report the find? someone had asked. Why tell anyone about it? Only the four of them knew the truth, and no one would prospect this area ever again once they filed their reports. They could return to Moscow, go about their lives for a few years, and then return and mine the reef themselves. They'd all be rich.

Savich stepped from the Ilyushin jetliner at PK's Elyzovo Airport, smiling as he recalled their naïveté. Akademik Strakhov allowed them to carry on for an hour or two before bringing them back to reality. He never told them it was wrong, what they wanted to do, for even the respected professor couldn't help his greed. But he also knew what they discussed was idle fantasy. It took just a few words to explain how they would never be allowed to return to Kamchatka, and even if they managed, how it was impossible for the four of them to mine enough material to make any sort of impact on their lives. He went on to tell them how world markets actually operated and how they would never be able to sell the ore they'd dug from the earth. He'd quickly cooled their ardor and dashed their hopes. The vodka went flat on their tongues.

Savich remembered that at that very moment the rain had started again. Strakhov doused their hissing gas lantern and for a few minutes the men listened to the rain pelt their canvas tent before crawling into their sleeping bags. He was sure the rest of them continued to think of the possibilities as they drifted to sleep. Many minutes passed before he heard their breathing settle into somnolence. All except his own. He had intuitively realized that with one additional element their plan would work: Time.

They were thinking in terms of years. He knew that it would be decades before anyone could come back. No one could return until the entire Communist government had collapsed and capitalism took root in the *Rodina*. Maybe they couldn't consider such an event, but Savich already knew it was an inevitability. Propaganda couldn't shorten breadlines or produce spare parts for automobiles, and eventually the leadership would just stop trying. He predicted a quiet implosion, not revolution, but eventually the Soviet Union would collapse under the weight of its own inefficiency. If he managed to position himself for that day, then all the other pieces could fall into place.

There was one more component that the others hadn't envisioned – that Savich had no intention of sharing his eventual wealth with any of them.

Their extraction helicopter wasn't due for another four days, more than enough time for him to put his plan into action. They had been assigned a sixty-kilometer-square search area and had been autonomous since their arrival five weeks earlier. When it arrived from PK, the chopper would fly box patterns across the grid and wait until the team launched flares to pinpoint their exact location.

Savich had to get the team as far away from their strike as possible, but Strakhov would want to keep them where they were until the helicopter came, ready to bask in the glory of their find. Without a weapon to compel them to move on, Savich would have to act now in order to get away from the site.

He lay in his bag for another couple of hours. It wasn't guilt or remorse that made him wait. He just wanted the team as deep into sleep as possible. He rose at four, the night's darkest hour, and by the glow of a penlight he opened their medical case. The supplies were rudimentary: bandages, antiseptic, some antibiotics, and a half dozen syringes of morphine.

Black flies were so prevalent that the men no longer bothered to swat them away or react to their nasty stings. Each of them was so covered in angry red welts from numerous bites that their arms, ankles, and faces were mottled red.

Savich emptied the morphine from one of the syringes into the ground and drew back the plunger to fill the cylinder with air. Mikhail was the biggest man on the survey team, a heavyset Ukrainian who had once been a wrestling champion in Kiev. Savich thought nothing of it as he sank the fine needle into Mikhail's throat where the carotid artery pulsed faintly. He slowly depressed the plunger, sending a lethal bubble of air into the wrestler's blood-stream. So used to the flies, Mikhail hadn't even felt the small sting. Savich waited just a few seconds before the bubble became an embolism inside the man's brain and he stroked out silently. He repeated the procedure twice more. Only old Yuri Strakhov struggled at the end. His eyes flew open at the prick of the needle. Savich clamped his hand over his mouth and pressed his weight on the geo-logist's chest, pumping the air into his artery with a savage thrust. Strakhov thrashed for just a brief moment before he went limp.

By the light of the gas lantern, Savich thought about his next move. He recalled that about five kilometers closer to the coast was a tall, steeply angled slope covered in talus and scree. The footing was treacherous, and a careless man could slide nearly a kilometer to its base. A tumble down the slope would do enough damage to a corpse to dissuade even the most iron-stomached forensic doctor in the unlikely event there would be an autopsy.

That first night Anton Savich went through his team-mates' notebooks and field journals. He tore out any page that made reference to the strike or any observation about terrain or geology from after they'd trekked past the gravel-strewn hillside. He excised everything that could be questioned during the investigation and made certain none of the journals mentioned anything interesting in their current search grid. He doctored his own journal to make it appear they had covered more ground than they had so no one would have reason to return here.

At dawn he began to carry the sleeping bags containing the bodies to the top of the slope. The Ukrainian, Mikhail, was too heavy to shoulder, so he fashioned a litter out of branches and straps from a backpack and dragged the corpse. He was exhausted and drenched in sweat and cursed himself for not waiting until the next day to move the last body. Rather than return to camp in the darkness, he spent a miserable night huddled next to his victims.

On the second day he broke down their tent and portaged all their gear to the slope. He had to repack the camping equipment and load it into the assigned backpacks before securing the packs to the bodies. He decided to wait until dawn the next day before tumbling the bodies down the slope. It wasn't that he particularly wanted to watch the men disintegrate against the sharp rocks but he needed to know where they landed. Only Professor Strakhov carried the flares he would need to alert the chopper coming in the next afternoon.

Mikhail went down the slope after Savich had a hearty breakfast of coffee, tinned meat, and a can of Crimean oranges. He watched through binoculars as the body first rolled, then tumbled, and as it picked up speed, began to cartwheel. Centrifugal forces caused blood to spray from numerous deep gashes, and limbs became rubbery after breaking against the stones. If possible, the other two were even more mutilated by the fall.

He took more than an hour to pick his way down the mountainside, scraping meat from his hands so they stung from his own sweat. Once at the bottom he removed gear and food from the packs and emptied a few tins so it would look like he'd been at the bottom of the hill for days.

When he estimated the helicopter was an hour away, he injected the two remaining morphine syringes into his arm and waited as the narcotic took effect. When he sensed a creeping numbness working its way up his extremities, Savich took a deep breath. To make things as authentic as possible it didn't seem right that three men died during the fall while he merely scraped up his hands.

Leaning against a rock outcrop he grasped a stone nearly the size of his head and held it as high as he could. He lay his left arm against the hunk of basalt and before he could give himself time to reconsider, he smashed the stone against his arm. The radius and ulna cracked audibly, and Savich bellowed in pain. Fueled by adrenaline and morphine he then took up a smaller stone and pounded it against his head hard enough to split the skin. Spittle drizzled from his slack lips as he fought the waves of agony and prayed for the drug to deaden the pain.

He was nearly unconscious when he heard the helicopter in the distance, and it took several tries to launch the flare. The arcing ball of white phosphorus rose on a column of smoke and must have been spotted immediately. The next thing Savich remembered was a hospital bed in Petropavlovsk.

The inquiry was perfunctory. The grisly scene the chopper crew described mirrored Savich's account of the slope giving way as the men crossed it and how they all tumbled to the valley floor. The investigator was amazed

Savich had only sustained a mild concussion, a few scrapes and bruises, and a broken arm.

'Just lucky, I guess,' he'd told the man as he'd closed his book of notes on the case.

Savich rubbed his left forearm as he crossed the tarmac to the airport terminal. In the past few years it had started to ache a bit on damp days. Maybe not quite as disquieting as Poe's Telltale Heart, but a reminder of his deeds nevertheless.

The immigration agent recognized him in the queue and motioned him to the head of the line. A few locals grumbled, but no one challenged him.

'Back again, Mr Savich?' the friendly guard asked, pocketing the twenty-dollar bill Savich had folded into his passport.

'I could get some work done back at my office in Moscow if your damn volcanoes would stop erupting.'

'It's the gomuls,' the guard replied with an air of mock conspiracy. 'They're the native spirits who hunt whales at night and return to the mountains to roast the meat on giant fires.'

'When I find whale bones in a volcanic caldera, I'll blame the gomuls, my friend. For now I suspect it's tectonic activity.'

Savich had returned to Moscow following his recovery in the hospital and lived and maintained his silence concerning his find, all the while continuing his work for the Bureau of Natural Resources. He led an unremarkable life through the waning days of the Soviet Union and managed to keep his position secure during its collapse. In the wild aftermath he had actively sought foreign contacts, cultivating some he thought would eventually allow him to see his plan to fruition.

His chance had come through a Swiss metallurgist he'd met at a symposium who in turn eventually led Savich to the banker, Bernhard Volkmann, and the current deal he had under way. Backed by Volkmann, and using the companies controlled by the loathsome Shere Singh, Anton Savich had returned to Kamchatka countless times over the past year, laying the necessary groundwork under the cover of a volcanologist. With the numerous eruptions all across Kamchatka, he had become a common sight at the airport and maintained a standing reservation at the Avacha Hotel, just a short walk up Leningradskaya Street from what was possibly the only Lenin Square in Russia still dedicated to Lenin.

He collected his bags and went straight to a counter run by a heliski company. The sport had grown popular along the rugged peaks of the peninsula, and there were several companies willing to take skiers up the mountains by chopper. The company, Air Adventures, actually did book ski trips to maintain legitimacy, but it was a dummy company Savich had funded through Volkmann in order to have rapid but unobtrusive transportation to the site. A private helicopter at Elyzovo would have drawn too much attention.

The woman behind the counter put away a Japanese fashion magazine when she saw him approach. Her smile was fake and perfunctory. He didn't recognize her, and he certainly didn't look like a thrill-seeking tourist.

'Welcome to Air Adventures,' she greeted in English.

'My name is Savich,' he grunted. 'Where's Pytor?'

Her eyes registered surprise, then fear, as she blanched. She vanished into a curtained-off section of the kiosk.

A moment later, Savich's pilot, Pytor Federov, stepped from around the curtain. He wore an olive drab flight suit and retained the cocky air he'd earned over the missile-filled skies of Afghanistan.

'Mr Savich, good to see you. I assumed you'd go to your hotel for the night and we would fly out in the morning.'

'Hello, Pytor. No. I want to see this latest eruption for myself before it gets dark,' Savich replied in case anyone was paying attention.

'Say the word, and I'll file a flight plan.'

'Consider it said.'

Forty minutes later they were racing down a twisting valley. The rugged mountains flanking the Air Adventure's MI-8 helicopter towered some eight thousand feet above them. Several peaks on the Kamchatka Peninsula topped fifteen thousand. The air was hazy with fine ash particles from the eruption farther north. Even with headphones it was difficult to speak in the forty-year-old chopper, so for the two hours it took to get to the site, Savich was content to let the landscape unfold around him.

He hadn't drifted off to sleep, the helo was too loud, but his mind had gone so blank he was surprised when Federov tapped him and pointed ahead. He hadn't been aware that they were about to arrive.

From above and at a distance, the area looked pristine except for the spreading brown stain that bloomed in the black waters of the Gulf of Shelekhov. A ring of containment booms had been strung along the coastline, but sediment from the workings drifted far beyond their reach. The reason the site looked so good was that much of it was hidden by acres of tarps strung atop metal poles. The tarps had been painted to look like snow, and the ash that had drifted onto the upper surface furthered the illusion. The ships had been beached and had also been camouflaged, first with dirt and rock from the workings and then with more fabric coverings to break up their shapes.

The only sign of life for a hundred miles was the thin wisps of smoke that coiled from the ships' funnels to provide heat and warm food for the workers.

Savich looked out to sea. A trawler was returning to the site, its wake a fat wedge, for she ran low under the weight of her catch.

With the ships' bunkers full of fuel, fresh water available from a nearby glacial river, and food provided by a pair of trawlers, the site could remain self-sufficient for months, perhaps years. He was rightly proud of his accomplishment, but then he'd had half a lifetime to refine every detail.

All except one, Savich thought grimly. There was one obstacle he hadn't been able to easily overcome, a commodity the site used up at a voracious pace and was the most difficult to replace.

Federov had radioed ahead, so the site manager was at the helipad to greet Savich when he stepped from the chopper into the biting cold wind. It was May, but the Arctic Circle was only four hundred miles north.

'Welcome back, Anton,' greeted Jan Paulus, a broadly built South African mine engineer.

The two shook hands and headed for a waiting four-wheel-drive. 'Do you want to go see the workings?' Paulus asked, putting the truck in gear.

Savich had seen that aspect of the project just once and never wanted to repeat the experience. 'No. Let's go to your office. I have a decent bottle of Scotch in my bag.' The Russian didn't much care for his site manager but knew he had to keep the man happy. Of course, Paulus's five million dollar salary did more for their relationship than the occasional drink.

The three ships they'd brought north and beached below the site were all old cruise liners that Shere Singh had provided through his ship-breaking business. Though past their prime, they were functional and served Savich's needs perfectly. Paulus had ensconced himself in the Ambassador Suite of a 380-foot cruise ship that had once plied the Aegean.

The gold and blue décor had once been considered chic, but the carpets were worn and scarred with cigarette burns, the furniture scuffed, and the fixtures tarnished. Savich used the bathroom and when he flushed, a god-awful stench erupted from the toilet. His image in the mirror appeared sepia because the glass had lost much of its backing.

Paulus was seated on the couch in the suite's living room when Savich returned. He'd already filled two tumblers with the Russian's Scotch. 'There was an accident on one of the drydocks.'

Savich paused in mid-sit. 'Which one?'

'The *Maus*. Two of your Spetsnaz commandos decided to ignore procedure and walk across the tarp covering the hold. The fabric gave way, and both fell to their deaths.'

The Russian took a sip of his drink. 'Any sign they were, ah, helped?'

'No. Your men swept the drydock and the ship in her hold as soon as the pair didn't return from the patrol. No one had come aboard, and there were no signs of struggle. The only vessel nearby was an Iranian-flagged freighter, so unless the mullahs in Tehran got wind of our little operation, I doubt they're involved.'

Savich cursed under his breath. All the men he'd hired to guard the ships were ex-special forces, the vaunted Spetsnaz. It went against their considerable training to deviate from a patrol route, but he could also understand why they might. Once they'd seized their prize, maintaining a high sense of alertness guarding a quiet ship at sea would be nearly impossible. He could easily imagine them cutting their perimeter patrol by crossing over the hold. It was a careless mistake that would teach the others vigilance in the future.

He considered this an unfortunate accident and put it out of his mind. 'How is everything going here?'

The South African had horrible teeth, so his smile looked like a gray grimace. 'Couldn't be better. The reef you found has the highest assay I've ever seen. Hell, this whole region is loaded with minerals. Production is above expectations by twelve percent, and we're still working the alluvial beds downslope. We haven't even started in on the main strike.'

'When do you anticipate sending out the first shipment?'

'Sooner than I expected, actually. The *Souri* is scheduled to arrive in ten days. Because of her cargo, she's carrying a triple complement of guards, so I want to send it out when she heads back south.'

'That should work out. I spoke with Volkmann two days ago. The processing center is ready. The last of the correct dies and stamps came in this week.'

'And the banks will take delivery?'

'As soon as possible.'

Paulus freshened their drinks and held his glass up for a toast. 'Here's to greed and stupidity. Find that combination in the right group of people, and it can make you very rich.'

Anton Savich could drink to that.

# 14

It was nearing midnight by the time Eddie left the Xang home. It had been an exhausting emotional ordeal. They had lost their son once, when he left with the snakehead, and Eddie told them they'd lost him again to the sea. He had introduced himself as a merchant sailor for COSCO, China's military-run shipping line, and said that his ship had come across a container on its return to Shanghai. The captain had ordered it hauled aboard, thinking there might be something of value inside. He spared them the grim details of what had really been found but said he'd discovered their son's diary and vowed he would inform the family.

It had taken several hours to coax out where the snakehead, Yan Luo, had his headquarters. Eddie was relieved the family didn't ask him to explain why a merchant sailor would want to know, because there was no ready answer.

He left their house above the bicycle shop armed with directions to a bar in a warehouse district and went in search of the snakehead who had sent Xang and his extended family on a journey to their deaths. The streets were quiet. It was late, and with the military encamped in the town square, the locals had prudently decided to remain indoors.

The bar was located on Long March Street, a potholed strip of crumbling asphalt that ran parallel to a tributary of the Min River. There were few lights, and the air was heavy with the smell of decay and rust. Most of the buildings along the river side of the street were corrugated metal, and all seemed to lean against their neighbor. It made Eddie think that if the lynchpost was removed, several blocks of warehouses would tumble like dominoes. Thorny weeds grew from grease-blackened soil in the few areas not paved over.

The other side of the street was crowded with three-story apartment blocks. Every time Eddie passed the alley separating two buildings, he got a whiff of the communal dung heap. From the numerous garbage piles came the sound of cats and rats competing for food. He heard the occasional wail of a child from one of the darkened apartments.

Nearly to the end of the street, garish light spilled from a storefront, and as he approached he heard muted music coming from within. This had to be the place. His pace slowed as he approached. He was planning on retracing the steps that Xang had taken, a route that had ended in tragedy. Once under the control of the snakehead, Eddie would have few options but to go along with the tide of humanity seeking to escape China. As the light grew brighter and the pop music louder, Eddie's breath became short, and he felt sweat trickle down from under his arm.

He knew his fears, had faced them over a distinguished career in the CIA and during his time with the Corporation, but knew that each time he forced himself to overcome them it had a corrosive effect on his psyche. It took something from him, weakened him. Like the cumulative effect of concussions, there was always the risk that the next one would be fatal.

Eddie clenched his fists and forced himself to stride those last few yards to the bar. There was no bouncer, so he threw open the door and stepped in. The music blared from a pair of speakers mounted behind the bar. The fog of cigarette smoke was as dense as a tear gas attack and just as irritating to his eyes. The wood-planked floor was slick with spilled beer and was moldy in spots. The patrons were mostly young toughs in black leather and overly made-up girls in miniskirts and belly-revealing tops. Despite the infectious beat of the music, the bar's atmosphere seemed charged with something ugly.

Eddie spotted the problem as his eyes swept the men seated at the bar along the room's back wall. Three of them wore uniforms. The army had come into the local oasis of Western decadence, and no one seemed willing to do anything about it. Yan Luo, if he was here, wouldn't invite trouble for his smuggling operation by confronting a trio of drunk soldiers in town for one night. And if the snakehead wasn't going to evict the soldiers, no one else would either. The men would remain until they'd had their fill.

No one paid Eddie much attention as he moved to an open seat at the far end of the bar. He ordered a beer, making sure the bartender saw the wad of money he carried. He had the situation figured out and a plan formulated by the time he'd downed half the bottle.

If the soldiers didn't leave before closing time, Eddie was in trouble. Once the soldier he'd killed turned up missing the next day and the army began to tear the town apart, Yan Luo would fade into the background. He'd close down his smuggling ring until after the body was found and an appropriate number of arrests had been made. It might be weeks before he felt safe enough to resume trafficking people out of the area. Eddie needed to be in the smuggling conduit tonight if he hoped to discover if there was a connection between the snakeheads and the pirates preying on shipping in the Sea of Japan. His solution was simple.

He had to get the three armed soldiers out of the bar before closing, which by the sour look on the bartender's face wouldn't be too much longer.

Of the three soldiers, only one was drinking heavily. He was a corporal, a couple years older than the two privates flanking him. He regaled his pals with wild stories as he drank beer after beer. His two companions had the look of peasants just off the farm and appeared overwhelmed by everything that had happened to them since stepping from behind the plow ox. The corporal sounded like he was from a city. It was possible that he was a friend of the would-be rapist; maybe they had joined up together. He held his comrades enthralled with tales of sexual excess and debauchery and made boasts that by the end of the evening his companions would have such stories of their own. He said this and leered at the closest girls.

Eddie waited for any of the locals to react. One man at the bar wearing black jeans and a motorcycle jacket made of vinyl glanced at a table in the darkest corner of the room. It was a quick flicker that the soldiers didn't notice, but Eddie did. At the table were three men and a pair of girls who could be twins. Two of the men looked like muscle, bodyguards. The third had to be the snakehead, Yan Luo. He wore a dark suit jacket over a black T-shirt and impenetrable sunglasses. He gave the barest shake of his head. It seemed he didn't want trouble with the soldiers.

The snakehead sensed Eddie's gaze. Eddie did nothing to mask his intentions. He stood. He'd finished his beer and grabbed the bottle around the neck. Yan Luo slid his Ray-Bans down his small nose to watch what was about to unfold. His expression remained neutral, and the bodyguards seemed oblivious.

Eddie moved so he was behind the soldiers and tapped the corporal on the meaty shoulder. The big man didn't react, although one of the privates shot Eddie a wary look. The din of patrons' conversations became a muted, expectant silence. Only the stereo continued to play on. Eddie tapped the corporal again, harder.

He whirled around on his barstool and shot to his feet. He was much steadier than Eddie had expected. His small, piggy eyes narrowed as he looked down at the creature who dared to interrupt his drinking.

'You owe those young women an apology, and I think it's best if you and your friends left the bar,' Eddie said in his most cultured voice.

The corporal roared with laughter. 'You think it best.' He laughed again. 'I think it best if you piss off.' He put a heavy hand on Eddie's chest and shoved with all his strength.

Rather than fall back, Eddie twisted so the force of the push made the corporal take a staggering step forward. As he'd anticipated, the two farm boys remained in their seats, though they watched expectantly. The corporal threw a lightning punch at Eddie's head. Eddie barely had time to duck as another shot bored in, a left jab to his ribs that connected solidly. He had wholly overestimated the corporal's level of inebriation, or else the man was a natural drunken brawler.

The corporal grabbed up his own beer bottle and smashed it on the bar. The jagged ring of glass he waved at Eddie's head was as sharp as any knife. Eddie could have broken his own bottle to even the fight, but killing the soldier wasn't an option. He wanted the men out of the bar, not a police raid.

'I think it best if you bleed a little,' the corporal snarled and swung the broken bottle at Eddie's throat. Had it connected, the glass would have torn through cartilage and arteries and nearly taken Eddie's head off. He rocked back and let the broken bottle whisk an inch from his skin. He jammed his own bottle under the soldier's ribs, digging the neck into the slab of muscle so the corporal had to step back, roaring in pain.

Both young privates got to their feet.

Eddie pegged the farm boys with a hard stare. 'You don't want any part of this.' His warning came in a hoarse whisper, and he refocused on the corporal. He moved into a martial arts stance, his motions so fluid it seemed his body was made of water. He let the bottle drop from his fingers.

The bigger man also crouched down, his hands weaving in front of his face, his eyes locked on Eddie's.

Big mistake.

Eddie's upper body didn't move as he threw three successive kicks: ribs, knee, and a shot to the groin that didn't properly connect. The corporal should have been watching Eddie's torso to be able to anticipate his blows.

The soldier staggered under the onslaught, but Eddie gave no quarter. He glided in close, launching a series of quick strikes, his hands almost blurring. Throat, ribs, solar plexus, head, ribs again, nose. By the time he stepped back again, five seconds had elapsed, and the corporal was a bloody mess.

One of the privates made a jerky move as if he were going to defend his comrade. Eddie had a hand to his throat before the boy was even sure he was going to commit.

'He isn't worth it,' Eddie said evenly, his breathing unaffected by the adrenaline or the fight. He gently pushed the soldier back into his seat.

The corporal was still standing, barely, but there was hatred in his eyes. In this condition, the soldier would most likely return to the bar with reinforcements. Eddie spun like a dervish, firing two brutal roundhouse kicks to the corporal's head. The first bent him double and rolled his eyes back into his skull. The second drove him to the floor so hard his insentient body bounced off the wood planking. He wouldn't wake for hours, and at least a day would pass before he would be coherent enough to consider revenge.

Eddie looked back at the privates. 'Do yourselves a favor and find a new buddy. This guy's got a big enough mouth to get you into trouble but no way to get you out. You understand?' One of them nodded mutely. 'Take him back to wherever you're encamped. Tell your sergeant he fell down a flight of stairs, and don't come back again.'

Grateful they'd been spared, the two privates scooped the unconscious corporal from the floor and slung his limp arms over their shoulders. They dragged him from the bar without a backward glance. Eddie turned to the bartender and indicated he wanted another beer. As if a dam had burst, everyone was talking at once, conversations floating over his head as the youths recounted what had just happened.

Eddie managed to take his first sip before one of Yan Luo's bodyguards ambled over. 'Mr Yan would like a word with you.'

Eddie eyed the bodyguard, took another sip, and got to his feet. Once he committed himself there was no turning back. The snakehead would have complete control of his life. Yan Luo could turn him in for reward money once Eddie made his play as a deserter. He could have him killed on the spot just for the sport of it, or he could pass him along the chain that could ultimately end in a shipping container on the high seas. He squared his shoulders and followed the bodyguard over to Yan's group.

Yan ordered the teenage twins away as Eddie approached. One of them purposely pressed her backside against Eddie's groin as she and her sister moved over to the bar. Eddie ignored her and sat opposite the snakehead. Yan Luo removed his sunglasses. Eddie estimated he wasn't yet thirty, but the smuggler had an aura of world-weary disdain found in someone who'd only known life's darker side.

'I suspect there was a reason behind your demonstration,' Yan Luo said.

'I couldn't speak with you with them in the bar.'

'Why is that?'

Rather than answer, Eddie pulled the stolen dog tags from around his neck and tossed them onto the scarred table.

Yan Luo didn't pick them up or even touch them. His gaze turned speculative. 'Are you with the troops in town for the election?'

'No. I was stationed outside Fouzou.'

'And you came here?'

'You helped a friend's cousin a while back.'

'I help a great many people. What did I help this person do?'

'You got him to Gold Mountain.' That was the name illegals had given the United States. Eddie let the words hang in the smoky air for long seconds. 'I want to go, too.'

'Not possible.'

'Why?'

'I get paid for favors,' the snakehead replied.

At that, Eddie pulled a thick roll of money from his

pocket. 'I know how the system works. I give you money now and work off the rest when I reach America. Only you have no way to guarantee I'd pay since I have no family here to threaten.' Eddie peeled several yuan notes from the outside of the roll to reveal an inner core of American dollars. 'Five thousand right now. Another two when I leave China, and you forget you ever met me.'

The corners of Yan's mouth lifted slightly, and his eyes narrowed. 'And what's to stop me from taking your money now and forgetting we ever met?'

Eddie spun the table forty-five degrees with a flick of his foot and rammed a corner into one of the bodyguard's chests, just hard enough to knock the wind out of him. He launched himself to his feet and drove his elbow onto the tabletop, splitting the wood in half. As it collapsed, he kicked the spot where the leg met the top, snapping the three-foot leg free. He had it in his hand and thrust against the second bodyguard's throat before the man had even thought of going for the gun hidden behind his back.

Yan remained in his seat but couldn't hide his disbelief at how quickly his two best men had been subdued.

'I could have killed all three of you,' Eddie said just loud enough to be heard over the driving rock beat from the speakers. 'I'm making you a fair offer. If you don't want it, I walk away.'

'I think you will do well in Gold Mountain,' Yan said, breaking into an insincere smile.

Eddie dropped the stump of table leg on the floor and retook his seat. The bodyguard massaged his throat and glowered but made no retaliatory move. 'How does it work from here?' Eddie asked.

'I have two others ready to make the trip with you.' The

snakehead checked his watch. 'I wasn't planning on leaving until tomorrow night, but things might get hot if that soldier decides to make trouble. I have a truck. I'll pick you up at the end of the block in an hour. We'll meet with my contact in Fouzou tomorrow. They'll have documents made up and take you on from there.' Yan paused, his stare hardening. 'Let me give you a little advice. Don't screw with these people. You pull the kind of crap you did tonight, and you'll find yourself trying to stuff your guts back into your body.'

Eddie nodded. He knew he could get away with intimidating Yan because he was low on the snakehead chain of command. He was a recruiter, a foot soldier with little clout. He would remain a big fish in the small pond of Lantan, while the people Eddie really wanted were much higher up. From now on he'd pretend to be a model immigrant, compliant, grateful, and a little afraid.

The fear he didn't have to fake.

# I5

By the time the jumbo jet's tires screeched against the tarmac at Zurich's airport, Juan Cabrillo had filled in the outline of his plan. Admittedly it was one of the most insane he'd ever thought of, but given the mission parameters and the short timeline his instincts told him he was under, there was nothing left for him but insanity.

He'd spent most of the long flight from Tokyo in communication with the *Oregon* through a secure laptop. Max Hanley had assembled the team Juan wanted with him in Switzerland as well as the equipment they would need from the ship. The *Oregon* was running at flank speed for Taipei, the closest anchorage with an international airport. It was a calculated gamble to break the surveillance with the *Maus,* but at four knots Juan was sure his crew could find the floating drydock again. He and Max estimated that they'd be off-station for less than a day provided there were no troubles in Taiwan. Juan had pulled in an old favor with the harbormaster in Taipei to make sure there wouldn't be.

Equipment that couldn't pass an international customs inspection would have to be improvised once they were in Switzerland, but Juan didn't think it would be a problem. He had numerous contacts in and around Zurich from his days with the CIA, and they only needed a couple of guns. They could mix the explosives themselves with household chemicals, and everything else they would need was either available for rental or sale.

With his team twenty-four hours behind him, Juan's first priority was to find a safe house and reconnoiter the route between Regensdorf prison and the courthouse downtown.

Twenty minutes after clearing Customs, he was behind the wheel of a rented Mercedes ML-500 sport utility vehicle. He doubted he'd need the truck's off-road capabilities, but it was anonymous enough in the affluent city, and it came equipped with a GPS mapping system. It was a beautiful spring morning, so he had the windows rolled down and the sunroof retracted.

Unlike Tokyo, Cabrillo enjoyed Zurich, with its seamless blend of old and new. Baroque and modern architecture stood side by side, not in competition but in a calming harmony. It was in Zurich that he'd first slept with a contact while working for the Company. She was a low-level Russian embassy employee who couldn't provide any valuable information, but that didn't make Juan feel any less like James Bond. The memory brought a smile as he circled the city on the ring road and found the exit that would take him to the prison. The safe house would have to wait until he had found the best spot for what he had in mind.

Just before he reached the turnoff for the prison, Juan turned around and headed back into the city. No sense in showing off the car to the guards at the entrance gate since he was pretty sure he'd have to cover this route a few times before he knew where his team would stage their strike. He drove straight to the courthouse where Rudolph Isphording was playing star witness in the trial of the century.

The streets around the courthouse were cramped and full of traffic, mostly because there was a new building under construction next door, and the trucks hauling materials to and from the work zone blocked intersections. The new building was still just a steel frame with concrete slab floors stacked seven high. A tower crane lorded over the construction site, its horizontal boom arm able to swing far over the plywood and chain-link fence ringing the construction site. Juan paused at a red light to watch it hoist a bundle of I-beams into the air and was startled into motion when the driver behind him gave a polite tap on his horn. The light had changed. He waved an apology and drove on.

He tracked back and forth between the prison and the courthouse six more times, taking six different routes. If he were in charge of the security team that drove Isphording into the city for the trial, he would select a different route at random each day, making it much more difficult for someone to attack the armored caravan. But the problem was that the destination was the same every time. The closer the van came to the courthouse, the more predictable and vulnerable it became.

Juan found a parking spot a few blocks from the court and spent the next two hours walking the neighborhood, sipping black coffee from a Starbucks. He felt he should have bought his coffee from a local vendor instead of an international franchise, but it had been months since he'd had a taste of his favorite brew. He made a mental note to contact the company's Seattle headquarters and see if it was possible to buy their special equipment for the *Oregon*.

While traffic was heavy all around the courthouse and the adjacent construction site, the main street behind the two buildings was relatively quiet. He would need to post people here for a few days to get a better handle on the traffic patterns if this was the location they would use. So far everything looked right. He only needed to make a few changes to his original plan.

A little after noon he rented an apartment in a four-story building about six blocks from the courthouse. He explained to the leasing agent that he and a group of American lawyers were in Zurich for several months as part of an ongoing lawsuit against an insurance company. The apartment had three bedrooms and an office. The furniture was a bit threadbare, but the kitchen had been recently remodeled, and the bathroom contained a tub big enough to swim laps. Most important, it was on the building's top floor and Juan could tell that, if they needed it, they could gain roof access from the back alley fire escape. He'd been forced into a six-month lease, which meant he'd need to keep the unit occupied well after the job was done in order to deflect suspicion.

Too often a criminal would establish himself in a neighborhood, stay close to the bank he planned to rob, then vacate the area as soon as the crime had gone down. A police canvass a couple days later would reveal the person had left, and the cops had themselves a solid lead. By rotating a few Corporation operatives or outside contractors through the apartment for a couple months, no one would suspect anything was amiss. It was this level of detail that ensured the Corporation's anonymity as well as its success.

After making calls to procure weapons, Juan had nothing to do but wait for his team to arrive. He grabbed a meal at a nearby restaurant. He hadn't planned on polishing off the carafe of wine, but each sip seemed to work magic on the tension in his shoulders and neck. Juan rarely worried about his own safety; it was his people who concerned him.

He'd always had a leadership style of commanding from the front, to never ask a subordinate to do what he was unwilling to do himself. For that, his people gave him their loyalty. In return, Juan knew he could trust them in any situation. But it never got easier, asking them to put themselves in harm's way. Yes, each member of the Corporation shared in the profits of their work. Each was a millionaire at the very least, but like he'd discussed with Max back on the *Oregon,* this wasn't about money, not really. It was about the dedication to doing the right thing. It was an ideal that drove Juan and his people, an ideal that someone had to face the new dangers of the twenty-first century.

People were needed on the ramparts of freedom to stand the dark watch against any and all who were against it.

His team had taken it upon themselves to become those gatekeepers, those standers of the dark watch. And it seemed each time Juan read a newspaper or caught the news from a satellite feed and learned of some new atrocity, he realized they would need to stand their posts for a long time to come.

Dr Julia Huxley was the last to arrive the next day. Rather than have her stay in the safe house, Juan had told her to take a hotel room near Zurich's famed Bahnhofstrasse, the bank- and shop-lined street that as much identified the city as Fifth Avenue did New York or Rodeo Drive did Beverly Hills. Although Julia had proven herself on several covert operations, her primary function was as medical officer. Juan would much rather have used Linda Ross for this job, but she wasn't the right body type or height for what he had in mind, nor were any of the other half-dozen women aboard the *Oregon*. Julia had readily agreed to come to Zurich, yet Juan made sure she was as insulated as possible from the rest of the team.

He barely recognized her when Hali Kasim escorted her

into the safe house living room. Gone were her soft, dark eyes. She wore tinted contacts that made them look watery blue behind large-framed glasses. Her customary ponytail was hidden under a wig of gray hair that curled around her head like a thinning bush. Julia normally had the curves of a 1950s pinup model, but her travel-wrinkled clothes now hid the doughy body of a prison matron. The frown lines across her forehead were deep enough to be considered corrugation, and two laugh lines alongside her mouth were like trenches.

She looked nothing like Julia Huxley, M.D., and everything like Frau Kara Isphording, wife of convicted embezzler Rudolph Isphording.

'Good God,' Juan greeted her, 'you're ugly enough to scare a bulldog off a meat wagon.'

Julia curtsied and smiled. 'You sure are a charmer, Juan Rodriguez Cabrillo. I must admit Kevin outdid himself.' Kevin Nixon ran what the Corporation had dubbed the Magic Shop, a large space aboard the *Oregon* where he and his team could throw together any number of uniforms, disguises, and all manner of dirty tricks.

'We might be here for a while,' Juan said as he circled his medical officer with a critical eye. 'Can you re-create this effect?'

'Kevin showed me how to do it.' Julia shook her ample hips. 'This oh-so-flattering body suit is no big deal, but doing the makeup so you can't notice the facial appliances is tricky. I think I have it, though. It's a little creepy. Kevin knows more about cosmetics and skin care than a counter girl at Bloomie's.'

'He was just nudged out for an Oscar for best makeup a few years before joining us,' Juan told her. He didn't add that Nixon had turned his back on Hollywood following September 11. His sister was on her way to see him from Boston when her plane smashed into the North Tower.

'Plus,' Julia added, 'he packed me enough frumpy clothes to open my own secondhand shop.'

'You don't need to bother with the costume until we're ready. No need to advertise there's a Kara Isphording clone running around Zurich.'

'What, and deny all the men a gaze at my beauty?'

'The only head you're going to turn looking like that is the head of a screw, and even then you're going to need a pneumatic wrench.' Juan called out to gather his people together. In total there were five members of the Corporation present, including himself. It was a small team, but once Julia had done her thing, she could act as backup when they made their move.

'I've had a chance to go over the ground, and think I found the perfect spot. We'll need a few days for additional recon just to be sure. I'm not married to the site, so if something doesn't feel right, don't hesitate to bring it up. We'll go over the ground together later on.

'Once we're comfortable and we have all our equipment ready, we'll move on to phase one, and that's snatching the real Kara Isphording.'

'Is she guarded?' Hali asked.

'Don't know yet. That'll be part of our reconnaissance.'

'What's gonna be our cover?'

'All the dummy companies Rudy Isphording set up for the purchase of the *Maus* have Russians on their boards of directors. We'll use that and pretend to be Russians out to spring Isphording from jail.'

'Why would he want to go?' asked Franklin Lincoln, a

SEAL vet. 'As I understand from the briefing Max gave, this shyster has a sweetheart deal with the prosecutors.'

'Because we're going to play up the rumor about how Isphording had his hands in the Palestine Liberation Organization's cookie jar.'

'Has he?'

'I've got Murph confirming it, but it appears old Rudy might know where some of Yasir Arafat's missing billions are. Either way, we convince him that the PLO believes it, and he'll know his only chance is with us.'

'And once we have him?' Julia asked.

Juan's tone darkened. 'We sweat him. Hard. Eddie's still in China last I heard.'

'Near Fouzou,' Hali interrupted.

'So we need to learn what we can on our end and pray we're in position to intercept the boat they're using to smuggle him. I'm convinced Isphording's the key to whoever's behind the *Maus* and the pirates.'

'What if he's not?' Julia asked. 'What if he doesn't know anything beyond the shell companies he set up?'

As much as he didn't want to face that possibility, Juan knew he had to answer. 'Then Eddie's as good as dead, and we're back to chasing individual pirates across the Sea of Japan.'

For the next several hours Cabrillo laid out his ideas in detail, refining them with suggestions from his people. They all had sharp intellects and years of covert experience. No one deluded themselves that this would be a simple job, but by the time they finished, they knew they had the best possible plan. Juan gave each of them their orders for the next several days. Some would chart traffic flows and activity around the construction site. Others were to procure and modify equipment, the most critical being a ten-wheeled truck and trailer. Juan would scout out the Isphording home and determine what, if any, security they would need to overcome as well as rent a warehouse outside the city.

Today was Tuesday. Mark Murphy had learned that Rudolph Isphording was scheduled to appear in court on the following Monday. For what Juan had in mind, they could lay a lot of the groundwork but would need the week-end to have everything in place for Monday morning. That meant they had to get to Frau Isphording no later than Thursday night if Julia was going to double her during Friday's regular visiting hours. Juan hated the tight timeline, but there was no helping it. He didn't dare wait another full week. God knew where Eddie or the *Maus* would be by then.

It was now or never.

'Com check?' Juan said into the voice-activated throat mike.

He received the ready signal from Linc and Hali Kasim. Julia merely placed a hand on his shoulder, since she wouldn't leave his side for the next twelve hours. The night was dark and moonless because of cloud cover. Dew shone silvery white on the lawn surrounding the three-story brick house. The upscale suburban neighborhood had been quiet since an elderly man had returned to his own mini-mansion after walking what had to be the most constipated dachshund in history.

Cabrillo knew after watching her for three days that Kara Isphording lived alone. She had a maid during the day, but at night she was her home's sole occupant. He also knew she had an alarm system. The doors and windows were all wired, and he'd once spied the maid deactivating the system when she'd shown up for work in the morning. He guessed it would have been installed after her husband had been arrested, so it wouldn't be too deeply integrated into the grounds, no motion detectors or IR cameras, but then again, all it took was Isphording's wife to push a panic button, and all hell would break loose.

'Okay, Hali, you're up. Once Linc pops the door, you have sixty seconds to deactivate.' This was an estimate on Juan's part but a calculated one. Kara Isphording was in her late fifties and would doubtless have little experience with electronics. Whoever installed the alarm would make sure a client had ample time to shut the system down so as to avoid false alarms.

Once the ex-SEAL and the Corporation's communications specialist did their job, they were to return to the Mercedes. Juan was approaching Frau Isphording as a member of the Russian mafia here to save her husband from Palestinian terrorists. It would be a little hard explaining the presence of a Lebanese and an African-American.

'Think of it as affirmative inaction,' he'd joked as they finalized the plan.

Frank Lincoln towered over Hali Kasim as they dashed from cover behind a thick hedgerow bordering the Isphording property. Both wore black. Hali carried a small duffel for his tools. Linc had his lockpicks in a slim billfold jammed into his back pocket.

They reached the heavy oak door. Curtains were drawn over the flanking sidelights. The house was completely dark. Kara Isphording's bedroom light had gone out three hours earlier, long enough to enter deep REM but not so long as to need to use the bathroom.

Hali hung back as Linc readied his picks. He'd practiced on an identical lock that he'd bought from a building supply store on the other side of the city. His fingers were large, but they moved with the delicacy of a surgeon's as he eased in the tension pick, then began to set the pins with another smaller tool. It took him eight seconds to snick back the dead bolt and a further fifteen to turn the main handle.

He shot Hali a glance. The smaller man had his bag open and wore a tiny light mounted on a headband. He nodded. Linc eased open the door. An electronic tone sounded and would continue at five-second intervals until the alarm was shut down or went active.

The entry floor was polished wood. A dark Oriental rug covered the space between the door and a massive staircase that rose to the second floor. To right and left were other rooms, a living room and a dining room large enough to seat ten. Hali saw all this in a fleeting glimpse. The alarm panel was to the right of the door. A red light on its cover blinked accusingly.

He pried off the face with a screwdriver. Within were bundles of wires. He ignored them all. The circuit had already been cut. He needed the numerical key that would deactivate the system. He spotted two computer chips embedded on a small motherboard. He popped them both, then clamped a tiny wire to the broken leads as a bypass. The light and chime continued. Linc posted himself at the foot of the stairs, straining to hear if Kara Isphording had been disturbed.

With such a system, the owner had three tries to enter the right code in order to prevent the alarm from sounding. After the third attempt the system would automatically trip.

By removing the logic circuits from the panel, the security system had no way of knowing how many attempts Hali was about to make.

Kasim dusted the alarm's touchpad with fingerprint powder. Actually, it was finely ground pencil lead and worked just as well. He let out a relieved breath when only four of the keys showed they'd ever been pressed. The fingerprints were smudged, but that wasn't the point. With just four numbers to reset the alarm, there were thirty-six possible combinations and not nearly enough time to run them all. Except that the four keys used by Frau Isphording were one, two, three, and four. It was the most common alarm code in the world, a convenience for homeowners and thieves alike. Hali pressed them in sequence. The little red light continued to wink at him and the chime sounded that another five seconds had passed.

He hit the keys in reverse order and still the alarm remained active.

'Time,' Hali hissed into his microphone.

'Twenty-three seconds,' Juan answered from outside.

Hali had no choice but to punch in the progression. 1243 Enter, 1324 Enter, 1342 Enter, 1423 Enter, 1432 Enter.

'What's happening?' Juan asked.

'Random number. I haven't hit it yet.'

'You've got ten seconds.'

2134 Enter, 2143 Enter, 2314 Enter, 2341 Enter.

'Hali,' Linc whispered, 'Try 3142.'

'Five seconds.'

Kasim didn't question Linc's guess. He hit the numbers and stabbed the Enter key.

The chime sounded again and the light began to blink at double speed.

'We gotta go,' Hali said, his voice strained with the tension.

'Reverse 'em,' Linc ordered. 'Try 4231!'

'One second.'

Linc's suggestion wasn't a reversal of the numbers, but Hali punched them in anyway: 4231 Enter.

The light stopped blinking. The alarm had been disabled. Hali shot a questioning look at his partner.

'Hey, man you should have paid more attention to Max's briefing.' Linc's smile was that of the Cheshire Cat. 'Isphordings have two grown children. One born on April second and the other March first. Four/two, three/one. Elementary, my dear Hali, elementary.'

Hali spent a few more minutes with the alarm panel to disable the panic buttons. One on this control and no doubt one next to the Kara Isphording's bed.

'All right, clear out,' the chairman whispered as he and Doc Huxley entered the foyer. 'If we're still inside after twenty minutes, assume everything's okay and you can head back to the safe house. Julia will take Mrs Isphording's car to Regensdorf tomorrow. Once she's back she'll babysit her over the weekend, and I'll borrow the car to get back to the city.'

After Hali and Linc returned to the SUV, Juan stepped outside and dialed the Isphording residence from his cell. He heard the phone ring in his ear and through-out the house. After the third ring a sleepy voice croaked, 'Allo?'

'Frau Isphording, my name is Yuri Zayysev,' Juan said in Russian-accented English. 'I am an associate of your husband. It is important that I see you tonight.'

'*Was? Nein.* That is not possible,' Kara Isphording

groused, switching to English. '*Mein Gott*, it is two o'clock in the morning.'

'This concerns your husband's safety, Frau Isphording.' Juan had deepened his voice, adding menace. By now she must have realized that many, perhaps all, of her husband's clients worked the other side of the law. 'I am just outside your home. Please meet me downstairs. I have already disabled your alarm system. If I wanted to harm you, I would have done so already.'

'Who are you?' Fear had crept into her tone.

'Someone who is trying to help you and your husband. He is a trusted member of an organization I work for, and we have learned that he's been targeted for assassination on Monday morning.'

'Assassination?'

'Yes, Frau Isphording. By members of the PLO.'

'What did you say your name is?'

'Yuri Zayysev. I have been sent from Saint Petersburg to help your family.'

She had to know Rudolph did a great deal of work with Russians, because after a moment's pause she agreed to meet. Juan was relieved. He could have simply bound and gagged the woman in her bed, had Julia send away the maid when she arrived in the morning, and put his plan into motion. However, that wasn't his style. The woman was an innocent in this affair, and he wouldn't put her through any more than absolutely necessary.

A light at the head of the stairs came on. Made up and properly dressed, Kara Isphording was not an attractive woman. But fresh from her bed with her hair awry and her face puffy with sleep, she was downright scary. She'd donned a heavy robe over whatever she wore to sleep in, and Juan fervently hoped it wouldn't slip open. For this meeting he was dressed in black jeans, a black shirt, and a large black leather jacket, the de rigueur uniform of an enforcer in the Russian Mafia. He'd dyed his hair and five days' worth of beard a ginger red. He also wore tinted contacts that darkened his bright blue eyes.

'I am sorry to disturb you, Frau Isphording,' Juan said when she reached the first floor. Neither made a move to shake hands. 'There was no other way. Plans are in motion to free your husband, but we need your help. You are the only one allowed to see him at Regensdorf, and he needs to be made aware of what is happening.'

'You said someone wants to kill my Rudy?' She dumped herself into a chair. Tears were already in her eyes.

'Yes. You may not be aware, but factions within the Palestinian movement believe your husband is the key to a great deal of their money. Perhaps billions of dollars.'

'But . . . but he said that what he did for the Palestinians was legal.'

Juan knelt in front of the frightened woman and took her trembling hands in his. 'That may be true, but for these people rumor is as good as fact. They are either going to kill him on Monday or try to abduct him. We must act before they do.'

'I don't . . . I don't know what to do. Shouldn't you tell the police?'

'Your husband's testimony has already ruined the careers of several prominent people in business and the government. There are even more powerful people who would like nothing more than for your husband to be silenced.'

Juan could see he was being too circumspect. Kara Isphording was already at the end of her mental and emotional rope and couldn't grasp what he was saying. He couldn't blame her. A year ago she was married to a success-ful lawyer and enjoying the genteel life of a Swiss *hausfrau*. Today she was bombarded with reporters and dosed daily with stories about her husband's criminal activities.

'What I am trying to tell you is the police won't prevent an attack on your husband.'

'But that's just not right!' she cried indignantly. 'We pay taxes.'

Cabrillo almost smiled at her naïveté. 'As the Americans would say, your husband has stirred up a hornets' nest. I am here to make sure he isn't the last one stung.'

She dabbed at her eyes with a tissue that looked like it had been in her pocket for as long as she'd owned the robe. She tried to square her shoulders. 'I don't know what to do. What do I tell Rudy? What is your plan?'

'You don't have to do anything, Frau Isphording.' Juan turned his head and called into the dining room. 'Ludmilla.'

Julia stepped into the light cast from the fixture atop the stairs. Kara gasped at seeing her twin and jammed her knuckles against her mouth. For a moment Juan was afraid she'd faint, but she gathered enough composure to get to her feet. She crossed to where Julia stood and studied her doppelganger.

'This is my associate, Ludmilla Demonova. She will go to Regensdorf in your place tomorrow. I do not mean to insult you, but it is safer operationally for her to pretend to be you than it is for us explain the details of our plan. Had we had more time, you could have gone to your husband yourself, but . . .' Juan's voice trailed off, letting the woman draw whatever conclusions she wanted. 'Are you allowed to give your husband anything?'

Kara Isphording continued to stare at Julia, forcing Juan to repeat the question.

'No, not really, but I pass him little notes. The guards haven't made me stop.'

'Okay, that is good. I need you to write to your husband. Tell him that we haven't harmed you and that he is to listen carefully to what Ludmilla tells him. Can you do this for me?'

'*Ja,* yes, I can.' She was regaining her senses and seemed to accept that Juan and Julia were there to help her. 'What happens afterward?'

'You mean once we free your husband? I do not know. I am only to take him to a safe house. After that' – Juan shrugged like a soldier just doing his job – 'it is up to your husband and my boss. I'm sure they will send for you, and the two of you can retire to the south of France or the Costa del Sol.'

She gave him a wan smile as if she knew that the rest of her life would never be so idyllic.

Julia left for the prison the following morning a little past nine. Juan chafed at having to wait around, but there was always the risk that Kara Isphording would lose her nerve and phone the police. After giving the maid the day off, the two of them sat in the dining room over a cold coffee service. Juan continued in his role of a Russian gangster so there was little conversation, and for that he was grateful. Only three days remained until they would snatch the lawyer, and he felt every minute tick by. The modifications to the truck weren't complete, although they'd done run-throughs in rental cars and had the timing down. What worried him most was the work they had to get done over the weekend at the construction site. Fortunately, the company overseeing the building didn't post night watchmen, so that wasn't a problem. However, they had ten tons of cement to get into position tonight if they were to make their deadline.

By eleven Juan's wrist was sore from checking his watch. He'd spoken with Linc and found they'd finished with the semi at the warehouse and were now loading the fifty-pound sacks of cement.

The sound of the automatic garage door opening launched Juan out of his seat. He was at the door to meet Julia when she stepped from the Isphordings' 740 BMW.

'Well?'

'Piece of cake.' Julia smiled. 'It actually took him a few seconds to see through the disguise, and none of the guards even looked twice.'

'Great job. Is he all set?'

'More than all set. He's eager. I guess he really was hooked up with the PLO. As soon as I mentioned they were gunning for him, he agreed to everything.'

'And you laid out the whole plan?'

'He knows where and when we're making the grab. He'll tell the prison administrator that he needs to meet with his attorney early on Monday morning. That'll put his convoy at the construction site before the work crew shows up.'

'Did he give up any information?'

'About the *Maus*? No. And I didn't press. But when I told him the Russians sent me, he asked if I worked for Anton Savich. I played dumb and agreed. Isphording seemed relieved. Savich must be his principal contact.'

'Savich?' Cabrillo said the name aloud as if tasting it, trying to draw out a memory. He shook his head. 'New one to me. I'll contact Murph and have him do a search. Are you all set to watch the real Kara Isphording?'

'Got everything I need.' Julia patted her shoulder bag. Inside was a syringe that she'd administer Sunday night after Kara went to bed. She'd be out for twenty-four hours, long after Juan and Julia were headed back to the *Oregon*.

# 16

No matter how often Doc Huxley admonished him, Max Hanley refused to give up his pipe or dessert. He figured that by his age he'd earned the right to know what was best for him. The thickening around his middle added only ten or fifteen pounds, and while he couldn't run a mile in under ten minutes, his job rarely required him to run a mile. So what was the big deal?

His cholesterol was just about normal, he wasn't showing any signs of diabetes, and his blood pressure was actually on the low side.

He swirled his fork through the raspberry drizzle pooled on his plate and made sure he got the last few crumbs of the chocolate cake. The fork was spotless when he returned it to his plate and pushed back from the mess hall table with a satisfied groan.

'All finished?' the white-jacketed mess steward asked.

'Only because I'd need a microscope to find the few remaining cake molecules. Thanks, Maurice.'

Max had dined alone this evening but nodded to the personnel at the other tables before leaving the mahogany-paneled mess. His sturdy brogans sank into the almost inch-thick rug. A squall had kicked up from the north over the past several hours, so he decided to take his pipe in his cabin. He'd just settled into an easy chair with a week's worth of the *International Tribune* that had been choppered back to the *Oregon* when his intercom rang. He let his cheater glasses dangle around his neck and set his pipe into an ashtray.

'Sorry to bother you on your day off.' It was Linda Ross from the operations center.

'That's okay. What's the trouble?'

'No trouble, but you wanted to know if we got anything from Eddie. It appears he's left Fouzou and might be headed back to Shanghai.'

Max digested the report. 'Makes sense from the snake-head's perspective. Shanghai is one of the busiest ports in the world. Much easier to slip a bunch of illegals onto an outbound freighter amid the confusion than at a smaller harbor like Fouzou.'

'That's what Murph and Eric Stone think, too. Do you want me to call the chairman?'

'No. Last I spoke to him he has enough to worry about. If we get any better intel, I'll have you pass it along. What's our position, and how's our wallowing friend?'

'They've picked up a current so they're now making six knots. That'll put us about a hundred miles due east of Ho Chi Minh City in another five hours.'

The name always caught Max off guard. Vietnam's largest city would always be Saigon to him. But that was from another time and another war. Every so often when a chopper approached the *Oregon,* a flood of memories would leave Hanley shaken for days.

Actually, the memories were never that far from the surface. It wasn't the sound of the Vietcong's RPGs exploding or the chatter of their AK-47s that stuck with him. And the screams as his patrol boat was raked from stem to stern were just a background noise. What remained sharpest in his mind was the sound of the Huey's blades pulsating over the black jungle, homing on the stream of flares Max launched into the night with one hand as he used his other to keep his newbie bow gunner's intestines inside his body. God, the blood was hot, even in that stinking hell. The Huey's door-mounted minigun sounded like a buzz saw, and the jungle flanking the estuary peeled back under its three-thousand-round-per-minute onslaught. And when that RPG arced up at the Huey –

Max yanked himself from the past he'd never stop reliving. The newspaper was balled in his fist. 'Ah, any course change?' he finally asked.

'No, she's still on one hundred and eighty-five. Projected either she's headed for Singapore, which isn't likely since they've got the most incorruptible harbor workers in this region, or she'll turn due south soon and make for Indonesia.'

'Seems a better bet,' Max agreed. With several thousand islands to patrol, the Indonesian Coast Guard was stretched thin. The pirates would have an easy time eluding them and finding a secluded spot to unload the ship they'd hijacked off Japan. The ship-wide betting pool had been evenly split between the Philippines and Indonesia as a final destination since before they'd reached Taiwan.

'Okay, then,' Max said, 'call me if the *Maus* turns or you get anything from Eddie or Juan.'

'Roger.'

Max straightened out the rumpled pages of his newspaper and set them aside. He relit his pipe and let smoke dribble past his lips until his cabin was perfumed with the aromatic blend. As yet he couldn't figure out why the pirates hadn't found a quiet spot of ocean to disgorge their stolen ship. They'd had enough time to give her a new name and make enough cosmetic changes that no one would recognize her, especially if they ran her in different waters, say, off the coast of South America. So why risk keeping her in the drydock this long? Unless they had a specific destination in mind. Someplace close to shore where they felt safe. Max hoped the *Maus* was leading them to the pirates' lair, but it couldn't be that easy.

There was another level to this operation, another peel to the onion they hadn't seen. He knew he wouldn't find it by merely shadowing the *Maus,* but he was confident that either the chairman or Eddie Seng would. Confidentially, he was betting on Eddie finding the key. There was no real reason, just a strong feeling of confidence in the tough, independent ex-CIA operator.

Had Eddie Seng known at that moment that Max was placing a mental wager on him, he would have told the Corporation's president to put his money on Cabrillo and his team in Switzerland.

During his training for the CIA, Eddie had undergone a grueling program to teach agents how to deal with imprisonment and torture. It had been run by army specialists at a corner of Fort Bragg in North Carolina. Before he left for Bragg, his training instructor at the Farm had given him a random code word: aardvark. It was his job to keep it a secret and the soldiers' to get it out of him.

For a month they owned Eddie body and soul. They used hoses to beat him on a regular basis, confined him in an iron box in the sun for hours without water, and often poisoned his meager food rations so he couldn't keep them down. They tried to break his will by keeping him awake for six straight days and screaming every racial slur they could come up with. They once dumped him naked onto a fire ant nest, and one night they poured half a bottle of Scotch down his throat and questioned him for an hour before he passed out. They pulled out all the stops in their interrogation, but Eddie never gave up his code word. He was able to keep a small part of his mind focused that no matter what they did to him, it was only an exercise, and he wouldn't die.

Eddie held no such illusions now, and as the truck lurched, the throng of illegals packed in with him swayed so that those closest to the rear doors were almost crushed. He whispered, 'Aardvark.'

Six days in the hands of the snakeheads made that month at Fort Bragg feel like a Club Med vacation.

There were about a hundred men packed into the sweltering box truck. They hadn't been fed or been given water in at least two days, and the only reason many were still on their feet was that there was no room for them to fall. The stench of sweat and body waste was overwhelming, a cloying film that coated Eddie's mouth and seared his lungs.

It had been like this since Yan Luo had turned him over in Fouzou. The next link in the smuggling ring were members of a triad, China's version of a Mafia crew. Once they'd taken his picture for forged travel documents, he'd been locked in a cell under a cement factory with sixty others. There were no bathroom facilities. They stayed there for two days, and each night guards came down to select a couple of the more attractive women. The girls would return hours later, bleeding and shamed.

On the morning of the third day a group of South Asians arrived. They spoke to the snakeheads in accented Chinese, so Eddie couldn't tell where they were from. They could have been Indonesian, Malay, or even Filipino. But he was sure their presence was a deviation from the normal channels for getting immigrants out of China and suspected they were connected to the pirate ring.

The immigrants were brought out of their cell in groups of ten and paraded in front of the Asians. The Asians made his group strip naked and then subjected them to a humiliating scrutiny. Eddie felt like he was a slave on the auction block. They checked his teeth for decay and his genitals for obvious venereal disease. He and the others had to prove they could lift a pair of cinder blocks suspended from a bamboo pole. The Asians singled out three of the men from Eddie's group, himself included. They were the biggest of the lot, the strongest. The others were sent back to the cell.

Of the original sixty from the cell, ten were loaded into a truck. The Asian guards had to use wooden planks like bulldozer blades to pack them into the already overcrowded vehicle. The bodies were so tight there wasn't enough room to take a deep breath.

Before closing the rear door a fire hose was turned on the crowd. In the frenzy to slake their thirst, several people were hurt. Eddie managed a mouthful and was close enough to the side of the truck to lick a little more water from the hot metal. Then the door slammed shut, and the immigrants were left in total darkness.

What got Eddie, what made this so difficult, was the silence as the vehicle began its journey. No one cried or complained, no one demanded to be released. They were willing to put up with any privation if it meant they could get out of China. To them anything was worth the chance for freedom.

They drove for what felt like days but couldn't have been more than twenty hours. By the continuous swaying and jostling Eddie was sure the snakeheads kept to back roads. To compound their misery, many of the men became motion sick, adding the acrid smell of vomit to the already overwhelming stench inside the truck.

The truck squealed to a halt after a particularly smooth stretch of road. No one came to open the doors. Eddie thought he heard the sound of jet aircraft, but the noise was muffled and indistinct. It could have been thunder. They were left packed and sweating in the truck for at least another hour before someone outside unlocked the rear door.

It swung open, and glaring white light blinded the immigrants. Eddie's eyes filled with tears, but the pain was worth the first breath of fresh air he'd had in a day. They were inside some kind of huge, modern warehouse, not at all the seedy dockside facility he thought the snakeheads would use. Had Eddie not been so disorientated, he would have noticed there were no support columns for the metal building's arching roof, a clue as to his real location.

The men were allowed to jump from the truck. Many were so weak they fell to the polished concrete floor and had to crawl away to make room for the next. Eddie was proud that he managed to keep his feet. He took a few shuffling steps away from the truck and tried to squat to ease his aching knees.

There were four guards inside the warehouse. Eddie was pretty sure they were Indonesians. They wore cheap cotton pants and T-shirts, and plastic sandals on their feet. All carried the Chinese version of the AK-47. Out of habit he burned their faces into his memory.

As his sinuses cleared he became aware of another smell, not the tangy saltiness of the sea but a recognizable chemical taint. Casually, so as not to arouse the guards, he crossed back around the truck. On the far side he saw towering doors that reached nearly to the ceiling. But what gripped his attention and sent a jolt of fear to his very marrow was the functional shape of a commercial airliner. It had four engines mounted on its tail, an old Russian-built Ilyushin Il-62.

They weren't taking this group out of China on a cargo ship. They were going to fly them out. Eddie realized he was in more trouble than he'd anticipated. These people weren't connected to the pirates at all. This really was a legitimate, albeit illegal, smuggling operation. His whole trip to China was a dead end, only he had no way of contacting the *Oregon*. The jetliner's door was opened, and the guards were forming the men into a line to board. The hangar doors were still securely closed, so there'd be no escape that way.

The truck that had brought them here was quiet, its engine was off, but Eddie thought that maybe the keys were still in the ignition. The last of the immigrants were out of the cargo box and shuffling toward the Ilyushin. Eddie joined the end of the line. The truck's cab was only ten yards away to his right. He could cover that in seconds, swing himself into the seat, and try to ram his way out of the hangar.

He braced himself for the attempt, planting one shaky foot, and was about to start running when he saw that the driver was still in the cab. For another fraction of a second he thought about trying for it anyway, even though he would lose time subduing the man. One of the guards saw he'd paused and barked something that was plain to understand in any language. Eddie released a long breath, allowed his body to relax, and adopted a posture of defeat.

He took one last glance at the truck when it was his turn to mount the stairs to the aircraft's cabin. He had no idea what awaited him and the others at the end of the flight, but he saw fear in the eyes of those he passed on his way to an empty seat. They were also realizing they'd gotten more than they bargained for.

Fifteen minutes later, the Ilyushin was towed out of the hangar, and after another delay its engines fired and it began to taxi. Judging by the size of the airport complex and the time they'd driven, Eddie guessed they were near Shanghai. His theory was confirmed after the plane took off and arrowed over the city before turning northward.

'How long do you think it will take to reach America?' his seatmate whispered. He was a big farm boy who had no idea what he'd gotten himself into.

The boy still thought they were going to the United States, a land of prosperity and opportunity called Gold Mountain. Eddie didn't know where they were headed, but he knew it wasn't the States. The Ilyushin didn't have anywhere near the range. He also had a sinking feeling that before long he'd come to believe the illegals they'd found drowned in the Sea of Japan were the lucky ones.

'You'll know it when we get there, friend,' Eddie said as he closed his eyes to the inevitable. 'You'll know it when we get there.'

Cabrillo and his team spent the weekend setting up for the snatch. They worked at the construction site under the cover of darkness. Moving the tons of cement was backbreaking labor that took all of Friday night and part of

Saturday evening. The risk of their activities being detected by a foreman checking the site over the weekend was negligible, since the sacks of portland were common at the work zone. They left the placement and wiring of the explosives for Sunday night. Because of their demolition expertise, this went quickly, and by midnight they were ready to return to the warehouse Cabrillo had rented in a town about twenty miles north of Zurich.

Juan sent the others ahead in the cars they'd use during the operation while he and Linc remained behind with the tractor trailer for one final test. At this late hour there weren't any pedestrians on the street to question why the truck's driver locked his partner in the back of the box trailer. Once Linc closed the doors, Juan wedged himself into a corner of the modified trailer to keep from being tossed around. He was exhausted, and his joints creaked as he eased himself to the floor. A moment later he heard the big MAN diesel grumble, and the truck started to move. He carried a flashlight, but the echoing metal container remained mildly claustrophobic. The motor and pulley system attached to the roof looked perfect, a simple design that Linc could operate from the cab.

Juan turned on a portable radio but couldn't get a station on any frequency, and when he powered up his cell phone it couldn't acquire a signal. 'Can't hear me now,' he said into the mute device. 'Good.'

They'd installed baffles and jammers inside the trailer to isolate it from electronic signals. Linc and Hali Kasim had tested the equipment at the warehouse, but Juan wanted to make sure the system worked inside the city limits where cell coverage would be more complete. It was one more detail that he wouldn't leave to the vagaries of Murphy's Law.

Every five minutes during the thirty-minute ride he checked to make sure the phone remained useless. Linc let him out after Hali closed the warehouse doors behind the ten-wheeled truck.

'Anything?' the big man asked.

'Nada,' Juan answered, noting that once he was outside the truck his phone could connect to the nearest cell tower. 'We're good to go. We'll grab a couple hours of sleep. The van carrying Rudolph Isphording should be in position no later than eight fifteen. I want us ready by seven thirty. Has Julia checked in?'

Hali nodded. 'She called me when you were in the truck. Isphording's wife is out cold, and she's on her way back to her hotel. She'll be waiting at the prison at seven and will report in as soon as the van leaves the gates.'

'Okay, good. She'll shadow them into the city. Linc, you'll wait with the truck behind the construction site. The crash car's in position?'

'Parked it myself,' Kasim said. 'And I triple-checked the cables are in the back.'

Juan nodded. He'd expected no less. 'Now, up until tonight the only thing illegal we've done is impersonate a lawyer's wife, and even that probably isn't against the law. Come tomorrow morning, however, we're going to break about every law written into the Swiss penal code. If this operation goes south, anyone who gets nabbed is looking at a few decades in Regensdorf prison.'

His people understood the danger. It was what they were paid for, but Juan always reiterated the risks before they went into action. Hali, Linc, and the other Corporate mercenary, an ex-pararescue jumper named Michael Trono, looked primed.

The following morning broke gray and cold. A light drizzle had begun to fall by the time the team reached their prearranged staging posts. The few people out on the streets were huddled in trench coats or under umbrellas. Rather than a problem, the foul weather was a blessing because it seemed to have delayed the morning traffic.

Juan had little trouble breaking into the construction site. After all, it was his third incursion, and hot-wiring the big engine that powered the crane was a snap. The climb up the tower left him wet and shivering but, fortunately, the crane's cab had a heater. He fired it up and drank coffee from a thermos as he waited. Around his neck dangled infrared goggles.

Julia checked in again, informing the team that the armored van bearing Rudy Isphording into the city would be there in another ten minutes. From his vantage high above the streets, Juan would be able to see them five blocks before they reached the construction site. Linc had parked the tractor trailer behind the muddy area. Juan could see smoke pumping from its stack as Linc waited with the engine idling. Hali and the others were in the crash car, a small van they'd bought secondhand from a moving company in Lucerne. Juan couldn't see them but knew they also had infrared goggles as well as gas masks.

The chairman scanned the work zone once more. Piles of building materials littered the site alongside overflowing trash containers the size of trucks. Excavators and bulldozers remained silent. There was no activity around the construction trailer because no one had yet shown up for their shift. If they held to the schedule the Corporation team had observed the past week, the first worker wouldn't arrive until a half hour after the snatch had gone down. The seven-story building was dark in the murky storm, a skele-ton of steel and concrete. From the high vantage he couldn't see where he and his people had wired it to blow.

His cell rang. 'Juan, it's me.' Julia Huxley. 'Isphording's van just stopped. One of the cops in the lead car got out to confer with its driver. Hold on. I think it's okay. The cop's getting back into his car. All right, they're on the move again. You should see them in a second.'

Far down the street a police car came into view followed by the armored van and a second cruiser. They didn't have their bubble lights or sirens on and crawled along with the regular traffic.

'Okay people, it's almost showtime,' Juan said over his encrypted phone's walkie-talkie mode.

He wiped the sweat from his hands and let them rest lightly on the crane's joystick controls. Although he'd never operated a tower crane, and the height made depth perception a bit tricky, he'd run more than his share of derricks and cranes over his years at sea to feel confident he could manage the behemoth. He'd already swung the hundred-foot horizontal boom over the street, and the trolley where the cable descended was positioned directly above the roadway. The heavy steel hook was lowered to within fifty feet of the cobbled street.

'I got 'em in my mirror,' Hali announced from the crash car.

'Goggles on, everyone.' Though distorted, Juan could make out details well enough, most notably the infrared strobe lamp they'd mounted on the crane's hook. Invisible without the goggles, the IR lamp glowed like a flare through the sophisticated optics. This was similar to the technology that allowed stealth fighters to drop bombs with pinpoint accuracy in any weather.

A flash of movement caught Juan's attention. He looked up the street as a Ferrari rounded a corner and shot up the road. It had to have been doing eighty miles per hour as it rocketed down the wrong lane of the two-way street. The sound of its throaty exhaust echoed up the canyon of baroque buildings and reached Juan's perch a hundred feet up in the control cab. He calculated speed and distance and realized that the low-slung sports car would be abreast of the lead police cruiser at the critical moment. If Hali pulled out in front of it, the kinetic energy of the impact would not only destroy the Italian-built car and kill its driver, it would also push the van carrying Isphording out of the path of the police car, allowing the convoy to pass through their carefully laid ambush.

'Juan?' Hali called anxiously.

'I'm on it.'

As much as he hated to move the crane from its carefully calculated position, he had to act. He flexed a joystick and the long boom arm began to swing across the horizon. He thumbed off a safety cover from a toggle, and as the boom reached what he thought was the right position, he hit the switch. The three-thousand-pound hook assembly plummeted from the sky.

The Ferrari's driver never saw the weight falling from above, so he only had seconds to react as the mass of steel smashed into the street, gouging a two-foot crater less than two car lengths in front the wedge nose of his F-40. He stood on the brakes and twitched the wheel to the right, sideswiping the trailing police cruiser. Juan activated another switch, and the hook tore free from the street, pulling up clots of dirt. The hook smashed through the million-dollar car's windshield and peeled off its roof like a sardine can as it passed below. The Ferrari's rear wheel fell into the hole, and the supercar pitched sideways, slamming into the cruiser again so both vehicles shuddered to a sudden stop.

Hali Kasim might have seen the whole thing unfold behind him in his rearview mirror, but it didn't distract him from his job. As the first cruiser passed the van, he accelerated out of his spot, barely clipping the Swiss police car's rear bumper. It was enough of a nudge to spin the vehicle so it completely blocked the narrow street.

The armored car carrying Rudolph Isphording braked hard and barely avoided hitting the cruiser. Julia Huxley, trailing the convoy, spun her car to block the van from reversing out of the trap.

Juan triggered the homemade explosives they'd laid inside the unfinished building.

The shaped charges had been carefully positioned for the maximum effect. As each went off, its force was funneled into sandbaglike redoubts of cement powder the men had stacked on every floor. From the ground level up, each sequential explosion sent a blooming gray cloud of dust blasting from the building in a scene reminiscent of the Twin Towers collapse. In seconds the fine powder had formed an impenetrable curtain of dust that lofted from street level to nearly two hundred feet and covered a two-block radius. It would take at least ten minutes for the light breeze to clear the dense fog from the area. Until then, no one would be able to see anything happening on the streets around the construction site.

Hali Kasim ignored the screaming pedestrians as he

and his men dashed from the van, each carrying lengths of braided cable. The gas masks filtered out the worst of the cement dust, but he could still taste it with each breath. As for the IR masks, they allowed him to see the descending hook and the infrared lamps wired to the cable in his hand, but for the rest, it was like running through a forest fire.

The driver of the armored van would be trained to ram his way out of the accident and was probably in the process of doing so when Cabrillo kicked off the explosives. Now, like everyone else on the street, the driver and his men sat paralyzed by the enormity of the explosions that appeared to have leveled the adjacent building.

Hali fumbled to the front of the truck and looped the wire around the axle. He used a parked car to leap onto the roof with the two loose ends. Looking up, he saw the IR lamp on the hook gliding through the gray clouds like a tiny star amid the darkness of night. Kasim's men had passed their cables around both rear axles and handed the ends up to Hali. Their job done, each stripped off their gear and vanished into the panicked crowd. The fleeing pedestrians were coated with cement dust and resembled ghosts stalking a foggy moor.

Up in the tower Juan maneuvered the hook so it was directly above the multiple bundle of IR lights atop the armored van. He could see them move a bit as Hali steadied himself on the vehicle's roof.

'Okay, that's got it.' Hali's voice was muffled by his gas mask. 'You're right above me. Lower the hook about ten feet.'

'Lower ten, roger.' Juan paid out more cable, watching closely as the two points of infrared light merged. Without

245

the lamps, finding the truck in the turbid swirl of dust would have been impossible.

'Hold there.' Hali fed the eyeholes at the ends of each cable through the heavy snap hook so that all six were secured. 'Okay, Chairman, she's all yours. Give me a second to get clear, and haul away.'

The Lebanese-American jumped to the ground and was about to let the current of running people to carry him away when a cop from the lead cruiser suddenly reared out of the dust cloud. For what seemed like forever the two regarded each other. The officer's eyes widened in his dust-streaked face as he finally recognized the object in Hali's hand was a gas mask. That was as much of a reaction as Kasim would allow him. Because he lacked Eddie Seng's martial arts training, Hali had to settle for a swift kick to the cop's groin before he took off running.

He managed just a few yards when he spotted another officer getting out of the rear-guard cruiser's passenger side. The man was dazed by the car crash and explosion but had the presence to carry his big flashlight and a blocky automatic pistol. He was halfway out of the car when he saw Hali running through the storm of cement powder. He recognized Hali's Arab features despite the dust and made a snap assumption. He tried to raise his weapon above the doorframe, even though the angle for a shot was all wrong. Hali threw himself bodily against the cruiser's door, breaking one of the cop's ankles and pinning him momentarily. Hali reached for the gun, realized the cop had an iron grip on the SIG Sauer, and rammed his elbow into the cop's face until his fingers went slack. Kasim wrenched the weapon away and took off again, leaving the unconscious officer in a heap on the pavement.

High above the fight, Juan Cabrillo put pressure on a joystick to raise the hook, tensioning the cables for a moment before lifting the seven-ton armored truck from the ground. Once he'd hauled it thirty feet off the street, he flicked the joystick to rotate the tower crane counterclockwise. He watched as the bright flare of IR light turned through the roiling dust. He slowed the rotation as the truck swung over the street where Franklin Lincoln waited with the semi.

As part of their preparations back in the warehouse, Linc and Hali had cut off the top of the trailer, split it lengthwise with cutting torches, and then remounted the two pieces on long hinges so the entire box could be opened to the sky. An IR light had been mounted on each corner of the trailer. While the dust had begun to settle at his elevation and his view out the cab windows was clearing, down at the truck the cement dust still billowed. Yet Juan could clearly see the rectangular pattern of lights with his goggles, and he gently lowered the armored van once it was positioned within the grid.

Linc had been waiting atop the tractor cab, and as soon as the van's tires flattened slightly under the vehicle's weight, he scrambled to release the hook. As soon as it was free, he radioed Juan to clear out, then returned to the cab. He put the transmission into first gear and hit the remote device to seal the trailer roof.

The guards were now isolated, and even if they'd called for help during the grab, they hadn't seen anything in the dust storm, and the local police would be busy for several hours as they pieced together that this hadn't been a terrorist attack.

Juan checked his watch just before descending the long

ladder that ran down the tower crane's single support column. From explosion to securing the armored van had taken one minute, forty-seven seconds. Thirteen less than he'd expected, but then he was working with the best. He could barely see to grope his way across the construction site, moving like a blind man through the dust storm. Grit filled his eyes and choked his lungs. It took five long minutes to find the gate. He climbed the chain-link fence and lowered himself to the sidewalk.

The street was at a standstill, and the curbs were empty of people. A fine, pale powder covered everything, like ash from a volcano. He had to brush his hand against the cars parked along the street to guide him out of the worst of the swirling storm, and it wasn't until he was two blocks from the ambush site that he could finally see enough to pick up his pace. Police cars were fast approaching, their lights slashing through the clouds like lighthouse beacons.

'What happened?' asked an Englishman standing outside a café. His clothes were clean as opposed to Juan's dust-covered work clothes.

'I think some sort of construction accident,' Cabrillo lied, coughing.

'Dear God. Do you think anybody was hurt?'

Juan looked back at the settling cloud. 'Not a soul,' he said, knowing this time he was telling the truth.

Rudolph Isphording knew a little about how the Russians were going to pull off his rescue, so he wasn't as stunned as the guard in the back of the van with him when they heard the screech of brakes and the crash of metal from a traffic accident. The big truck came to a sudden stop. But when an instant later the building next to the courthouse seemed to collapse, Isphording's fear was genuine.

Neither he nor the corrections officer could see anything out the small view ports that had been installed into the side of the vehicle, nor could they comprehend what was happening when the truck suddenly began to sway. They could both feel the slight centrifugal force, as if they were going around a gentle curve. Then the motion stopped, the truck pendulumed for a moment, and there was a slight bump followed by a low-pitched mechanical whine and a loud crash over their heads.

Just seconds later came a new sensation of movement, only this time Isphording was sure that the van was on the road again. Outside their armored box they could see nothing but darkness. The guard tried his cell phone but couldn't get a signal and could only communicate with the two men in the cab by banging on the bulkhead that separated them.

For thirty-five minutes they could feel the motion as the van was moved out of the city. They could sense and hear the truck accelerate as it reached a highway and later slow and twist around curves as it left the major thoroughfare. Not long after, all motion stopped. Wherever the Russians, Yuri Zayysev and the woman, Ludmilla, who'd pretended to be Kara, were taking him, Isphording assumed they'd arrived.

He and his guard waited in silence for something to happen. The minutes crept by slowly.

What the lawyer couldn't see from the back of the armored van was that Linc and the others were waiting for Juan to arrive. As soon as he pulled his Mercedes SUV between the tractor trailer and Julia's Volkswagen, Hali closed the big overhead door. Because of the overcast sky, the light coming through the opaque skylights cast the big warehouse in murky shadow. Hali snapped on a few overhead lamps, but it did little to soften the building's gloomy air.

Cabrillo's SUV was powdered with cement dust, and the chairman himself was grimy. He accepted a damp cloth from Julia to wipe the worst of the dust from his face. He also drank down a half liter of water. 'So far, so good,' he congratulated his people. 'Looks like no one had any trouble getting here, so let's open this tin can and finish it. Linc, I couldn't tell when I lowered the truck into the rig, which way is it facing?'

'It's facing the rear doors.'

'That should make this a little easier.' Juan grabbed a Heckler&Koch MP-5 machine pistol from a workbench and slid the strap over his shoulder. He also palmed a pair of round grenades. They were dummy practice grenades but would look indistinguishable from the real things to the guards in the van. He passed around black ski masks to everyone and lowered his over his face so only his eyes and mouth were exposed. The others had also armed themselves with an assortment of pistols and machine guns.

Once everyone was ready at the rear of the trailer, he unlatched the door. He gave his people a five-second count-down and swung open the door with a jerk. All five of them swarmed up inside the trailer, jumping onto the van's long hood, waving their weapons and shouting incoherently. The Swiss driver and the guard riding shotgun had service pistols in their hands, but through the bulletproof glass they were at a standoff. Before the driver could start the engine and try to drive out of the trailer, Juan leered into the windscreen and showed off the grenades.

He pointed at each man and then at the doors before pulling the pin from one of the grenades. There was no mistaking his intention.

The guards maintained their defiant look but knew there was nothing they could do. They laid the weapons on the dashboard and slowly reached for the door handles. As soon as the doors unlocked, a member of the team was ready with plastic-tie handcuffs, blindfolds, and gags. Hali yanked the key ring from the driver's polished belt and tossed it to Juan.

The chairman climbed over the top of the armored van and jumped lightly to the floor of the trailer. On the fifth attempt he inserted the correct key into the lock, but before he turned it, he nodded to one of his men.

If anything went wrong there was no reason for Kara and Rudolph Isphording to be able to give the same description of Yuri Zayysev, so he had General Operations specialist Michael Trono call out in Russian-accented English, 'To the guard in there with Herr Isphording. Your two comrades have already been subdued. They will not be harmed, and neither will you. I am going to open the door just enough for you to toss out your weapon. If you do not, I will be forced to use tear gas. Do you understand?'

'I understand,' the guard responded.

'Herr Isphording, how many guns does the guard have?'

'Just a pistol,' the lawyer replied.

'Very good. Has he removed it from its holster?'

'Yes.'

'That is very wise of you,' Trono said. 'Herr Isphording, take the gun from him and move to the rear door.

I am opening it now. Toss the weapon onto the floor.'

Cabrillo cracked open the heavy door, and a black revolver clattered off the rear bumper. Hali and Julia had joined them, their weapons at the ready. Juan nodded to them and heaved the door all the way open. The frightened guard sat on a bench that ran along one wall of the van. He understood enough of the situation to have already laced his fingers on top of his head. Hali cuffed, gagged, and blindfolded him while Julia helped the paunchy lawyer from the vehicle. The other two guards were shoved into the back of the van, and Juan locked them in.

Isphording saw five armed commandos, some wearing work clothes, others all in black. One had the curves of a woman, and he guessed it was Ludmilla. 'Is one of you Yuri Zayysev?' he asked eagerly.

'Da,' one of the commandos answered. His work clothes were streaked with gray powder, and when he stripped off his mask, his face was still streaked with dust. His hair was red, like Isphording had been told to expect, and his beard had been trimmed to a ruddy goatee.

'Mr Savich sends his compliments, Rudolph.' The man used the name Isphording himself had provided. 'Of course, he couldn't meet you in person, but you will see him soon enough. There is an office at the back of the warehouse. Ludmilla will take you there. We'll leave here in a few minutes.'

Julia had taken off her mask so that the attorney could see that she was the woman he knew as Ludmilla, although she wasn't wearing the disguise.

'Thank you.' Isphording pumped her hand. 'And my wife? What about Kara?'

'Another team is fetching her now,' the woman called Ludmilla replied.

'Thank you,' the lawyer repeated. 'I thank all of you for saving me.'

'You were not harmed?' Ludmilla asked as Isphording followed her out of the trailer. Linc had placed a stepladder at the rear door to make it easier for him.

'No. I am fine. A little frightened perhaps. Until you came on Friday I had no idea the Palestinians were after me. I'm grateful to you all.'

Julia gave him a smile. 'You have Mr Savich to thank. We are just doing as he ordered.'

'I know he's a powerful man, but I had no idea he could arrange something like this.'

'Here we are,' Ludmilla announced.

The office was spartan, just a couple of desks and filing cabinets and a worn vinyl couch under a frosted glass window. The floors were scuffed linoleum, and the room smelled of cigarettes. Curtains were drawn over the large piece of plate glass that overlooked the warehouse floor. Isphording collapsed onto the couch and accepted the bottle of water Ludmilla handed him.

A few minutes later Yuri Zayysev strode into the office. He'd left his machine pistol out in the warehouse, but he'd belted a holster around his lean waist.

'What happens now, Herr Zayysev?' Isphording asked.

'We're waiting for some more of my people, and then we are leaving. The man who drove the truck thinks he might have been followed, so we're hurrying our schedule. We don't know if the Palestinians are on to us or not.'

'They haven't operated outside the Middle East in years,' Isphording said. 'They must truly be desperate.'

'A lot of money is unaccounted for since Yasir Arafat's death,' Zayysev countered, 'enough to make anyone desperate.'

The lawyer was about to reply when everyone jumped at a crash outside in the warehouse. A second later came the unmistakable sound of silenced weapons fire. One of Zayysev's men gave a choking scream that was cut off by another burst of gunfire. Zayysev tore his pistol from its holster and racked the slide. 'Stay here,' he ordered Ludmilla. He crossed to the open door, keeping low. More gunfire echoed outside. He eased around the jamb, his pistol outstretched, probing. He cursed and fired four rounds to clear a way out of the office. Taking a cautious step out, he fired again at a dark shape running behind the semi. He turned to give Ludmilla another order when he was caught by a sustained and brutal burst of autofire that stitched him from knee to chest. The impact of a half-dozen rounds blew him back into the office, where he fell crumpled against a desk. His chest was a mass of blood.

The plate glass window overlooking the warehouse exploded in a rain of silenced gunfire. Bullets impacted all around the room, sparking off the metal furniture and tearing gouges from the cheap paneling. With the reactions of a cat, Ludmilla threw her body over Isphording, shielding him until she could unholster her own weapon. She twisted off him as a figure loomed in the shattered window frame. Around his face the gunman had wound a checked kaffiyeh like those favored by Palestinians. He spotted Ludmilla and raised his assault rifle to his shoulder. She fired first, and Isphording saw the Arab's head literally come apart. Blood and pink clots of brain matter sprayed the wall next to him in an obscene Rorschach ink blot. Another Muslim gunman took his place and raked the office with his assault rife. A chunk of Ludmilla's arm was blown off, and then she caught two more rounds to the stomach. She managed a low keen of pain as she fell to the dirty linoleum surrounded by a spreading lake of her own blood.

The attack had been so lightning fast and savage that Isphording was too stunned to move. The smell of blood and gunpowder overwhelmed the small office. The attacker, who must have been the one that killed Zayysev, entered the room. He stepped over to Ludmilla's crumpled body, using a foot to turn her corpse so he could better see her wounds. 'Nice shooting, Mohammad,' he said in Arabic to the gunman at the window. The terrorist leader unwound the kaffiyeh from his face and glanced at Isphording. His features were sharp and dangerous, and his dark eyes blazed with hatred. 'I know you speak my language,' he said to Isphording, continuing in Arabic. 'You did work for the late Chairman Arafat, hiding money that should have been spent fighting the Americans and the Jews.'

'The others are all dead, Rafik,' Mohammad reported from outside the office. 'The building is ours.'

'Did I not tell you someone would try to free this pig from prison?' Rafik gave Isphording such a superior leer that the lawyer couldn't stop his bladder from releasing. 'All we had to do was wait.'

Rafik snicked open a switchblade knife, its keen edge glinting in the fluorescent light. 'Now, let's talk about the money.'

## 17

Rudolph Isphording never gave much thought to the people whose money he laundered. He'd insulated himself from his clients so they were nothing more than pass codes on bank account ledgers or vague signatures on legal documents. He had always considered himself a numbers man, a person most comfortable behind a desk protected by a paper fortress. Now the evidence of what he'd done was sprayed across the walls of the office and pooled under Ludmilla's body. He couldn't bring himself to look at the carnage that had been Yuri Zayysev's chest.

Rafik had been called out to the warehouse before asking the lawyer any questions. Mohammad watched him from the office doorway, his eyes looking like chips of obsidian. Isphording could see that the Palestinians were maneuvering a ramp to the back of the trailer to unload the armored van. The Russians who'd snatched him had taken great pains to make sure no one had been injured or killed. He felt certain that Rafik and his thugs wouldn't be so scrupulous. Isphording's entire body trembled like he was in the grip of an epileptic seizure.

The terrorist leader called out for Mohammad to join him for a moment. He pinned Isphording with a menacing glare and stepped out onto the warehouse floor.

Minutes crawled by, allowing the lawyer's fears to kaleidoscope in ever more horrifying thoughts, so when the sound penetrated his mind, he wasn't sure what he heard.

It sounded like someone was calling his name, but the voice was distorted and wheezy, like they were a great distance away or it was coming from a dream. He turned his eyes toward the doorway. No one was there. He looked around the room. Ludmilla lay faceup, her clothes sodden with blood.

'Isphording.'

He heard it again, and had he not been turning his head to check on Zayysev he never would have believed the Russian's lips had moved. By some miracle Zayysev was still alive. He was ghostly white, and blood continued to drool down his chest like crimson molasses. Isphording felt hope surge inside him like a dose of adrenaline.

'Keep them talking,' Zayysev mumbled, his eyes flickering from shock.

'What?' the lawyer whispered urgently. Mohammad or Rafik could be back any second.

'Tell them anything they ask. Just keep them talking.' Zayysev's voice was so faint Isphording had to cup a hand to his ear and tilt his head to hear him.

'I don't understand,' he pleaded.

'More of my men are on the way ...' Zayysev's voice trailed off. His eyelids fluttered and rolled back into his skull as he fell unconscious once again. How he had survived the multiple gunshots staggered the imagination.

Rudolph Isphording recalled what the Russian had said prior to the attack, that they were waiting for more of his companions. No doubt they would be armed. His first rush of hope became a torrent. He was going to be rescued. He was going to get out of this alive!

A bellow of exhaust echoed from the warehouse, and the armored van slowly emerged from the trailer, guided by one of the masked terrorists. Rafik strode back into the office an instant later. His face was contorted in a cruel mix of hatred and self-satisfaction. He dragged a chair from behind one of the desks and sat astride it in front of Isphording. His breath smelled of carrion.

'Now, pig, you will tell me what you did with the money you stole from my people.' He spoke in English, his accent somehow making him even more intimidating.

'I will tell you what you want to know,' Isphording replied in Arabic.

Rafik slapped him across the face hard enough to leave a red print on his skin. 'You will not defile the language of the Prophet again. Speak English, Isphording. Isphording? That is a Jewish name.'

'I'm Catholic.'

Rafik slapped him again, his eyes going wide with insane rage. 'You will speak only when asked a question.'

Isphording glanced to the motionless form of Yuri Zayysev, praying that his men would come soon.

'We know you used part of my people's money to create fake companies,' Rafik began. 'One is called D Commercial Advisors. Another is Equity Partners International. You used these companies to buy a large ship, called *Maus*, that is someplace in the Far East. You will tell me who controls these companies and who profits while my people suffer.'

For a long second Isphording didn't know what to say. The Palestinian had it all wrong. None of the PLO money he'd hidden away had gone into that deal. That one was set up solely for Anton Savich and the Sikh, Shere Singh. Then he thought that it didn't matter if he told Rafik all about it. Zayysev's men would be here any moment, and the kidnappers would be dead.

'That is correct,' he said in a scratchy voice before clearing his throat. 'There were actually two ships, floating drydocks. One called *Maus*, the other *Souri*.'

'Who has control of these vessels?' Rafik demanded.

'A Russian named Anton Savich and a Sikh named Shere Singh.'

'You are wise not to lie.' There was little praise in Rafik's voice. 'We know about Savich. Tell me where we can find him.'

'I – I do not know,' Isphording admitted miserably. 'He travels all the time. I don't think he has a home, only a post box in Saint Petersburg.'

Rafik made to strike the lawyer again.

'It is true, I swear,' Isphording cried. 'I have only met him once, over two years ago.'

'We will return to him in a moment. What about this Sikh? Who is he?'

'Shere Singh. He is Pakistani but now lives in Indonesia. He is a wealthy man. His holdings are vast – timber, shipping, real estate. The largest company is the Karamita Breakers Yard on the west coast of Sumatra. I believe he controls the two drydocks through it.'

'Have you ever met this man? What does he look like?'

'I've met him through a video conference last year. He appears to be a big man and like all Sikhs has a long beard and wears a turban.'

Mohammad suddenly burst into the office, jabbering in almost incoherent Arabic. 'Rafik!' he shouted. 'Rafik, the police arrest Fodl. He knows our, our, eh . . .' He drew silent.

'Location,' Rafik snarled in his native tongue. 'Fodl knows our location.'

The terrorist got to his feet. Isphording gave a startled cry and cowered into the couch cushions, expecting to be beaten. 'Please don't hurt me. Please.'

'Silence!' Rafik snapped. He took a blindfold and a pair of hard plastic ear protectors from Mohammad.

'What – what are you doing?' Isphording sniveled. Tears coursed down his cheeks. They were going to execute him right here and now.

'I said, silence,' Rafik roared.

Before Rafik tied the blindfold around Isphording's head, Mohammad jammed soft rubber plugs deep into his ears. Then came the blindfold and finally the ear protectors. Isphording couldn't stop shaking. He could neither see nor hear anything. He was then gagged, but surprisingly, not too tightly. One of the terrorists hauled him to his feet, and together they guided him from the office. He had no idea what was happening, couldn't tell where they were taking him. After just a few steps he smelled the exhaust from the idling van. A moment later he was unceremoniously dumped into the back. Though disorientated, he could sense the presence of the three guards charged with driving him to his court date. His ankles were bound with some kind of plastic tie, while his wrists and hands were taped as tightly as a mummy's wrappings. He couldn't wiggle a single finger, which meant he'd be unable to worry the tape off his hands. Rafik's men were as efficient as they were deadly.

Isphording imagined the guards had been similarly bound.

The doors slammed shut as soon as he was secure, and the van took off, but they went only a short distance. Judging by how he and the guards rolled across the floor, they'd made three tight turns. As near as he could tell, the

Palestinians had merely stashed the van behind the warehouse. The driver killed the ignition. A few minutes passed before Isphording felt the driver slam his door.

He and the guards were isolated from each other by the gags and ties, unable to hear because of the ear protectors. He could not imagine a worse feeling of deprivation, and while he was alive for the moment, he had no idea how long it would be before the van started up again and the four of them were taken away and killed.

Chairman Cabrillo had slammed the armored van's door hard enough for the men inside to feel it, then tossed the keys onto the roof. He checked the street fronting the warehouse one more time. No one had seen him hide the vehicle behind the building. He twirled the spray bottle of bleach around his finger as he walked. Certain that no one had left behind fingerprints, he'd taken the precaution of dousing the inside of the cab with bleach to dilute any trace DNA.

Linc greeted him at the door. The ex-SEAL had unwound the kaffiyeh he'd worn to hide his black face and let the checkered head cloth drape around his wide shoulders. Artificial blood from when Julia had shot him dripped from the fringed edges.

'Well done,' Juan said, and the two men exchanged toothy grins.

'You must have a thing for playing Arab bad guys, Chairman,' the big man teased. 'First you were Colonel Hourani of the Syrian Army, today you're Palestinian terrorist leader Rafik. Who are you going to be tomorrow, Ali Baba?'

'Only if you play Scheherazade and do the Dance of the Seven Veils.'

Mike Trono, who'd taken over the role of Yuri Zayysev for Rudy Isphording's benefit, was plucking the spent remains of devices called squibs from a special vest he wore under his shirt. The squibs were made of tiny explosive charges and an ounce or two of fake blood. These devices had been a staple of Hollywood effects wizards for years. A more sophisticated device had been placed inside Linc's headscarf to make it appear that Julia had shot away half his skull. The office had also been rigged with small charges along the walls and on the furniture to further the illusion of bullets striking the plasterboard and metal. Of course all the weapons they'd used to stage the assault had fired blanks.

When Isphording and the guards were found, the story they would tell would be too bizarre to be anything other than the truth. After being grabbed by the Russian mob, the lawyer's rescuers had then been attacked by rogue members of the PLO looking for money missing since Arafat's death. The attack had been savage, and none of the Russians survived. Then the terrorists ran off when they learned one of their men might have been picked up by the police. What couldn't be so easily explained is what happened to the Russians' bodies and why the terrorists hadn't taken Isphording with them. Nor would they be able to trace how the 'Palestinians' got into the country in the first place.

Juan wasn't too concerned with those details. The Swiss authorities would rattle their sabers about tighter border restrictions, but in the end they'd be satisfied because no civilians had been hurt throughout the ordeal, they had their star witness back in custody, and the world was minus a few gangsters from Saint Petersburg. And as a bonus, he thought that they would probably put pressure on Isphording to explain where the former head of the PLO *had* stashed the billions he'd stolen from his people. Who knew, maybe they'd even get some of it back.

The one thing he couldn't control was if the lawyer revealed what he'd said under interrogation. He didn't want the Swiss looking into Anton Savich, whoever he was, or a Sikh shipping mogul named Shere Singh. He could only hope that the lawyer was as frightened of Savich as he was of the PLO and would keep silent.

Dr Huxley stepped out of the warehouse's only lavatory. She'd washed away the fake blood from her face. She'd also stripped down to a black tank top that barely contained her curves to clean the mess away from her arm. The squib that had made it appear her arm had been blown nearly off had left a livid purple bruise on her otherwise flawless white skin.

'Are you okay, Ludmilla?'

'*Da,*' Julia deadpanned, rubbing the spot. 'Is nothing.' Then she arched a teasing eyebrow. 'Why is it everyone but you and Hali look like extras from some zombie B-movie?'

'Because none of you either speak Arabic or look Arabic.' He laughed. 'Although Hali's portrayal of the steely-eyed terrorist, Mohammad, left a lot to be desired. He had just a couple of lines to learn, and he managed to mangle both. On a brighter note, I have to hand it to Kevin and his team in the Magic Shop. They really outdid themselves this time. Especially Linc's effect. For a second I thought it had gone wrong and his head really had exploded.'

'Scared me, too,' Julia admitted.

Juan called out to gather the rest of the team. 'Okay everyone, listen up. First off I want to commend each and every one of you on a job well done. This little caper was a long shot from the beginning, and you pulled it off flawlessly.'

'That mean we're getting bonuses?' Hali asked.

'You most of all, Hali. I'm sending you to a Berlitz so you can at least fake speaking Arabic.' This earned a round of good-natured laughter at Kasim's expense. 'Julia, head back to your hotel as soon as you're ready. You've made your flight reservations?'

'I'll be in Istanbul by two o'clock. From there I can hook up with you anywhere. Judging by what Isphording said, I take it we're going to Indonesia?'

Cabrillo nodded. 'Shere Singh sounds like the next link in the chain.'

'As soon as I reach Ataturk International I'll book a flight to Jakarta.' She slipped into a dark blouse. 'All of my disguise stuff is in a suitcase in the office.'

'I'll make sure it's burned,' Juan assured her and gave her a kiss on the cheek. Julia waved good-bye to the others and settled into her rental car. Linc opened the garage door, and she roared out of the warehouse.

'Okay then, I've wiped down the armored van for prints and hit the cab and door handles with bleach. Even though we're torching this building, make sure you go over everywhere you've been, especially the bathroom. Not that any of our DNA is at Interpol, but I don't want to take any chances.

'You all have your escape routes planned. Stay loose, and we'll all be on the *Oregon* by this time tomorrow.'

Although he'd used disguises each time he'd made most of the rental arrangements, Cabrillo was the most likely to be identified, so he would be the next to get out of the country. While the others cleaned up the warehouse, he changed clothes and used a bucket of water and a rag to wash the concrete dust from his Mercedes SUV. By the time he finished, Hali, Linc, and Trono had finished scrubbing down the warehouse and placing incendiary bombs throughout the structure.

'How long should I set the timer?' Linc asked.

'Hold on.' Juan used his cell phone to call the *Oregon*.

'Law offices of Dewey, Cheatem, and Howe,' Linda Ross greeted in her high-pitched voice.

Cabrillo calculated the time difference between Switzerland and the South China Sea. 'Good evening, Linda.'

'Chairman, how'd it go?'

'Smooth as silk. Listen, have Murph and Eric been monitoring the news here in Zurich?'

'Sure have. Let me get them.'

Mark Murphy came on the line a moment later. Juan could hear the speed metal music blaring from the headphones Murph had pulled down around his neck. It sounded like someone using a chain saw against a piece of railroad track. 'Chairman, from what I'm getting from CNN and SkyNews, the Swiss don't have a clue what happened. At first they thought it was a structural failure of some kind, and then they thought they were having their own 9/11. From what I can get from local police chatter, there's been a couple mentions about the missing armored car and unknown gunmen at the scene when the explosions went off.'

'Are they closing borders or delaying flights?'

'No. They think this is a local thing.'

'So we're safe for the time being.'

'It'll take them so long to add two and two they'll need to include interest.'

'Huh?'

'It's a joke. You know, Swiss banks? Interest? Hey, that was funny.'

'Stick to being a connoisseur of fine music and leave the humor to the professionals, like Max. How far are you from Sumatra?'

'A few days still, why?'

'Rudolph Isphording said the guy who controls the *Maus* is named Shere Singh. He owns a company called the Karamita Breakers Yard. Check them both out. Also track down another floating drydock called the *Souri*. Singh owns it, too.'

'How do you spell that?'

Juan did and added, 'It's French for mouse.'

'Got it.'

'Thanks, Murph. Tell Max I want you to break off from the *Maus* and make best practical speed for the Karamita Yard.' Best practical speed was far slower than the *Oregon*'s top speed, but running that fast during daylight hours or without radar jamming would give away one of the ship's most important secrets.

'I'll pass it along.'

'See you in a day or so.' Juan killed the connection and turned to Linc and the others awaiting orders. 'It seems the police don't know what happened, so we're in the clear for now. We'll all be out of Switzerland within six hours, so set the charge for eight p.m. Isphording and the guards are in for an uncomfortable day, but they won't dehydrate by the time the local fire department arrives and discovers the missing armored car.'

Cabrillo fired up the SUV's throaty V-8. He had a long drive to Munich ahead of him where he'd catch his own flight out of Europe. He hoped that by the time he got there, the adrenaline still pumping through his body would dissipate, because his hands remained shaky and his stomach was still knotted. He also hoped that Mark would find that the *Maus*'s sister ship was operated as a legitimate drydock and not involved in hijacking on the open seas, but he knew the chances of that were longer than Hali Kasim giving the keynote sermon at next year's *hajj* to Mecca.

# 18

Juan Cabrillo knew the type. The man behind the desk opposite him dressed poorly and took little pride in his personal appearance other than to follow the tenets of his faith. His turban was wound tightly around his head, but the fabric was frayed and stained with sweat. His shirt was of cheap cotton, and the dark circles under the arms looked permanent. Bits of food clung to his beard and mustache.

The office was also staged to present a particular image. The desk was covered with papers, and the file cabinets were filled to bursting. The furniture was cut-rate and uncomfortable, and the posters on the wall were most likely given away by the Indonesian tourist board. The computer behind the desk was old enough to be in a museum of ancient technology.

The woman who had shown Juan into the office was perhaps the only genuine article about the whole setup. She was an elderly Indonesian woman, stick thin and tired. Her clothes were as cheap as those worn by her boss, but Cabrillo suspected it was because he paid her a pittance and not because she was putting up the front of a struggling business.

After reading a complete dossier put together by Mark Murphy prior to the meeting, Cabrillo knew more about Shere Singh and his family than he'd ever wished to. He knew their estimated net worth was nearly half a billion dollars. He knew that the family's patriarch lived in a five-hundred-acre compound in a house large enough to keep his eleven children and their families under one roof. He trusted his sons-in-law only to a point. It seemed that the sides of the business they were in charge of were for the most part legitimate. It was Shere Singh's own sons who ran the illegal operations. Abhay Singh, the eldest, was the representative for the Karamita Breakers Yard.

He maintained their offices in a run-down district of Jakarta, near enough to the docks to occasionally hear a ship's horn but far enough that one had to search to find it.

Setting up this meeting with Abhay Singh had been simple. Cabrillo had contacted the company while en route from Munich to Jakarta, representing himself as the captain of a ship he wanted to sell for scrap. He wanted to know what Karamita Breakers Yard would bid for the hulk.

Juan wasn't dressed much better than the ship broker. He hadn't shaved since the day before snatching Rudy Isphording and wore a greasy black wig under a yachtsman's cap. His duck trousers had never seen an iron or a press, and the blazer stretched over his enormous gut was missing several buttons on the sleeve. If the wealthy Singh family wanted to present themselves as struggling workers, Juan could just as easily play the part of a down-on-his-luck captain.

Abhay Singh read over the report Juan had handed him on the *Oregon,* although he'd listed a false name that was currently being painted on the old freighter's hull. The papers gave her dimensions, tonnage, and lists of equipment and appointments as well as several dozen photographs. The Sikh's piggy eyes scanned the documents rapidly and thoroughly. The only sound in the dilapidated office was the rattle of a black oscillating fan and the traffic on the street one floor below the open window.

'There is one thing I do not see here, Captain, er, Smith,' Singh said, shooting Cabrillo a penetrating stare. 'And that is your ownership documents. It appears that perhaps you do not own this vessel you want to sell for scrap.'

Cabrillo, playing the part of Jeb Smith, one of his regular personas when dealing with officials, matched Abhay Singh's dark gaze. 'There is something else you don't see there.' He handed over another sheaf of papers.

Singh glanced at them skeptically, got halfway down the top sheet before his head shot up, his eyes glinting with avarice.

'That's right.' Juan nodded. 'Her holds are filled with eight thousand tons of aluminum ingots we brought aboard in Karachi. How about we make ourselves a bargain, Mr Singh? You forget that my ship is owned by someone else, and I forget that when you take possession I know she's carrying ten million dollars' worth of raw metal that doesn't belong to any of us.'

Singh set the papers flat on his desk and folded his dark hands on top. He gave Juan a speculative look. 'How is it, Captain, that you came to us at Karamita?'

Cabrillo knew what he was really asking is how did Captain Jeb Smith know that the owners of the Karamita yard were open to corruption and bribery. 'Poets often write about how vast the ocean is, and that's true, Mr Singh, but don't you know the world can also still be a small place. One hears things.'

'And where does one hear things?'

Juan looked around furtively. 'Different places from different folks. I can't quite recall who told me about your fine facility, but word of mouth spreads faster than dysentery and can be even uglier to deal with.' His eyes settled back on Singh's, and his expression had turned to stone. Abhay Singh understood the subtext of what Cabrillo was saying: Ask any more questions, and I'll make sure the authorities take a closer look at Karamita.

Singh flashed an insincere smile. 'It gladdens my heart to hear that others speak so highly of our business. I think we can come to an arrangement, Captain Smith. You must know the price of scrap steel is up in the markets, so I can see you receiving a hundred and ten dollars per ton for the hulk.'

'I was thinking more like five hundred and fifty dollars,' Juan countered. By rights he could have quadrupled that price because of the aluminum ingots he was pawning, but he wanted to get the negotiations over with and shower away the stench of dishonesty.

'No, that won't do,' Abhay replied as though Juan had just insulted his sister. 'I can perhaps go as high as two hundred.'

'You can go as high as four hundred, but I will take three.'

'Oh, Captain,' Singh moaned theatrically, acting like Cabrillo was now insulting his mother. 'I wouldn't even break even at that price.'

'I think you will more than break even. We both know the value of her cargo. Why don't we say two hundred and fifty dollars a ton, and I will deliver the ship to your yard in two days.'

Singh paused to consider the proposal. Juan knew that the *Maus* would most likely reach Karamita at the same time he delivered the *Oregon,* and he wondered what would win out in the Sikh's mind: greed or prudence. A cautious man would lock down the facility until after the drydock had disgorged its cargo and they'd scrapped the evidence of their piracy, but Singh would stand to make a fortune off the prize Juan was offering.

The Sikh made his decision. 'The yard is full right now. Bring your vessel in seven days, and we'll have room.'

Juan got to his feet and stuck out a sweaty hand. 'Deal, but just in case the ship's owners have spies in Jakarta, I'll be at Karamita in two days anyway.' He was out the office and past the reception desk before his comment even registered in Abhay Singh's mind.

He met George Adams at the airport, and the pilot choppered them back to the *Oregon,* where she held station well outside the shipping lanes. George had racked up twenty hours in the past few days ferrying the team Juan had used in Switzerland back to the ship. At last the whole crew was together with the notable exception of Eddie Seng.

In his cabin, Cabrillo stripped off the Jeb Smith outfit, sealing the foul clothes and wig in a plastic bag that he tossed in the back of the walk-in closet for the next time he'd need to play the part. He lathered his face with a shaving brush and carefully went over his skin with a straight razor.

In the mirror above the copper sink he saw the glint in his eye, the look he always got when he was nearing his quarry. That Singh had agreed to buy a vessel without clear title was reason enough to have the man arrested, but more importantly it told Juan that the scent he'd picked up from Rudy Isphording was running true. Abhay Singh and his father were in this up to their necks. Juan's job now was to make them expose just enough for him to track down Anton Savich and then hang them all.

After his shower and smacking his cheeks with bay rum, he dressed in a pair of charcoal trousers, a crisp white cotton shirt, and soft dark moccasins. He called down to the galley to have some food brought to the boardroom, then called all the ship's senior staff to a meeting.

The boardroom was on the starboard side of the ship aft of the superstructure and large enough to hold forty people, although the table only accommodated a dozen. When there was no need for stealth, large rectangular portholes were opened to bathe the room in natural light. Juan was the first to arrive, and he settled himself in the high-backed leather chair at the head of the cherry finished table. Maurice, the Corporation's chief steward, appeared with a steaming dish of samosas and a pitcher of his famous sun tea. He poured a glass for Juan and handed him a plate.

'Welcome back, Chairman.'

Because the dossier on the Singh family had been e-mailed to Juan during his flight from Europe, and George Adams had met his flight in Jakarta with the Jeb Smith disguise, this was his first time on the *Oregon* since leaving for Tokyo with Tory Ballinger almost two weeks ago.

'Good to be back. What's the latest?' Maurice was an incurable gossip.

'Rumor has it that Eric Stone is currently involved with a woman in Spain over the Internet. I hear their little chat sessions are rather torrid.'

Eric was a first-rate helmsman and had a mastery of the ship's systems that rivaled Juan's and Max Hanley's, but when it came to the opposite sex, he was absolutely hopeless. In a bar in London following the Sacred Stone affair, Eric had gotten so flustered over a woman's brazen approach that he'd rushed outside to be sick.

'You wouldn't be using my override to check the ship's computer logs, would you, Maurice?' Juan chided mildly.

'I didn't even know there was such a thing, Mr Cabrillo. I merely overheard him discussing it with Mark Murphy.'

That fit. Juan chuckled to himself. Murph, Eric's partner in crime, had even less luck with women than Stone, if one overlooked the occasional Goth girl he hooked up with. But a girl with more piercings than a pincushion and who was impressed with a guy who could catch air on a skateboard half-pipe wasn't much of a catch in Cabrillo's mind.

'Well, you know what they say, Maurice, any love is good love.'

'Don't ask, don't tell, Mr Cabrillo.'

The steward bowed out as Max, Linda Ross, and Julia Huxley entered the room. They helped themselves to tea and plates loaded with the spicy samosas. A few seconds later Hali Kasim came in with Franklin Lincoln. Linc normally wouldn't have been in on the meeting, but he was taking the place of the absent Eddie Seng. Eric and Murph arrived last, arguing about some obscure line from an old Monty Python movie.

'First things first,' Juan said after everyone had taken their seat. 'Any word from Eddie?'

'Still nothing,' Hali replied.

Juan cocked an eyebrow at Doc Huxley.

She answered immediately. 'The subcutaneous transmitter I surgically implanted in the muscles of Eddie's thigh checked out perfectly before you and he took off for Tokyo. In fact, that one's only been in there three months.'

A few key members of the Corporation had special burst locaters implanted under their skin, Juan included. The electronic devices were the size of postage stamps and drew power from the body's own nervous system. Every twelve hours they were supposed to send a signal to a commercial satellite that was then relayed back to the *Oregon*. It was a covert way of keeping tabs on operatives in the field without having them carry bugs that could be discovered and confiscated.

The technology was new and far from perfected, which is why Juan didn't necessarily trust the devices; however, in Eddie's case, there had been no other alternatives.

Hali added, 'The last transmission we received from him showed he was on the outskirts of Shanghai, someplace close to the new airport.'

Juan digested the information. 'Any chance they planned on flying him out?'

Max Hanley tapped the stem of his pipe against his teeth. 'We considered that option, but it doesn't jibe with what we know of the smugglers. Eddie's following the trail of the illegals we found in the container. By rights he should be following the same route.'

'But if they were losing too many people to the pirates, wouldn't they change their tactics?' Eric Stone asked from behind the laptop he'd set on the table.

'We don't know how many the pirates have taken,' Hali replied. 'The ones we found on the *Kra* could have been the first batch that were intercepted.'

'Or the last straw,' Eric countered, 'and now the snakeheads have switched to airplanes.'

'If they already had seaborne resources, it would be cost prohibitive to switch to aircraft. They would need all new infrastructure.'

Juan let the debate circle the table but knew there were no answers. Until they received something from Eddie's transmitter, they were just jawing in a vacuum. 'Okay, that's enough,' he said to end the futile debate. 'Hali, broaden the number of satellites you've been checking. It's possible that somebody else's bird is getting Eddie's signal. Think outside the box on this one. Check anything capable of relaying an electronic burst transmission.'

The *Oregon*'s communications expert bristled. 'I've checked the logs. My people have looked at every satellite that comes within a thousand miles of Shanghai.'

'I'm not doubting the competence of your staff, Hali,' Juan soothed. 'If Eddie was within that thousand-mile circle, they would have found him. But I don't think he is. Now I want you to double the area, search for him within two thousand miles of Shanghai, and if he's not there, expand the grid until you find him.'

Hali jotted a few notes on a notepad bearing the Corporation's logo. 'You got it, boss.'

Juan paused until he had everyone's attention. 'As for my meeting yesterday, Shere Singh, his son Abhay, and anyone else affiliated with the Karamita Breakers Yard is on our official list of suspects. They own the *Maus* and its sister ship.' He caught Mark Murphy's attention. 'That reminds me. Anything on the sister drydock, *Souri*?'

Murph grabbed Eric's laptop and moused through a few screens. 'Here we go. She was Russian-built and bought at the same time as the *Maus* but under a different web of dummy companies. They did make the same mistake and used Rudolph Isphording to establish the fronts. Unlike the *Maus,* the *Souri* has yet to be engaged in any salvage activities. No one has rented her, no one has even seen her. She was on the Lloyds list, but the last they knew she was still in Vladivostok waiting for her new owners to take possession.'

Juan opened his mouth to ask a question, but Murph was ahead of him. 'Already checked. She was towed out of the harbor eighteen months ago. And no one remembers the names of the tugs.'

'Damn.'

Linda Ross spoke around a mouthful of samosa. 'So, for the past year and a half Singh and company could have been using her for anything. Even if they didn't go around snatching ships off the high seas, a vessel that size would be perfect for all sorts of smuggling operations. They could load her with a few hundred stolen cars. Hell, they could haul a couple of big corporate jets without dismantling the wings or cram a couple thousand immigrants into the hold.'

She meant her comment to be speculative, but the air in the boardroom suddenly became somber and chilled, as if a cloud had covered the sun and darkened the wood-paneled room. Everyone envisioned the massive vessel turned into a slave ship and filled with countless miserable souls destined for a life perhaps worse than death.

'*Jesus,*' someone muttered under their breath.

'Find it, Mark.' Cabrillo's voice was like steel. 'Whatever it takes, you find that ship.'

'Yes, sir!' the young weapons specialist replied.

'Okay, back to where I was,' Juan continued gravely. 'For those of you who don't know, I was just in Jakarta negotiating to sell the *Oregon* for scrap.' Normally this would have warranted a sarcastic remark or at least an appreciative chuckle, but everyone was too focused. 'Just like Isphording said, the men who own the Karamita Yard are as corrupt as they come. Until yesterday all we had was speculation, thirdhand accounts, and the word of a convicted embezzler. I am now satisfied that Singh is involved with the pirates and maybe the smugglers, too.

'He doesn't want us to deliver the *Oregon* for a week,

which would give him enough time to dispose of whatever ship is inside the *Maus,* but we're going to drop anchor outside the yard in two days. On the night the *Maus* shows up, we're going to blow the lid off this entire operation.'

'What's the plan?' Linc asked.

'That's what we're here to discuss. Everyone get together with your department staff and come up with some scenarios. Mark, have you gotten pictures of the yard yet?'

'From a commercial satellite. They're a year old, and it looks like the place was under construction at the time.'

'Get George to make a few passes in the chopper for some better shots. If the Robinson doesn't have the range, have him rent another helo in Jakarta. As soon as he's back, make sure everyone has copies.'

'Check.'

'Linc, I don't know how many guards the place will have or what kind of weapons they carry, so make sure all your gun bunnies have everything they need, up to and including shoulder-fired missiles.'

'Aye, aye.'

'Doc?'

'I know, I know,' Julia preempted. 'I'll double-check our blood supply and play vampire with the crew if we need more.'

Everyone stood, but Juan wouldn't dismiss them just yet. There was one more piece of business he had to address. 'Ladies and gentlemen, I want to be very clear here. This mission has gone far beyond what we were hired to do. So far we've put ourselves in danger and come out all right.' He gave Linda a significant look. 'You've been up against Singh's hired guns on a one-to-one and know their capabilities. The money we're making is nothing compared to the risk we face once we enter the breaker's yard. Actually it barely covers the cost of running the ship.' He got a few grins. 'The people under you draw salary plus bonuses. We don't. We only get paid when there's a profit.

'Each of you joined the Corporation with expectations of using your unique talents to make money. I'm afraid that there won't be much on this caper, so if any of you want out until we're done, you have my permission. Your jobs will still be open after we're through, and there'll be no questions asked and no recriminations later.'

He waited for a reaction, his eyes meeting each of his senior staff's. No one said a word until Max cleared his throat.

'It's like this, Chairman. We've all had a chance to talk about this ever since we started following the *Maus*. And the truth of the matter is, some jobs are worth more than money. We all pretty much agree we'd pay for the chance to nail these bastards to the nearest outhouse door. We're backing your play one hundred percent.'

The crew gave a few 'hear, hears' as they followed Hanley out of the boardroom.

Juan could only smile his gratitude to his people.

Sporting his Jeb Smith disguise again to foil casual observers on the beach, Juan leaned against the rail of the *Oregon*'s bridge wing. He'd been there long enough for the coat of scaly rust on the railing to turn his callused palms orange. The sun was a waning fireball setting slowly behind the mountains that rose in the distance behind Shere Singh's Karamita Breakers Yard. The air was heavy with the smell of scorched metal, industrial solvents, and spilled bunker fuel. While coming north along the Sumatra coast he'd observed pristine white beaches and lush jungle. Most of the land was unspoiled and primeval. But around the yard it looked as though a cancer was eating away at the earth. The beach was a tarry morass, and the sea was the color of dishwater. With the exception of a new warehouse built out over the bay, all the buildings were dilapidated and coated with black dust. He had never seen a more depressing or dehumanizing place.

The massive scale of the buildings, cranes, and pieces of construction equipment rendered the workers almost to insignificance. The derricks towering over the yard swung slabs of steel from the beached ships to fenced-in areas where grimy men attacked them with torches, hammers, and their bare hands. From Juan's vantage a quarter mile from the beach, they looked like ants devouring the carapace of some giant beetle.

And around the *Oregon* floated an armada of the damned. The fleet of derelict ships destined to be torn apart at the yard stretched nearly to the horizon. They comprised an archipelago of rusted hulks as haunted and forlorn as the spirits of the dead awaiting entrance into hell. The container ships, oilers, and bulk freighters reminded him of a herd of cattle in the pens of a slaughterhouse. The *Oregon*'s decrepit state was artful camouflage, but around her was the real thing, the consequence of salt air, raging seas, and neglect.

'Will you look at that,' Max Hanley said, stepping out from the bridge. He wore a pair of grease-stained coveralls. The oil was fresh. He'd just come from the engine room. 'Compared to some of those tubs, I'd say the old *Oregon* looks shipshape and Bristol fashion.'

A deafening roar from inside the large warehouse reverberated across the bay and drowned out Cabrillo's reply.

'What *is* that?' Max exclaimed after the noise faded.

'Murph's new stereo?' Juan laughed. 'I think there's some kind of saw inside the warehouse. I read about them once – big chain-driven machine that can cut a ship like a slicer going through a loaf of bread.'

Max ducked into the bridge to retrieve a pair of binoculars from their cradle under the chart table. After a few minutes, the warehouse's landward doors cranked open. Small diesel locomotives emerged towing a twenty-foot-thick slice of a ship. The segment had a graceful flare, almost like a sculpture, and had come from near the unknown vessel's bow. A mobile crane lifted the section into the air once the train engines had reached the end of the tracks. The piece was open in the middle. Whatever ship it had come from had cargo holds rather than decks, most likely a bulk carrier or a tanker.

'Looks like a freighter-shaped cookie cutter,' Max remarked.

'Big cookie,' Juan said as the chunk of steel was laid on its side for workers to continue the disassembly process.

Something about his distracted tone caught Hanley's attention. 'What's going on in that cesspool you call a mind?'

'We know Singh is involved. But I've been up here a couple of hours, and the place looks like it's on the up-and-up except what might be going on inside the shed.'

'Where the ship saw is?'

'Uh-huh.' Juan studied the building from the binoculars he'd taken from Max. 'I want to take a peek inside tonight.'

'What about the *Maus*?'

'She'll be here soon enough. In the meantime, knowing what ship they're tearing apart in there might tell us something.'

'It's possible that it could be one of the ships the pirates hijacked before we were hired to stop them,' Hanley agreed. 'Could be they brought her down here inside their other drydock.'

Cabrillo looked at his old friend. 'I won't know until I get inside.'

One of Max's bushy eyebrows went up. 'Just you?'

'No sense risking any of the crew on this. I'll be in and out before they know I was there.'

'Linda Ross thought the same thing when she and her team boarded the *Maus*.'

'Take a look at the seaward side of the warehouse.'

Max took the binoculars and studied the sprawling structure. 'What am I looking for?'

'The building's built on pilings. I suspect that the metal siding doesn't extend all the way to the sea floor, and even if it does, I'm sure the doors don't. It would cause too much drag opening and closing them.'

'You plan to swim under the doors.'

'Once inside I should be able to identify the ship. It won't take more than an hour, and most of that is just swimming there and back.'

Max stared out at the massive shed, judging odds and risk. He came to a quick conclusion. 'Use a Draeger rebreather,' he advised just as a horn sounded to end the workday onshore. 'That'll eliminate the trail of bubbles on your way in and out.'

An hour after midnight, Juan Cabrillo was in the amidships boat garage wearing a head-to-toe wet suit. The water surrounding the Karamita Yard was as warm as blood, but he needed the thin black Microprene as cover once he reached his goal. He wore thick-soled dive boots and had his fins ready on the bench next to where he sat. He was going over the Draeger unit. Unlike a scuba rig that provides fresh air for a diver with every breath, the German-made rebreather used powerful filters to scrub carbon dioxide when a diver exhaled in a closed-loop system that allowed for great endurance while eliminating the telltale stream of bubbles.

The Draeger could be dangerous at depths much below thirty feet, so Juan planned to stay close to the surface. In a slim waterproof pouch strapped under his right arm he had a minicomputer, a flashlight, and a Fabrique Nationale Five-seveN double-action automatic. The pistol fired the new 5.7 mm ammunition. The advantage of the small, needle-like cartridges was that the matte-black weapon's grip held twenty rounds with one in the chamber. Also, the bullets were designed to blow through most ballistic vests while at the same time not overpenetrate a target.

A dive knife was strapped on the outside of his right thigh and a dive computer to his left wrist.

A dive technician hovered nearby. 'Just for the fun of it, I had Doc Huxley analyze a water sample,' the tech said as Juan finished his inspection. 'She said the sea here is more polluted than the Cuyahoga River when it caught fire back in the sixties.'

'That's your idea of fun?' Juan asked sarcastically.

'Rather analyze that gunk than swim in it.' The man grinned.

'You all set?' Max asked as he entered the darkened garage. Linda Ross was at his side, a slip of a girl compared to Max's looming silhouette.

'Piece of cake.' Juan got to his feet. He nodded to the tech, who doused the red battle lamp.

'Eric's at the helm,' Max told the chairman, 'and Mark is at the weapons station just in case something goes wrong. Also Linc and a few of his SEALs are kitting up now and will be ready with a Zodiac by the time you're halfway to the warehouse.'

'Good idea. But let's hope I don't need 'em.'

The garage's door rattled open, and without another word Juan stepped down the ramp, slid into his fins, and silently rolled into the sea. As soon as the water enveloped him, he felt the cumbersome weight of his gear vanish. This was Cabrillo's element. Here his mind became focused. He could forget about Eddie Seng, the pirates, the smugglers, and the thousands of details it took to run his company. It was as if nothing else in the world existed except him and the sea.

He adjusted his buoyancy until he was ten feet below the surface and checked his dive computer's integrated compass. With his arms dragging at his side, Cabrillo effortlessly finned through the inky water, his breathing even and smooth. After a minute he could no longer sense the *Oregon*'s presence to his left. He'd passed her bow.

Even with the Draeger's large mouthpiece, he could taste the foul water on his lips. It was metallic, like sucking on a penny, and when he touched his wet suit he could feel a greasy sheen of spilled oil. Juan was no tree hugger – he understood that civilization was bound to have an impact on the environment. But, if for no other reason, he wanted Singh shut down for the ecological damage his operation had done to the region.

He didn't dare use a light, so he had to rely heavily on his other senses. He'd been in the water for twenty minutes, swimming against a mild tide, when he heard a hollow whooshing sound. It was water sluicing under the doors of the mammoth building. He changed course slightly to compensate for a minor drift, and a minute later his hand brushed against rough concrete. It was one of the many pilings holding up the huge building. He swam around so he was directly behind the shed. While gantry lamps illuminated a great swath of the beach, the seaward side of the structure was in total darkness. Cabrillo flicked on his dive light. The red lens produced a feeble ruddy glow, but it was enough for him to get his bearings.

He doused the light again and allowed himself to float upward, breaking the surface with the merest ripple. The doors were as tall as an eight-story building and stretched nearly two hundred feet wide. All but the largest cruise ships, container ships, and tankers could easily pass inside on their way to be broken up.

Juan ducked back under the water, kicking down only a few feet before feeling the underside of the door. He rolled under the door and resurfaced inside the hangarlike shed. He spat out his regulator and pushed his dive mask onto his forehead. The tang of scorched metal burned his nose when he took a breath.

For a moment he thought the warehouse was completely black, far darker than the near moonless night, but he realized he'd surfaced under a catwalk. Once he moved out from its shadow he could see there were a few bare bulbs strung along the distant ceiling, revealing the dark outline of a ship. He swam along its length. Unlike the vessels out in the bay, this ship wasn't scaled with rust. The hull was smooth and free of growth and had a fresh coat of either black or dark blue paint.

This was no derelict at the end of its useful life. This was a new ship that wasn't more than a few years from coming down the ways. Cabrillo's pulse quickened.

He found a set of open metal scissor stairs that rose from under the water all the way to the walkway circling the building near the ceiling. He shrugged out of his gear and tied it so it remained submerged. He transferred his silenced automatic to a shoulder holster and made sure the minicomputer had survived the trip without damage. Leading with the pistol, he slowly eased his way up the stairs, placing each foot carefully before transferring his weight. He had no idea if Singh had posted any guards, but he knew the slightest sound would echo within the metal confines of the building, so he took every precaution to maintain silence.

A metal scaffold had been laid from the stairs to the ship's main deck. He paused in a shadow, listening for the quiet conversation of bored guards or an accidental cough. He heard nothing but the low hiss of water against the ship's hull and the occasional creak as a large wave surged in from outside.

He padded across the scaffold and found cover on the ship next to one of the ship's capstans. He brushed his fingertips against the metal deck. Like the hull, it was smooth and newly painted. From what he could tell, the ship was a small tanker, what in the profession was called a product tanker because it usually hauled refined products like kerosene or gasoline rather than crude oil. The first sixty or more feet of the tanker was gone, carved away by the ship saw and hauled outside. It went against his seaman's sense to see such a new and beautiful vessel get treated like this.

Juan ignored the slight superstitious chill and made his way aft toward the superstructure. The four-story accommodation block sat right at the stern, and he could see that workers had removed her bridge wings and hacked off her funnel so she could fit into the shed. He found an open hatch and stepped inside, making sure he was well away from any portholes before turning on his light. The deck was clean linoleum, and the walls were paneled in wood. He felt along the wall. Instead of finding the plaque that would give the ship's name, registry, and other information, he found four screw holes. Someone had taken pains to erase the ship's identity.

He found a stairwell and climbed to the bridge. Keeping his light shielded, he discovered that all her electronics had been stripped out. Her radios, navigation aids, weather computer, it was all gone. The empty racks, where the gear should have been, looked like whoever had done it had taken their time. There were no torn wires or any indication the workers had been rushed.

They had also removed anything that might list the ship's name. He searched the rest of the superstructure. The galley was nothing more than a room sheathed in stainless steel. The refrigerators and stoves had been removed as well as all the pots, pans, and utensils. They'd taken the place settings as well, which usually carried the owner's corporate logo and the name of the ship. The cabins were devoid of furniture but somehow retained a hint that they had been recently occupied. One smelled of cigars, while the bathroom of another carried the aroma of aftershave.

His next stop was the engine room.

A pair of big diesels dominated the space, each the size of a bus, and fed by miles of wiring, ducts, and pipes. He checked each engine carefully, cursing where he saw someone had removed all the identification tags. And where serial numbers had been stamped into the engine blocks someone had used a hand grinding wheel to polish them away. In their wake the metal was shiny silver and smooth.

Juan holstered his pistol and began a more thorough search. It was laborious work because of the engine room's cavernous size compared to his light's puny cone of illumination. And no matter where he shone the lamp, shadows dominated his view. Still, he pressed on. He got down on the floor to squirm under a freshwater condenser only to find that someone had already beaten him there and peeled off the manufacturer's decal. He played his flashlight beam over every nook and cranny and found nothing.

Singh's people knew what they were doing, he thought. Then he spotted an area where a thick coating of spilled oil had congealed under the starboard engine. It would be next to impossible to reach the spot, which was why he felt like ignoring it, but if he was unwilling to check it out so, too, might the men who'd erased the ship's identity.

Moving his body like a contortionist, he slithered under the cold engine. The space was tight, the engine mounts barely giving him enough room to breathe, and he rapped his hand against an unseen conduit and had to suck the blood from three knuckles. Once he reached the spot, he used his hand to scrape away the tarry grime. As his fingernails peeled back trenches of thick oil, he felt the slightly raised outline of a metal plate. They'd missed one!

It took him a few minutes' more work to rub away enough grease to read the tag. It said the engine had been built by Mitsubishi Heavy Industries, and there was a fifteen-digit ID number. Juan committed it to memory and squeezed back out from under the engine. He retrieved his computer, powered it up, and began cross-referencing the number.

Their client, his friend Hiroshi Katsui, had provided a wealth of information about the ships that had gone missing in the Sea of Japan, dossiers on all the crews, including pictures, and the serial numbers of dozens of each ship's principal components. Had the pirates not swiped the oven from the galley, Juan would have been able to check his database and match it to the vessel it had been installed on by its ID number.

Using a stylus, he typed in the fifteen-character number, chose the icon for engines, and pressed the Search button.

When the ship's name came up, Cabrillo's jaw literally dropped.

'We've been had,' he muttered to himself.

'Understatement of the year, Captain,' a familiar voice whispered in his ear at the same time the muzzle of a gun was pressed to the back of his head.

A second later, men's voices and the dancing glow of several flashlights approached from one of the engine room's few entrances.

## 19

Too many years had passed since Eddie Seng sat through his freshman lit class at NYU for him to remember how many circles of hell Dante described in the *Divine Comedy*. He was sure, though, that he had discovered one below whatever the medieval Italian poet had envisaged.

As soon as their plane landed after its six-hour flight, Eddie and the other illegals were herded inside a shipping container. By interpreting the motion that followed, Eddie knew the unventilated steel box was trucked to a port and loaded onto a ship for another ten-hour trip. The only clue that gave Eddie a sense of his location was the cooler temperatures. Factoring in the weather and a six-hour flight at roughly five hundred knots, he put their position within an arc that included northern Mongolia, southern Siberia, and the Russian coast. And since there were no lakes in the hinterland large enough to necessitate a ten-hour boat trip, he figured he was someplace on the Kamchatka Peninsula or along the coast of the Sea of Okhotsk.

The container was offloaded and dropped to the ground hard enough to tumble the men inside. Moments later the doors were opened, and Eddie got his first look at hell.

Dark mountains rose in the distance, their tops obscured by soot of some kind so the rugged peaks looked smeared. He had to blink his eyes to keep them in focus. The beach where he stood was water-worn rock ranging in size from pebbles to bowling balls. The surf made the stones clatter with each wave cycle. The ocean behind was flat and dark, gray, with a menace Eddie associated with the calm before a storm.

These details weren't what caused Eddie's mind to go numb. It was the human misery that toiled on the hill rising from sea. It was a scene out of the Holocaust. Emaciated figures, so streaked with grime it was impossible to tell if they were clothed, covered the hillside so the whole expanse seemed to be squirming, like a bloated carcass being devoured by maggots. They were rendered sexless and inhuman by their wasted condition.

There had to be two thousand people forced to work along the slope.

Some climbed up the hillside laden with empty buckets, while others staggered down under their loads. On a level section three-quarters of the way up the hill, shovelers filled the buckets with mud. They moved like automatons, as if their bodies could no longer perform any other act but scoop and dump. Farther up the hillside, others manned water cannons. The cannons were fed by hoses that snaked across the landscape to where glacial runoff from the distant mountains had been diverted into an earthen retention pond. Gravity forced the water through the lines so when it exploded from the cannons it was an arcing jet that the workers cut back and forth across a dirt embankment, sluicing away layers of soil with every pass.

Excess water from the guns poured down the hillside, gathering the topsoil until it was a liquid slurry as treacherous as quicksand. In those first moments that Eddie watched, dumbstruck by what he was seeing, a thick wave of mud suddenly shot down the slope. Those not quick enough were caught in the swell and tumbled down the hill.

Some rose quickly back to their feet. Some more slowly. And one not at all. He was soon buried alive.

No one paused from their labor.

Strung over the workings on wooden poles were acres of camouflage netting that had been dyed in the same hues of gray and black and brown as the landscape, so from above, the site was completely hidden.

Near the beach where Eddie and his group gaped, haunted-eyed workers dumped their buckets into a series of mechanical sluice boxes, devices little changed from their introduction more than a century ago. The mud was washed down a long table by a gentle rocking motion. The bottom of the trough was lined with baffles that would trap and separate the heavy material from the lighter overburden. The waste fell away at the end of the boxes and eventually reached the ocean, where it spread in a brown stain, while the concentrated ore would need to be scraped away and taken for further refining.

A bucket brigade of workers formed a human chain from the tables to a three-story building a short way down the beach. Like the undulations of some enormous worm, buckets of ore that had been cleaned out of the sluice boxes were passed hand-to-hand toward the building. Eddie saw that what he assumed was the processing plant had been bolted down to a flat, oceangoing barge that could be easily towed away from the site. Tendrils of white smoke rose from a short stack next to the structure, telling him that whatever process they used to get their final product required heat.

Overseeing the sprawling site were armed men. They were dressed for the weather in thick pants and jackets. Their boots were knee-high and made of rubber to protect them from the ubiquitous mud. Most had gloves. All had

AK-47s over their shoulders and carried either clubs or short whips. There were only a few guards positioned up the hill, but there were more closer to where the mining process came to its conclusion. Four men watched over each of the dozen sluice boxes, while it appeared there was a guard for every ten laborers manning the bucket brigade. The lash of whips rising and falling was the work chorus that kept the laborers in motion.

A razor-wire fence prevented the Chinese workers, and from what he could tell they were all Chinese, from approaching the far side of the building where a tracked vehicle similar to an arctic snow cat had direct access to a partially buried cruise ship that had been beached farther down the coast.

There were other beached ships on the workers' side of the barbed wire. They were small cruise ships that were so badly decayed it was astounding they had survived the trip here. They, too, had been buttressed with rubble and their decks strung with netting to break up their outlines.

Dormitories, Eddie realized, for the workers.

Even as he thought it, he corrected himself. These weren't workers. They were slaves, forced to mine the hillside in the most deplorable conditions he could have imagined.

There were only a few things on earth valuable enough for such insatiable greed. And he instinctively understood what they were after: gold.

It seemed even longer ago that Eddie had sat in a geology class, but he remembered enough to recognize that someone had discovered gold-bearing strata up the hillside. The water cannons used hydrokinetic pressure to crumble the soil so it could be fed into the sluice boxes. From there the concentrate was spun in centrifuges to further separate out the lighter waste. The final process was to dump what was removed from the bottom of the centrifuges into mercury, the only substance in the world that attracts the precious metal. Once bonded to the microparticles of gold, the ball of mercury would then be boiled away, leaving pure molten gold.

In most modern smelting facilities the mercury vapor was recaptured, condensed, and reused in a closed-loop system that prevented workers from coming into contact with the deadly metal. Judging by the deplorable conditions of the men working the hill, he imagined the poor souls in the refinery being subjected to untold amounts of mercury vapor, one of the most savage toxins in the world.

Those few seconds taking in the enormity of the workings were the last moments he was spared the depravity of his captors. He and the others that had followed the snake with him from Shanghai were ordered into a line. An Indonesian guard locked a small chain around his neck. From it dangled a tag stamped with an identification number. Another guard noted the number in a ledger book, and the batch of them were led off to one of the derelict cruise liners. They were assigned unheated cabins. While the ship had never been luxurious by any standard, the rooms were crowded with bunk beds so ten men occupied a room designed for two. From the stench it was clear the ship's plumbing no longer functioned, and even this deep into the vessel Eddie could see his own breath. Each bunk had a single mud-caked blanket, and the mattresses were soaked through and molding. There was no place for the workers to dry themselves, so at the end of their shifts they merely collapsed into their beds, wet and covered in slime.

A guard prodded him on. He and the others were shown where they ate. It had once been the cruise ship's main dining room. All the furniture was long gone, and any ornamentation had been stripped from the walls. The floor was bare metal, and that was where the workers took their meals. The group was ordered into a line, and each took a filthy metal bowl from a pile. A Chinese man with his arm in a sling used his free hand to scoop a palm full of rice into the bowl. Next to him another disabled worker ladled in a grayish pink slop from a huge drum.

The concoction retained just a trace of warmth and was barely fit for human consumption. Eddie would later learn that the operators of the mine sent out a pair of fishing boats to drag the oceans. Anything and everything that got caught up in their nets was fed into a giant shredder to rip apart the bigger chunks and was then liquefied.

Five minutes after finding a place on the floor to choke down the sickening gruel, their guard cocked his weapon and shouted, 'On your feet.'

Knowing he'd need to keep his strength, Eddie tipped the remainder of the bowl into his mouth, wolfing down the rank paste as well as his own bile. Bits of fish scale scraped at the back of his throat.

'You were fed now because you are newly arrived,' the guard continued. 'From now on you only get food at the end of your shift.'

The men were led outside once again. For the first time Eddie became aware of the wind, a constant breeze that blew in from the sea and passed through his clothes and seemed to buffet against his bones. It also carried fine particles of ash, volcanic, he guessed, which confirmed for him that he was on the Kamchatka Peninsula. They were ordered to begin lugging buckets up the hill, and as Eddie began what would be the first of a hundred torturous climbs that day, he patted the meaty part of his thigh where Doc Huxley's homing device had been implanted.

He was a long way from the *Oregon*, but he knew he wasn't alone. It would be a day, or two at the most, before Juan had a team on the ground, and the nightmare would end before it really got started.

That night he got a chance to talk to the men assigned to his cabin. There was no electricity, so the exhausted workers whispered in the dark. They all had similar stories about being smuggled out of China as illegal immigrants inside shipping containers. They had paid the snakeheads to take them to Japan, but when the containers were unsealed, they found themselves here.

'How long have you been here?' Eddie asked.

A disembodied voice replied from his bunk, 'Forever.'

'Seriously, how long?'

'Four months,' the same man said, shifting in the dark to find a less damp spot on his mattress. 'But the mine has been in operation much longer. Years maybe.'

'Has anyone tried to escape?'

'To where?' another answered. 'We can't swim away. The water is too cold, and the fishing boats are heavily guarded when they return, and they are only here long enough to dump their nets on the dock. You've seen the mountains. Even if you get past the guards, which no one has been able to do, you wouldn't last a day out there.'

'They own us,' a third man remarked. 'From the moment we said we wanted to leave China, they own us. Does it matter if we work ourselves to death here, in a textile factory back home, or in a sweatshop in New York City? This is what the gods meant for us, for all Chinese peasants. We work and then we die. I have been here ten months. All the men originally assigned this room are now gone. Go ahead with your fantasies of escape, my friend. In the end there is only one way out – and that is death.'

Eddie wasn't sure if he should tell them who he really was. From what he saw as the men shuffled to the cabin, they were all in terrible condition, so he doubted the mine's overseers had planted any informants within the ranks. However, he couldn't discount the idea he'd be exposed by one of them for an extra ration of food or a dry blanket. As much as he wanted to give these wretched souls a glimmer of hope, it went against his years of training and experience. In the end he allowed exhaustion to overcome his wet bedding and the knots of pain radiating from every joint in his body. Two of his cabin mates coughed and hacked throughout the night. Pneumonia or worse. He imagined the squalid conditions and meager food rations meant disease was already rampant throughout the operation.

It was on the third day of shivering cold, and constant wet that pruned and paled his skin, and backbreaking work, that Eddie began to realize rescue might be a long time in coming. Surely Juan could have flown someone to Russia where they could rent a helicopter and at least fly over the area? But there had been no such overflight. Instead, he'd worked with the others, mindlessly hauling mud down the mountain, like ants who know nothing but to follow their instincts.

He'd already lost his shoes, and every time he took a deep breath he felt a slight rattle in the depths of his lungs. He's started off in much better shape than the others, but his body was used to regular food and rest, unlike the peasants who had lived their entire lives on a starvation diet and knew nothing but hard labor. Two of the men from his cabin were already dead. One of them had been buried by an avalanche, and the other was beaten by a guard so severely he died with blood dripping from his ears and from around his eyes.

By the fifth day, his back stinging from a particularly brutal whipping that he'd done nothing to trigger, Eddie Seng realized two things. One was that the burst transmitter in his leg had failed, and the second was that he was going to die on this forlorn coast.

On the morning of the sixth day, as the work crews were being led outside into the predawn chill, a huge ship had appeared in the bay. Eddie paused on the ramp leading to the beach to note that it was a floating drydock but mistakenly assumed it was the *Maus* and not her sister. Even at a distance the stench emanating from the black-hulled behemoth was overpowering, and flocks of gulls swooped around open ports to pluck the human waste that had spilled out from within.

As a guard prodded Eddie with a baton jab to the kidneys, he realized she was a slave ship, loaded with workers to replace the ones who'd died or were so weak they could no longer rise from their bunks no matter how hard they were beaten. How many hundreds or thousands had already perished, he wondered, only to be replaced with a steady supply of hopeful immigrants thinking they'd bought their one chance at freedom?

'That is how I was brought here,' Tang, one of his roommates, remarked as they trudged up the slick hillside. Tang was the one who'd said he'd been here for four months already. His body was stick thin, and Eddie could clearly see his breastbone and rib cage through his torn shirt. He was twenty-seven years old but looked sixty. 'We were loaded onto an old ship, and then it was swallowed up inside an even bigger ship like that one. If you can imagine, the journey here was worse than the work they force us to do.'

By the time they'd filled their buckets for the journey down to the sluice boxes, a rust-coated ship was slowly emerging from the belly of the drydock, and workers were throwing large bundles off its deck.

'Bodies,' Tang said. 'I was forced to do that. We had to dump over the corpses of those who didn't survive the journey.'

'How many?'

'A hundred, perhaps more. I myself had to dump the bodies of my two cousins and my best friend.'

Tang didn't slow his pace, but Eddie could tell the memory was taking its toll. 'So they will beach the boat and use it to house more workers?'

'First they will pile rocks around it and cover it with nets so it can't be seen from the air.'

'What about the water? This whole operation is exposed to the sea.'

Tang shook his head. 'Other than the two fishing boats, I haven't seen any other ships since I arrived. I think we are too far from anywhere for ships to pass close by.'

They had just reached the sluice boxes when Eddie suddenly fell flat on his back as though a rug had been yanked out from under him. Stunned, he looked around to see hundreds of others had also fallen. That was when he felt the ground shaking.

Even as he realized it was an earthquake, the shaking

subsided, but a deep roar continued to echo like distant thunder.

He got to his feet, wiping the worst of the clinging mud from his tattered clothes. His attention and soon that of every person at the mine was drawn upward toward the central-most mountain peak that dominated the workings. Steam and dark ash gushed from near its peak in an ever-expanding cloud that would soon blot out the sun. Lightning crackled around the summit like Saint Elmo's fire.

The separating plant's door burst open, and a man rushed out, stripping off a gas mask as he ran. He was the first white person Eddie had seen this whole time at the mine.

'That is Jan Paulus,' Tang whispered as the man ran toward them. 'He is the overseer.'

Jan Paulus was a solid-looking man, broad across the shoulders with weathered features and hands as big as anvils. He stopped just a few paces from Eddie and Tang and studied the now-active volcano that towered above the bay. He watched it for only a moment before pulling a clunky satellite phone from a holster strapped around his waist. He flipped up the antenna, waited a beat to ensure he had a signal, then dialed.

'Anton, it's Paulus,' he said in English but with a Dutch or Afrikaans accent. He listened before saying, 'I'm not surprised you felt it in Petropavlovsk. Shook the shit out of us. Worst one yet, but that's not why I called. The volcano above the site is active.' A pause. 'Because we've talked about this possibility a dozen times, and I'm looking at a bloody great cloud of ash and steam, that's how I know. If that thing really lets go, we're finished.'

As if to punctuate his sentence, the ground shook again in a mild aftershock. 'Feel that one, too, Savich?' the South

African asked sarcastically. He listened for a beat. 'Your assurances don't mean anything. It's my arse out here while yours is sitting in a hotel sauna three hundred kilometers away.' He glanced around as he listened again. Eddie quickly dipped his bucket into the sluice, hoping that the mine's foreman hadn't noticed him eavesdropping. 'Yeah, the *Souri* just arrived. They're offloading the latest batch of Chinese in another of Shere Singh's rustbuckets. As soon as they're ready, I'm going to load the first shipment like we talked about last week.'

Paulus shot Eddie a scowl. He had no choice but to move on, but still he listened for as long as he could. 'We just finished another run with the mercury smelter, so now would be a good time to think about at least towing the processing plant off the beach until we know what's happening with the volcano. You have the influence to stop your fellow Russkies from sending any scientists over to have a look-see, but you sure as hell can't stop that mountain from blowing. Why don't you chopper over and take a look? In the meantime I'm going to make plans to get out of here.' The miner's voice rose, as though the connection was fading. 'What? Who cares about them? We can evacuate the guards using the *Souri*. Singh can get us more ships, and there's a million Chinese a year trying to get out. We can replace the lot of them . . . So what if we lose a month or two, we've already got enough raw material to keep the minters going for at least that long . . . All right, see you in a couple of hours.'

Tang had gone on ahead, ascending the mountain with the dull gait of a pack animal. Eddie made no effort to catch up. He watched the ballooning ash cloud high above, digesting what he'd just heard. The foreman wanted to evacuate his people and the guards, but it sounded like he needed the permission of someone named Anton, someone with enough pull to keep Russian volcanologists from visiting the area. The South African had argued that now was the perfect time. The drydock was here with its powerful tugs ready to go, and it sounded as though they had already amassed a large stockpile of gold destined to be struck into coins. The separating plant, arguably the most important and expensive piece of equipment, could be towed to safety. The beached ships being used as dormitories were worth only their scrap price, and it sounded like they had a line on how to obtain more. That just left the workers, and as Paulus had said, with a million illegal Chinese riding the snake every year, replacing their slave force would be simple enough.

Eddie understood their twisted logic. The only thing of value they would really lose is time.

Another temblor struck. Eddie knew there was a real danger that the volcano would erupt, and he envisioned a cataclysmic explosion like the one that leveled a couple hundred square miles around Mount Saint Helens. There was no way he or anyone else left behind could escape such a blast. Over the past few days he'd resigned himself to work the weeks or even months it would take Juan to find him, and of his eventual rescue he had no doubt. The Corporation did not leave its people behind.

But the one thing Paulus and Savich could afford was the one thing Eddie Seng no longer possessed: time.

# 20

The thought popped unbidden into Cabrillo's mind. *Of all the engine rooms in all the ships in the world she had to walk into mine.*

The unseen gunman pulled the weapon from the back of his head at the same time Juan shut off both his computer and flashlight. 'Are you wearing night vision?' he whispered into the gunman's ear.

'Yes,' came the near silent reply.

'Lead on.' He took the gunman's hand. It was slim and delicate despite the leather gloves.

The lights carried by the approaching men gave just enough glow for Juan to avoid jamming a knee or bumping his head amid the forest of pipes, but he couldn't see enough to know if they were headed in the right direction. He would just have to trust someone who a moment earlier had a pistol to his skull.

He had been aboard the ship for nearly forty minutes, so he figured his presence hadn't been detected, meaning it was his companion who had drawn the guards. The smart thing for him was to separate, make his way to the side of the vessel, and swim back to the *Oregon*. However, that left too many unanswered questions. For the time being they were in this together.

They reached a hatchway that led to the steering gear room. As soon as they crossed the threshold and made a sharp turn down a utility corridor, Juan could no longer hear their pursuers.

'So who are you?' he asked as they silently padded toward the bow. 'MI-6?' That was the British equivalent to the CIA. His question was met with silence. 'Royal Navy?'

'No,' replied Victoria Ballinger. 'I'm a field investigator for Lloyd's of London, fraud division.'

If Lloyd's was taking insurance hits because of the Sea of Japan pirates, it made sense they would send someone out to investigate, which explained her presence on the ill-fated *Avalon*. Most likely there had been an entire team on board to repulse the pirates and get their own answers about who was behind the attacks. Unfortunately, they had vastly underestimated the pirates' sophistication, and as a result Tory had been the sole survivor.

'How about you?' she asked. 'Are you still claiming to be a tramp freighter captain with fish-finding gear, a couple of scuba tanks, and a knack for being at the right place at the right time?'

'We'll talk about that as soon as we're out of here.' Cabrillo's tone was clipped. He wasn't happy about her presence or the larger implications of what he'd discovered moments before her arrival. There was time for recriminations later. First he had to get them back to the *Oregon*.

He chanced turning on his flashlight but dialed down the beam so it was as dim as a guttering candle. Tory stripped her night vision goggles from her head and stuffed them in a shoulder bag. She had to resettle her mass of black hair under her watch cap. Juan gave her a look to catch her eyes. They were blue, steady and resolved, without a trace of fear. He had no idea what kind of training she had received during her career, but the way she'd handled her ordeal on the sunken *Avalon* and her current composure told him she was ready for anything.

The corridor ended in a ladder that rose to an overhead hatch. 'So, Captain, I assume you have a plan?'

'My original plan didn't include finding you and the goons who obviously followed you. I want to get past these guys without a firefight, then I've got a Draeger rebreather stashed out in the shed. Do you know how to dive?' Tory nodded sharply. 'Then we'll swim back to my ship.'

'I'm not leaving here until I know what vessel this is.'

Cabrillo caught the stubborn lift of her chin and knew she meant it. 'We're on a ship that shouldn't be here called the *Toya Maru*. She was snatched while the pirates were attacking the *Avalon*. That big ship you remembered seeing was a floating drydock called the *Maus*. They concealed the *Toya Maru* inside her and towed her here. All the while under near constant surveillance by my people, I might add.'

'So why shouldn't she be here?'

'Because the *Maus* is still a couple days out.'

A look of confusion swept across her beautiful face. 'I don't understand.'

Juan was growing frustrated. They had to get out of there, and Tory wanted to play twenty questions. But the truth was he was more angry at himself than her. Like everyone involved, he, too, had failed to anticipate the pirates' cunning. 'It means they knew they were being shadowed the whole time and waited for their chance to offload the *Maru*, which came when I had to call the *Oregon* away for a day near Taiwan. They put a crew aboard this ship and sailed her down here under her own steam, while my people followed the ballasted drydock. Gauging the amount of disassembly work they've already accomplished, I'd say they've had her in this shed for a few days at least.'

He touched her sleeve. 'I'll tell you everything, but later. We have to get going.'

Without waiting for a reply, Cabrillo tucked his pistol into his holster and climbed the ladder. The hatch wheel gave a chirp of protest as he broke the seal, then spun freely. He eased the cover up, got his gun in position, and ducked his head through to the next level. It was pitchblack and silent. He pulled his body through and waited for Tory. Once she was at his side, he risked using his light again.

He recognized the space as the main ballast control room. From here the crew could use a system of pumps to transfer their load from tank to tank in order to maintain trim. He briefly considered finding the sea suction inlet, a breach in the hull where seawater could be pumped into the ship for ballast, but it would take too long to find and open an inspection hatch. Plus there would be heavy mesh to prevent the pumps fouling on a large fish or kelp when it drew in the water.

Now that he had his bearings, he turned on his mini-computer and called up a set of the *Toyo Maru*'s blueprints. On the tiny screen the schematics were tough to make out, so it took him a few minutes to trace their escape route.

'Got it,' he said at last. 'Okay, stay close and stay behind me.'

'Chivalry, Captain?'

'Practicality. I'm wearing body armor, and unless you dropped twenty pounds in two weeks, I know you're not.'

She shot him a cheeky smirk. 'Touché and lead on.'

Cabrillo checked the corridor outside the ballast control room and edged out. With no light to amplify, Tory's goggles were useless, forcing him to rely on his flashlight and trust the guards would give themselves away before they saw it.

At the end of the hall they came to a set of steep stairs. Juan was halfway up when he heard voices and saw light from above. Without turning he stepped back again, feeling Tory right behind him. From the bottom of the stairs he caught a glimpse of two men armed with assault rifles passing by. He and Tory waited a full three minutes after the voices faded before making the climb again.

They had reached the level just below the main deck. Once they reached the outside, Juan planned to just jump over the side and find the rebreather. In the darkness Shere Singh's men would never spot them.

From down the hallway came the unmistakable mechanical ratchet of a weapon being cocked. Cabrillo threw Tory to the deck as lights snapped on all over the place. His finger was working the trigger before he had a target, laying down suppression fire to maximize confusion. In the first seconds of the ambush he didn't care about the danger of a ricochet. Getting out was all that mattered. Tory added her own pistol, an unsilenced 9 mm that boomed like a cannon in the metal confines of the ship.

He wanted to get back down the stairs, but when he glanced over the landing, autofire ripped up from below so close he felt the heat of the bullets and the muzzle flash was like an explosion in his face.

He fired a blind shot at the downstairs gunman and crawled across the passageway, seeking cover where the hall turned ninety degrees. Once out of sight of the ambushers, he dragged Tory to safety. He hadn't been hit, which was a miracle, and now wasn't the time to worry about the Englishwoman.

He tossed his minicomputer out into the hallway. Immediately an automatic weapon opened up. Good. The guards were jumpy. He levered his pistol out into the hall and fired three shots, moving his body as he pulled the trigger so he was exposed by the time he pulled the trigger a fourth time. He spotted his target, a turbaned guard lying on the deck and cringing behind his AK-47. Cabrillo put a pair of bullets through the top of his head, then dashed for cover as another guard farther down the hallway unloaded his magazine in a wild sustained burst.

He grabbed Tory's hand, and together they ran away from the ambush, all pretense of stealth forgotten.

Juan rounded a corner and saw the flicker of movement an instant before a rifle butt crashed into his skull. He fell flat, poleaxed, but didn't lose consciousness as Tory came up behind him and double tapped the guard as he was recovering from the swing. The guard was blown back by the kinetic energy of her nine millimeter rounds and the wall behind him was painted in his blood.

His head feeling as fragile as glass, Juan let Tory help him to his feet. His vision was blurred, and blood oozed from where skin had been smeared from his forehead. It hung like a flap over his left eye. Juan ripped away the slice in a savage jerk that caused a fresh rush of blood but allowed him to see. Tory gasped.

'I know a good plastic surgeon,' was all he said, and the pair started running again.

That's when a metallic scream unlike anything Juan had ever heard began. He knew immediately it was the ship saw. A moment later the thick band of the chain saw cut into the ship just ahead of the superstructure, no more than twenty feet in front of Cabrillo and Tory. Water from the lubricating jets turned to steam, spiking the humidity to a hundred percent, and slivers of metal filled the passageway like shrapnel. The saw changed directions and began to cut horizontally toward them, shredding metal bulkheads as though they were tissue. The thick chain burst through the wall next to them, its teeth cutting the ship as easily as a can opener. The chain came at them four feet off the deck, moving through the vessel almost as fast as they could run. The stench of scorched steel was overwhelming, and an occasional filing blew off the chain and landed on Cabrillo, melting holes in his wet suit.

They came to another staircase and raced up, their focus on staying away from the deadly saw. As if the machine knew where they were headed, it started to angle up after them, chewing apart the stairwell like some prehistoric predator. The railings ricocheted off the wall as the sawing action tore them from their mounts.

Juan could barely see. The combination of the blood and what he knew was a mild concussion slowed him. But Tory didn't leave his side. Together they raced from the ravenous charge of the ship saw. They ran past crew cabins, and when they rounded another corner, both began to sprint for an exterior hatch. It was a race because they were running parallel to the thick cutting chain and could no longer see it as it sliced apart the *Toyo Maru*.

Ten feet from the open door, the wall to their right began to glow and vibrate as the chain's teeth took their first taste of the bulkhead. Because the Japanese tanker wasn't exactly square in the shed, the saw first ate through the corner they had just turned and, like a zipper being pulled, it started to split the wall.

Juan glanced over his shoulder. The chain had already cut through the first ten feet of the hallway and as he watched, another few feet were torn apart. Metal filings filled the hall like a nest of enraged wasps as the chain began to span the width of the corridor.

With five feet to go before they were clear, Cabrillo pounded Tory between the shoulder blades. The blow made her tumble, but her inertia kept her rolling. Juan threw himself after her as the thick chain passed directly over them the instant they burst out onto the open deck.

And into another ambush.

Four turbaned men had been waiting for them, eyeing the duo's fall over their AKs' iron sights. Juan and Tory had landed in a tangle of limbs that parodied intimacy. Before either could get their gun hand free, the Sikhs had weapons to their heads. The ship saw rattled to silence.

'I was hoping the saw wouldn't get you just yet,' an accented voice boomed from a catwalk suspended over the ship.

Juan and Tory had their weapons taken away and were allowed to their feet, their fingers laced at the back of their heads. Cabrillo studied the man above him. Judging age and his resemblance to Abhay, Juan guessed that the man was the leader of the pirate ring.

'Shere Singh,' Juan growled.

'I hope you found what you were looking for,' the Sikh said. 'I would hate to think of you going to your graves still filled with curiosity.' He gave an order in a language Juan didn't recognize, and he and Tory were shoved toward the ship's bow.

Overhead an unseen operator was resetting the chain blade of the ship saw. Tracks built near the ceiling allowed it to be maneuvered almost anywhere within the shed. The segmented blade now spanned the deck about fifteen feet behind where the bow had been cut off, held so taut that despite its length of nearly two hundred feet, it didn't sag. And in the glare of overhead lights the tips of its special alloy teeth glinted like so many hundreds of daggers.

A moment later, Shere Singh reached the *Toya Maru*'s deck and approached, flanked by two more guards. He carried an odd metal pipe with long, perpendicular handles. Juan and Tory were each held by a pair of men in such a way that their toes barely touched the deck. Cabrillo tried to shift his weight to find leverage to break free, but each movement caused his captors to lift him even higher. When Singh was close enough to smell, he passed the length of pipe under Juan's arms and behind his back. The guards shifted their grip so they could hold him in place by grasping the handles.

Cabrillo now understood the device's purpose. This had to be a favorite way for the pirate to dispatch his enemies. The handles allowed the guards to hold their victim so when they pressed his body against the ship saw they were in no danger of being caught in the whirring chain.

When she realized the full horror of what was about to happen, Tory Ballinger screamed like an enraged lioness and jerked her body to get away. The men holding her laughed and lifted her even higher, so her entire weight pulled awkwardly against the tendons in her shoulders. The agony quickly drained the fight out of her, and she seemed to deflate.

'You're not going to get away with this,' Cabrillo said.

The threat sounded as hollow to him as it did to Shere Singh, and the heavyset Pakistani laughed. 'Of course I am, Captain Jeb Smith. But I must say you have lost a lot of weight compared to what my son, Abhay, described.'

'Jenny Craig.'

'Who?'

'Never mind. Listen Singh, we know about the *Maus,* and we know about the *Souri.* As soon as either vessel tries to enter a legitimate port, they will be seized. You're finished, so why not give up now and spare yourself a pair of murder charges?'

'So you would not charge me for the deaths of the *Toyo Maru*'s crew, eh?'

Juan hadn't held much hope that the pirates were merely holding the tanker's crew, and now he had his confirmation. 'In about ten minutes a special forces team is going to rush this building and kill everyone inside.'

Singh laughed again. He was enjoying his complete dominance over his captives. 'They will be five minutes too late for you and your nubile friend. There is nothing you can say to stop me and nothing you can do, either. I have men approaching your boat as we speak. At most you have a small mercenary force. They will be dealt with.'

Cabrillo knew that even if he didn't make it out of this alive, his people would cut down Singh and all his men like so much wheat. But he wanted to keep Singh talking. Buy himself some time until he could think of a way out of this mess. 'If we are going to die, at least tell me about the Chinese. How do they fit into your plan?'

Singh stepped close again. He possessed the piercing hazel eyes of a goat, and they never blinked. He smelled of cigarettes and at about six foot four stood half a head taller than Cabrillo. Using just the strength of his arm, he rammed a fist into Juan's solar plexus, a blow that expelled every molecule of air from his lungs. Had the Sikh used the full force of his body, Juan's ribs would have been stove in. It took several struggling breaths until his lungs felt at least partially inflated.

'You never knew I discovered you were following the *Maus* from the Sea of Japan. You didn't know I offloaded this ship' – Singh stamped a foot onto the deck – 'when I had the chance. I have been ahead of you every step of the way, so what makes you think I would be so stupid as to tell you anything now? Knowledge must be earned. I taught my sons that. Anything given to you is worth exactly what you put in to deserve it. Nothing. What we do with the Chinese we've captured is none of your concern.'

That at least verified for Cabrillo that Singh was connected to the snakeheads. 'Aren't you at least curious who we are and why we've come after you?'

A lupine look crossed Singh's face. 'You have me on that account, my friend. I indeed do want to know who you are, and if you came here a week ago I would have delighted in extracting that information. But now, today, it doesn't matter. I will permit you to go to your grave with your secrets as I go about my business with mine.'

Singh made a spiraling gesture with his finger, and the powerful motors that drew the ship saw through its massive gears came to life. The chain soon became a blur as it whipped by just above the deck. The sound was staggering but nowhere near as bad as when it was chewing through a derelict hulk.

Juan looked around for something, anything, to forestall the inevitable. He'd come up with the germ of a plan, but at most he could hope to take out two, maybe three of the guards before he was gunned down. His only hope was that Tory would have the presence of mind to get herself over the side of the tanker and the hell away from the shed. He looked over to her. Their eyes met with such intensity that it was as if they could read each other's minds. She knew he was going to try something crazy, and her gaze told him she would make the most of his attempt. That brief exchange told him that in another world he would have enjoyed knowing her better.

The guards maneuvered Juan closer to the whirring chain saw, and no matter how he tried to resist he couldn't stop himself from taking halting tiptoe steps toward the industrial guillotine. Even from five feet away he could feel its power. Like the tingle of atmospheric electricity during a storm, it was a living force that split the air.

He tried to twist his shoulders, but that only made the guards shove him even closer.

Shere Singh moved up next to Juan, keeping enough distance that there was no way he could reach the Sikh. Singh held a length of wood in his hand. Making sure he had Juan's attention, he lowered the piece of timber onto the spinning chain. There was a brief pop and an explosion of sawdust. It took a fraction of a second for the saw to pulp the heavy piece of mahogany. Singh grinned again and stepped back, shouting over the roar of the machine, 'I think I will let my men enjoy the woman before they feed her to the saw.'

Juan gave no outward sign that he was about to act, but in his mind he planned out every move, choreographing the actions so when he went into motion there would be no hesitation. There was, however, a glaring variable to his plan. And that was if he survived the first instant.

He kicked both legs into the air, relying on the goons behind him to hold him steady as the limbs inexorably fell back toward the saw. His right calf made contact with the top of the serrated chain. He was dimly aware of Tory's stunned scream as the fast-moving saw bit into something hard in his leg and ripped the pole handles out of the guard's grip.

The shock and savagery nearly ripped Juan's leg from its socket and the straps securing the prosthesis below his knee were stretched to their very limit. But it had worked. The men hadn't fought the saw in a tug-of-war that would have allowed the blade to slice through the titanium struts of his artificial leg. The saw's relentless momentum tossed Juan like a rag doll fifteen feet across the deck. He landed in a perfect shoulder roll, and as his body came to rest, he was reaching into the ruin of what he called his combat leg for the Kel-Tec pistol secured within the composite limb.

The Kel-Tec was one of the smallest handguns in the world, weighing just five ounces when empty. But unlike other small pistols that were limited in their caliber to .22 or .25, the Kel-Tec was designed to fire P-rated .380 cartridges. They were man stoppers, and the armorers on the *Oregon* had hot-loaded the rounds to within a few newtons of their maximum tolerance.

As much as Cabrillo wanted to put the first bullet through Singh's head, the compact weapon only had room for seven rounds. He took aim at the startled guards who'd been holding him a second earlier and fired. The first round went wild. His breathing was coming too fast and his stump had begun to throb. The next two found their marks, and one of the guards had his throat blown open. He fell forward into the ship saw.

The chain severed his body in a fountain of blood. His head and torso fell to the deck with an obscene wet smack while his lower extremities were kicked into the air when a tooth snagged on his spinal column. They cartwheeled through the air and caught the second guard in the chest, knocking him flat and for the next few seconds out of the fight. Juan shifted his aim at the men holding Tory. They held her in such a way that he couldn't get a clean kill, so he put a round into the kneecap of one of them. As he spun away shrieking, Tory managed to twist out of the other's grasp. Juan dropped him with a double tap to the chest.

The two turbaned men that had boarded the *Toyo Maru* with Shere Singh were scrambling for cover and preparing to open up with their AK-47s. Juan emptied his three remaining rounds in slow succession to keep them down while screaming for Tory. She raced at him, and together they ran for the railing. Juan's leg could barely support him so he and Tory moved with the lurching gait of a couple entered in a three-legged race.

They reached the railing at the same time the guards took aim. The jacketed 7.62 mm bullets pinged and sparked as the men adjusted the hosing barrels of their weapons. Without pause and as ungainly as a pair of corpses being dumped from a bridge, Cabrillo and Tory allowed their speed to fold them over the railing, and headfirst they plummeted toward the water. There was nothing either could do to right their trajectory, and they slammed into the murky surface in a tremendous splash. They sank deep, and even though his lungs hadn't recovered from Singh's sucker punch, Juan made sure he and Tory stayed under as they swam away from the impact wave.

Juan could hear that someone had cut the power to the ship saw, for the building no longer echoed. He counted to ten in his head, promising his punished body that at the end of the count he would surface for air, but when he reached the magic number, he forced himself to count another slow ten and then another. It was Tory who first needed air, and they surfaced together as close to the hull as they could. Juan gulped a lungful and forced them under again, not knowing if they'd been spotted.

When they surfaced for the second time, he took a moment to get his bearings. They were less than twenty yards from the railing where he'd tied off the Draeger set. Bullets began to stitch the water around them, shooting little jets of white water into the air. The pair ducked back under without getting their breath but somehow managed to cover the distance.

Juan's mind was too fogged with the pain radiating from his leg and head to attempt untying the simple knot he'd fastened. Instead, he reached into his shattered prosthesis for a flat throwing knife. The ship saw had shredded one side of the blade, but the other still retained its keen edge. He sliced through the lines and fed the regulator to Tory as he made them both sink deeper. Because the rebreather didn't produce bubbles, the gunmen above couldn't see where they lurked ten feet below the surface. The Sikh fighters fired indiscriminant volleys into the water, hoping to get lucky but mostly just venting their anger that two of their comrades were dead and a third would limp for the rest of his life. Juan held no sympathy for any of them.

He took the mouthpiece from Tory, careful not to let water enter the system where it would cause a caustic reaction in the $CO_2$ scrubbers. Despite the polluted salt water, he could taste her on the rubber. He gave her hand a reassuring squeeze and then maneuvered the Draeger pack over his shoulders. The mechanical parts of his artificial limb were completely destroyed, so he fitted his fin onto his good leg, giving the other fin to Tory.

Once he had cleared water from his mask and they were

both settled, he became aware of another sound: gunfire. And not the maddened fusillades fired by the guards. It was the rhythmic pulse of a weapon he knew well. He couldn't suppress a smile. Singh's men were attempting to board the *Oregon*, and he could imagine Mark Murphy ensconced behind his video screens as he opened up with the ship's Bofors 40 mm autocannon.

That's when the men above him must have seen their motion through the water, because suddenly bullets were striking all around them, cutting cavitation trails that looked like white arrows.

## 21

Max Hanley ordered Franklin Lincoln and his SEAL assault team to launch their Zodiac as soon as he heard the ship saw whining from inside the shed across the bay. Max hurried from the boat garage to the operations center buried below the *Oregon*'s superstructure. The red battle lights were on, which blended with the blue computer screens to make the room glow an awful shade of purple. Why Max had never noticed this detail before was just one of the million things swirling through his mind.

With the rest of the breaker's yard quiet so late at night, Max was certain that Shere Singh had fired up the ship saw because he had caught the chairman. Eric Stone was at the helm, Murph had the weapons station, and Hali Kasim and Linda Ross were watching the threat board. Max settled in the command chair, hooking a hands-free microphone over his balding head.

'Linc, you on the net?'

'Roger, *Oregon*. We're approaching in stealth mode. ETA seven minutes.'

Max was about to ask why they didn't open up the Zodiac's big outboard, because the sound of the saw would surely mask the engine's throaty roar, but then remembered that in the moonlight the Zodiac's wake would show as a white crescent on the otherwise black sea.

Lincoln continued, '*Oregon*, be advised that there is a lot of traffic pulling away from the beach. I count four, repeat, four utility boats. Thermal scan shows they're loaded to the gunnels with men.'

'I have 'em,' Mark Murphy called from the weapons station. His screen showed the feed from the thermal/IR/low-light camera mounted on the *Oregon*'s main mast. 'I estimate fifty soldiers in total, armed with automatic weapons and rocket-propelled grenades.' He typed commands into his computer to call up the ship's vast arsenal. His screen split so that each forty-foot boat approaching from the beach was on its own display. A sight reticle appeared over each dark-hulled craft. 'Targets designated tango one through four. I have tracking on all inbound.'

'Where's the Zodiac?' When the *Oregon*'s batteries opened up, the last thing he needed to worry about was a friendly fire accident.

'Linc's angling out of the way, but he's moving slow.'

Max brought up a wide-angle camera shot on his screen. Singh's men were coming straight for the *Oregon* as the Zodiac slowly motored off to the starboard. The ex-SEAL couldn't gun his engine because the guards would open fire as soon as they saw his wake. Max was forced into a waiting game between Linc's progress out of the line of fire and the speed of the approaching utility boats.

'Incoming!' Linda Ross called out from her station. 'Missile launch from the beach.'

In the two seconds it took her to shout the warning, the RPG had covered half the distance to the *Oregon*, and before anyone could react, it finished the other half. The five-pound missile struck the anchor fairlead high on the bow and exploded. The Soviet-made RPG mangled a good-sized chunk of steel and blew a hole up through the deck but didn't damage the anchor chains or machinery.

'We've got more. Multiple launches!'

Wallowing this close to the beach, the range was too short for the ship's automated defensive systems to engage the incoming missiles.

Max had no other choice. 'Helm, all back full!'

Eric Stone had anticipated the order, and his hands were already drawing back the dual throttle controls. Deep within the ship the four massive magnetohydrodynamic engines came to life. Like flicking a light switch, the revolutionary engines were running at full power in an instant, drawing seawater's naturally occurring electric charge, amplifying it through the cryo-cooled magnets, and creating a force wave that pumped water though her drive tubes with unimaginable power.

The backward acceleration was enough to send dishes tumbling in the galley and toss a batch of files on Cabrillo's desk into the air. But they weren't quick enough to avoid the incoming volley of RPGs.

Six of the notoriously inaccurate missiles fizzled harmlessly into the sea. Another impacted one of the *Oregon*'s dummy cargo derricks, dropping it like a felled tree. The heavy steel mast crashed against the deck hard enough to make the eleven-thousand-ton vessel shudder. The eighth missile slammed into the superstructure below the bridge. The shaped high-explosive warhead was designed to punch through a tank's thick armor, so when it exploded through the half-inch steel, much of its force remained. Two of the mock-up cabins the Corporation used during harbor inspections were gutted by the kinetic force of the explosion, but the damage was mostly cosmetic. The damage control computer activated the fire suppression system without need for human intervention, and it also directed damage control teams to the area.

'I want a report in thirty seconds,' Max said over the ship's emergency channel.

He checked the GPS display and speed indicators. They were backing out of the breaker's yard at twenty knots and accelerating. A few seconds more, and they'd be out of range of Shere Singh's RPGs. But if he had more sophisticated weapons, Stinger missiles, for example, they still needed more room to shoot the rockets out of the air.

'Linc, give me a sit rep.'

'They're on to us,' the SEAL called back. Over the voice channel Max heard the bellow of the Zodiac's engine and the crackle of machine gun fire. 'One boat is chasing us. The other three are still closing on you.'

'Give us a minute to get out of those missiles' range, and we'll provide cover fire. Gomez Adams is about to launch our second UAV, so we should have a good view of the battlefield in a few minutes.'

'Roger.'

Arrowing across the bay at nearly forty knots, Linc couldn't hope to hit anything as he sprayed rounds at the utility boat with his M-4A1. The three-round bursts were intended to keep the pursuers from firing at him. So far, the few return volleys had been wild. The men had simply propped their weapons against the utility boat's gunwales and fired without looking.

He couldn't believe the hits the *Oregon* was taking and realized that they had been expected. But it didn't matter if the Sikh owner of the breaker's yard was on to the Corporation. What mattered now was finding the chairman and then beating a fast retreat.

The ship saw had stopped its ungodly racket a moment

earlier, and Linc didn't know if this was a good sign or bad, but until the *Oregon* took out the utility boat chasing in their wake, they couldn't risk making a run for the shed. Or could they?

Mike Trono was at the Zodiac's helm, and Linc used his hands to indicate what he wanted to do. Trono nodded wordlessly and sent the lightweight boat skidding in a tight turn that would take them past the back of the huge shed.

The maneuver allowed the utility boat to cut the distance between it and the Zodiac, and the guards on board were emboldened by the opportunity. A dozen guns opened up at the same time and had Trono not juked the Zodiac, its rubber hull and the four men riding in her would have been cut to ribbons.

Linc and the others fired back. Even Trono fired his pistol with one hand while gunning the throttle with the other. One of the guards on the utility boat clutched his throat as he fell forward over the rail. He struck the roiled water of the bow wave and was sucked under. Even if the wound wasn't fatal, the props would dice his body into hamburger as the boat motored over him.

The utility boat peeled away, giving Trono the opportunity to slow as they passed behind the warehouse just as the ship saw came back to life – quieter this time because it wasn't cutting through metal.

Clutching his rifle tight to his chest, Linc rolled over the soft side of the Zodiac, absorbing the impact of the water on his massive shoulders. He was left bobbing in the wake as Mike brought the Zodiac back onto plane and rocketed parallel to the beach.

He ducked under the shed's metal skirt and came up inside the structure.

There was enough light to see that the name of the ship inside had been removed from her stern. But, with the chain saw whirring farther toward the beach, it was impossible to hear any voices that would tell him what was happening.

'*Oregon,* this is Assault One,' he radioed. 'I am inside the shed preparing to look for the chairman.'

'Roger that,' Max replied instantly. 'We're almost ready to engage, so your extraction will be clear. Good luck.'

Linc clicked his radio in response and began to swim down the length of the ship, searching for a way to reach the deck. Then he heard the distinct crack of a pistol up near the ship's truncated bow.

Seconds later two bodies tumbled over the ship's rail. Both wore black, one in a combat uniform and the other wearing a wet suit. It had to be Cabrillo. Linc didn't know the identity of the other person but wasn't surprised the silhouette had a woman's curves. Only the chairman could find a date in a place like this.

No sooner had the pair sunk below the water when two guards appeared at the rail, their gun barrels tracking back and forth as they searched for the two people who'd leapt overboard. The range was too long for Linc to guarantee his shot, so he silently swam on, keeping near the catwalk that ringed the shed a few feet above the tide mark. Twice he watched Cabrillo and a woman who looked vaguely familiar bob to the surface for air. Linc was sure they were headed for an open metal stairwell. *That's where Juan must have stashed his rebreather,* he thought.

The guards fired down into the water, but Linc could see they had no idea where Cabrillo had fled. By Linc's estimate, a full minute had passed since the last time Cabrillo had surfaced. He knew the chairman to be an excellent free diver capable of staying under for two minutes or more but not after a shoot-out on a ship and having fallen thirty feet from her deck. He must have reached the Draeger set.

Just as he reached this conclusion, he heard Max's voice over his radio say they were engaging at the same time he heard the 40 mm automatic cannon mounted on the *Oregon*'s fore quarter start to pound away.

Undistracted by the cannon outside, the guards began concentrating their fire at a spot about ten feet from the staircase. Something had drawn their attention. In a move that took tremendous strength because he was wearing combat boots rather than swim fins, Linc kicked his legs to thrust his upper body out of the water and brought his M-4A1 to his shoulder. Before gravity dragged him back down again, the former SEAL got off a pair of three-round bursts. One of the guards had his AK shot from his hands. The other's head vanished in a crimson mist.

He sank back down under the surface and waited for any other gunman to rake the water. What he got instead was a hand clamped around his ankle. He resisted the urge to kick it away. The chairman.

Linc felt Cabrillo thrust the regulator mouthpiece to his lips and took a few grateful breaths before passing it back. Juan must have then given it to the woman because he could feel her chest moving against his shoulder. Together the three of them began an awkward swim that was more dog paddle than any other stroke with each taking turns at the regulator. It took several minutes to retreat down the length of the tanker.

Once at the shed's rear doors, Cabrillo brought his party to the surface below the catwalk. His forehead stung from where he'd torn away the flap of skin, and his right leg throbbed from the groin all the way to the toes he'd lost years earlier.

'Your timing couldn't have been better,' he told Linc. 'I think my fin broke surface and gave away our position.'

'Any more in here, boss?'

'Shere Singh took off the instant I pulled my gun, and if you capped the last two on the *Toyo Maru,* then that's all I know about.'

'Let's not wait for reinforcements, shall we?' Tory said.

'I'm with the missus.' Linc keyed his tactical radio. '*Oregon,* this is Assault One. I've got the chairman and the mermaid we pulled off the *Avalon.* We're ready for extraction by Zodiac.'

'You have to wait. There's still one more utility boat out here. We're tracking it now with the eye in the sky, but we need a few minutes to try to destroy it.'

Cabrillo took the Linc's headset. 'Negative, *Oregon.* Shere Singh could be escaping as we speak. We need him.'

'Okay, Juan. I'll vector the Zodiac to your position.'

A moment later the Zodiac roared over to the spot where Linc had performed his roll-off and throttled down to a low burble. Juan abandoned the Draeger rebreather and followed Tory and Lincoln under the door. Linc's SEALs easily plucked her from the water and helped Cabrillo and the team leader into the rubber-hulled craft. Juan wasn't fully inside before Mike Trono opened the throttle gates and shot the nimble boat across the waves.

They came under immediate fire from men on the beach, their weapons winking in the darkness like angry fireflies. Trono twisted the boat away from shore and out toward the open bay where the *Oregon* was trying to find the final utility boat. The other three were flaming wreckage that would soon sink to the bottom of the harbor. The fourth had to be hiding amid the dozens of rusted hulks awaiting their turn in the shed or on the beach for dismantling.

Juan moved to the Zodiac's bow to call directions to the helmsman as they entered the flotilla of derelict ships. He'd donned a pair of night vision goggles. The outboard reverberated between the decaying hulls as they threaded their way toward the *Oregon*. With this many vessels, it was like running full speed through a maze. Trono bobbed and weaved the Zodiac, following Juan's hand signals, barreling past a supertanker that had to be a thousand feet long and between a pair of car ferries that still carried the livery of the English Channel company that ran them.

They rounded the bow of the ferry, and were angling for a gap between a partially sunken tugboat and another container ship when the last utility boat appeared from behind another ship. The Corporation team responded a second quicker and raked the utility boat from stem to stern with well-aimed fire.

The utility boat cut a tight arc in the water and took off after the Zodiac. With the tide changing, the bay was growing rougher. Both boats buffeted in the rising swells, making it impossible to engage with their weapons. In calm seas the Zodiac could more than outrun the heavily laden work boat, but the waves were acting as a great equalizer.

Every time Trono tried to break out of the forsaken armada, the utility boat was there to cut off their escape back to the *Oregon*.

The outboard coughed, dropping power for a moment before rehitting on all cylinders. Mike Trono felt around the big engine cowling and cursed when his fingers felt a bullet hole. They came away wet, and he sniffed at the liquid clinging to his skin.

'Juan, they got the gas tank,' he shouted over the engine noise. 'I don't know how much longer we can play cat and mouse.'

The utility boat had broken off pursuit, but the Zodiac was headed away from the *Oregon* and still boxed in by so many ships they couldn't tell where Singh's men would attack from next.

'Did they head back to shore?' Tory asked.

'I doubt it,' Juan replied just as the work boat leapt from behind a big commercial fisherman.

More gunfire stitched the seas around the Zodiac as Trono tried to squeeze another half a knot out of the engine. He could smell oil burning inside the cowling. The bullet had done more than hole the gas tank. They zigzagged past the ferry boats again when something caught Cabrillo's eye.

'Mike, take us back to that sunken tugboat. I have an idea.'

They raced across the bay toward the dark shape of the sunken ship. She'd settled awkwardly on some obstruction on the seafloor so that her bow was thrust out of the water and her back deck was awash. A broken crane dangling over her deck was nearly invisible in the moonlight.

Cabrillo concentrated on the course he wanted to take, ignoring all other distractions, including the fire coming from the utility boat. He had one shot to make this work. With his arms outstretched he called minute direction changes that the helmsman responded to instantly, feathering the hurtling Zodiac with a light touch.

'Okay, slow us down, draw them in.'

Everyone heard the crazy order, but no one questioned it. The Zodiac dutifully slowed, which allowed the utility boat to cut their separation to seventy feet. As if sensing the moment of victory, the utility boat's driver hammered his throttles to their stops in hopes of running down their quarry.

Juan continued to feed course changes to Trono, guiding them so they would pass astern of the sunken ship. He looked over his shoulder to see the utility boat bearing down on them like a shark making its final lunge. Through his goggles' enhanced optics he could even see the delight on the helmsman's face as he prepared for the kill.

A few more seconds, Juan told himself, studying his target once again. A few more seconds. Now!

He dropped his left hand to order Mike to make a hard turn to port. The Zodiac was now racing for the gap under the tugboat's broken crane. The larger utility boat was cranked over in pursuit, its driver never seeing he was being led into a trap.

'Down,' Juan shouted as the Zodiac crossed behind the tug's sunken rail and shot under the ruined crane boom. There was barely three feet of clearance, and had they not ducked to the floorboards, the rusted steel derrick would have taken off their heads.

Juan looked back as soon as they were through. The utility boat was following in their wake but at the last second the helmsman must have seen the crane. He threw the wheel to its lock, but it was too late. They were going too fast. The boat smashed into the crane, and the metal easily ripped through the fiberglass hull. A gouge was torn down her entire length, and one of her big fuel tanks was ripped from its mounts.

None of the men aboard the doomed craft had time to brace themselves, and all twelve of them on the deck were launched over the bow by the sudden deceleration. Most landed safely in the water, although one hit the crane boom headfirst and died instantly.

The diesel spilling from the ruptured tank pooled inside the filthy bilge, but before enough seawater could dilute it, a spark from the ruined electrical system detonated the mixture in a ballooning fireball of orange and black.

'Scratch the last utility boat,' Cabrillo said over the tactical radio. 'We're headed home.'

The Zodiac's engine died when they were still a hundred yards from the *Oregon,* forcing them to man the paddles. With the motor silenced they could hear continuous gunfire from the beach as Singh's men fired blindly out to sea.

Juan threw the painter to a waiting deckhand as the rubber craft reached the ramp. By the time the last of Linc's SEALs had piled out, Juan had limped to where Julia Huxley waited with a spare prosthetic leg. He'd radioed ahead. She used surgical scissors to cut away part of his wet suit and examined the stump. Apart from some purple swelling, his leg seemed okay, so she let him strap on the second prosthesis as she examined his head wound.

'What happened?' she asked, peering at the gash with a penlight.

'Rifle butt.'

She flashed the light into his eyes, checking if he had a concussion. She grunted, unsurprised that his pupils reacted normally. 'You have a head like a cannonball. How do you feel? Dizzy? Lightheaded? Nauseous?'

'None of the above. It just stings a bit from the salt water.'

'I bet.' Julia knew that like most men, Juan was down-playing the pain. She swabbed out the four-inch-square wound, making sure that the antibacterial made him wince a few times before putting a large sterile dressing over the cut and swathing the top of his head with a gauze wrap. 'That should hold you. Sorry, but I'm fresh out of lollipops.'

'Then I guess I should have cried more.' He dry-swallowed the painkillers she'd handed him.

Julia noticed Tory Ballinger standing nearby. 'Do I even want to know what you're doing here?'

'Tory works for Lloyd's of London,' Juan said, getting to his feet and testing his weight on his artificial limb. While the stump was sore, he had full mobility. 'She's working the same case we are but from the other end.'

'And I thought it was my bedside manner.' The two women shook hands, and Julia asked if Tory needed any medical attention.

Tory was toweling off her hair. 'Thanks, Dr Huxley. I'm fine. Bit shaken maybe, but unharmed.'

'Juan has a good bottle of brandy in his cabin. I'm prescribing at least one snifter.'

'Chairman, you there?' It was Max Hanley over the ship's intercom. Cabrillo hit the switch mounted to a nearby bulkhead.

'I'm here. What's the situation?'

'They're still firing at us from the beach. Just small arms. No RPGs. George Adams has the UAV circling the compound. A few minutes after the ship saw kicked off for the last time, he spotted someone running from the shed. They hopped into a jeep and tore out of the facility headed for a cluster of houses a mile or so up the coast. There's a chopper on a nearby pad, but so far there's been no activity around it.'

'What about our bird?'

'Crew has it on ten-minute standby,' Max replied, meaning the four-passenger Robinson helicopter could be in the air in ten minutes.

'Tell George to turn over the UAV to Eric Stone. The kid has enough hours on the Microsoft flight simulator to qualify for his commercial pilot's license. I want to be airborne as soon as possible. We need Singh alive if we're going to get to the bottom of this.'

'You sure you're up to this?' Julia asked.

'I'm more pissed than hurt,' he told her. 'Singh knew we were coming.' He snapped on the intercom again. 'Max, it's me. Listen, Singh's been a step ahead of us. He unloaded the *Toya Maru* from the *Maus* a while ago. Probably when you broke off at Taiwan. Hiro's tanker is already inside the shed and halfway to becoming razor blades.'

'How?'

'It doesn't matter now, but I think the *Maus* has better radar than we thought. She must have known you were tailing her. Have Hali get ready to file a report with the Indonesian authorities. I suspect Singh's plugged in with the government, so he'll have to cut through a lot of red tape, but bottom line is we need this place raided by the navy or coast guard as soon as we're clear.'

'I'm on the circuit,' Hali Kasim interrupted. There was a manic edge to his voice. 'Chairman, you're not going to believe this, but I just got a signal from Eddie's transponder.'

'When?'

'Just now! Two seconds ago.'

'Jesus. Where is he?'

'It doesn't make any sense.' Doubt crept into the communications officer's tone.

'Talk to me, Hali.'

'Russia, sir. The western coast of the Kamchatka Peninsula. What the hell is he doing there? I thought the snakeheads had their conduits running into the U.S or Japan.'

Juan went still and turned his mind inward so he could no longer hear Linc and the other SEALs stowing the Zodiac and their gear or feel Julia's concerned look or Tory Ballinger's intrigued scrutiny. Eddie Seng had been taken to Kamchatka. While the question of why worried at part of his mind, the bulk of his intellect was forming a plan, calculating speed, distances, and the priorities of the mission. He factored in the *Oregon*'s speed, the maximum speed of the Robinson R-44 with various payloads, and the need to interrogate Shere Singh.

He was sure Eddie wasn't the only Chinese immigrant that had been taken to the isolated part of Russia, a volcano-strewn jut of land that had been closed off to the world for the better part of the past century. How many more had ended up on its rugged shores was something he couldn't know, but instinct told him there would be a great many.

What was Singh's connection? Transportation was the obvious answer. He could move men and ships inside the pair of floating drydocks with virtual impunity. He could hijack vessels carrying illegals from the open seas and make sure any witnesses, like Tory's hapless *Avalon*, never survived long enough to file a report. All Singh needed to know was which ships were carrying immigrants, and he could target them at will. That would mean that someone in China was supplying that information, Cabrillo realized, but was the smuggling the only crime taking place, or was it a means to an end?

'They need cheap labor,' he said aloud.

'What was that?' Tory asked. She'd stripped off her wet jacket and wore only a thin black T-shirt. A fluffy towel was draped over her shoulders to cover her breasts. Her dark hair was damp and untamed and somehow incredibly attractive. If she had any questions about what she'd seen of the Corporation so far, she had the good sense to keep them to herself.

'This is about cheap labor; slaves. The night we saved you we also took out a pirate boat that was carrying a shipping container. We sank the ship and managed to recover the container, but not in time to save the people who'd been locked inside. We later learned they were illegal Chinese immigrants. I had one of my men follow the route those poor bastards had taken in hopes of learning what they were up to and how it related to the pirates. He just turned up on the Kamchatka Peninsula.'

'We at Lloyd's only suspected Singh of hijacking shipping in the region and using his facility here to eliminate the evidence.'

'There's more than that,' Juan said. 'He's also hijacking ships carrying Chinese immigrants and transporting them to Kamchatka. And if he needs transporters as big as the *Maus* and her sister drydock, it leads me to believe they've probably seized hundreds, or maybe thousands of illegals. They're using them as slave labor.'

'What on earth for?' Tory asked.

'It could be anything.' Juan hit the intercom again. 'Max, make preparations to get us out of here. I'll take Linc and

Mike Trono with me to find Shere Singh. I want you headed for Eddie's location with every knot the old girl can give. We'll catch a flight to . . .' He needed a second to recall Kamchatka's capital. 'Petropavlovsk.'

'Not gonna happen, Chairman,' Mark Murphy said over the open circuit. 'I've been on the Internet since Hali said that's where Eddie is. The government is reporting a major volcanic event is under way. I confirmed it through the U.S. Geological Survey's Web site. The Russians are saying there's so much ash falling that they've been forced to shut down the airport. No one's going in or out.'

Juan cursed under his breath. 'Okay, that doesn't change anything. I still want the *Oregon* under way as soon as possible.'

'What about Shere Singh?' Max asked.

'My window to catch him just narrowed, that's all. Even with the *Oregon* moving at maximum speed, we should have a half hour here before you steam out of the Robinson's range.'

'May I say something, Captain Cabrillo?' Tory asked.

Juan nodded.

'I infiltrated this facility from the landward side, and I have to say it's bloody enormous. I've been observing the place for a week, and even I don't know the full scope of Singh's operation.'

'What's your point?'

'My point is that if you're only giving yourself thirty minutes to find him, then I think I can lead you to where he keeps his residence when he's here.'

Juan hesitated for a fraction of a second. Tory Ballinger was a virtual stranger to him, but he felt like he knew her because he recognized a great deal of himself in her steady gaze. She'd handled herself well just moments earlier, and he still didn't know how she'd kept her wits when she was trapped aboard the *Avalon*. He saw in her the same indefatigable British spirit that had once made their island the most powerful nation on earth and had seen England through the blitz during World War Two. While in Winston Churchill that look came across as pugnacious confidence, in Tory it was alluring drive.

And to top it off, Juan thought, her own investigation had led her to the very same place his had taken him, and he doubted she'd blown up a building and kidnapped a corrupt lawyer to get here.

'You're on.'

Tory had expected an argument. It was in the storm clouds building behind her bright blue eyes. Juan's quick acceptance of her offer left her off balance for a moment and her mouth agape.

'We've got about five minutes to change and kit up. Come with me. You, too, Linc. We're not done yet.'

Moments after the Robinson R-44 lifted from its hydraulically operated pad, the *Oregon* cut a tight circle in the bay using her athwartships bow thruster, and Linda Ross gave Eric Stone the order for full speed. Max Hanley was down in his beloved engine room. As soon as the order came through, the quad magnetohydrodynamic engines spooled up like aircraft turbines, and almost instantly the water at her stern boiled up with the raw force of her revolutionary propulsion system. Linda also ordered Mark Murphy to rake the sea just short of the beach with the Gatling gun to give the departing chopper a few moments of cover fire.

George Adams sat in the Robinson's left-hand seat with

Juan at his side. Linc and Tory took up the rear bench seats. With their personal weapons and equipment as well as the Barrett .50 caliber sniper rifle lying across Linc's lap, the chopper was crowded. Adams looped them out to sea and crossed the shoreline well north of the breaker's yard.

'There's a compound up the beach about a mile,' Tory said over the helo's intercom. 'It's where the executives live. I watched them for a couple of days over the past week. One of the houses is much larger than the others, and now that I've seen Shere Singh up close and personal, I remember him living there.'

'Any guards?' Juan asked.

'A few, but after tonight I expect the area to be lousy with them.'

Juan smiled at her turn of phrase, but inside he knew to expect the worst. 'What about access to the facility?'

'There is a road that runs north and south behind it. There's a hydro dam and a smelting factory to the north.'

'Much traffic?'

'Mostly lorries hauling the steel plates to be melted. And almost nothing after nightfall.'

'Okay, folks, we're coming back over the coastline.' Adams's helmet was integrated with a night vision camera mounted on the Robinson's nose to give him greater visibility. 'I see the compound she just mentioned. A lot of lights and a lot of people milling around. And, as luck would have it, a few of them aren't armed.'

'Keep us out of their range and let's see what's happening.'

'I see a chopper pad a little farther away from the compound,' Adams said. 'It looks like they've got a JetRanger, and her rotors are starting to turn.'

'Can we follow them?' Tory asked.

'She's got us by forty or fifty knots and at least a hundred miles of range,' Juan told her. He looked back at Franklin Lincoln. 'How about it, big man?'

'I'm on it, boss.'

'George, hold us steady,' Lincoln said as he loosened his shoulder harness. He opened his door, ignoring the frenzied hurricane of downwash from the rotors that whipped into the small chopper's cabin. The Barrett was an ugly weapon, nearly five feet long and heavy. In the hands of an expert the half-inch bullets it fired were accurate up to a mile.

Adams turned the Robinson broadside to clear Linc's view. A few guards in the distant compound fired at the hovering helicopter, but the distance was too great. Lincoln fitted the big rifle to his shoulder and checked the sight picture through the night vision scope. The world was an eerie green through the optics, but somehow intimate. He could see the frustration on the guards' faces as they fired at the chopper. He scanned the scene and settled the reticle on the idling JetRanger helicopter. His view was so sharp he could see the air shimmering from the heat that poured from the turbine's exhaust.

The crack of the gun sounded like a cannon, and Linc absorbed the brutal recoil without taking his eyes from the sight. The bullet arrived long before anyone on the ground heard it, so the destruction came as a stunning surprise. It struck the JetRanger's rotor mast, the most vulnerable part of any helicopter. The whirling mast came apart so that her blades were launched like a pair of deadly scythes. One cut through a cluster of men who were setting up a shoulder-fired missile. The dismemberments were something even a veteran like Franklin Lincoln had a hard time stomaching.

The other blade hit a large fuel tank mounted on stilts. The highly volatile aviation gas went up in a towering explosion that overwhelmed the scope's light filters. Linc looked over the rifle and saw flames mushrooming outward and upward. Anyone standing within a hundred feet of the tank was knocked back by the concussion. Anyone within fifty feet had been immolated.

'I've got movement,' Adams called out. 'Rear door of the JetRanger just opened. Guy wearing a turban is running for it.'

'That has to be Shere Singh,' Tory said. 'Where's he going?'

'Hold on.' A few tense moments passed. 'Okay, he's getting into a car. Looks like a big Mercedes sedan. He's getting into the backseat. There's only him and the driver.'

'Want me to take him out, Juan?' Linc asked, bringing the sniper rifle to his shoulder again.

'Not here. Let him get out onto the highway and away from all these guards.'

'Singh must have radioed someone,' George announced. 'Another car is pulling away from the residential compound. Looks like at least three armed men inside.'

'We knew this wouldn't be easy.' Cabrillo checked his watch. A third of their thirty-minute window to catch the *Oregon* had gone by.

A moment later they all saw the headlights of the pair of cars race out the facility's back gate and head south. The road was hemmed in by dark jungle, so the lights reflected as though the vehicles were speeding through a tunnel. George opened the throttle to the Robinson's engine and quickly overtook the vehicles.

The drivers maintained a fifteen-foot separation. It was a

little tight for what Juan had in mind, but he had no other choice. He plucked a grenade from the web harness over his shoulder and opened the small window set into the chopper's right-hand door. Optimally the grenade should have a five-second fuse; however, each incendiary's timer varied by as much as a second – not a big deal when throwing one into a foxhole or trying to take out troops advancing on foot – but with the cars hurtling at ninety miles per hour, they could cover more than a hundred feet in a single tick of a watch.

Cabrillo pulled the pin, maintaining a firm grip on the spoon, and held the grenade outside the window. The toss was more experience and instinct than calculation. He released the spoon to prime the weapon, waited a few moments, and let it drop.

The grenade was instantly swallowed by the darkness, but a second later the Mercedes swerved as the driver reacted to something heavy bouncing off the trunk. The grenade rolled off the car, hit the road, and momentum kept it tumbling down the asphalt. The trailing car raced over it as though they hadn't seen it or didn't understand what it was. Another second passed, one of the longest in Juan's life. He was sure that the guards' car had safely passed the grenade and was reaching for another when it detonated directly under the vehicle's gas tank.

The two explosions came an instant apart. First the low crump of the grenade and then the second spectacular detonation of the gasoline. The rear of the car lifted off the road, and it pivoted on its nose for a heartbeat before slamming onto its roof. It rolled seven times, shedding sheet metal and waves of burning fuel. It ended up careening off the road and slamming into a utility pole, the force of the impact bending the car in two around the teak pole.

Shere Singh's driver unintentionally slowed as he watched the destruction in his rearview mirror. This gave Franklin Lincoln all the opportunity he needed. George passed the Mercedes flying ten feet above the low jungle canopy and fifty feet to the right of the road. Linc nestled the Barrett to his shoulder and fired. While a normal bullet might have only punctured the Mercedes's tire, the .50 caliber slug shattered the spline where the front axle met the wheel. The entire assembly, wheel, hub, and tire were torn from the car. The heavy Mercedes dropped onto the shattered axle in a shower of sparks, and the car instantly began to decelerate as the driver fought to keep it on the road.

For good measure Linc put two bullets through the front of the hood and gave a satisfied nod when steam erupted from the mangled radiator.

Adams brought the Robinson over the road, keeping just behind the dying limousine, and when it finally came to a stop, he had the skids on the macadam. Even before the machine had settled onto the road, Cabrillo, Linc, and Tory Ballinger were rushing ahead. Linc and Juan carried M-4A2 assault rifles while Tory had borrowed a Beretta semi-automatic pistol from the *Oregon*'s armory.

The team had covered half of the twenty yards when the driver heaved open his door. He was out and around it before anyone could get a shot off. From his covered position behind the door, he sprayed the roadway with fire from a machine pistol. The driver was panicked, and his shots went wild, but still the trio fell to the ground. Linc opened up with his M-4, concentrating a withering stream of 5.56 mm into the open door. The high-powered rounds ricocheted off the armored door and turned the bulletproof glass opaque.

Having assumed that the big Mercedes would be armored, Juan fired under the door. His first burst missed the driver, but the second tore apart the calf and ankle of one of his legs. As he fell the door closed, exposing him to a double tap from Tory's Beretta. The impact threw him bodily into the car's fender before he slid to the ground in a disjointed heap.

Juan checked the Mercedes's rear door. Locked. He loosed his nearly full magazine into the glass at point-blank range. The first dozen bullets couldn't penetrate the tough laminate, but by clamping the barrel tightly he was able to bore a hole through the pane. Linc stepped up as Juan backed away to reload and expanded the hole, sending chips of glass arcing though the air like glittering diamonds.

Once Juan had his weapon reloaded, he tapped Linc on the shoulder to cease firing.

'Singh, I'm giving you three seconds to place both hands outside the window.' There were no sounds coming from inside the vehicle. 'One. Two. Three.' Linc and Juan opened fire at the same instant. Bullets passing through the shattered glass started to disintegrate the opposite window. Several imbedded in the seat back, and a couple pinged off the armored plating and rattled around the back of the car until burying themselves in a soft target. A sharp cry of pain cut above the rifles' chatter. Both men held fire.

'Singh!'

'I'm shot.' His voice remained strong. 'Oh, praise to Allah, I am going to die.'

'Put your goddamned hands outside the window now, or I throw in a grenade.'

'I cannot move. My legs, you have paralyzed me.'

Juan and Linc exchanged a look, both certain they couldn't trust the Sikh but knowing they had no alternative. Juan reached his hand into the car and opened the door with Linc in position to cover as much of the interior as he could. As the door came open, the interior lights came on. Singh was on the floor and as soon as he could draw a bead he fired with his own machine pistol. His aim was even worse than his driver's. The stream of bullets plowed into the armored door, saving Linc's life. The former SEAL did what tens of thousands of hours of training had instilled in him. As he dodged out of the way he put two rounds into Singh's face, one below the eye and the other straight down the man's throat. His turban uncoiled like a striking snake, and the back of his head came apart in a blooming flower of blood and tissue.

Linc cursed, twisting away in frustration and self-recrimination. 'Damnit, Juan, I am so sorry. It was just —'

'Instinct,' Juan finished for him, peering into the car to survey the carnage. 'You had no choice. I would have done the exact same thing.'

Tory shouldered past them and stepped into the back of the stretch Mercedes. Ignoring the blood she patted down Shere Singh's corpse, handing out his wallet, a leather billfold. She plucked a briefcase from where Singh had wedged it into a seat cushion, looked around to see if she'd missed anything, and backed out once again.

'Well, lads, this turned into a dead end, eh?' She wiped her hands on the seat of her pants and gestured up the road behind the idling Robinson helicopter. 'It won't take long for more of Singh's forces to get organized and come looking for their boss. Discretion being the better part of valor and all that, I think we should get the hell out of here.'

As they started for the chopper, George Adams added power in preparation for takeoff, choking the air with fine grit and forcing them to bend double. Juan tapped Tory on the shoulder and jerked his thumb back toward the Mercedes limousine.

'Just an investigator for Lloyd's?'

Tory intuitively knew what he was talking about. She gave him a cocky grin. 'Before that I was employed by Her Majesty's government.'

'Doing what?'

She placed a hand on her holstered Beretta. 'Trouble-shooter.'

# 22

Juan Cabrillo slouched in the master's chair on the *Oregon*'s faux bridge. Although the tall seat's leather was torn to make it appear as old as the rest of the tramp freighter, he'd had it custom fit so it was perhaps the most comfortable on the ship. Any watch officer was expected to use the central workstation in the op center, but this chair was reserved exclusively for Cabrillo's use.

The sun was sinking fast to port, a dramatic play of color and light made more intense by the stratospheric curtain of volcanic dust billowing from peaks far to the north on Kamchatka Peninsula. The heat of the day lingered on the bridge. Metal was still warm to the touch, and the band of Juan's shorts was damp with perspiration. He wore no shirt and had only boat shoes on his feet. With the speed the *Oregon* was making over the water, opening a door would have invited a hurricane into the bridge, so the room remained hot and stuffy.

Rather than risk running up through the East China Sea and the Sea of Japan, where shipping traffic was as thick as a Los Angeles rush hour, he had decided to vector to the east once they cleared the northernmost of the Philippine Islands and race along Japan's Pacific coast. Shipping lanes were more regulated, so he didn't have to worry about other vessels reporting a ship steaming through the region at over fifty knots. With their radar jamming on active mode, it was visual reports that concerned him. In another few hours they would cross the Tokyo shipping lanes, and traffic would drop precipitously, ending their need to steer around car carriers, container ships, and the dozens of other vessels plying the Pacific routes.

They lost only a few minutes whenever they had to detour, but time was the one thing that Juan could no longer afford. Eddie was another two days away, and already the scant reports coming from the Russian volcanologists trapped in the capital city of Petropavlovsk were disturbing. The peninsula was being rocked by nearly continuous earthquakes, and three volcanoes along the same chain were belching ash and noxious gas. So far there had been no reports of deaths, but most of the settlements on Kamchatka were so remote it might take weeks to get word.

The only bright spot, if it could be called bright, was that Eddie's transmitter continued to send out a signal that Hali could receive through the satellite umbrella. But there was a problem with even that. According to the satellite data, he was on the beach in the shadow of one of the erupting volcanoes. Juan could have asked Dr Huxley how long the batteries in the transmitter would last after the wearer was dead, but he knew the answer already. Eddie could have died a week ago, and no one on the *Oregon* would be the wiser.

'Penny for your thoughts.'

Juan whirled around before recognizing the voice, his face a mask of anger at being disturbed.

'Whoa, sorry,' Tory said. 'Didn't mean to startle you so.'

'You didn't.' He turned back to gaze at the horizon once more as if watching it would somehow bring it closer.

'I thought you might like one.' Tory held out a bottle of

San Miguel beer, what Juan regarded as the Philippines' only worthwhile export.

She wore a white linen skirt, a teal polo shirt, and flats. Her dark hair was brushed away from her face, highlighting the graceful curve of her high cheekbones, and artful cosmetics deepened the already arresting blue of her eyes and the fullness of her mouth. As openly as Juan studied her, he could feel her attention on him. She took in the breadth of his shoulders and the dense muscles of his chest and how even lounging in the chair, his stomach was rippled. But when her glance shifted farther south, to his artificial leg, she quickly looked away.

Because he was so adept at hiding his prosthetic limb, usually by never wearing shorts in public, Juan had encountered few awkward moments since losing the leg. Although he barely knew her, Tory's sudden discomfort made him very conscious of the leg, especially because the one he was wearing made no effort to look real. It was all tubular steel and black carbon fiber. He suddenly wished he'd either worn long pants or at least one of his legs that looked more human.

He took his feet off the rail beneath the forward windows and sat up straighter in his chair so his leg was better hidden. He was both annoyed and intrigued by why he felt Tory's opinion of him was important.

Juan accepted the proffered bottle and rolled the dew-blistered glass across his forehead before taking several healthy gulps. Julia had rebandaged his wound so he no longer looked like he was wearing a diaper on his head. He was putting off a skin graft until after the mission was over. 'Thanks. Sorry about the glare of death I just shot you. I was lost in my own world there.'

'Thinking about your man? Eddie, is it?'

'Eddie Seng, yes. One of my best.'

'Max told me a bit about him. Actually, he told me a bit about all of you.' She smiled. 'Quite a collection of pirates you've put together.'

He chuckled. 'Brigands and privateers every man jack of them, and in all my life I've never worked with a finer team. I'm sorry I haven't been able to give you the nickel tour and introduce you around.'

'I know you've been busy. Linda was kind enough to play docent.' She waved her hands down the length of her body. 'And to let me borrow some clothes from your Magic Shop.'

'And your cabin. Is it all right?'

Her eyes went wide with delight. 'All right? It's bigger than my flat in London, and if you find the marble tub missing after I'm gone, don't be surprised. You do seem to enjoy life's finer things. The food rivals Cunard, and Maurice, the steward, is an absolute love.'

'Just because we're in a savage business doesn't mean we have to act like savages.'

'How did you become, well, mercenaries, I suppose?'

Juan indicated for Tory to take the closest seat. This one was Max's and it seemed to swallow her. 'When the Cold War ended I knew that the global polarity that had kept the world in check for a half century was over. Regional conflicts were bound to erupt, and the need to provide security services would grow. That's why I created the Corporation. As for the *Oregon,* well, rather than base my outfit in some country where I'd be subjected to their laws, I decided that using a ship would give me the freedom we would need.'

'And you do this for the money?'

'I'm as much a capitalist as the next man, but I'm also particular about my clients.'

'I think you are more particular than you are capitalistic.'

Juan laughed again. 'Maurice has been gossiping.'

'He thinks the world of you.' Tory smiled. 'Actually, your whole crew does. I've heard you've turned down some very lucrative offers in the past few years.'

'And accepted some, too.'

'You know what I'm saying. This isn't all about the money.'

'Let's just say it's pretty gratifying to get paid to do what you know is right. How about you, madam investigator? Did you take your job with Lloyd's because their ad in the *Financial Times* promised more pay than becoming a stockbroker?'

'Touché.' She sipped from her own bottle of beer. 'So, do you have any theories about what what's going on?'

'Theories, yes. Answers, no. Especially since we lost our last link in the chain.'

'Franklin hasn't forgiven himself, you know.'

'He and Eddie are best friends. He won't forgive himself until he knows Eddie's safe. That reminds me.' Juan jumped down from his stool and grabbed a portfolio from the deck. He handed it to Tory. 'The computer finished with this about an hour ago. You might find it interesting.'

'What is it?' Tory asked, opening the crisp leather cover.

'Translation of what we found in the briefcase you recovered from Singh's car. In a nutshell it lists every ship his group has hijacked over the past several years from all over the Pacific. I imagine it can close a number of your cases. Most of the ships were scrapped at Karamita, but some are still sailing under flags of convenience for dummy companies Singh controls.'

'Controlled,' Tory corrected without looking up from the book.

'Unfortunately,' Juan continued, 'there's nothing about what the *Maus*'s sister ship, *Souri*, has been doing since Singh bought her. I suspect that there are other ships she's transported, perhaps a great many, that Singh kept in another ledger to compartmentalize this particular aspect of his criminal fiefdom.'

She looked up. 'Why would he do that?'

'No idea.'

'What if he doesn't control this aspect of his criminal fiefdom?'

Juan leaned forward in his chair, sensing she might have something. 'Anton Savich?'

'Max told me that's a name that has cropped up all during your investigation, although I confess I never came across his name during mine.'

'All we've learned is that he was a functionary for the Soviet Bureau of Natural Resources, and after the collapse he worked for the Russian equivalent. We have no clue how he got tangled up with a smuggler like Shere Singh.'

'Are there any natural resources on Kamchatka? Maybe something he came across in a report when he worked for the bureau? Like precious gems or metals or something?'

'Mark Murphy checked a bunch of databases and found nothing in any appreciable quantities.'

A light shone in Tory's eyes. 'What if it's something that never got reported? What if when he was working for the Soviets a report crossed his desk that indicated a major find of some kind, and he quietly buried the discovery?'

Juan nodded. 'That's a distinct possibility. We all believe that they've brought a lot of Chinese labor up there. It could be he has them working in a mine of some kind.' Then he got a sudden burst of inspiration. He plucked his encrypted cell phone from his pocket and dialed. On the third ring of the *Oregon*'s private cellular system, Mark Murphy answered. 'Murph, it's Juan. Where are you?'

'Down in the Magic Shop fixing my skateboard,' the weapons specialist said.

'Hop on a computer terminal and tell me if mercury is used in any kind of mining techniques.'

Used to obscure requests, Mark said he would get right on it and killed the connection.

'What's this about mercury?' Tory asked.

'Julia found heavy doses of mercury poisoning when she performed autopsies on the pirates who tried to attack my ship – the ones who dumped the container carrying those Chinese immigrants.'

'You think they picked it up on Kamchatka?'

Cabrillo nodded. 'The Chinese weren't contaminated, just the sailors. If they'd been up there a lot, say dropping off other workers or on guard rotation, then its possible that's the source.'

A companionable silence passed while they waited for the couple of minutes until Juan's cell chimed. He answered it by saying, 'What did you find?'

'Mercury is the only element that bonds with gold,' Mark replied. 'It's been used to separate raw gold from ore. The practice is banned in a lot of countries because of environmental and health concerns, but it is still widely employed by indigenous miners in South America.'

Juan mouthed the word *gold* to Tory. 'Thanks, Murph. You can get back to your skateboard now.'

Tory leaned back in her seat. 'So Anton Savich is using Chinese slave labor, provided to him by Shere Singh, to mine gold on the Kamchatka Peninsula, most likely under the nose of the Russian government.'

'I think that about sums it up,' Juan agreed, taking another healthy swallow of his beer.

'That solves that mystery, then. We know the who, the how, and now the why.'

'Appears that way.'

Something in Juan's tone made Tory wary. 'What is it?'

'I was just thinking, with Shere Singh out of the piracy business, your end of this investigation is over. I don't know what we're going to find when we get up there, but if our run-ins with Singh and his gang are any gauge, it's going to get bloody.'

'And?' she asked, already suspecting what Juan was about to say.

'And you don't need to come with us. We'd only lose an hour or so by choppering you off when we pass the northern tip of Japan and enter the Sea of Okhotsk.'

Her fury was at full gale by the time he'd stopped speaking. She came out of her chair, placed both hands on the armrests of his seat, and leaned in so her face was inches from his. 'I've dedicated the last six months to this investigation. This has been my life, my every waking moment. I had to fight to get the Royal Geographic Society to let us join their expedition, only there wasn't anything I could do once the pirates hit. I had friends on the *Avalon* who were butchered by these monsters, so don't think for one second I'm not going to see this through to the bitter end, Mr Chairman of the bloody Corporation.'

For several long seconds their eyes were locked, neither giving an inch. Juan had known her strength, understood her intelligence, and now saw her passion. If he could forget that he had grown attracted to her, he would have asked her to join the Corporation right then.

'Just so you know,' he said in a low, intimate voice, 'I can't guarantee your safety.'

Tory sensed the shift in tone, and her anger was replaced with something softer, gentler. Their mouths were still inches apart, but for both of them it was an insurmountable distance. 'I'm not asking you to. I just want to be there when you put an end to this once and for all.' She straightened reluctantly.

Cabrillo's throat was suddenly dry, and he needed to finish his beer. 'Deal.'

# 23

If nothing more, Eddie Seng had to respect his captors' efficiency. The volcano looming over what had been dubbed Death Beach continued to rumble and belch ash that fell in a choking black blizzard across the facility. Earthquakes were an almost hourly occurrence, and the sea had turned into a writhing sheet of lead. Yet the overseers never relaxed the pace of work even as they implemented their evacuation plans. The boilers in the separating plant remained lit so that the last precious gram of gold could be extracted before they left. Guards exhorted the workers with clubs and whips to keep toiling up and down the hillside burdened with baskets of gold-bearing ore. And at night the slave laborers were locked in the beached cruise ships dreading the call to start working again in the morning.

Out in the bay the crew of the tugboat had succeeded in ballasting the huge drydock so that the ship in its hold could be floated free. The rough seas had caused numerous delays in the tricky operation, which explained why the evacuation had gone slower than Eddie had anticipated. He had seen a young turbaned Sikh arguing with the Russian, Savich, and assumed that he was refusing to sacrifice the expensive drydock when the volcano finally blew. Unloading the ship meant they wouldn't have any incriminating evidence when they sailed away.

Like the other ships already littering the beach, the

newest vessel brought to Kamchatka was a cruise liner. At around four hundred feet it wasn't large, but she had rakish lines, a classic champagne-glass stern, and balconies for nearly all the cabins. In her prime she would have filled a niche market for only the wealthiest passengers, those willing to pay anything for a chance to visit the Galapagos or explore the Antarctic wastes.

Today she was just another derelict, her once bright hull smeared with the excrement of those poor souls who'd endured the harsh journey to Russia. Hundreds of Chinese immigrants crowded the rail as the cruise ship was left to drift in the bay. Because her engines had been removed and she was unballasted, she rode so high that a thick band of antifouling paint could be seen above her waterline. Even the smallest waves made her roll dangerously. Eddie could hear the cries of the people trapped aboard her when a big wave sent the vessel reeling.

Fortunately, the tide was coming in, and it drove the ship closer and closer to the beach. With the winds whipping up the frigid bay, Eddie knew that a storm was coming. Hopefully the vessel would soundly ground herself onshore before it hit; otherwise she would drift back to sea. If that happened he knew the liner would turn broadside to the wind and capsize when the swells hit above ten feet. She carried no lifeboats.

Eddie switched his attention from the drifting cruise ship back to the drydock. Her massive bow doors had been closed once again, and water jetted from pump outlets along her hull. It would take several hours for her hold to be drained of seawater and make her light enough for one of the tugs to take her away. The second of the two tugs that had brought the drydock north had been maneuvered into position about a hundred yards from the ore processing building.

As Eddie had noted earlier, the processing plant had been built on a flat barge that had been towed to the bay. They had used heavy equipment to drag the large structure high above the tide line. Under the watchful eye of armed guards, workers were now clearing debris and rocks that had washed onto the beach behind the plant so the tugboat could haul it back into the sea. Drums of machine oil were standing by to be poured onto the rocky shore to ease the barge's progress back to the water. Paulus, the South African supervisor, had ordered that all the excess mercury be dumped in an area beyond the processing plant. Lakes of shimmering mercury collected in pools that eventually drained into the sea. Already wave action had claimed hundreds of gallons of the toxic metal.

The Chinese laborers given this dangerous job were those who had already been exposed to fatal doses of mercury vapor working in the plant. Most moved like zombies, their brains destroyed by the cumulative effects of mercury poisoning, while others were so afflicted with tremors they could barely stand. If by some miracle they survived the next few days, they would never recover from the exposure. And even if they did, they had received such high doses that generations of their children would suffer unspeakable birth defects.

Eddie burned the image of the brain-damaged workers splashing about amid the mercury puddles into his mind. He was so intent that he didn't realize the worker next to him had finished filling his plastic bucket with muddy ore. The young Chinese tried to catch Eddie's attention, but a guard noticed the lapse first. He lashed out with a weighted piece of hose that caught Eddie behind the knee. His leg buckled, but he refused to allow himself to fall. He knew not to even glance at the guard, because such defiance would send the Indonesian into a frenzy that in his condition Eddie didn't know if he could survive.

He hoisted the fifty-pound bucket onto his shoulder, smearing old abrasions that wouldn't heal in the constant damp. Eddie's roommate from the cruise ship, Tang, had timed his work so the two of them would trudge down the hill together. Of the original ten men crammed into the cabin when Eddie first arrived, only he and Tang were still alive.

'I think they are leaving today,' Tang said out of the corner of his mouth, his eyes downcast on the treacherous footing.

'I believe you're right, my friend. The drydock will be empty soon, and it won't take them long to drag the processing plant off the beach. And have you noticed the fishing boats haven't been around for a while?'

'How can I not?' Tang replied with a sparkle in his voice. 'The only thing worse than ground-up fish paste is three-day-old ground-up fish paste.' They maneuvered around a particularly tricky spot before Tang remarked, 'There is also what is happening around the ship the guards use as their dormitory.'

For the past few days a double-ended tender had been making trips between the dormitory ship and the tug they were going to use to take away the processing plant. The area around the dorm ship had always been off limits to the Chinese, but since the transfer had begun the number of guards had doubled. Most of them were Indonesian, but there were also a handful of hard-looking Europeans who

357

reported to Savich and not the Sikh. Judging by their discipline, Eddie thought they were ex-special forces, Russia's elite Spetsnaz. He could also tell that the Russians were as suspicious of the Indonesian guards as they were the laborers.

It didn't take a genius to know that they were transporting the gold they had already processed. Judging by how low the thirty-foot tender was in the water when she motored out to the tug, Eddie estimated they'd moved a hundred tons of bullion. The gold was being stacked in two shipping containers lashed to the tug's deck.

'What do you think will happen to us?' Tang asked.

'I told you what I heard Paulus tell Anton Savich, that they're going to leave us behind.'

'So, we die on this forsaken stretch of coast whether they are here or not.'

Eddie could tell from the sorrow in Tang's words that the younger man had reached his emotional and psychological limit. Like in any survival situation, keeping a positive attitude was half the battle to stay alive. In the past week Eddie had seen people endure unbelievable hardships because they would not let it penetrate their souls, while others had died in a few days, almost as if they willed their deaths to come quickly. Eddie knew that if Tang lost hope now, he wouldn't last the day.

'Listen to me; we are not going to die here.'

Tang shot Eddie a wan smile. 'Thank you for your strength, but I am afraid your words are empty.'

'I'm not Chinese,' Eddie said, and then corrected himself. 'Well, I am Chinese, but I was raised in New York City. I am an American investigating illegal immigrant smuggling. There is a team of people looking for me right now.'

'Is this true?'

Using his best De Niro, Eddie said in English, 'You talkin' to me? You talkin' to me?'

Tang stopped and stared, unable to believe what he'd just heard. 'I know this movie!' he exclaimed.

'You've seen *Taxi Driver*?'

'Yes! We were shown it in school because it was so decadent that it drove one of your people to try to kill the president.'

Eddie chuckled, imagining some Communist party official putting a spin on how Hinckley's attempted assassination of Reagan related to a breakdown of our running dog capitalist ways.

'You really are an American?'

'Yes,' Eddie said. 'And very soon a ship's going to enter the bay.'

Tang looked over his shoulder at the smoldering volcano. It was a couple miles up from the beach but seemed to blot out half the horizon. Ominously, the ash had stopped spewing from the caldera, though it continued to drift over the work site.

'I know,' was all Eddie could answer to the unasked question.

'Hey, look,' Tang pointed out to sea. The pair of fishing trawlers was headed back toward the beach. 'Fresh slop tonight, eh?'

Eddie watched the squat boats for a moment. Gulls swarmed around their fantails. There was no logical reason for them to return. Savich was abandoning the Chinese in the shadow of an erupting volcano, so why would he bother to feed them? Then he noticed that they were moving faster than normal; white foam boiled around their blunt bows, and the seabirds had to wing hard to keep pace. Their holds were empty, Eddie realized, and he saw, too, that they weren't headed for the jetty but angling more toward the tugboat in position to pull the processing plant from the beach.

Eddie's senses went on high alert, sending a jolt of adrenaline that could make him forget, at least temporarily, his exhaustion and misery. The Russian guards must have felt the same thing. They clutched their weapons a little tighter and instinctively moved to cover positions.

'Follow me,' Eddie ordered.

He and Tang were near the sluice boxes, twenty yards from the separating plant. If his fears were correct, the two of them were much too exposed. He led Tang around the far side of the long metal tables and up the hillside, trying to put as much distance between them and the coming crossfire.

'What is happening?' Tang panted.

Before he could reply, automatic gunfire rippled from the nearest trawler. The dozen Spetsnaz had already found sufficient cover, so they could ignore the incoming rounds and instead concentrate on taking out the Indonesian guards who'd turned their weapons on them. The battle reached a fever pitch in less than five seconds. Tracer fire cut the smoggy air like laser beams, and laborers too slow or too disorientated to dive out of the way were cut down indiscriminately.

There had to be fifty or more Indonesians with more joining the fight in an attempt to overwhelm the Russians, but the Russians' superior training and better weapons more than evened the odds. None had been hit in the ambush, and as the fight became more fixed, they were picking off their foes with near impunity.

The timing of the betrayal was nearly flawless. Savich and Jan Paulus were on the cruise ship where the gold had been stored. The Sikh, the likely architect of the double cross, was already on the tug with a few of his guards overseeing the transfer. With the oceangoing towboat securely fastened to the processing barge by inches-thick cables, the vessel's captain couldn't make a run for it.

A jet of black smoke erupted from the funnel of the other tug, the one connected to the drydock, and the black water under her stern turned into a whirlpool as her isopod screws dug in. They were making their escape before the drydock was completely empty.

A swarm of guards came running down the hill past Eddie and Tang. They had been on duty up where workers blasted ore from the hillside with the water cannons. Hidden by a boulder, Eddie waited until one of the guards came too close. In a lightning move, he rammed the heel of his hand into the man's nose. The guard's momentum, more than Eddie's strength, shattered the nose and sent shards of bone into his brain. He was dead before he fell to the muddy ground.

Eddie checked to make sure no one had seen his attack and grabbed up the fallen AK-47.

With adrenaline still coursing through his veins, he turned to Tang and said, 'Payback time.'

The *Oregon* found herself in the teeth of the worst storm to hit the Sea of Okhotsk in a quarter century. It was the confluence of two low-pressure areas, ravenous holes in the atmosphere that sucked in great draughts of air from every point on the compass so the wind shrieked with a banshee's wail and the tops of the waves were ripped clean off. The sky was an oppressive gray curtain that clung to the sea, split occasionally by electric blue forks of lightning. The temperature had dropped to the forties, so hail fell with the rain that pummeled the freighter in horizontal sheets.

The ship would rise up the backs of the tallest waves, driven by her high-tech engines until her bow pointed straight at the roiled clouds. Her bow cleaving a fat wedge through the crest was marked with explosions of seafoam that mushroomed as high as her funnel. She stood poised atop the wave for what seemed an eternity, exposed to the worst of the wind, and then her stern would rise as she plummeted down the back of the roller, her engines suddenly silenced because there was no water to force through her jets. In the sheltered lee of the towering wave the sound of the wind fell away, so an eerie quiet descended on the ship. Down the eleven-thousand-ton ship would drop so that all the bridge crew could see was the surging black of the ocean.

The *Oregon* plowed into the sea so that her bows were buried up to her first set of hatches. The sudden deceleration buckled everyone's legs and made dangling radio cords slap the ceiling. The magnetohydrodynamic engines screamed as they rammed the ship through the sea, their sheer power able to push aside the water and raise her bow. A waist-high surge of seawater raced across her deck, swamping her derricks and pounding into the superstructure with enough force to shake the entire vessel. The water sloshed over her railings and poured from her scuppers like opened fire hydrants.

As the last of the water finally drained away, the bow would begin the laborious climb up the next wave, and the cycle would repeat.

Two things enabled the *Oregon* to make any speed in the

naked face of such a powerful storm: her remarkable power plants and the sheer will of her master.

Cabrillo was strapped into his command seat in the operations center. He wore jeans, a black sweatshirt, and a watch cap. He hadn't shaved since the *Oregon* plowed into the storm, so his cheeks and jaw were heavily stubbled. His blue eyes were rimmed red with exhaustion and tension, but they hadn't yet lost their predatory sharpness.

The senior bridge staff had the watch, which put Eric Stone at the helm. His station's flat-screen displays gave him a panoramic view around the ship so he could anticipate and compensate for the bigger waves. He had such a fine touch on the rudder and throttles that he could coax more speed out of the *Oregon* than her sophisticated autopilot.

Juan watched him work the ship, keeping an eye on the speed indicators above the central display screen. Her speed through the water, speed over the bottom, and drift were all measured using the global positioning system, and only when the big freighter bottomed out in the wave troughs did she lose any momentum.

Cabrillo had thrown caution to the wind, literally, in this mad dash up the Sea of Okhotsk. He was trying to outrace the fast-moving storm. The prize would go to the first to reach the coastline where Eddie Seng's transponder said he was stranded. With the storm tracking northward at eight knots, the *Oregon* and her crew had been subjected to two full days of constant punishment. Juan didn't want to contemplate the strain the engines were going through, and he'd politely told Max Hanley where he could shove his disapproval.

He'd had no choice but to suspend most routine maintenance and with it too rough to cook, the crew had subsisted on U.S. Army issue MREs, meals ready to eat, known affectionately as morsels of recycled entrails, and coffee.

But the gamble was paying off. The latest meteorological information showed them nearing the storm's leading edge, and already the barometer was rising. To his seasoned eye the freezing rain seemed to have lost its needle edge, while the swells, still towering, were coming with less frequency.

Juan called up their position on the GPS and did some mental calculations. Eddie was sixty miles away, and once they broke free of the storm, he could probably increase speed to forty knots. That would put the *Oregon* off the coast in an hour and a half with the storm barreling in on them less than six hours later. If he was right about there being thousands of Chinese laborers being used in a gold mining operation, then the window to rescue them was just too tight. They could pack maybe a few hundred onto the *Oregon*, a thousand if they jettisoned the submersibles and the Robinson helicopter, but given the ferocity of the storm, the impending volcanic eruption, and the weakened condition of the people he expected to find, the death toll could be staggering.

He had worked with guys in the CIA, mostly senior case officers, who could imagine such loss of life with the indifference of an actuary reading columns of numbers, but he had never developed skin thick enough for that. In truth he wouldn't let himself lose that much of his own humanity even if it meant paying for it with nightmares and guilt.

'Chairman, I have a contact.' Linda Ross spoke without straightening from the radar repeater.

'What have you got?'

She glanced over at him, her elfin face looking even

younger in the glow of the battle lights. 'Storm's playing havoc with the returns, but I think it's the sister drydock to the *Maus*. I'm getting two hits forty miles out in close proximity. One's a lot bigger than the other, so I think it's the *Souri* and a tug.'

'Course and speed?'

'She's headed due south from where Eddie's transponder has been pinging, and she's not making more than six knots. She'll pass at least ten miles to starboard if we don't change course to intercept.'

Juan called over to Hali Kasim at the comm station. 'Any change on Eddie's signal?'

'Last sweep was eight hours ago. He hasn't moved.'

Again Juan ran the numbers. It was possible given the *Souri*'s speed and the amount of ocean she'd covered that Eddie was aboard her, but his gut was telling him his crewmate and friend was still on the beach.

'Ignore the *Souri*.'

'Chairman?'

'You heard me. Ignore her.' Juan knew he could leave it at that, and his orders would be followed implicitly, but he felt he had to give them more. Since his conversation with Tory before heading into the storm he hadn't uttered a sentence with more than five words. His concern, even fear, at what they'd find on Kamchatka had sent his thoughts inward. Now that they were getting close, he needed his crew to understand his logic.

'Once she hits the storm,' he said, 'the tug is going to have to haul that pig against thirty-knot winds with the drydock's hull acting like an enormous sail the entire time. Even if they ballast her down to reduce her profile, they won't make any headway in this slop. There's a good chance they even might be driven northward again. All this will give us enough time to reach Eddie, do whatever the hell we can, and then cut back south and take the *Souri* on the high seas.'

Juan saw that everyone on the bridge agreed with his logic, although he could see in their faces they wanted to take the easy prey first. He expected no less from them.

'Now,' he continued, 'we were burned the last time we shadowed one of Shere Singh's drydocks. They have radar capabilities that probably rival our own, so I want full jamming on her, a complete radar blackout.'

Linda Ross raised her hand slightly. 'If they have the kind of sophisticated gear we think they do, they'll have to know they're being jammed.'

'Not if we hit them now,' Juan answered.

'He's right,' Hali added. 'Their radar is looking into the storm and is picking up so much backscatter from the waves and lightning that they can't see us yet, and if we hit the jammers, they never will.'

'Hit them with everything we've got,' Cabrillo ordered. 'Full spectrum across the board, radar, radio, satellite uplinks, the works. Mr Stone, I still want to give them a wide berth. Change course so they don't come within twenty miles of us just to be safe.'

'Aye, aye,' the helmsman replied, punching in the course correction on his computer.

Thirty minutes later the radar began picking up strong returns from the beach. There were six distinct metallic contacts. Five of them were actually grounded on the coast while another, presumably a tugboat, held station in deeper water a hundred yards from shore.

Juan wanted to send up their last aerial drone to photograph the area, but George Adams told him the light radio-controlled plane wouldn't last ten seconds in the wind. Juan considered his offer to risk a quick scout flight in the Robinson. Having the tactical data about what they were getting into was important; however, the element of surprise was just as crucial. Also, the atmosphere was still heavy with ash that would likely overwhelm the helo's air filtration system and bring the chopper down.

'Thanks, but I want to keep you in reserve,' Cabrillo spoke into a pin mike headset. Adams was in the *Oregon*'s hangar. 'Maintain ten-minute alert but be ready to push it to five once we engage.' Five-minute alert meant the hatches over the hold were opened and the Robinson had been lifted up to the deck with her engines running and up to temperature.

'Roger that, Chairman.'

'Senior staff, give me a status report.' One by one his people called in. Murph at the weapons station had lowered the plates covering the Gatling gun and the 40 mm auto-cannon. The deck-mounted gimble .50s were locked and loaded, and a pair of torpedoes were in the twin tubes with the outer hull doors closed. He also reported all cameras were up and functioning. Hali was going to run double duty on the communications and radar systems so Linda Ross could accompany the assault team. Max Hanley was grumbling his way up from the engine room where he would take overall command as well as direct the damage control teams. Linc and his gun dogs were kitting up in the boat garage and reported Linda had just arrived. Doc Huxley was ready in the medical bay, having co-opted the entire kitchen staff for nursing duty.

Juan switched to the ship-wide channel. 'Attention all hands, this is the Chairman. Here's the score. One of our own is on that beach. Each and every one of us has owed our life to Eddie Seng at some point since we started serving together, so his rescue is our top priority. Secondary to that is saving as many of the Chinese immigrants as we can. We don't yet know their number or condition, so our response to them has to remain flexible. Number three is the volcano above the site that's about as stable as the psych ward at Bellevue. That, along with the storm that's barreling down on us like the hammers of hell, means speed is of the essence. We're in and out as quickly as possible. I will not risk the ship or crew if it looks like we're running out of time.

'I'm not going to give you Henry V at Agincourt or Nelson at the gate. Each of you knows your duty and knows that every other crew member is relying on you. We're facing an unusual situation for us. This contract has gone far beyond what we were hired to do. This is no longer about pirates preying on ships in the Sea of Japan. It is about traffickers smuggling the most precious commodity on earth, human life. We're here not to line our pockets but because it is our duty as members of a civilized society to stand up and be counted among those who believe in what is right.

'All of you have had time to think about this, knowing that this moment was coming. Well, the moment is now, ladies and gentlemen. In less than an hour we engage an unknown force with the fate of untold lives depending on us. I know you will not let them down.'

He clicked off the radio and immediately got back on the net. There was humor in his voice this time. 'Sorry, that did come off a bit like Nelson. Now let's go out there and kick some ass.'

# 24

Cabrillo stopped at his cabin on the way to meet the assault team. He changed out of his clothes, donning black fatigues, a Kevlar vest, and a combat harness. While most of the Corporation's small arms were kept in a weapons locker, Juan kept his in an antique safe in the corner of his office, a relic from a long-defunct railroad's Santa Fe depot. He fitted a pair of his FN Five-seveN pistols into kidney holsters, sacrificing a small amount of weight for the seconds he'd save not having to reload. Because he was leading a large force of seven operatives, they'd already decided to standardize their assault rifles. He grabbed up an M-4A1 and slid six spare magazines into the appropriate pouches. He didn't bother carrying a second knife, just the four-inch Gerber hanging inverted from his shoulder strap.

He strapped on a pair of knee pads, flexing a couple of times to settle them properly, and slid his hands into fingerless gloves with thick leather patches to protect his palms. He caught his reflection in the bathroom mirror. The determination and drive that had sustained him through the CIA and led to the creation of the Corporation was in his eyes, hewn flint-hard and focused. Game face, they'd called it, that single-minded convergence of training, experience, and will.

Once again Juan was going to step beyond himself, sacrifice for others by maybe sacrificing himself. He looked hard into his eyes, saw an unforgiving gleam, and abruptly laughed aloud.

Game face or no, Juan also knew he thrived on the danger. Why else would he be in this business? Adrenaline and endorphins were starting their siren song, humming at the base of his skull, giving him that high that only those who'd been there understand. Facing an enemy meant facing yourself. Conquering that enemy gave affirmation of what you always believed about who you are.

The boat garage was cold and clammy, crowded with men and women making final preparations. Rather than use a Zodiac, most of the garage was taken up with a SEAL assault boat, a rubber-rimmed polycarbonate-hulled craft with a modestly protected central wheelhouse and twin outboard engines. The boat could handle any sea thrown at it and could reach speeds approaching fifty knots.

The lights in the garage had been dialed down to match the outside overcast, so everyone's face looked drawn and pale. Their eyes, however, were bright and their motions swift and sure as they checked over each other's equipment. The sound of magazines being slapped home and actions being cocked was a reassuring symphony to Cabrillo's ears.

He caught Tory Ballinger's eye across the room. She had agreed, reluctantly, to stay with the assault boat when the team hit the beach. The Corporation mercenaries had trained together more times than any of them could count and been under fire more than any wanted to remember. In combat they moved and thought as one by seeming to read each other's minds. He made her realize that her presence among them would jeopardize that hard-won unit cohesion.

He couldn't dissuade her from coming on the raid, and he hadn't really tried that hard. He saw that she needed to be part of this because of her survivor's guilt over the attack on the *Avalon*. Until she'd exacted some measure of revenge, that incident would haunt her for the rest of her life. And he planned to help by making sure she'd see a little action as everything unfolded.

Tory gave him a thumbs-up and a silent nod. He shot her a cocky grin that made her smile.

Cabrillo's headset crackled. 'Juan, it's Max.'

'Go ahead.'

'Murph says the video is about to come online. I'm piping it down to you.'

'Roger.'

Juan vaulted the assault boat's gunwale and flipped on the cockpit flat-panel display. Autostabilizers built into the camera mounts compensated for the constant pitching and rolling, and Murph was doing a good job zooming in on what was unfolding as the *Oregon* steamed into the bay.

The feeds flipped at a steady pace, first showing Juan an intense firefight near a large metal building built on a barge, then men who were clones of the pirates they'd taken out weeks ago attacking a tugboat that was in place to tow the barge; next he saw hundreds of Chinese workers running across the sloping moonscape of mud and boulders to get away from the expanding gun battles. He saw that the ships they'd picked up on radar were old cruise liners. All but one had settled deep into the beach, driven almost to their load lines by waves and tidal action. The lone exception might be a new arrival. Although the breakers that slammed her hull couldn't make the vessel rock, she had yet to settle into the rocky beach. Finally Murph showed him a quick shot of the volcano in the distance. Its peak was wreathed in steam and smoke.

Cabrillo quickly sized up the tactical and strategic situation and began relaying instructions. His orders sent every member of the crew scrambling. Their shouts and calls echoed down the ship's long passageways as they made their preparations. The Chairman had called for a desperation Hail Mary-type play, and for it to work he needed everyone at their sharpest.

A few minutes later the ship was close enough to the fighting to attract attention. The troops dressed in identical black uniforms, all of whom were Caucasians, ignored the *Oregon,* while the ragged-looking Indonesians fired hasty pot shots at the ship.

As soon as a pair of deckhands manhandled a large beam with lengths of chain on each end onto the assault boat, Juan ordered Eric Stone to turn the freighter away from the shoreline. While this presented a larger target to the gunmen, it allowed Cabrillo and the shore team to open the boat garage without being seen.

As the door rose smoothly upward, the shore team leapt into the assault boat, locking their arms through purpose-made restraining loops. Each team member called out as soon as they were secured. The driver, Mike Trono, fired the engine, and Juan nodded to the garage boat master. Like a giant slingshot, a series of hydraulic pulleys launched the boat down the ramp and out of the garage. The acceleration was brutal and got worse as Trono lowered the props into the water. The massive outboards bit deep, throwing a rooster tail of water back into the *Oregon* as the nimble craft came up to plane.

Cold air ripped at any exposed skin like sandpaper, and the sting of drops of water that hit them were cold enough to burn. The assault boat rocketed around the rust-streaked freighter, carving a fat wedge into the black sea. By the time anyone on the beach noticed the boat, they were moving at fifty knots, much too fast to accurately engage.

Trono constantly juked the boat across the sea as he made for the spot where Juan had indicated he wanted to land. It was in the shadow of one of the beached cruise ships, one that was so heavily grounded that workers had built a stone ramp up to the main deck. The area around the ship was strewn with trash too heavy for the surf to take away.

The boat arrowed through the breaking surf and had such a shallow draft that the team had only a couple of yards to wade to find cover on the boulder-strewn beach. Juan and Linc dropped behind a house-sized chunk of stone that had been blown from the volcano during some pre-historic eruption. The assault boat had already worked its way back off the beach. Juan looked to make sure Tory had followed his orders to stay aboard, and his estimation of her rose another few notches as he saw her standing in the open pilothouse between Mike Trono and an ex-marine named Pulaski.

'What do you think, boss?' Linc asked.

'Looks to me we dropped in the middle of a little war here. I bet Singh is paying the Indonesians while Anton Savich's guys are the ones in black.'

'So the enemy of my enemy ain't necessarily my friend, eh?'

'That's the attitude I'm taking.'

The team worked their way up the hillside, keeping the cruise ship between them and the main area of combat. Dozens of wide-eyed Chinese workers lay on the ground, cowering. They didn't know what to make of the armed patrol. Juan tried to urge them to find cover, but they were all paralyzed with fear, and he gave up.

If he hoped to rescue any of the Chinese, he knew they'd have to put an end to the fighting.

'Chairman, we're ready,' Max called over the tactical net.

The *Oregon* had shifted position. The doors covering her Gatling gun were still closed, although the ship had maneuvered to give it a clear line on the two fishing trawlers lashed to the tug.

'We're about set, too. Any luck finding Eddie?'

'Negative. Hali's taken over the cameras from Murph so he can concentrate on weapons control. He's getting good shots, but there are so damned many people on the beach that it takes a few seconds for the computer's facial recognition software to sort through them all.'

'Check the area closest to the fighting. If Eddie's in any kind of shape, that's where he'll be.'

'Good thinking. Hali?'

'I heard,' the Corporation's comm officer said. 'Shifting focus now.'

Cabrillo and his people reached a level strip of land several hundred yards above the beach. Further toward the center of the site was an area that had been heavily dug up. Water cannons for blasting the tough soil lay abandoned, their nozzles pointed skyward. The ground was littered with shovels and buckets. All the workers had fled, and their guards had gone down to join the fight.

They approached the workings cautiously, weapons held at the ready, eyes never settling on one spot for more than a second.

An explosion echoed up from below, a grenade blast behind the barge that momentarily drew their attention. The black-clad body of one of Savich's men pinwheeled in a lazy arc before falling to the beach in a broken-limbed heap. At the same second came the chatter of an AK-47 firing at point-blank range.

Cabrillo dropped flat as clods of mud were thrown up all around him. He stitched the area around one of the water cannons in a reflex shot that emptied half a magazine. It was poor fire discipline but it forced the attacker to dodge for cover, and his gun fell silent.

Linc had a better bead. He fired a three-round burst that sent the Indonesian pitching backward into a coffee-colored retention pond. His body vanished under the surface while his blood stained the water. The team found cover behind an earthen berm as more Indonesians appeared out of nowhere. The sheer volume of gunfire made the air ripple.

'We don't have time for this,' Linda Ross shouted over the din, changing out her magazine.

Juan looked down the hill. The assault boat was getting into position, and they would need the cover fire from the *Oregon*'s Gatling gun, but he couldn't afford to remain pinned down. The oldest adage of warfare, that no plan survives first contact with the enemy, had never felt more true.

He called the boat over his throat microphone. 'Mike, can you hear me?' When there was no reply, he called again. The boat was still moving at fifty knots, enveloped in a cocoon of engine noise that made communications impossible.

He cursed and called up Mark Murphy. 'Murph, we need you. There's about fifty bandits above us. We're pinned.'

'Mike's about to hit the tug,' Murphy pointed out.

'And the longer you question me, the closer he's getting.'

'Roger that,' he replied, then muttered under his breath, 'Sorry, Mike.'

As soon as the last of the assault team jumped over the gunwales, Mike Trono reversed engines and drew the boat off the beach, maneuvering backward until he had the sea room to spin around.

He pulled down his headset to talk to Tory as the boat built speed. 'Can I ask you something, ma'am?'

'Only if you promise to never call me ma'am again.'

'Sorry.' Trono grinned. 'Force of habit.'

'What's your question?'

'Do you know how to operate a boat?'

'I work for Lloyd's of London. My entire life revolves around boats. I'm a licensed captain on anything up to twenty thousand tons, which includes your *Oregon* before you turned it into something out of *Star Wars*.'

'So this assault craft?' He stamped the deck.

'Seems to handle as well as the Riva speedboat I rented on my last holiday in Spain. Why the inquiry?'

'Because we have a little job to do, and I need you to man the helm while Pulaski and I take care of it.'

'I assume it has to do with that piece of steel that was loaded before we left your ship?'

'Captain's orders. He thinks we can salvage a bit more than a bunch of immigrants from this nightmare.'

A smile lit Tory's eyes, and her cheeks blushed more than what the wind caused. 'Why am I not surprised?'

They had shot across the bay, circling behind the *Oregon* again for cover, and now were headed for the tugboat. One of the trawlers was drifting away from the tug's flank, while the other remained tightly lashed. There were men scrambling all over the decks. Most were pirates, but a few were crewmen desperately trying to defend their ship. Some of the pirates had added another level to their butchery by switching to machetes to dispatch the last of the crew.

The timing was critical, but with Murph watching their back over the Gatling's sights, the assault boat charged into the battle. They were twenty yards out when Mike remembered he'd taken off his headset. As soon as he settled it over his ears, he heard the shrieking scream of the six-barreled Gatling gun, and he goosed the throttles a little more.

The expected destruction as the 20 mm shells ripped apart the pirates' boats and cleared the tug's deck never came. Instead, pirates began shooting at the lightly protected assault boat from over the tug's railing. The boat ran into a steam of gunfire. Rounds from their AK-47s punctured the inflatable curtain ringing the craft, raked the deck, and ricocheted off the outboards, miraculously missing everyone. Trono tried to wrench the wheel to get away from the tug as fast as possible, screaming to Mark Murphy to find out what went wrong.

The ground between Cabrillo and the Indonesians exploded, churned up by five hundred depleted uranium bullets. A four-foot-thick layer of earth was stripped away by the onslaught, exposing the gunmen where they'd been hiding behind the rim of the pond. Those that weren't hit directly were torn apart by flying rocks. The entire group was blown into an oblivion of bloody mist and debris.

Linc took point to check for survivors, and while his search was thorough, he also knew it was unnecessary. Nothing could have survived that.

'We're clear.'

Juan drew his people together. 'From here on out our element of surprise is blown, but we'll stick to the plan, flank the fighting down below, and try to find Eddie. I only hope he's built a level of trust with some of the other Chinese because if we're going to save any of them, we're going to need him.'

They started off down the slope.

Eddie Seng had remained hidden, watching to see how the fighters would react to the *Oregon* steaming into the bay. As he'd expected, the Russians ignored the distraction and continued to fight with skill and discipline. They had made a sizable dent in the number of Indonesians, but the sheer numbers were becoming overwhelming. Of the dozen who'd been caught in the initial ambush, four were dead and three were wounded, although they could still defend their position. The tide of Indonesians continued to hammer at the hillock the Russians had taken as a crude fort. The outcome of the gun battle was inevitable, and the Russians knew it. They weren't fighting for their lives anymore. This was now all about dying with honor.

Something caught Eddie's attention on the far side of the processing building. The range was extreme, but he thought he saw Jan Paulus emerge from the dormitory ship. It was Paulus, and he was starting to climb up to the helipad where Anton Savich's helicopter sat idle. He was with another man, and by the way they walked it appeared that Paulus was holding a pistol to his head. It was most likely he had taken the contract pilot hostage to fly him out. There was no sign of Anton Savich, and Eddie wondered if the South African had already killed him.

Pursuing the mine overseer was a tactical mistake, but the

flame of rage that ignited in Eddie's chest blocked out any chance of rationality. The weeks of pain, starvation, and deprivation had exacted a toll on his soul that would take a long time to heal. Killing the sadistic miner would at least start him on the journey. He'd already told Tang to gather as many of the other workers as he could and head for the newly grounded cruise ship. Of any of the vessels littering the forlorn beach, it had the best chance of surviving the eruption if Juan didn't think of a way out of this mess.

His body was in no condition to chase Paulus, and yet when he started after the man, Eddie's legs felt as powerful as coiled springs and his lungs pumped air like a black-smith's bellows. He felt alive for the first time since turning over his life to the snakeheads back in Lantan village. If any of the fighters noticed him as he dashed around rusted shipping containers and other equipment left lying about, they quickly dismissed him as just an anonymous worker trying to save himself. He'd hidden the AK-47 under the loose shirt he'd scavenged from a dead guard.

Once he was beyond the worst of the fighting he stumbled across the motor launch that had been used to transfer the gold out to the tug. It was in a secluded bay well sheltered from the rest of the beach by massive boulders, and as he stepped into the open, eight pirates who had been making ready to launch the craft looked up in unison. They should have ignored him like the others, but one went for his gun. Eddie dashed to his left as a stream of bullets chiseled at the boulder near his shoulder. He unlimbered his AK, waited for the firing to stop, and stepped back around the corner.

The gunman had turned to laugh with his comrades at the sport of it all. The first three-round burst sent his lifeless corpse sprawling into the startled arms of his friend. The second blew that man to the ground. Eddie killed one more before they got organized and made to fire back. He ducked out of the way again, quickly slinging his rifle, and began to climb the slick side of the boulder.

It was only eight feet tall, but Eddie barely had the strength to make it. His arms quivered at the strain of lifting his own diminished body weight, and the AK-47 felt like a hundred-pound rucksack. The boat's motor roared to life just as he reached the summit. He slithered over the rounded top of the boulder, trying to bring his weapon to bear. The engine's beat changed as the prop dug into the surf.

One of the pirates must have guessed his intentions, because chips of rock were suddenly blown from the boulder as at least four guns opened up from below. Eddie clamped his hands over his head as stinging chips of stone struck his skin like he'd fallen into a wasps' nest. They maintained their fire until the boat was so far away that they couldn't keep the boulder steady in their sights.

Eddie chanced looking up. The pirates were headed for the tug where a SEAL assault boat from the *Oregon* was coming under heavy fire from gunmen aboard the large vessel. Whatever plan Juan had devised had seriously come apart. There were only a couple of people on the assault boat. They needed cover fire from the *Oregon* if they were going to attack the tug, and yet the Gatling remained silent.

Then the multibarreled machine gun opened up. A ten-foot tongue of flame jetted from the weapons bay, and a section of hill where there were a bunch of retention ponds high above the beach vanished in a hammering volley that sent dirt flying thirty feet or more into the air.

Unable to warn the assault boat about the approaching tender, Eddie slithered down the boulder and took off again after Jan Paulus.

Firing with one hand while the other worked the wheel, Mike Trono added to the gunfire pouring off the assault boat as they countered the pirates' initial barrage. Tory was hunkered low on the floorboards, firing precisely aimed shots at the pirates lining the tug's rail. She had the accuracy of an Olympic marksman and the patience of a sniper.

The weapon felt perfectly balanced in her hands as she squeezed the trigger for a fifth time. Her target had ducked behind the railing's metal plating, but the shot would keep his head down for a few critical seconds. Another gore-spattered gunman raised himself suddenly, hosing the sea with his AK-47 before homing in on the fleeing boat. Tory aimed carefully, her body anticipating the wave action, and she pulled the trigger. The light bullet sparked off the railing just in front of the Indonesian and ricocheted into his chest just below the sternum, lifting him high off his feet.

'Hold on!' Trono shouted. 'We're going back in. Cease fire.'

He twisted the wheel once again and set the boat on a collision course with the squat tugboat. Because they weren't being fired on, many of the pirates stood up to draw a bead on the craft.

'Showtime,' Murph said over Trono's radio.

The *Oregon*'s weapons officer shifted the Gatling from the hill and sent a few seconds' burst into the drifting trawler. The boat was ripped to pieces in a hail of wood splinters and shredded netting. The pilothouse disintegrated. Seabirds gorging themselves on offal left to slop on the deck took flight as their world came apart. Then the stream of bullets penetrated the engine room, tearing the big diesel from its mount before puncturing the fuel tank. The resulting explosion sent a greasy fireball climbing into the sky, and the seas were raked with shrapnel.

What little remained of the trawler sank instantly, snuffing out the flames in a gout of steam.

The destruction on the tug was less dramatic when Murph pivoted the Gatling gun and gave the trigger another squirt. As though caught by a broadside of grape shot, the pirates were scythed down by the fusillade. A hundred ragged holes appeared in the big shipping containers lashed to the deck, and glass from the aft-facing secondary bridge, used by the crew to check their charges under tow, fell in a glittering cascade that further mutilated the corpses. Murph hosed the deck with autofire, making certain that no one was left alive.

'That should hold 'em,' Murph whooped.

Mike Trono danced the assault boat up to the lowest section of railing and turned the controls over to Tory. 'Just hold it here. We won't be a minute.'

'Why are you doing this, anyway?' she asked, standing aside while Pulaski and Trono manhandled the heavy steel girder onto the tug's low deck.

He handed her his tactical radio and gave her a wolfish smile. 'Chairman thinks there's booty aboard, and not the kind a Hollywood hottie's packing.'

The men levered themselves onto the deck. Hard years of training forced them to visually check to make sure no one had survived. It was a gruesome task, something out of a horror movie, because the Gatling had minced the bodies into what Trono could only describe as a sort of chunky paste. Leaving the assault boat burbling along the tug's flank, they hoisted the beam onto their shoulders and waded through the carnage toward one of the containers.

Trono pulled his Glock and shot the lock off one of them while Pulaski maneuvered the beam so they could drag it up to the top. The hinges screamed as Trono swung open one of the doors and just as quickly closed it again. Pulaski shot him a questioning look.

'Chairman's right again.'

'Gold?'

'Gold.'

He hoisted himself up the container with a boost from his partner, and together they levered the two-hundred-pound beam to the top. Trono looked up as they began to thread the lengths of chain through the lifting hardpoints. A small runabout was racing out from shore, hidden from Murph's vantage by the bulk of the tugboat. He counted a half dozen armed men bobbing in the craft as it crashed through the surf line and into smoother water.

'We got trouble.'

Pulaski looked over his shoulder. 'Damn!'

The boat would reach them in seconds, not the minutes they needed to secure the beam to the container, but they weren't about to abandon their prize. Mike shouted down to Tory, 'We've got company. Bunch of goons in an open tender. Get the hell out of here.'

'I'm not leaving you behind.'

'We're not being heroic. We need you to draw them out so Murph can hose 'em with the Gatling.'

Tory understood and slammed the throttles to their stops. The assault boat shot away from the tug, turning sharply so she passed behind the ship. She'd forgotten about the thick tow cables still securing the tug to the barge on shore. With no time to maneuver she shot under the first cable, ducking as the thick steel tore the standing cockpit from its mounts. Had her reactions been an instant slower, the hawser would have decapitated her.

The boat flashed under the second cable, angling to cut off the approaching tender. She was going so fast that the men on the boat could only stare as she bashed her boat into theirs. One of the men tumbled over the tender's side, and by the time any of them thought to reach for their guns, Tory was twenty yards away and accelerating like a greyhound.

She slalomed the assault boat as the men began firing on her. She was exhilarated by the adrenaline pumping through her veins. 'I know, I know, bloody women drivers. Hit you then try to run away. How about you come and catch me, and we'll exchange license and insurance information.'

She looked back to see if they'd taken the bait but was horrified to see they were intent on reaching the tug. She whipped Trono's radio set over her head. 'This is Tory. I'm with Trono and Pulaski on the assault boat.'

'Tory. It's Max Hanley. What's the problem?'

'There are six terrorists in a small boat about to reach the tug. Your guys are trapped on board with only pistols. They haven't a chance.'

'Where are you?' Max asked in a reassuring tone to calm her down.

'On your SEAL boat. Mike wanted me to draw them away, but they weren't having any of it.'

'Okay, just you hold on for a second. Pulaski? Trono? You there?'

The reply came in a faint whisper. 'Max, it's Ski. We're on top of one of the shipping containers. The pirates just came aboard.'

'Do you think they know you're there?'

'Negative. Mike grabbed a tarp just before they got here. Unless they check the top of the container, we're hidden. And it doesn't appear they're searching the ship.'

'What *are* they doing?

'It looks like they want to release the tow cables and get out of Dodge. What do you want us to do?'

'Help them,' Juan Cabrillo said over the open comm channel.

'What?' Max and Ski said in unison.

'I said help them. Ski, you and Mike hang tight. Max, I want you to cut the tow cables.' Juan's radio carried the sound of the gunfight raging on the beach – the sharp crack of rifle fire, the staccato bursts from AK-47s, and the agonized screams of the wounded.

'I can do it with the Gatling,' Mark Murphy chimed in. 'A direct hit on the big cable drums on the tug's stern should do it.'

'But why?' Max asked.

'Because there are a thousand or more Chinese workers caught in the crossfire down here, and the longer this battle lasts, the more of them are getting killed. The Russians look like they can hold out for hours still. Right now that tug is the pirates' only way off the beach, and if they see it's about ready to make way, you can bet they're going to forget all about their fight and hightail it over there.'

'Which gets them away from the civilians . . .'

'Which gives Murph the opportunity to hose 'em down,' Juan finished.

'What about the Russians?'

'We'll give them a chance to surrender and get off this beach alive. If they don't take it, you can take them.'

As if to underscore the urgency, a tremendous crack split the air. A fresh explosion of ash spewed from the top of the volcano, billowing ever higher like a nuclear mushroom cloud. Juan had no idea how long they had. Hours or minutes. They still hadn't located Eddie, and if his plan to end the gunfight quickly didn't work, he had to seriously consider evacuating his people from the beach and making a run for it.

Hali Kasim's excited voice cut through Cabrillo's grim thoughts. 'Chairman, I found Eddie! He's on the far side of the barge. It looks like he's tracking two people, one of whom appears to be a hostage.'

'Where are they headed?'

'Up away from the beach. The range is pretty extreme, but I think they have a helicopter up there.'

'Take it out,' Cabrillo ordered, and then he and Linc exchanged a look. It was all the communication they needed. Linc was now in charge of the field team while Juan took off in a ground-eating run. He had only covered forty yards when his ankle caught on a loose stone. Had it been his real leg, the ankle would have broken or at least suffered a major sprain. All that happened was the chairman fell hard, but his clumsiness saved his life as the air above him came alive with automatic fire. He combat rolled a dozen times to find cover behind a pile of stones. The gunman was below him, hidden behind a pyramid of fifty-five-gallon drums.

Juan checked the load on the grenade launcher slung under his M-4, steadied the rifle against his shoulder, and fired. The weapon made a comically hollow sound, and a second later the grenade impacted behind the drums. The grenade's primary explosion detonated the fuel. Three hundred-pound drums were launched into the air like rockets, some exploding in flight, while others hit the ground and spilled their flaming contents across the beach.

Juan scrambled to his feet as a drum arced high and began to fall straight at him like a meteor. It landed five yards from him and slightly higher on the hill, so when it split, a burning lake of gasoline roared over him. He fought the instinct to run down the hill. He ran at a diagonal instead, flames licking at his knees and the heat enough to sear his lungs, but in just moments he was through the conflagration with nothing more than singed hair.

'Out of the frying pan . . .' he wheezed as he continued after Eddie Seng.

A one-second burst from the Gatling was enough to shred the steel tow cables, and the timing couldn't have been better, because the pirates on the tug had just bumped the engines to high idle, sending a thick plume of smoke from her funnel. The reaction on the beach was exactly as Juan had predicted.

The pirates almost instantly disengaged the Russian holdouts and began running for the shore. Some kept their weapons, but most dropped them as they plunged into the frigid water and began to swim out to the tug. Watching them reminded Linc of rats deserting a sinking ship. He and the rest of the shore party swept down from their position. There were a few gunmen so intent on the fight that they didn't know their ride was about to leave.

Linc took out a pair of them with a grenade and had a

bead on a third when what he thought was a corpse at his feet sprang to life. The pirate knocked away his M-4 and tried to ram a wickedly curved knife into his chest. Linc blocked the blade's fatal thrust, but the knife sliced a long gash into his arm. He sank a fist into the pad of muscle under the fighter's arm, paralyzing the limb for the second he needed to cross-draw his pistol and put a bullet between the man's eyes. He ignored the torrent of blood streaming down his arm and continued his patrol.

Eddie realized he was never going to catch Jan Paulus. The burst of energy that had gripped him so tightly had now flickered to nothing. He was nauseated by hunger, and he couldn't draw enough oxygen into his lungs, but still he pressed on, driven by raw emotion. Paulus and his hostage were a minute away from reaching the MI-8 helicopter, and no matter how Eddie willed his legs to move faster, he knew he was slowing. Then from out on the *Oregon* came the distinct pop from the 40 mm autocannon. Five rounds went sailing high over the beach, passing directly over Eddie and blasting the area around the chopper. When the dust settled, Eddie could see that the cockpit had taken a direct hit. Flames licked from around the shattered Plexiglas, and the ground around the craft was littered with mangled electronics.

He looked back over his shoulder to give the ship a congratulatory salute and spotted a figure running toward him. There was no mistaking the distinctive silhouette: Cabrillo.

Paulus summarily shot his hostage as soon as he realized the helicopter was ruined and started running back down the hill, maybe thinking he could reach the tug and broker some kind of deal or maybe just in blind panic.

Knowing that Juan would have his back, Eddie started running after him, letting gravity do the work that his legs no longer could. They were thirty yards from the beach when Eddie skidded to a stop and threw the AK-47 to his shoulder. He was shaking so badly that he could barely see through the sight. He squeezed the trigger, and the rifle recoiled into his shoulder, but only one round had fired. Paulus turned at the sound, then continued on as Eddie checked the weapon. At some point he'd unseated the banana magazine from the receiver. He jammed it home, cocked the gun, and sprayed the remaining clip at the fleeing miner.

A feather of blood spurted from Paulus's calf, and he staggered and fell. He was slow to get to his feet, giving Eddie the time to cover the distance. He crashed into the South African, sending them both sprawling across the rocks. Though injured, Paulus was a big man, used to the punishing life of mining, and could absorb a tremendous amount of pain.

'You're going pay for that, mate,' he said through gritted teeth, goading Eddie to hit him again.

'Don't bet on it.' Eddie used the moment of confusion at his American accent to whip the AK-47 at Paulus's head. The miner ducked just in time but gave Eddie an opening for a brutal kick to the knee.

Paulus took the hit without even wincing and wrapped his arms around Eddie's chest, squeezing with machinelike strength. Eddie slammed his forehead into Paulus's nose, feeling the bone crackle, but the miner only seemed to redouble the pressure. Eddie hit him again, and this time the South African roared in pain, loosening his grip enough for Eddie to get one hand free. He grabbed the man's ear and gave it a savage yank. Paulus let go. Eddie got one leg behind Paulus's and shoved him. Paulus reached out as he fell, taking a handful of Eddie's shirt.

Hitting the ground with Eddie on top of him should have driven the air from Paulus's lungs, but it didn't. The impact had been cushioned. It reminded Eddie of falling on a waterbed. To his horror he realized they'd landed in a huge puddle of mercury.

Before Paulus could recover, Eddie rammed his knee into the man's crotch at the same time he forced his head below the surface. Paulus involuntarily gasped at the pain, sucking in a mouthful of the toxic liquid metal. He started going into convulsions, but Eddie stayed on him like a cowboy riding a bull. Paulus managed to wrench his head above the surface. He coughed up great silvery globs of mercury before Eddie jammed his head back under. It took a minute more for him to stop struggling. When Eddie got off the body, it rose back to the top of the pond. Paulus's mouth and nostrils were little glimmering pools of mercury, and his eyelids looked like someone had already laid coins over them.

'That is definitely on my list of top ten ways not to die,' Juan said, placing a hand on Eddie's shoulder.

'For a while there,' Eddie panted, 'I thought I had to take on all these goons by myself.'

Juan helped him to his feet. 'What, and deny us a share of the glory?' He nodded at the corpse. 'Anton Savich?'

'No, a South African hired to oversee this nightmare named Paulus, Jan Paulus.'

'Any idea where Savich is?'

Eddie shook his head. 'Last I knew, he was in that big cruise ship down the beach. Paulus had Savich's pilot hostage, so I think he's already dead.'

'Damn.'

'Why? Saves us the trouble.'

Cabrillo went silent for a moment then said, 'The fence.'

'Fence?'

'Like the guy who buys stolen goods from a thief,' Juan explained. 'Until gold is properly assayed and stamped by an official mint, it's worthless. No one legitimate will touch it. Savich had to know that before putting this caper together, which means he already has someone lined up to buy it from him. Someone who could get the gold authenticated and trickle it into the system. It has to be someone big to handle this much, a major banker with serious connections.'

'Sorry, boss, I've got no idea who it is.'

Juan smiled. 'Don't worry. We'll find the greedy bastard.'

Linc called Juan over the radio. 'Beach is secure, Chairman. The Russians saw the writing on the wall and surrendered in exchange for a ride out.'

'It's time for us to get out of here.' Cabrillo looked around. Hundreds of Chinese workers seemed to have materialized from the ground. They'd found cover among the boulders, and now that the fighting had stopped and the tug had motored a mile down the bay, they were milling around in shock. 'All of us.'

Once Juan issued his orders it took only a few minutes for the word to spread that the workers were to board the newest ship to arrive on the beach, but it would take an hour or more for them to climb the only ladder tall enough to reach the ship's rail.

Juan was waiting at the pier the trawlers used when Tory motored up in the assault boat. 'Going my way, sailor?'

He jumped down into the deck and impulsively kissed

her mouth, but the kiss was interrupted by another booming explosion from the volcano that sent foot-high ripples dancing across the water.

'My, my, you made the earth move.' Tory laughed huskily.

For Juan the mood had already passed. They were in a fight against the clock, and every second counted. Tory correctly read his expression and gunned the throttles.

On Cabrillo's orders, Max had swung the *Oregon* around so her stern pointed at the grounded cruise liner. Deckhands had run out the ship's own towing cables from recessed hatches under her fantail. Using a pair of Jet Skis, thick ropes attached to the cables had been transferred to shore where a hundred of the most able-bodied Chinese immigrants were in position to haul the big hawsers to the cruise ship.

'Max, you reading me?' Juan called over his radio.

'I'm here.'

'What's the situation?'

'They're about ready to haul the cable over to the cruise ship. Her name's *Selandria,* by the way. Linda and Linc are over there directing everything. She says the bollards are nothing more than mushroom-shaped rust, so we're going to thread the cable around her anchor capstans. They should be able to handle the strain.'

'Okay. I'm almost back. As soon as they have the cable secure, I want all our people back on the *Oregon.*'

'I'm going to have to sit on Doc Huxley. She wants to take a team over there right now and start helping the worst of the Chinese.'

'Then sit on her,' Juan snapped. 'If this doesn't work, the grim truth is we're going to leave those people behind and pray we can get some help up here before the volcano blows its top.'

'On that front, once the fighting stopped I tried to raise the Russian Coast Guard, but the mountain's pumping out a lot of electrical interference. All our communications are out except the short-range tactical net.'

'We're on our own.'

''Fraid so.'

'I want you to stay in the op center. I'll be up on the flying bridge. Have someone meet me there with some clean clothes.' He shot Tory a glance, and she nodded enthusiastically. 'Some for Tory, too.'

Juan stripped out of his filthy battle jacket as he made his way through the ship, feeling bad that the housekeeping staff was going to have a hard time getting his muddy boot prints out of the plush hallway carpets. He reached the flying bridge just as Maurice stepped off the elevator from the op center. He was pushing a silver mess trolley. He handed a bundle of clothes to Juan and another bundle to Tory. Tory stepped into the radio shack to change while Juan undressed where he stood.

'That feels better,' Juan said.

Maurice pushed back the trolley's gleaming cover, and the aroma of hot food made Juan's mouth swim. 'Shredded jerked beef burritos and coffee.'

Around a mouthful of the spicy, foot-long Mexican specialty Juan said, 'Maurice, you just doubled your salary.'

The elder waiter then tipped a flask into Juan's coffee cup. 'From my stock of brandy. Just enough to take the edge off.'

'Tripled it.'

The storm they had raced up the Sea of Okhotsk had caught up with them. Rain began to pound the windscreen, and lightning crackled overhead. From under the trolley Maurice pulled out a matching pair of rain suits, baseball caps, and Juan's rubber sea boots. 'I had a feeling, sir.'

Juan slipped into the slicker as Tory came out of the radio room. She wolfed half a burrito in just a couple of bites. 'God, I didn't know how hungry I was.'

'Chairman?' Max was calling through a walkie-talkie.

'Go ahead.'

'They have the cables across. Linda says she needs ten more minutes.'

'Tell her she has five. This storm's about to hit, making a tough job near impossible.' He stepped out onto the flying bridge and into the gale. The wind had picked up to force five, and volcanic ash mixed with the storm so clots of mud fell from the sky. He looked aft. The heavy cables had been fed through the *Selandria*'s fairleads, and all looked in order – except that the *Oregon* had drifted in the wind and wasn't straight on to the cruise ship. He called a correction down to Eric Stone and looked to see the swirl of water at the bow thruster port.

'That's good. Stations keeping, Mr Stone.'

The assault boat roared off into the choppy sea to pick up the shore party, her rubber pontoon flexing as she crashed through the waves.

'Think we can do it?' Tory asked, joining him out in the open.

'We can generate the horsepower of a supercarrier with our engines, but if that hulk is stuck fast, we'll have the classic dilemma of immutable force and immovable object.'

'Would you really abandon them?'

Juan didn't answer, but that was answer enough. Despite

what he'd said earlier, she could see the determination in his eyes and knew he'd tear the guts out of his beloved ship and risk his people for the chance of saving even one of the Chinese immigrants.

A couple of minutes later the SEAL boat pulled away from the beach, loaded with the last of the Corporation people left behind. Juan waited until it was clear of the tow cables before bringing the walkie-talkie to his lips.

'Okay, Eric, put some tension on those cables.'

The *Oregon* crept forward, and the cables slowly rose out of the sea, sheeting water as the bundles of wire clamped tighter and tighter.

'That's it,' the helmsman reported. 'Speed over the bottom is zero. We're at full stretch.'

'Dial us up slowly to thirty percent and hold it.'

There came the distinctive whine as the magnetohydro-dynamics spooled up. The angle of the tow and the power of the engines made the *Oregon* settle heavier into the sea so that waves split over her bow in raging sheets.

'I've got movement,' Eric cried. 'Gaining five feet a minute.'

'Negative, we're just stretching the cable a bit more.' Juan had spent a summer on a tugboat during college and knew how easily cable stretch could look like they were already under way. 'In a minute you'll find we're sliding back. When that happens bring us up to fifty percent.'

Juan watched waves slamming into the *Selandria*, trying to see if she was riding them or just being punished by them. There was some movement as walls of water passed under her bows, but each time the foreward section of the ship rose up on a wave meant her stern was being ground deeper and deeper into the beach.

'Fifty percent,' Eric announced a moment later. 'No movement.'

'Bring us to eighty.'

'I can't recommend that,' Max Hanley warned. 'You've beat my babies pretty bad already.'

Theoretically there was no limit to the power output from the magnetohydrodynamics, but there was a weakness in the system: the high-speed pumps that kept the banks of magnets cooled to superconductive temperatures with liquid helium. The extreme cold played havoc on the impellors, and after the prolonged abuse they endured to reach Kamchatka, their failure weighed heavy on Max's mind.

'Those engines are maintained by the best engineer afloat. Bring us to eighty.'

The *Oregon* dug in even deeper, allowing waves to wash over her railings. The water at her stern became a boiling caldron as the pump jets forced hundreds of tons a minute though the tubes.

'Nothing,' Eric reported. 'She's stuck fast. We're never going to haul that pig off the beach.'

Juan ignored his pessimism. 'Give me full starboard lock.'

Eric complied, wrenching the controls so the *Oregon* sheered off a straight line like a dog straining at a leash, adding a couple more tons of pressure to the tow.

'Port lock!'

The ship swung around, straining the cables so they vibrated with tension. A haunted moan escaped from the *Selandria* as her hull pivoted on the rocks and then came a rending scream of metal as she shifted further.

'Come on, baby. Come on,' Juan urged. Tory had her

hands to her mouth, her fist clenched so tightly her fingernails were a bloodless white. 'Anything?'

Eric sent the *Oregon* careening back to starboard before answering. 'No. Speed over the bottom remains zero.'

Max interrupted. 'Juan, I've got temperature spikes showing in engines three and four. The coolant pumps are starting to go. We've got to shut down and try to get as many of those poor souls aboard as we can.'

Juan looked back. The Chinese had been warned to stay off the deck – a tow cable parting under tension would whip back with enough force to cut a man in two – however, the *Selandria*'s bow was a sea of pale, frightened faces, huddled and shivering in the cold rain. A rough count put the number of immigrants on the liner at over three thousand. The *Oregon* could take maybe a third of that number. 'Okay.'

Max must have had his hands on the engine controls because they wound down to low idle the instant the word left Juan's mouth. Free of the strain, the *Oregon* bobbed up, shedding water like a spaniel.

Tory gave Juan a sharp, disapproving look, a stinging rebuke at his giving up so easily, but she hadn't let him finish speaking.

'Take the tension off the cables and spool out another hundred yards. Creep us ahead and prepare to weigh both anchors.'

'Juan, do you really think . . .'

'Max, our anchor winches are powered by four-hundred-horsepower engines,' Cabrillo pointed out. 'I'll take every pony we can muster.'

Down in the op center Max used computer keystrokes to disengage the clutch on both cable drums, allowing them to run free while Eric Stone engaged the engines again to move the ship farther out into the bay. When they reached the hundred-yard mark, Max let go the anchors. They sank quickly to the bottom, which was only eighty feet deep.

'Now back us gently and set the flukes,' Juan ordered.

The big Delta kedging anchors dragged along the rocky bottom, cutting deep furrows in the loose rock and boulders until their hardened steel flukes snagged bedrock. A computer control automatically adjusted the tension on the anchor chains to keep them from slipping.

'We're ready,' Max announced, but his tone was less than enthusiastic.

'Tension the tow cables, then bring us up to thirty per-cent.' Juan snapped a pair of binoculars to his eyes, purpose-fully avoiding looking at the men at the *Selandria*'s railing. Waves continued to pound the ship's bow, causing her to saw up and down, grinding her stern ever deeper.

'Thirty percent,' Eric announced. 'No movement over the bottom other than stretching the cables.'

'Ramp it up to fifty,' Juan said without taking his eyes off the cruise ship. 'Anything on the anchors?'

'Zero recovery on the winches,' Max answered. 'Heat's already building in three and four. We're thirty degrees from red line and automatic shutdown.'

The forces acting on the tow were titanic, brute horse-power against twenty thousand deadweight tons of steel that had been pounded into the beach. Pulled taut by the cables, the *Selandria*'s bow stopped responding to the waves, so water washed under her, causing volleyball-sized rocks to dance back and forth.

'Anything?' Juan called.

'No recovery on the winches,' Max said grimly, 'and zero movement over the bottom.'

'Eighty percent!'

*'Juan?'*

'Do it and take the safeties off the engines.' Juan's voice was charged with anger. 'Bury them past the red line if you have to. We're not leaving those people.'

Max complied, typing a few commands that told the computer to ignore the heat building up in the massive cryo pumps. He watched his screen as the columns indicating temperature turned red and then climbed above the safety limit. He reached out deliberately and shut off the computer monitor. 'Sorry, my darlings.'

Juan could feel his ship's torment through the soles of his boots as she fought the tow. The vibrations were tearing her apart, and each shudder sent a lance into his chest.

'Come on, you bitch,' he snarled. 'Move.'

A rumble built across the bay, so deep and resonant that it was a feeling across the skin rather than a sound that hit the ears. The top of the mountain was hidden by a dense cloud of ash, and the ground shook so strongly that the beach seemed to become a liquid. This was it. The main eruption. The volcano was going to blow like Mount Saint Helens, and a wall of superheated ash and gas would tear down from the summit in a deadly avalanche that scientists called a pyroclastic flow, one of the most destructive forces on earth. Juan had gambled all and was about to lose everything. It was too late to go back and save any of the Chinese. Tears stung his eyes, but the firm line of his jaw never slackened.

'We've got to cut the tow,' Max said.

Cabrillo said nothing.

'Juan, we've got to go. We need a couple of miles between us and that volcano if we're getting out of here alive.'

He didn't doubt the words. The pyroclastic flow would reach far out to sea in an enveloping noxious cloud that would smother anything in its path. But still he remained silent.

'Movement!' Eric shouted. 'Port winch is recovering, five yards a minute.'

'Must be slippage,' Max countered. 'She's dragging across the sea floor.'

It was as if the sun had been eclipsed. Darkness came so swiftly that it left Juan's eyes swimming. He could barely see the *Selandria* through the swirling ashfall. Hot ash stung his bare hands as he held the binoculars to his face. He just couldn't tell if the liner had moved or whether Max was right and the anchor had slipped.

No one spoke for what felt like an eternity. Stone's eyes never left the speed indicators, which remained stubbornly at zero.

Then over the sound of the eruption, the *Selandria* screamed, a mortal, almost human sound, as if she could no longer endure the tremendous pressures of tow and storm.

'Got her,' Eric shouted as his speed indicators tickled ever so slightly.

Max turned his computer screen back on. 'Recovery on both winches.'

'Speed over the bottom is ten yards a minute. Fifteen. Twenty.'

As more and more of the ship's weight felt the buoyancy of her natural element, the speed continued to increase. Tory clutched Juan's hand as they watched the *Selandria* get drawn back to the sea, her hull plates shrieking in protest as she was dragged over the rocks. And when a particularly large wave pounded the beach, she gave it a squeeze as the ship rode up its face, her stern coming high in her first moment of freedom.

'She's free,' Juan called down to the op center and heard a roar of approval from his crew. Someone, probably Max, who was a rank sentimentalist under his tough veneer, sounded the ship's horn – a keening celebratory note that echoed and echoed.

'We're not out of the woods yet,' Juan said and led Tory back inside the bridge. They descended into the op center. Another cheer rose from the throats of his people, and his back was slapped black and blue.

Now that the *Selandria* was refloated, Juan ordered the power output cut to fifty percent and had the view from the aft-facing cameras brought up on the main screen. Already water frothed along the liner's waterline as the *Oregon* continued to accelerate down the bay.

'Dear God,' Tory gasped.

The top of the mountain had been vaporized. A solid black wall of ash was pouring down the mountain, a swirling, choking mass that seemed alive. Everything before its fury was cut flat. Trees that had stood for a hundred years were ripped from the ground and tossed like matchsticks. A second later the sound of the explosion reached the ship, a painful assault on eardrums that was the loudest yet.

Workers on the *Selandria* scrambled to get back inside the ship as the pyroclastic flow finally reached the surf line in an explosion of steam, and still the ash roared onward, spreading outward so it swallowed the other ships left abandoned on the beach. One of the smaller ones was blown onto its side, while the barge carrying the processing plant was flipped completely upside down.

'Hold on,' someone said unnecessarily as the ash

enveloped the *Selandria* and completely filled the camera's view.

It hit the *Oregon* like a sledgehammer blow, a hurricane of ash and pumice that shattered windows and heeled the ship over so her starboard rail was buried into the sea. But she kept driving, shouldering aside the fresh onslaught of nature's fury until she burst out of the cloud and into shadowy daylight.

No one moved or even breathed as they watched the screen. Seconds dribbled like molten lead. Then suddenly the bow of the *Selandria* emerged through the curtain of ash like a ghost becoming real. Her hull was covered in clinging dust, but she'd never looked more beautiful. But still the crew waited, watching. A tiny movement caught everyone's attention. Mark Murphy quickly zoomed in as a door on the upper deck opened tentatively. A small figure stepped out, looked around, and then motioned at someone inside the ship. In seconds there were a dozen people on the deck, kicking up clouds of ash in a spontaneous game to celebrate their survival.

Maurice appeared in the op center as if by magic. The tray in his hand held a trio of Dom Perignon bottles and enough cut crystal flutes for everyone on duty.

Amid the raucous celebration, Tory whispered into Juan's ear, 'So who was the bitch?'

'Huh?'

'When we were on the flying bridge you said, "*Come on, you bitch, move.*" Who was the bitch you were talking about? The *Oregon* or the *Selandria*?'

'Neither.'

The corner of her mouth turned downward as she thought about his answer. And then her lips parted in a beaming smile. 'Max is right. You are a crafty bastard. You were talking to Mother Nature.'

He couldn't keep the satisfied smile from his lips. 'I knew there'd be a major earthquake just before the main eruption. Water-saturated soils undergo what's called liquefaction. Basically, the shaking causes the ground to turn into quicksand. That broke the suction that had built under the *Selandria*'s hull and allowed us to drag her off.'

'Cutting it awfully close, weren't you?'

'You only get the big rewards when you're willing to face the big risks.'

'Chairman.' Mark Murphy was still at his weapons station. 'I've got a radar contact six miles dead ahead, moving at seven knots.'

'The tug,' Max said.

'Speaking of rewards.'

Even with the *Selandria* in tow it took the *Oregon* only fifteen minutes to come within visual range of the fleeing tugboat. Juan scrambled the deck crew to get in position as he ordered Eric to take the squat tug down the port side. There were only a handful of pirates on the tug, so they were almost on top of them before anyone realized they weren't alone. Two of them raced out onto the tug's flying bridge with their AK-47s, but they quickly ran for cover when Murph opened up with one of the gimble-mounted fifty-calibers housed in hidden bunkers on the *Oregon*'s deck.

'Mike, Ski, can you hear me?' Juan called over the radio.

'I thought you'd forgotten all about us,' Pulaski replied over the tactical communications channel. 'Mike and I were thinking we were in for a long cruise vacation.'

'Sorry, boys. You're not up for leave for while yet. I can

see the two containers on the tug's stern. Which one are you on top of?'

'The rearmost.'

'And the lifting assembly?'

'Ready to go.'

'We'll be alongside in about one minute.' Juan then addressed Murphy. 'Disable the tug's rudder assembly, would you please.'

'With pleasure.'

He called up the Bofors 40 mm autocannon, waited for the weapon to be deployed from its concealed bay, and put a half-dozen rounds under the tug's fantail. Her speed dropped off instantly, and a trail of oil began to seep from where her hull had been penetrated.

Eric Stone kept his hands loose on the controls as he brought the *Oregon* alongside the tug, slowing to match speed as the gap between the two ships shrank to just a few feet. He used rudder and bow thruster to keep the vessels in virtual lockstep. Murph never took his eyes off his cameras, waiting to provide cover fire if any of the pirates showed themselves.

Up on deck, a pair of deckhands swung the boom of the *Oregon*'s main derrick across the gap, feeding out line so the hook dangled scant inches above the shipping container. Trono and Ski finally emerged from under the tarp and attached the hook to the beam they'd secured to the metal box. Mike made a circular gesture with his hand, and the crate came free of the deck.

Mohammad Singh, Shere Singh's second-eldest and therefore second most trusted son, had survived the initial assault on the tug because he'd hidden in a cabin while his father's men fought and killed the crew and were later gunned down by the Gatling. Fighting was something that his father paid others to do. However, when he saw the crane swing over the side of his ship, he immediately understood that someone was trying to rob him. He raced down from the bridge, brandishing a pistol, and burst out on the afterdeck, screaming curses at the top of his lungs.

Mark Murphy saw the man dash across the deck but was a fraction too slow training one of the .50 calibers.

Singh leapt for the container just as it began to pendulum from the wave action. He scrambled to find a grip and was forced to drop his pistol in order to hold on tight.

The winchman drew back cable so the container cleared the railing and had just started to pivot the boom back over the *Oregon* when a heavy rolling wave surged past the two ships. Stone did an excellent job of keeping the vessels from crashing against each other, but the deckhand couldn't stop the container from arcing across open space and slamming into the tug's bridge with a wet slap. When it swung back, all that remained of Mohammad Singh was a meaty red stain.

Most of the crew not on duty assembled in the hold where the container had been lowered once the *Oregon* was well beyond weapons range of the floundering tug.

Ski and Trono doused everyone with a cascade of champagne froth when Maurice handed them each a bottle.

'It's kind of anticlimactic,' Juan shouted over the revelry, 'because these two clowns had to sneak a peek on the tug, however . . .' He drew the word out as he swung open the big doors.

The lighting in the hold wasn't particularly conducive for examining treasure, but the golden reflection that radiated from the container was the most beautiful color any of them had ever seen.

Juan hefted one of the bars, pumping it over his head like a trophy, while around him the men and women of the Corporation went wild.

# 25

Juan Cabrillo leaned back in the sofa with an exhausted sigh and took a sip of the brandy he'd bought from the duty-free shop at Zurich's airport. For the first time in nearly two weeks he felt he could finally relax.

He gazed into the fire burning in the open hearth, losing himself in the flames' hypnotic dance.

When they'd dragged her off the beach, the *Selandria*'s hull had been holed by sharp rocks. They managed to tow her twenty miles down the Kamchatka's west coast before maneuvering her into a shallow inlet and letting her sink. They transferred as much food as they could spare and emptied nearly all the supplies from the medical bay. Juan allowed Doc Huxley and her team just twenty-four hours to evaluate and treat as many people as she could before he ordered the *Oregon* to continue south.

They came across the second tugboat and the drydock *Souri* only 150 miles from what Eddie said the workers called Death Beach. As Cabrillo had said, she'd had a hard time making headway in the storm. They put a torpedo into the *Souri* as they passed her by without so much as a warning and blew the rudder off the tug's sternpost with a blast from the 40 mm.

It was only then that Cabrillo contacted the Russian Coast Guard. He routed the radio call through a half dozen satellite relays to mask their position and reported that there were several ships in distress in the Sea of Okhotsk and gave their GPS coordinates. He explained about the Chinese refugees, which the operator he spoke to didn't seem all that concerned about, and how there was a fortune of illegally mined gold on one of the tugs, which seemed to get more of a reaction.

News of the dramatic rescue and incredible find following the worst volcanic eruption in Asia for a decade broke as the *Oregon* limped into Vladivostok. They turned the Russian mercenaries over to the authorities and laid up the ship for much-needed repairs.

It was there that Juan phoned Langston Overholt, their principle CIA contact, and told him the whole story. He also called Hiroshi Katsui to inform him that the pirate menace that had overwhelmed the waters off Japan was over and gave instructions for their final payment.

He considered the fortune in gold they'd made off with a bonus that their client didn't need to know about.

Two weeks after the eruption, Lang sent Juan an e-mail. The first rescue workers to reach the bay reported that someone had survived the eruption aboard one of the cruise ships. He'd barricaded himself in a food locker as the pyroclastic flow buried the vessel under five feet of searing hot volcanic ash. Lang thought Juan would like to know the survivor gave his name as Anton Savich, a volcanologist well-known in the region. Savich was currently staying at a hotel in Petropavlovsk

Juan wanted to go himself, but he felt that Eddie Seng needed it more. Franklin Lincoln went along for the ride. They were back two days later with the name Bernhard Volkmann. He was the banker who was going to fence Savich's gold.

'How'd you do it?' Juan had asked his two officers across the desk in his cabin.

'Simple, really,' Eddie had said. 'Once we broke into his room and kidnapped him, we drove him to the airport and promised that we wouldn't kill him if he told us what we wanted to know.'

'And?'

'He had nothing to lose and everything to gain, so he told us.'

'*And?*' Juan repeated, feeling like he was pulling teeth.

'Well, when the Russians rescued the Chinese off the *Selandria*, there weren't enough beds around Petropavlovsk to house them, so they put about a thousand men into a hangar at the airport until they figured out what to do with them. So after Savich told me the name, I went into the hangar with him, explained to a few of the men there that Savich was responsible for what had happened to them, and, well, let nature take its course.'

Juan glanced at Linc.

'Like the man said, we promised not to kill him. Never said anything about turning him over to his victims. Guy had already stopped screaming by the time we were out of earshot.'

That was what had sent Juan back to Switzerland for a meeting with Bernhard Volkmann, which, as Juan recalled while sipping at his brandy, had gone as well as he'd expected.

Volkmann had agreed to buy the sixty tons of gold that had followed Juan to Switzerland in a couple of airfreight containers. He agreed to establish a trust with half the proceeds on behalf of the Chinese workers who'd mined the gold, and he agreed that he would then sell his bank and

409

retire to the slums of Calcutta, where he would devote the rest of his life to charity.

For his part, Juan agreed not to put a bullet through the greedy bastard's head.

A light knock on his door jerked Juan back to the present. The press interest in the explosion and kidnapping of Rudolph Isphording had long faded, and he looked nothing like the dark-haired, dark-eyed, and mustached Spaniard he'd pretended to be when he'd rented the safe house, so he walked calmly across the living room and swung open the door.

'Hi, sailor, remember me?' Tory wore her hair up, accenting the long line of her neck, and her blue eyes captured the glow of the fireplace and reflected it back at Juan. She wore a loose gray suit over a white oxford shirt buttoned low enough to catch his attention. Her lips were brushed with gloss and were poised in an unsure smile.

'I never expected to see you again,' Juan finally stammered. She'd disappeared soon after the *Oregon* docked in Vladivostok without so much as a word of good-bye.

Her smile faded slightly. 'Are you going to invite me in?'

'Sure, sure.'

He fixed her a drink and was careful to sit opposite her in a chair rather than next to her on the couch facing the fire.

'I didn't think you *were* going to see me again,' she began, 'but Max called me in London and dispelled some of my preconceived notions. I saw you as the rakish sea captain with your merry band of swashbucklers and figured you would have a girl in every port. I realized that I didn't want to be another notch on your sword belt, so rather than let myself get hurt for falling for the wrong kind of man – again

– I decided to go home and spare myself a touch of heartache.

'Then Max called me. He told me that you don't keep a woman in every port, and in fact in all the years he's known you, he's never seen you even go on a date. He told me you were widowed and that your wife was killed by a drunk driver. He says you don't have a single picture of her and only told him about her one night years ago, but that since her death you've cut yourself off from relationships.'

Juan made to speak, but Tory silenced him by crossing to the chair and placing one delicate finger across his lips.

'Max also told me that since I left, you've been an insufferable sod, which is why he called me. He seems to think you might like me, and was pretty certain I liked you. So here I am, flying in on a wing and a prayer. How about it? Remember what you told me. Only big risks can bring you big rewards.'

'Only Max ever knew I was married, and I didn't tell him the whole truth,' Juan said softly. 'She was killed by a drunk driver, but what I didn't say is that she was the drunk. It was ten, no, eleven years ago. She had been to rehab twice already, but it never really stuck. I didn't know she'd relapsed this time. When I saw the cop standing outside my door that night, I knew immediately what had happened.'

'I'm sorry.' Tory's hand rested on Juan's chest. 'And you still carry a torch.'

He stared into her eyes. 'I still carry the anger.'

The silence stretched for several seconds. 'You're not angry at her, are you.' It wasn't a question. 'It's yourself you blame.'

'Who else can I?'

'Her, for one.' Tory shrugged out of her jacket. 'Listen,

Juan. Max told me you've already have another job lined up, and I've only a week's leave from Lloyd's. I'm not asking that you drop everything and marry me. I'm not even asking that you love me. I'm asking that for once you stop taking the blame for everything bad in the world and let yourself enjoy some of the good. When was the last time you were intimate with a woman?'

The frankness of the question sent a stirring jolt through his lower body and inside him a dam he'd spent half a lifetime erecting crashed down in a swirl of emotion. His hand wrapped around the back of her head of its own volition, his fingers entwined in her hair. 'Since . . .'

'Don't you think it's about time?' she asked and kissed him.

Juan lifted her easily from the chair, cradling her in his arms as he moved to the bedroom, his heart beating like a trip-hammer. 'It was never about time,' he whispered in her ear. 'It was just waiting for the right person.' He smiled against her skin. 'And I have to warn you I'm probably a bit rusty.'

'Don't you worry. We'll work the kinks out.' Tory gave a throaty chuckle. 'And maybe even work a few kinks in.'